Family Secrets

A NOVEL BY

RONA JAFFE

SIMON AND SCHUSTER · NEW YORK

COPYRIGHT © 1974 BY RONA JAFFE
ALL RIGHTS RESERVED
INCLUDING THE RIGHT OF REPRODUCTION
IN WHOLE OR IN PART IN ANY FORM
PUBLISHED BY SIMON AND SCHUSTER
ROCKEFELLER CENTER, 630 FIFTH AVENUE
NEW YORK, NEW YORK 10020

DESIGNED BY EVE METZ
MANUFACTURED IN THE UNITED STATES OF AMERICA

2 3 4 5 6 7 8 9 10

LIBRARY OF CONGRESS CATALOGING IN PUBLICATION DATA
Jaffe, Rona.
Family secrets.
I. Title.
PZ4.J2Fao [PS3519.A453]   813'.5'4   74–9893
ISBN 0–671–21842–5

FOR THE PEOPLE I LOVE

Prologue

An hour after you leave New York City everything is green; even though you are still on the highway you know you are in a different place. You know the air is clearer because you can see the sky and it is blue. If you turn off the highway on to Hill Avenue you will see on one side of you, where the zoning is more relaxed, rows of fifty-thousand-dollar houses, looking all alike because they *are* alike, built by the same builder; only the outside trim of each is different. The grass is new and the trees are small. Nobody bothers with a garden. The houses are all new, on the grounds of what was once a great estate, a common sight here.

On the other side of Hill Avenue, where the zoning is still strict, there are public buildings with more land around them, a grade school, a church, a seminary, and some little farms that sell produce all summer to the local people. In the old days, if you were looking for the turnoff to Tetley Road you would almost always miss it, hidden as it was behind trees and walls. But now it is clearly marked by a brand-new cement parking lot servicing the church. For years the land lay bare and brown, once the property of The Crazy Russian, dead now for twenty years, who sold first the trees for lumber, then the turf, and finally the topsoil, leaving the rocky barren land, the desecration a local joke, until his heirs finally got rid of it. It was perfect for a parking lot.

Tetley Road is just a mile and a half long and is known to the local people as The Valley because it is a valley, swooping down below arches of tall ancient trees, cool in summer, fragrant with grass and leaves and wild flowers. In the 1940s, during the war, it was known as The Polish Corridor, because even though the town itself was restricted, Jews had bought land in The Valley. The

Crazy Russian had done it—stripped the topsoil and sold to Jews. The Valley holds the fog like a teacup. It is misty in the mornings, and in the late afternoons when the sun goes down the fog begins to rise until at night only the people who have lived there all their lives can find their way home. The fog comes from the rivers and ponds and lakes of this vicinity; it is what makes everything so green.

Almost half of The Valley belongs to one deserted estate: Windflower. There is the sign, "Windflower—Service," and then much later, "Windflower," although you can see no house, only a road that seems to stretch for miles. On either side of the main entrance are stone walls, then there are the acres of grass surrounded by the electrified barbed wire that could stun a large animal and kill a small one. There is the field where the third Mrs. Saffron used to land her private plane. The grass is high now in the outer field, studded with the tiny white flowers that gave the estate its name. "No Trespassing" signs are tacked up on the large trees near the entrance, but no one pays much attention to them any more. Most people think the place is a public park. The families who live in the new houses along Hill Avenue come to picnic here sometimes, or to ride their sleds down the hills in winter. The pond is fine for ice skating on cold winter days, and in summer the little boys come to fish in the lake and to dare each other to walk across the slippery stones on top of the waterfall.

The houses are empty here, except for the one where the care-taker lives, and they have been empty for so long that the local people just ignore them, as if they were another useless convenience like the pool house by the empty swimming pool or the ivy-choked pavilion by the lake. The tennis court has no net and no tapes, but sometimes there are little paw prints in the en-tout-cas, what is left of it. Small animals live here freely now, skunks and wood-chucks and rabbits and raccoons. Nobody ever kills them except occasionally a car on the road in the fog. Once there were timid deer that came to drink from the edge of the lake at dawn, but they are long gone, and so are the horses that ran and played in the lower field. The stables across the road are still there, that boarded the neighborhood horses, but now there is only one horse in the corral, wearing a muzzle and fixing you with a mean eye. The horses from the riding academy on Green Street still cut across the bridle path that runs along the edge of the woods in Windflower. The bridle path came with the estate, and the Saffrons left it open as a gesture of good will, although no one ever knew it belonged to anybody because the estate was so large.

The Saffrons were rich, so rich that they seemed almost not to exist: rich and aloof and strange. Hardly anyone ever came into the estate, but when they did they either stayed forever or went away and never came back. There were no casual relationships in that family. They did not know how, they did not dare.

PART I

Adam's Dream

ONE

In March of 1902 the rains never seemed to stop; there were floods all over the eastern part of the United States, and the part of Brooklyn the immigrants called Mudville was a sea of mud. The fixers, the peddlers, the people who worked out of doors, were driven inside, not only to keep from being drenched to the skin but because there was no business outside. Only a fool or a starving man would stand in such a rain. The coffee houses were full. Not only the men who sat there all day talking their business deals were there, but also those for whom the coffee house was ordinarily only an after-work luxury. It was better than the crowded rooms in which they lived, filled with the shouts and gabble of women and children and the smells of cooking and bodies and poverty and everyday life.

Adam Saffron had been sitting in the coffee house for nearly two weeks now. He was a fixer: a mender of chairs mostly, although his fingers were blessed and he could fix almost anything you gave him to repair, quickly and neatly. It was not his wish to be a chair mender, and certainly not his life's ambition, but it was the first job he had fallen into when he stepped off the boat, and it fed him and his wife, Polly, and the baby, Leah Vania, who was almost two and walked and talked already. He was twenty-four years old, he could speak English, and he had a small apartment with an indoor toilet for himself and his family. But he was not meant to remain a fixer for the rest of his life and he knew it, and so he sat in the coffee house and listened to the men who made business. These men bought and sold land without even setting foot on it. They knew where each lot was and what could be built on it, and so they bought and sold and never got their hands dirty. That was a job for an intelligent man, a clever man. It seemed to Adam, as he sat there nursing his cup of tea, that the only thing a man needed to do such business was a persuasive tongue and money. But if a man had no money, as he had none, then an intelligent man needed a persuasive tongue and a stupid partner who had money but no charm, no brains, and no gift of talk—in other words a man who needed someone to make deals for him with his money. Adam had considered several such possibilities, but the best one seemed to be Yussel, a big loksch who wanted to be liked and always made stupid deals that lost money. If anyone was to buy a piece of land that was impossible to sell, it was Yussel, and that was a feat, for they were buying everything, buying in the morning and selling that night. A man could make three hundred dollars in a single day.

Adam bit into the piece of sugar and holding it in his teeth sipped the tea through it, as he had done as a boy in Russia and would probably always do, although the Americans preferred to stir the sugar into the tea. That was what a rich man would do, not afraid to waste sugar; an American, who did not have to spend his life scheming of ways to make every little good thing last longer. There was Yussel in the corner with friends, his broad flat face beaming, slurping his tea from the saucer like a cat. A Hungarian, a peasant, but rich in this rich land, and so he could do as he pleased. There were those who drank their tea from a glass, and those who drank from a cup, and those who slurped from saucers, and there were those who drank coffee, and each showed his national origins and his wish to assimilate or to remain apart by this simple, natural act. Adam knew that what he saw everyone else also saw, and so he had begun to drink his tea from a cup instead of a glass, thus remaining somewhere in the middle, a man who could adjust but a man no one would really know.

He kept his eyes on Yussel, knowing that after a while the other men would drift away to join other groups, and then he could make his move. Yussel already liked him; Yussel liked everybody. And Adam had been listening to and learning the business talk around him until he knew exactly how to buy and sell a piece of land. But he had done one thing more, because he was new at this and had much to learn—he had left the coffee house every evening before supper and walked through Mudville, getting drenched and dirty and cold but hardly feeling it, walking and looking and imagining what could be done with such a place. It was a dreadful-looking place, even uglier in the rain. But a clever man could build cheap houses there, rent them to immigrants who would live anywhere as long as the rooms were big enough to house their large families and there was an indoor toilet. The houses could be ugly, they could be built all in a row and attached, which would be much cheaper than building separate buildings, and the immigrants would rent there because the apartments would be clean and new and the idea of being close to their own landsmen made them feel safe. These businessmen in the coffee house were clever, but they lacked imagination. To them Mudville was not real; it was a piece of paper, a handful of money, a deal, an abstract. But Adam saw it teeming with life, with sidewalks, with children running along those sidewalks and horse-drawn carts filled with produce being hawked along those streets. He saw the immigrant women coming out of their row houses, drying their reddened hands on their aprons and haggling with the peddlers for their family's dinner. He could hear them shrieking at their children to come in because dinner was ready, and he could see the immigrant husbands coming home from the factories, tired, sweaty, looking forward to a bath in their own kitchens.

This was his vision, but he would tell nobody, not because they would laugh at him but because it was none of their business. He would do it, step by step, and then when it was done they would wonder why they had not thought of it themselves. When he came home every night, soaked and muddy, Polly was upset because she thought he had been out trying to find chairs to mend, and she worried for his health. She filled the bathtub with hot water for him and dried and pressed his suit, cleaning it as best she could. She sighed over his ruined shoes, stuffing them with old newspapers as they dried to keep them from warping out of shape, cleaning and polishing them when they were dry, shaking her head sadly over her good man and watching him go out into the day to ruin his shoes all over again and not come back with a penny.

"Must you go out today?" she would ask softly. "We have enough saved to last until the rain stops. There's enough to eat, Adam. Stay. You'll be sick."

He would silence her with a look and pick up the baby, squeezing it hard in a hug until it screamed. Then the baby would wave at him from the doorway, one fat hand in her mother's thin one, the other waving at him. "Papa, Papa, Papa," the little voice would pipe, and Polly would smile.

It was Polly who had been taken sick, not he, and now she had been in bed for a week, burning with fever and coughing. It was the influenza. Everyone had it; it spread from house to house in the rain and the damp. She was a good woman, intelligent, tall but not strong, and she was his first cousin. His family often married cousins; they met each other at family occasions, were attracted, fell in love. If you married a cousin you knew the family, you were not likely to end up with bad blood. It was safer than marrying a stranger. Her family had come to America about the same time as his, and because he had known them back in the old country it was natural to become close with them here in the new one. Polly was as talented with her hands as he was with his. She sewed and embroidered ladies' clothes at home, and so helped him make a living. She always wore clothes she had made, and they were a living advertisement in the neighborhood when they went for a walk. Now that she was sick in bed it was lucky they had the family; there was always a cousin or an aunt in the apartment, tending to Polly, feeding and dressing the baby. He never had to worry about them, and that was good, for a man's work was in the world and he should not have to spend his time worrying about what was going on in his home. If he could make his first business with Yussel today he would have something good to tell Polly at last, and although perhaps she might not understand it, it would make her happy because she would know it was good. If he had some money in his pocket he would bring the doctor. Even though the cousins and the old aunts had all their home remedies from the old country, this was the new country, and maybe the doctor knew something they didn't know.

He saw the men who had been sitting with Yussel say their goodbyes, and Adam stood slowly and walked over to Yussel's table. "So nu, Yussel? Vas machst du? May I sit a minute?"

Yussel beamed. He was happy to see anybody who would be nice to him, and he was not a snob. A fixer was as good as a businessman because a fixer was needed too. How would life go on without those who worked with their hands? His father was a wealthy merchant of yard goods, and as Yussel saw it, how could he sell those yard goods if someone else hadn't first made them? It was the only clever thing Yussel had ever thought of all by himself, and so he liked to repeat it to anyone who would listen, hoping they would think he was a philosopher.

"Please sit," Yussel said. "Will you have tea?"

"Why not?"

Yussel laughed. "Why not? Yes, why not? There's nothing else to do today but drink tea until a man floats away."

"I have an idea for you and me to do a little business," Adam said.

And so the first part of his plan happened. He persuaded Yussel to put up the money to buy a lot, and then Adam sold the lot at a profit to one of the dealers in the coffee house, and by the end of the day Adam and Yussel were three hundred dollars richer, half of it for each of them, and not one of them had gotten their hands dirty, not one of them had set a foot out of doors into the mud. Yussel was as delighted and proud as if he had done it all himself.

"We make good partners, you and I," he said.

"We do," Adam said.

"You have the gift of gab. When I talk, I put my foot in my mouth. With you talking and me being the financial power, we could do very well together."

"That's true," Adam said. "But we could do more than trade one lot. What *is* a lot?"

Yussel looked blank. "What's a lot? Everybody knows what a lot is."

"I mean," Adam said patiently, "what is it for?"

"It's for . . . for trading."

"But why do we trade it?"

Yussel brightened. "To make money!"

"But why, besides making money?"

"I don't like it when you talk in circles," Yussel said.

"We trade it," Adam said, "because it is a piece of land that someone, some day, will build houses on. Now, we have been trading land that everybody wants, and it's easy to sell a piece of land to a man who already has another piece of land next to it, because when he has enough land he wants to build on it and then he really makes money. So, my plan is this. Why don't we buy some land that nobody wants, get it very cheap, and then *we* build on it?"

"Why do we want something nobody wants?"

"Because we have imagination. We see what it could be."

"But who would build there, on this land nobody wants but us?"

"We would," Adam said.

"I thought you said that," Yussel said. "But would somebody want it after we built on it?"

"Of course. The people who would rent apartments from us."

"You mean we would be landlords?"

"We would be landowners and builders and landlords."

Yussel breathed a heavy sigh. "Oy, that takes a lot of money. Where could we get it?"

"From the bank."

"What would we use as collateral?"

"The land."

"What land?" Yussel said. "What is this magic land that nobody sees is wonderful but us, that we will get cheap and that will make us rich men?"

"Mudville."

Yussel's excited face turned glum. "You've been making fun of me."

"I'm serious," Adam said. "We buy a big piece of Mudville. You with all your bad luck, and me, a fixer with no brains, how could anyone do anything but laugh at us? They will sell us as much land in Mudville as we want and think good riddance. And the bank will give us money, not as much as we would like, because they will think we're fools too, but enough. We won't be building palaces, you know. We'll be building good, cheap houses for people who have no homes to live in."

"If you say it can be done I believe you," Yussel said. "I'm willing to put up the money if you do the rest. But I wouldn't tell anybody. I'd be too embarrassed."

"They'll find out soon enough," Adam said.

With a hundred and fifty dollars in his pocket and wet feet Adam got off the streetcar and walked the two blocks to his apartment house. What a story he had to tell Polly tonight! First the story, then the doctor. No, first the doctor, then the story. He walked up the steps to his front door and suddenly there were women all around him—wailing women in babushkas and sheitels, crazy women, strangers, neighbors, all of them weeping and babbling like lunatics. He tried to push his way through them but hands grabbed at his sleeves. He recognized one of them at least, Tanta Yettel, his ancient aunt.

"Oh, my Adam," she said, and burst into tears. Her eyes were red as if she had already been crying for hours.

"What is it?" he said, and the first thought that popped into his mind was that something had happened to his mother.

"Polly is dead."

TWO

The day of the funeral the rain stopped, and Adam thought that life was strange because it was the rain that had started him on his great plan to become a success in life and it was that same rain that had taken his wife away. Afterward the small apartment was filled with friends and relatives. The women brought cakes and pies they had baked, platters of noodle pudding, chicken, beef, potato pancakes, cookies, bread. They sat and stared at each other and tried to think of things to say, and sometimes one or another of the women cried. They had every intention of sitting shiva for the entire prescribed time, and as far as Adam was concerned it was a waste of part of his life. Dead was dead. The dead lived on in the minds and hearts of the living. God had not made heaven and hell, the goyim had, and if they wanted to believe in such things and frighten themselves to death it was their pleasure, not his. Heaven or hell were here, on earth; he had seen plenty of evidence of both. He had seen plenty of devils who were human, without worrying about one with horns and a tail.

He left the apartment, and the women were sympathetic, thinking he needed to be alone with his grief. He went to the coffee house to find Yussel, and told him what had happened. Yussel was full of sympathy.

"I'm a bachelor myself, but I feel for your sorrow."

"Ya, ya." Adam nodded solemnly. "Now, you remember that we are still going to buy that land. Next week, on Monday, I'll be here to meet you and we'll start to work."

Yussel nodded and clasped Adam's hand. "Work is good medicine for grief. My mother used to say that, may she rest in peace."

"Your mother was a smart woman."

It was not so bad in the apartment in the evenings, for then the men came back from work and Adam had someone to talk to. He could never talk to women. He looked around at the faces of the people he had known for years, so many of them married to relatives, so many of the faces alike, all of them looking for security in a hard world and a strange land. A man should be married. A man should not live alone like a dog.

The baby screamed in her bed in the night. Polly's younger sister, Lucy, rose immediately and went into the dark room to comfort her. She came out carrying the baby, soothing her with soft words and little kisses. Adam watched them. Lucy was so young and small, only twenty. She almost never spoke, which he liked, and when she did her voice was gentle and she never said anything stupid. She was small, but she was not frail looking. Polly's height had been deceptive; she was thin and she had not been strong and she had died of an illness that took old people and babies. Looks could fool you. He followed Lucy into the kitchen.

"I'm making tea, Adam. Would you like some? Or would you prefer coffee?" She was speaking to him in Yiddish.

"You don't speak English?" he asked.

Lucy blushed. "Oh, yes," she said in English. "I studied at night school. But sometimes, with the family, I feel more comfortable when I speak Yiddish . . ." She smiled shyly and buried her face in the baby's soft hair. She still had the child cradled in one arm, the child half-asleep now, her face cuddled in Lucy's neck, drooling on her clean white shirtwaist. With the other hand Lucy kept on measuring the spoonfuls of tea. It was a small, square, capable hand.

"There's nothing wrong with that," Adam said.

"I'll put her back to bed soon," Lucy said. "She had a bad dream. She misses her mother and she doesn't understand what happened."

"She needs a mother."

Lucy nodded and hoisted the baby higher on her hip.

"She's too heavy for you," Adam said.

"No, it's all right."

"I'll take her. You make the tea." He took Leah Vania from Lucy's arm and realized how heavy the child must have been for her. He liked a woman who loved children. The baby recognized him in her sleep and put her fat arms around his neck. Lucy smiled at them.

"What a pretty picture that makes," she said.

"A sad picture," Adam said. "A young man alone, twenty-four years old, and an orphan child. I suppose they'll put her in an orphanage now."

Lucy paled. "Oy, no! We would never let them do that!" She put her fingers delicately to her lips and made a soft puffing sound into them: her way of spitting on the floor to keep away evil, her gentle New World version of the coarse Old World custom she still believed in.

"I have to work hard all day to make a living," Adam said, "Who would take care of the child?"

"We will! All of us. I promise you, Adam, they would have to kill me first before I would let them take away your child." The color had returned to Lucy's face and she was having trouble catching her breath. He hoped she wouldn't cry. He hated women who cried. She didn't cry: she turned to the kettle in which the water had begun to boil and deftly wrapped a dish towel around the handle, then poured the freshly boiling water over the tea leaves and put the cover on the teapot so the tea could steep. Then she looked at him again. She was breathing normally.

"I think I would rather have coffee," Adam said.

"Yes? All right," she said calmly, and took the tin of coffee from the shelf.

"No, don't bother," he said. He put his hand on her hand. He was glad that she didn't recoil. Her hand was very cool.

"If you want coffee, of course you shall have it," Lucy said matter-of-factly. He saw how quick and neat she was, without a wasted motion. She was shy, but she was not uncomfortable with him; she was, after all, his first cousin as well as his sister-in-law. She respected him and was fond of him, but Adam sensed that she was not afraid of him, and he liked that too. A shy, quiet woman was good; a frightened, silly one was a trial for life.

"So, nu?" he said pleasantly. "What are you going to do with your life?"

"Do?" She looked at him in open amazement. What else was there for a woman to do but hope to have a good husband and healthy children? Her look searched him to see if he was teasing her, and then she seemed satisfied that he was not. "I don't know how to talk philosophy," she said.

"I wouldn't want you to."

"Good." She smiled almost mischievously. "See, the coffee is boiling already. Would you like a piece of cake with it? There is some which is fresh today and I put it aside for you."

"Did you make it?"

"No."

"But is it good then?"

"Yes."

"Tomorrow is the last day we all sit shiva," Adam said. "It will be lonely here."

"I know," she said softly. He liked the way her moods shifted along with his, as if she were his own shadow; instantly, instinctively sympathetic, following the lights and darks of his spirit. "Please will you come spend Shabbas with us?" she said. "Both Friday night and Saturday."

"That is not what I want," he said. "I will *not* live in other people's houses."

"We're not 'other people'—we're family."

"No."

"Then no," she said.

"Will you marry me?" Adam said.

She looked at him for a long moment and he noticed that her eyes were green. "Yes," she said. "But on one condition."

"A condition you're giving me?"

"Yes. I know that in time, please God, we'll have children, and I want them all to be equal. I want Leah Vania to be my child. She's so young, soon she won't remember her mother. I want all our children to be true brothers and sisters. I don't want anyone to tell them."

Adam felt a great wave of contentment wash over him. He had chosen well. "I promise," he said.

Lucy held out her arms. "Now give me my daughter," she said, "It's time I put her back in her bed."

When Adam married Lucy in six weeks, everyone felt it was a good move; it was the old, respected way for a man or a woman who was widowed to marry quickly, and preferably marry the next of kin, for it held the family together even more tightly, and the family was safety. In the meantime, Adam had begun to buy land in Mudville, using Yussel's money, and there were very few in the coffee house who were loyal enough friends to come forward and tell them what fools they were. This pleased Adam, for he knew people were talking about him and Yussel behind their backs, laughing at them, and the more they laughed the easier the land in Mudville became to buy. Soon they owned enough to start a small community. Then he went to the bank, where the people told him it was a risky venture but seemed impressed by his confidence in himself. He knew which men were the best builders; they had to be fast and cheap, but their houses had to be safe. He would not build houses that fell down or burned down and killed people. A man did not have to be a killer to make money.

In August, when the land was dry and hard from the summer sun, the builders began to build on what had once been a sea of mud and now was nothing worse than a barren and ugly foundation which could be quite serviceable. The fact that there was nothing around it did not bother Adam. He would also build some suitable stores and perhaps even plant some trees. He would take out a few ads in the Yiddish language newspapers, and between that and word of mouth, the apartments would be rented in no time.

Lucy was pregnant, and remembering his promise to her, Adam moved their little family to a new neighborhood. No neighbor women remembered Polly in her stylish dresses walking down the street with Leah Vania, nor the funeral, nor his remarriage. Lucy was his wife, Leah Vania was their child, and he noticed with approval that the little girl was going to look exactly like him. She had his clever little eyes and his clear, intelligent forehead. She remembered everything she heard, like a little monkey, both English and Yiddish, and babbled and prattled away in both interchangeably.

There was only one problem with the child, which Lucy told him about sadly. Polly had been fond of wearing a long purple cape, which she had sewn herself, and during the spring which had passed after her death it had become stylish for many women to wear such a long purple cape—and so when Lucy took Leah Vania out for a walk often the child would see a tall woman in a purple cape from the back and run after her, screaming: "Mama! Mama!"

"I am your Mama," Lucy would say, and the child would look at her with those clever little eyes filled with confusion.

"When will she forget?" Lucy would ask him.

"Nu, she'll forget. An adult forgets, so a child can forget."

"She screams at night, Adam. You sleep, you don't hear her."

"All children scream. That's why I snore, so I can't hear them scream."

He would take the child on his lap and bounce her up and down. "Nu, nu, nu, my little monkey. You will be good to your Mama? You will obey your Papa?"

"Yes, Papa."

"Then give me a kiss."

"Nooo . . ."

"Why no?"

"Moustache!" the child would shriek, putting her hand gingerly on its bristly surface, and then she would put her arms tightly around his neck as if she was determined never to let him go. He would have to pull those little arms open, comfort her screams, and hand her to Lucy, thinking how glad he was to be a man and so not have to take care of children.

When Lucy's child was born and it was another girl he was not too disappointed. It was good for two sisters to be close in age; then they could be friends. The baby was beautiful, with giant clear eyes as green as grass, much prettier even than her mother's. Her nose seemed to turn up, and her hair was golden. A regular goy, he thought, amused. Now he hoped the next one would be a boy.

But the next child was a girl also, plain-looking but placid. Leah Vania was six, ready for school in the fall, and they had moved to a larger apartment in the same building. Lucy's mother was living with them now, the son she had been living with having died and no one else in the family financially able to care for her. She was an Orthodox old woman who wore a sheitel and kept strictly kosher, poking around the pots and pans to make sure she was not being poisoned by tref, speaking only Yiddish and making a general pest of herself. But family was family, and it was good that she was there to watch over the two older girls while Lucy was busy with the new baby.

Adam's dream of Mudville had come true. The row houses were filled with immigrant families, the streets were filled with children playing and peddlers hawking their wares, and the stores were rented too, one a kosher butcher, one a store for yard goods and things for making clothes, and one a grocery. Adam was pleased with his new tenants. He went by there every day to check on things, to make sure a toilet had not broken or a naughty boy had not smashed a window playing ball in the street. He was making money, and he was respected. Even Yussel was respected.

Yussel would have been happy to spend the rest of his days in the coffee house, telling and retelling the story of how he and Adam Saffron had been great visionaries who had foreseen all this when other men had not. But Adam was ready to buy more land and build again. This time his credit was good, he was known, and he had his choice of men who wished to invest with him and a loan from the bank. He decided to stay with Yussel, but in the back of his mind he was not sure how long it would last. Yussel was of small mentality, he was content with what they had now and although he was excited at the prospect of something new he was also afraid it would all be taken away from them. Because he did not understand business or finance, Yussel regarded it all as a sort of magic. They had magically been lucky, and he could hardly understand that, so they could magically be unlucky, and although he could not understand that either, at least it was something he was used to.

Adam decided to build more houses with Yussel, and in the meantime look around to choose other men with more money and more vision. He already had a vision of his own. The next building he built would be tall, maybe even ten stories, with an elevator in it, such as very rich people had in their homes, and it would be used only for business. Doctors and lawyers could have offices there, companies could do business—not dirty business like a factory but clean business with paper work and figuring and clean girls in starched white shirtwaists typing business letters on typewriters. Men in suits and hats would have appointments, and there would be serious conferences in quiet rooms with desks that shone of good wood and carpets on the floors so not a footstep could be heard. That was beyond Yussel's imagining, and also his purse, so Adam did not speak of it to him. He concentrated on the new family dwellings he was building and bided his time. He hired a young man he liked and trusted to take his place as watcher in Mudville, to go there every day as he had done and see that everything was all right. The people liked knowing that their landlord cared about them, and having the young man there was the only way Adam could be sure they would be good tenants and not turn the place into a pigsty. He hoped that it would not be a long time before his wife started having sons. By the time they grew up there would be a great deal for them to do.

THREE

It was fall, and it was Leah Vania's first day at school. School! How long she had dreamed of it, wishing to be old enough. Now she could learn to read. She had seen the grownups with their books, studying English, squinting over the pages, and she had longed to be able to read a book. She could speak English already, so it could not be too hard for her to learn how to read words. Her heart was pounding with happiness as she skipped along the street with her hand in her Mama's. She was all dressed up in the dress her Mama had made for her first day at school, and her Mama was all dressed up too because it was the first time a child in the family, born in America, an American child, was going to an American school. Leah Vania knew she had been born in Brooklyn, New York, United States of America, and was a citizen.

They approached the large red building and suddenly Leah Vania was afraid she was going to cry. She choked back the tears and looked at her Mama, who was smiling proudly.

"Will you come for me at three o'clock, Mama?"

"Yes, of course, mein kind."

"You won't forget me?"

"I'll think about you all day and be happy."

"You promise you'll come?"

"I promise. I'll wait outside here until you are in. You go in this door here with the girls. Go. They look like nice girls. You'll meet friends. Go, and be good and do everything your teacher tells you."

Her home room was cool and smelled of dust and chalk and feet. There were boys and girls both in the class, all the same size and age, the ones who had been noisy in the street quiet and frightened now, all of them awed by their first day in the first grade. They had to line up and walk to the teacher single file. She was a tall, stern-looking woman with a huge bun, red. Leah Vania had never seen red hair before and she stared at it. It sat on the top of her head like a big tomato, and under it her face was long and white like a radish, the kind you made horseradish from. Her name was Miss White. She sat behind her huge desk with papers and pencils on it.

"Name?" she said.

"Leah Vania Saffron."

The teacher shook her head as if she were trying to get a fly out of her bun. "No, no, your American name."

"It *is* my American name. Leah Vania."

"Yes, well, from now on your name is Lavinia. We don't have foreign names here. Go sit in that row with the S's."

"Yes, ma'am," Leah Vania now Lavinia murmured, and went to the row where she was supposed to sit. The teacher had already forgotten her and was changing the next girl's name. Lavinia, Lavinia . . . it was pretty. It sounded like a flower of some kind, a scent. It sounded like lavender, that's what it sounded like. Mama kept lavender sachet in the dresser drawer with her secret things. Lavinia . . . it was so American!

Lavinia sat at her desk. Her old name sounded foreign now. She wanted to be like everybody else here and to be liked. She had been named after old dead relatives back in Russia, but this was Brooklyn, and Lavinia Saffron was the most beautiful name she had ever heard.

Miss White was standing now, talking to the class. "Keep your hands on top of your desk at all times. If I don't see your hands at all times I will hit them with this ruler." She waved the ruler menacingly. "No talking. You will answer questions when I call your name. If any of you has to go to the bathroom you will raise your hand and wait until I call on you, then you will ask permission." She pointed with her long, wooden ruler at the American flag hanging limply from a tall pole in the corner near where she stood. "Now, children, we will learn the Pledge of Allegiance to the Flag."

At three o'clock when the bell rang Lavinia raced out of doors with the other children, bursting with the need to shout, to giggle, to run, to move her aching legs and arms and back. She had never

27

sat so long, so stiffly, in one place in her life. It had been horribly embarrassing to raise her hand to ask to go to the bathroom in front of the boys, but worse to think of what would happen if she wet her bloomers. She had been so afraid someone might whisper to her and make her get hit by that big hard ruler that she had kept her eyes looking straight ahead at Miss White every minute, never even glancing at any of the other girls, and so she had not made any friends but she had not gotten hit either.

But it was all worth it even so, because finally, after learning that long boring pledge that they would have to recite every day, they had been given their first glimpse of the mystery of life: Miss White had written the alphabet on the blackboard. Lavinia had a notebook and some pencils which her Mama had bought her, and she had copied the letters into the notebook to study and learn. Soon they would be put together into words, and then she would be able to learn everything in the world.

"I love school!" she said to her Mama.

"I'm so glad. You must tell Papa. He'll be proud of you."

That night while he ate supper she told him. "I love school, Papa. We got the alphabet and we learned to pledge allegiance to the flag, and my teacher's name is Miss White."

He was obviously pleased with her. "Good, good. It's good that you should learn. I want you to be good and listen to your teacher."

"I do. And Papa, my name is Lavinia now. That's what Miss White said. It's my American name."

"Nu? American name?" he seemed amused.

"So please, Papa, could everybody in this house please call me Lavinia from now on?"

"You like it better than Monkey?"

"Yes, Papa."

"Very hoity-toity." His eyes twinkled and he pounded his fist on the table. "From now on everyone in this house will call Leah Vania Lavinia!"

"Vus? Vus?" her grandmother, the old witch, grumbled from her seat at the end of the table. She couldn't stand it when they spoke English.

"The child is telling us about school," Papa spoke in Yiddish.

"She talks too much," the old lady said.

For once Lavinia couldn't care less what the old witch said, because she was so happy that her Papa was pleased with her.

But such happiness had to end, and afterward she wondered how she could have been so dumb and innocent. School was a place where the teachers were always watching for ways to be cruel to the children, and the children always had to be on guard not to get hit or slapped or made fun of.

One day Lavinia knew her tooth was going to fall out. She moved it with her tongue, back and forth, trying to tell how long it would be before it came out altogether. She liked losing teeth because it meant she was growing up. This one was nearly ready to pop. If she just gave it a little nudge with her finger . . . she did, and it came out white and tiny in her hand. The hole filled with blood, which did not disgust her at all because she was used to it, and she swallowed it so it wouldn't mess her dress. But of course some did get on her dress, it always did.

"Ooh," the girl sitting next to her whispered, "you're all bloody!"

"Lavinia Saffron!" Miss White shrieked triumphantly, striding down the aisle between the desks, waving her famous wooden ruler. "You were talking!"

"No, ma'am," Lavinia said. "I didn't say a word." She held up the tooth. "I lost my tooth."

"You pulled out your tooth—*in class*—and then you had to tell your friend, didn't you?"

"I didn't tell her, she saw it."

"Liar! Liar!" Miss White grabbed Lavinia's arm and pulled her up out of the seat. "I hate a liar."

"I'm not a liar."

She was dragging her now, almost pulling her arm out of its socket, the ruler smacking her on the bottom, on the shoulder, on the backs of her legs, wildly. "I'll show you what I do with liars, Miss Liar."

The school room was completely silent. Miss White dragged Lavinia out into the hall, down the hall, and then opened a door and shoved her into a dark closet.

"In you go, Miss Liar," Miss White said, and slammed the door shut.

It took a few seconds for Lavinia's heart to stop pounding, and then she realized that her eyes were never going to get used to the dark in the completely dark closet. She couldn't tell which was front and which was back. Fuzzy shapes brushed the top of her head and she screamed and jumped away, hitting her shoulder on one wall. They were only coats, not bats. They smelled. There was no air in there, none at all. She was going to smother. She tried hard to breathe, but her terror and the closed-in darkness choked her and she knew she was going to die. It was so unfair! She began to cry, great gulping sobs, and felt the blood from the empty tooth socket running down her chin. She still had the little tooth clutched in her hand. Her tooth, a part of her, part of her life, her growing up. Now she would never grow up, she would die at six years old, and nobody would save her ever. Papa and Mama thought she loved school, they thought she was good, they didn't know that she was going to be murdered by Miss White. It would be a slow death, by suffocation. She lay on the floor and it felt fuzzy with dust. Maybe there were bugs there, maybe rats or spiders. She sprang to her feet in fear and felt the fuzz stuck to her chin, her face. She wiped her face with the skirt of her clean dress and tried to breathe, but the harder she tried the more she couldn't. She began to feel dizzy, and knew she was going to fall down.

And just before she fainted on the floor of the dark coat closet Lavinia knew one terrible last thing: she had wet her bloomers.

At three o'clock Miss White opened the door and pulled her out and told her to go home. Lavinia went to the girls' bathroom first and vomited into the toilet. Then she washed out her mouth and washed her face, drying it with the awful towels they gave you. She tried to wipe off as much of the dust and dirt and blood from her dress as she could. She smoothed her hair and then hurried downstairs and out of the building. She went home alone now, because she knew the way and Mama was busy with the other children.

She was relieved that no one she saw along the way paid her the slightest attention. They all seemed used to the sight of a little girl in a terrible mess and assumed she had been playing.

In the front of the apartment building where they lived there was a small yard—not much, just enough for some grass and a few flowers which the ladies like Mama planted to make the place look nice. There was Grandma, the old witch, in her black dress and her black wig which was always crooked, revealing some wisps of white hair, and her black kerchief tied over it, kneeling down in the front yard mumbling angrily to herself and burying something.

"Vas machst du, Grandma?" Lavinia called.

"Tref," the old woman snarled, "Tref, tref."

She was burying the silverware in the front yard, in front of the whole world to see!

"Grandma, why are you putting the silverware in the ground?" Lavinia asked her in Yiddish.

"The milk forks she used for meat, I saw her, and the spoons too. All of it, poisoned."

"Mama?" Lavinia said, surprised.

"No, the girl, stupid. They have a girl now, to help, a Polish, a goy. She tried to poison us all."

"But if you bury them we won't have anything to eat from."

"I'll take them out tomorrow, stupid. Then they'll be clean again."

"How can they be clean from being in the dirt?"

The old woman looked at her for the first time. "Dirt? You talk about shmutz, you, queen of shmutz, shmutz-face? How did you get so dirty? Your poor mama doesn't have enough to do without washing your dirty dresses too, and you're not even her daughter?"

"I am so her daughter, you old witch," Lavinia said, being careful to say 'old witch' in English so the old witch wouldn't understand her.

"You're not her daughter. You're an orphan. Orphan. Orphan."

"Oh, you're crazy," Lavinia said in English.

"Speak Yiddish!" the old witch said, furious at missing something.

"Why do you call me an orphan?" Lavinia said in Yiddish.

"Because your real mother is dead and your Mama is not your mama, she is only the mama of your sisters. You have no mama. I *know*, because I am the mother of both of them!" she finished triumphantly.

Lavinia felt a terrible fear. She couldn't remember, but somehow she knew that what the old witch said was true. She remembered the dreams she sometimes had at night of a woman without a face, tall, in a dark cloak, running away from her, and of herself running after this faceless woman, not knowing who she was but somehow feeling herself choking with pain and knowing that she needed this stranger. The woman in her dream must have been her dead mother, but she could not remember her and she knew only her own Mama, whom she adored, and who loved her. If her Mama wasn't her mama, why did she act as if she was? Maybe she didn't know either. Maybe only the old woman knew. If Lavinia didn't tell her then she would never know. Did Papa know? She was tired from her horrible day and it was all too much to figure out. She went into the house.

By the time anyone noticed her she had put the soiled dress and stockings and bloomers into the wash hamper for the new girl to launder and had washed her face and hands very well with good soap and dried them with her own clean towel. She brushed the top of her hair—luckily not much could happen to braids—and put on clean bloomers and stockings and her play dress. Mama was in her room, lying on the bed.

"So, mein kind? How did it go today?"

"Good, Mama."

"Did you learn well?"

"Yes, Mama." She could not bear to wait another minute; she threw herself on top of her mother and buried her face in her neck, the way she used to when she was a baby. "I love you, Mama."

"I love you, too, shaina maidel. Oooh, what's this, such a big hug? You have to be careful now, Lavinia, my big girl. I'm going to have another baby."

"A boy?"

"Maybe."

"That's why we have the Polish girl to help out?"

"You saw her?"

"Yes," Lavinia lied.

"You can help teach her English," Mama said. "Now that you're such a good student."

"All right. And look, I lost a tooth. I saved it for you." She held out the tooth proudly.

"Thank you."

She noticed how tired her mama sounded, as if it were hard for her to breathe. Her face was flushed but her hands seemed damp and cold. It must be hard to have babies.

"Are you having the baby now, Mama?"

"No, no, not until the spring. I want to rest now a little. You go in the kitchen and see the Polish girl makes the baby's food right."

"Yes, Mama."

She went to the kitchen to help out. She would be good, she would help, she would be smart in school, and she would never tell either Mama or Papa anything bad that ever happened to her, ever again. Then they would think she was perfect, and even if she really was an orphan they wouldn't want to give her away. She would be the best one of all their children.

FOUR

The immigrants were coming in torrents. The ships disgorged them from steerage, tired, seasick, frightened, hopeful, excited. Some had come to join family, some for an arranged marriage, some just because it had been unbearable where they had been and America had to be better. Some of them had nobody to meet them. But those who were related to Adam Saffron, no matter how distantly, always had a scrap of paper with an address on it clutched in their hands and knew when they got there they would have a place to stay.

"Another greenhorn is coming," Adam would say to Lucy, and then she would find someplace for the foreigner to sleep, even if it was the floor. Adam would find a job in a factory for the greenhorn, and at night there were classes in English at night school, so that although the apartment was always filled with strangers babbling in strange tongues and wearing odd-looking clothes, they were really hardly ever there, and so it did not disturb the pattern of family life very much. Although there was another mouth to feed there were also two new capable hands to help out, to wash dishes, to cook some special dish remembered from home with nostalgia, to hold a cranky baby.

When Adam had any extra money he sent it home to his family in Russia, for he knew Jews were having a hard time there and he believed America was to be his family's salvation. His family in Russia saved too, and they came one by one, in order of age. First Isaac, his oldest brother, thirty-eight years old and set in his ways, who hated America with all its strangeness and went back to Russia as soon as he could save the passage money. A waste, the ingrate, everyone said; but then he was so old, and it was hard for a middle-aged man to learn new ways.

Next came his brother Solomon Saffron, with his wife, a cousin. They had been intelligentsia in Russia, spending long hours talking of intellectual things with their friends, respected. Now they were not respected, for they could no longer express their thoughts in this new tongue, and even when they spoke in the old one no one had time to listen. Solomon refused to work in a factory, so Adam set him up with a small candy store. Solomon felt humiliated.

Adam had better luck with his placid older sister Hepzibah, whom he brought over with her husband and their two children. They stayed, grateful and content, moving into a small apartment in Mudville. Hepzibah's husband was a tailor, and did well enough.

Zipporah came over soon afterward, so close in age and temperament to her sister Hepzibah that they might have been twins. The two sisters were overjoyed to be together again, and Zipporah and her husband moved into an apartment right next door to Hepzibah's.

Now there were only two more whose turn was to come: first it would be Bena, and finally, when the money was saved, the youngest sister, Rebecca. Adam had already spoken to a cousin about Bena, how good she was, how capable, how pretty. This cousin had a good job as a foreman in a factory, and he seemed interested in an arranged marriage, although he insisted on meeting the bride first. That didn't bother Adam. It was better that two people should be compatible. He wrote to his mother, explaining his plans for Bena, and enclosed the ticket for the boat. It would be good timing, for it was spring, and Lucy had finally given him his first son, a fine lively boy.

Lucy seemed to have more and more trouble breathing. At first she had thought it was from carrying the child, who was a large one, but after the birth she was no better. One doctor said it was her lungs, another her heart. Neither seemed sure, but both agreed she should have rest and not have to care for her children until she was stronger. Bena could help with the baby, and in this family setting she could meet the young man who was intended for her, and he would be sure to be pleased. There was nothing like the sight of a pretty young woman with a child in her arms to inspire a man who was thinking of marrying; Adam knew that as well as anyone. He hadn't seen Bena for a long time, but his mother wrote that she had grown up to be the prettiest girl in the family, and his mother was a wise and critical woman whom Adam trusted.

FIVE

It was not a very long journey from their town to where the ships would leave, but long enough so that Papa couldn't go with them because he would miss four days of work. Rebecca helped her Mama pack Bena's things, while Bena hurried to finish the tiny stitches on the fine new woolen dress she would wear on the ship. It would do for the cool days at sea, and would not be too hot for the nights below in steerage, for the girls had heard frightening stories of how crowded it was.

"Is it true people bring their goats with them?" Bena asked. She was not happy, and had not eaten anything for two days. She was nervous about the adventure. Becky envied her; if it were she who was going she would be singing with happiness.

"Goats?" her Mama said. "Of course not. Who would bring a goat on the ship with people?"

"Well, that's what Fanny told me," Bena said, looking near tears. "She said her brother wrote her that there were goats and chickens on the ship and it wasn't fit for pigs."

"And how would Fanny's brother know about a pig?" Mama said. That was her way, to talk sideways, always to get out of things. She often said that it was her brains that had made Adam become such a success in America.

"You could bring your cat then!" Becky said. "Couldn't she, Mama? It would be company for her and she wouldn't get homesick."

"She will bring no cat," Mama said.

Becky knew that was true; there would hardly be enough room for the hamper of clothes and personal things Bena was bringing with her to America. It was hard to believe that once there she would never come back, and Papa and Mama would probably never see her again. In a few years, maybe sooner, Becky herself would be joining her, and then she would never see her parents again. She didn't want to think about that. Mama and Papa could go to America if they wanted to, but they were too old and they didn't want to. Her oldest brother Isaac had come back with a long face, saying the new land was no place for people of their age, and if he had not been able to adjust there then certainly their parents could not. Isaac the old bachelor lived with them, and helped Papa out in the store. Isaac and Papa liked to sit and read, and talk for hours about things which Becky couldn't understand, like the philosophy of the Torah.

"Daydreaming again," Mama said, giving Becky a nudge. "Go get the bread I made, and the cheese and fruit. Bena, go drink some milk. You won't have fresh milk again until you get to America, and by then you'll be so skinny and ugly that no man will want you, unless you fatten up now."

Becky giggled. Bena was the sleek, plump, pretty one, and it was unlikely that the voyage would make much difference. All the boys in their village were after Bena. It was she, Rebecca, who was a scrawny little vons, twenty years old and looking sixteen, nothing to speak of on top and not much more below, and such tiny little bones that Papa could put his hands around her waist and his fingers would meet. Their Mama traveled around the countryside in her wagon, selling calico and woolen materials to the peasant women, and she had saved the best of all for Bena's hamper.

"You're a lucky girl," Mama said to Bena. "Most girls go to America with hardly more than the dress on their backs, but you have everything you'll need for years and years. A young man will be happy to marry a girl who's not only pretty but won't cost him a penny for clothes. And who has her wedding sheets so beautifully embroidered."

For they were there, at the very bottom of the hamper: the beautiful wedding sheets, the finest linen, a fortune they cost. There were pillowcases too, everything made over the years by Mama and Bena.

How lucky Bena was, and she didn't even seem to care. She had always had everything she wanted. It was Becky who had climbed trees when they were children, to pick the sweetest fruit, and Bena who was content to wait until they dropped on the ground.

It was Becky who ran down the road when she saw their Mama's wagon in the distance, excited to find out what stories she had to tell of the far-off places, even if they were only farms that were not so far away at all. It was Bena who helped Mama count the money, and Becky who begged for stories. Bena had a pet cat, a white one, while Becky indiscriminately loved every cat in the neighborhood; but Bena was leaving her pet cat behind and didn't even seem to care. It was Becky who had dreamed all her life of going to America, and Bena who was going. No one had ever bothered to make beautiful clothes for Becky's wedding because Becky was still growing, Mama said. But she was twenty years old! They all still thought she was a child because she was so small.

Bena finished the last stitch on her new wool dress and Mama heated the heavy iron in the fireplace to press out the wrinkles. Papa and Isaac came in and washed their hands, and then they all sat down to eat their last meal together as a family.

When they finished the meal the men went out in front of the house where it was cool to rest and talk, and Bena took a bath. "Your last bath until you reach America," Mama said. "Soap yourself twice."

Then she put on her new dress and the fine, new leather shoes Mama had bought to go with it. Becky watched Bena brushing her long, shiny hair, and wondered what she was thinking. She was so quiet. Well, it was a moment both happy and sad.

During the long trip in Mama's wagon Mama treated Bena like a piece of glass. Don't touch this, don't touch that, don't get yourself dirty. She wouldn't even let Bena peel a piece of fruit; Becky had to do it for her. Bena sat stiffly in the back of the wagon, her hat on her head, the hamper strapped in beside her, looking straight ahead as if she were dead. Why, I would be singing, Becky thought.

None of them had ever seen anything so enormous as that ship—except Mama, of course, who had seen such a ship take away all her children but these two and Adam, who had been the first, the one who ran away. Imagine, Becky thought, he ran away and had no idea what he was going to find! She hardly remembered him because he had started running away when he was nine years old, first to another town, then to relatives, then home for Pesach, then away again, and finally when he was younger than she was now, to America.

Some men hoisted Bena's hamper on board the ship. She had her ticket and her papers clutched in her hand, everything in order. Mama was smiling, but for the first time there were tears in her eyes.

"Go," Mama said. She hugged and kissed her daughter. "Go." Bena just stood there.

"Hurry," Mama said. "You'll lose your luggage in all that crowd." There were people pushing their way on board the ship, whole families with children and babies. Becky was looking for goats.

"Go, go," Mama said.

Suddenly Bena turned very pale and she thrust her ticket and papers into Becky's hand. "You go," she said. "I'm not going."

If she had been crying or hysterical they would not have believed her. They would have comforted her and finally pushed her up the gangplank, for Mama knew how to handle tears. But this calm Bena, this pale Bena with clenched teeth and out-thrust jaw, was a stranger to them. "I am not going, Mama," Bena said in a low, firm voice. "I have thought about it and I will not go, I cannot go. If you make me go I will jump overboard and drown myself."

"Bite your tongue!" Mama whispered.

"I mean it," Bena said, and they knew she did.

"The papers . . . so long to get . . . the passage . . ." Mama was saying, but they were only words, for she was looking at Becky, looking up and down to see if she was suitable, if she could survive.

"Let me go, Mama!" Becky said. "Oh, please!"

"All those clothes . . ." Mama said sadly, looking at the hamper where it glistened in the sun on the deck with all those other, battered pieces of luggage from all the peasants.

"America is the land of milk and honey and I'll grow fat in no time," Becky said. "Then they'll all fit me."

"So young . . ." Mama said. She looked at both girls: the strong one who had turned weak and the weak one who had turned so unexpectedly strong. "All right," she said. Her voice was decisive now, the voice both girls knew so well. "The papers say Bena Saffron, so Becky, you are Bena now. From now on you must tell everyone that is your name. When you get to Immigration you just show them your papers and they won't pay any attention to you. You go to Adam's house and you obey him just as if he were your Papa. You help with the home and the children and make yourself useful."

"Yes, Mama."

"God knows, that poor boy, he won't want to marry you, expecting your sister, but Adam will find you someone else."

Becky giggled.

Her Mama hugged and kissed her. "Maybe God has his plans," she said.

Becky kissed her Mama and Bena, and then ran up the gangplank, worried the ship might leave without her. She stood at the rail as the ship pulled away, waving at her Mama as long as she could still see her in the crowd on the wharf. She was so excited that she didn't feel the slightest bit homesick or sad. If she didn't like it in America she could always come home. The truth was, she didn't have the slightest idea how far away America was, or what she would find there, but she knew it would all be wonderful. God had his plans, and it had been planned all along by God that *she* would go. And all those lovely things in the hamper would be hers, and the happy life that went with them. She was Bena now, and she felt as if she had taken on her sister's skin with her identity papers. She actually felt herself becoming pretty.

"Oh, thank you, God," Becky-Bena breathed, and she had never been so happy in her life.

SIX

It was Lavinia who took the younger children to school on their first day, one by one, and Lavinia who named them. First her beautiful blonde sister: "When the teacher asks your name you tell her Melissa."

"Why?"

"Because when you go to school you have to have an American name, and if you don't say one she'll give you one. How would you like it if you had a horrid name for the rest of your life?"

"Melissa."

"Melissa Saffron."

Melissa shrugged. She wasn't anxious to go to school; she liked playing out of doors with her friends. There was never a child who had so many friends. She climbed trees and jumped rope, she made up little plays to act out with the other girls, she gave tea parties for her dolls and invited the whole neighborhood.

School was different for Melissa than it had been for Lavinia, for Melissa didn't care. She hated studying and hardly ever did her homework, but because she was so pretty the teachers were partial to her. Whenever she did get hit she really didn't seem to care; she loved to whisper to her friends and if she got caught, well, that was the price you had to pay. She loved to sing and dance, and dreamed of learning to play the piano. When the class sang "The Star-Spangled Banner" it was Melissa's voice that soared out above the rest of them, a sweet, pure soprano. She was the essence of everything that was feminine, and if she stumbled over her reading or did not remember her multiplication table, her huge, guileless green eyes said that after all, what business did a little girl have with such matters?

Lavinia knew that Melissa was a fake. She was a little devil, and she was smarter than most of them, but she was lazy. She did exactly as much schoolwork as she had to, and she was always testing her teachers to see if she could get away with doing a little less. She was all energy and dreams. Yet, although she was so different from her sister, she adored Lavinia. They were very close, two sides of the same universe; one the sad, serious moon, the other the bright insouciant sun. Melissa knew that she had Papa and Mama and Lavinia and the world. Lavinia feared that she had no one. If Papa gave Melissa a smack for disobeying, Melissa knew it was only a smack. It was Lavinia who brooded over slights and injuries, who promised herself never to forget. Melissa cried whenever she couldn't have her way. Lavinia never cried any more.

Lavinia loved books. It was from her books that she chose the children's names. After Melissa came Hazel. Hazel neither looked nor acted like her two sisters. She had a flat, sullen face, with little bewildered eyes, neither green like Melissa's nor brown like Lavinia's, but a sort of muddy combination of both. She thrust her jaw out like a turtle, stubborn, slow. She couldn't understand what they understood, and she was angry because no one waited to listen to her. But she was so slow! She could hardly get the words out. At first she screamed when she found herself ignored; later when she was older and stronger she devised a simple method of being noticed: like a turtle she snapped hold of the victim's arm with her two strong hands instead of jaws, and held on until her mind and tongue could form the words, no matter that it was finally nonsense.

The family simply ignored Hazel's problem. It was the easiest way, and they did not really understand it. Only Lavinia, "the orphan," felt compelled to defend her. "She has a fat tongue," she would say, and everyone accepted that.

The first-born boy was named Andrew by Lavinia, and that is what the family called him, except of course for the old witch, who was still living with them, and who called all the children by their Hebrew names except Lavinia. She called Lavinia "Orphan." There was a curious bond of hate between Lavinia and her grandmother. Lavinia was the only one of the children who knew Yiddish, therefore she was the only child who could ever communicate with the old woman. She felt compelled to fight with her, and the old woman felt compelled to pick on this child, simply because she was an old woman whom everyone ignored. Her daughter Polly was dead, her son was dead, her youngest daughter, Lucy, lay panting and sickly in bed for weeks at a time, and her son-in-law kept her on in his house out of pity, not respect. The old woman knew this, and she knew that the only person who was in the natural order to receive less respect than she did was this argumentative child.

Although her life was ruled by superstitions she was clever. She knew that the matter of the orphan was between herself and the child and Lucy and Adam would not tolerate it, and so she kept it their secret, hissing "Orphan!" at this fierce little girl, pulling her braids, smirking when the child went running to her Papa to tell.

"Grandma pulled my hair again."

"And what did you do to deserve it?"

"She was rude to me," the old woman would say.

Adam would cuff Lavinia then, always taking the side of the older one, who was due more respect. "Don't back talk your Grandma!"

41

"I didn't!"

"She did, she did," the old woman would crow. Why wouldn't the child cry? She could see tears in the blazing little eyes, but the jaws would clench and the child would stand there rigid, glaring at her, wishing for her death, longing for the day she could pretend to cry at the old woman's funeral.

Such hate! But it was better than being ignored, and at the end of a long life when one was lonely and ignored, it was interesting. If one could be hated then one was still worth reckoning with.

When Mama had a second boy, Lavinia began naming the children when they were born, without waiting for them to reach school age. She named this one Basil. She wanted the whole family to be American now, to fit in. Basil was a distinguished name, graceful. Basil Saffron . . . he could become a famous businessman. It was an English name, and it was also the name of an herb. Lavinia had found books about flowers in the school library.

When Mama had a little girl, Lavinia named her Rosemary.

"That's a Catholic name," Melissa said. "There's a Catholic girl in my class and her name is Rosemary Feeney, and her family comes from Ireland."

"Don't be silly," Lavinia said. "If she was Catholic she would be in a school with the nuns."

Melissa chewed her lip. "I guess you're right."

"Rosemary happens to be the name of a beautiful-smelling herb," Lavinia said. "It was a name celebrated in poetry and beautiful stories."

"It's pretty, anyhow," Melissa said.

The photographer came to take a picture of all of them for their Papa's thirty-sixth birthday. There was Papa, stern and distinguished, and next to him Mama, always frail, but having one of her better days. Beside them was Lavinia, then Melissa, with a great bow in her hair, and in front the smaller ones: Hazel, sturdy Andrew, Basil holding a ball, and little Rosemary, sitting on a chair holding her pet kitten. It was the gray and white kitten Basil had tried to cook by putting it into the oven in a pot, and it was only by luck that the servant girl had discovered it and saved its life. Now Rosemary wouldn't let it out of her sight.

"Smile," the photographer said. "Hold still. Look at the birdie." He would crouch under a black cloth and set off a flash of light and a puff of smoke, but there was no birdie. Lavinia didn't like him because he was ugly. His skin was pockmarked and his teeth were broken and brown. Her Papa didn't like ugly people, and neither did she. She wanted to be exactly like her Papa when she grew up.

Papa was very pleased with his birthday photograph, and had a large one made and framed to sit on top of his bureau. They were going to move to a private house in the spring, where there would be enough room for all of them including Grandma and Aunt Becky, and any greenhorns who came to stay for a while, and there would be a whole top floor just for the two Irish girls who worked for them now, cleaning the house and doing the laundry. In the new house they would have a grand piano in the living room, and on top of the piano there would be a fashionable fringed Oriental shawl, and on top of the shawl would be the framed photograph. None of them was smiling in it, no matter what the photographer said; they knew better than that. Suitably solemn and dignified, they were the very image of a refined, intelligent, prosperous American family.

Aunt Becky had been with them for a long time now. Lavinia remembered when she came, looking like a little girl, with a big box full of pretty dresses that were all much too big for her. Papa had gotten Aunt Becky a job in a factory, but she hadn't liked it, and so she would come home in the middle of the day, saying: "I had a vision that one of you children fell out the window and so I had to rush home." After doing that once or twice Aunt Becky would lose the job, and Papa would have to find her another one, but it was always the same. She would be back home by lunchtime, insisting she'd had "a vision." Finally Papa just gave up and let her stay home. She learned English at night school, and Lavinia tried to help her, although she was too young to be of any real help. Mama helped Aunt Becky fix the dresses so they would fit, taking them in at the seams and shortening them. Aunt Becky told the children the story of Aunt Bena, how she wouldn't get on the boat at the last minute and so Aunt Becky had come in her stead. The cousin who had been intended to marry Aunt Bena had taken one look at Aunt Becky and run away, which was fine as far as Aunt Becky was concerned because she didn't like him either.

The years went by and Aunt Becky stayed on in their home,

content, but Papa had begun to worry about her, and thought it was time she had a husband. Since she couldn't seem to find one on her own, he would have to find one for her. She was nearer thirty than twenty, no longer a silly girl, and some good man would be glad to have her.

The children split into cliques: Lavinia and Melissa were together, Hazel had no one, Andrew chased after Lavinia; and Basil and Rosemary, being close in age, were close friends. Lavinia would have thought that Andrew and Basil, being brothers, would have been close, but they were very different in temperament and there was jealousy between them. Andrew was a worrier, a conniver, a planner. He wanted a pony and he asked for one; Papa gave it to him. Basil, on the other hand, wasted his time feeling sorry for himself. "Andrew got a pony," he would whine. "I wanted a pony, but Papa never gave me one. Papa gave Andrew a pony, not me."

"You never *asked* him for a pony," Lavinia said.

"Papa likes Andrew better than me."

"Quitter," Lavinia said. "You'll never get anywhere in life if you don't fight for it."

"Andrew gets everything. I never get anything."

Much as he delighted in his pony, Andrew was busy thinking of something new to wish for, to ask for, to get, to prove that he, not his brother, was the favorite.

He admired Lavinia because she was older and had a way of taking over. Because he admired her, he teased her, pleased to have found a way of getting close to her. Andrew knew that Lavinia wanted them all to be American, that she hated it when anyone spoke Yiddish in front of strangers. He only knew a few words, but it was his delight to chase her down the street in front of amused onlookers, imitating a goat. "Tsigeleh maaaaa!" he would bleat, while Lavinia, all dignity forgotten, ran away from him, her face red. It was not the goat baa she minded, it was the "tsigeleh."

"Play with Hazel," Lavinia would tell Rosemary. Rosemary had her kitten in the doll carriage, and Lavinia had put a doll's dress on it.

"No," Rosemary said.

"Don't be selfish."

"She's stupid," Rosemary said.

"Shh! Shame on you. Sisters should love each other."

"Then you play with her," Rosemary said. "My kitten has an appointment to see the doctor. She's going to have puppies."

Before they moved to the new house the old grandmother died. She had been their link to an old and vanished time, and now she was gone and buried. Gone her musty black dresses, her permanent mourning, gone the black sheitel, gone the spitting on the floor and the tossing of salt over the shoulder to keep away evil, the endless search to root out tref, the prayers, the curses. Gone the old witch, gone the snarls of "Orphan!" Now they were all one family. Lavinia was very relieved.

SEVEN

Adam had found a prospective husband for Becky. His name was Isman Levine, and he was two years younger than she; a short, ruddy-faced, timid, eager young man. Adam had told him that if he decided to marry Becky, and she would have him, then he would set Isman up in his own business, with a haberdashery store. Not a big one, of course, but a nice one with prospects for a young man who was willing to work hard. As their family grew, so the business would grow, and Isman was grateful and eager to try.

Becky looked at herself in the glass, waiting for her first meeting with Isman Levine. Isman meant "a good husband" in Hebrew, which was a good sign. She hoped he would find her pretty. Bena had written to her from back home, telling her that she had married Mattis Andreyov, the handsomest young man in town. Now Bena had two handsome little sons and a daughter as beautiful as herself. It was time for *her* to marry, to have children. She could not go on forever pretending Lucy's little ones were her own, content to dream of her mystery husband as if she were still sixteen.

Melissa came to the bedroom door and knocked.

"Come in."

"He's here, Aunt Becky." The child had a little smile on her face, half mischief, half awed envy. She knew the man downstairs was Aunt Becky's future husband, and *she* had seen him before his bride had!

"What is he like?"

"He has light brown hair."

So. Not black. Not Mattis Andreyov, but then she was no Bena.

"Curly?"

"I think straight."

Ah. Straight. Well, perhaps he had a happy disposition and could make her laugh. It didn't matter if a man was no beauty if he could keep laughter in the home. "Do I look all right?"

"You look like a queen, Aunt Becky."

Becky kissed Melissa. Such a little liar! Such a flatterer, such an imp! Like a queen, imagine!

Becky walked down the stairs and went into the front parlor. Isman Levine was sitting on the green velvet chair, but when he saw her he stood up. She noticed that he was not much taller than she was. His light brown hair was combed back very straight and smelled faintly of pomade. She was touched. He must have wanted to make a good impression on her as badly as she had wanted to make one on him.

"Please sit," she said, and sat across from him on the chair's twin. She noticed that Lucy had put a bowl of fruit and some plates and napkins on the low table between them, and a small silver bowl of almonds and raisins.

"I am Isman Levine," he said.

"I know," Becky said gravely. Who did he think she thought he was? The man in the moon? Ah, no, but she should not be so critical. He was as shy as she was, and he probably couldn't think of anything to say. "A piece of fruit?" she offered.

"Not right now, thank you."

She held out the silver bowl of almonds and raisins. "Oh, thank you," he said. "My favorite." But he took only a few, and then he held them in the palm of his hand, tossing them up and down. His eyes met hers for a moment and he looked away. Why, the man is blushing, Becky thought, and her heart went out to him.

"Perhaps you're thirsty?" she said.

"Oh, please don't trouble yourself."

"It's no trouble." She was relieved to go into the kitchen for a moment to collect her thoughts.

Lavinia and Melissa were hiding behind the kitchen door. "Scat!" Becky whispered fiercely. "Don't you dare listen." Melissa was stifling a giggle and Lavinia's eyes were as big as saucers. "What do you think you're going to hear? Grown-up secrets? Go away." The two little girls ran up the back stairs. Becky filled a pitcher with cold lemonade and put it with two glasses on a tray.

"It's a warm night," she said to him. "I thought cold lemonade would be better than hot tea."

"It looks very nice."

They drank lemonade solemnly and both of them looked at his shoes. What small feet he had, Becky thought. She imagined those feet dancing, graceful, lively, and pictured herself dancing with him.

"I like to dance," Becky said. "We used to have dances back home. People don't dance so much here, and I sometimes miss it. Do you like to dance?"

This time she was sure he blushed. "I . . . not much," he said.

"You don't know how?" she said kindly. "But that's nothing to be ashamed of. I would be glad to teach you, not that I'm so good myself."

"No, it's not that."

"You're not Orthodox?"

"Oh, no."

"Then you're shy," Becky said. "That's nothing to be ashamed of either. I myself am more shy than I seem to be."

"Yes, I am sometimes shy too," Isman Levine said. "But I must tell you the truth, because you would see it anyway. I don't dance because . . . because, you see, I have a small limp."

A cripple! Oh, God forbid, Adam wouldn't bring her a cripple to marry, never! She must have had a terrible look on her face because suddenly Isman Levine stood up.

"Look," he said. He began to walk from one end of the room to the other, and it really was quite a small limp, nothing to shock a person. "See, it's really not a big limp, but my foot hurts a little, and so I don't like to dance. But I'm not a cripple. I can make a good living, and I would be a good husband and father. It's not because of the limp that I haven't married before this, it's simply that I wasn't ready."

Oh, the poor man! Becky felt a lump in her throat and tears filled her eyes and, before she knew it, spilled out for this gentle young man who was demeaning himself by walking before her so she could see his limp.

"Oh, please sit down!"

"I have disgusted you."

"Oh, no, no. It's not right that a man should have to shame himself in such a way in front of a woman. Please sit down, I beg you. If you hadn't told me about the limp I wouldn't even have noticed it."

"Really?"

"Of course not."

"I'm so used to it," he said. "I hardly ever think about it. I never had time to play games as a boy, anyway, because I had to go to religious instruction after school, and then I had to help my family."

"You're a scholar, then?"

"No, no. My parents were religious, but I suppose all parents are more religious than their children."

"Yes," Becky said, not really ever having thought about it one way or the other.

"Things are different today," he said. He was quite comfortably settled into the green chair again, one leg crossed over the other, the shiny leather boot dangling gracefully. She could not even remember which foot it was which was lame. "When my father married my mother, he never even saw her until after the ceremony when she lifted the veil. But today we can not only see our intended bride, we can even pick her."

"It must have been quite dreadful in the olden days," Becky said.

"For me," Isman Levine said, "I'm happy to be living here and now. I am sitting in this comfortable house, with this lovely young lady, and I am thinking . . . do you know what I'm thinking?"

"No. What?" Becky said.

"Well, I'm thinking: I wonder if she would be willing to marry me?"

At that moment Becky thought she was almost in love with him. Imagine, the tact of the man, the humbleness of him, to pretend that she had a choice, that he was her suitor, that it had not all been arranged already by Adam. It would never have occurred to her to say, no, I will not marry you. Adam had chosen this man, Adam had brought him here, and that was enough for her. Yet here he was, this Isman Levine, asking her if she was willing to marry him!

"I think I would be most willing to marry you," she said.

He smiled, a sweet smile, and her heart began to pound. Isman Levine would be good to her. They could have a life together.

"Then I am very happy," he said.

Becky smiled. "So am I."

She went then to call Adam and Lucy and the children, which was not difficult because everyone was listening already, except for the smaller children, who were asleep. Lucy sent Lavinia and Melissa to bed, and then Adam and Lucy and Isman and Becky sat there in the front parlor and made conversation, just like two couples. Isman now gobbled up three pieces of fruit, and Becky was pleased.

After a nice little visit Isman said goodnight and went home. Adam said that he lived alone in a room because his parents both were dead. Becky had seen those advertisements in the newspaper: "Room for refined, single Jewish lady or gentleman. Good meals." She had always thought it was sad to have to live that way, and she could hardly wait until she and Isman were married so she could make him a good home.

When she went upstairs to her bedroom Becky found Lavinia and Melissa cuddled together on her bed in their nightgowns. "What are you bad girls doing here?" she whispered, delighted to see them and share some of her joy.

"Do you like him?" Melissa whispered.

"Yes, of course."

"Tell us everything he said," Lavinia said.

"No, I won't," said Becky. "Some things are private. And besides, I heard you little mice sniffing behind the door."

"We couldn't hear anything," Lavinia said. "The kitchen is two whole rooms away."

"Did he get down on his knees to propose?" Melissa asked.

"Where did you get such an idea?"

"They always do that in novels, don't they, Lavinia?"

"Yes," said Lavinia. "But that doesn't mean real people know how to do it."

"Did he?" Melissa said. "Did he? Tell us, Aunt Becky, don't be mean."

"I never even heard of such a silly custom," Becky said.

"And afterward," Melissa said, "did he kiss you?"

Becky felt her face flush. Kiss her? Why, she had not even thought about that. Isman Levine had walked into that house a total stranger, and to leave it having kissed her . . . it was a shocking idea.

"It's all right to kiss if you're engaged," Lavinia said.

"I bet he did," Melissa said. "Aunt Becky's blushing."

"How do you children know about such things?" Becky said, amazed.

"Everybody knows about kissing," Melissa said airily.

Everybody but me, Becky thought.

EIGHT

The Great War of 1914 brought changes to the Saffrons, but none that the children were really aware of. The boys were much too young to be drafted, and the girls were too young to know any of the young men who went off to war. Lavinia, the oldest, after all, was only seventeen when the war was all over. The major changes that came about due to the war were in Adam Saffron's business, and he seldom shared any of this information with the family.

Because of the war, the building business was, as Adam's new partner Klein said, "lou-say." There were no materials, no labor force, nothing. So Adam's family found that he was in the shipping business. He had been studying and learning the mechanics of running ships, and he was a good organizer as well as a man who traveled in different circles and was not afraid to go into a new business if an old one looked unprofitable. Ships were needed during a war to carry cargo as well as soldiers. If a man owned a freighter he could lease it to the government at a better price than he could get from private jobs, and if he could manage other people's freighters more economically and efficiently than other men could, then the government would be glad to hire him. So Adam ended up both owning a freighter of his own and managing several others. When the war was over he resumed building, but decided to stay in shipping as well.

Becky had married Isman Levine and was living in the Bronx with him and the three children they had had, three in four years. Isman's business, the one Adam had set him up in, had failed. It was due to the war, everyone said sympathetically, but Adam knew better. The man had turned out not to be a manager at all. But Becky was not young, she was not pretty, she was not rich, she was not exactly a catch, and at least Isman had a good character. So Adam set him up with another small store, this time shoes. People always needed shoes, and it would be as easy to get rid of his stock as it would be to dispense bread to the hungry.

But somehow that didn't seem to work either. The bookkeeper juggled the funds, the customers stayed away. "What did you expect?" said sharp-tongued Lavinia. "Getting a man with a limp to manage a shoe store! People will think he limps because the shoes pinch."

So Adam found Isman a job in a company owned by a friend who owed him a favor. A small job, one not requiring managing ability or even initiative. He was to do as he was told, and since Isman was ever eager to please, he would fit in well. He would never become a rich man now. But at least his children would not starve. Adam hoped Isman and Becky would restrain themselves and not have any more children.

Lucy was not well. She spent more and more time in bed, fighting for breath, and the doctor said she should have sea air. So she went to the seashore, accompanied by a widowed cousin and a maid. When she came back, no better, the doctor said mountain air was what she needed. So Lucy packed up the cousin and the maid and went to a resort hotel in the mountains. She could not even take her youngest, Rosemary, for the care of a child was too much for her in this exhausted state. Besides, Rosemary was at school all day now, and it was not good for a child to miss any of her education.

All the children took piano lessons, even the boys. Lavinia did as she was told, although she did not enjoy it, and rather fancied herself playing a mandolin. Melissa adored piano and had a natural talent. She could play both from sheet music and by ear, and liked to sing while she was playing. She dreamed of going on the stage. Her idol was Isadora Duncan, the Divine Isadora, and she liked to dress in flowing scarves and dance around the house, pretending she was already a star. She had grown up to be the beauty in the family. Her blonde wavy hair hung to her waist, and her large green eyes were set off by naturally dark lashes. She was slender and graceful, although not skinny, and boys already liked her, though luckily she couldn't care less for them.

Hazel was so hopeless at the piano that Adam decided to stop wasting money on her, hoping instead that she could just manage to get through grade school. She was thirteen and in the fifth grade. She could read and write, but her mind wandered, she could not manage her homework, she could not speak in class. She could neither cook nor sew. It would all have been bearable if she had been an ornament, but she was plain; and she was sullen and ill-tempered because she was just intelligent enough to know that she could not do what the others did, and that none of them had the patience to wait for her.

"Why doesn't anybody listen to me?" Hazel screamed once in one of her rare moments of coherence. "I'm not stupid! You all think I'm stupid, but I'm not."

"Of course you're not," Lavinia said. The others said nothing.

It was assumed that Andrew and Basil would go to college, then hopefully to law school, and then join their father in his businesses. There was not to be a doctor or a dentist in the Saffron family; a good doctor or a dentist you could hire, but every family needed a good lawyer of its own, loyal, honest, devoted, and filled with initiative.

As for the girls, they would marry. All of them had good characters, come from a strict moral upbringing, and each of them had some special quality of her own. Lavinia was exceptionally bright. Melissa was as pretty and graceful as a fairy princess. Hazel was easy to please. And little Rosemary was a musical genius. Only seven and a half, and she could play "The Minute Waltz," imagine! Her little fingers couldn't even reach an octave, but how they moved! And of course, God willing, they would all grow up to be rich, so it would not be hard to find them good husbands.

Lavinia, however, had plans of her own.

"Well, now, Lavinia," Adam said to her, a week before her graduation from high school, "You know I never give birthday presents because I can't remember birthdays and I think they're foolish, but a school graduation is a big event. So, you tell me what you want, whatever it is you're dreaming of, and I'll give it to you."

"Anything?" Lavinia said.

"Anything. You want even a motor car, I'll buy you one."

"All right," Lavinia said, "I would like you to pay my tuition at college."

"College?" He was amazed. "Why do you want to go to college?"

"I want to study psychology."

"What's that?"

"It's a new science."

"Science? We have a scientist in the family?" He was amused, but good-natured about it. After all, he had given her his word. "So how much does it cost, NYU or Hunter?"

"I'm going to Cornell."

"Cornell?" he said. "Where is that?"

"Ithaca, New York."

"Ithaca? Ithaca? Two days by train, you'll sleep away from home, you'll live in a strange place by yourself? What if you get sick? I won't allow it."

"I've already applied," Lavinia said calmly, "and I've been accepted. I will live in a dormitory with other girls, and older chaperones. I'll be perfectly safe."

"Chaperones?" he said. "There are boys there, too?"

"Of course. It's a university. But they have their own dormitories and they can't come in to bother the girls. Papa, I'm going to college to study, to get a degree, not to meet boys. I can meet boys at home."

"I never said it was wrong to want an education," he said. "I always admired intelligent people. But you're a girl—a girl doesn't go away from home to live with strangers."

"I want to go to college, Papa. I want to go to *this* college. I sent for all the booklets and this one has the best psychology department. Please."

"To go away from home . . ."

"You went away from home when you were younger than I am

now, and you went much farther away."

"Nu, so a boy is different."

"These are modern times, Papa."

He was thinking. He had made up his mind, but still, it was good to wait, to see what she would say, if she was really sure about this. She waited too, calmly: she was wise to him, she knew his ways and she knew he admired her. "And if I don't pay this tuition?"

"Then I'll have to get a job. I can wait on tables at college, other girls do. And I can apply for a scholarship. My marks are high enough. It's too late for this term, but I can work this term."

"A waitress? Adam Saffron's daughter a waitress?"

"And of course I'd have to wash dishes too," Lavinia added casually. "But I'm quite good at that."

"With two maids at home you want to wash dishes."

"I want to have a degree in psychology from Cornell."

He looked at her, his little spitfire, his third son. He noticed that she had grown up to be quite pretty, with a softness to her face that compensated for the shrewdness that sparked from her eyes and burned everyone it landed on. The boys would chase her. But he was secure in the way he had brought up all his girls, and he knew she would stay out of trouble. He knew perfectly well that Lavinia would wash dishes all night, every night, if it gave her what she had set her heart on.

"All right," Adam said. "I'll pay for your college."

"Oh, thank you, Papa!" She flung her arms around his neck, the way she had when she was a little girl.

"And see that you study hard and get good marks," he said, pretending to be stern, but he already knew that she would.

NINE

Lavinia knew that they were the elite. In the evenings, snuggled in flannel nightgowns and robes and slippers, homework finished, they would all sit in someone's room, six or seven of them, gorging on packages from home, giggling, gossiping. They were college girls. That meant not only that they were bright, but that they had guts. They had all come here from far-away places, some of them from as far as the South, most of them over the protests of their anxious parents. Most of them were homesick. In the first month she was at Cornell Lavinia chose her group of closest friends, the girls she would be close to for the next four years. They were not all from the same background as hers. Some of them were not even Jewish. Two of them were on scholarships, which made her respect them more because they had to be bright. One of them was from her own neighborhood in Brooklyn, and one of them was from Alabama. Only one other girl besides Lavinia was a psychology major, and she changed her mind after the first term and switched to English. None of them really planned to teach when they graduated; they had simply come to learn. And that was what, in Lavinia's mind, made her group of friends the elite, because they cared about knowledge for knowledge's sake.

There were serious girls who seemed almost angry, who did not try to look clean and neat and who never smiled. Lavinia kept away from those girls, who always seemed to have something to protest, some cause to get riled up about. They had come to college out of a kind of vengeance for having been born female, or poor, or ugly, and they made Lavinia nervous. Then there were the frivolous girls, who had come to college to get away from home and have a good time. They chased the boys and spent very little time thinking about their studies. They were known as wild, and Lavinia avoided them too, because she was scrupulous about her reputation.

Although she loved her friends and enjoyed her classes, there were times when Lavinia was so homesick she wondered why she hadn't chosen a school near home, so she could eat dinner every night with her own family instead of slops in that cold dining room, and sleep in her own warm bed instead of that hard, lumpy one. But then, on cold clear mornings, with the white snow shoulder high and the sky so blue, muffled up to the eyes in her wool scarf, her hat pulled down to her eyebrows, she would peer out at this academic world that had become her world and she would feel a great joy. She wondered if there would ever be time to read all the psychology books that had been written, time to unlock all the mysteries of human behavior. All her life Lavinia had been told that people were as they were, either good or bad, but now she knew it was not so. People could be shaped.

She was not yet ready to understand herself, because so much of it was so painful, but she knew that in time she would.

It was in college that Lavinia learned about sex. She had always known about sex in the sense that men and women got married and had babies: Mama had had all her babies at home and although no one but the midwife had been allowed into the bedroom, the children accepted pregnancy and birth as natural happenings of life. Rosemary's kitten had grown into a cat, had had litters, and they in turn had grown up, all of them a nuisance, those which did not run away had to be given away. But beyond the fact that birth was a natural part of life, Lavinia did not know much else, and there was no one at home to ask. Mama would have been too embarrassed. It was out of the question to ask Papa, because he was a man and both he and Lavinia would have been too embarrassed. The only thing he ever said about sex was when he told Melissa: "If I find out that any of my daughters is not a virgin, I'll throw her out of the house." This was because Melissa was so popular, and Lavinia was a little annoyed that such unnecessary advice had been given to innocent, prudish little Melissa when she was the older one, the one who was about to go away from home into the dangerous world. Did Papa think she was *that* ugly, that boys wouldn't want to take her out?

The one to whom Lavinia had been closest was Aunt Becky, and now that Aunt Becky had three children she would have been the logical person to ask about such things, but the truth was Lavinia couldn't bring herself to do it. Besides, Aunt Becky was so old-fashioned, she probably didn't know what she had done to have those babies. Lavinia, in fact, would rather not have known, when she came to college and discovered that there were girls who did know; not only knew, but had done it, and were willing to talk about it to their closest friends.

These girls claimed to like it, but Lavinia suspected most of them were lying. How could you like something that was so furtive, so forbidden, so dangerous? She couldn't figure out why those girls had not become pregnant. When she had a class with one of the boys who had slept with a girl in her dorm, Lavinia could hardly look at him. He must be a skunk. If he had slept with that girl and wasn't in love with her, then he must have slept with lots of other girls. Who would ever marry those girls now? Certainly not a skunk like him. A nice boy would never marry them if the word got around. Why, he wasn't even handsome. And when one day after class he actually came up to her and tried to start a conversation, Lavinia just stuck her nose up in the air and walked away, leaving him staring after her. That was how she treated skunks, gave them what they deserved.

She did not date much. Some boys asked her to football games and dances, and sometimes she went, but she did not particularly like any of them. She went to the games and the dances because they were a part of college life. She had a slight crush on one of her professors, but she would never have dreamed of having anything to do with him because he was married. That was another thing Lavinia discovered at college that shocked her: some married professors sneaked out with girls. She could understand admiring a man, but what had happened to decency, to self-control? She was terrified of all these new things she was discovering. The old safe world she had grown up in was vanishing before her eyes. She had lived all her life with her family, with their friends, with the girls on the block and around the corner, whose parents were friends of her parents. Now she was in a community of strangers from all over the United States. If a boy whose life before this moment was a total mystery to you wanted to come up to you after class and ask for a date, he was allowed to do so. And you could accept, and find yourself alone at night with a strange man—yes, they were men now, not boys—and you had to rely on your wits and your natural decency to see that he treated you with respect. But some of these strangers were only after one thing. Papa would have had a fit if he had ever known, he would have dragged her right out of college. But Lavinia had a natural reserve, and there was something about her that seemed to frighten off the boys with the worst reputations. Perhaps it was her own good reputation.

A girl didn't need to go out with a boy to have a good time. You could go out in groups, which was more fun anyway, besides being safer. And you could go places with your own clique of girlfriends. When Lavinia was pledged to the sorority she most wanted to join, she was delighted. Now she really belonged, and she felt safe. The sorority house was so much nicer than the dorm, and the girls were all like sisters to each other. Most of the boys in their brother fraternity treated them with respect. You knew, at least, that they weren't total strangers.

She kept up good marks and studied hard. When she came home for vacations she sometimes brought a friend with her, one girl or another from her sorority whose home was far away and who wanted to see New York. She never accepted invitations to visit them, always making up some excuse; her mother was sick, her father needed her. The truth was, Lavinia had no desire whatsoever to visit anyone else. Vacations with her family were a treat she looked forward to. Who knew what kinds of homes those other girls lived in, if she would have to share a bathroom with strangers?

By her junior year at college Lavinia had learned another hard truth about life: not all her sorority sisters were what she had thought. Some were petty, some were slobs, some were dishonest, some disagreeable, some vengeful. One stole things. Another cheated on exams. One, she knew for a fact because everyone knew it, slept with boys. Not just one boy, but *boys*, plural. And when that girl left college in the middle of her junior year to get married, everyone knew why. She was darn lucky the boy was willing to marry her.

So this was the world. There were dangers in it, and not everyone was what he or she seemed. Knowing these things, Lavinia felt wise and worldly. Not all the interesting case histories were to be found in schoolbooks.

At the start of her senior year her adviser told her she should think about staying on to take a master's degree, then a doctorate.

"You have a great potential," he told her, "and there's a need for women in this work. You could teach, or you could work with sick people. I don't think you should let being a woman block you off from an academic career. So many bright students let their potential go by, just from lack of confidence."

But Lavinia had had enough of college. She was homesick and she was tired. She would graduate with honors, her Papa and, please God, her Mama too would see her graduate in her academic gown and mortarboard, and then she would go back to Brooklyn. Her Papa could frame her college diploma and put it on the wall of the room in their house he used as a study. She had all her schoolbooks, and she would always keep them. But enough was enough.

TEN

Melissa knocked timidly on the door of Papa's study. How she wanted him to say yes to her! Everyone said yes to Melissa; yes, and please, because she was so pretty and so winning. But with Papa you could never be sure what he would say. And she wanted this one thing more than anything else in the world.

She had wanted to go on the stage ever since she could remember. She knew she sang beautifully, she played the piano and sang for everyone, and they always begged her to perform for them. She loved to dance, and she knew she was graceful. Her idol was the Divine Isadora, and she imitated her, dressing in scarves, dancing in that flowing, free, Greek way. Isadora was an American, just like her, and she had performed throughout Europe. Melissa even thought perhaps they looked alike; at least she hoped so.

"Come in," Papa's voice said.

Melissa entered. Whenever she came into Papa's study she felt a little awed. It was not a big room, and it looked even smaller because it was dominated by the largest desk anyone had ever seen, huge, of dark shiny wood, with heavy carving along the sides, and heavy curved legs. It was always covered with Papa's paperwork from the office and his household accounts. Along the walls of the study were dark wooden bookcases with glass doors— little panes surrounded by curved dark wood frames, in the fashionable and dignified manner of the day. Inside those bookcases were worn and cherished books, some classics, some dealing with the lives and struggles of accomplished Jewish leaders. There were all of Lavinia's college textbooks. And on one wall, above the bookcase, there was Lavinia's college diploma, in a thin black frame with glass on the front.

Oh, Lavinia, Lavinia! So she was the genius in the family, so what? There was a place for everyone in this world, Melissa knew, and her place was in the world of the arts. She could perform and make people weep and applaud. Not everybody had to be an intellectual. Someday her own framed portrait would hang on one of Papa's study walls, right beside Lavinia's diploma—Melissa starring in a musical comedy, or perhaps even an operetta.

"So, nu, Melissa?" Papa didn't like to be interrupted when he was working in his study. But when else could one speak to him alone?

"Papa, I've come to talk about my future," Melissa said.

"Good." He didn't seem to be taking any of this very seriously.

"I would like to take singing and dancing lessons."

"All right," he said pleasantly.

"And acting lessons."

"Acting? For what, acting?"

"I would like to go on the stage."

Suddenly he was taking her very seriously; he was angry. "Who has been putting such foolish ideas into your head?"

"Nobody," Melissa said. "It's my idea. It's what I've always wanted, all my life. I know I'm talented. I feel this is my vocation."

"Vocation? To go on the stage like a whore?"

"The stage isn't for whores, Papa. The stage is for talented people who work hard. You're thinking of vaudeville. I mean the *real* stage. The *theater*."

"Whores," Papa said. "All whores and bums and no-goodniks. I say no and that's the end of it."

"Papa . . ." She had tears in her eyes, she knew he would never understand her.

"You want to sing opera, you want to give concerts, recitals, that's different. That I approve of. For opera I'll give you lessons."

"I'm not good enough for opera," Melissa said. "My voice isn't strong enough."

"You'll go to Juilliard, they'll make it strong. That's my final offer."

"Please, Papa. Please let me take acting lessons. Please."

"Don't be silly. Go away." He turned back to his work.

"Papa!" She was almost shrieking now, this was her last and only chance and she knew it. "Papa, this is what I want to do with my life! What will I do?" It wasn't coming out right at all. What she meant was: What will I do with all my dreams? But how could she say that? He would only laugh at her.

"Do?" he said. "You'll take singing lessons or you won't. You don't want singing lessons, you'll do social work or you won't. You don't want to do social work, you'll go around with your friends and have a nice time and then when you meet a nice boy you'll marry him. That's what you'll do." He went back to his work, and it was final.

Melissa turned and left the study, closing the door quietly behind her. She knew she couldn't fight him. It wasn't in her. He had said no and closed off forever a part of her life, and there was nothing she could do about it. Could she leave home, support herself? No, because then she really would be a whore. She didn't have the courage. It was one thing to be "a gentlewoman of modest means," but to be an eighteen-year-old girl who ran away from home to go on the stage when she didn't even know if they wanted her there—never. Without her Papa's permission and support she was trapped. She felt her throat close. She was being smothered. She rushed upstairs to her room, screaming, and tore all her scarves to pieces, stamping on the ones she could not tear. Her nails were all broken and her toes were sore right through her shoes from kicking the furniture. No one paid the slightest attention or bothered to come up to see what was the matter—Melissa was having another one of her famous tantrums, that was all.

Two weeks later Melissa enrolled in a music theory class at Hunter. It didn't interest her, but it was better than staying at home doing nothing, and it gave her a chance to get out of the house. There was no one home during the day but Mama and Hazel and the maids; Mama spent most of the time in her room resting, and Hazel was driving Melissa crazy. Lavinia had a job teaching English to foreigners; the boys and Rosemary were in school all day. Hazel was home, alert and eager as some pesty child although she was seventeen. "What'cha doin'?" "Where ya goin'?" You couldn't go out for a walk without her running after. "Lis! Lis!"

When she was not in class, Melissa was at some friend's house, or she surrounded herself with girlfriends at home. When she had a group of her friends in the living room, gossiping and giggling and drinking hot chocolate, playing the Gramophone and dancing with each other, Hazel stayed quietly in the corner, content just to watch. It was only when Melissa was alone that Hazel struck. Out came the claw, out stuck the jaw. "Lis . . ." What a pest.

"You should be nicer to Hazel," Mama said. "You should take her with you sometime when you go out. It would be nice."

You couldn't say no to Mama, she was so sweet and she asked for so little. And sometimes Hazel was useful as a companion, for instance, to go to the theater. Melissa liked to go to matinees, and Hazel would sit through anything, even if she didn't understand it. Hazel just liked to get dressed up and go. She could stare at all the people and make what she liked of what was happening on the stage, and Mama was always glad to give Melissa the money for tickets for the two of them. And best of all, Hazel didn't care if you took her to see the same show five times in a row. In fact, she preferred it. It pleased her to know in advance what song was going to be sung or what would happen at the end of the love scene.

For Melissa, the theater was an anesthetic. She could sit there and dream her dreams, pretend she was the heroine on the stage, imagine herself receiving the applause at the end. In her room she could practice the dances in front of her mirror, trill the songs, arrange her hair in the style of the ingénue of the last show she had seen.

Boys she had known all her life asked her out, and sometimes she went with them, if they would take her to a concert or to the theater. Just to have a boy come to call and sit in the living room making conversation bored her to death. She preferred parties. There was always singing around the piano, and dancing, and it was very gay. She wondered if she would ever meet a boy she liked.

When the new shows opened in the fall Melissa was delighted. Between her classes and matinees her days were full, and she didn't have to think. The first show she decided to see was a new romantic play called *All My Daughters*. She took Hazel. After she saw *All My Daughters*, that was the only play she ever bothered to see; she saw it every Wednesday afternoon. The reason was that for some idiotic reason (since she didn't know him) she had developed an enormous crush on a young actor in the play named Scott Brown.

He was about twenty-four years old, tall, with blondish-brownish hair, and a sweet, handsome face. The only thing that kept him from being too handsome was that he looked somehow familiar, as if he might be someone you knew. He was a good actor, too, with a lovely speaking voice. Melissa wondered if he was married.

After she had seen the play for six Wednesday matinees in a row, she decided it was ridiculous not to be courageous and go backstage to ask him to sign her program, just as everyone else did. She washed her hair that morning and brushed it dry so that it shone. She wore her new bottle green velvet suit, the one that matched her eyes. She had even bought a little bottle of perfume, and put some on just before she and Hazel left for the theater. Not cologne, real perfume, so it would last until after the show.

"You wait here," she told Hazel in the alley outside the stage door.

"Why?"

"Because it's too crowded."

Hazel stuck her jaw out and followed her.

It was mean, Melissa supposed, but when they got inside the stage door it was so crowded that she was away from Hazel in a minute. She saw her sister looking around in the crowd, and turned away to the doorman who was guarding the dressing rooms.

"Scott Brown, please."

Scott Brown was not a star, just a player, and Melissa looked so refined that the doorman simply waved her upstairs. She had her playbill clutched in her hand and her heart was thumping with excitement and fear. What could she say to him? Well, she would just ask for his autograph and leave, and no harm done. He could only be flattered . . . no, he might be annoyed because girls were always pestering him. So then, let him be annoyed. If he was nasty then she could get over her crush on him and think about other, more important things. There were a lot of plays she hadn't seen yet this year.

His dressing room door was open. He was sitting in front of his dressing table, wearing a dressing gown and taking off his stage makeup with cold cream. Melissa realized she had never seen a strange man in his bathrobe. Why, this was almost like being in his bedroom!

"Excuse me . . ." she said softly. He turned around. Up close, with most of his makeup off, he looked even younger and nicer.

She caught a glimpse of herself in the mirror and was reassured at how pretty she looked. She held out her playbill.

He smiled. "Would you have a pen?"

"Oh, no . . . I thought you would." Then she giggled.

"How about an eyebrow pencil?" he said. He rummaged around the clutter on his dressing table and found one. "To whom do I sign it?"

"To me, Melissa Saffron."

He wrote and handed it back to her.

"Thank you," she said.

"Thank *you*."

That was all, then. She would have to leave. "I thought there would be about a million people here," she blurted.

"No," he said, and smiled. "They don't want to see me when they can see Elvina Dare."

"Well, I saw the play six times, and I didn't come to see Elvina Dare."

"Six times?"

"I'm a fanatic for the theater."

"Gee, that's really something," he said.

"I thought you would have a dresser," she said.

"There's an old lady who takes the costumes away to be pressed. Only stars have dressers."

"That shows you how much I know," Melissa said.

"Someday I'll have a dresser," he said.

"I'm sure you will."

"You didn't come here all alone, did you?" he said.

"No, my sister's downstairs."

"Well, uh . . . if you're not doing anything, I always eat a sandwich after the show, at this restaurant where a lot of actors go, and it's very nice and fun, and as long as you saw the show six times, well, I would be glad to take you and your sister out for supper if you want, if you're not doing anything . . ." He shrugged like a clown and looked shy.

He was asking her out! He was an actor and a shagetz and Papa would kill her! On the other hand, Melissa thought, if she didn't go out with him she would kill herself and save him the trouble.

"I have to take my sister home because she's very young and I promised to bring her right back," Melissa said. "But then I could meet you at that restaurant if you tell me where it is ."

"Oh, that would be swell," he said, looking genuinely pleased. "It's two doors down from the theater on the right. It's called The Saloon. It's not a speakeasy though, it's just that they have it fixed up kind of Gay Nineties style. I could get my makeup off and dress and then I'd wait for you there in a booth, okay?"

"Okay," Melissa said, jauntily. Okay. Why not? He was the first boy she had ever liked and she was going to sneak right out with him and she didn't even feel guilty.

Hazel was in the alley, sulking. "Where'd you go?"

"I don't know why you had to get lost," Melissa said. "I was looking all over for you. Now you're going to make me late for my class."

"Class?"

"My night class. Advanced music theory is at six o'clock now. Come on, hurry up." She practically dragged Hazel to the subway. "Now you go right home, and don't forget to tell Mama that I'll be late for dinner because of my class and not to wait for me. They can leave something for me in the kitchen."

When the train bearing Hazel was rattling safely on its way toward Brooklyn, Melissa breathed a sigh of relief. She was sure Hazel would get off at the right stop; she'd been there often enough. Now there was no one to snitch on her. She was free! She skipped back toward the theater district like a little girl, all dignity forgotten. And Scott Brown was a nice boy, she could tell. He didn't seem at all fresh. What a funny name, Scott Brown. She bet he hadn't even made it up. He would have made up something fancier for the theater if it weren't his real name.

He was waiting in a booth at The Saloon, just as he had promised. He was wearing a sweater instead of a jacket, and a shirt with no tie. All the other boys in the place were dressed the same way, or if they were wearing jackets they were disreputable ones. He smiled when he saw her, and when she sat down across from him he reached over for just a moment and took her hand and squeezed it, not hard, just nicely. It was fresh, but it didn't seem fresh when he did it.

"I'm glad you came," he said.

"I'm glad you invited me."

"Would you like a near-beer? I'm having one."

Beer! Oh, gosh, that was what shagetzes drank, beer! Beer was for goyim and lower classes and . . . actors.

65

"I'd love one," she said.

The near-beer tasted terrible so she just sipped at it, and then they ordered roast beef sandwiches and talked about themselves. He was a boy like the other boys she knew, but he was as different as if he came from the moon. His parents came from England, which was why he spoke so nicely, and his father drove a milk wagon. They were poor, compared to the other people she knew, and his parents were proud that he had become an actor.

"I want to go on the stage but my father won't let me," Melissa said. "He's very strict."

"Oh . . ." He thought for a moment. She hoped she hadn't embarrassed him or hurt his feelings by implying that the stage wasn't good enough for her. "I bet he doesn't know you're out with me," Scott said.

"Well, actually . . . he doesn't. It's not that I lied to him; I just haven't seen him yet."

"But I bet you won't tell him."

"No," she said. "No, I won't."

"Does he let you go out with boys?"

"Yes. Boys he knows. They're sort of like brothers. Boys I grew up with, friends of the family. It's not very interesting."

"How old are you?"

She thought of lying and decided honesty was the best policy, "Eighteen and a half."

"I'm twenty-three and a half." They both laughed because it sounded so silly.

"You're awfully innocent for an eighteen-year-old girl," he said. "Your father's probably right not to let you go out with strangers. But he doesn't have to worry about me. I promise to treat you with the utmost respect."

"I didn't think you wouldn't," Melissa said.

He looked at her to see if she meant it. "You're so strange," he said, rather admiringly. "I never met a girl like you before. You're right out of another century."

"I beg your pardon!"

"Well, you are. Gee willikers, this is nineteen-twenty-two, and you're Victorian. Not that I don't like it. I love it. It's just unusual, that's all."

"Everybody I know acts exactly like me," Melissa said.

"Nobody I know does."

They looked at each other for a while, and then he shrugged in that clown way she found so sweet. "I like you better for it," he said. "Do you like me even though I'm strange to you?"

"You're not so strange," Melissa lied.

"I'm an actor—grr, that's a dirty word—and a stranger, and I asked you out the minute I met you. Now that's strange, isn't it?"

"I went, didn't I?"

"Yes. And you never had beer before and you hate it."

"How could you tell?" she cried, amazed.

"I'm an actor, my business is observation. I observe all sorts of different people so I can imitate them. How do you know I'm playing me right now?" he said. "Suppose this was all a part?"

"I don't think it is."

"How do you know?"

"I just feel it," Melissa said. "After all, I wanted to be an actor too, so I also observe people."

"Touché."

"Could I have a sarsaparilla, please?" she said.

He grinned and ordered one for her. "Now we're always going to be honest with each other from now on, okay?" he said.

From now on? He had said "from now on." He wanted to see her again! "Okay," Melissa said, her voice trembling a little.

"What are you going to tell your father when you get home?"

"I'll tell him I had a class."

"Then you would have that class every Wednesday at this time, right?"

"I suppose so."

"Then you could meet me between shows, just like today."

"I guess I could."

"Would you?"

"Would you want me to?"

"Yes," he said. "I really would."

"Then I'd love to," Melissa said.

He looked at his watch. "I have half an hour till I have to get back. What would you like to do?"

"Could you take me backstage and show me how everything works?" Melissa said. "Oh, I'd really like that more than anything!"

So he did. He not only showed her backstage but he let her walk on the stage, among the furniture that was set up for the first act, and as she faced the closed curtain Melissa could imagine that empty theater filled with people, all of them looking at her. Imagine speaking lines to other actors, right here, and walking around this chair, and sitting on that one, and crossing to the mantle . . .

"We have to go now," Scott said.

"Oh . . ."

"Careful, don't trip on that rope." He took her arm to help her. A man who was standing in the wings wearing overalls gave them a jaunty little wave. Scott waved back. With him holding her arm that way they looked like a young couple in love. Well, maybe they were. Why not? Stranger things had happened.

"I could just see the show all over again," Melissa said, "Now that I know you."

"Do you want to? I might not be able to arrange a ticket, but I could get you standing room for tonight."

"Oh, no. I can't stay out that late."

"I forgot." He grinned. "Old-fashioned."

"I should hope you wouldn't want your sister walking around all alone in the middle of the night," she said indignantly.

"I would take you home."

"Oh, no! I mean . . ."

"You mean he'd throw me right out of the house."

"Well, he's old-fashioned," Melissa said. It was the first time she had ever uttered such a blasphemy.

"I still can't figure out what's so disgraceful about being an actor," Scott said.

"It's not just that. It's that you're not Jewish."

"You're Jewish?"

"What did you think I was?"

"I never even thought about it, to tell you the truth," he said.

"Do you mind?" Melissa asked.

"Why in the world should I mind? I can't figure out why he minds. It's not as if I'm an atheist or an anarchist or a socialist. I'm a good, God-fearing Episcopalian."

Melissa didn't even know what that was, except that it was some sect of goyim. She thought that most of the people who came from England must be Episcopalians. She hoped it wasn't as strict as Catholics.

"Are you religious?" She asked, fearfully.

"Do you mean do I go to church every Sunday? No, I sleep every Sunday, because I give two performances every Saturday and I'm tired. My mother goes to church and my father doesn't, except of course for special holidays like Christmas and Easter."

"Well, we're the same, then," Melissa said happily. "We all went to Sunday school when we were younger, and the boys were bar mitzvahed, and my parents go to temple on the big holidays like Yom Kippur and Rosh Hashanah and Passover, but they don't go every Saturday morning either."

"So then it doesn't matter," he said happily.

"Not a bit."

But it did matter. It mattered a very great deal, as Melissa knew and had been taught, but it was something she wasn't going to think about now. After all, she had just met the boy, and he had asked her out again, but who knew if they would hit it off and if it would last? There was no point in worrying about religious differences when they had just met and neither of them had the faintest idea if anything would come of it. She was too young to get married. She couldn't picture herself running a house and raising children. She wouldn't dream of getting married until she was at least twenty-four. When you got married you were stuck together for ever after, and twenty-four was a much more sensible age than nearly nineteen. She wasn't going to worry about it now.

He walked her to the subway entrance. "Thank you for a lovely time," she said.

"Thank *you*."

"I'll see you at The Saloon next Wednesday at about a quarter to six."

"Could I . . . no, I don't suppose I could."

"Could you what?"

"Telephone you sometime in between?"

"Oh, no!" she said, panicked.

"I bet your father doesn't even have a telephone," Scott said.

"Of course we do," she said indignantly, and then she realized he was kidding. "Oh, you!" she said, and flounced down the subway steps. She was so happy she wanted to skip, but she wasn't going to skip in public any more, ever. She was a grown-up young lady with her first real boyfriend, and from now on she would behave with more dignity. No more tantrums; at least she would try. She would be kinder to Hazel. She would be pleasant around the house and would try not to sulk. She might even learn to cook. Scott Brown . . . ooh, what a beautiful name, and what a handsome boy he was! She'd just love to take him around the neighborhood and show him off; everybody would just die. Lie down and die from shock and envy. But it had to be her secret. No one could ever know, not even Lavinia. No, especially not Lavinia. It was Melissa's secret—Melissa's and Scott's. And that somehow made the whole thing even better.

ELEVEN

In a family constellation each member has his place, and Rosemary's was The Good Soul. Nobody had designated her the good soul; she had simply chosen it as her way of gaining attention and appreciation. If you didn't notice, she would remind you how good she was. It was she who was always first to offer to run an errand, to take care of Aunt Becky's children, to take care of Hazel, for gosh sake, who was older and should be taking care of *her*. And then later she would remind them all. "I wiped your behind," she would say to little Ned, who stared at her at a loss as to what he was supposed to do to repay her for this favor. "Don't you forget it," she would say. "Someday . . ."

Someday they would all pay her back. She was saving up her IOUs, doling them out to each of them from the oldest to the youngest. Went to drugstore for medicine for Mama. Lent Melissa her hair ribbon. Returned library books for Lavinia and repaid fine, two cents, out of her own money. Let Hazel come with her to Prospect Park. Lent Basil her roller skate key, which he lost. Gave Andrew her dessert when there wasn't enough for seconds. The Good Soul. What did they ever give her?

It was no fun to be the youngest. Nobody appreciated her. She was the one stuck with all the jobs no one else wanted. Lavinia was at work every day with those foreign women, dragging them around, speaking Yiddish to them and teaching them English, so everybody thought she was noble. The boys were supposed to concentrate on their studies because they were going to grow up to help Papa in his business. Melissa was always running off to her music theory lessons, and at night she was allowed to go out on dates, so she got all the new dresses. Nobody expected anything from Hazel, who could just laze around the house and play with her doll. Oh, Rosemary knew Hazel still had a doll. She had walked in on Hazel one day when she was actually talking to it. "Baby," Hazel called it, "my baby." Seventeen years old and she had a baby doll. But what did she, poor Rosemary have? She wasn't even pretty. She hated her hair—it was too curly—and she hated her freckles, and her eyes were too small, and she loathed her little tiny pointed teeth. She was too skinny, and her feet were too big. She was fourteen years old and she had pimples on her face.

She just knew she was going to grow up to be the family old maid, the good soul forever, hanging around other people's houses like the relatives who came and went, the greenhorns. Now they had Aunt Becky's three kids staying at their house because Aunt Becky was sick or something, and who had to wipe *all* their behinds? Who else?

Rosemary was so glad when they went back home to the Bronx and the house was peaceful again, and then just when she was setting out for her very favorite thing: a whole day of ice skating with her friends on the frozen lake in the park, another burden descended on The Good Soul, in the person of her sister Hazel.

"Where ya goin'?"

"Ice skating."

"C'n I come?"

"You don't know how to skate."

"I c'n watch."

"You can come the next time."

Hazel gripped Rosemary's arm in that unbreakable grip of hers. "Ro . . . Ro . . . take me."

"Next time."

"Ma!"

"Never mind, don't bother Mama, I'll take you. But you can't take your doll."

"Don't have a doll."

"Good. Then you won't take it. Put on your warm coat, hurry up, and wear your mittens."

Hazel disappeared into her room and Rosemary thought for one wild moment of running out of the house and leaving her, but then the conscience of the good soul overcame her and she waited impatiently on the stairs. Why did everything always take Hazel so long? The kids would all be waiting on the corner and they would leave without her. Rosemary was a good skater. She could skate backward and forward and do a turn and a figure eight, all of which she had taught herself. For Channukah she was going to get real figure skates, Mama had promised her.

Hazel came out of her room with her coat neatly buttoned, her hat set squarely on her head, her scarf wound around her neck and properly looped, her mittens on her hands, and her doll wrapped tenderly in her arms.

"I told you you can't take that doll," Rosemary snapped.

"Don't have a doll."

"What's that thing, then?"

Hazel looked at the doll. "My baby."

"You can't take that baby, everybody will laugh at you."

"Why?"

"Because you're not married." Hazel looked bewildered. "Oh, put that thing in your room," Rosemary said. "It's either the doll or me. Make up your mind. Do you want to come or not?"

Hazel went slowly into her room and came out without the doll. Gee willikers, what a pest, Rosemary thought, and rushed out of the house to catch her friends before they left without her, hearing Hazel's footsteps in hot pursuit behind her and wishing with all her heart that Hazel wasn't so tall and didn't *look* seventeen.

Hazel was happy. She was happy because she had fooled Rosemary and she had her baby doll wrapped right up in her coat where no one could see her. Rosemary didn't have to be so mean. Everybody was always mean to her and Hazel couldn't understand why, because she wasn't mean to them. If she had any place to go she would invite them. She just didn't have any place to go. But they always had places to go and they never wanted her to come. It was fun to play a trick on somebody. When they got to the lake in the park Hazel would sneak away and hide her baby doll and then nobody would know about it. Ha ha, Ro!

Rosemary was running so fast that Hazel had a hard time keeping up with her. By the time Hazel got to the lake all the kids had their ice skates on and were playing on the ice. She didn't know why nobody ever tried to teach her to skate or asked her to play with them. They were all mean. She walked around the edge of the frozen lake until she got to a clump of pine trees. The trees still had leaves on them even though it was winter and none of the others did, and they made a fine, dark, cozy hiding place for her baby doll. Hazel propped her doll up under a tree, leaning against the trunk.

"Go to sleep, baby," she said. The doll closed its eyes.

She walked back to the lake where the other kids were all skating. Rosemary was all the way in the center of the lake doing her fancy ice tricks and didn't even care about her. Hazel sat down heavily on one of the benches at the edge of the lake and looked around to see if there was anybody to talk to.

There was a boy sitting there by himself, just hanging around, drinking a bottle of beer he had taken from a paper bag. He was taller and bigger than the other kids and Hazel thought he was probably her age. That was good, because then he could be her friend. He was looking at all the girls, and once in a while he'd kind of try to get one of them to look at him if she was an older girl, but none of them did. They all had friends of their own and didn't want to be his friend, but Hazel did. She could go talk to him and tell him about the trick she'd played on Rosemary by bringing her baby doll and hiding it under the tree. Then maybe they could play house, or if he thought he was too old to play house maybe the two of them could think up some funny trick to play on the other kids.

Hazel walked over to the boy. "Hi," she said.

He looked her over. "Hi, yourself."

"What'cha doin'?"

"Not much. What are you doing?"

"Wanna see somethin'?" Hazel said. "Come on."

She beckoned to him, and he stood up, looking a little surprised, but not mad at her the way all the other kids always did. Just to make sure she wouldn't lose him, Hazel grabbed hold of his arm, and then she pulled him toward the clump of pine trees. She was getting excited because he was coming with her and not trying to get away, and she wanted to show him how smart she was.

"Come on," she said. "Just for fun."

"Okay," the boy said. He looked really pleased.

"We'll have a good time," Hazel told him.

"Oh, you kid!" he said admiringly. He went right with her into the dark, secret place under the trees, and then, before she could even show him her baby doll he grabbed her and started hugging her. She tried to struggle to get away, but he was very strong. He was trying to push her down onto the ground, with him on top of her, and Hazel didn't like that a bit. She didn't want to play rough, and he was scaring her. Then he put his mouth on hers and pressed hard. She could feel his teeth. She jerked her head away and started to scream loud.

"Hey!" he was saying, "Hey, what's the matter?" He wouldn't let go and she wouldn't stop screaming until he put his hand over her mouth and then she bit him and started to cry.

"Bitch!" he said, real mad, and slapped her face.

It was then a whole bunch of kids found them and everybody started yelling and Hazel didn't pay any more attention because she was crying too hard and she couldn't understand why that boy had turned out to be so crazy and so mean and tried to hurt her when she had just wanted to be friends with him.

"Listen, Mama," Rosemary said, sitting on the edge of her mama's bed, "we have to do something about Hazel." She had brought Hazel home and made her stop crying and wash her face, and now she had Hazel put away in her bedroom, calmed down and sniffling just a little, with her baby doll on the floor beside her and a big plate of cookies and two glasses of milk. "It's serious, Mama."

So she told Mama about what had happened that afternoon, the way the kids had pieced it together. Hazel had just wanted to play with the boy, but the boy hadn't known how dumb she was and he had thought she wanted him to get fresh with her, so he had.

"We can't let her go out alone, Mama, and I can't watch her every minute. It isn't fair."

"Poor Hazel," Mama said.

"What's the matter with her anyway?" Rosemary asked.

"I don't know—she's just different. I think she's like a child that didn't grow up yet."

"Is she going to grow up?"

74

"She's better. Slowly, slowly, she's always better."

"But she's too old now to go out alone, Mama. She could talk to some other boy and there wouldn't be anyone around to save her. She just doesn't understand."

"I know. Poor Rosemary. Poor Hazel. You have to love your sister; she's family. We all have to love each other. That's what a family is for, to stick together and help each other."

"Yes, Mama."

"But you're right, you're too young for all that responsibility. I'll talk to Hazel. I'll keep her more with me."

"I'm sorry, Mama," Rosemary said. "I know you don't feel well. I'm sorry this has to fall on you."

"Nu, so what's a mother for?" Her mama smiled. "Go, go get me the knitting basket from the closet and then send Hazel in here. I think I have an idea."

Thus it was that Mama taught Hazel how to knit. Hazel turned out to have a positive genius for knitting. It was simple and repetitious, and she could see results, so she loved it. Scarves flowed from her needles, then squares that Mama crocheted together into afghans; the house was covered with afghans, every bed and chair and sofa had one, then Hazel gave them for presents. Then she got orders: "Oh, Hazel, please make a blue one for the new baby boy," "Oh, Hazel, one for Cousin Leah's trousseau would be so nice."

It made her important. Mama tried to teach her how to make sweaters, and Hazel tried, but they never seemed to come out right. One side was always crooked, or one sleeve was longer, or the pieces didn't fit. Hazel kept forgetting to count the stitches. But her talent was afghans, and somebody always needed one, wanted one, was happy to be surprised by one. With such a chore to make her popular and keep her occupied, Hazel bloomed; she became placid and quiet, content to sit on the periphery of the family activity with only the click-click-click of her knitting needles signifying her presence. She liked to pick the colors and the combinations. Her only outings were to the local knitting shop to pick up more wool, always accompanied by one of her sisters.

She gave her baby doll away to Aunt Becky's younger girl. It was a baby toy, and Hazel was a young lady now, knitting just like Mama and the other grown-up ladies. Everyone said it was a talent. It made her feel proud.

TWELVE

"Come, ladies!" Lavinia called, "Come on, hurry, ladies." She always called them ladies, but to see them you would think they were a herd of rumbling rhinoceroses. Huge, fat, dressed in all their clothes in case, God forbid, someone at home might steal them—who knew why they wore so many clothes? And with their babushkas over their heads, like her hated grandmother (well, you shouldn't speak badly of the dead, but Lavinia still hated the old witch), and all those parcels and paper bags they dragged with them in case, God forbid, they happened to get hungry, they were a sight. There she was, barely five feet tall, a hundred pounds, and herding the whole lot of them. "Follow me, ladies! Single file, please!"

Today she was taking them to learn how to use the subway. It had been her own idea: learning to speak English was not enough if they did not also learn how to use it in this strange city. So she would take them on field trips and give them confidence. Most of them lived within walking distance of the Adult Education Center, and those who didn't had a son or daughter to bring them there so they wouldn't get lost.

"Does everyone have her nickel?"

Nickel, nickel, they were all scrabbling through their parcels and handbags to where they had hidden their money. She had already taught them currency, which coin was which and how to make change.

"I got this," one of them called, holding up a crumpled bill.

"What is this?" Lavinia asked.

The old woman peered at it. "A dollar."

"Good. Now, you will go to that booth over there, which is called the change booth, and you will give the dollar to the man inside, and he will give you nickels, dimes, and quarters."

"How do I know he won't keep my dollar?" the old woman grumbled suspiciously. Well, you couldn't blame her; she'd probably been cheated blind since she came here, not knowing the language or the ways.

"Because it is his job to give correct change," Lavinia said. "And if you wish, you can count it." She was immediately sorry she had said that, because Mrs. Tannenbaum (she finally put the name to the lumpy face) was slow and stingy and would probably take half an hour to count her change while they all stood there.

The subway roared into the station and several of the old women put their hands over their ears. The younger ones looked at it with interest and some fear. While Mrs. Tannenbaum got her change, all in nickels, which she had requested, and was counting them, Lavinia counted heads. She was always afraid of losing one of her charges and never seeing her again, lost forever in the heart of the city, murdered in Chinatown, dead under the wheels of a trolley, who knew? They were worse than children.

"All right, ladies, follow me." Lavinia put her nickel into the slot in the turnstile and walked through. The ladies set up a chorus of oohs and ahs. They loved mechanical things.

Click, turn, click, turn, click, turn, click, ouch! It was fat Mrs. Buchbaum (or was that Mrs. Rottenberg?) stuck fast in the turnstile. She just couldn't get through. The ladies were giggling and clucking with concern, some of them biting their fingers. The other fat one (the one who was either Mrs. Rottenberg or Mrs. Buchbaum, whichever wasn't stuck in the turnstile) was pushing at it, trying to get her friend free. There but by the grace of God go I, she was probably thinking, or some version of that homily.

That was stupid planning of the transit system, Lavinia was thinking. How could a fat person get through that turnstile? All people weren't the same size. She was looking for a guard to call for help when the turnstile turned and Mrs. B. or Mrs. R. was through on the other side, and now the other one was afraid to try. Well, she'd just have to try, or else she would never be able to use the subway.

"You can do it," Lavinia called. "Hold your breath."

The ladies all applauded when Mrs. R. (or Mrs. B.) was through. They were so good-natured, they liked their outings, and Lavinia could never get angry at them even when they tried her patience. But the job was just such a bore, that was all. It was not what she'd had in mind when she completed her training in psychology at Cornell, but Papa wanted her to do social work because she was well off and didn't need the money. Jobs, he said, were too hard for women, and the jobs offered to women were not worthy of her. She could have taught, but it would have meant more schooling, and she didn't want that. There was such a need for trained women in social work, and she would be such a gem, Papa said. When she found this job working with middle-aged immigrant women Papa was delighted. It was good to help your own. Lavinia didn't feel they were her own at all, but she was making everybody happy so she stayed with it.

When they were all through the turnstile she counted heads again. Good, all there. "We are going to take the train marked Atlantic Avenue," she said to them. "When the train stops and the doors open you must go inside *fast*, because it doesn't stay a long time in the station. When you are inside we will count four stops, and then we will all get out. After that I will show you how to change trains to come back."

"I want to go to Delancey Street," one of the women said. "My daughter said there's a bargain there on an iron."

"No shopping today," Lavinia said sternly. "Today we master the subway. When you learn how to travel you can go shopping all by yourself."

"Ooh." The women looked pleased. Already they were dreaming up places they could go when they learned how to travel alone.

The train marked Atlantic Avenue roared into the station. The doors opened, the women rushed on, Lavinia followed them, the doors shut, the train lurched off, and she counted heads.

One of the women was missing.

"Who's not here?" That was a dumb question! If she wasn't there, how could she say she wasn't there? But someone knew.

"It's Hannah Shindel," said Mrs. Levey, a bright, birdlike little woman who knew not only everybody's name but the names of their children and grandchildren as well.

"We have to get off at the next stop and go back," Lavinia said. She tried to sound calm, but inside she was frantic. Who knew what Mrs. Shindel would do? She could get on the next train and ride on forever into oblivion, she could wander around the station, she could get hysterical, she could end up at the police station and that would be the end of Lavinia's altruistic unpaid job. If there was anything worse, more disgraceful and unbearable than failing, it was failing at something you didn't even care for in the first place.

The ride to the first stop seemed endless. As soon as the train stopped Lavinia herded her charges off, then led them to the track where the return train would come, barking at them like the meanest teacher she'd ever had in grade school. She was so nervous she was developing a headache. All the time they were waiting for the train she was praying Mrs. Shindel was not sitting stupidly on the train that was passing them on the opposite track. Their train screeched to a stop, she herded the women on, and they went back to the place they had started from. She couldn't even remember what Mrs. Shindel looked like. It wasn't fair; they should have more help. How could one young woman take care of fifty others, each of whom had a keeper of her own at home?

"So we're back?" said Mrs. Tannenbaum. "That wasn't much of a ride for the money."

"We'll all go look for Hannah Shindel," Mrs. Levey said brightly.

"No, we won't," Lavinia said. "You ladies will all stay right here. Do not move. I will look for Mrs. Shindel. I don't want to lose any more of you."

She had them all lined up obediently against the wall, away from the tracks so they wouldn't fall on them and be killed by the next train or trampled by passengers getting off and on. Luckily it was afternoon and the station was not crowded. Lavinia started to walk toward the most populous place, the concessions that sold food and drink and magazines, when a bulky woman dressed in black, who could only be Hannah Shindel, came rushing toward her, parcels and handbag in one hand, a bottle in the other. She was fat and panting.

"Oy, I was so thirsty! I had to get a seltzer." Hannah Shindel took a big gulp of her soda to prove her point, then smiled happily. "I knew you wouldn't go without me, Miss Saffron. You're a good girl."

After dinner Lavinia approached Papa in his study. "May I come in?"

"Of course."

"Papa, I want to talk to you about my job."

"You don't like your job?"

"It's too hard for me. Physically. It's too tiring. Today I lost one of the ladies on the subway and I nearly lost my mind. I just can't drag them around like that, and there isn't enough help at

79

the center so I have to take on too much myself. I'd like to do it, I care about them, but I'm not up to it. I haven't the strength."

She knew he would understand that. Your health was the most important thing in life.

He shook his head sympathetically. "It's horse's work."

"Exactly."

"We were never peasants, any of us. We never did hard physical work. Your ancestors were all scholars, intellectuals, some tradespeople, but all artistic. We weren't ever horses. You have to be born a horse to work like a horse."

"Exactly."

"So tell them you want to go back to working in the school room."

"Papa, now they have me doing this they won't let me do anything else. They think this is such a good idea that I'm sorry I thought of it. Next week I have to take them to the Statue of Liberty and that will be even worse."

"So then why don't you quit?"

"That's a good idea," Lavinia said. "I knew you would come up with the right idea. I think I *will* quit."

He laughed. "Nu, you, you think you fooled me. I know you. Why shouldn't I know you? You're just like me. Make the other person tell you to do what you were planning to do all along. You're my smart one, Leah Vania, you're as smart as a man."

Joy flooded her until she thought she would burst into tears from it. Papa hadn't called her by her baby name for years, and he had said she was just like him! That was the greatest compliment she could think of: to be like him. He was a genius. He had said she was as smart as a man. Did that mean she was the smartest one in the family? He wouldn't have said she was like him if she weren't his favorite. Oh, how much she wanted to be his favorite, the one he loved the most, the one he was proudest of!

"But now I'll tell you something," Papa said happily. "It's me that wanted you to quit that job. So you think you got what you want, but really I got what I want and you think you fooled me into letting you get your way."

"Oh, Papa!" But she wasn't angry, she was delighted that he was playing this game with her, as if they were equals vying for position. "So now I'll put my cards on the table," Lavinia said.

"So put. I'm ready."

"I would like to work in your office."

"Yes?"

"I would like to work for you, to help you."

"I have a secretary already."

"Then something else. When the boys finish school and college they'll work for you and you'll have plenty for them to do. You must have a little something for me to do now."

He was quiet, thinking.

"You are interested in business?" he said finally. His tone was neutral, noncommittal.

"I don't know. I know I would like to learn, and then I'll see."

"I don't pay people to learn," he said.

"Then I'll work for nothing. Please, Papa. Give me something to do in the office."

"Business . . ." he said thoughtfully. "Don't you want to get married like other girls, have a companion for your life, give me grandchildren? You're a pretty girl, Lavinia, and smart. Pick a nice boy before they're all gone."

"I'll get married when I meet the right man."

"Nu? So who said you should marry the wrong man?"

"You know what I mean. I'm looking, but I'm not searching."

"As long as you're not just sitting."

"I'll meet more men in the business world than I will taking old ladies on the subway."

"I could have introduced you to some nice fellows," he said. "I could have, but I never did, because I know you. Nobody forces a husband down your throat. When the time comes, you'll pick your own husband. I trust you. I have faith in you. I know you'll pick a fellow with a good character."

"That's the first thing I'll look for," Lavinia said solemnly.

"Na, I know you, the first thing you'll look for is looks. But you won't be fooled. Looks *and* character. I wouldn't expect less."

"You won't get less, Papa. I promise."

"And if he's not such a millionaire, I wouldn't stick my nose up at him if I were you. Potential is what matters. Brains and potential for the future. I wouldn't mind taking a smart young fellow into my business if he was your husband and had a good character and was willing to work hard and learn. Brains. I want brains."

"So do I," Lavinia said. "I wouldn't accept less."

"To tell you the truth," Adam said, "I personally could never stand to have ugly people around me. I only hire good-looking men in my office. So don't be ashamed to stick your nose up at a funny-looking fellow, he asks you out. It's no shame to like beauty."

"I've always known that, Papa."

"Good. So when do you want to start working for me?"

"I'll give them two weeks' notice," Lavinia said. "No, the heck with it! I'll start with you on Monday."

"*For* me," Adam said. "Not *with* me, *for* me. You're not the big boss yet."

"Yes, Papa."

"You'll ride to work with me in the car. Go, shut the door behind you." He turned away to his paper work. When a conversation was over he never even bothered to say goodbye, he just ended it. You knew, and he knew, so why waste time?

Lavinia shut the study door efficiently behind her and went upstairs. Free! Free! She was free, and she would work in the office with Papa! Now she had only one other piece of unfinished business and then she would consider things well settled for the time being. The unfinished business was Melissa's sneaking around with what was obviously some boy she was ashamed to bring to the house, and Lavinia intended to get to the bottom of it and fast.

She had called Hunter and asked them if their six o'clock advanced music theory class was filled, and they had said she must be thinking of the beginners' class because the advanced class was at three in the afternoon. Maybe . . . maybe Melissa was still taking the beginners' class and was ashamed to tell them so, but Lavinia doubted it. Melissa wasn't the kind of person to pretend to be smarter than she really was. It didn't matter to her. No, it must be some boy. She advanced to Melissa's room with a firm step and rapped on the closed door.

"Entrez!" Melissa sang out.

Lavinia entered. The room was a mess. Melissa had been trying on her entire wardrobe, tossing every dress on the bed or the floor when she was through. She must be in love.

"I haven't seen you for a while," Lavinia said. "With my job and your classes. How is your music class?"

"Oh, fine."

"It must be very hard for you."

"Why?"

"Well, advanced theory. A friend of mine, Esther Meyers, takes advanced music theory at Hunter—maybe you know her? Big eyes and black hair?"

"No . . ."

"She says it's very hard," Lavinia said. "I'm surprised you haven't met her. You would like each other."

"I never heard you mention any Esther Meyers," Melissa said. "How come you never invite her to the house?"

"I knew her at college. I just found out she was here. But maybe she isn't in your class after all. She says her class is at three in the afternoon, and yours is at six in the evening, isn't it?"

"That's right."

"Maybe you didn't say you took advanced after all. Maybe it was intermediate or beginners and I heard wrong. Was it?"

"I said advanced," Melissa said calmly. Not even a flicker in the steady green eyes. Not for nothing did the girl want to be an actress.

"Well, maybe she doesn't go to Hunter," Lavinia said. "Maybe it was NYU."

Melissa shrugged and held up another dress, deciding if she should try it on.

"You remember when Aunt Becky's kids had to stay here that time?" Lavinia said.

"Which time?"

"The last time. When she was sick."

"Mmm . . ." Not interested.

"Well," Lavinia said, "I didn't want to tell you because I thought it might upset you, but after all, you're old enough now to know about these things. Aunt Becky was up in the Bronx having an abortion."

"What's that?"

"That's when they take the baby before it's born so it won't live. When the mother is just a month or two pregnant."

"Ugh," Melissa said.

"It was very sad. But Aunt Becky just can't afford to have another child because Isman is out of work again."

"What's the matter with that man?" Melissa said.

"Some men just can't make a go of it," Lavinia said solemnly. "Some can and some can't. When you're in love it's hard to tell which man is going to make a good provider and which one isn't. It's easy even to fall in love with a no-good bum who would get a girl in trouble and run away. When you're in love, and you're young, you can't see these things so clearly. It's better to have someone to give you another opinion, like a sister."

"Well, Papa fixed up the whole thing with Aunt Becky and Isman," Melissa said, "so let her blame him."

"Let's not talk about Papa!" Lavinia said sharply. Melissa was slipping out of her hands like a fish, and on top of that she was being disrespectful about Papa. It was obvious she had come under the spell of someone very no-good.

"Do you think I should give this dress away?" Melissa asked. "It always made my skin look green."

"I don't see anything wrong with it."

"I'll give it to Rosemary." She tossed it on the bed. "Well, it was nice to have a talk with you, Lavinia, but I have to take a bath now."

"Oh? You're going out?"

"Goodness," Melissa said, "You'd think I never took a bath in my life. It isn't exactly an event around here."

"You're not going out?"

"Of course I'm going out," Melissa said. "You know I sing with my choral group on Thursday nights."

"Oh? Where is this choral group?"

"At Gertrude Solomon's house."

"Gertrude Solomon?" Lavinia said. "I never heard you mention any Gertrude Solomon."

"Well, I never heard you mention any Esther Meyers," Melissa said cheerfully.

Darn her! "I wish we could be better friends," Lavinia said.

"You're practically my best friend," Melissa said. "But you know, being someone's friend also means trusting them."

"I trust you!" Lavinia snapped. "Who said I didn't trust you?"

"I know you trust me," Melissa said, her eyes wide and pure.

"I hope you also trust me," Lavinia said.

"I do."

"And that you'd feel free to come to me if you were unsure about anything, or if you wanted a little friendly advice."

"Oh, I would," Melissa said. "I would."

"I hope so."

"Do you want to scrub my back?" Melissa asked cheerfully.

"No, I do not. I have things of my own to do." Lavinia turned and left her sister's room. Darn her! Sneak! Actress! But what could she do? She would think of something. She never gave up when she had her mind set on something. But for the moment she was so happy at the thought of working with Papa in his office that the problem of Melissa's mystery boyfriend faded into the background. Let her stew in her own juice.

There was something in Lavinia that made her want to protect Melissa from the others, just as she protected all the others when it was necessary, as she always protested that there was nothing wrong with Hazel, that Hazel was not stupid, that Hazel had flashes of brilliance which the others just happened to overlook. She would never dream of telling Papa or Mama of her suspicions about Melissa. To tell Papa and incur his wrath would be worse than anything bad that Melissa could bring on herself. Maybe the boy was a perfectly nice boy and Melissa was just biding her time, hiding him so the others wouldn't rush her. It wasn't fair to jump to conclusions. Patience . . . and no one had more of that than Lavinia did.

THIRTEEN

The New Year's Eve Revel at the Jewish Center was one of the few occasions that allowed all the generations to mix: the pillars of the community and the young folks. Also the sexes: the men who attended the Beefsteak, Smoker, and Movies evenings, and their wives, who usually stayed home. The serious-minded, timid, and religious, who attended the lectures on such subjects as "Whither Jerusalem?" appeared, and the frivolous, the ones with fragile health, and the jolly jokesters, who never attended those lectures, showed up at the New Year's Eve Revel. Prohibition didn't bother any of them very much; they were all proud that they could have a good time without liquor.

There were funny hats and noisemakers for all, and lots of good food. Creamed chicken (none of them were kosher; they were proud to be Conservative Jews, not Orthodox, which was more fitting for these modern times in this new land) and cold roast beef, stuffed derma, fluffy noodle pudding, little meatballs swimming in tomato sauce, mixed green salad with tomatoes in it, fruit salad with sweet pink dressing, cold cuts and rye bread to make big sandwiches (ham, of course, was missing; there was something disgusting about ham), white bread, Bialy rolls, good sweet butter, bagels, cream cheese, chopped liver, lox and Nova Scotia, olives and pickles, celery strips and carrot curls, macaroons and schnecken, butter cookies, brownies with nuts in them, lemon roll, white cake with chocolate filling, chocolate cake with white filling, and all the sweet punch you could drink.

Adam Saffron had a big table for his family. There was Lucy, risen from her sickbed and smiling, in a beautiful black beaded gown; Lavinia, whose date was her younger brother Andrew; Melissa, who had disdained to accept a date although five young men had asked her; Basil, who had been forced to escort a young cousin, Hermine (fat, shy, unfortunate cousin Hermine, who thought sixteen-year-old Basil was a sophisticated man of the world and who worshiped him); Hazel and Rosemary, both without dates because they were too young. Already Hazel and Rosemary had been grouped together as if they were the same age, although Hazel was eighteen now and Rosemary fifteen.

Adam was proud and happy to be seen with his family around him. The girls all had new dresses, the boys had new suits. His friends from the Jewish Center came up to greet him, paying him court, for he was a respected man in the community. Men introduced him to their wives, and he introduced them to his. He presented his children. They were polite, well-groomed, attractive children, not all of them exactly beauties, but good enough to show off. When the well-wishers began to trickle off, Adam became restless, and then he took Lucy by the arm and they began to make a tour of the room, greeting old friends who had not greeted them, stretching their legs so to speak. Just taking a little walk.

"How do, how do," bobbing the head ever so slightly. Speaking only English. Dignified.

At the table Melissa was miserable. She missed Scott. It was

New Year's Eve, and they should be together because they were in love, but he was working, giving a performance, and she couldn't be with him anyway because he was forbidden, a shagetz. How she loved him, and how she wished he were here! They could hold hands under the table, and at midnight when everyone kissed everyone else, maybe he could give her their first kiss.

She had been seeing him twice, sometimes three times a week, but he hadn't kissed her because he had promised to treat her with perfect respect. He thought that was funny. He laughed at her, and said he had never gone with a girl he hadn't been allowed to kiss, but Melissa was afraid. She knew that if you kissed a boy you sometimes couldn't stop, and so it was better to wait until you became engaged. If he was here tonight she would kiss him! Yes, she would. Right in front of everybody. Maybe she was being a prude to stick to the old rules, maybe she should let him kiss her when they were on a date. How much could he do, kissing her goodnight in the shadows outside the subway? Just a kiss . . . but how she had dreamed of it, how it would feel to kiss Scott. He was so beautiful. She sat there, toying with her punch, and she couldn't eat a thing. She felt like crying. New Year's Eve was a horrible holiday. People should be with the people they loved on New Year's Eve. Oh, she didn't mean not with family, because she loved her family, but a girl should be with the boy she loved and then they could all be together, she and the boy she loved and family and all. It wasn't fair.

Andrew and Lavinia were scouting the food-laden table.

"I detest stuffed derma," Lavinia said. "Do you know what they make the outside of? Intestines!"

Andrew put the piece of stuffed derma he had been about to take back on the platter. "How awful," he said. "Why did you tell me that? Now I'll never be able to eat it again."

"Just as well," Lavinia said. "It's lower class anyway."

"I have this theory about food," Andrew said. "When you're eating it, it's food, but the minute you put your fork down it's garbage."

Lavinia laughed. "Eat the creamed chicken," she said. "It's good, I tasted it. But I wish they wouldn't put pimentos in it."

"Why?"

"They're goyish."

"*Pimentos?*"

87

"We used to have them at college in the creamed chicken. All the food at college was goyish."

"Well, that doesn't bother me," Andrew said cheerfully, and helped himself to a big spoonful of the creamed chicken, pimentos and all.

"Why didn't you bring a date tonight?" she asked him.

"I didn't feel like it."

"You're seventeen years old—you could go out with a nice girl. You shouldn't be shy."

"Shy?" Andrew said. "Me, shy? Are you kidding? I just don't like any of the girls around here as well as you."

"Me?"

"You're the most *upper* class."

"Oh, Andrew!" They both laughed. "You always liked to tease me."

"Well, I do think you're pretty swell. And I have good taste."

"Thank you."

"Just look around at these girls," he said. "I don't see anybody worth asking out, do you?"

"Oh, some of them aren't so bad."

"You and Melissa are the best-looking girls in the room."

"Well, I won't argue with you if you insist," Lavinia said, smiling and blushing a little. She didn't think she was pretty at all, but she was flattered that her brother thought so. Younger brothers could be so critical, and Andrew the most of all. Nothing was good enough for him. He didn't like the rug, he didn't like the color of the living room walls, he hated the lamp on the side table, he thought Rosemary's new dress was too long and had too many bows on it, he didn't like the way Hazel wore her hair, he wanted Melissa in green to match her eyes, he wanted Papa to get a bigger car, he wanted a car of his own, he wanted this, he wanted that. Lavinia was the only one he seemed to approve of.

"Why did Papa make Basil take Hermine out tonight?" he asked her.

"He thought it would be nice if they got to know each other. Basil is so shy, and Hermine is sweet."

"Well, I think she's dreadful-looking," Andrew said.

"You would."

"Basil does too. Just watch him. He won't give her a tumble."

"He doesn't have to be rude," Lavinia said. "That's the trouble with both of you, you won't give any nice girl a chance."

"When the time comes," Andrew said, "Basil and I will both pick our own girls. Nobody is going to change that."

"Nobody's trying to!" Lavinia said sharply.

He didn't answer. Andrew simply didn't bother to answer if you tried to get into an argument with him. He thought he was right and that was that. Lavinia had some hope for what Andrew would pick, but she couldn't imagine what Basil would like. He was still so young, and so self-conscious. Look at the way he was treating his cousin Hermine. He wouldn't even talk to her. He was actually dancing with other girls and letting her sit there. He hadn't asked her to dance all evening! That was unpardonably rude. Lavinia strode over to the family table and put her filled plate down at her place, then she went over to Basil.

"Are you having a good time, Basil?" she asked.

"Sure," Basil said, unconvincingly.

"And you, Hermine?"

Hermine's heavy-featured face crumpled. She really should do something about those eyebrows, Lavinia thought, but except for being a little too heavy, which was just baby fat, she was a very nice-looking girl. "When can we go home?" Hermine asked. She looked as if she was about to cry.

"Oh, you can't go home until after we bring in the New Year," Lavinia said cheerfully. She took hold of Basil's arm and gave it a pinch. He winced and glared at her. "Why don't you two dance?" she said. "Go on, don't just sit here like old folks."

"I'm very tired," Basil said.

"Shame on you," Lavinia gave his arm a tug. "Go dance with Hermine."

Basil rose dutifully and, scarcely glancing at Hermine, walked out to the dance floor as if it was to his execution. Hermine rushed after him. The hired band was playing a waltz.

"Oh, I love a waltz!" Hermine said. "My father sent me to dancing class and we learned how to waltz, so that's what I do the best."

Basil didn't answer. He held her at arm's length and they waltzed.

"You waltz very well," Hermine said.

"Why don't you just dance?" Basil said.

89

Hermine burst into tears.

Basil was so embarrassed by this public display in the middle of the dance floor that he ran off and disappeared into the men's room. Lavinia couldn't possibly rout him out there, and he was safe from that fat pig.

He looked into the mirror and combed his hair with the pocket comb he always carried. He was growing up to be a handsome boy, with straight dark hair and a smooth oval face. He was shaving every day now, and his dark beard (the bane of his existence the way it grew back so fast!) and dark skin made him look almost Greek. He was a head taller than Papa already. He knew girls liked him, and he had no intention of being stuck, even for an evening, with any girl he didn't like. All his life Basil had felt like the sixth finger. He was sorry for himself. He could feel the partiality Papa showed to Andrew—no, that *everyone* showed to Andrew. Andrew complained and Andrew got. Andrew asked and Andrew got. Andrew had but to speak and the world was his. But who listened to Basil? He never even bothered to ask because he was so convinced no one would listen to him. The words never came out right. All right, he had as much money as he could want; Papa was very generous. His marks at school were adequate, but Andrew wasn't at the top of his class either. But Andrew had talents. He painted and sketched, and sculpted in clay. Andrew was always making drawings of his sisters and their parents and giving them the pictures for presents, and everyone was always thrilled. He, Basil, had no such talents. He played the piano fairly well, but Rosemary was much better. He didn't bother much with sports because sports weren't respected in that family; intellectual achievements were.

As Basil preened into the mirror he knew one thing. He had a talent to make girls chase him. So his family didn't think the sun rose and fell on him the way they did on Andrew. So what? Girls thought he was wonderful. Every person had his talents, and his talents were girls. *I will never marry*, Basil thought. *I will grow up and have a mistress!*

The thought delighted him and he began to feel cheerful again. All right, he would go outside and dance with that impossible Hermine if it made them feel better. He could be charitable.

But when Basil emerged from the men's room he discovered that Hermine's parents had taken her home because she wouldn't stop crying, and everyone was mad at him. Mad at him again, as usual. First they wanted him to spend his entire New Year's Eve being nice to an impossible, fat, funny-looking little girl, who was his cousin on top of that, so there was no possibility of even thinking of trying to kiss her had she been beautiful instead of that little pig, and now they were all acting as if he was a villain.

"You are so rude!" Lavinia said.

"Really, Basil," Rosemary said, "Hermine is a friend of mine. You could have tried to be nice to her. You were horrible."

"Oh, poor Basil, for goodness sakes!" Melissa said to the others. "Let him alone. He has a right to pick his own girlfriends. Hermine was much too young for him."

"One year!" Lavinia said.

"Gee, Basil, you really destroyed that poor girl," Andrew said sweetly.

Basil didn't know what to say to restore his ruptured reputation so he turned away from them and went over to a table where twenty-year-old Rachel Fenster was sitting. She was beautiful and slim, and she was four whole years older than he was. He asked her courteously to dance, and to his delight she accepted. That would serve them right.

Poor me, Melissa was thinking. She looked at her little watch. Only eleven-thirty. Scott would be out of the theater now, makeup off, the show long over, and he would be celebrating New Year's Eve with his friends. She wondered which girl he would kiss when the clock struck midnight, and she didn't want to think about it. To some people kisses didn't mean anything anyway. And to others they meant too much . . .

"I don't believe I've met your daughter." A tall, thin, older man was standing next to her seat at the table, talking to Papa but meaning her.

"This is my daughter Melissa," Papa said. "Dr. Lazarus Bergman."

"How do you do?" Dr. Bergman said.

"Pleased to meet you," Melissa said politely, as she had to a hundred other strange faces passing through her life that night.

"Would you care to dance?" Dr. Bergman asked.

It was so funny, the way he talked in that old-fashioned way, so proper. She was rather flattered that a man of his age would ask her to dance; why, he must be almost forty! He wasn't old enough to be those boring old married men who asked her to dance because they thought she was a cute little girl, while their fat wives looked on with amusement and no jealousy at all, and he was old enough to seem mysterious and sophisticated. She stood and glided into his arms. She knew she was the most graceful dancer in the room, and to her surprise he was pretty good himself.

"Which of these ladies is your wife?" Melissa asked.

"None of them. I'm a bachelor."

A bachelor? Goodness, he must have a sick mother at home, the poor man. She tried to remember if she'd ever heard Dr. Bergman mentioned at home. No, the one with the sick mother was someone else, and there was someone with a sick sister, but he was a dentist and he was crazy anyway. Yes, yes, she remembered now; Dr. Lazarus Bergman was a German Jew and very rich, and both his parents were long since dead. She felt quite sophisticated, dancing there with that nearly-middle-aged bachelor.

When the music stopped, Dr. Bergman steered her expertly to her table, and then to her surprise he sat down next to her in the empty seat. "I understand you're a music student," he said.

"Yes, I am."

"I'm very fond of opera," he said. "Are you?"

"Yes," Melissa said. "I once considered singing opera, but my voice isn't strong enough. I'm afraid it's more suited to less difficult work."

"And who is your favorite composer?"

"All of them," she said.

"Indeed? You have very catholic tastes."

"Catholic?" she said in horror.

"Eclectic. 'Catholic' used in this sense means to enjoy all sorts of music in the broad sense. The word was not always used to mean the Church, you understand. Originally, the Church was all-embracing, thus the word 'catholic' means to embrace all."

The man was taking her breath away!

"Oh," Melissa said, at a loss to contribute anything more intelligent in the face of this man's extraordinary knowledge.

"I am quite enamored of linguistics," Dr. Bergman went on. "And I think it's a shame the way so many useful and evocative words are allowed to lie dormant in our vocabularies."

"Yes," Melissa said. She felt like a fool.

"But then, this must be tedious for you," he said, and smiled at her. "May I bring you some punch?"

"Oh, please."

"I'll be back in a nonce."

When Dr. Bergman had gone to the punch bowl, Melissa poked Lavinia. "Did you hear that man talk? I couldn't understand half of what he said."

"Serves you right for falling asleep in school," Lavinia said.

"Well, you may be smarter than I am, but he picked me."

"Tut!"

"And tut to you!"

Melissa stuck her tongue out, and then popped it back into her mouth and composed an angelic expression on her face as Dr. Bergman returned carrying two glass cups of punch.

"Oh, thank you," she said.

"You shouldn't be drinking this stuff," he said, settling himself back beside her. "It's full of sugar, and sugar is bad for your teeth."

"I eat tons of sugar," Melissa said ruefully.

"You couldn't eat a ton of sugar. Do you know how much a ton is?"

"It's how much I eat," she said, flashing him a grin. "You never saw me attack a candy box."

"Only after meals, I hope."

"Is that better?"

"Of course it's better."

"Oh. Then I will from now on. Thank you for your free medical advice."

"It's not exactly free," he said. "I'm going to extract payment, in the form of your pleasant company at the opera next Tuesday night. It's *Tosca*. I think you'll enjoy it. Some people find it heavy going, but of course, they're not aficionados."

"The Metropolitan Opera?" Melissa said, excited. "I've never been!"

"Then you'll allow me to escort you?"

"I'd be delighted."

"Good. Then it's settled. I'll pick you up at seven, so that we won't be late."

People started ringing their little bells, clanking their toy clackers, and blowing on their noisemakers. Happy New Year! Happy New Year! Melissa looked at her watch: it was midnight.

People were kissing each other. She looked around in panic. Oh, gosh, she hoped nobody tried to kiss her!

"Happy New Year," Dr. Bergman said. He extended his cool, dry hand, and Melissa took it. Solemnly, they shook hands. "May your wishes come true this year," he said.

"Thank you, Dr. Bergman," she said. "And yours."

"Please call me Lazarus."

"Lazarus."

"You see, I've risen from the dead now that I've met you."

Melissa giggled.

Papa stood up. "All right," he said. "We go now."

His children came running: Basil, Andrew, Rosemary, Hazel, and Lavinia. He took Mama's arm.

"Oh, my goodness," Melissa said to Lazarus, "do you know where I live, for Tuesday night?"

"Yes, indeed I do."

"Then, à *bientôt*," she said gaily.

Sitting in Papa's car on the drive home Melissa thought about Dr. Lazarus Bergman. Lazarus. She had never known such a grown-up man who asked her to call him by his first name. It seemed almost impolite. She felt like the romantic heroine of a novel. An older man, brilliant, educated, a doctor, enamored of linguistics and an aficionado of opera, was smitten with her. It made her feel very glamorous. She wouldn't tell Scott. After all, it would make him feel badly, and Dr. Lazarus Bergman really wasn't a date; he was just an adventure. And an adventure was exactly what she needed to get her out of the dumps.

FOURTEEN

Dr. Lazarus Bergman appeared promptly at seven o'clock, in formal attire, to call for Melissa. He had a taxi waiting, because he did not drive. A taxi! She had never had a date who could afford to take her all the way from Brooklyn to New York in a taxi. She was glad that she had worn her sea green chiffon tea gown with the handkerchief hem, because it looked very formal and appropriate beside his tuxedo. Around her head was a matching sea green chiffon scarf, tied in the manner of The Divine Isadora, and floating down her back in a graceful streamer. Her golden hair was still worn long, which was not exactly à la mode, but then, The Divine Isadora wouldn't cut hers, either.

"You look very lovely," Lazarus said. "Like a muse."

"Which muse?"

"The muse of terpsichore."

"Well, that's exactly who I am!" Melissa said gaily.

On the ride to New York he told her about his trip to Europe in 1903. It all sounded very glamorous: the big, elegant hotels and spas, the famous paintings in museums, the strange habits of the natives in France and Germany and England. Why, in 1903 she hadn't even been born yet, and there he was, a young man of twenty-one, on a trip to Europe all alone. Melissa was wonderstruck. In 1903 her own Papa was still just an immigrant, and Europe wasn't a glamorous place to visit on a big luxury ship, it was a sad place to run away from, in steerage.

The inside of the Metropolitan Opera House reminded her of a giant wedding cake, all in tiers, all lit up. She had never seen anything so grand in her life. Everyone looked so elegant, and so much older and more sophisticated than she was. She hoped she wouldn't be bored by the opera; that would be a disgrace.

Lazarus had little mother-of-pearl-covered opera glasses, even though they had excellent seats. He handed the glasses to her and told her she could use them. The orchestra began the overture. Melissa felt her spine tingle. This was so different from the faraway music she played at home on her Gramophone. This was so loud and clear and . . . real! Oh, it was so lovely. The music was so beautiful it made her want to cry.

To her relief, she liked *Tosca*. It would have been difficult to lie to Lazarus, although she usually found it easy to fib to anyone else. But he was so wise. She was quite disappointed that the leading lady was so fat, but in a way she was also glad, because now she knew she could never have been an opera singer, no matter what Papa said. She simply wasn't fat enough.

"I loved it," she said to him when it was over.

"I knew you would. Are you hungry?"

Actually, she was ravenous. She had been too nervous to eat dinner before he came to call for her, and now it was so late. "Well, I suppose I could eat just a little something," she said daintily.

He hailed another taxi and gave the driver an address. When the cab stopped in front of an unimposing-looking building, Melissa was confused. She had rather imagined that the restaurant he took her to would look like the Metropolitan Opera House.

"I was considering going to Sherry's," Lazarus said to her, "but I thought this might be more amusing for you. We could perhaps go to Sherry's on another occasion, for dinner."

He rapped on the front door and a little peephole opened. The man who looked out recognized him, and opened the locked door. Lazarus led Melissa in.

She had never been to a speakeasy, and she was overwhelmed and delighted. The music was so bright and cheery, and everyone was so gay, and so . . . so drunk. It was so funny to see drunk people. They were dancing wild dances and laughing and talking too loudly, and some of them were even kissing. There was a lot of smoke in the air, and Melissa noticed that some of the girls were smoking too. The head waiter led them to a small table at the edge of the dance floor, and Lazarus ordered champagne.

"Unless, of course, you would prefer whiskey?" he asked her.

"Whiskey? Oh, no thank you, I never drink whiskey. Champagne would be just lovely." She had never had champagne either.

The champagne appeared, along with a silver bucket on a stand, filled with ice, and two champagne glasses. The waiter poured Melissa's first glass of champagne.

She tasted it. It was rather good. It was certainly better than beer, and although it was different from the sweet holiday wine they had at home, which she liked very much, it was quite pleasant. Yes, quite pleasant. It was disloyal to have such a thought, but this was certainly a far cry from The Saloon with Scott, with all those mangily-dressed actors and sloppy girls, and that dreadful near-beer, and the perspiration smell you just couldn't avoid. Here it smelled of perfume from all those sophisticated ladies, and of cigarette smoke, and Lazarus smelled faintly of tangy after-shave lotion and good hair pomade. Scott never smelled of perspiration. He smelled nice and clean, like a child. He was like a puppy; you wanted to hug and fondle him, but she had grown used to him and he was no longer someone to be in awe of. Lazarus really kind of scared her because he was so sophisticated and older, but not an *old* man, just someone way out of her league. The champagne was making her giddy and she felt her cheeks flush.

"I would suggest a white meat of chicken sandwich," Lazarus was saying. "That's light but nourishing. It isn't good to ingest anything heavy just before retiring—it gives you indigestion and keeps you from sleeping well."

"A chicken sandwich would be lovely," Melissa said.

The waiter brought two small white meat of chicken sandwiches, on white bread with the crusts cut off. Melissa started to pour salt on hers.

"You don't need salt," Lazarus said. "If God had meant meat to have salt on it he would have made it that way."

"Did God mean chickens to end up in sandwiches?" Melissa asked.

"God created the beasts of the field and the birds of the air and the fish in the sea for man to eat," Lazarus said. "The law of nature is the survival of the fittest. Man eats meat. He is a carnivore. Animals prey upon each other. If we choose to eat fowl in a sandwich or in a pot it is all the same in the law of nature."

"Oh," she said. She put the salt shaker down.

"Salt is bad for your health," Lazarus said. "It raises the blood pressure and retains fluids, creating edema, or swelling, particularly in the lower limbs."

"Oh, I wouldn't want that," Melissa said. She could just imagine her pretty ankles swelled up like tree trunks, like some of those old fat ladies she knew.

Lazarus refilled her empty glass with champagne. She certainly wouldn't want to get drunk in front of him and disgrace herself.

"I really shouldn't have another," she said tentatively.

"Alcohol in moderation is good for you," he said. "It's relaxing, and good for the circulation. It's particularly beneficial for older people, for whom I always recommend a small glass of whiskey just before retiring."

"Whiskey for medicinal purposes!" Melissa said. She had read that on the label of a bottle once, which belonged to Papa. Anyway, it had said something like that: a skull and crossbones and "For Medicinal Purposes Only" on it, and then it said "Scotch Whiskey." Papa called it schnapps.

"Don't worry, Melissa," Lazarus said. "I won't let you get drunk."

"I know that. I can tell a gentleman when I see one."

"I bet you tell that to all the fellows."

"I do, and it always works." She smiled at him. "If someone knows you trust him, how can he betray you?"

"Oh, how innocent and naïve you are!" Lazarus said. "The world is full of bums just waiting to take advantage of a beautiful young girl like you."

"Just all lined up," Melissa said, and giggled.

"They are. They are."

"Then how can I tell who they are?"

"You can't always tell. That's why you need someone older and wiser to protect you."

"But I have to go out, don't I?" she said.

"Of course. But what I am trying to imply or infer is that you should choose such an older and wiser person as your companion or escort. In other words, I am suggesting myself. I would like to see a great deal of you in the near future, Melissa. May I?"

"Oh. Well, yes, of course," she said, stunned. Her life was certainly going to be full for a while, keeping company with two men at the same time.

"I would like to take you to the theater," he said. "And to the opera, and to concerts. There are many fine restaurants in this city which I am sure you haven't yet had the pleasure of encountering, and I would like to show them to you."

"Oh, I'd love that!" Melissa said.

"And I as well."

When Lazarus escorted her to the front door of her family's house, telling the taxi to wait, he saw her safely inside and did not try to kiss her or even shake her hand. He simply touched his fingers to the brim of his hat in a polite and jaunty way, bobbed his head to her, and left. Melissa thought it was just perfect. If he had tried to kiss her she would have been disappointed in him, and if he had shaken hands it would have been too formal. Men shook hands with each other. She didn't like it much. Lazarus made her feel like a precious little thing to be protected. A china figurine. A goddess. The muse of terpsichore. She danced around the vestibule, in front of the long mirror, watching her chiffon streamers trailing gracefully out behind her, light-headed from the champagne but not drunk. It was delicious to have two suitors, both mad about her; one a handsome young actor who was going to be famous someday, and the other a distinguished, brilliant, rich doctor who was famous already. Dr. Lazarus Bergman was definitely a good catch, and he was after her.

The next day, red roses arrived, with Dr. Lazarus Bergman's printed calling card. Melissa put the red roses into a big vase on top of the shawl on the piano in the living room, and tucked the card into her memory book along with the ticket stub and the signed program from her first date with Scott Brown and a whole lot of other things that were really just junk. She liked beginnings. If life could always consist of just beginnings it would be wonderful. Nothing would ever be boring, and nothing would be sad because it would never end.

FIFTEEN

In that summer of 1923 Andrew was in his senior year at Boy's High and a junior counselor at Camp Kinnewanah. He had liked the camp when he had gone there as a camper, and he liked being a junior counselor even more. He taught arts and crafts. Arts and crafts was a joke: it consisted mainly of teaching the boys to braid lanyards and paint colors on plaster plaques with Indian heads on them in bas relief, all premade, something a five-year-old could do easily. Or, if they were particularly adventurous, they could hammer a circle of copper into a copper ashtray, something any seven-year-old could do. The fact that they kept on doing these dumb things until they were fourteen, then brought them home to show their parents what they had spent so much money on, made Andrew indignant. But what he did like about arts and crafts was that every summer there were a few boys who were actually interested in painting and drawing, and so he could teach them the thing he loved best.

Andrew loved nature as much as he loved anything, but the trouble was he always wanted to improve on it. The bridle path through the deep woods was lovely, but he would have made it wider in a few places, and narrower in another, and he would have liked to take it up on the high ridge overlooking the lake so that a rider could pause a moment to rest his horse and gaze down on the view.

When he painted pictures of scenic places around the camp he improved upon nature as he would have wished to see it, so his paintings although representational, were also fantasy. The colors came from Andrew's head, and the landscape from his dreams. The boys to whom he taught painting enjoyed working with him because his pictures didn't look right any more than theirs did. Painting was fun and no one felt inferior. Painting made Andrew happy. Although he had learned charm, basically he was quiet, and he liked not having to talk to people.

There were many feelings Andrew kept inside. To the world (the world being his family and friends) he was the clever, charming golden boy who got everything he wanted. He was also a sometimes cranky perfectionist, who criticized and changed things. He knew all this. But what that same world did not see was the other side of Andrew, the secret side, the always frightened Andrew who knew the world was going to come to an end and could not figure out how to stop it. He worried that he was not handsome enough, that his father would lose all his money, that he himself would not be accepted into Columbia with all his friends, that he might disgrace himself, that people didn't really like him, that his father would find him wanting in some way. The motor car, the horse, the things he asked Papa for and got, were only props to keep the fragile roof of his world from caving in. In nightmares he was alone, weak, afraid, trying to run through water and finding that his legs pained and failed him. In the daytime he sometimes had headaches so painful he would strike his head against the wall.

His plan for life was to go to Columbia and law school and enter his father's business, do well, be respected, make a lot of money. Nothing would ever be enough for him, he wanted to be rich beyond measure so that he would never have to be poor. He wanted to marry the prettiest girl in the world, with the sweetest disposition, and protect her. He wanted bright, happy children. He wanted his father to be proud of him and what he made of his life. He wanted people to look up to him and say: "Andrew Saffron is an honor to his father and his family."

His secret plan (his silly plan he thought of it, because he would never do it) was to run away to Paris and study painting, live on the Left Bank in a studio with north light and paint in oils, know other young artists and even the more established ones —well, this was a dream, so he might as well include Picasso as his close friend—and he would have lovely girls to admire him, and in the evenings, tired and satisfied from a good, long day's work, he would go to a cafe or a cheap restaurant with those other artists and those lovely girls, and they would all talk of art and their feelings, without shame or pretention.

Now at Camp Kinnewanah he was enjoying his last summer before he would have to put away boyish things and become a man. By next summer he would probably work in Papa's office, learning the business from the bottom up so that when the time came for him to take his place there he would be able to fit in. Although it would be only a summer job, to learn the ropes, he would have a better position than Lavinia, who was there biding her time until she got married. Lavinia did the little things Papa's secretary was too busy to do, and she liked to feel she was a help, but no one there took her seriously. One was sorry for Papa's secretary, who was an older woman with no husband and no parents, who had to support herself, and certainly no one would ever imagine a girl like Lavinia would want to end up like that. She was twenty-three, and soon she would find the right fellow. She was very picky, and no one was good enough for her, but Andrew thought she was right. He would hate having an ordinary brother-in-law.

He cheered himself up this last summer by swimming in the cold lake, walking in the cool, dark woods, or watching the kids playing sports. Lucky kids, nothing to worry about yet. There was Jonah Mendes, the head counselor, an interesting guy, pitching a spitball to one of the older boys. Jonah Mendes was the kind of person Andrew would ordinarily never have known because he lived in a slum and was very poor. He was a math teacher and an athlete, an Orthodox Sephardic Jew who kept kosher and wouldn't eat half the things they served at the camp. But he didn't sit around reading the Bible or anything; he was really a great guy who loved baseball and diving and hikes. He had taken the job as head counselor because he needed the money. Teachers didn't make anything and had no future. The funny thing was that even though they came from opposite ends of the earth, in a way,

Jonah Mendes had always been in Andrew's life, first because Andrew had been in his math class in high school, and later because of the camp. At school he had been Mr. Mendes, who really felt sorry when he had to give Andrew a bad mark, not because a bad mark made it harder to get into college but because Mr. Mendes thought math was art. At camp he was Jonah, the boss but still a nice guy, reticent but pleasant, with a big happy smile. You couldn't swear in front of him—he would practically faint because of his religious upbringing—but Andrew made it a practice never to swear anyway because he felt it was bad taste. The worst thing you could do was use certain Yiddish words in front of Jonah; then he would hit the roof. For instance, to Andrew "shmuck" meant a dunce, but to Jonah it meant a dirty street word for penis, and if you called someone a shmuck in front of Jonah he would nearly choke. It was funny in a way.

Andrew sometimes felt sorry for Jonah. He was tall, he had looks, he had a great build, he was an intellectual, but he would never make it in life. He would always be poor, always have to struggle. What a dumb job to pick, a math teacher. A shmucky job! Jonah Mendes just didn't have any future at all. And he was a wizard at math, too. Jonah with his math was sort of like what Andrew would have been with his painting, but Andrew was practical enough to know that his painting and the whole poor-in-Paris fantasy was just a dream, a diversion, but Jonah had gone and committed himself to being a poor math teacher, not because he was brave but because he didn't ever know or dream of anything better. Or maybe he *was* brave. How could you tell? You couldn't sit down with him and tell him you thought he was strange and ask him why he had done it. He was either very brave or very limited. He was either someone to envy or someone to pity.

That was another thing Andrew would miss when he left camp: being able to meet and know people who were so different from the all-the-same people he would meet when he went into his own world for keeps.

But as it turned out, no one, even Andrew, could ever really plan life.

Afterward, he liked to tell the way it happened, and so did Lavinia, until in the telling it became something entirely different although essentially the same, something out of a storybook. It was visitors' day at Camp Kinnewanah, and Lavinia and Basil and Papa had driven up to see Andrew, in Papa's chauffeur-driven car. Basil did not go to camp. Basil hated camp.

It was a yellow car with a black top, and the sun was shining. Lavinia was wearing a white dress and white stockings and white shoes, and she and the car looked all gold and white, the car hard and shiny, Lavinia small and soft and gauzy. Her dark hair was bobbed, and because it was naturally wavy it looked marcelled and very stylish. And Jonah Mendes was standing there to greet all the parents as the cars drove up, because that was what a head counselor did. And of course, Andrew was standing there too, because he wanted to see his family. And so it happened that Andrew was standing next to Jonah when Papa's car drove up and stopped, and Lavinia climbed out. And Jonah, seeing Lavinia for the first time in his life, sucked in his breath as if he had seen a vision.

"That girl!" he whispered to Andrew. "See that girl? Someday I'm going to marry her."

"You mean," said Andrew, "my stupid sister?"

SIXTEEN

When Jonah Mendes asked Lavinia for a date that summer after camp was over for the season, she accepted because she liked his looks and Andrew said he had a good character. She had never seen a young man who looked like Jonah. Black hair in fat curls like black grapes, and skin so dark from the sun that he looked like a Spaniard. He tried to comb his thick hair down with pomade so he could look like everyone else, but it sprang right up again. He had good, strong features, and large, kind black eyes, a happy smile with dimples, and good, strong, white teeth. He looked clean. Cleanliness was very important to her. He was twenty-nine years old, but in many ways he was an innocent. She was not afraid of him, not afraid to admit to herself that she found him handsome.

However, he was crazy. The first thing he did on their first date was propose to her.

"You don't even know me!" she said.

"Yes I do. I know enough to know that I love you and I want to marry you."

"How can you love me when you don't know me?"

"I loved you the minute I saw you."

"Well, you're crazy, that's all," she said.

They went for a walk because he had no money. A walk! Lavinia had never been out with a poor boy, and her high heels hurt her feet. She should have known better than to wear her brand-new shoes on a date without breaking them in first. While they walked he told her a little of his life, that he had grown up in a good Jewish neighborhood in Harlem, but not a rich neighborhood, on the fringes of it, where the poor people lived. All the men in his family had been scholars, teachers, rabbis, and professors. His father was deeply religious, and because he would not work on Saturday he had ended up in a menial job in a factory, he a scholar! And his sons were all school teachers because it was a five-day week, enabling them to go to temple not only on Friday night but on Saturday, as good, Orthodox Jews did. And of course, they kept kosher.

I certainly would never marry a religious fanatic, Lavinia thought to herself. *But then, of course, I suppose men can be made to change.*

"When I was a kid, I used to swim in the East River," Jonah said. "I always liked the outdoor life, but I had to go to school, and Hebrew school, and also I had to work to help my family, so I never had as much time for sports as I wanted. Although we used to play ball in the street when we had a chance."

"I always enjoyed bicycle riding at college," Lavinia said.

"You see how much we have in common!" he said, delighted.

"No, I don't see."

He wanted to take her somewhere for a bite to eat, but this place looked suspicious, and that one looked doubtful, until finally he found a nice clean cafeteria. He had a swiss cheese sandwich because it was kosher. Lavinia had a ham sandwich and a glass of milk to drive him away, but he pretended not to notice.

After they ate, he lit up a cigarette. "I can't stand the smell of cigarettes," Lavinia said. "To me, they're a dirty habit."

"I'll get a pipe," he said.

"Well, you certainly don't have to do that for me."

"No, I like a pipe. If you don't like cigarettes, I wouldn't want to disgust you."

Lavinia smiled, flattered. "That's really very nice of you," she said. It occurred to her that by allowing this lunatic to spend some of his hard-earned money on a pipe, just to please her, she was committing herself to seeing more of him, but the thought rather pleased her. He was stubborn, and she admired a stubborn man. But he also gave in, and she liked that.

"I want to take you out every night," he said.

"Oh, I couldn't do that."

"Then as often as possible. Although, since I know we're going to get married eventually, there's no point in dragging it out."

"Who *says* we're going to get married—*ever?*" Lavinia said.

"I say."

"Ha!"

"You'll see."

After he walked her home, she was bathing her sore feet in hot water and epsom salts when the telephone rang. It was Jonah.

"What's the matter?" Lavinia asked.

"I just called to say good night," he said. "And to tell you I love you."

"You nearly scared everybody out of their wits," she said. "Don't you know that when you phone someone after ten o'clock at night it could only mean that somebody's in the hospital or *dead?*"

"Oh, I didn't know that," Jonah said cheerfully. "You see, we don't have a telephone."

"Where are you?"

"In the candy store on the corner."

"Well, you ought to go to bed. It's late."

"I will. What are you doing? I want to imagine you."

She certainly didn't want him imagining her soaking her sore feet in a basin of water and epsom salts. "Oh, I was just reading a little before going to bed."

"What were you reading?"

"Freud."

"What do you think of Freud?"

"Jonah, I'm not going to get into a discussion about Sigmund Freud in the middle of the night. It's nearly eleven."

"I just wondered if he was your favorite psychologist."

"I don't really have a favorite. Each one has something interesting to say, although sometimes I can't really agree."

"What does Freud say?"

"Jonah!"

"Can I see you tomorrow night?"

"I told you I have a date."

"What time?"

"Eight o'clock."

"All right, then I'll call you around six. Will that be okay?"

"Fine. Good night, Jonah."

But the next night he called her at a quarter of eight instead of six, and then kept her on the phone for forty-five minutes so that her date was twiddling his thumbs in the living room waiting for her for half an hour. It occurred to Lavinia that she didn't have to talk to this transparently devious young man for forty-five minutes unless she really wanted to, and therefore she must really want to. But what a pest he was! In order to spare herself the repetition of another such phone call she was obliged to accept a date with Jonah for the following night.

But it also occurred to her that she didn't have to accept a date with him unless she really wanted to. Lavinia never did what she didn't want to.

She also did exactly what she wanted to. And so, because she wanted to, when Jonah came to call for her she handed him a little present she had bought for him that afternoon. It was a pipe.

SEVENTEEN

It was hot that summer, well into September, but Melissa was glad that the family hadn't gone away to the beach or the mountains because she was having such a good time at home. Being wined and dined by Lazarus, and sneaking off to see Scott, her time was full. Lavinia had stopped bothering her about her mysterious excursions because finally Lavinia had found a fellow she liked and her mind was on herself. Actually, with Lazarus so respectable and appearing at the house so often, no one would ever suspect that Melissa was seeing an unrespectable young man on the side.

"I think you're really swell, Melissa," the unrespectable young man said. "I'm serious about you. I'd like you to come home and meet my folks."

Since she was so busy making sure that he was not just toying with her, it never occurred to Melissa that perhaps she was the one who was toying with him. She dressed in her most refined and ladylike manner to impress his parents. They were all to have an early supper together at his parent's apartment before Scott had to go to the theater.

Melissa had never seen anything like Scott's parents' house. Aunt Becky was poor, but her apartment didn't look like that. To start with, everything seemed to take place in the kitchen, an ugly small room with flowered oilcloth on the table, torn flowered linoleum on the floor, and rings and stains on top of everything. His parents were English all right, but they didn't talk a bit like the actors she had seen on the stage, nor like Scott for that matter. They were Cockney, and she couldn't understand half of what they said. There was beer and whiskey in the kitchen, in plain view, and both his parents drank it. His mother even offered some to her. They were so strange, so different, but what made them particularly frightening was that basically they were so ordinary; they didn't think they were odd, they didn't have wicked thoughts or swear or act unkind, and they were really trying to be nice to her and make her feel at home, and that was terrifying. If they were eccentrics, the Parents of an Actor, then she could have understood. But they were ordinary. His mother was a drab little housewife and his father was a drab little milkman, and their son the actor was just a nice ordinary boy.

Melissa saw it all in a flash. Ordinary! Not only was Scott ordinary, but he was unforgivably different: he came from another world, one which she had never seen before and which she had no desire whatever to enter. No wonder her Papa forbade her to go out with goyim. What in the world would goyim have to offer her except confusion? She felt homesick, although home was only within a subway or trolley ride away, and she wanted to cry.

She was stuck there and had to eat supper with them, and she knew she would not be able to get a bite beyond the lump in her throat. His mother was putting it on the table already: some boiled grayish meat that smelled nauseating, some big boiled carrots, and boiled potatoes.

"What is this?" Melissa asked sweetly.

"Mutton," the father said, his mouth already full of it.

"I hope you like mutton," the mother said.

"Oh, yes," Melissa said. She had never even heard of it.

She couldn't eat anything that smelled and looked like that, she just couldn't, but she couldn't insult them either. There was his mother, looking at her with concern.

"You don't feel well?"

Melissa shook her head.

"It's the heat," his mother said understandingly.

"I'm particularly susceptible to heat," Melissa said. "It's my metabolism." These were things Lazarus had said to her, and now suddenly she missed him. He would have told these people that greasy, fatty mutton was bad for them to eat in this intolerable heat. She put her head down, feeling faint.

"Oh, Melissa, you should lie down," Scott said, full of concern.

"Put her right on my bed, ducks," his mother said.

Melissa allowed herself to be led into the parents' bedroom, and lay on the tacky flowered spread (they were flower mad in this house!) while Scott brought her a cold, damp cloth for her forehead. There was flowered linoleum on the bedroom floor too, and over it was a small, oval, braided rug, rather dirty. Across from where she lay she could see the dresser, painted and chipped, with a dirty lace antimacassar on top of it, and on top of that a tray filled with gewgaws. She noticed a hairbrush, full of hair.

"I'd better go home," she whispered to Scott.

"Oh, poor Melissa, I hope you aren't coming down with something," he said.

"My cousin has chickenpox," Melissa said.

"Oops! I'd better get you home."

For once she didn't protest. She apologized to his parents and let Scott lead her away. In the subway she sat with her head on his shoulder, feeling better but very sad and nostalgic. She felt as if he were her brother, or perhaps a cousin. She liked him. But she knew it was over. There was no future for them, none at all. He wasn't glamorous any more, and she was tired of sneaking around. When they got off at her stop she let him walk her right to her front door, because after all she didn't want to faint in the street, and then she gave him her hand.

"Thank you, Scott," she whispered. "Good night."

He was looking at her house with some amazement. Perhaps where she came from was as big a surprise to him as his origins had been to her. "May I call you tomorrow to see how you are?" he asked.

"If you like." She gave him her phone number. It didn't matter now, not at all. He wasn't her boyfriend. She could tell whoever asked that he was just a boy she knew from class.

"I hope it isn't chickenpox," he said.

"Oh, I'm sure it isn't. Don't worry. I'll see the doctor tomorrow."

She watched him walk away. It was still light out, and as he grew smaller and farther away she wanted to run after him and hug him because she was sorry that she had been mean to him, and that she was going to be meaner still because she would never see him again. But he would forget her. She was sure of that. There were lots of other girls who wanted him, and he would have a happy life.

The next day she did see the doctor—Lazarus. He took her to the theater, to see *Cyrano de Bergerac,* and afterward they went dancing and had a light, cold supper. She did not mention her brief illness. She felt fine now, and they hardly noticed the time fly by.

When Lazarus proposed to her, Melissa said yes, and when he asked Papa for her hand, Papa said yes too. They planned to be married in January, at the temple, with a reception afterward at Delmonico. There would be chauffeur-driven cars to take all the guests who did not have cars of their own. Melissa was the first girl in her crowd to have a reception all the way in New York, but then, no one had married anyone nearly as distinguished as Dr. Lazarus Bergman. The girls who were already married were no older than she was, and they had all married young neighborhood boys, whose parents were friends of their parents. She spent weeks planning the wedding and changing her mind about her wedding dress. She bought an etiquette book to make sure everything was just perfect, from the invitations to the seating arrangements. By the time she and Lazarus and Papa had finished compiling the list of people to be invited there were two hundred guests. Those were just the people they simply had to invite. There were a great many more whose names had finally been stricken regretfully from the list. Imagine! Two hundred close friends and relatives!

She had never dreamed there were so many things to be done before a wedding, and she had only four months to do them in. Papa told her to go to town and buy anything she wanted for her trousseau. She and Lazarus found a nice apartment, but then she had to furnish it, and what did she, a girl of twenty, know about furnishing a whole apartment? Mama simply didn't have the strength to go shlepping around to department stores with her, so they hired a decorator. That was terribly très chic. The decorator was a hatchet-faced old woman, but she had the strength of a man, and she and Melissa spent many days finding exactly the right things. There was a lovely bedroom set, and a wonderful, modern dining room set, and the living room had an Oriental carpet and a grand piano in it. That was nice; Melissa could play and sing for her friends. Then the wedding invitations went out and the wedding gifts came pouring in, the silver tea set with the coffee pot to match, the everyday silverplate (Mama gave her the good silverware, of course), and the good dishes and the everyday dishes. Melissa thought, amused, that they might as well be kosher with two sets of everything like that, but that was what grown-up people did: they gave parties and they had good things, and then they had normal things. Oh, and there had to be two sets of glasses too, the ones with stems and engraving on them, and the regular ones. And there had to be linens, sheets and towels and tablecloths and doilies and blankets and pillows and a bedspread, and there seemed to be no end to it. No wonder people had long engagements. It obviously wasn't to get to know each other better, since she and Lazarus hardly had time to see each other, she was so exhausted; it was to buy things.

Wallpaper or paint? The decorator said paint was more modern. Melissa thought wallpaper was romantic, but then she remembered all those horrible flowers in Scott Brown's parents' apartment and she decided to make everything very simple and gracious. It would be paint. Simple red velvet draperies would be nice in the living room with the Oriental rug, and a sofa to pick up one of the other colors. She was learning. There had to be bookshelves, of course, for all of Lazarus' books. They would be in the living room, so that everyone could see them. Besides, there was no place else to put them.

She even bought a painting to go over the sofa, a romantic, sweet oil of a summer country scene with sheep in it. Sheep looked so nice and gentle. Darling Andrew made her a painting for a wedding present, a portrait of herself in her wedding dress. It actually looked like her. Basil gave her a clock. That seemed like a strange present until she remembered she would need one when she was cooking . . . and she didn't even know how to cook! There were all those brand-new pots and pans in her new kitchen-to-be, and she couldn't make one single thing without consulting a cookbook. At least she wasn't stupid, she could cope.

It was nice of all her sisters and brothers to give her presents they bought with their allowances (of course, Lavinia had a salary, if you could call it that, although it was hardly more than an allowance). Lavinia chipped in for some of her everyday silverware. Rosemary gave her a cookbook. And Hazel made her something odd which she said was supposed to be an egg warmer: it was a little knitted cap for a boiled egg.

Lazarus had decided that for their honeymoon he and Melissa should go to Dr. Kellogg's Health Farm in Battle Creek, Michigan, a veritable winter wonderland, where he could hopefully gain a few pounds and Melissa could lose a few. She had rather dreamed of seeing Niagara Falls, but they could do that some other time, and after all the work of preparing for the wedding she supposed she would need a nice rest.

It would be a beautiful wedding, a glamorous reception, a sensible honeymoon, and then they would come home and move into their very own apartment, within walking distance of Papa and Mama's house. What girl could possibly ask for more?

EIGHTEEN

Adam was well satisfied with Melissa's marriage. She had always been a giddy girl, too pretty, too wild and immature, and he was glad she had chosen an older man who would take care of her and help her settle down. Other fathers were sometimes jealous of the men their daughters married, but not Adam Saffron; he was too secure in his position of patriarch of the family. A family was like a pyramid, with the father at the top. Since Adam believed much more in the equality of women than most men did, he did not feel that the husbands of his daughters should be higher on the pyramid than their wives; no, they should be equal. But of course his sons should be ahead of the daughters, for the simple reason that they would run the family business and carry on the family name, thus if any of the daughters should remain unmarried, or marry a man who turned out to be a disappointment, the brothers would always have the responsibility and the means to take care of her. This was natural. The sisters would love each other and care for each other and for each other's children, as sisters should, but the boys would bear the burdens of the outside world.

Adam had been watching Jonah Mendes paying court to Lavinia, and it amused him. He liked the young fellow. Jonah had guts, he would not give up even when Lavinia flaunted her other boyfriends in his face, but Adam knew that Lavinia liked Jonah the best and was simply making up her mind. She was like him: she tested things and people, she knew what she wanted and how to get it, but she was patient, stubborn, and careful. She was also unlike him, because she was a girl: she did not trust her own instincts in a split second as he did. She felt something, but had to make sure. This was not a bad trait. Adam knew that once Lavinia had decided, she would be as a rock. Like him.

It did not disturb Adam that Jonah Mendes was poor. The young man was intelligent, and he had a future. It was no disgrace to be a school teacher; it was an honorable profession. It was to the disgrace of the school board or whoever was in charge that teachers were so poorly paid. Scholars never made money. They were supposed to eat air, and feed their children air. Never mind; if Jonah was serious about Lavinia, and if she decided to accept him, then Adam could take him into the family business. He would do well. It would be good to have three sons to help him instead of two. He was doing better every year, and there would be plenty for them to do.

Jonah was so persistent it was funny. He telephoned Lavinia every time she had a date with someone else, and kept her on the phone while the other fellow waited. And then, of course, Jonah took Lavinia out every time she would let him, even though he had no money to spend on her. Adam was sure Lavinia liked Jonah the best, because she seemed happier just taking a walk with him or sitting in the living room talking with him than she was going out someplace fancy with anyone else. Young people today thought they were so intellectual. They could sit for hours talking about themselves, their plans and dreams. In his day you didn't waste time telling a girl about those things. Genug! Who had to sit and talk? Talk was cheap.

Well, his Lavinia was a special girl, and she deserved a special man. Adam hoped she and Jonah would get on with it.

"Papa," Lavinia said finally, "Jonah wants to talk to you."

"So? Then I'll talk."

"But first I want to talk with you."

"All right," Adam said pleasantly.

"I would like to marry him."

Adam nodded. "Good."

"I wouldn't do it without your approval."

"You want my approval?"

"Yes, Papa."

"You love him?"

She actually blushed. "Yes, Papa."

"He loves you?"

"Oh, yes."

"Then I approve."

Lavinia beamed. "I'll send him in."

Jonah entered Adam's study and Lavinia tiptoed out, shutting the door behind them. Jonah was respectful but not frightened. He had—this was strange, Adam thought—a kind of great affection about him: a warmth, almost a love for him just because he was Lavinia's father. Most young men were ready to respect a father-in-law, or even fear him, and sometimes to hate him and fight with him, but this young man was ready to give his love. He was too good. He would learn hard lessons in life. He was lucky to have Lavinia, for she would protect him with her caution, just as he would warm her with his recklessness.

"I would like your permission to marry Lavinia," Jonah said.

"Yes, I know. But you will have to understand a few things first."

"Yes?" Eager, earnest, he would understand anything, even the impossible to understand.

"Lavinia is a very stubborn, strong girl," Adam said. "She has to have her way. If you marry her and you don't give her her way you will never be happy. She'll drive you crazy."

"Then I'll give her her way," Jonah said.

"There is the matter of religion," Adam said. "You know Lavinia is not religious. Not *without* religion, you understand, but not religious. She will not be Orthodox."

"I know."

"She will not keep kosher."

"I know."

"You are ready to accept these things?" Adam asked.

"If it makes her happy."

"Will it make you unhappy?"

"I can accept it," Jonah said.

"Then you have my permission and all my good wishes," Adam said.

Ah, how the boy beamed! He looked impatient to run out of the room and tell his beloved the good news. Adam was not ready to let him go yet. "I have a proposition for you," he said.

"Yes, sir?"

"Give some thought to coming into the business with me. There would be a place for you. I can use a man who is good with figures."

"Thank you. I'll think about it."

"You don't accept right away?"

"No, sir. I'll have to think about it, and discuss it with Lavinia."

"Good, good. And call me Papa. Sir, it's for the Army."

"Thanks, Papa. I *was* in the Army, you know."

"Oh? You fought in Europe?"

"No, I was lucky. They kept me here. They said: 'Oh, you're a school teacher? Then you must be smart. So you can drive the Colonel around on his motorcycle.' That's their idea in the Army of what to do with a smart man."

Adam laughed. "You knew how to drive?"

"No. But I learned on the motorcycle."

Then they both laughed, and Adam shook Jonah's hand. "You'll have dinner with us tonight."

"Thanks, Papa."

"You don't have other plans?"

"No."

"It's Friday. You don't have to go to temple tonight, go home to your parents and light the candles?"

"I have to, but I won't," Jonah said. "I want to be here."

"Consider us your family too," Adam said.

"Thanks, Papa. I do already."

"So go, go. What are you doing here with me when a pretty girl is waiting for you?"

Jonah fairly ran out of the room. Adam smiled. Love . . . well, it was good. Lavinia had chosen well. It might seem a strange choice to someone else, but he knew better.

He sat at his huge desk and took a key from the top drawer. Then he unlocked the bottom side drawer, the one where he kept secret papers of a financial nature which were no one's business but his own. Among them was a folder, and he took it out, his fingers holding it tenderly. It was Adam Saffron's dream.

Adam had had this dream for many years now, kept it to himself, planning to make it come true some day. All his life, ever since he was a small boy in Russia, there had been two needs battling each other in him: the need to seek out new frontiers and the normal need for family love, companionship, and security. The need to find new frontiers had triumphed. When he had gotten a ride on a farmer's wagon to the big town when he was only nine and small for his age, to live with strangers just so he could go to the good school there because he was already beyond his own small village school, his parents had been as proud of him as they were concerned. They knew he was different and they accepted it. They understood man's need to better himself through education. And when his education had shown him even finer frontiers, across the ocean, Adam had gone to America. He was eighteen, and he knew that he would never see his parents again, that the moment he stepped on the ship he would be swept into the next generation, a man. A man . . . and alone. When he married and his family grew, and he busied himself with his work and later what became his financial empire, Adam still remembered the sad pain of loneliness he had felt as a child, always driven to succeed, to find, to build, and yet longing for closeness and home. The two seemed so incompatible, but Adam determined that someday he would have it all, the frontiers conquered, the warm family all around him. The All was in this folder he held in his hand.

In the folder were the blueprints for four elegant, comfortable houses, to be built someday somewhere deep in the country, near enough to New York so that he could drive to work every day, but far enough away so that there would be peace, quiet, and beauty. Four houses. One for him and Lucy and any of their yet unmarried children. One eventually for the boys and their wives and children.

Two eventually for the four girls and their husbands and children. Little Rosemary was only sixteen, but she wouldn't be sixteen forever. A family should stay together. Please God he would have the money to make this dream come true. Someday they would all be together forever, in such a place of beauty and bliss that it could truly be called a paradise.

Adam took out a fountain pen and carefully, on the plan for one of the houses, he inked in four names. Melissa and Lazarus. Lavinia and Jonah.

In a week or two, when the excitement died down over the engagement announcement and a date was being discussed for the wedding, he would suggest that Lavinia be a June bride. Jonah would have the whole summer off, being a teacher. He wouldn't be able to afford much of a honeymoon. Perhaps a weekend in the mountains somewhere. So Adam would suggest that Lavinia and Jonah take a small cottage with Melissa and Lazarus, for the summer. He, of course, would help, if needed. It would be nice for the four of them to get to know each other better as couples and it would make the finances possible. Lazarus could go back and forth to the city, and then he could take the month of August off. Doctors could do anything they wanted to.

He put the blueprints back into the folder and locked the folder away in the drawer. Dreams should not be exposed too soon. They had to be handled gently.

NINETEEN

That summer the two couples had their first beach house together: Melissa and Lazarus, Lavinia and Jonah. It was actually a cottage, tiny, with two bedrooms, one bathroom, a living room, a kitchen, and a minuscule porch surrounded by screens and shaded by awnings. On the porch were heavy white wicker chairs with flowered cushions, and outside the house purple and violet hydrangeas bloomed. A sandy path led the four blocks to the beach and the ocean. But you could hear the ocean from the house, and if you stood in front of the house you could see it. Lazarus and Jonah braved the icy water—Lazarus because it was good for him, Jonah because he enjoyed it. Lavinia and Melissa hated both the sea and the sun. Melissa's skin was too fair and delicate to bear even five minutes on the beach, and she had never learned how to swim. Lavinia had learned to swim at college, but she was afraid of jellyfish, the undertow, and whatever mysterious creatures or castaway garbage lurked out there in the waves.

Besides, Melissa was pregnant. She was doing well, only a minimum amount of morning sickness, and she felt secure with Lazarus around to protect her and her own obstetrician in the city less than an hour away. She spent her days lolling on the cool porch, taking care of herself and the unborn child. She had hardly gotten used to the idea of herself as a wife, and now she had to get used to the idea of herself as a mother. It seemed funny now that only six months ago she hadn't even known where babies came from. Oh, she knew how a pregnant woman looked, she'd seen enough of that. But what did men and women do together to make babies anyway? She hadn't known until her wedding night, when she and Lazarus had gone to their bridal suite, and as she was sitting there, quite nervous, Lazarus had sat down next to her and told her gently that there was nothing to worry about. He knew that she hadn't the faintest idea of what people were supposed to do on their wedding night.

"Now, Toots," he'd said, "I'm not going to jump on you. First I'm going to tell you everything you ought to know. Now, you mustn't be embarrassed, because I'm a medical doctor as well as your husband."

And then, slowly, simply, patiently, he had told her everything he felt she ought to know. And then he showed her. Melissa was very happy. She'd had no idea it was so nice. No wonder no one ever told her anything. They were obviously afraid she might go out and do it! And of course, if she'd done it, she might have had a baby, which would have been dreadful with no husband. So here she was, a woman of the world, and a mother-to-be, rocking on the little front porch of her summer beach cottage, thinking up names.

Adam and Lucy had taken a larger house four blocks away, right on the ocean front. Hazel and Rosemary were with them, and Basil, and Andrew commuted with Papa every day in the car to his summer job in the family office. It was a huge, white, airy house, good for Mama's lungs with all that ocean breeze blowing in the open windows and a fine, big lawn to sit on, protected from the wind by a sea wall. They had brought the two maids, Lena and Letty, twin sisters from Poland. Lena cooked and Letty cleaned, and both of them were trying to learn English.

Many evenings Melissa and Lazarus, Lavinia and Jonah went to Papa's house for dinner, but whenever they ate in their own house they always went to Papa's to visit afterward. It was a nice way to spend the evenings, all the family together. Lavinia and Jonah were still newlyweds, really on their honeymoon if you wanted to be technical, and they were quite shameless, holding hands and kissing whenever they thought no one was looking. Everyone teased them.

Rosemary was taking tennis lessons during the day, and at night she went gallivanting around with the other young kids whose parents had summer homes in the neighborhood. Hazel spent her days knitting for Melissa's expected baby; a little afghan, a carriage cover, a summer crib cover, a winter crib cover. She had even mastered a cap, although Mama had done most of it. Basil spent his days swimming, sunning, and playing tennis, and in the evenings he chased girls. In his white suit, with his hair slicked back, his face freshly shaved, smelling of eau de cologne, he fancied himself quite a devil. Especially when he could borrow Papa's car. There was no place to take a girl in the car, but a drive in the car with Basil was quite thrill enough.

Andrew had two close friends, but his life was quieter, more mysterious. When he took a girl out he did not discuss it, he simply got dressed up and left the house. Since he had to get up early in the morning on weekdays, he usually stayed out late only on weekend nights. He was doing his best to live a moderate, dignified life.

If Jonah had been given his choice, this would not have been the way he would have chosen to spend his honeymoon. He would have preferred to get a job as head counselor at a camp in the mountains somewhere, and he and Lavinia could have a little cottage there for just the two of them. They would be able to ride bicycles together through the lovely, wooded bike paths and pick wild berries when they got thirsty. He was sure she wouldn't be afraid to swim in a clear mountain lake, and he would be right by her side to protect her. But this summer plan was what Papa wanted, and what Lavinia wanted too, and so it was not up to him to disagree. He was really very lucky. Certainly he could not have afforded a cottage like this all by himself. He liked the beach and the ocean. And he was so fond of his in-laws that they seemed his own dear family. That is, Papa and Mama did. About the others he had varying opinions. But then, that was the way one felt about one's own brothers and sisters too. You didn't love them all alike, you couldn't, because they weren't all alike as people. Some of them you even had a hard time liking at all.

He was not too fond of Lazarus. He didn't like the way Lazarus kept making fun of him for being "just a poor school teacher." Sometimes Lazarus and Papa talked about the stock market, as both of them owned a great many stocks, but whenever Jonah tried to venture an opinion Lazarus laughed at him, so he stopped. The truth was that Jonah knew a good deal more about the market than any of them except Lavinia suspected. During the school term, whenever the teachers had time off, they would sit downstairs in the basement boiler room (which was the only place where they were allowed to smoke) and talk about the market. It was all wishful thinking because none of them could afford to buy any stocks, but perhaps because he was being intellectual and not emotional about it, Jonah had found that the market was as fascinating to him as any mathematical problem, and even more fascinating, because it concerned real businesses. It could be a lifelong study. It *had* to be, to make it pay off. Jonah supposed it didn't make much difference to rich people if they lost a little money, but a little money was a lot to him. He couldn't understand people like Lazarus buying on margin, even though the economy was booming. A small margin, yes, but the big margin everyone bought on seemed dangerous to Jonah. But try to say a word to Lazarus! "Oh shut up, what do you know?" was the answer.

Women were strange, Jonah thought. Melissa worshiped the guy. She thought he was a genius. She took his part even before he could open his mouth, which was pretty fast. She actually mothered her husband, and he seemed to demand it. Although Melissa was totally dependent on Lazarus, he was also totally dependent on her. It was a symbiotic relationship, to use one of those big words Lazarus was always showing off with. Both of them were the child, but if Jonah had to pick the one who was more the child he would pick Lazarus.

Jonah didn't know much about women, never having gone out with girls before Lavinia, but he knew about people. His impression of women was that they were usually hysterics. The only girl he'd ever met whom he could really respect as a sensible, brilliant person was Lavinia. And his mother-in-law, although she hardly ever said a word, being a quiet person, was sensible too. Whatever Lucy did say made sense. The rest of them would hock you a chainik, by the hour. You had to be polite, to converse with them, but women just didn't know how to shut up. It was one of the things that had driven him away from girls before he met Lavinia, the way they could bore you to death without even trying. Besides, you couldn't do anything with them anyway. A nice girl wouldn't kiss you until you were engaged, and then you couldn't do much else so it was hardly worth it, and the kind of girls who ran around sleeping with guys, well, you never knew what you would catch from them. Who wanted somebody's castoffs anyway? Jonah was proud that he had been a virgin when he married Lavinia. His very religious upbringing had helped, but his actual fear of being dominated by a shrew and trapped into an unwanted marriage had helped more. He didn't intend to stay a poor school teacher forever. The slobs in his neighborhood didn't attract him in the least. Lavinia was a princess. She was his dream. When he saw her he was glad he had waited.

"Jonah!" It was Papa. "Why don't you let me teach you to play pinochle? You'll like it."

"Okay," Jonah said, smiling, flattered to be noticed.

He had been watching Papa play pinochle with Lazarus for so many evenings now that he had more or less gotten the hang of it himself. He listened attentively as Papa showed him the game, and tried a few hands, finding it easy.

"Why don't you play with Lazarus?" Papa said.

They seated themselves opposite each other at the card table. Lazarus shuffled and dealt. Jonah won.

"You cheated!" Lazarus screamed, his face red with rage.

"I did not!"

"You did!"

"Please, Lazarus," Lucy said quietly. They all turned to look at her because she spoke so seldom. "I was watching. Jonah did not cheat."

"I won't play with him again," Lazarus said sullenly.

Papa touched Jonah on the arm. "We still have something to talk about, you and I," he said quietly.

120

"Yes, Papa?"

Papa looked around. Melissa had taken Lazarus to cool off on the porch, and Hazel didn't count. Lavinia and Lucy were family and entitled to hear this secret. "I offered to take you into the business. Have you been thinking about it?"

"Yes, I have."

"You could start in the fall. You get a nice vacation, then you quit the school, say goodbye, and come to work with me. Well?"

"It's hard to say no," Jonah said. "But I love teaching . . ."

"Then you should teach," Lucy said. They all looked at her again, the soft, firm voice startling them as it always did. "A man should have something of his own."

There was a silence. She was right, of course. What was a man, if he did not have something of his own?

Papa nodded. "Nu, it's not a bad business, the school business. Good times and bad times, it goes on. The children always have to learn. It has security. I tell you what, Jonah. You stay in the school business, and every afternoon at three o'clock you come downtown and work for me. I'll teach you *my* business."

"What will you pay him?" Lavinia asked.

"Pay him? I don't pay people to learn."

"I don't want to be paid," Jonah said quickly. "I'd like to learn business."

"It's worth it," Lavinia said. "Papa is a genius."

Jonah smiled. "Maybe I should pay you, Papa."

"Nu, so I'm a teacher too," Papa said cheerfully.

"Don't make him work too hard," Lavinia said. "You know Jonah. He'd kill himself for you."

"Don't worry. You think I want a widow for a daughter?"

So in the end, each of them thought he had won.

TWENTY

Everett Bergman was the first baby in the Saffron family to be born in a hospital. He missed being a Christmas baby by one day. Melissa brought him home proudly, to his new white room, with a temporary nurse named Miss Gibbs. After discussing it with Lazarus, Melissa decided not to breast-feed. She really hadn't wanted to anyway. Everett was a bad feeder from the start, cranky and always throwing up. It was assumed that he was allergic, but that he would grow out of it. Eventually he did stop throwing up, but he remained a picky eater, skinny and pinched-looking. Still, he was a beautiful child. He looked exactly like her, except that his hair was dark like his father's. He had her lovely large eyes. At one he looked like a girl, at two a pretty little boy, at three a pale and skinny little boy, and at four years of age he somewhat resembled a little animal.

He was hyperactive, furtive, and nervous. He wouldn't eat. He sometimes stammered. Melissa got rid of Miss Gibbs. Everett cried for two weeks, then seemed to forget her. He still stammered.

The two couples, Melissa and Lazarus, Lavinia and Jonah, had been coming to the beach cottage every summer now. They had worked out a kind of life style: Melissa planned the meals, based around what Lazarus liked or disliked, or what Lazarus said was good for you; Lavinia fought with her, based on what she and Jonah liked or disliked; and a compromise was reached, based on what Lazarus liked and Jonah could tolerate. Then the two young wives would shop together and cook. Neither of them cooked very well, but the cottage was too small to accommodate a sleep-in cook. Many nights they solved the food problem by dining at Papa's and Mama's beach house, where there were always two in help and the food was good.

But before the evening meal, whether it was in their own house or at "the big house," there was always the battle of feeding Everett. Usually Everett's dinner consisted of what he had rejected at lunch. Melissa had been studying child psychology books, and the newest theory to make a stubborn child eat was to keep giving him what he had rejected until he gave in from hunger, or the food rotted, whichever came first. Everett would never give in from hunger. He liked meat and hated vegetables and all other foods. But Melissa's child psychology book said that you had to give the child the food he hated most first, leaving the food he liked best for the end as a sort of bribe. Everett refused to be bribed.

So meal after meal he sat there, thirty pounds of hatred, and stared at his stringbeans.

"Hold his nose and stick it down," said Lazarus, not really meaning it, but bored with this child, this irritating little disappointment. Lazarus did not like children. He had produced this son and heir because that was what a man did, but he resented the time and attention Melissa lavished on it—he would have to remember Everett was not an It—and he could not even remember to hug or touch the boy. Melissa was always hugging and kissing the brat, because she was so loving, but Lazarus liked hugging and kissing only Melissa. Someday the boy would grow up and he would be able to have an intelligent conversation with him, but now, what could you do with a kid? How could you amuse it? *Why* should you amuse it? It tore at the pages of his books when he was reading peacefully, it destroyed property, it tried to flush its new beach sandals down the toilet. Then Lazarus shrieked, and Melissa spanked, because that was what the book said to do. Then Everett cried and sulked and thought up something even more annoying to do.

Lavinia watched all this with pity and annoyance. Pity for the child, annoyance and pity for her sister, only annoyance at her brother-in-law. The man was a baby himself. He was obviously jealous of his son, resenting Melissa's attentions to Everett. But poor Melissa, so dumb, so stubborn, insisted on doing everything wrong. Trying to be both mother and father to this boy, she was a failure at both. Lavinia had her own child psychology books.

"Give him the meat," she said to Melissa. "For heaven's sake, at least let him eat something. Look at him!"

"He has to learn," said Melissa, near tears from pity for the boy and frustration at the world.

"So if he eats the meat, what harm is there?" Lavinia said. "Look how skinny he is. You make every meal a battle. Let him enjoy eating."

"He'll get spoiled," Melissa said.

"Spoiled! He'll starve!"

"They never starve," Melissa said, sniffing.

Everett stared at his stringbeans. They were a grayish color, four days old now, entering their fifth.

"Throw that stuff away and start over, Melissa," Lavinia said. "*I* wouldn't even eat it. It looks disgusting. Give him the steak and some nice fresh carrots. Then he can have ice cream."

"Everett hates carrots," Melissa said.

"We're all having carrots tonight. He'll eat if he eats with us."

"Children shouldn't eat with grownups," Melissa said.

"I don't mind."

"Lazarus minds. He works hard in the city all day, and at night he should have peace and quiet. Besides, it's too late for Everett. He has to go to bed."

"To bed hungry again," Lavinia said. "You don't know anything. That book is ridiculous. Use your mother's instinct. A mother's instinct is always right over a book, any time."

"I only want to do what's right," Melissa said, and burst into tears. She hurled the plate of gray stringbeans to the floor.

Everett stared at her. She was doing exactly what he wanted to do, but why then was she crying? Nobody in this house liked him. He didn't like them either. His left eyelid began to twitch. His stomach hurt sometimes, but he wasn't really hungry. He wished he had a dog. They wouldn't let him have a dog. They said dogs were dirty and brought fleas. Dogs messed the furniture. He wished he had a big, bad dog that tore up the whole house and bit everybody and he could just stand there and watch it and say: "Oh, what a surprise! I'm so sorry, everybody." Inside he would be laughing. He would give the dog a big steak bone and they would eat it together.

"He's your child," Lavinia said. "So you have to do what you think is right, but I would give him that steak."

"If he eats the carrots, too," Melissa sobbed.

Lavinia put some carrots on the plate beside the beautiful rare steak, and put the plate in front of Everett. He didn't like her for making his mother cry. He folded his skinny arms and stared at the steak, pretending to himself that it was poison.

"See?" Melissa said. "See? See?"

"Let's all leave the room," Lavinia said. She took Melissa's arm and led her out of the kitchen.

"At least drink your milk!" Melissa shrieked after Everett as she was being dragged away.

When they were gone, Everett pulled his chair over to the kitchen cabinet and grabbed the box of oatmeal cookies the grownups kept there for themselves. He took two and stuffed them methodically into his mouth until his cheeks were bulging. Then he washed them down with a swallow of his glass of milk. The rest of the milk he poured out the kitchen window.

It was not his fault that the front porch curved around the

house just enough so that the grownups sitting on the porch could hear the milk strike the hard ground below the window.

"What's that?" his father yelled. He jumped out of his chair, waving his evening newspaper. "Toots, it's that rotten kid again! He just threw something out the window."

Melissa came rushing back into the kitchen. "What did you do?"

Everett stared at her silently with round, innocent eyes. His left eyelid was twitching again. He would name his big dog Toughie.

"Why can't you be good?"

Toughie would grab his father's newspaper and run away so fast that no one would ever catch him.

"I'm going to have to spank you now."

She swatted him a few times. She hated hitting him. Toughie would bite her anyway, but not really hard. Just enough to make her scared. He, Everett, would be the only one to have the power to tell Toughie what to do. Bite, Toughie! Stop, Toughie! Come here, Toughie! Get 'em, Toughie!

TWENTY-ONE

Adam had always wanted at least one of his two sons, either Andrew or Basil, to go to law school after graduating from college, because they were both going to go into the family business and he felt that it never hurt to have a lawyer in the family, albeit a nonpracticing one. Andrew, as the elder, graduated from college first, and went right to Columbia Law School, going into the summer session to get through faster. With Andrew, everything had to be faster, faster, more, more, better, better. He had grown up to be even more of the perfectionist he had seemed as a child: picky, critical, aesthetic. He liked elegance. He was offended by a job poorly done. Yet, he retained his shy, boyish charm, which made these qualities—which might have been annoying in someone else—seem admirable in him. Adam sometimes even asked Andrew's opinion on things.

With Basil it was always tomorrow. Although he was now a

grown man in the eyes of the law, he was still the little brother in his own family, and the more he saw his Papa leaning toward Andrew the more Basil drew into himself. Basil's closest friend in the family was still his younger sister Rosemary, not his brother. He didn't have to compete with Rosemary. She could just be his pal. Basil had fulfilled all his youthful indications of growing up to be a very handsome young man. Some of the girls he knew even told him he looked like a more masculine version of Rudolph Valentino. He combed his hair back with a lot of pomade to further the resemblance. No, Basil would not go to law school and compete with Andrew. He would have a good time. Not that Basil really was a Good-Time Charlie, it was just that he needed an identity that was different from anyone else's in the family. At heart he was morose—that was the true Basil—but he created another Basil for the world, the amiable, high-living ladies' man.

The summer of 1929 Basil was traveling through Europe with a friend, Maurice Weinstein, as a college graduation present to both of them from both their families. Rosemary missed him. Her sister Hazel, still at home and just as dumb as ever, was certainly no company. Rosemary had finished studying piano at Juilliard, but she did not want to give recitals although her teachers urged her to. There was something in Rosemary that cringed from competition. She could not even bear to play the piano in front of anyone but the immediate family, and her teachers, of course. If a visitor entered the house while she was playing, and she heard the strange voice in the hall, she would stop playing immediately, her face would compose itself into the grim semblance of a smile, and her fingers would clench into fists.

At home during the winters, she practiced the piano four hours a day. Practice makes perfect, she had been told, but she knew she would never be perfect, not even near it. Nothing she did would ever be spectacular. She was ordinary. This made her bitter. Why couldn't she be beautiful so that people noticed her? Why couldn't she be charming so that she could enchant a roomful of people? Why couldn't she have confidence so that she could do the one thing she did well—play the piano—for people to admire? Why did she feel this hatred choking her when she was really trying to be nice? She could hear her own voice: a high, nasal sneer, offering derision, when she had meant to offer a compliment. There were two people inside her, the Rosemary she really was and the other one. Which one was the real one? The argumentative, sharp-tongued Rosemary who could not agree even when someone said it was going to be a fine day out, or the good soul, the Rosemary who only wanted to please and be liked? The more the good soul took over—staying with Everett, for instance, so that Melissa and Lazarus could go to the opera on the maid's night out—the more the other Rosemary demanded payment. When an ordinary, tactful white lie was called for, her tongue failed her. The truth came out, bitter, cruel. Why had she told her best friend, Ruth, that her yellow dress was unbecoming? Now Ruth was angry at her. But wasn't truth beautiful? Wasn't it worse to pretend the dress looked well? But perhaps the yellow dress wasn't so bad, maybe she had only said it was unattractive because Ruth had a date that night and she didn't. Who *was* the real Rosemary?

Hazel was twenty-four now and had never had a date. It didn't seem to bother her. She had discovered a new passion: crossword puzzles. Puzzle books had to be fetched for her from the drugstore, more and more. She sat engrossed in them by the hour. She would never let anyone see what she had done, not that anyone really cared. She kept her crossword puzzle books with her, and put them into the bureau drawer in her bedroom when she was not working on them. They were her pride.

"You see?" Lavinia told everyone, "Hazel is a lot smarter than you give her credit for. She's doing puzzles. Look how fast she does them! If she didn't have a fat tongue, she would be able to express herself and you'd see . . ."

"There's no such thing as a fat tongue, Lavinia," Rosemary said. "Hazel has a fat tongue."

"Then how do you account for what comes out of her mouth?"

"Oh, I can't talk to you!"

Lavinia had stopped working in Papa's office, realizing she had no future there, and with Jonah's help had been able to get a job as a substitute teacher during the school year. She liked being in his world. She taught first grade, which was easy. Anyone could do it. She read to them and taught them the alphabet, and how to count. She tried to make it fun. School was much different from when she had been a pupil. You didn't hit the children for being children. She remembered her own school days with horror, and remembered how even Andrew, a boy and tough, had quaked with fear every day at the thought of going back to that horrible place. As a child she had approached school with a certain stolid fatalism, but Andrew had really dreaded it. When he was very young he had sometimes even cried in the mornings. And now he was such an eager scholar! It was terrible the way the school system had destroyed sensitive children, bright children, gentle children. It was a system of brutish mediocrity.

There were certain teachers like Jonah (and herself, she hoped) who made learning an exciting experience for the children. His students loved Jonah. Papa had given her some money, and she had given it to Jonah to invest in the stock market for her. He was a student himself, learning more about the market every day, and she trusted him. The stocks he had bought had done very well.

But now Jonah wanted to sell them. He wanted everybody to sell their stocks. "It's not a real economy," he told Papa and Lazarus. "I don't like it. I don't trust it. It's fake, it's inflated."

"Oh, what do you know?" Lazarus said. "A poor school teacher thinks he knows more than my own broker."

"There are three kinds of investors," Jonah said calmly. "Bulls, bears, and pigs. A bull can make money, a bear can make money, but a pig will never make money."

"Who are you calling a pig?"

"I would never call anybody a pig. I'm just telling you a saying they have in the market."

"This little pig went to market," Melissa said, and giggled.

Papa studied the market and sold his stocks at a huge profit. Jonah sold the ones he had bought for himself and Lavinia, and put the money into the savings bank. The only stock he kept was a few shares of a utility. "You can always trust a utility," he said. "No matter what, people need lights, they need phones."

Lazarus refused to sell any of his stock. He had more than any of them. In fact, the dividends he received from his investments were most of his income. They enabled him the luxury of being a neighborhood doctor, for the poor, the immigrants, whoever came to his door. He didn't have to scuffle for the society trade. No one woke him up in the middle of the night. He had an office, and office hours, like a businessman. He had a low overhead. One nurse doubled as a bookkeeper-secretary. Most of his cases were very simple: a cut, a bruise, a broken arm, an attack of appendicitis which he sent to the hospital. Anything requiring complicated care or surgery he referred to another doctor, receiving his share of the fee. Lazarus hated blood. He loved book medicine, and had gotten high marks in medical school because he was a fanatic for memorizing. He had been a perfect little boy, with As in all subjects including deportment, and Ds in sports, and then he had been the perfect scholar all through college and medical school, but he lacked a love or compassion for humanity. Medicine interested him, his patients did not.

Melissa took Lazarus' side about holding on to their skyrocketing stocks. They were rich. She dressed Everett in little white suits with sailor collars, and white sandals. He had two suits for each day so he would always be clean. He had a roomful of toys. He had books and records. She had learned to drive and Lazarus had bought her a motor car. Lazarus did not drive. "If God had meant man to drive a car . . ." but he never finished the sentence, for what could he say? "He would have given him wheels?" However, he gave Melissa whatever she wanted.

Basil wrote many glowing letters home from Europe. He was having a wonderful time, meeting old friends and new ones, seeing all the famous cultural sights, eating strange new foods, drinking wine for the first time. There was no Prohibition in Europe. The one thing that disturbed him, he wrote home, was the obvious and growing anti-Semitism in Germany. It was this that had made him and Maurice decide to leave Berlin a week earlier than planned to go straight to Paris. He had trouble with the language, but people seemed kinder. Of course, he was used to anti-Semitism at home, but the kind he had seen in Germany was frightening, different. There was anger in it. At home, people simply didn't like Jews, and Jews knew it and avoided people who were not their own kind. But people didn't go out deliberately to make life difficult for you at home, the way they were starting to do in Germany.

He planned to stay on until the holidays, Basil wrote, although Maurice had relatives in London, and they had invited him and Basil to spend Yom Kippur with them. It might be broadening to see how Jews celebrated Yom Kippur in London. Perhaps he would stay on until Thanksgiving, or until the weather got cold, if nobody minded . . .

After Labor Day everybody packed up and left the beach houses for another year. They took up their autumn lives again in Brooklyn. Melissa was thinking of enrolling Everett in prekindergarten, but he was such a cranky child she wondered if he would do well. Lavinia said it would be good for him to have friends. He had no friends. "Four-year-olds don't have friends," Melissa said. She knew this was true because even though some of her own friends had children of Everett's age, when they brought them over to play Everett never wanted to. Obviously if four-year-olds were supposed to have friends he would have wanted to. He was too young.

The problem of whether or not to send the child to school was solved when the stock market crashed in October. Lazarus lost everything. There was no question of private school, or anything else for that matter. People were jumping out of windows. Melissa sold her beautiful car, for a fraction of what it was worth, but they had to pay the rent.

Papa's business toppled along with everything else, but he was not worried. He had money saved, and he had been poor before and had survived and become rich. He had a perspective none of the others had except Jonah, for none of the others had ever had to do without.

Jonah still had his job. Schoolteachers were still needed in this time of crisis. But now the poor teachers were the rich, for they had work. Any man who had a job was an aristocrat.

"That bastard!" Lazarus muttered.

The crash had been a terrible blow to Lazarus. It shook his world. He had been the bon vivant, the big spender, Mr. Generous, and now he was dependent on the poor people he treated who always whined and pleaded and promised to pay him "next week." He put a lock on one of the closets in his apartment and filled the closet with the only thing of value he had left: bottles of Prohibition whiskey. Those were still worth money. Someday he might need them.

Frightened, adrift, he became stingy. He stole slivers of soap from public toilets and brought them home. He never bought a newspaper any more, but furtively snatched one whenever it was left behind, read and discarded, on the subway seat. He would refold it neatly, as if it were new, and bring it home proudly. Then he would sit in his chair and read it, snapping at Everett if the boy tried to touch it. A newspaper cost money. Everything cost money. Food cost money.

"Don't make him eat if he doesn't want to, Toots," he would

say now, the good father liberating his son from the disciplinary mother. Good, the kid didn't eat. More for him.

Papa sent a telegram to Basil telling him to come home. Basil said goodbye to his happy life and came home. When Lavinia and Rosemary met him at the ship Lavinia cried because she was glad to see him. Basil cried too, because he didn't want to be there.

TWENTY-TWO

Andrew's best friend at law school was named Ferdinand Bader, Jr. After the crash both Ferdinand and Andrew stayed on in law school, because both their fathers believed that no matter what the sacrifices, education came first for a boy. Ferdinand had found a part-time job, and Andrew was being subsidized by Adam, for even though times were hard a landlord could still collect some rent. There was no money to spend and no place to go, so whenever Ferdinand and Andrew had free time they spent it at the home of one or the other of them. It was at Ferdinand's family's apartment that Andrew met Cassandra, Ferdinand's little sister.

When the crash came, Cassandra Bader was at finishing school in Switzerland. She was eighteen years old and had been there for two years, studying French, French literature, gourmet cooking, needlepoint, piano, riding, and skiing. She disliked all of them.

It was not so easy for a Jewish girl to get into a finishing school like the Lycée Capuchine. They would take a Loeb, a Lehman, a Straus, a Schwab. And of course, they would take a Bader. Ferdinand Bader, Sr., was a New York banker, of German extraction, with a little French thrown in. The little French had been thrown in by his mother, who had no French blood herself but had named him Ferdinand after her favorite uncle, Fredl. Cassandra Bader was an only daughter, a girl of exceptional delicate beauty. She was small and thin and chic. Her eyes were blue; her soft brown hair was so straight her barrettes slid right out of it. Her hands and feet were tiny. Her skin was white and poreless. Her posture was perfect. Cassie could get in anywhere.

Because she had always been an aristocrat of sorts, Cassie

couldn't care less. She liked pretty clothes, she liked to spend money and had no idea of the value of anything, but when her father lost his money overnight she took the shock with a shrug, came home, and went right to work in his office to replace the secretary he could no longer afford to pay. Being a secretary was much more interesting than doing needlepoint, and she immediately taught herself how to type. She didn't miss her friends from the Lycée Capuchine, and she enjoyed seeing her older brother Ferdinand, who had been remote and uninterested in her when she had left home at sixteen, but who treated her almost like an equal now that she was eighteen and a working woman.

She also liked Ferdinand's friend Andrew Saffron. Andrew was five years older than she was, and she was impressed by that, but more by his sweet gentleness. She loved his eyes. He treated her with amusement, because she was his best friend's kid sister, and with respect because he saw her as a potential woman. The two young men let her tag along after them, and soon Andrew was spending all his free time with her, having told Ferdinand to find something else to do. Cassie was delighted when Andrew told her he was in love with her, and horrified when he proposed. She wouldn't marry for years and years, at least until she was twenty-four. Marriage was forever. How could she live with one man forever, love anyone forever? But she was madly in love with Andrew.

When she had been going with Andrew for a year Cassie finally decided to brave marriage. On her wedding day, a simple ceremony in Adam Saffron's house (because the apartment her parents had moved to after the crash was too small to invite all the relatives), Cassie looked at the rabbi, the assembled family, and her groom, and thought: "Well, if it doesn't work I can always get divorced." She figured it would last about a year, because she was so young and immature. A year was a very long time. She had been going with Andrew for a year and look at her now, a veil on her head, a bouquet in her hand, and in five minutes she would be a married woman. Good lord, the things that could happen in a year! Why, only a little over a year ago she'd been sitting in school in Switzerland, practicing her French conversation. Now she was stumbling over her Hebrew, and Andrew was putting the ring on her finger. Oh, well, if it didn't work . . .

But how handsome he was! Cassie thought Andrew Saffron

must be the handsomest, kindest, most intelligent, most interesting, sexiest man in the world.

After Andrew married Cassandra Bader, Adam inked in their names on his blueprint, on the house that was meant for the two boys and their wives and children to share.

Cassie and Andrew rented a small apartment in New York. Every day Rosemary got on the subway and went there to see Cassie. Her new sister-in-law had opened a new life for her. Rosemary was awed and worshipful as well as envious of this girl who came from another world and yet seemed to love her just as she was. There Cassie stood, ready to go out for a day of window shopping, slim and immaculate, a little hat pulled down over her neat, straight hair, a chic little suit with a real fur collar fitting perfectly on her flapper figure, a tiny golden Pekingese in her arms. The puppy was the final touch. Who else could get away with it?

And there was Rosemary, knowing everything about her clothes and hair was wrong and ready to die before she would ask for advice. She couldn't copy Cassie. That kind of suit would never fit over her hips, the hat would make her big nose look worse, and with her luck if she carried a puppy it would shed. But Cassie was her dearest friend. Andrew was working all day in Papa's office, and Cassie had quit her job to stay home and keep house. Who else but Cassie and Andrew would go to New York to live? And not even anywhere near Cassie's parents either! They had gone to live in New York because New York was fun, it was alive, there were things to do there.

Of course there was no money, but two girls could walk for hours and gaze into the windows of the elegant New York stores, even go inside and touch things, pretend. Cassie looked as if she could afford to buy whatever she wanted, even though she and Andrew were as poor as Rosemary. Everything Andrew made went for rent and food. Cassie didn't have new clothes, but her old clothes came from Paris, France, and everyone knew you kept those forever.

Sometimes Rosemary was afraid she was making a nuisance of herself, but Cassie insisted she come to visit, every single day, even when it rained. And then, most nights, Cassie would insist that Rosemary stay on and have dinner with her and Andrew. Sometimes she even invited a boy for her. But it never worked out.

Rosemary couldn't think of a thing to say, and she knew the boy was comparing her with Cassie, finding her lacking. She began to look at the boys she knew and to find them lacking. The ones at home in Brooklyn who asked her out all had something wrong with them. Why hadn't she noticed it before? This one was boring, that one was funny-looking, one was too fat, one too skinny, that one too short, that one too tall, that one didn't know anything about music, that one was stingy, that one was a showoff. What it all meant was that none of them, not one, was good enough to bring to New York to visit Cassie and introduce as her boyfriend.

It was all right to go to a concert or a movie with a boy as just friends, but Rosemary made it clear that she was not interested in anything more serious. The man she picked would represent her, just as Cassie represented Andrew, and he would have to make up for everything she lacked. She couldn't imagine how she would find such a man, and if she did, why he would want her. She supposed she would end up an old maid, hanging around, everyone sorry for her and bored with her.

She met Earl Fischer at Cassie and Andrew's apartment. They invited him to dinner for her as a blind date. He was the worst of all their offerings; Andrew was running out of old friends from law school and Cassie hadn't known that many boys before she left home. But he was better than anything Rosemary had been able to dig up for herself. He was a lawyer, just starting out as a clerk in a law office. He still had pimples on his cheeks. He was rather cute otherwise, although Rosemary didn't like them so thin, and she was not partial to blond men. He was a German Jew, his family had had money before the crash, and he was taller than she was. It was a start.

He liked movies and so did she. They went to movies twice a week, and had dinner at Cassie and Andrew's twice a week, and after four months of this they became engaged.

Rosemary wasn't sure what she had expected from being engaged, but it wasn't this. She had thought she would have status, and indeed she did; people congratulated her, she brought Earl home to dinner with Mama and Papa and everybody was nice to him, she brought him to dinner at Lavinia and Jonah's and they had a bottle of champagne they had managed to scrounge somewhere (bought it from Lazarus, it turned out later), and she brought him to dinner at Melissa and Lazarus', where Lazarus said he seemed intelligent and Melissa asked her why he still had pimples. It was not at all as she had dreamed.

Rosemary had somehow imagined in a vague way that if she managed to hook one of Cassie's offerings then it would automatically transform her into Cassie. But she was still Rosemary, and Earl Fischer instead of making her look better had started to look worse. She didn't think she had ever loved him for a minute. She didn't care whether he loved her or not. How dare he love her? How dare he try to make her a part of his life, and worse, enter hers?

She broke the engagement. Goodbye, Earl Fischer. Nobody seemed heartbroken. Melissa giggled and said that Rosemary and Basil were two of a kind, fickle heartbreakers. That was the biggest compliment Rosemary had gotten since her engagement. She realized then that breaking an engagement gave a girl a lot more status then entering one. Fickle heartbreakers! She looked around with new interest for new men to entice and ruin. Ah, how she would drag their hearts in the dust! But they couldn't be too terrible, or else people would just think she was a fool. No more men with pimples. She would have to find a good one, and then say he wasn't good enough for her. If she kept on doing that then people would have to believe her. They would think she had some mysterious power to fascinate men that wasn't apparent to just anybody.

Of course, she had to find the good one first, and then he had to want her. It wasn't as easy as she had hoped, but it gave her something to do. If she was going to be an old maid, at least she would go down fighting.

TWENTY-THREE

In 1931, the worst year of the Depression, Lavinia decided to have a baby. She and Jonah had been married for six years, they had some money saved, and she wanted to have her baby while she was still young. Always, from the start, it had been "her baby," singular. It would be an only child, loved and petted and given everything she had lacked and wanted, and it would be a girl. She prayed night and day for a girl, and never even considered what she would do if it was anything else.

It was a difficult pregnancy. She had morning sickness for seven months, and threw up not only in the morning but after lunch and dinner as well. Her weight went down to ninety-seven pounds. Melissa said she looked like the toothpick had swallowed the olive.

She and Jonah were thinking of names. "I'd like to name it after my father," he said, "if it's a boy." His father had died.

"It's not going to be a boy," Lavinia said.

"If it's a girl, maybe we could name it after my mother," he said. His mother had died a year after his father. People said it was from grief. When two people had lived together for so long . . . "You're lucky both your parents are alive," he said to Lavinia.

"Mmm." Of course now she knew whom she must name her daughter after, and she could never tell anyone. She wouldn't for the world hurt Mama, but the dead must be remembered. Mama would be the first one to agree. It had to be a P, for Polly, and there had to be a good reason, some logical reason that made everyone believe it.

Melissa gave her the reason. Silly, romantic Melissa, always dreaming of her Isadora Duncan. "A name I adore," Melissa said one day, "is Paris. You remember Isadora's lover, Paris Singer? The rich dashing one she refused to marry although she had his child? Isn't Paris a lovely name? For a girl or a boy, either one."

"Paris!" Jonah said, appalled.

"Why not?" Lavinia said. "Singer is a Jewish name."

"Oh, Paris Singer wasn't a Jewish Singer," Melissa said.

"How do you know?"

"Paris is a place," Jonah said.

"So what?" Lavinia said. "You'd rather name her Becky?"

"I didn't say Becky. My mother's name wasn't Becky."

But my mother's name was Polly, Lavinia thought. For a moment she tried to remember the tall figure in the long purple cape, but the image eluded her. She could only remember being told about it. Her eyes filled with tears for the lonely little girl she had been, the sad, earnest little girl, the orphan. Her daughter Paris Mendes would have two loving parents.

"Don't cry, Vinnie," Jonah said quickly, putting his arm around her. "I didn't mean to yell at you. If you like Paris for a name, then so do I."

"I like it," Melissa said. Since she had been married to Lazarus she no longer referred to things she liked as "terribly très chic." She had become more subdued, and she never used words improperly.

"Don't you think Paris Mendes is a lovely name, Jonah?" Lavinia said. "It sounds like somebody important. It goes together so well."

"I hope he's not a schoolteacher," Jonah said. "They'd laugh at him."

"She will never be a schoolteacher," Lavinia said. "She'll go into the arts. Our family is very talented in the arts."

"What are you going to do if you have a boy, Lavinia?" Melissa asked. "Drown it?"

"Give it to you as a brother for Everett," Lavinia snapped.

"Don't snap at me. I was just teasing. When I was pregnant I was never grouchy like you are."

"Well, everybody's different."

In the eighth month, just when she was enjoying her first month without morning sickness, Lavinia went into labor. Paris Mendes, female, was born a month prematurely, weighing three pounds, twelve ounces. She was a perfectly healthy baby, beautiful but scrawny, and she went into an isolette instead of an incubator.

From the start Lavinia never had a feeding problem. Melissa was astounded. Lavinia was unable to nurse (although she had planned to) because she was so thin and run down there was not enough milk, but Paris thrived on her bottle and was soon fat and rosy. She gobbled down her cod liver oil as if it were candy. Anything you gave her, she ate. She was born starved, and in a few months she was overweight.

Little skinny Everett, six and a half years old, had been waiting for this baby, who would be his cousin but really more his brother or sister. They could play together. Lavinia and Jonah were now living in an apartment only a block away from Melissa and Lazarus, and Everett was running in and out all the time. He was in first grade at public school, but he never brought little friends home to play after school or asked to be allowed to go to their homes to play with them. He seemed to think of Baby Paris as a kind of squeezable toy, one you could feed, make laugh, or pinch and make cry. He was very devoted.

Paris began to speak at seven months. Lavinia wrote down every word. She had a book called "Baby's First Year," and it contained a record of everything Paris said or did, her weight, her length, her first tooth. At the end of baby's first year Paris said so many words that Lavinia could not record them all. The baby stood but couldn't walk, but this was not unusual considering that she was obese.

At two, she not only walked but ran, singing out her favorite tongue twisters. Lavinia knew she had a very intelligent child. She was also beautiful, rosy cheeked, fat, with curly brown hair. People stopped Lavinia in the street to compliment her on the baby's clothes. There were dozens of little dresses and bows Lavinia had made to go with each outfit, tied in the silky ringlets. Jonah said the baby looked exactly like him, but Lavinia knew she looked exactly like her only much prettier.

"Now a bite of lamb chop," Lavinia said, feeding Paris. Down went the bite of lamb chop. "Now a bite of carrot. Oh, please, Mr. Carrot, the lamb chop is saying, come down here and join me!" Down went the spoonful of carrots.

Dessert was junket. Paris took one taste and threw the bowl of junket on the floor. "I don't like junket."

"Neither do I," Lavinia said. She gave the baby a bowl of chocolate pudding. Paris gobbled it up.

"Gee, are you lucky," Melissa said to Lavinia.

A fat baby was a healthy baby. Paris laughed and giggled all the time. At night she threw up. This was undoubtedly due to some allergy, just as Everett had had at her age, and eventually she would be sure to outgrow it. She threw up in cycles, every night for a few weeks, then not at all for a few weeks, then it started again. It was hard to tell what she was allergic to. But it didn't matter, as long as she stayed fat and healthy. Lavinia didn't mind having to change the sheets every night. She would do anything for that child, because that child was her.

TWENTY-FOUR

Climbing out of the Depression was more than a challenge to Adam, who liked challenges; it was a rebirth. He was like a phoenix climbing out of the ashes, and he reveled in it. Here he was, a man in his early fifties, and he remembered the young man he had been at the turn of the century, so ambitious, so hopeful, so careful and painstaking, and so lucky. He would be lucky again. This time there was no coffee house to linger in as an outsider, no stupid rich partner to help him because he had no means, no baby to feed. His children were all old enough to take care of themselves, and he was a famous man to whom the banks would give money, to whom the sellers and buyers paid attention. He would stay in real estate, but he would do exactly as he had done so long ago in Mudville. He would develop a joke and make it a miracle.

He looked around, and he had friends and information. He decided on the swamplands of Miami, near Miami Beach. Naturally, everyone told him he was crazy. He bought swamplands as he had bought the muddy land in Brooklyn, for a song, and he also bought land which was good but was so far away from the places which were developed and full of life that no one could conceive of them as a place where anyone would live or work. Swamplands could be filled in and reclaimed, and if a man built a community in the middle of nowhere other men would rush to fill in the empty spaces between.

He went back and forth by airplane even though everyone told him he was crazy to take such a dangerous, uncomfortable means of transportation when he could be having a pleasant trip on a nice, safe train. Adam did not have time for trains. He was a fatalist, and he felt it was not his time yet to die in a plane crash. In Miami he stayed in a Miami Beach hotel. He noticed that a good part of Miami Beach was restricted. The newspaper ads made this obvious: Restricted. Sometimes they were more tactful and said it was "near churches." But what all this meant to Adam was that there was a need for a Jewish community, this time not for those poor immigrants whom he had housed so long ago in Mudville, but for their children who had made good, for their children to come on their honeymoons and for their vacations, to spend their new money, to bring their own small children on school holidays. And yes, it was also for some of those poor immigrants who had made good themselves, as he had, to spend their middle years and their retirement years, to enjoy warm weather all winter, to have sunny beaches to sit on and nice hotels to live in among their own kind, where they could dress up as they wished without being laughed at, festoon themselves in sequins and satins and garish colors, high heels on the sand, fur stoles in the eighty-degree heat, good jewelry with bathing suits, yes, anything they wanted, because they deserved it. These men had made good, and if their wives wanted to deck themselves out like freaks, and if it made the husbands happy to pay for it and see it as a measure of the goods they had been able to earn in this hard world, then what was the harm? For himself, he despised such rubbish. He liked simplicity and refinement. But if someone else wanted to be ridiculous, who was he to look down his nose? Let them dress as they wished and dance the ridiculous new dances with their fat wives shaking their big rear ends, let the old men make fools of themselves with their young chippies, let them all make merry, and he, Adam Saffron, would build them a pleasure palace.

He built his pleasure palace in the middle of nowhere, on the beach, and he also built an arcade of shops and restaurants, for he remembered that people never really change, and just as those immigrant families in Mudville so long ago needed food and clothes, so did his newly rich ex-immigrants need food and clothes, close to their dwelling places.

His pleasure palace was beautiful, with fountains and statues and mosaic tiles. The word went out, as he had planned it to: this kike builder is making a Jewish community. And so his people came to see it, to stay where they would be welcomed and made comfortable. The economy was turning around. Other builders, seeing what he had done, began to build. And so the two worlds, the Jew and the Gentile, began to move toward each other, each enlarging, slowly crawling together, each protecting its own, filling in the open beachfront with large hotels, covering the empty roads with streets and houses, and then Adam did what he liked to do best: he built an office building.

Business! Business brought people, business made them stay. An office building in the middle of nowhere was a joke, everyone said, but Adam knew the joke by heart. The office building would bring stores, the stores would bring customers and the transportation for them, and that would build another community. There would be a bank, and a movie theater. Another pleasure palace, with giant golden statues holding up the imitation sky studded with imitation stars. A building for men to work in, a bank to hold their money, stores to take their money, and the movie theater to bring them back at night to spend more.

Now men were calling him a genius instead of a crazy man. Adam was pleased but not surprised. They were unimaginative and they were afraid. He had thought of it, and now he accepted the praise with a modest nod and a little smile. He looked around meanwhile for a nice house to buy for himself and Lucy and the children. He could stay there during the cold winter months and manage his Southern properties, and then when the weather was clement he could take care of his business in New York. He had good men working for him, men he could trust. He had his two sons now, Andrew with a lovely young wife who had just become pregnant with their first child, and Basil the bachelor. Basil lived with Adam and Lucy, of course. And he had Lavinia and Jonah with their lively little daughter Paris (funny name, well, Lavinia was always independent) and Melissa and Lazarus with little Everett. They could visit on holidays. Rosemary and Hazel would of course live with him wherever he lived. He would need a big house.

The warm Florida climate would be good for Lucy's lungs, or heart, or whatever it was. Just now, when things were going well again financially, she had taken a turn for the worse. Why couldn't a man have some peace? Give, take away, give, take away. It made a human being nervous, made a man want to hold on to his family, to what he had, because it was all so fragile. Someday he would have his land in the country not far from New York City, and they would all live together. He wanted them close. They didn't seem to understand how important it was, but they did what he told them, they respected his wishes. He liked that even now, given their own choices, they all chose to live close to each other, visiting each other. Why, Lavinia and Melissa visited his sister Becky more often than he did. In fact, the truth be told, he never had time to visit her up there in the Bronx, but she sometimes visited him, bringing her children, four of them now. Four children and four abortions. He knew because he had to pay for it all, the children she had and the ones she had agreed not to have. Why couldn't she and Isman control themselves? The man could hardly make a decent living, but he certainly could produce children! Adam was not shocked by abortions. The midwife was clean. The practice, although it was not a happy event, was an old one, and he had always known about it. If you could not afford to have a child you had to get rid of it. But he also knew that it was not safe, it couldn't be, to have so many abortions. One or two, yes, those things happened, but four was enough. Silly Becky would kill herself one day.

It was time for him to have a man-to-man talk with Isman, much as it repelled him to have to discuss such things. He invited Isman to meet him downtown for lunch.

Adam had not seen Isman for some time and he was surprised at how small and pale he looked. He still remembered the ruddy, eager young man who had come to marry Becky. But this man was almost servile, nervous but not in a charming way, in an almost doglike way, a frightened man, and he was no longer a boy. Ah, how dreams flew out the window. Isman seemed ill at ease to be here downtown in this fine restaurant with its wood-paneled walls, white tablecloths, and neat, silent waiters. Perhaps Adam should have taken him to a delicatessen, but he disliked delicatessens.

"A schnapps?" Adam asked kindly. He thought it might put Isman more at his ease.

"No thank you, Papa."

"Since Prohibition was repealed nobody drinks any more," Adam said.

Isman managed a weak smile.

Adam had a whiskey, downing it straight, the way he always had his schnapps. One, just one, and swallowed straight from a little glass. It was good for a man but did not blur the mind. Then he read the menu, although he knew it by heart, and ordered. He recommended to Isman what he thought the man might like, and Isman accepted his suggestions docilely. Adam thought with disgust that if he had suggested horse, Isman would have agreed.

"So how is Becky?"

"Fine, thank you, Papa."

"Recovered?"

"Oh, yes."

"And the children?"

"Fine, thank you, Papa."

"And your job, it goes well?"

"Yes, thank you, Papa."

"Managing inventory, it's not boring for you?"

"Oh, no, not boring."

"Good."

Silence. The food came, and Adam ate quickly, silently, as was his custom, enjoying his lunch, paying it the respect it deserved. Isman ate in little nervous bites, also silent, but his silence was out of respect for Adam, not for the food. When Adam's plate was clean he put his finger into his mouth and removed an offending morsel of meat that was trapped between two of his molars, and then he delicately wiped his lips and fingers with the thick, clean white linen napkin. The waiter removed the plates and brought coffee. Neither of them wanted dessert, or at least Adam didn't and Isman said he didn't. Adam wondered if Isman liked coffee. He supposed the man hated it, but was afraid to order tea. Well, too bad.

"You know, Isman," Adam said, "When a man is an adult he is responsible for his own life and that of his wife and his children. He can't be a child forever, depending on other people."

Isman turned even paler.

"I'm sure," Adam went on in front of this pale, perspiring man, "that you feel responsible for your family. It is you who has to feed them, to put a roof over their heads, to send your children to school so they can make something of themselves. You are the man of the house."

"I'll pay the loan," Isman whispered. "I promise. Give me more time, just a little more time . . ."

"Sha! Forget the loan. The loan is a present."

Isman seemed to come back to life, the color returned to his cheeks, he began to breathe normally again. "I thank you with all my heart," he whispered. "Becky hasn't been well . . ."

"I know. That's what I want to talk to you about."

"Florida . . ." Isman said. "It would be good for her in Florida. Maybe you could use me in one of your stores?"

"Why, you're planning to lose your job?"

"Oh, no!" Isman paled again. "You didn't hear anything?"

"What should I hear?"

"Nothing, Papa. I have the job, it's secure."

"Then why should I take you with me to Florida?"

"For Becky's sake. No, no, I apologize. You've done enough for us already."

"Becky wouldn't like Florida," Adam said. "She likes New York, she has her family and friends. I can't use you in Florida. That isn't what I wanted to talk to you about."

Isman seemed to stop breathing altogether. His eyes darted to Adam's eyes, then away, afraid to read the answer, afraid not to know. Adam knew he was imagining all sorts of horrors. No job? No home? Adam deserting him, leaving him to struggle along all alone? What could it be?

"Please, Papa, tell. . ."

"Four children are enough children for a poor man. You have two fine sons and two lovely daughters. Genug! Now you stop."

"We tried to stop . . ."

"I don't mean the woman in the Bronx. I mean you and Becky at home. I mean you two stop. No more. No more children."

Isman knew what that meant. No more nights of comfort and love in the bed, no more pleasure, no more forgetting the humiliations of his day as a failure in the warm, sweet nights. No more sending Becky to suffer in silence and pain under the instruments of the woman in the Bronx who removed unborn babies from poor women who could not afford to have them. No more putting Becky's life and health in danger. No more lovemaking. No more comfort and joy. His eyes filled with tears. No more money was coming from Adam. He knew this. The words did not have to be spoken.

"I won't pay for any more children, Isman."

He had said it. Had he really said it at last? Isman felt his head singing, he was dizzy. But Adam had only said no more money for more children. He had not said no more money at all. He would not desert them.

"Yes, Papa," Isman said.

"When Ned is ready for college, if he wants to go I'll pay for it. You tell him that. Tell him to study hard."

"Yes, Papa. Thank you."

"He's a good boy."

"Thank you, Papa."

"You should be proud of your fine children. You should concentrate on giving them everything you can. You must not be selfish. You brought them into the world and they look to you. When you're old, they can pay you back with devotion and care."

"Yes, Papa."

Adam stood and pushed back his chair. Isman, watching him, did the same. The conversation was ended. They walked to the door of the restaurant and Adam received his coat and hat from the checkroom attendant. Isman retrieved his threadbare coat. He did not wear a hat. The two men walked out to the street, where Adam's chauffeur-driven car was waiting. His office was five blocks away. Isman could take the subway back to the Bronx.

"My best to the family," Adam said.

"Thank you, Papa. Thank you for that good lunch."

Adam nodded and stepped into his car. He watched Isman walk to the corner and turn it, and then he forgot about him.

TWENTY-FIVE

Next to their Papa, their Mama, Lucy, was the most important person in the children's lives. She was their moon, waxing and waning with her illness, but there.

Lucy thought that perhaps this time she might be dying. It did not frighten her, but it made her infinitely sad. What would all of them do without her? True they were adults now, and she had never been with them as much as she had wanted to when they were little, but still they always knew that she existed, that she was somewhere where they could reach her, that she was ready with her advice and words of love. She had spent her life with Adam, and their children had spent their lives with her, and now they would all be alone.

She had never believed in heaven as a place. Heaven was if the people who were still living remembered you with love. Thus you lived on as a part of them. What else could she have told them? What had she forgotten? Who was she anyway to be telling other people what to do? She knew she was old, fifty-one, an old woman, but inside she was still a girl. She had not changed. Old people only grew old on the outside. They couldn't walk quickly, they had arthritis and couldn't move their arms and hands the way they once did, their backs ached, the mirror showed them the face of an old, wrinkled, white-haired person, but inside there was still the young person who didn't understand all these changes and resented them. Why do I look like this? Why do I feel so different? What has happened to me? That was the secret of old age, Lucy thought, you only grew old to the outside world, but not to yourself, and so it was sad.

There were two nurses in her bedroom now instead of one, and the doctor came to see her twice a day, in the morning and the evening. The shades were drawn and the room was dark so she could rest. How could she rest when each breath was a torment? She was literally dying from lack of air, and her chest hurt with the effort of trying to get it. Sometimes she slept, or thought she slept, but she knew she had been unconscious from the lack of air, half-asleep, half-dead. There were no drugs for this illness, no pills. She would not go to the hospital and they did not force her to. Hospitals were to die in, and now to be born in too. Everett and Paris had been born in hospitals, and it had made Lucy happy to see that a hospital could also be a place of life, not just of sickness and death. Her strength had left her and she could no longer fight. This was what being old meant. Unable to handle your own destiny. Unable to fight. Weak . . .

Her children came to see her, one by one, and that made Lucy sure that she was dying because they came with long faces, pretending to be cheerful but obviously worried and holding back tears. She wanted to tell each of them something nice that they could remember but it seemed pretentious. They would remember all of her and all of their lives, and what could she say anyway except that she loved each of them? What would become of them? What would happen to poor Hazel? Would her sisters and brothers care for her when they were all old? Would any man ever marry her? Lucy doubted it. And what of poor Basil, her grown-up crybaby, pretending to himself and the world that he was so much the man of the world? She knew better. Basil was soft. She hoped he could take care of himself. At least Lavinia and Melissa and Andrew had chosen partners to help them through life. But what of little Rosemary? A girl her age should be married by now, but nobody seemed to suit her. She would wait and wait until there was no one left for her to marry. At least she had the family. Adam would have her for company when she was gone. Rosemary could keep house. Lavinia and Melissa would visit, but they had such small children of their own to care for . . . It was strange how young children made Lucy tired now. Their noise and liveliness got on her nerves. She was too old to enjoy little children any more, and too sick. It was probably for the best. Children belonged to their mothers.

There had been so many changes in the world since she was young. She was not exactly an educated woman but she spoke three languages and had been in two countries. In her lifetime she had seen the miracles of indoor plumbing, hot water, trolley cars, subways, telephones, automobiles, the radio, motion pictures, movies that talked, the airplane. She could hardly count the miracles they had happened so fast. This should be enough for any one person, to have lived to see all these miracles, but she didn't want to leave the world.

There had been bad things too, the Great War, and weapons, and killing, and crime here in the city, and all those dreadful things you could read in the newspaper, but even these ugly things could not make her want to leave the world. The moment of death was supposed to be peaceful. They said that people died with a smile of bliss on their faces. She was not ready to feel peaceful. She wanted air, she wanted to be able to breathe, and she wanted to live.

When Lucy died, strong Lavinia took it the hardest. She was hysterical. Her Mama's death brought back to her, as a grown woman, all the baby terrors she had forgotten from the time she was two years old and her other Mama had died. She didn't remember them as her baby feelings, but she knew that she was enveloped in terror and grief and bewilderment which made no sense even as much as she loved her Mama. She felt completely unhinged. She was in a panic. She clung to her Papa as if he were the one thing of safety in this terrifying world, and Jonah and her own baby were unable to comfort her.

A few days after the funeral she began to find herself again. She played with her baby, Paris, she tried to be nice to Jonah, and slowly the blurred world around her began to take shape again. But at night she had nightmares and woke up crying. Then early in the morning she would phone Papa, just to say hello, to make sure he was still there, alive and well. Then she would call Melissa, or Melissa would call her, and the two sisters would chat for half an hour, an hour, until they had run out of trivia and were literally speechless. They would say goodbye and Lavinia would phone Cassie, to see how she was, how her pregnancy was progressing, if she needed anything. Lavinia had become very close to Cassie during the past few years. She was glad that Andrew had married such a sweet, loving girl, and she thought it would be nice if Cassie would have a girl so that Paris would have a little cousin who was also a friend.

Then Lavinia would call Rosemary, to ask how Papa was, what

was happening. Papa would be at the office with Andrew and Basil, and after she spoke with Rosemary sometimes Lavinia would think of an excuse to call him there. She always had to keep in touch. By lunchtime Jonah would have phoned from school, to see how she was getting along, and then she would have to make lunch for Paris and herself. While Paris napped, Lavinia phoned Melissa again, knowing that Everett was also sleeping, and she would report the results of her other phone calls. Then Paris would wake up and Lavinia would put her into the stroller and take her on the rounds of the grocery store, the butcher or the fish store, the bakery. She would always pick up some nice little cake or cookies for Papa. Jonah would go straight to Papa's office after school, but he would be home around five or five thirty, and they would eat promptly at six, after Paris had been fed and given her bath. Lavinia was not as anxious during the afternoons as she always was in the mornings, because she was further from her nightmares of the night and because she knew in a few hours she would be seeing Papa again. Jonah would carry the sleeping baby (Lavinia did not trust any stranger to come to stay with her child) and they would walk to Papa's house. Papa's house now, although Lavinia knew it would always be Papa and Mama's house. It was Mama's bedroom, and Mama's presence was throughout the other rooms. Lavinia would put the cake or cookies on a plate, and see that the maids had brought out fruit and candy. Rosemary and Hazel were there, often Melissa and Lazarus (there was a girl hired to take care of Everett whenever they went out lately), and sometimes Andrew would bring Cassie, but only for a short time because she was nearly ready to have the baby and she got tired early. Sometimes Basil would be there, sometimes he would be out. A few relatives would drop in, a few old friends. Lavinia felt she hardly knew her father's brothers and sisters; the old aunts from the old country spoke no English and seemed at a loss for anything much to say. She felt closest to Aunt Becky, whom she had known so well for so many years. The others were nearly strangers, because they were from another world. It was hard to think they were her Papa's own older sisters because they were so different from him.

Although many evenings Mama had not been feeling well enough to leave her bedroom, they had always known she was there, and so there was warmth in the house. Now they knew she was not there, and pretend as she tried Lavinia felt a chill go through her. The bed was flat.

Poor Papa, alone in this house. Those old relatives were boring him, she knew it. They were boring her, too. She wished they would go away so she could be alone with Papa, like in the old days, and they could talk of interesting things instead of trying to entertain all those old foreigners who did not want to be entertained.

"So," Papa said. "Friday I go to Laurel Pastures."

"What's Laurel Pastures?" Rosemary asked.

"A fancy resort hotel in the mountains," Melissa said, "Lazarus went there once."

"What's there, Papa?" Rosemary asked.

"I need a change," Papa said. "Finklestein from the Center, he went there last year with his wife, he liked it. I'll go by car."

"We'll go with you, of course," Lavinia said quickly. "Jonah can stay for the weekend, and then Paris and I will stay with you as long as you need us."

"Who needs you?" Papa said. "I'm a grown man, I go alone."

"Well, I just meant for company . . ." She had never felt so rejected.

"It's full of old people like me and Finklestein," Papa said cheerfully. "I'll get a good rest."

"Papa needs a rest," Melissa said sympathetically.

"But do you have reservations?" Lavinia asked. She could call them, she could request the best suite . . . wasn't there anything she could do for him?

"What do you think, I learned everything from you?" Papa said, amused at her. "You learned from me."

So Papa went to this fancy Laurel Pastures to rest and recover from his grief, and Lavinia worried herself sick. She called him every evening at ten minutes to six, after he had finished his afternoon of pinochle and just before he went in to dinner. He sounded cheerful. Andrew and Basil called him too, during the day, to report on things at the office, and he called them. Lavinia always called each of the boys in the evening to find out if there was anything new with Papa; was he taking care of his health, was he well? He shouldn't eat too much salt, she reminded them, tell him, tell him, he thinks I nag him.

Cassie went into the hospital and had an eight-pound baby boy.

She and Andrew named him Christopher. Christopher Saffron. Chris. Lavinia was not too pleased with the name. It seemed so . . . goyish. It had no roots. Not that she had any right to complain, naming her daughter Paris, but still, wasn't Christopher a saint? He was an absolutely exquisite baby, with straight light brown hair and slightly uptilted eyes, the image of Cassie. They should have named him after Lucy. Well, they would have if it had been a girl. It seemed heartless.

They were already, slowly, moving out of the family circle, these two. Andrew had found a piece of land in upstate New York, two hours from the city, and he and Cassie's brother Ferdinand had bought it for a song. Andrew hadn't told Papa; he was saving it for a surprise, that he was a man, that he had done this all on his own. It had a huge lake on it and many old, beautiful trees. They were going to build two houses on it. Andrew liked traditional architecture and Ferdinand favored modern, so the two houses would be far from each other so that neither would clash with the appearance of the other. Ferdinand's would be built into the side of a cliff overlooking the lake, and it would be small because he was still a bachelor. Later he could enlarge it if he married and had children. Andrew's would be deep in the woods. Andrew was wild about nature, and he already had men hacking down this and moving that so his view would be artistic and the mood peaceful. Two hours from New York City; what a trip! Lavinia wondered when anyone would ever get to see them now. But they planned to spend every weekend there, winter and summer. Cassie had a nurse for baby Chris, a great strong German girl, a refugee, and the nurse would stay with them full time.

Andrew's face lit up like a little boy's when he talked about his place. It was still just a piece of land and some plans, but he could see it all in his head. He and Cassie had driven up on a sunny day, taking the Pekingese.

"You should have seen Muffin," he said, grinning. "She looked like a little golden streak, running in and out among the trees. I wanted to paint her."

He hardly had time to paint any more, what with going to the office all day and then attending to things at home. His land would be his painting now.

There was Papa, sitting up at that hotel, missing everything. He had been there four weeks: a whole month. It wasn't like him to vegetate like an old man. He didn't seem to miss them at all.

"Let's go up there," Lavinia said to Melissa.

"I can't get Lazarus to budge."

"It's the money," Lavinia said.

"Well, he's busy with patients. He can't just up and leave them."

"He certainly leaves them on weekends. We could just go up for a weekend."

"I'll talk to him," Melissa said.

"And I'll talk to Jonah. I'll call you tonight."

Jonah would go anywhere. He was always ready to pack and go on any adventure. He and Lavinia and Paris could stay in one room. There were all sorts of outdoor sports at Laurel Pastures and he would have a good time. Lavinia knew Jonah would agree to anything she asked. She had only said to Melissa that she had to ask him so that Melissa couldn't pretend Lazarus was the patriarch in her family. Patriarch, what a joke!

Lavinia called the hotel and made reservations for two rooms. There was a train that left four times a day and then the hotel car would pick you up at the station. She made train reservations too, and told the hotel what time to send the car. She felt better. Poor Papa would be glad to see them. It would be a nice surprise.

TWENTY-SIX

Adam liked Laurel Pastures. It was still too early to be the season, so the place was not crowded, just enough people for company if you wanted them and enough space to be alone with your thoughts if you wanted that. The dining room service was excellent and the food was very good. He particularly admired the buffet spread they offered every day at lunch, every platter so tastefully decorated. He tried to stick to his pot cheese and raw vegetables in order not to ruin his digestion, but sometimes he tasted a little piece of herring, or tongue, or sometimes even a blintz smothered with sour cream and oozing thick jam with whole cherries in it. Who could resist such a treat?

The hotel was situated among green and blue mountains, with

acres of manicured lawns and gardens to stroll through. There was a lake, of course, with small rowboats. The main part of the hotel, where Adam had chosen to stay, was a huge Victorian house with a wide shady veranda all around it, overlooking the lake and the lawns and the mountains in the distance. The house was painted white. On the veranda, at intervals for private conversations, were groups of comfortable outdoor rocking chairs so that the guests who did not care for sports (which at this off-season time was most of them) could sit all day and rock and chat, waiting for the next meal. The wan spring sun warmed them outside, the good, old country food warmed them inside, and the view alone was worth every penny of the cost.

Inside the hotel there were two card rooms, which were kept busy day and night. One was for the ladies, and one for the men. The card room for the men was heavy with stale cigar smoke, while the one for the ladies was lively with chatter. The ladies detested cigars, and the men detested chatter, so everyone was happy. There was a music room, where recitals were sometimes held for the pleasure of the guests, and there was a piano lounge, where a thin, effeminate man played and sang old favorites and requests from five to seven while guests sat in plush armchairs and sipped drinks. There was also a room for dancing and drinking at night, a night club really. There was a floorshow on weekends, with well-known entertainers brought up specially. Usually it was a comedian who told jokes and anecdotes liberally sprinkled with Yiddish, sometimes slightly off-color, and the guests laughed heartily.

Adam had gone there the first night, alone, to the early show, and although he had no coat or hat with him, coming from the main building, he gave the coat check girl a dollar when he left because she was trim and refined-looking and he felt sorry for her. It was a shame for a woman to have to stand on her feet all night and work like that. She had gray hair. Her sons should be supporting her, it was a shame.

During the weekend Adam met several people he knew, and he occupied himself with pinochle games, and walks, and talks about business. There were the usual old widows chasing him, but he managed to evade them. None of them was at all his type. At night he slept well, alone, with his windows open to the clear mountain air, and he thought that this was somewhat the sort of place he would want his estate to be in the years to come, when all his children would be around him with their children, sleeping peacefully at night with clean, cool country air coming in through their open windows. Yes, he had done well to come away from the city, to peace and contemplation.

On Monday evening the night club was closed. Many of the people had only come up for the weekend. Adam did not mind that there were fewer people, for it made him feel that the place was his. It was always easy for him to make a new friend if he wanted one for a game of cards. He was rocking in a chair on the veranda, watching the sun set over the lake, when a woman approached him. He recognized her but was not quite sure from where. She was trim and neatly dressed, with gray hair.

"Mr. Saffron?" she said.

He stood politely. "How do?"

"I'm Etta, from the coat check concession."

"Oh, yes."

"It's such a lovely evening, isn't it," she said pleasantly.

"Yes," he said. He was not surprised that she knew his name; she had probably asked someone.

"Would you like to take a little walk, Mr. Saffron?" she asked.

"Why not?"

Side by side, not touching, slowly, solemnly, they walked around the veranda, taking their evening constitutional. The night was clear and not yet cold.

"You can make a living that way, in a coat check?" he asked her.

"I also supervise the salad decorations."

"Ah. Very nice. I admired them."

"Thank you. My husband died several years ago, leaving me without means," she said. "But now my son is married and I have only me, so it's easier. Naturally I wouldn't live with him. It wouldn't be fair."

"Children are a blessing but sometimes also a nuisance," Adam said. "If they live with you it's one thing, but if you live with them it's a tragedy."

"Oh, I agree. How well said!"

They walked around the veranda again in silence. He liked that she did not speak, but he suspected that her silence was because she had nothing to say. She didn't seem like an intelligent woman, not an intellectual, but a man his age couldn't be bothered with an intelligent woman, it was too tiring. She seemed a peaceful woman, and resourceful, and clever with her hands. No, he was sure she was not very intelligent. An intelligent woman would die of boredom standing in a coat check closet all night. An intelligent woman would have found work in some office somewhere. On the other hand, this Etta was not stupid. She knew a hotel like Laurel Pastures had rich men who gave good tips, and perhaps even rich men who were looking to marry.

She had found out his name, which was not difficult, and she had probably also found out that he was recently widowed, and she had sought him out this evening. No, she was not stupid. But he did the choosing, not the woman. She had to find that out immediately.

"Good evening," he said pleasantly, when their stroll took them to the front entrance of the hotel. He nodded his head politely, then he turned and went in.

"Good night, Mr. Saffron," Etta said pleasantly to his back, "Sleep well."

He went into the men's card room, but found it empty. Ah, these old men, in bed already at eight o'clock! Even he, a man of moderate habits, wouldn't go to bed at eight o'clock. What did she mean, "sleep well"? Did she think he was so old? He walked into the lobby and looked at the bulletin board announcing the social events of the night. Bingo, that was for the ladies. Movies, an old laugh-filled Festival of Silent Films. Couldn't they afford to get something new? Boring place. He bought the evening newspapers from the lobby newstand and went upstairs to his room.

The following evening after supper he was sitting on the veranda when she approached him again. He realized that the night club did not open until eight o'clock and so she was free. She pretended to be casual but Adam knew she had been looking for him.

"Well, Mr. Saffron," Etta said. "How are you feeling tonight?"

"I'm feeling well," he said. "And you?"

"Well, thank you. Would you like to take a little walk?"

"Why not?"

He stood, and again they conducted their ritual of the slow, leisurely walk around the veranda in companionable silence. If the woman was after him, why wasn't she chattering? She should be trying to draw him out, flattering him, telling him how wonderful she was. This woman was either very stupid or very smart. He decided he liked her.

"How old are you?" he asked abruptly.

"I'm . . . forty-six."

He shouldn't have embarrassed her. Women didn't like to tell their ages. "You shouldn't be ashamed," he said. "You look good for forty-six. Myself, I'm fifty-six, so you see to me you're just a young girl."

"Ten years isn't so much among adults," she said.

"Nu, so what's age anyway if you've got your health?"

"Very wisely said, Mr. Saffron. Health is everything. My husband was much older, but he was just like a young man. He died on the tennis court."

"The tennis court!"

"Yes. Heart attack. I told him not to play singles."

"A man plays tennis like a gentleman and he leaves his wife without money?"

"He always liked to enjoy himself."

"You have only the one son?"

"Yes."

"He has children?"

"No, he's a newlywed." She smiled.

"You like the bride?"

"Yes."

"Good."

They walked in silence again. He thought tonight he might go to bed early. The mountain air made him feel tired and the evenings were empty. Four days, and already he was nudgy.

"You live in New York?" he asked Etta.

"Yes."

"I too."

"Actually, I used to lived in New York," she said. "Now I live here."

"Here?"

"My room and board are part of the job."

"But there are no coats to check during the summer."

"We're very busy in the kitchen. And we do weddings here in the summer, especially in June."

"Ah . . ."

"You must find it restful here, Mr. Saffron," she said.

"Restful, yes. Also boring. And you?"

"Also boring." She looked at him and smiled.

She was an attractive woman, he thought. He liked a woman who kept herself neat and immaculate. She had well-chiseled features and very fair skin. What he could see of her legs beneath her skirt hem was trim and nice, and she had small feet with a high arch. Her fingernails were perfectly manicured, and she wore a simple gold wedding ring. The youngish face with the gray hair made a striking combination. She was not a woman a man like himself would be ashamed to be seen with, for she was refined and not too young, yet young enough to still be a woman. She glanced at her wristwatch.

"I have to go now, Mr. Saffron."

"I'm sorry you have to work," he said. "Otherwise I would invite you to be my dancing partner."

She smiled. "I'm sorry too."

She left for her job and Adam strolled around the veranda by himself. It was not good for a man to be alone.

The next evening after supper he found that he was looking forward to her appearance. She did not disappoint him. Before she could ask him, Adam stood up from his chair and offered her his arm. She took it, and slowly, sedately, they set off on their walk. It was the first time he had touched her. It was his gesture of acceptance, for Adam did not like to be touched except by people he chose to touch him. She seemed to recognize this.

"Did you have a nice day?" she asked.

He nodded. "Restful. And you, what do you do all day?"

"I read in my room, I take care of personal things, and then I'm very busy decorating the salads."

"Yes, of course, the famous salads. But then, you must also have some free time."

"Oh, yes."

"You don't mind being alone?"

"No. I'm used to it. There are so many little things to do the day goes by."

"What do you read?"

"Mostly mysteries."

It was the time in his life for a simple woman. "You have family, besides your son?" Adam asked.

"No. They've all passed away."

Good. He didn't like supporting relatives. "Your son enjoys his job?"

"He works for an airline. He likes it very much."

"Ah, an airline."

"He's in the office right now, but he's learning to be a pilot."

"You're not afraid?"

"I can't run his life."

"No," Adam said, "that's true."

"How long are you expecting to stay here, Mr. Saffron?" she asked.

"I don't know yet. I would like to know you better."

"There's not much to know," Etta said with a rueful little smile.

"Then I won't have to stay long."

"Then I wish there was more to know."

"Why?" he said. "Maybe when I go I'll take you with me."

"Oh, you're teasing me!"

"Why did you ask me to take a walk with you that first night?" Adam asked abruptly.

"You looked lonesome."

"I was. My wife had passed away."

"I know. I'm very sorry."

"You knew?"

"Everybody knows about everybody here," she said.

It's no crime to want to marry a rich man, Adam thought. There isn't a widow here, even the ones with diamonds on every finger, who doesn't want to marry a rich man. Did he think for one minute they were all chasing him because he was so handsome? So Etta was human, so what? She would get something and he would get something.

He would bide his time and see if she wore well. It would be indecent to bring her right home, and there was no point in leaving her here by herself. He was already thinking of her as his. Things were going well at the office, and the boys could run it for a while, keeping in touch with him faithfully every day as they did. He was not anxious to return to the long faces of his family in Brooklyn. They tried to do too much for him and it annoyed him; it was as if they were trying by their constant ministrations and hovering to make him weak, their prisoner. No, a house should have an older woman in it, for balance. Then his children could return to being children again and his silly daughters would stop playing house.

Once he had made his decision, Adam began enjoying his vacation. The weather was beautiful every day, and he took long walks, building his strength. Long ago he had walked for miles, first because he could not afford any other means of transportation than his two legs or some kind farmer's wagon, and later because he was looking for work. Now, through the years, he had become lazy. It was a good feeling to become strong again. One afternoon he even took Etta out in a rowboat, although she was pale with fear because she couldn't swim. He was not too disappointed to have to bring the boat back to shore after half an hour. He was not meant to row a boat anyway.

In the afternoons he usually played pinochle, always able to find a partner, and he made sure to read all the New York newspapers, particularly the *Wall Street Journal*. Jonah had been buying stocks for quite a while now, penny by penny, and Adam thought it would be a good idea for him to start buying some too, while the prices were still low. Lavinia called him every evening, if not more often, and he had word of all the news from home. He always asked her what Jonah had bought, what Jonah had sold, what Jonah was considering buying. She always knew.

The food at Laurel Pastures was delicious and varied. Adam realized at the end of a month that he would have to be careful or he would put on weight. He was spared the unpleasantness of going on a starvation diet by Melissa.

"We'll be up this weekend, Papa," she said happily on the phone.

"Up here?"

"Lavinia wanted it to be a surprise for you," Melissa said, "But I think that's silly. Besides, Lazarus was thinking that since you've been there so long, their best customer so to speak, and must know everybody by now, that you might be able to get us a discount."

"Who's coming?"

"Lazarus and me, Lavinia and Jonah, and the kids."

"You can see me for free," Adam said. "I'm coming home."

Melissa squealed with joy. "Oh, good! When?"

"Before the weekend. You stay put."

That evening when he met Etta on the veranda he told her to quit her job and pack. They would get married.

"But what will I do?" she asked. "I have no place to live until . . ."

"They have weddings here, don't they? You told me."

"Yes . . ."

"Good. Then tomorrow morning we take the car and go into town and get a marriage license. Then the hotel doctor can give us our blood tests and the hotel rabbi can marry us. You care about your own rabbi, it's important to you?"

"No, no," she said.

"Good. It's settled."

It was the moral way, the only way. He would bring Etta home as Mrs. Saffron. There had never been a breath of scandal surrounding him and there never would be.

Adam had kept his car and chauffeur on at the hotel while he was there, so he could keep his independence and mobility, but he hadn't used them and so he hadn't seen the chauffeur for a month. The man had grown so fat Adam hardly recognized him.

"Moishe, you eat too well here," he said.

"Yassuh, yassuh, Mist' Saffron," the fat colored man said, laughing. His name was Maurice, but Adam called him either Morris or Moishe.

"You be careful, I'll have to get a bigger car."

"Yassuh, heh, heh, heh." They both knew there was no bigger car to be found.

The chauffeur drove Adam and Etta into the small town to get the wedding license. Etta was wearing a navy blue dress with a white collar and cuffs, and she looked very nervous. She had removed her wedding ring and she kept clenching and unclenching her hands.

"Do you swear," the clerk said dispassionately, "that everything you say here is true, so help you God?"

"I do," said Adam.

"I do," Etta whispered.

"Name?"

"Adam Saffron."

"Age?"

"Fifty-six."

"Any previous marriages?" On and on, blah blah.

"Name?"

"Etta Weinstein Palinski."

"Age?"

No answer. Etta's face was dead white. You had to swear to tell the truth or the marriage wouldn't be legal . . .

"Age?"

"Thirty-five," Etta said.

Adam did not make public scenes. He listened carefully to the rest of her answers, his face betraying no emotion, watching her from the corner of his eye. She was nearly in tears and afraid to look at him. When they had finished the legal folderol they each signed the paper and the license was theirs. They went back to the car in silence.

"The hotel, Moishe," Adam said.

The car climbed the road between the green and blue mountains. "The marriage is off," Adam said.

Etta began to cry, softly, wiping her eyes with a little white handkerchief.

"You told me you were forty-six," Adam said. "Why did you say that?"

"I was afraid you would think I was too young for you if I told you the truth."

"But you are too young for me. My oldest daughter is only a year younger than you are."

Etta cried harder.

"You're twenty-one years younger than I am. You could be my daughter."

She never answered. He looked at her. Her legs were crossed and her skirt pulled slightly up. She had not bothered to pull it down demurely as she usually did because she was so distraught, and Adam took a good look. Then he looked at the rest of her, carefully, weighing the pros and cons of such a relationship. Thirty-five was a lot better-looking than fifty. A woman of the proper age to make his wife would never have such legs, nor even such a bust or such a trim waistline. Nor such a nice smooth face. She had managed to fool him with her lie and her gray hair, maybe she could fool everyone.

"The gray hair," he said, "how did you get the gray hair?"

"I've had it since I was fourteen," Etta said, sniffling.

"And the married son? There really is a married son?"

160

"Oh, yes."

"How old is he, then?"

She gave a small sob. "Seventeen."

Thirty-five years old. It was outrageous, embarrassing, not to be considered, but there was something quite delicious about it. A man of his age was entitled to some pleasures. He was always doing for others, giving to others, seeing that they were taken care of, and what of himself? Who did for him, gave to him? Why shouldn't he have a young wife? He was far from dead. Fifty-six was not ready to retire from the living.

"It's not good to start a marriage with lies," Adam said.

Etta sobbed into her handkerchief.

"Stop crying and listen to me."

She controlled her crying to a few little noises and wiped her eyes and nose. She looked at him.

"If I go through with this marriage you must first promise me no more lies. You understand?"

"Yes, yes."

"You swear it? No more lies, ever?"

"I swear it."

"Nothing is so bad it has to be a secret between two married people."

"You're right. You're always right."

"You have anything else you want to tell me?"

"No, no."

Adam looked at her and chuckled. She looked back, surprised. "Every woman lies about her age," he said, amused, "but backwards—that's a new one on me!"

When she saw that he was no longer angry at her she smiled at him gratefully. Then she put her head on his shoulder. He patted her neat little hand, lying there on her neat little silken knee.

After the necessary legal waiting period Adam and Etta were married in the Laurel Pastures Wedding Salon by the hotel rabbi. She wore a beige dress and he wore a dark business suit. She held a small bouquet of yellow and white flowers from the hotel gardens and her temporary wedding ring came from the nearby town's only jewelry store. It was a simple gold band. When they got back home he would get her a big diamond from New York, maybe wholesale from Finklestein. Finklestein always gave him a good bargain. If it hadn't been for Finkelstein he would never have come here to Laurel Pastures and he never would have met Etta.

They spent their wedding night at the hotel. Then the next day Adam and Etta Saffron and all their luggage went in the car to Brooklyn, where he would present her to his children. It was exactly six weeks since their mother had died.

TWENTY-SEVEN

Hazel was the first to know although Adam had planned on telling Lavinia because she was the oldest and most level-headed of his children. But when he arrived at his house with Etta, there was Hazel, sitting at the window seat waiting for the first sight of his car.

"It's my daughter Hazel," he said to Etta in the driveway.

"Hazel." She nodded, trying to remember the name with the face.

Hazel opened the door before the maids could get there or Adam could use his key. She was neither excited nor joyous, she was simply glad for the diversion of her Papa coming home.

"Hazel, this is Etta," Adam said.

"Hello, Hazel," said Etta nicely.

"Hello," said Hazel, without curiosity.

Adam and Etta came in and he helped Etta off with her coat and handed it to the maid. "Take Mrs. Saffron's coat upstairs to our room," he said to Lena, the maid. Lena's mouth fell open. "There's luggage in the car," Adam added. "Help Morris."

Hazel was looking at Etta. "Are you related to us?" she asked.

"Etta and I just got married," Adam told her kindly.

Hazel frowned, trying to digest the news. She nodded. "You knit?" she asked Etta.

"Yes, very well," Etta said.

"Me too," Hazel said contentedly.

Adam showed Etta around the house quickly and then left her in their room to unpack and settle herself. It had once been his room, now it would be their room. Not the sickroom, not Lucy's room, not his lonely room, but their room. There would be life in it now. He went downstairs to his study and telephoned Lavinia.

He told her that he was back home, that she should come over with Jonah after dinner, and that while he was at Laurel Pastures he had met a nice widow named Etta and he had married her. He wanted Lavinia and Jonah to meet her. He told Lavinia to telephone Melissa and tell her the news and tell her to come over after dinner with Lazarus. As for Andrew and Basil, Adam told Lavinia, he would inform them in a minute when he called the office. Rosemary, apparently, was out of the house.

He called Andrew then, found out whatever news had transpired in the business since they had spoken the day before, and told Andrew about the marriage and to come over that night with Cassie and to tell Basil, since Basil might well have made a date. If Basil had a date, naturally he would have to postpone it, since this family event took precedence.

Both Lavinia and Andrew had sounded shocked, but Adam realized they would have the whole afternoon and evening to compose themselves, and would put on a friendly, pleasant air for Etta no matter what they felt. It would be a civilized evening. He would not have expected less, nor would he accept less.

When she hung up the phone Lavinia burst into tears. She had been crying easily ever since her Mama had died, which was not like her, and now she cried bitterly at the heartlessness of it all. How could Papa do that to Mama? How could he?

Jonah tried to comfort her, and finally, because she knew there was no other way, Lavinia composed herself. She telephoned Melissa, pretending to be very calm, and told her the news. Melissa shrieked.

"How can you be so calm, Lavinia?"

"I'm not calm, I'm very upset."

"You're so strong. You were always so strong. I'm having a fit."

"I know. But we have to be nice to her, I suppose."

"Maybe she's nice."

"Melissa! What difference would that make? It's *six weeks*."

Melissa began to sniffle.

"Stop crying and listen to me," Lavinia said. "Can you get me a girl to stay with Paris tonight?"

"I think so. I'll ask Bridie."

"Good. Call me. And tonight, for once, don't be late."

Lavinia hung up and cried again for a minute or two, then pulled herself together and concentrated on looking as well as she could for the meeting. She wished she'd had time to have her hair done. This was some way to tell them, to spring it on them at the last minute. She would wash her hair herself and set it. Luckily it was short and dried fast, and she was handy. The yellow dress was her most becoming one. Mama had always said not to wear black to funerals, Mama hated black, but tonight Lavinia felt like wearing a black dress to remind both Papa and that woman that there was someone who remembered. Should she wear her black dress to show them what was what, or should she wear the yellow because it made her look pretty?

Melissa called back to tell her that Bridie had found a friend of hers to come stay with Paris, and the girl would be there at seven o'clock promptly.

"You sound peculiar," Lavinia said.

"Lazarus gave me a drink to calm me down and I'm a little giddy," Melissa said cheerfully.

"You're drunk now, is that it?"

"I'm not drunk, I'm just a little giddy."

"Don't show up drunk, Melissa, and don't be late. We have to be there all together."

"I know . . . Lavinia, what are you wearing?"

"I don't know."

"Do you think we should get dressed up?"

"Wear what your conscience dictates," Lavinia said.

After she hung up she tried on the black. It made her look older, and too pale. Even pearls didn't help enough. But the yellow looked like a celebration. She would be dignified, she would be civilized, but she would not celebrate. She decided on a subdued brown print. Refined, she would look refined. What kind of woman could that be, to get her hooks into a widower before his wife was cold in her grave? Etta. What kind of name was Etta? Cheap. She must have married Papa for his money. But nobody fooled Papa.

Lavinia bathed and fed Paris and covered her with kisses. She hated leaving her with a stranger, but this was an emergency. It was not the time or place to bring a baby.

"Jonah, you can't wear that tie."

"Why not?"

"I never liked that tie. Wear a blue one. You look best in blue."

"You pick it, Lavinia," he said.

She chose his tie and shirt and suit. Simple and refined. Both of them would be the epitome of what Adam Saffron's family represented, and then this Etta would see what she would have to be.

The minute she saw Etta, Lavinia knew she was young. Young! What could Papa have been thinking of? They all sat in the living room trying to make polite conversation, all of them dying to ask this Etta every detail of their meeting and not daring to because their interest was so obviously suspicious instead of enthusiastic or even friendly. Rosemary had come home to find Etta right in the house and hadn't gotten over the shock yet. She sat there with her hands in her lap, her lips tightly together, and didn't even look at Etta. Hazel was pleased that they were all there and the house was full of life again, but what did Hazel know? Maybe Hazel was lucky to be so oblivious to things. Hazel and Rosemary would have to live in this house with Etta, and it was Rosemary who would suffer.

Andrew and Cassie were being very polite and civilized. No one could do this better than Cassie. She was bringing Etta out with her subtle little questions that were really very pointed. Etta seemed intimidated by Cassie, and well she should be. She wasn't one bit in Cassie's class. Lavinia was pleased with the appearance Andrew and Cassie were making.

Melissa sat there next to Lazarus, looking quite content, the little actress. This was her performance, and she was doing it very well. Once in a while she made a flighty remark or asked a trivial question, just to be polite, and because she managed to put Etta at ease more than any of the others Etta answered her easily and soon they knew everything.

Papa had married a thirty-five-year-old coat check girl!

Who had a seventeen-year-old-son, God knows what kind of a scavenger!

Who had no background and no education and had already married one older man who had died, God help him!

Oh, poor Mama, please God there shouldn't be a heaven where she would be sitting now, looking down on them and crying!

Lena and Letty were in and out of the room serving cookies and fruit and ice water and hot tea. Lena and Letty, who had loved Mama and served her and been trained by her when they came over without knowing a word of English or even how to lay a place at the table. There was Mama's favorite plate, the one with the blue flowers on it, filled with thin cookies, and Etta was offering it to Basil as if she owned it, holding it daintily in her hand. Etta had nail polish on her nails. Etta had a gold wedding ring on her finger. And Etta didn't even know how important that blue flowered plate was to all of them, what memories it had.

Basil shook his head and ran upstairs to his room.

"My goodness," Etta said, surprised.

"Go after him," Lavinia whispered to Andrew.

Andrew rose and went after Basil, not fast, just casually, as if both of them had been merely going to the bathroom.

"These are delicious cookies, Papa," Cassie said sweetly to cover the embarrassed silence.

"Yes?" Papa said, pleased. "You like them?"

"These are Papa's favorite cookies," Lavinia said to Etta. "Papa likes home-made cookies in the house all the time to nibble on. And for bought cake, the only bakery we ever use is Ebinger's. We always feel that you should never serimp on your stomach." She almost said: "My Mama used to say that," but then she bit her tongue. Papa would remember who always used to say that.

"That's what I always tell them," Papa said. "Don't save on food."

When Andrew entered Basil's bedroom, Basil was sitting there in the dark crying. Andrew stood in the doorway. "Basil?"

Basil choked back a sob.

Andrew didn't turn on the light; that would be cruel. Poor kid. Basil really missed Mama. He didn't have anybody. Those women he was always running around with didn't mean anything to him. There wasn't one of them he would dream of marrying. He, Andrew, had been lucky. He had the best wife in the world and a lovely little son. But Basil was so immature for his age, clinging to Papa, afraid to assert himself in the office, afraid to make decisions. Sure, *he* worried too, all the time, but Basil was the little brother.

"We all miss her," Andrew said. Basil didn't answer. "But Papa is human too, and he must have been very lonely. You have to think of him, Basil, even though it's hard right now."

"It's not Mama," Basil said. "It's us. What's going to become of us?"

"Papa loves us," Andrew said. "Why, you could get married next week and leave him, and then where would he be? If you met the right girl, would you worry about leaving Papa alone?"

"It's not Papa," Basil said.

"Then what is it?"

"It's the money. She's going to get her hands on all the money and there won't be anything left for us."

"You're twenty-seven years old, will you grow up? Papa is the smartest man in the world. Nobody, nobody ever fools Papa. Do you think Papa hasn't thought about the money? Don't you think he knows Etta's story? What's the matter with you? Papa will never let us down."

"I'm worried," Basil said.

"Well, don't you worry. I have complete faith in Papa, and if you don't too, then you're being disloyal and a fool besides."

"Do you think he loves her?"

"Who cares?" Andrew said, because he didn't even want to think about the possibility.

"Papa loved Mama, didn't he?"

"Yes, of course."

"And Papa loves all of us, doesn't he?" Basil went on.

"Of course he does."

"Then Papa won't let her get the money, will he?"

"No, no, no. I know him. And we're in the office every day. We know everything that goes on. Come on, Basil, come downstairs. You're being rude."

When Andrew and Basil returned to the living room everyone pretended that nothing had happened. Melissa was laughing and describing a party she and Lazarus had been to and everyone was acting interested.

At ten o'clock promptly, as they always did, everyone looked at the large grandfather clock in the corner while it chimed, then they looked at Papa, Papa yawned, and they all stood up. Good night, good night, good night. Lavinia and Melissa and Cassie kissed Papa good night, as they always did, and everyone made sure to say good night to Etta, calling her by name so she would be sure to notice they had done their duty and paid attention to her. Then the three couples left.

"Good night," Rosemary said, as if the words were choking her. They were the first she had said all evening. Then she dashed upstairs.

"Good night, Papa," Basil said, and dashed after her.

"Hazel, go to bed," Adam said.

Hazel got up and lumbered up the stairs. She was very tired, but she would stay up all night if someone didn't send her to bed. She hated to miss anything.

Alone with Etta, Adam looked at her, pleased. "Nu?"

"Nu?" she said.

"Everything went very well," he said. "Now you know my family."

She nodded. "So let's put out the lights and go to bed, Papa."

Until their marriage she had always called him Mr. Saffron, or else nothing. She had never called him Adam, not even after they were married. Something about him seemed to restrain her. Now she had found the proper and perfect name, and quite naturally, without even thinking, she had called him what everyone else did: Papa. Adam rather liked it.

Yes, he was Papa to his whole family, even his older sisters who had fallen into the habit following his younger sister Becky, who had called him Papa for years, as did her husband. The little children called him Grandpa. His business associates called him Mr. Saffron, and his old cronies from the Center called him Saffron, as he called them Finklestein, Marx, and so on.

Now there was no one left alive who called him Adam.

PART II

Papa

ONE

Now it was not only Rosemary the good soul who made lists; all of them made them, and compared them. They were verbal lists, of course, all of them concerning the lapses of taste of Etta, the grievances and afflictions Etta had brought upon them, their kindnesses and thoughtfulness to her and her nasty responses. Etta buys store cake. Etta gets it at the corner, not at Ebinger's. Poor Papa hardly ever gets his favorite cookies. Etta serves burned leg of lamb when the family comes to dinner. When Papa gives a party or a get-together for his friends Etta serves her fancy salads, but when we come we get the dregs. Did you notice that last week there wasn't enough to go around? I spent seven dollars for a bottle of cologne for Etta's birthday, but do you think she ever remembers one of ours? A handkerchief that must have cost fifty cents, that's what she gave Rosemary. Not even a card to Melissa. Sure, she gave Paris a doll, but that was the first and last present she ever gave one of the kids, and Papa must have told her to. And do you know what she said to Paris? Paris was running around like she always does, so happy and cheerful, and she said to Etta: "I'm a pretty little girl." And Etta said to her: "What makes you think you're pretty? You're not pretty. You're conceited." What a nerve! Poor Papa.

Etta brought her seventeen-year-old married son to meet Papa. Everyone heard about it. She wanted Papa to take him into the business. A langer loksch, a shlump, a nothing. Papa said no. No outsiders in the business. Let him go be a pilot. Stanley his name was, or Sidney, or something. What a nerve! Poor Papa.

Etta can't buy enough fancy clothes, she has fresh flowers in the house all the time, expense means nothing to her. Etta has two fur coats and a boa. Ha! I suppose that's the first time she ever had fur on her back. She certainly came to Papa in rags. She said the dead husband spent all his money before he died.

There probably wasn't any money, and if there was, she was probably the one who spent it. Did you see the diamond Papa bought Etta?

Did you notice how Mama's things are disappearing? Do you think she sells them? Etta said the samovar was too old-fashioned, but I bet she did something with it. We'd better go over there and collect some of what's coming to us before she gives it all to that son of hers. Remember all those hand-embroidered linens? What do you think became of them? Remember the red vase? I haven't seen that around for a long time since she came. There are so many things in that house you can't count them, but I remember what was there, don't you? What a nerve! Poor Mama.

Every Sunday the family came for dinner at noon. All except Andrew and Cassie and little Chris. They went up every weekend to the country, where they stayed at a nearby inn and Andrew supervised the building of his house and the landscaping of his property. Andrew had been so pleased when he broke the news to Papa. It was at the office, the first day Papa came back.

"Papa," Andrew said with a big smile, "I have something to show you." He laid out the blueprints of his dream house on Papa's desk.

"What is this?" Adam asked.

"It's my house." And Andrew babbled on, telling him all about the land, and the good deal he had gotten, and Ferdinand, and Adam felt the shock and pain in his chest like a physical blow and could hardly breathe. "It's the first thing I ever did on my own," Andrew said. "I want you to be proud of me."

Adam could tell that it had never occurred to Andrew that his Papa wouldn't be proud of him. He pretended to be busy in thought so that Andrew wouldn't see the pain on his face, and then, slowly, Adam began to ask Andrew questions: was the deal final, what were the terms of the financing, did they intend to live there forever or build and sell, was the house equipped for winter too, what sort of land development did Andrew expect would go on in the vicinity in the next few years, and later on, what then? Andrew was happy to be able to tell him that he had thought of all this already by himself. He planned to live in the house for years and years, probably forever. It was not to sell, it was to love.

Oh yes, Adam knew about a dream and about love. It had never occurred to him that one of his children would do something like this. And that it should be Andrew! He could not, of course, reveal his disappointment and sorrow to Andrew, nor could he force Andrew to sell. This house, this land, was Andrew's dream, and if he had kept it a secret it was because he had meant it as a surprise—look, Papa, I'm a man!—and not because he was being devious. It had been a mistake not to tell the children about his dream of all of them being together some day on their own land in the country.

Adam nodded finally, solemnly, and patted Andrew's hand. He wanted to hold it, but he didn't, he just patted it because it was clenched there on the edge of his desk, the knuckles so white, the hand actually trembling with Andrew's excitement and need for affirmation. "You're showing a real talent for the business, Andrew."

"Thank you, Papa." Andrew beamed at the great compliment.

"I'll drive up with you one day and look at your land. You'll show me everything. We'll go for the whole day, take our time."

Andrew fairly glowed. He looked like a little boy again. But he would never be a little boy again. "Any time, Papa!"

When Andrew left Adam took his blueprints out of his desk drawer and sadly inked out Andrew's name. Now it was necessary to give his plan new thought. Perhaps it would be wise to buy a great deal of land and build slowly, a house for himself and Etta and the unmarried children, a house for Lavinia and Jonah and Melissa and Lazarus and their children, and space for whatever the future might bring. He would have to think about it. Meanwhile he would have to reveal the surprise before he had planned to, but it was imperative. If he had told all of them his plan before this then Andrew would never have bought that land and started to build on it.

He told the children his plan after they had finished Sunday dinner at his house. They were all delighted, as he knew they would be, except for Lazarus, who was worried and grumbled that it would be too expensive.

"But share and share alike won't be expensive!" Melissa said gaily.

"Humph."

"I like the country much better than the beach," Lavinia said. "It's so much cleaner. You aren't always tracking in sand."

"And the sheets won't always be damp," Melissa said. "Oh, and I worry so about Everett running into the ocean and drowning! When are you going to do this, Papa?"

"When the time is right," Adam said.

"Soon?"

"Not soon. But I want you all to have something to look forward to. Meanwhile, I bide my time, and we see."

There would be no more mistakes. But Adam would not cry about it, for it was as foolish to cry about something which was done as it was to make mistakes. Andrew was a good son, a devoted son. But he was the son of a builder, and the son of a builder built.

TWO

Paris was six years old and had been at school for two years. It was a private, progressive school, and she was there on scholarship, as were many of the other children during the Depression. She knew that some of the children were poor and some were richer than she was by their houses. The poor ones lived in row houses in Mudville, and the rich ones lived on Eastern Parkway and had doormen in front of their large buildings. She lived in a nice building sort of in-between, a block away from Aunt Melissa and Uncle Lazarus and Everett. Everett was twelve, and she had known him all her life. They told her he had been waiting at her house when her parents brought her home from the hospital the day she was born. Since both she and Everett were only children, and saw so much of each other, she thought of him more like a brother than a cousin. If anyone asked her if she had any brothers or sisters she sometimes said yes, she did, a brother named Everett. She liked pretending that he was her brother, although she also liked that it was just pretend and she was really an only child. She would have loved to have a dog or a cat. But her parents didn't seem to like animals.

Her father brought her as many frogs and toads as she wanted, and a big bottle of tadpoles that turned into frogs, and she liked them, but after all, you couldn't hug and kiss a frog, could you?

She had to content herself with hugging and kissing her toys.

She thought everybody in the world was Jewish, like her. When she found out that her favorite teacher wasn't Jewish she felt very sorry for her. Poor Miss Martin! She was so pretty and so nice, and so young, and not only wasn't she Jewish but also she wasn't married, so she must be very lonely. Paris knew that Jews had lots of relatives like she did and always had people around to care about them. She didn't know her father's family and she assumed they lived far away. Her mother had a great big family and some of them lived far away, so you only saw them on holidays or at parties. But on Sundays most of them went to Grandpa's house for dinner at noon, and that was really boring. Paris drove everybody crazy by talking so much, and Daddy would give her a penny for every minute she could keep still, but she never made more than a nickel. Then they would let her go outside to play in the yard, which was what she liked, and she was perfectly content climbing trees and digging up worms and chasing the white dog that lived down the street.

She had a lot of friends at school, girls and boys both. She loved school. The two things she hated about school were Playground and being fat. Being fat was what made her hate Playground. She wasn't any good at games, and whenever they had to choose up teams she was always the last one picked, which was humiliating. At meals she tried to eat the meat and vegetables and leave over the rice or potatoes and the buttered bread, but the teachers always made her eat everything. Couldn't they see how fat she was? Everybody teased her. If you wanted seconds on meat you had to have seconds on everything. That was a dumb rule the school dietitian had made. You either had to eat everything or nothing, and it was hard to eat nothing when you got so hungry.

She was the third fattest girl in the class. The other two were much fatter than she was, which was a relief. Her best friend was very skinny and the other kids teased *her*. You obviously had to be just in-between, just like everybody else, what her mother angrily called Average, not to be picked on.

Her mother often talked about Average, with scorn, especially when it meant Average Mentality. She told Paris that she was very smart, and that most people were Average and didn't appreciate people who were superior. It sounded as if Average really meant stupid, the way her mother talked about it. Paris could write stories and poems and draw and paint, she usually had the lead in school plays, and she always painted the scenery and even made up the music. She couldn't play the piano but she would hum her tune and the teacher would write it down. She was terrible at dancing class, naturally, being clumsy and self-conscious, just like a horse. She was tall as well as fat, so that even though she was the youngest one in the class she was always one of the tallest. That was lucky, because she sometimes got into fights with the boys and she had to beat them up. In a fight she was completely fearless as long as it was only one person. If it was a gang she would run for her life. Since they went to a progressive school they were allowed to have fights, although the teachers lectured them on being kind to others. She tried to be kind; she really didn't want to hurt anybody's feelings and sometimes she worried for days that she had. Why didn't words come out the way you wanted them to? She knew that words could really hurt. If you had a fight, if you hit someone or knocked them down and sat on them until they cried, it was just a fight, and maybe the next time they would win. But if you said something that hurt somebody they might never forgive you, never forget it, and it was hard for you to forget it too because you felt so guilty.

She knew there were a lot of things people had said to her mother that her mother had never forgotten, mean things that had hurt. It was important to be kind to people, her mother said. But you were not to confuse it with being Average. It was a little hard to understand.

Brooklyn was a paradise for kids. You could go to the park and there were so many places to play and pretty things to look at, like the Japanese garden, and the flower garden, and of course there was ice skating in the winter if the lake was frozen hard enough. Most of the time though they went to the Ice Palace, which was indoors. In good weather you could roller skate on the sidewalk, and Paris could even roller skate all the way to Everett's house, which was at the bottom of a big hill and a very thrilling ride with the bumpy sidewalk coming right up through the metal wheels of your skates until it made your teeth rattle. Halfway down the hill was the candy store, with penny candy, which she knew she shouldn't eat but which sometimes she couldn't resist. Her favorite was the chocolate-covered sponges, which cost two cents but were worth it.

You could also play ball in the street and against the walls of buildings, and you could skip rope and play hopscotch. Even though she was the worst one at sports in school Paris was very active and full of energy, so her afternoons were always spent in some sport or other with her friends, which wasn't at all like the horrible things they made you do in Playground like hang from a sideways ladder and climb across it holding on like a monkey. If you were with your friends in the street and didn't go far from home or talk to any strangers, especially men, it was safe for kids to play outside alone. Paris knew her mother was always somewhere very near, watching her and pretending not to. It was fun to try to run away and hide from your mother, but she was also glad her mother was there.

There was also the museum, where Paris went with her mother and a friend and the friend's mother at least once a week. Her favorite thing was the dinosaur bones, and her second favorite was the armor. Her third favorite was the museum restaurant, where they went for lunch on Saturdays. Her least favorite was the woman who read stories to the kids on Saturday afternoons after lunch. Paris hated to be read to. She was a good and fast reader and loved books. They were her favorite present. No one had read to her since she was four years old; she wouldn't let them.

She had just started being taken to the movies. Her parents had told her she would be allowed to go to the movies when she could sit through the whole picture without asking to go to the bathroom. Movie bathrooms were dirty.

They were going to build a big new library across the street from her house. In the meantime there was the school library, which let you take books home. Everett didn't like to read, or play any sports, or even ice skate. He only had one friend, and he hardly ever saw him after school. Everett was the smartest person Paris knew. (She didn't include grownups in her list of who was smart, because they were so different from kids.) Everett could build anything mechanical in the whole world. He could build a telegraph and even a radio. Sometimes he took apart the telephone and showed her how it worked, and then he put it together again. He said he didn't like books because he knew everything in them, but Paris knew you could never know everything that was in books because there were too many of them. He was probably a bad reader.

At least once a week Paris went to Aunt Melissa's house with her parents for dinner. She and her mother usually went over in the afternoon and then she could watch Everett in his room where he was always making something new and wonderful. He could sit over his things for hours, soldering, tinkering, putting things together, and she could sit there and watch him, fascinated. She just wanted to watch. She felt flattered that he let her. He was usually nice to her.

Her father would come there later, in time for dinner, because he had been at Grandpa's office, and Uncle Lazarus would come from his office at around the same time. The food at Aunt Melissa's was very boring. It was always what Uncle Lazarus liked, and he liked what was good for you. Everett never ate anything, and Paris ate to be polite.

The nicest thing about Everett, besides that he was so brilliant and always doing interesting things, is that he wasn't scary at all. Older boys and grown men were scary. They had something in their pants that you weren't allowed to see, and when Paris rode on the subway with her mother that thing was just on her eye level and it scared her to think of it. She tried not to look at where it was, but she couldn't keep her eyes away. She didn't remember where she had heard about that thing, or who had told her, but she knew it was there. When they left her alone with any older boy cousin who she didn't know she kept looking at where it was and wishing she didn't have to be in the room alone with him. She knew that strange men in the street who tried to kidnap little girls had that thing. That was why if she was ever alone in front of her house without her friends and she saw a strange man coming, even if he was all the way down the street, she would duck inside the lobby, where she felt safe. The doorman was there, but she never thought about him having one. Men who had them were strangers and enemies, but the nice men like her father and her uncles and the few men teachers at school and the doorman and the man who owned the candy store and people like that, they had one but you didn't have to be afraid or even think about it. The boys in her class had them, but you didn't have to think about that either because those boys were her friends, the same as girls, and most of them she could beat up if she felt like it.

She was never going to get married. She wouldn't marry a grown man or a stranger. Maybe when they grew up, if he still didn't have any friends, she would marry Everett. It would be nice, because then nothing would change.

THREE

In 1938 Adam had bought a nice big house in Miami Beach, a few blocks from the beach itself, and Etta had furnished it in the most modern style. The house nestled among all sorts of tropical foliage, with tall emperor palms outside, and behind the house were orange trees, with both regular and mandarin oranges, and lemon trees with lemons on them as big as a fist. There was a goldfish pond and a shuffleboard court, flowering bushes in profusion, and many palms. Right at their back porch there was a banana tree with dwarf bananas on it. It was a garden of Eden to a Northerner; you could reach right out and pick your own snack.

Inside, the house was done in pastel colors, with a white piano in the living room and navy blue glass walls in the bar like a real cocktail lounge. The bathrooms all had tiles of gray or navy or maroon, for white was commonplace. The master bathroom even had a navy blue bathtub. Adam took showers.

Fat Maurice was still with them to drive the Cadillac limousine, and Etta had hired a gem of a cook named Henny, a scrawny colored chain-smoker with an enormous family who seemed to appear out of nowhere whenever an extra maid or gardener or serving girl was needed. Was it possible for someone to have so many relatives? No matter, they were there and they were good. Besides Henny there were two of her daughters to clean and serve, not always the same two, but she always managed to produce two of the right age and appearance. Henny's family had a strange, earthy, literal sense of humor which shocked Adam's family. One day one of her daughters began to appear listless, and her stomach was protruding rather significantly.

"Oh," Etta said, "maybe she's pregnant."

"Naw," Henny said, her Camel wobbling under her upper lip, "she had a hysterectomy."

Everyone was shocked that Henny hadn't said that her daughter couldn't be pregnant because she wasn't married yet.

There were bedrooms for Rosemary and Hazel and Basil and enough left over for all the others if they decided to visit at the same time. Rosemary and Hazel stayed with Papa and Etta all winter, while he managed his growing Miami Beach real estate interests, while the boys, as Andrew and Basil were still called in their thirties, managed the New York office and took turns visiting down South. Cassie had had another son, Paul, who was an infant. He had blond hair.

"His mouth looks like a tunnel," Cassie said. "I can't wait till he gets some teeth. He's so ugly."

Chris and Paul were exactly four years apart, as had been recommended as the best way of spacing your family according to a child psychology book Cassie followed. Everyone used to have children every year, whenever they appeared, and that, the book said, led to jealousy and sibling rivalry. At four a child was nearly on his own; he would not be so insecure. She still kept the German girl, who was more of a governess than a maid or a nurse.

Adam had realized his dream of putting up a big office building, and he had become well known and respected in the Jewish community, and even, grudgingly, in the Christian one. He stayed with his own socially, but when it came to hiring he always chose the best man for his needs, regardless of social caste or religious beliefs, and everyone wanted to work for him because he was successful and paid well. His employees were mainly tall, handsome young WASPs, glib showpieces, who preferred Palm Beach to Miami Beach and were uncomfortable on their mandatory yearly visit to Adam's home for cocktails. They overdressed, expecting Adam's friends to overdress, and then found they were conspicuous. But they had been chosen to be good at business, not to be like him or his friends socially, and Adam was satisfied with his choices, who were all bright, hard-working, and ambitious although not treacherous.

None of them ever asked to date Rosemary, who had just turned thirty and was still single and looking, and she wouldn't have gone out with them if they had. She was painfully self-conscious with any young man who seemed too different from what she was used to back home. On the other hand, she was a snob. And as she was not particularly pretty, although she had a trim, athletic figure, she spent many evenings at home with the family. During the day she took tennis lessons and went to the beach, where Papa had rented a big cabana. She hated cards and mah-jongg, and had not made any friends among the young married women of her age, whom she considered dull. In the afternoons she played the piano for several hours, and then it was time for dinner and the boring evening. She considered social work, but never considered taking a job, not that there was anything for her anyway. But the social work was dull, and the women who did it were all rich and dull too. Her favorite times were when Basil came to visit, for then they did things together. Sometimes they would take the cruise ship to Havana for the weekend, and visit all the night clubs. Once they were forced to take Hazel with them, because she nagged so, but luckily she didn't nag after that one weekend. Hazel didn't drink and she didn't dance, so the night clubs weren't much fun for her except as an observer, and anyway, Papa took them all out to dinner and night clubs every once in a while in Miami Beach, whenever a new hotel was opened, just so he could see it. And, of course, when Melissa and Lazarus came down there was always a round of restaurant going and night-clubbing. Everett was thirteen, and old enough to accompany the family, although naturally not old enough to drink. He was having a big fight with his parents because he was too shy to have his bar mitzvah, and they of course insisted that he go through with it after all those years of study. He didn't want to speak in public, nor be the center of attention, and all Lazarus' promises of watches and fountain pens did not convince him that it would be worth the agony of having people notice him for the first time.

Not have a bar mitzvah? It was like a Christian not being baptized: unthinkable. Terrible. What would people say? He would be a lost soul in the eyes of God, not to mention in the neighborhood. Everyone knew that Melissa and Lazarus would win, because a thirteen-year-old child never won, and of course they did win, and everyone said Everett's bar mitzvah was lovely. It was held in Brooklyn, and they all went.

Hazel's life in Florida went on as it had in Brooklyn, with one big exception. She was thirty-three now, and looked forty-five. She had nothing much to do at home, so she ate, and Henny was a good cook. Hazel was portly, matronly, although not fat, and with her slow ways she seemed more like a calm young grandmother than a single girl who still had private dim hopes of finding a husband. She dressed carefully every day in her boned all-in-one and expensive dresses, smeared on her lipstick, and purse in hand (filled with money Papa had given her) set out in Papa's car, driven by Maurice, who had dropped Adam at the office and was not needed again until afternoon. She made the rounds of the stores. It was her favorite hobby now, more fun even than knitting or crossword puzzles. She loved to browse and window shop, go inside and touch and look, but she never spent much money. It was too hard to choose. If Papa had told her to buy a dress or a handbag, she would have dutifully bought a dress or a handbag, but since he had given her the money and told her to have a good time, she preferred to just look and come home with the money. Sometimes she bought a cheap little thing, a joke or novelty. She did not really wonder why they let her go out as she pleased here in Miami Beach, when she had spent her younger life kept in the house in Brooklyn unless she had a chaperone, but she supposed it had to do with the warmer climate. You wouldn't catch a cold here. It never occurred to her, nor would anyone ever dream of discussing it among the family behind her back, that now that Hazel was a large, distinguished-looking matron, no boys would ever try to take her into the bushes. She still chatted with strangers—salesgirls, women she met at the cabana—but she didn't speak to strange men. She knew men didn't like to chat about the same things that women did, and she didn't know how to talk about men things.

During school holidays Lavinia and Jonah and Paris came to visit. They always took the train, as did everyone else in the family except impatient Papa. Lavinia would ask Paris' school to let her have several weeks off besides the holiday, and as Paris was so bright and always able to make up the missed work, the school would agree. Paris had a friend in Miami Beach, whose grandparents also lived there during the winter, and she and her friend Lucille drove everyone crazy with their pranks. The two little girls could stay out of doors for hours, endlessly inventing things to do, like putting a brick in Etta's daughter-in-law's pillow case the one time Etta's son and his wife came to visit. It was already clear to Paris, at seven, that this tall, blue-haired lady whom no one ever let her call Grandma or even refer to among her friends as her step-grandmother, but only as Etta, Aunt Etta, or "my Grandpa's wife," held a special place in the family. She was the boss in the house, responsible for the menus and most of the household discipline (for example, she yelled at Paris all the time, but Grandpa never did), but nobody really thought of her as the boss. They were very polite to her, but they didn't seem to like her at all. She wasn't like a relative, she was more like a teacher they were a little afraid of because she represented the school. Paris thought Etta was pretty dumb for a grownup. She had a blank look in her eyes. She liked to play the horses with Henny. The bookie would come to the back door every morning and take fifty-cents or one-dollar bets instead of the two dollars you had to bet at the track, and Etta and Henny would always bet with him. Then they would listen to the radio to see who had won and get all excited. If you bet a dollar you only got back half of what the racetrack paid if you had won with a two-dollar bet. Paris could understand Henny betting only a dollar, because she was just the cook, but Etta was rich and Paris thought it was silly for her not to bet the whole two dollars and get twice as much.

Paris was not in the least afraid of Etta. Whenever Etta yelled at her, her mother got very angry, but Paris didn't mind because she knew that some people just didn't like children, and Etta was one of those. She didn't take it personally. She didn't like Etta much, nor did she dislike her; Etta was just there and you had to be very polite and nice to her because that was what everyone did in this house. You couldn't kid around with her like you could with Aunt Hazel, who was very patient and like a child, or with Aunt Melissa, who was so sweet and pretty and loved Paris and Everett very much. The other person who didn't like children was Uncle Lazarus. He couldn't stand children, even his own son. He was always yelling at Everett, or else ignoring him. Paris thought Uncle Lazarus was the most boring person in the world and she kept away from him, which was what he liked. He referred to her as "that rotten kid." That made her mother furious. But since he also called Everett, his own son, "that rotten kid," Paris paid no attention.

Sometimes the grownups took Paris with them when they went out at night, and sometimes they left her home with all the maids. When they left her home she knew they were going to a very boring grownups' thing called a charity affair, which she would hate. They went to a lot of those, and everybody ate dinner and then stood up and promised to give money to the charity. Why they all stood up and announced out loud how much they were going to give was beyond her. Why didn't they just have someone go around with a bag and collect it, or else let them all stay home and mail it in? Some of the things grownups did that they thought were fun were so boring that Paris wasn't sure she ever wanted to be a grownup at all.

Adam enjoyed the charity affairs, because he could see all his cronies and business associates and have his fine family with him. It was a part of life, he had taught his children: if you had, you gave to those who did not have. It was important to be a generous man, a philanthropist if possible.

The children, Lavinia and Melissa, Andrew and Basil, and Rosemary, were terrified of these charity events because Papa always stood up and pledged for them all, and he got carried away by the other people's pledges and always pledged more than he had planned to, more than they could afford.

"It's one thing to be generous, Papa," Lavinia said, "but not to the point of making *us* charity cases."

"Don't be silly," Papa would say calmly. "You can give it in installments."

And there went the fur coat Melissa had been dreaming of, there went Everett's camp (he would have to go to the Boy Scout camp again instead of Whip-poor-will, and everybody Melissa knew in Brooklyn sent their boys to Whip-poor-will), and Lazarus would worry himself sick as usual about his finances. There went the new dress Lavinia had been meaning to wear to her college reunion and Jonah wouldn't be able to send any money to his family (although Lavinia wished he had stopped that practice a long time ago). There went Basil's planned summer in Europe. As for Andrew, he would have to delay putting in the swimming pool for another year, and Chris would have to play under the garden hose.

When Adam Saffron stood up in the main ballroom of the new Neptune Palace and made his pledge to help the poor refugees from Europe, a buzz of admiration went through the room. What a pledge! What a generous man! He really must be rich to be able to give away so much. After the pledges were completed and the assembled guests had begun to dance to the music of the forty-piece orchestra and drink, and the old tired ones had begun to go home, yawning, friends came over to Adam Saffron's table to greet him and express their admiration. Ah, the poor refugees would be so grateful to Adam Saffron, if they only knew he existed.

The first to rush over was always Herman Winsor. Fat, bald, paunchy Herman Winsor, with the ever-present cigar in his mouth, the fine dollar cigar from Havana that Lazarus disgustedly called his stinkadoro.

"Here comes Weinstein again," Lazarus would say. "I can always smell his stinkadoros a mile away."

Melissa would kick him under the table. "Shh!"

"What are you kicking me for, Toots?"

"His name is Winsor now," Melissa would whisper.

"I know it."

Lazarus couldn't stand Jews who changed their names because they were ashamed of their ancestors. Having a fine family name like Bergman, which was often mistaken by Gentiles for Gentile, which he liked, made him even more intolerant of people who changed their names. "Thinks he's the Duke of Windsor, ha ha," Lazarus would say. "Couldn't even spell it right."

"Hello, Herman," Melissa would say warmly, to make up for Lazarus. Lavinia would stifle a giggle. She didn't like Lazarus, but she liked Herman even less.

Herman Winsor, né Weinstein, was in real estate too, like Adam. He was originally from Brooklyn, and everyone from Brooklyn knew about everyone else from Brooklyn, like Jews from a small town in Russia knew all about the other Jews in that town in Russia after they had emigrated to New York. Herman Winsor was very nouveau riche. But he was jolly and friendly. He paid his respects to Adam, greeted Etta and the children politely, and then managed to pull up a chair to sit next to the object of his heart's desire, Rosemary. Rosemary would move her chair away, just an inch, but not subtly.

"Hello, Rosemary," Herman would say, loudly. He always spoke loudly when he was trying to be particularly jolly.

"Herman," Rosemary would say, nodding her head. Her voice would drip icicles. She was very good at that.

"How about this dance?"

"I hurt my ankle this morning playing tennis."

"Oh. Better take it easy with that." He would lay his cigar carefully in the glass ashtray and beam at her. "You'd better go to a good doctor."

"I will."

"My doctor is good."

She wouldn't answer, but would occupy herself with great interest in watching the dancers. Herman would search his mind for something to say to impress her.

"I'm thinking of turning in my car for a new one."

"Oh?"

"It's only a year old, but I like a new car every year. You'll have to see my car when we leave."

She would see the car, in passing, when she left with her family and Herman managed to leave at the same time. The whole family would admire the car, and Herman would be pleased. They would tell her what a grand fellow he was, he was sure.

If it was not the ankle and the auto the dialogue always ran to something of that same nature. Herman would pursue, in his own way, and Rosemary would retreat, in her own way, and because neither of them understood the other Herman thought he was making progess and Rosemary could not understand why he didn't take a hint and go away. She wouldn't be caught dead going out with Herman Winsor. She thought he was terrible. He, on the other hand, thought she was shy, strictly brought up, and a nice old-fashioned girl. The more she rejected him the more impressed he was. As a forty-three-year-old bachelor he'd had his share of chippies and good-time girls, and still did, but when he was looking for a wife, as he had decided to do now, he wanted a nice old-fashioned girl, quiet, docile, and very rich. Adam Saffron's youngest daughter was perfect for what he had in mind. He liked that she was athletic, that was so goyish. It would impress his friends, all of whom were his age and spent their time playing cards, and of course their wives played mah-jongg too, but none of them would dream of playing tennis. Rosemary reminded him of a Jewish Katharine Hepburn: her lean sinewy legs, her freckles, her frizzy reddish hair. But he would never have considered any girl who wasn't obviously Jewish. At heart he was much more religious than he pretended to be for business and social purposes. He really would have liked to light the candles every Friday night before supper, the way his mother always had in Brooklyn.

Herman Winsor took a cabana on the beach near the one Adam Saffron rented. When Lavinia and Jonah and Paris, Melissa and Lazarus and Everett, the whole damn mishpuchah, were there, he seldom stayed for more than a moment to say hello. It was too hard to get any time alone with Rosemary when she was surrounded by her family. He would sit outside his own cabana, under the awning, and play cards with his friends, chewing on his cigar, dressed in a cool white suit. Herman Winsor would never appear on the beach in a bathing suit. He was not that big a fool. Of course, he confined his cabana visits to weekends, as during the week he had his real estate interests to attend to.

Adam would sit outside his cabana under the awning, watching the passing parade and being greeted by friends. He enjoyed watching his family having fun on the beach. Everett, skinny and white, would be running around because his mother had commanded him to, although he would have much preferred staying in the house tinkering with some of his junk. Melissa and Etta, who seemed to hit it off quite well, would sit in the shade together, inside the cabana, for they both had fair skin and dreaded the Florida sun. Lazarus would be standing near the water's edge, facing the sun, timing his sunbath: ten minutes facing, then ten minutes sideways, then turn with the back to the sun for ten minutes, then ten minutes on the other side. He never sat down, he never walked, he never swam, and he never seemed to enjoy his carefully timed sunbath either. He did it because it was good for him; the sun had vitamin D. As soon as he had finished his sunbath Lazarus would go into the cabana, take a shower (first hot with soap, then cold for the circulation), and dress. He would sit in the shade and read his medical journals. After lunch and a rest he would get back into his bathing suit and take his afternoon sunbath, the same as his morning sunbath.

Jonah had taught Paris to swim and they would spend a lot of time in the water. Lavinia did not trust this ocean any more than the one on Long Island—hadn't someone said there was an invasion of man o'wars, and they could sting and kill you?—and she spent her time in the shade or running along the water's edge warning her husband and child of their imminent injury. She would never say death. God forbid, bite your tongue, spit. "Watch out for the man o'war!" she would shriek. "Don't step on a jellyfish!"

Paris was beginning to dislike swimming. She didn't like jellyfish. Everett had showed her a man o'war once, on the sand near the water, and it was blue and looked scary. It looked like a big glob, but the thing that stung you came out, wham! It was probably like a long needle with electric sparks.

"Jonah! Be careful of the undertow!" Lavinia was standing carefully away from the foaming tide. Paris was scared of the undertow. She didn't like to get water in her eyes either because it stung. If the undertow got you it carried you right out to the open sea and no one could save you. You drowned.

"Jonah! Don't let Paris get tired! Don't let Paris get cold! See if she's cold. She looks cold to me. That's enough now."

They would go back to the cabana. Wash off the salt, dry off with a clean towel, get dressed in a dry suit, eat lunch. You had to wait an hour and a half after lunch before you went into the water again or you would get a cramp and drown. If you even ate a banana, nothing else, you could get a cramp and drown. Paris would go in back of the cabana after lunch, to the place where the cabana stuck up on stilts in the sand, and throw up. Then she would bury it in the sand with her foot. She had been throwing up a lot since they came to Miami Beach. She thought it might be the pickle she ate with her hamburger the first day they came. Her mother said never to eat pickles, but she had anyway. Eventually, in a couple of weeks, it would have to go away. Nothing could stay plugged there forever, even a pickle.

When the two families went back to Brooklyn the cabana was peaceful. Etta often did not bother to come, relieved now of her job as hostess, and she preferred to stay in the cool house, reading her murder mysteries, arranging flowers, planning the menus with Henny, knitting. She also liked to go shopping, so the only time she appeared at the cabana was on Sunday for lunch, if she could not persuade Adam to have a nice lunch at home. Bagels and lox, Adam! Nice fresh smoked nova, mmmm! Sturgeon! Whitefish, Adam. You can't have that in the sun.

Hazel enjoyed the cabana on weekends because there was so much to watch. All those people doing things. She would busy herself with her knitting or her crossword puzzles.

When Herman Winsor came to his cabana on weekends and looked eagerly toward Adam Saffron's cabana to see who was there and who was missing, he was now pleased to see that it was nearly deserted: only Hazel, Adam with a friend playing pinochle, and his Rosemary in a white bathing suit. Herman went over to her.

"Good morning, Rosemary."

"Morning."

Herman reached into the pocket of his white jacket and took out a hundred-dollar bill. "Look what I have for you, Rosemary." He handed it to her.

She looked at it, holding it in the tips of her fingers as if it were contaminated. What kind of a crazy man gave a nice girl money?

"Look at it!" Herman crowed. "Don't you see anything different?"

She looked at it more carefully. "No."

"Look at the picture!"

There in the center, instead of the picture of whoever was on a hundred-dollar bill, was a picture of Herman Winsor.

"Very cute," Rosemary said coolly.

Herman roared with pleased laughter. Hazel looked up. "Watcha got?" Hazel asked.

Herman strode over and handed her one too, grandly. "Here's a hundred-dollar bill with my picture on it, Harriet."

"Hazel," Hazel said. She scrutinized the bill. Then she looked up at Herman Winsor. It certainly did have his picture on it. He must be a very important man. She was very impressed.

"Hazel," he corrected himself. "You may keep it. But don't try to spend it, ha ha."

"I wouldn't," Hazel said. She put the hundred-dollar bill into her purse. She had no idea it was fake. But she certainly wouldn't dream of spending a bill with the picture on it of someone she knew. That would be a dumb thing to do. Then you wouldn't have it any more.

Herman pulled a chair up to Rosemary's. "Did anyone tell you, Rosemary, that you look like Katharine Hepburn?"

She looked at him. What a slush artist!

"Why, thank you, Herman," she said sweetly. "And did anyone ever tell you that you look like Spencer Tracy?"

He was beaming, the jerk! He believed her!

"Thank you, Rosemary," Herman said. She had made him a very happy man. Victory was near at hand, he felt it, and it was time for him to make his master move.

That Monday morning Herman Winsor telephoned Adam Saffron at his office and made an appointment to come in to see him.

"Yes, Herman?" Adam said pleasantly. "What can I do for you?"

189

He pushed the large ashtray toward Herman, who was puffing on a brand-new cigar from his latest shipment. They were both comfortably seated, Adam behind his large desk, Herman in the chair in front of it. Adam's office had wood-paneled walls and thick, pale-colored carpets. The prints on the walls were all guaranteed good.

"We know each other in business and socially," Herman began. "You know me, I know you. No mystery. We're friends, right?" Adam nodded. "So, I'll get right to the point," Herman said. "I want to marry Rosemary."

Adam put his fingertips together and studied them for a moment. He nodded. "Mmm. There is, however, a problem. I could never let my youngest daughter get married while her older sister is still unmarried."

Oh yes, the other one. Herman could understand Adam's feeling, for it was the old, traditional way, and he himself was at heart, a traditionalist. "She has any prospects?" he asked.

Adam shook his head. "None that I would approve of."

"Ah."

"Now, you, Herman, are a prospect I would approve of."

Hazel. He had never considered Hazel. He thought about her now. She wasn't Rosemary, but she was Adam Saffron's daughter.

"Hazel has a good soul and a kind nature," Adam said. "She has a good disposition. She's the sort of woman who would respect her husband and cater to him. He would be the boss in the house."

"I like that," Herman said.

"She has been strictly brought up and because of that is unworldly."

"Nothing wrong with that," Herman said.

"All my daughters are equal to me," Adam said. "Equal. I never favor one above the other."

Herman knew what that meant: they all shared alike. "As it should be," he said.

"Personally, in my opinion, Herman, I think Hazel would be a better wife for you than Rosemary. Hazel is more settled; she would enjoy your kind of social life, the dinners and charity affairs and so on. Rosemary is still a bit giddy."

Yes, Herman thought, Hazel had a dignified air about her. She looked more like the wives of his friends than Rosemary did. That was why he had been attracted to Rosemary. On the other hand, if he couldn't have Rosemary . . .

"I wouldn't want you to make a snap decision," Adam went on. "You think about it. Take your time. We're going back to New York next week."

Herman nodded and rose. "A marriage, that takes some serious thought."

"Of course."

"I suppose it would be best if we decide everything before you go back north."

"It would seem sensible," Adam said calmly.

"May I call Hazel tonight for a date?"

"Why not?"

"Thank you for your time."

"I'm always at the service of a friend," Adam said.

So that night Herman called Hazel, who was surprised and thrilled at his unexpected attention. He invited her to a charity affair and she accepted with pleasure. Adam and Etta decided which of her many pretty dresses would be most suitable, and Hazel spent the afternoon at Etta's favorite beauty parlor. She even had a manicure. Herman called for her in his big new car, which Hazel admired. Rosemary was nowhere to be seen. The charity affair was held in a big hotel, as they usually were, and Herman knew everybody there. He left Hazel sitting docilely at their table while he table-hopped, greeting all the people it was important to greet, and then it was time for the speeches. After the speeches were over it was late, so Herman took Hazel home, and she thanked him for the nice time. Altogether they had not said more than ten sentences to each other, but they were both pleased.

The next day Herman telephoned Hazel and asked if he could come over to see her in the evening, and when he got there he asked her to marry him. Adam had already told her that Herman was interested in her, and that if anything serious came of it he would be glad to give his permission, so Hazel accepted happily. Cute, famous Herman Winsor wanted to marry her! Wasn't she lucky?

Before the Saffron family left to go back to Brooklyn, Herman arranged everything with Hazel, which is to say he told her what they would do and she agreed to everything. He would announce their engagement in the New York and Miami papers. They would be married next fall in Miami Beach so that all his friends and business associates could be there. Adam and the rest of the family would have moved back to Miami Beach by then for the winter, so it would be good timing for them all. His rabbi would marry them. They would live in Miami Beach. In the meantime, Hazel would stay in the nice cool North for the summer, while he, noble Herman, would find a suitable big house for them to live in, which he would buy. He would hire the finest decorator to "do" it, and the decorator would mail Hazel samples of the wallpaper and material and paint colors so she could chose the ones she liked best. Everything else would be left to the decorator. Herman would also hire a cook and a maid, although his life style demanded that they go out nearly every night for business purposes and public appearances. Still, Hazel wouldn't have to lift a finger in the house because Herman would hire the best help.

Herman presented Hazel with a big diamond engagement ring and his photograph. He was unfortunately unable to see her off at the train because he had to be at an important convention that afternoon, but Hazel didn't mind because she had the ring on her finger, glittering, and his photograph in her purse to take out and admire along with that hundred-dollar bill he had given her at the beach.

Rosemary told everyone that Herman had wanted to marry *her* and that he was marrying Hazel because Papa told him to, but luckily Hazel never found out about that because no one told her.

FOUR

Hazel Saffron's wedding to Herman Winsor was one of the social high points of the early winter Miami Beach season. Even though both the bride and the groom were a little old for that sort of formal, elaborate wedding, it was the first for each of them and therefore if they wanted it, what was the harm? Hazel wore a long white lace dress; she had insisted on it, and when Lavinia suggested that perhaps a pastel might be more chic, she burst into tears. So it was white, the same dress Hazel had seen long ago on a bride doll and had always secretly wanted. Herman wore a tuxedo and a yarmulke. Some of the younger men were starting to wear top hats instead of skullcaps to their own weddings, but Herman was a traditionalist. Hazel of course agreed with him in whatever he decided.

Adam gave the bride away. There were three hundred guests, and the reception afterward was at the Neptune Palace, in the grand ballroom, which was decorated with thousands of pink and white flowers. The guests were all friends and business contacts of Herman's and Adam's, who had made out the guest list together. Nobody asked Hazel if she had any special friends she would like to invite because she didn't. Her special friends were her sisters. Etta supervised the menu for the reception and saw that the caterers did everything the way it had been done at Laurel Pastures. All the guests raved about the food and the attractive way it was presented, and Hazel kvelled. They were complimenting her, because it was her wedding, wasn't it? It was a lovely, lovely wedding.

Hazel and Herman spent their honeymoon on a cruise to Havana and five days seeing all the night clubs and gambling. It wasn't a long honeymoon, but Herman was right in the middle of a new project and couldn't spare any more time.

Herman opened charge accounts for Hazel in the best stores and told her to buy nice dresses for when they went out. Since he had told her to buy, she bought dutifully. She went to the most expensive department and bought everything the other married ladies wore, so she could look like his friends. If they wore sequins, she wore sequins. If it was feathers, she wore feathers. Was cerise the color? Lime? Powder blue? Flamingo? Whatever was the most popular color of the moment, Hazel wore it. Herman was pleased with her fashionable appearance and didn't mind at all that the dresses were so costly. She also bought shoes and bags to match, and Herman gave her a mink coat and a mink stole and a lot of real jewelry. It was much more fun to play dress up than just to go looking and touching the way she used to do when she had no place to go at night. Now she had to dress up every night.

Sometimes she bought funny novelty things for their house, like toilet paper with money printed on it, or a wastebasket with a jeweled poodle on it, or a toilet seat that played the National Anthem whenever you sat down on it, so you would have to stand right up again, and Herman let her put them in the powder room off the bar. He thought they were funny too.

Hazel had her own car and had finally passed the driver's test after four tries, so she could go anywhere she wanted. She was careful to drive very slowly, and she only went to the stores or to the beach, because she knew the way to those places and didn't get lost. Besides, there was no place else she wanted to go.

At the beach she would sit and watch the wives of Herman's friends playing mah-jongg. Lots of times the women talked about their children and some of them showed around photographs of their grandchildren. Hazel wanted to have a baby so she could show off too. When she started feeling sick and went to the doctor she was very happy when he told her that she was going to become a mother too.

It was a difficult pregnancy. She felt sick a lot and Herman hired a nurse to stay with her during the last three months in case anything went wrong. The birth itself was very easy. The doctor just put her to sleep, and when she woke up Herman told her they were the parents of a fine little son.

They named him Richard. Richard Winsor. What a distinguished name! He would be called Richie for short. He was so cute and looked just like Herman. Nobody at the beach club had as many photos of their children as Hazel had of Richie Winsor. Of course Richie had a full-time nurse because he was just a little baby. Papa had insisted on that, and Herman had agreed. The nurse fixed all Richie's bottles and gave him his baths and changed him and did everything except cuddle him and play with him, which was Hazel's job, and one she loved. She could play with him by the hour. He was much better than her baby doll had been because he was alive and knew her and laughed when she tickled him under the chin.

The doctor told Hazel and Herman that they shouldn't have any more babies because Hazel had a bad heart and it would be too dangerous. Hazel didn't mind too much because she had Richie, and one baby doll was enough for anybody. Herman went right out and bought twin beds with a night table in between them, with a nice big reading lamp on the night table, and after that he never slept in her bed again. Hazel didn't mind that either. After all, your health was the most important thing in life, everybody knew that, and she knew that Herman loved her anyway.

Papa said he was beginning to look for land, and in a few years he would build a big estate in the country near New York City

194

where they could all spend their summers. Then she could come to stay in the summertime when it was so hot and awful in Florida, and she could see the family, whom she missed terribly even though she was having fun here. Naturally Herman wouldn't be able to spend the summers there because he had so much work in Miami, but he could come to visit her and Richie.

It didn't look like Rosemary was ever going to find a husband. Poor Ro! She was so independent. She'd better watch out or she'd be an old maid and she'd be sorry, Hazel thought from her high perch as a securely married woman. There was nothing like marriage. She felt sorry for anybody who was still single.

FIVE

Being an old maid wasn't as dreadful as Rosemary had envisioned. Here she was, thirty-three years old, still living at home, all her sisters and brother Andrew married with children, only herself and Basil still alone. But Basil had himself a heck of a good time. There was always some divorcee or widow, a touch shady perhaps (which meant that he slept with her), whom Basil was seeing. Rosemary kept busy and knew a lot of people, but men weren't exactly flocking to her door, for the good reason that any man worth looking at had already been taken. She would never accept a leftover.

She had joined a music society, which met twice a week in the evening to play chamber music. She had friends there and enjoyed that they all had a common interest. Brooklyn was more fun than Miami Beach because there were more people here with her feelings about things. People in Miami Beach were frivolous, always on vacation, playing cards and sunning themselves. Here you could go to concerts, theater, art galleries, museums—not that she went often, but they were available.

"Oh, Rosemary," her friend Jessie said one day, "let's go to the gypsy tearoom and have our tea leaves read! It's the newest thing; everybody's doing it."

"What's so new about it" Rosemary said. "It's a fake."

"Well, so what? It'll be fun anyway."

Jessie was little and birdlike and played the flute in the chamber music group. Rosemary liked to be with her because when they went places together she knew that she, not Jessie, was the more attractive one. There was always a pretty one and a not-so-pretty one with two girls. Of course, Jessie had an edge because she was younger, but twenty-six and not married yet was nothing to boast about either.

"How did you hear about this gypsy?" Rosemary persisted.

"Well, I know four girls who went already and they loved it."

"Who?"

"Well . . . Rachel, Bessie, Shirley, and Fay."

"Who is Bessie?"

"She's Fay's cousin. You met her once."

"No I didn't."

"Well, let's go, Rosemary. Come on. I made an appointment."

"You made an appointment without asking me? How did you know I would go?"

"I was hoping you would go."

"Gypsies steal. They rob your pocketbook while you're sitting right there. I heard about that."

"There's two of us; I'll hold your bag and then you'll hold mine."

"How much does it cost?"

"Just a dollar and a half. More if you want your astrology chart done."

"What's astrology?"

"You know," Jessie said. "It's the stars, and the sign you were born under and who your compatible mate will be and all that. They tell you what your nature is too, and what's going to happen to you."

"It's all fake," Rosemary said.

"Well so what? It'll be fun!"

So she went with Jessie to the gypsy tearoom, one flight up in a sleazy neighborhood, with red curtains on the windows and a red bulb in the lamp inside, and beaded curtains hanging over the doorway. It looked insidious, dirty, and naturally completely a fake. Jessie was excited and happy. Rosemary was a little nervous, because who knew what else that woman might do besides picking their pockets? She might have a brother or a man somewhere behind the beaded curtains who would drag them off into white slavery. Just the kind of fake silly fraud to trap middle-class girls like Jessie and all her friends.

"Who will be first?" the gypsy asked. Some gypsy. Probably just a refugee, a Hungarian or a Russian or something, who found a gimmick.

"Me!" Jessie chirped.

The gypsy looked at Jessie and then at Rosemary and shook her head. "No, first I read the doubter."

"Why?" Rosemary asked.

"Because I don't want your friend to influence you with her enthusiasm. I want you completely doubting. Then you will be more surprised when you see that I am right."

"Mmm," Rosemary said coldly.

"You want the tea leaves or the astrology?"

"Which costs less?"

"The tea leaves."

"Then I want the tea leaves," Rosemary said.

The gypsy shook the wet leaves around in the teacup and looked at them. Mumbo jumbo, Rosemary thought. "I see a man," the gypsy said. Ha ha, big surprise. They always saw a man. "Yes, a man who plays a musical instrument."

Jessie gasped.

"Do you know what an astral twin is?" the gypsy asked Rosemary.

"I thought this was going to be tea leaves, not astrology."

"An astral twin," the gypsy went on, unperturbed, "is someone who is exactly like you. In this universe, each of us has his astral twin. Most of us never meet him. But when you meet him you will both know each other."

"So?"

"This man, who plays the musical instrument, who I see here in the tea leaves, is your astral twin. When you meet him you will both know it, and you will fall in love and marry."

"When will this be?" Rosemary asked skeptically.

"You have already met him, but because you have not spoken to one another you have not had a chance to discover your twinship. You know him now, that is, you are acquainted, but you do not know him yet in the heart. That will come soon."

"What else?"

"That is enough, is it not? You are not interested in anything else."

"Who says I'm not? I'm interested in a lot of things."

"This is your only question about the future," the gypsy said calmly. She tossed the tea leaves quite nonchalantly into a large bowl full of wet leaves and turned to Jessie. "Now you, young lady."

"Oh, I want the tea leaves and the astrology!" Jessie said happily. "And find me a boyfriend too!"

The gypsy peered into her fresh supply of damp leaves. "Ah, you, I am afraid, will have to wait five years before you meet the man of your dreams."

"Five *years*?"

"Because at the present time he is living in a foreign country."

When Rosemary and Jessie left, Rosemary a dollar and a half poorer and Jessie out three dollars because she'd had both, Rosemary snorted. "What a fake! I told you." She put on a foreign accent like the gypsy's. "I see a tall dark stranger . . ." She laughed. "That's what they always say, and you believed her. I've seen better in the movies."

"She must have meant someone in our music society," Jessie said. "Who looks like your twin? Phil Levine! He has freckles and reddish hair."

"I wouldn't be caught dead going out with Phil Levine."

"She didn't say he looked like you . . . she said he was like you. I wonder who that could be. Come on, *think*, Rosemary!"

The last thing in the world Rosemary wanted was a boyfriend who was like her. All her life, as long as she could remember, she'd wanted a boyfriend who was better than she was, who could represent her and make up for her shortcomings. Any man she could fall in love with would have to possess all the qualities she lacked. If he was just like her, how could she possibly stand him? A man who was her astral twin, whatever that was, would be exactly the kind of man she would hate. She would have to be very careful in the meetings of the music society and never even talk to any man who looked at all like her. Not that she would fall in love with him. That was ridiculous. No one ever believed a gypsy fortune teller, except a silly romantic girl like Jessie. Now Jessie would sit around for five years waiting for Mr. Foreigner, Mr. Tall Dark and Handsome, the myth.

"Why don't *you* go out with Phil Levine, Jessie?"

"I would if he asked me," Jessie said. "Nobody in the music society ever asks me out. They all act like I'm their sister or something."

"It's just as well," Rosemary said. "There's nobody there anyway."

At the next meeting of the music society Rosemary found herself looking around at the young men with more curiosity than she wanted to. Well, she wasn't in the least like any of them, and they weren't like her either, so she was safe. None of them was her type. In fact, most of them didn't have any talent, as far as she was concerned. She was really the best. It was this knowledge which had given her the courage to join the music society in the first place. It wasn't that she really expected to find nice dates here; it was just that it was a congenial thing to do two evenings a week, and she really had met new friends here after all. Not special friends, just friends. Rosemary didn't have special friends. She would like them and then she wouldn't like them any more.

The only other person in the group who had any real talent at all, besides herself, was that man in the beige suit playing the violin. Jack Nature, his name was, from "Clothes Cleaned the Nature Way," which his father owned. Their name was formerly Natelson. Jack was very shy and very beige—the beige hair, the beige skin, the beige eyes. He even had beige eyelashes. She could just imagine him as a child, all pale and beige, practicing the violin in the afternoons while the other boys were out playing baseball. Poor Jack Nature. He seemed about her age, and he wasn't married either, but he never spoke to any of the girls, except once in a while to make a joke. Maybe he had a beige girlfriend.

When they stopped for a rest Jack Nature came up to her.

"Are you doing anything Saturday night?" he asked.

She was so startled that she said no before she realized what she was doing. The man hadn't said two words to her and now he was asking her if she was free Saturday night. Maybe he just wanted to rehearse or something.

"Would you like to go out with me, then?" he asked.

Why not? She was thirty-three and she couldn't hang around the house every Saturday night for the rest of her life. "All right," Rosemary said, trying to sound pleasant.

199

"I'll pick you up. How much do you weigh?" He gave a little half-smile. "Get it?"

"Yes."

"How about eight o'clock?"

"Fine."

"See you then."

What had she gotten herself in for? A whole evening with a shy drip!

When they were finished for the evening Jessie came over to her with a big grin on her face. "I saw that," she said.

"I'm stuck."

"Oh, Jack's a pretty nice fellow. My family knows his. You could go out with a lot worse."

"At least the gypsy was wrong," Rosemary said, and laughed.

Jack Nature came for her at ten minutes after eight, which was lucky because Rosemary wasn't ready herself either. She had decided to wash her hair, and then it didn't dry fast enough, and when it did she hated the way it looked. Oh well, they wouldn't see anybody she knew so it didn't matter. He had a tan car—what else?—and to her surprise he drove right to New York to a very lively night club where there was dancing to a Spanish band.

Rosemary ordered a daiquiri, which she'd first heard about in Havana with Basil, and Jack had one too. The drink made both of them feel much more at ease with each other.

"I didn't picture you in this kind of a place," Rosemary said.

"You ought to see me dance. Want to try?"

They danced, all the dances she'd learned in Havana, and Jack was as good as she was. "Have you been to Havana?" she asked him.

"No, but I've been coming to this club ever since it opened. I like Spanish music."

"So do I. I used to go to Havana for the weekend with my brother when we were staying in Florida. Havana's more fun."

"Yeah," he said. "There are all those Jews in Florida."

They both smiled.

During the course of the evening and three more daiquiris Rosemary learned that Jack Nature was the youngest in a family of seven girls, smothered, coddled, protected, ignored, and had grown up to feel just as cheated as she had. His mistrust of the world and people was as great as hers, but while she covered up her fears and hate with sharp remarks, he covered up his by his corny jokes. She felt a great kinship with him. Both of them were mistrustful, wary. The world was out to get you if you didn't get it first. It was a warm, relaxing feeling to be able to talk about this with someone who felt exactly the same way she did. He was nice, and she really felt that she liked him. He was starting to look not so beige, more a clean-cut type now, a type you wouldn't mind being seen with. She even liked his corny jokes. She'd never had a sense of humor, not even a corny one, and she admired him. It was better to be the clown at the party than the wet blanket.

"Did you ever want to be a musician?" she asked him.

"Oh, no. I never liked performing in public. My mother used to make me practice the violin every day because she thought it was important to be artistic, but I can't imagine playing in an orchestra. I don't mind being in business with my father, and we're expanding. Eventually I suppose I'll be stuck with the whole thing."

Rosemary knew that was his way of telling her that he would some day inherit a good business. She was amazed at how easily she understood him, and at how he seemed to know she would. "What do you dislike most about the cleaning business?"

"The stink in the plant."

"And what do you like the best?"

"The money."

They both smiled.

"It's funny how we got successful," he said. "When my father came to America he changed his name from Natelson to Nature because his best friend changed his name from Sinowitz to Simmons. So when my father started in the cleaning business he decided to put on his sign: 'Clothes Cleaned the Nature Way,' and what happened was that people started thinking it was some kind of new, natural way that was better than the old way. They thought we were using fresh air or something. So now we have four places instead of one."

"What happened to Simmons?"

"He's a chiropodist."

"Do you like to play tennis?"

"Yes, do you?"

"Yes, that's why I asked."

"I've got a friend whose family has a tennis court," Jack said. "They live on Long Island. I could ask him if we could go there next Saturday and play. He always has people over."

"I'd like that," Rosemary said.

"I'll have to polish up my game. I bet you're pretty good."

"Yes, I'm pretty good."

It was such a pleasant evening she was hardly aware that it was one o'clock in the morning until the band stopped playing. Jack drove her home in his car and promised to call as soon as he got hold of his friend with the tennis court. In the meantime, of course, they would be seeing each other at the next meeting of the music society, and he suggested they go out for coffee or a drink afterward. Rosemary agreed right away. He was so easy to be with she felt as if she'd known him all her life. He didn't try to kiss her goodnight because it was their first real date, but she had the distinct feeling he wanted to, and if he had she wouldn't have minded.

She tiptoed up the stairs so as not to wake anybody, but Basil's door was still open and she supposed he would either come creeping in at five in the morning or else, more probably, not bother to come home at all. He was so brazen about it. You could never get him to go out with any nice girl, any girl whom he might fall in love with and marry. All he wanted was those women who'd had a man and now couldn't get along without one. He was so immature. He was perfectly happy just going along like this. When he got old he'd be sorry. Then he'd be lonely, and who would want him? Who am I kidding, Rosemary thought. A man is always wanted, no matter how old he gets, especially if he has money. It's we girls who have all the bad luck. If you're not pretty, nobody wants you. If you don't have a dazzling personality, nobody wants you. If you're not young, nobody wants you. She wondered why a nice young man like Jack Nature hadn't been snapped up long before this. It was probably because he was shy. Or maybe he'd been taking his time, like Basil, having fun. She was sure Jack Nature liked her. He made her feel liked, admired.

It was funny about being out with someone who was a lot like you. She felt so comfortable. They were two against the world. She was sure he had confided in her that night things he hadn't told to other girls. The odd thing was that instead of making her feel insecure, it made her feel secure that Jack was like her. It might be a lot better than being with her opposite. This way there was two of them. Strength in numbers.

At the next meeting of the music society Jessie kept trying to get Rosemary's attention, and Rosemary ignored her. She knew Jessie was dying to ask her about her date with Jack Nature. It was none of her business! Rosemary was so annoyed that she missed her place in the piece they were playing and had to apologize to everyone and start over again. Darn Jessie, the pest!

As soon as the evening was over Rosemary dashed right out of there and Jack had to run to catch up with her.

"Where are you going?"

"Oh, I just wanted to get away from Jessie," Rosemary said.

"Well, I don't want to take her too, so let's run," he said, taking her arm, and they ran together to his car, which was parked at the corner.

They had coffee at a little restaurant where no one they knew ever went, and Jack made the arrangements about their tennis date on Saturday. He would pick her up at ten-thirty because neither of them liked to get up early. There was a nice, conspiratorial feeling about being in that little restaurant together, with none of their friends knowing. Rosemary felt the comfortable warmth again of just being with him. Was this what falling in love was like? No pounding of the heart, no blushes, no cold hands? Just warmth and comfort and feeling happy for perhaps the first time in her life? Well, if this was falling in love, then she liked it.

That night when he took her to her front door he kissed her. She liked that too. She was beginning to find him very attractive.

The next morning, too early for her taste, Jessie called her. "Well?"

"Well, what?"

"I saw you go out with Jack Nature. I saw the way he looked at you. How was your date? Was that your second date or have you been seeing him even more and keeping it from me? Tell all, Rosemary, do!"

"There's nothing to tell."

"Oh, come on, Rosemary! Is Jack Nature your astral twin?"

"Do you really believe that garbage?"

"Why not? It's fun. Is he?"

"Is he what"

"Is he Mr. Right?"

"No, he's Mr. Nature," Rosemary said, and chuckled, very pleased with herself because this was the first joke she had ever made. Jack would have liked it.

On Saturday they played doubles with Jack's friend and a date of his, on Long Island, and then they went to a seafood place and had fresh boiled lobster. Rosemary wondered what would happen that summer. The family was taking a beach house again and she wasn't anxious to leave the city if Jack was going to be there. Well, she could invite him for weekends. He had a car.

SIX

At ten years of age Paris was proud to be able to say that she had been going to camp for five years and was a veteran of five different camps. Lots of kids didn't even *start* going until they were ten! The only difference was that her parents were always with her all summer at the camp. At first, when they had no money, her father would get the job of head counselor so that she could go free, and her parents would live right at the camp and she would see them every day. Because her father was the head counselor the other kids never picked on her, and the counselors were nice to her even when she was bad. Everyone knew that every year you had to pick one girl in the bunk who was going to be the one you would torment all summer, but Paris was always secure in the knowledge that with her parents right at hand the victim would never be her.

Later on, when her parents could afford to send her to camp and pay, somehow her parents always managed to make an arrangement with the owners so that they could live right at the camp in a guest house. Her parents had a good time, riding their bicycles on the bike path, taking walks in the woods, playing Ping-Pong, and her mother managed to be around all the time to see what Paris was up to. Paris didn't have to dive or put her head into the water because she had sinus. Paris didn't have to sweep the bunk because she was allergic to dust. But it wasn't all good things. Paris wasn't allowed to eat afternoon cookies and chocolate milk because she was too fat. Her mother was always there, with her proffered paper cup of orange juice, while the other kids were gorging themselves on chocolate-iced cupcakes. Paris had to have weekly hay-fever shots at the infirmary. Paris had to have some smelly medicine put into her scalp every week by the camp nurse because her allergies made it scabby otherwise.

She had been to all sorts of camps with her parents. The first, when she was only five, had been a baby camp, and she didn't remember it very well. The next one was less of a baby camp, but boring, and the one after that was very interesting because the kids lived in tents and went on hikes where they caught fish in a stream and cleaned them and cooked them over fires they made, in pans they had brought along, and then washed the pans in the stream. They were supposed to sleep outdoors all night in sleeping bags when they went on the overnight hike, but Paris was afraid to go to the bathroom in the woods, so she got her mother to make them let her come back to the bunk to sleep so she could use the regular toilet. After that, her mother made them let her out of all the overnight hikes because it was bad for her flat feet. Paris sat in the bunk with the other girls who had something wrong with them, and read.

The next camp was the one Paris thought of as the eating camp. This time instead of tents there was sheer luxury. Each girl had her own closet, next to her bed, and in the back room of the bunk there were shelves where you had to put your clothes that folded. The ones that hung up went into the closet, and all the trunks had to be completely unpacked and then the camp handyman put them into a big loft sort of thing in back of the bunk. Paris missed her trunk because a trunk was fun, and part of camp. You could hide secret things in your trunk, like letters from friends, and forbidden candy, and just stuff you had collected that was personal to you and therefore important. You could sit on top of your trunk instead of always on the lumpy cot. At the eating camp there was a shower in each bunk, for just the six girls, instead of a wash house a long walk away, the kind they had in other camps, which was used by everyone only once a week. At the eating camp you had to take a shower every day.

After reveille there would be breakfast, then cleaning the bunk and a sport like baseball or basketball, and then there would be the midmorning snack, which consisted of huge onion rolls slathered with butter and strawberry jam, and milk or chocolate milk. The snack was served in a little gazebo in the center of the lawn, which was just for snacks, and Paris' mother was always around with the cup of orange juice, making sure she didn't cheat. Then there would be swimming, and then lunch, which was a long, big meal of several courses, served in the dining room. After lunch there would be rest and letter-writing time, and then the afternoon sport, or arts and crafts. Paris always chose arts and crafts, which she was good at. You could also work on the camp newspaper, if you were older. The girls mimeographed it themselves. Then there was the afternoon snack: chocolate-iced chocolate cupcakes or brownies, milk and chocolate milk. Paris' mother appeared again with the orange juice, although this time Paris was allowed to have white milk if she preferred. Then there was another sport, and then dinner.

Dinner was a phenomenon. It went on and on, with course after course, just like a grown-up restaurant, and if you didn't like what they gave you, you could always ask for a steak or lamb chops or anything you wanted grilled to order. One day Paris asked for six lamb chops, got them, and ate them. There were always two desserts. The kids were bloated and bored with food, and by the time the desserts came they usually occupied themselves with making balls of the cake and throwing them at each other, or otherwise making a mess. The night of the great angel food cake fight, when gummy balls of cake the kids had rolled between their palms until they had the consistency of putty were hurled around the room for half an hour, despite all the counselors' efforts to put a stop to it, was the first time the camp directors suspected that possibly they were feeding the kids too much. But it was an expensive camp, and the parents expected it. The camp was famous for its food. Better wretched excess than a smaller camper list next year because parents complained their children were losing weight from all the physical activity.

After dinner the kids went back to their bunks to get ready for the evening's activity. It was either a movie, skits presented by the camp's dramatics students, a sing, a campfire, or (three times a week) Foreign Night. Foreign Night was Chinese, Japanese, Spanish, French, Italian, Russian, or a repeat of whatever had proved most popular, usually Chinese. The social hall would be decorated in the manner of the nation to be represented, the kids wore costumes supplied by the camp, and the highlight of the evening was a feast featuring the foods of the native country. Gorged, stuffed, bursting, nauseated, the kids would walk happily back to their bunks, where they would fall into their cots without brushing their teeth, a handful of Tootsie Rolls and sourballs and licorice sticks for a good night present clutched in their hands, and all would be silent and peaceful by nine o'clock.

When Paris came home from the eating camp in the fall she had fourteen cavities in her teeth, and had gained weight. She thought she would have to spend the entire winter at the dentist, getting drilled. Her mother said no more eating camp for her, so the next summer she went to a music camp.

The music camp was quite normal except that there were compulsory recitals every evening on the lawn, while a trio played classical music and the kids swatted mosquitoes and passed each other notes. The constant presence of her parents at all these camps was becoming a little embarrassing to Paris; she wished they would let her come to camp alone like the other kids and be grown up. She didn't know exactly how they managed it— probably knew someone or had to pay—but they were the only parents allowed to stay all summer right at the camp. Maybe it was because her father had been a head counselor for so many years and had pull.

At the beginning of every summer you looked around your bunk to see who would be your best friend and who you would pick on. Then, when you had picked your best friend, it was time for the camp to put everyone on teams, and you and your best friend would pray that you wouldn't be assigned to opposing teams, or else you would have to be enemies all summer in the color war, even though you really loved each other. The day you came back to the bunk and found the little colored string on your pillow telling what team you belonged to, and compared colors with the other girls in your bunk, was the happiest or saddest day of the summer. It was funny about friendships at camp. You never saw the girls all winter—they came from other places and went to other schools—but for the two months you were at camp they were your closest friends and allies. It was sad to have to go away and know you might never see them again. Their parents took them away and yours took you away, and that was that. Into your real life again. Maybe someone you really liked wouldn't come back the next year, or maybe you wouldn't came back, and then you'd never see each other again as long as you lived. At home, at school, in your own neighborhood, you had your real friends, the ones you would always have. But your camp friends disappeared because they had their real-life school friends too. Paris thought about some of the girls afterward, wondering what had ever become of them.

There was Annette, the refugee from Holland, which had been occupied by the Germans in their war, and she came to camp the first day with a foreign accent and a box lunch, so all the girls thought she would be the one they would pick on for the summer. But by the end of that first day they had discovered that she was the leader, the best one of any of them: strong, funny, brave, pretty, a good athlete, generous, so much more grown up than any of them that they all adored her. At the end of the summer Annette had been picked Best Camper of the Year. She was also captain of the White Team, and Paris' best friend. But Paris went to another camp the next year, where athletics was not so important, and she never saw Annette again. She sometimes wondered where she was, what she was doing. She knew that Annette lived in some sort of suburb, Scarsdale or something, that was pretty far from Brooklyn. None of the girls ever wrote to each other, not more than just one or two postcards in September, even though they always promised faithfully to write when they parted. There was too much to do back home: school and your real friends, and your family, and homework, and then after a while you sort of forgot camp because it was winter.

It was nice to know that at least your school friends would be your friends forever. That was something you could count on. You missed camp terribly the first few weeks after you came back home, and you were so lonely for all the kids and the fun you had, and the one counselor you particularly liked, but then it disappeared like a dream. But your own friends at home, that was something you could count on. It never occurred to Paris that she couldn't, or that she might move to another place, or go to a different school, and that they all might just go on with their lives without her and that she might never see any of them again.

SEVEN

That summer Adam took the beach house again. It was a smaller family group around him now: Etta, of course, and Basil and Rosemary, but Hazel was married and spending the summer in Florida, Lavinia and Jonah were at camp with Paris as usual and not coming until camp was over at the end of August, and Melissa and Lazarus were at the beach without Everett, who was at camp too. There was a young man hanging around Rosemary whom she seemed to like, Jack Nature, and Adam thought this one might be serious. The time was right to find his perfect piece of land for his permanent summer estate, to stop living in this damp beach house like a gypsy. The children could stop going to camp and have a decent place to live with the family. Yes, it was time. Adam had made one mistake with Andrew, losing him to that place of his, and he was not going to make another. Who knew what plans Jack and Rosemary might be cooking up on their long walks together down the beach? And it was enough of Lavinia and Jonah following Paris to camp every year as if there was something wrong with the child. If they were so afraid to let her go away alone then let her stay with them in the country. People shouldn't run their lives around children. How could they stand hanging around a camp full of screaming children all summer?

The problem was, where was the piece of land? Adam had been looking all winter and spring, but whatever was available was not good enough—too small, not scenic enough, too far from the city, too near the city where it was apt to turn into a busy suburb, not quite right. And whatever he liked was restricted. If he had liked it enough he would have put up a fight, but he never really wanted the places he saw and so he went away tactfully. When he saw the place he would know it. He had decided only one thing in the course of his search: the place should be in Connecticut just over the New York border.

In the fall he began searching again, hearing of this place or that through friends in the real estate business, or agents, and finally he found it: Windflower. It was exactly what he wanted. He might have been imagining it all these years, so perfect was it. The only problem was, the area was restricted. This time Adam refused to let it be a problem.

It was an enormous amount of land, and it was expensive, but the man who owned it was known in the neighborhood as The Crazy Russian, and also known to love money. Adam knew he had a price. It was only a matter of time. In his limousine, driven by Maurice, Adam went to visit the Russian in his house. It was a mansion, really, set in a forest. The landscaping was not only haphazard, it was nonexistent. A narrow dirt road led from the main road to the house, and another narrow dirt road led from the house through the forest to a large, clear lake with a rushing waterfall. How could the man live in that house and not want to look at his waterfall? It was sheer stinginess. He should have cleared away the trees and made a vista. Beside the lake was a run-down little stone pavilion with some battered outdoor furniture in it, a fireplace that worked, and electricity that did not work. There was a ladder that let you climb into the deep lake, and a diving board. The water was cold and pure, and there were fish swimming in its depths. But how the pavilion was overgrown with bushes and poison ivy! Obviously the Russian took his baths in the bathroom.

Maurice parked the limousine in what passed for a driveway outside the mansion, and Adam rang the doorbell. He had an appointment, so there was hope. They were willing to see him. That meant it was possible to negotiate. There were no servants, but when the sound of the bell went through the house it was answered by the excited barking of at least a dozen dogs. Then the dogs themselves appeared, all sizes, from a Russian wolfhound to a Yorkshire terrier, and several mixed breeds that looked like accidents. Adam was not fond of dogs; they rather intimidated him. The dogs were followed finally by a tall, slender, beautiful woman of about fifty. The Russian's wife.

She shooed the dogs away with affection and let Adam come in. She had a very slight Russian accent. Russian, but not Jewish. Neither she nor her husband were Jewish or they wouldn't be allowed to live in this neighborhood, yet they were willing to see Adam to discuss selling their place. That was a good sign. They were either not anti-Semitic or else they were of the impoverished ex-nobility. The appearance of the inside of the house convinced Adam of the latter. There was not a chair or sofa in the huge living room that was not covered with dog stains. Right in front of his very eyes one of the dogs lifted its leg and added another. Mrs. Crazy Russian paid no attention.

The living room had a two-story-high ceiling with wooden beams, and a huge fireplace flanked by stone gargoyles. The walls were stone, covered with some sort of plaster in the Spanish style, and it was obvious that they were at least two feet thick. At one end of the enormous room there was a valuable-looking tapestry hanging on the wall over a battered piano.

"My husband will be with you in a moment," she said, and offered Adam a dog-stained seat. He accepted, gingerly. When he bought this house he would have it fumigated immediately. "He's on the property somewhere. He's usually late, but don't worry."

"Thank you."

"I know you've been all over the property, but I guess you'd like to see the house."

"Yes, I would."

"As far as I'm concerned, I'd love to sell," she said. "We have seventeen rooms, and there are just the two of us. I'd like to get something smaller and easier to keep up. But we're fond of this place. We've been here a long time. Still . . ." She picked up a spaniel, set it on her lap, and began to pick burrs out of its coat. Fumigate? Maybe he should gut the house and start all over.

The dogs set up their barking again and the Russian came into the room, dressed in jodhpurs and a tweed jacket. He had a large white moustache and clever little eyes.

"Oh, I was just going to show Mr. Saffron the house," the wife said.

"Yes, yes, well, so you're Mr. Saffron," the Russian said. "I hope you like the place."

"I do."

"Forty years old, this house. Everything put in modern—plumbing, heat, electricity. And the land, of course, the most valuable land within fifty miles. Beautiful land. Those trees, hundreds of years old. A work of God, those old trees."

So tell me how much, Adam thought, and nodded and smiled politely about the trees.

"The problem is," the Russian said, "I can't find anyone who can afford my price."

"How much is your price?"

The Russian paused, looking at him, assessing him. He would make the price too high, outrageous, unthinkable, and the unwanted buyer would go away and no one would be offended. The Russian cleared his throat. "Two million dollars."

"I'll take it," Adam said.

But that was not the end, no that was not the end. When the Russian had recovered from his shock and his greed began to take over it was easier, but it was far from the end. He had a lawyer and Adam had a lawyer, and daily the phone calls came, the changes, the demands, the concessions. There was no law that said the Russian could not sell to Jews. Everyone knew he was crazy anyway. But he would be a social outcast, and therefore he would have to move away. So it had to be worth his while to move away. He would miss his old trees. Therefore the old trees were numbered and discussed, and every day the Russian demanded another of his old trees, and Adam said the old tree would die if it were moved, and the Russian said he would miss it too much if he left it, and finally Adam said he could take it, knowing the man was as crazy as they all said. They hondeled and they argued. Adam came back to see the house, and liked it, and planned to do extensive changes. The Crazy Russian had built pieces onto the original beautiful old house, hit or miss, so that it resembled a toy put together by a clumsy child. There was a bathroom window looking out on an inside wall of the house because the Crazy Russian had closed up a balcony in order to make a hall leading to a new room he had built. A window looking at a wall! What kind of planning was this? Windows of some rooms looked directly into windows of other rooms, where once they had looked out onto the forest. But Adam would fix it. He just first had to get the papers signed.

Months went by, and then it was time to go to Miami Beach, so Adam went, as always, and left the problems to his lawyer and the telephone. And then, on December 7, war was declared, and the world fell apart. Adam was in the shipping business as well as the building business, and now there were more important things to think about than that estate. Ships were being sunk. The government needed ships to transport cargo and soldiers. Adam had ships. The world was at war. He was negotiating with the government to lease it his ships, and to manage them for it, and overnight had decided to come back to New York until this was all settled. When the phone call came from the Crazy Russian, Adam had almost forgotten about him.

But the Russian had not forgotten about Adam Saffron. A wartime economy was a treacherous one. Who would want to buy that big white elephant of an estate in the middle of a world war? The Russian was ready to sell.

"I'll have the papers drawn up."

"Good," Adam said.

"If you want, you can start to fix Windflower up or do whatever you want to by this summer."

"Good."

"Then you should get the papers within a week."

"Good," Adam said.

"Goodbye, then."

"Goodbye."

When the papers came they were all in order, and Adam signed them and arranged payment. The estate would be purchased as a corporation by all his children except Andrew. Each of them would have shares. Share and share alike. No one could sell his part except to another member of the corporation. In order to sell the entire estate there would have to be a unanimous vote, and the entire estate would have to be sold, not part of it. Thus, all Adam Saffron's children and grandchildren and great-grandchildren and great-great-grandchildren forever and ever would be together. No part could separate without all. And when it was finished, in all its magnificence according to Adam's dream, none of them would ever want to sell it or move away.

Jack Nature, Rosemary's young man, was drafted, and Rosemary announced to Adam (not asked, but announced!) that they were going to be married immediately. Fortunately, Jack Nature was given an office job in the United States, so Adam was pleased that his youngest daughter was happily settled at last. He got out his blueprints and printed in the names of Rosemary and Jack on the house where he had already printed the names of Hazel and Herman. Basil would live with him and Etta in the mansion. It would be hard to find building equipment during the war, but who could find it better than a builder?

Adam was not worried that there would be a direct enemy attack on New York. He was old enough, had lived long enough, and knew enough to be sure about that. Their lives would go on as usual, as best they could. In the meantime he needed to appear with his and his children's birth certificates in front of the government officials, to prove that they were all loyal American-born citizens of the United States, in order that his shipping business for the United States government could commence. He had made his children shareholders so that they could afford to buy Windflower, and live decently in the city as well now. He had all his children's birth certificates among his private papers, but for himself he had to show his citizenship papers. Who knew from birth certificates where he came from? He was lucky he knew his real birthday. The government certainly was careful nowadays, but you couldn't blame them. A slip of the lip could sink a ship. Adam didn't mind the inconvenience. No one in his fine family had anything to hide.

EIGHT

Lavinia was a nervous wreck. When she tried to brush her hair the brush flew out of her hand. She bumped her knee on the corner of the dresser and nearly burst into tears although it hardly hurt and she never cried. But she wanted to be the first to get to Papa's house for dinner tonight, before any of the others, because he had been to the government with all the children's birth certificates—and Andrew and Basil—and she knew her birth certificate was different. Oh God, she prayed silently, biting her lip. Maybe neither of the boys had looked. Andrew was so worried about getting the government contract and all that money that he wouldn't have anything else on his mind. Andrew was always a worrywart. The last thing on Andrew's mind would be to pick up all their birth certificates and read them.

As for Basil, he had already seen his own birth certificate because he had needed it to take to the passport office when he got his passport that time he went to Europe, so a birth certificate held no mystery and no interest for him. He would be interested in making a good impression, better than Andrew, and he would be so concerned with his own appearance and manner that he wouldn't think of anything else. No, she didn't have to worry about Basil. Why then was she so nervous? It was silly, it was just silly.

She couldn't make her fingers work fast enough, buttoning buttons and fastening snaps, and naturally she had to fight with Paris, who wanted to wear her school clothes instead of that nice jumper they'd just bought her. The child hated dressing up; she complained she was fat and her clothes were awful, which wasn't true. She was a little too chubby, that was all, and her clothes were the prettiest the Chubbette line carried. Would you believe a child who got nauseated in a department store? Actually nauseated! It was a problem having a child with an inferiority complex about her looks. Paris was the most beautiful child in the entire neighborhood and the entire school, and everybody knew it. If they teased her about being fat it was just because they were jealous of her lovely face.

Lavinia and Jonah and Paris (in her new jumper) arrived at Papa's house promptly at six. Melissa and Lazarus arrived with Everett a few minutes later. Basil was already there, of course. The fumes of leg of lamb drifted out from the kitchen. It was going to be Etta's old standby again: lamb, oven-browned potatoes, green peas, and a store-bought cake. The only one who was delighted with this meal was Melissa, because leg of lamb was one of Lazarus' favorite foods. Lazarus himself was not delighted; Lazarus was either annoyed or not annoyed, but never delighted, never grateful. Tonight Lazarus was not annoyed. Jonah hated lamb but was too polite to say so. He would eat everything you gave him, but put his foot down at the idea of pig. "I don't eat porrrrk," he would say, the word "pork" coming out as a sort of growl demonstrating his loathing and horror. Lavinia hadn't kept kosher for a minute since she was married, and there was often bacon or boiled ham in the house, for Paris and the maid. Jonah didn't have to eat it. If it was just sitting in the icebox it wouldn't poison him.

Everyone was nice and sweet and normal. Everyone kissed everyone else hello. Basil didn't seem any different. Lavinia decided he hadn't seen her birth certificate and she was safe. She breathed a sigh of relief and started to unwind for the first time that day. As long as she was sitting there in that loved, familiar room, with Papa there, kind, strong, brilliant Papa, always planning things to make them happier, then everything would be all right. They all understood that he was waiting for the proper time to tell them what had transpired with the government deal, and that proper time would be when Etta removed herself to attend to some household chore. No one ever came out and said that they would not talk family business in front of Etta, but they all understood that it would be that way. She was not family.

Jonah and Lazarus were family. Herman was not family. Cassie, of course, was family. Jack Nature, being new, would have to prove himself before they decided whether or not he was family. In order to be family you had to have certain qualities of sensitivity, intelligence, understanding, and . . . class. That was it: quality.

Etta? Well, Etta. She could be married to Papa for a hundred years and they would all be as sweet as sugar to her, but she would never be family. Never. She had no class, she was not intelligent, and no one would ever believe that she had married Papa for love. Naturally, they didn't think that he had married her for love either, but what he did was always excusable. He was entitled to do whatever he wanted to and they would make the best of it. He had been lonely. That was easy to make the best of.

Paris was begging Everett to play Chinese checkers with her, and finally he agreed and they went into the little back room behind Papa's office, where Etta stored the extra sets of china and linens, and where the children were banished to play so they wouldn't disturb everyone else. There were Chinese checkers and real checkers and backgammon and cards, both pinochle cards and regular decks. There were jigsaw puzzles and a card table to set them up on. You didn't have to hear the children's noise and they couldn't hear you talk about business.

Etta went into the kitchen to supervise the final touches on their evening meal. Now they were just family and they could talk. Papa told them with pleasure that the government deal had gone very well. All their ships were needed, and there would be others for him to manage too. They would all make money. And this money would be spent for their shares in Windflower, to buy it, and then to build and furnish their houses in it.

They had all had time to get used to the idea of buying Windflower, but somehow it had all still seemed like a fantasy. It was so glamorous, so expensive. Now that the money was at their fingertips it seemed more real. Melissa was excited, but also a little frightened, because she had become more like Lazarus through the years, being so close to him, and now she worried about money too. Lazarus was glum. The thought of spending money always put him in a foul mood. Jonah was pleased because Papa was optimistic, and he too felt that the war would not touch America. Wartime was boom time for everyone. His stocks would go up. Lavinia was happy because they would all be together, but at the same time she was certainly not looking forward to sharing a house with Lazarus for the rest of her life. A lifetime of eating leg of lamb. Oh well, it would be a big house with big grounds and plenty of places to be alone if you wanted to be. She decided to be optimistic too.

She looked at Basil. It was hard to tell what he was thinking. He ought to be delighted. Ought . . . but Basil didn't do what he ought to or think what he ought to. He was still a child.

Etta emerged from the kitchen to tell them to wash up because dinner was almost ready. They dispersed to the various bathrooms for their cleansing ritual. Basil followed Lavinia into the bathroom.

"It just doesn't seem fair," he said.

"What doesn't?"

"Having to put all our money into that place. I don't want to settle down yet. I was hoping to travel in the summertime, and now I'll be stuck living with Papa and Etta."

"Well, when you get married you'll have your own house," Lavinia said. She dried her hands neatly on the paper towels Etta always put out so they wouldn't mess up her linen guest towels.

"That's not what I meant. I'm not ready to settle down. Now I'm trapped. Why didn't Papa ask me before he bought that place? That was really selfish."

"Don't you criticize Papa! Papa is never selfish. He's always thinking of us and you know it, Basil."

Basil imitated her voice, making it sound insufferably sanctimonious. "Don't you criticize Papa!" He glared at her. "You're not even my sister. You don't deserve to have a share in that money. I saw your birth certificate today."

So it was out. "I am so your sister."

"Who was Polly?"

"Mama's sister," Lavinia murmured, humiliated. She didn't even remember her. Why did she have to be blamed, be considered not part of the real family, when she didn't even remember Polly? She only remembered Lucy. She was sure she loved Lucy more than any of them because she knew how precious a mother could be. None of *them* had lost one until they were adults, and then she had lost two.

"Then you're just my cousin," Basil said. "Like Ned and Fanny and . . ."

"You little twerp! We have the same father and I'm every bit your sister. You're the last one to have a right to complain about what you're given. You've been handed everything on a silver platter, and all you ever think about is yourself. If you didn't have Papa for a father I'd like to see the kind of job you could get, you little ingrate."

Basil's stricken expression showed that she had smashed him properly, so Lavinia turned and strode out of the bathroom, leaving him standing there. What a terrible thing he had said to her! She would forgive him because he was her brother, and you had to forgive your brothers and sisters no matter how they wounded you, but she would never forget. Never, never would she forget what he had said to her. Adam Saffron's children were special. She was one of Adam Saffron's children, and she was the best of them. Whiny little Basil had better watch his step around her.

They all knew so little about her, really. None of them knew her thoughts, her fears, her dreams. To them she was the strong one, the one made of iron, the one they could go to with their problems and the one they hid their secrets from because they knew she was not afraid to criticize them when she felt they were wrong. But it was she who had the recurring nightmare that made her wake up damp and crying. It was she who dreamed night after night of Mama's ghost wandering through the house moaning: "Where can I go now? Where is there a place for me?" Etta had taken Mama's place in the house and now Mama's ghost wandered through Lavinia's dreams. How could Basil say she wasn't one of them? None of them could be more one of them than she was.

Lavinia was proud of herself at dinner. She was calm and showed none of the turmoil that was inside her. She never said a word to Basil, but it was not obvious to anyone but Basil. She had taken her customary seat at Papa's right hand, a seat she always got simply because she slithered into it a moment before anyone else could get it. Paris sat on the other side of her, as usual, with Jonah beside Paris. The child safely flanked by her parents. Paris was lucky to be an only child, having all the love of her parents, sharing with no one, and Lavinia intended to keep it that way. There would be no brother or sister for Paris, no other child who could ever be jealous of her or hurt her. Paris would have everything Lavinia had never had. Her life would be a paradise.

The Mendes family was the last to leave, as always: Jonah yawning, begging, "Come on, Lavinia, I have school tomorrow." Paris was asleep on the sofa and they had to wake her up. Lavinia just couldn't stand to leave before they all left; she didn't want to miss anything.

They walked back to their apartment through the quiet streets.

"Hurry up, get washed and get into bed," Lavinia told Paris briskly, as if it were her fault they were still up so late. "You have school tomorrow."

As soon as Paris was safely out of earshot Lavinia told Jonah the horrible thing Basil had said to her. She always liked to think that Jonah couldn't exist without her, but the truth was she couldn't get along without him either. He was the only one who would understand and always be on her side. She went through the scene with Basil in Papa's bathroom, every cruel word. Jonah was properly sympathetic and disgusted at such a display of lack of brotherly love.

"I'm afraid he'll tell the others," Lavinia said. "I'm sure he will. What will I do then?"

"What difference does it make if he does?" Jonah said. "It doesn't matter. It's not going to change anything. Don't worry about it."

"Well, I can't help it if I'm a worrier."

"But it doesn't matter if he tells them," Jonah said. "They'll only have sympathy for you. Basil just has a strange sense of values, that's all."

"Maaaa!" Paris screamed from the bedroom. Too old to call Lavinia Mommy any more (under Lavinia's guidance) and too stubborn to call her Mother (Lavinia's suggested substitution), Paris had settled for Ma, the name she had copied from her friends in the street. She'd have to get the child out of Brooklyn, Lavinia thought, before her accent became impossible. A Brooklyn street accent. They would have to go to New York someday, before it was too late.

"Oh, I just don't know where to run first," Lavinia said. "I have to be everything to everybody."

"Just relax," Jonah said.

She went into Paris' bedroom to kiss her goodnight and have their little nighttime chat, and be sure the alarm clock was set for seven-thirty, not that it would help. "I don't know why, living in this house, you can't have better diction," Lavinia told Paris.

"What's wrong with it?"

"I don't want you to copy your friends. I want you to copy me. I was always very careful about my diction. It's important to speak well and not to fall into sloppy habits. People judge you by the way you speak."

"Okay," Paris said. Lavinia wondered if she had impressed the child at all.

"And don't call me Ma. Call me Mother."

"Nobody I know calls their mother Mother," Paris said.

"You are not the people you know. You are you. You are my child. You are better than they are."

By the time Lavinia had gotten Paris settled for the night Jonah was sound asleep, snoring. She poked him to make him turn over, and he stopped snoring. She knew that was only a short respite, and jumped into their double bed beside him, trying to fall asleep as quickly as possible before he turned over and started snoring again and kept her awake the whole night. It was a funny thing about marriage, she thought. You never knew in advance if you would marry a snorer. How could you know? You didn't even think to ask him, and even if you did ask him and he said yes, you couldn't possibly imagine how dreadful it was until you were right there in the bed listening to that loud sound. Jonah had a magnificent snore, the champion of snores. A wet, guttural, long-drawn-out, vehement steam engine of a snore. Sometimes she just wanted to hit him. But he couldn't help it, poor thing. He had a deviated septum from once being hit on the nose by a stray baseball, or a bully in his childhood neighborhood, or perhaps by both, and he couldn't breathe. She knew he'd had a lot of fights as a child. Jonah was never a sissy. He had grown up in a tough neighborhood and he had defended himself with the best of them. He was gentle, but he was not afraid. The religious young man who carried his Torah tenderly and hit out with a hard fist if anyone called him sheeny. They had both had to fight for their lives, he with his fists and she with her sharp tongue, and they had both survived, but he was an innocent and she had learned to be wary. He still trusted people. Well, he would learn someday.

She tried to sleep but she couldn't help reliving that dreadful scene with Basil in the bathroom. He would learn too, someday. Someday someone would hurt him the way he'd hurt her. It wouldn't be she. But he'd get his. That was how it worked out. Lavinia liked to believe that. It saved her from feeling guilty, because it wasn't she who had hurt the transgressor, it was fate.

Jonah began to snore again and Lavinia sighed. She poked him, and he mumbled and turned over. Oh, God, he was snoring again! How could that be? You weren't supposed to be able to snore on your side, only on your back. Apparently Jonah could snore in any position. She couldn't wake him up, he needed his sleep. But so did she, dammit!

She took her pillow and got the extra blanket out of the closet. Then she took them into Paris' room and made a nice little nest for herself on the daybed, the one they used to use when Rosemary was still single and slept over to take care of Paris if they were going out. It was warm and quiet in the room, the child's soft breathing almost inaudible. Lavinia looked over at the nice bed they'd bought her when she got too big for her crib. A pretty little Early American reproduction, with a dresser and desk to match. Someday Paris would appreciate it. There were toys and dolls lined up on top of the dresser, but none in Paris' bed. Lavinia was proud to be able to say that Paris had never slept with toys, not since she moved from her baby crib to her big-girl bed. All she'd had to do was drop a casual remark that sleeping with toys was a silly thing to do, and Paris had exiled her toys to the dresser top. It was better that way. Who knew, she might swallow one of the teddy bear's button eyes in her sleep and die.

Lavinia slept then, in the peaceful room with her child, and that night she did not dream, or if she did, they were soft dreams she never remembered in the morning. She woke up when Paris' alarm clock went off. Paris was still sleeping. That child loved to sleep; she hated to get up for school and always slept right through the alarm. She also hated to go to bed. Poor dear child, it was going to be hard for her in the daytime world when her favorite time was the night. She would just have to adjust if she meant to make anything of herself. Still, it was too bad. She could have taken after Jonah, up at dawn and ready to go, full of energy, and drooping at nine o'clock at night.

Lavinia went over to Paris' bed and looked down at her. How beautiful she was! She covered the sleeping child's face with kisses, to wake her up gently for the day. Paris' little fist came out and flailed at her, striking her. *She had hit her!*

"Jonah! Paris hit me!"

He came running. "What?"

"She hit me. That rotten kid *hit* me!"

Paris, still half-asleep, was looking at both of them with a look that was part anger, part bewilderment, part fear. Striking out at her mother had been an instinctive act, not premeditated.

"Oh, Lavinia," said Jonah, the peacemaker, "you know she's a grouch in the morning."

"I was *kissing* her," Lavinia said, hurt.

"Don't you ever hit your mother," Jonah said sternly.

"I hate it when you kiss me on the mouth," Paris said.

"Why?" Lavinia snapped. "Do I have bad breath?"

"No, I just don't like it."

"Little porcupine, you hate to be kissed. Porcupine."

Paris looked pleased. She liked to be called porcupine. How could anyone understand such a strange child?

"You'd better get ready for school," Jonah said.

"Come on, porcupine. I'm not leaving until your feet are on the floor."

Paris obediently got out of bed and shuffled into her bathroom. She left the door open, the way she had been taught to. At least they wouldn't have a fight about that this morning. Lavinia went back into her bedroom and Jonah followed her.

"I guess I snored again last night," he said.

"Oh boy, did you."

"I'm sorry."

"You can't help it."

"I can't hear it when I snore," he said.

"I know, but I can."

"Well, that's my aristocratic Mendes nose. My fine, big, Sephardic nose."

"Broken nose. Nobody in your family has a big nose. That's one of the only good things I can say about them. I wouldn't have married you if you had a big nose."

Jonah smiled. "It is not such a bad-looking nose, is it?"

"Fishing for compliments. You know you're handsome."

"Paris is going to look like me," he said proudly.

"She looks exactly like me."

"Well, she looks like both of us. Anyway, she's pretty."

"I wonder why she hit me. I didn't like that at all."

"You shouldn't try to kiss her in the morning."

"She hit her mother. I would never have dreamed of hitting my mother. I would have cut my hand off first."

"Children are different today," Jonah said. "I had great respect for my parents. Today they're different; I see it at school."

"Well, she's going to respect me. I'm going to demand it."

"You're right," he said mildly.

"You bet I'm right." Why were things always falling out of control? Everything was a battle. All she wanted was to keep control of her life, her family, her safe little kingdom, and everything kept falling out of place. A family should have order, with the parents at the head of it. Was it too much to ask that there be some kind of order in a life? It was such a little thing to ask. It was her right; she had earned it. She would get it. She always got what she set her mind to, eventually. Lavinia sighed. It was only eight o'clock in the morning and Paris had already ruined her day.

NINE

Basil and Andrew were deferred from the draft because they were involved in important government business, managing cargo ships for the war effort. Lazarus, Jonah, and Herman were too old to go. Jack was safely in Virginia with Rosemary, at a desk job during the day and living in a hotel room at night, writing funny letters home complaining about the unintelligible accents of Southerners and the stupidity of small-town life—but he was safe, and that was what mattered. They were all safe.

On a cold clear day in January, Adam and Andrew and Jonah went up to Windflower in Adam's limousine to look over their property. Basil said he was too busy to go with them. The girls didn't want to go, it was too cold. They had all seen the place already, when the trees were in full leaf, and they had all agreed that it was an earthly paradise but The Crazy Russian lived like a pig. It turned out to be just as well that only the three of them went there this day, because what they saw was a dreadful shock.

The land had been stripped bare. Before leaving, The Crazy Russian had sold the trees for lumber, all of them but a few giant trees near the house which were over a hundred years old, had them cut off at the root and sold them. So that was his sentiment for his old trees! And then he had sold the turf, neatly stripped away, and then he had sold the topsoil. The land was stripped down to its bare bones, stony, infertile, dead. The great expanse of view was revealed down to the lake, the waterfall frozen in ice, its water suspended as if in glass, and everywhere you looked were the stumps of trees, like pegs on a board. The cold and the gray icy sky above them only made it all look more desolate. Andrew gasped.

"That's something," Adam said. He shook his head. "A businessman like that I never saw. If you bought his pet dog from him he'd skin it first and sell it for a fur coat. You'd have to specify dead or alive. This is a kind of mind I never saw before."

"Terrible," Jonah said.

Adam brightened. "Still," he said, "it's not so bad. I would like to dynamite that hill and make it lower, so you can walk to the lake and back up without too much trouble, but still keep it a hill for the view. You can have your house there, Jonah. And the other one can be right next to it. Both equal. It's nice the Russian saved us the trouble of clearing the land. We can start from scratch, bring in a landscape architect, put the trees where we want them."

"He left the woods behind the lake, Papa," Andrew said.

"I wonder what's wrong with them," Jonah said.

"He probably only had a contract to sell so many," Adam said. "We can use some of the trees from the deep part of the woods. They'll be free of charge. We'll have to dynamite all those stumps, so we should dynamite the rocks too and make a nice lawn. The tennis court could go right there." He pointed.

"I'd make it higher, Papa," Andrew said. "We have trouble with ours when it rains. It takes too long to dry out. We had to change from clay to en-tout-cas. If you make it higher and cover it in en-tout-cas you can play a half-hour after it rains."

"Me, I wouldn't play at all," Adam said pleasantly. "But that's a good idea. I'll build up the valley there a little while I'm at it and then put in the tennis court."

"Then maybe it's a blessing in disguise?" Jonah said hopefully.

"A blessing I wouldn't call it exactly. But it's a lesson, and it's done, and it can't be helped. Someday we'll laugh and say it's funny. Thank God we can afford to fix it. A man who can kill trees like that is a sick man. To be so hungry for a dollar . . . he's a poor shnook so forget him. Andrew, what's the best kind of grass it shouldn't get crab grass in it?"

By the time the three men left Windflower and went back to Adam's house for a family dinner and report they were hopeful about the future and amused about the past. Although it was not to be his home, Andrew was delighted to have a new place to play with and was full of suggestions. He had even made some sketches. Adam was in good spirits. At last he was building for himself and his family, not for strangers, and he would make every dream come true. The electricity in the pavilion by the lake would be made to work, and the pavilion itself would all be cleaned and fixed up, the bushes and poison ivy cleared away, the place painted, and nice dressing rooms put in with slatted wooden floors, and benches to sit on while you changed your shoes. There would be a nice big glider and some comfortable chairs, and awnings to roll down if it rained. They would put in a refrigerator and then they could have lunch there. For the lake there would be a new diving board and they would have the best kind of steel ladder and a big float to swim to. There would be a rowboat and a clean dry place to store it in. There would be a wading pool roped off at the edge of the lake where the water was shallow, for the children. He would have a little sand beach built there too.

His house, the one The Crazy Russian had formerly lived in, would be completely refurbished. Not a trace of dog odor would be allowed to remain. Etta would have a decorator, and she would fix it up, expense no object. In back there would be a garden filled with flowers, and under the big old trees the Russian had had the decency to allow to remain there would be another big comfortable glider and chairs and tables so that the whole family could sit with him on the hot summer afternoons after they had come back from swimming in the lake. Basil could live in the downstairs suite and Adam and Etta would have the largest upstairs suite, with the other rooms used for relatives who came to visit. Henny and the maids would live in the room in back of the kitchen. One maid's room was enough; they could double up the way he was sure they did at home already. All the maids were related to Henny anyway, so it didn't matter which daughter or cousin or niece she decided to bring.

As for the two houses for his four married daughters, they would both be built from exactly the same architect's plan, exactly alike so no one would feel short-changed. The only thing that would be different would be the exteriors. Then the houses would be built backwards to each other, so that everything was reversed except for the front porch, which afforded the wonderful view, and no one would ever be able to guess that they had both been built from exactly the same plan.

There were four bedrooms and four bathrooms on the second floor of each house. In each house two of these bedroom-bath combinations had been planned as an adjoining suite. In Hazel and Rosemary's house Hazel and Herman could have the suite so that Hazel could be near baby Richie, and Rosemary and Jack could have the separate bedroom because they had no children. Later, when they did have children, the children would have the bedroom across the hall.

In the matching house, Lavinia and Jonah would have the suite because Paris was younger, and Melissa and Lazarus would take the bedroom across the hall from Everett. None of them was planning to have any more children, so the downstairs den would be a family room doubling as a guest room.

There would be eight bathrooms in each house. Eight! Four on the second floor, three on the first floor counting the one for the maids' room, and one in the basement for the handyman to use. That made more than one bathroom per person.

"I remember when we had only one bathroom for the whole family," Jonah said happily, "and the bathtub was in the kitchen and the toilet was in the hall."

"Well, you," Lavinia said, dismissing his whole family with a wave of her hand. "Bathrooms are very important, and thank God we can afford them."

Lavinia and Melissa had decided that they would hire a couple, so one maid's room was sufficient. Cassie had a couple and liked the idea very much because the man could double as a butler whereas a maid could only wait on table as a maid, which didn't have the same panache.

Windflower already came with a caretaker, who had stayed on when The Crazy Russian left. He was a young Irish immigrant, Tim Forbes, who lived with his wife, Molly (also an immigrant), and their two baby sons, Timmy and Mike, in a shack. Adam had been horrified by the shack The Crazy Russian had provided them with, no better than a chicken coop in his opinion, and had already made plans to build them a nice little house. He was also building a cottage for Maurice, a garage for all the family cars, and a tool house for Tim's equipment. Now that there would be such an enormous expanse of lawn there would have to be a tractor with an attachment to cut the grass, and it would stay in the garage with the cars. And there might as well be a vegetable garden—why not save money somewhere?—as long as Tim Forbes loved growing things and swore he had a green thumb. They could even try raising chickens, for the eggs. And your own chicken in the pot, made with your own fat hen and your own home-grown vegetables, wouldn't be bad either, would it?

They would start to dynamite the stumps and rocks that spring as soon as the frost melted. They could then level off the hill a bit and start to build the houses. With luck, if Adam's pull with building supplies held out, the houses would be finished before the first snow. The girls could spend the winter decorating, the spring worrying, and maybe by summer the things they had ordered for the houses would arrive. If all went well, Windflower would be ready to move into a year from this coming summer.

Lavinia and Jonah decided to send Paris to camp alone that summer for the first time. She was nearly twelve, big, and far superior mentally to anyone her age. If anything went wrong, she had a mouth, she could complain. With her safely out of the way Lavinia would be free to supervise the building and decorating of her house and all the other details she could never entrust to anyone else. Jonah thought it was a good idea for Paris to be on her own at last. He knew the owners and head counselor personally. As for Adam, he thought it was high time the child went to camp alone. No one asked Paris her opinion of this arrangement, but she was thrilled. She would be free the whole summer, just like everybody else. Nobody would ask her why her parents were hanging around.

Etta had the use of the department store decorator first because her house was already built. The decorator was a chic, skinny little woman who was obviously a Gentile, Miss Anderson. Between them she and Etta made The Big House, as it had come to be called, a riot of flowers. Sunny flowers bloomed on the drapes, the sofas, the chairs, the bedspreads, the wallpaper. The Big House had been transformed from a kennel into a giant flower garden. The only person who wouldn't live in a flower garden was Basil; his suite was painted white and filled with dark, heavy furniture, as befitted a bachelor of his age and taste. His suite consisted of a bedroom, a bathroom, and a library. In the library there were bookcases filled with the classics (supplied by Miss Anderson) and a desk with a ship model on top of it. There were comfortable chairs for reading and good lamps to read by. He even had a double bed. After all, Miss Anderson said, he might get married. You never knew.

The weather became nice, workmen began dynamiting the rocks and tree stumps, and Adam drove up in his limousine nearly every day to watch, taking whoever wanted to come with him. The waterfall was full and frothy white, flowing freely now that the sun had melted the ice, and the state of Connecticut sent a man to stock the lake with fish. Imagine, the state gave you fish! Jonah immediately bought his first fishing rod, having always fished at camp with borrowed ones, and bought a child-size one for Paris. They could catch and eat their own fish.

The land around The Big House still had its grass and trees, and Tim Forbes had put in a rose garden. Now the huge trees were budding, and then overnight they burst into leaf—large, young, pale green leaves, exuding a fresh odor and a promise of the great, heavy, dark green leaves that would shelter the house in summer. And suddenly, in the grass around The Big House and all along the edge of the woods, there occurred a miracle: thousands of tiny white flowers sprang up like dots of snow. They were something The Crazy Russian hadn't killed or taken away or sold, a miracle of courage and tenacity and nature. What were they?

"Those are windflowers," Tim said. "There used to be millions of them. They're why the place was named Windflower."

"Windflowers . . ." Adam said, liking the sound of the word on his tongue. He had never really wondered before why the place had been called Windflower, he had just supposed someone had made up the name, and as he hadn't minded it he had decided to keep it. But now it had meaning. Not the meaning of the flowers for which this place had been named, but the meaning of the miracle these little white flowers represented. They were his. All his life he had overcome odds, fought difficulty and doubt, and he had survived and flourished, just like these tiny flowers. They had come out of nowhere, like himself, and they were survivors too.

"When we put in the lawn," he asked Tim, "will they grow there too?"

"I don't see why not," Tim said. "We have plenty of bees."

"You'd better make us a sign for the front drive," Adam told him. "And get a lot of 'No Trespassing' signs and tack them up on the trees."

For the first time he was filled with an enormous, personal sense of possession, stronger than anything he had felt before.

TEN

That summer Paris loved camp. There was a polio scare so the two Parents' Weekends were canceled and the camp was quarantined. That meant that she didn't see her parents for the entire summer, but instead of missing them she was delighted. She felt grown up and independent. She had started getting her periods, and all of a sudden, even though she was eating the same as she always did, she shot up and got skinny. None of her clothes fit any more; her shorts were baggy at the waist and her shirts were too tight across the chest. When she had to run during sports she was self-conscious in her undershirt because those things kept bobbing up and down. To compensate for that was the wonderful transformation of her legs, from two roly-poly little pig legs with no knees to two knobby-kneed long legs rather like a boy's. She wasn't ashamed to wear shorts any more, even though she had to hold hers up with safety pins.

When she got off the train at the end of the summer her mother screamed, but her father was pleased. Actually, her mother seemed rather pleased too, even though she was afraid Paris was suffering from malnutrition, and she even let her have a chocolate soda. This was the last time though, her mother said, because if she ate chocolate she would get acne. From now on no milk, just that awful blue skim milk. She had to stay looking pretty because this winter she would be going for interviews at New York high schools. They were going to move, just for her. She wouldn't have to go to Midwood with all her friends, where it was so crowded they had to have classes in three shifts, and some of the kids had to be there at seven-thirty in the morning. Seven-thirty, ugh. Paris hated even having to be at school by nine.

Her mother had chosen two private schools she liked the best. One was where Everett went, but he had to commute every day on the subway. Paris certainly wasn't going to commute, her mother said. No wonder Everett didn't have any friends, shy as he was and then living so far away from school that none of the boys wanted to come home with him. Paris would live in New York and have lots of friends. It had been difficult to get the schools to agree to see her because she was so young—not even twelve yet—but she was so tall and looked so grown up. Her mother would let her wear lipstick. And now that she was thin she could have some real grown-up clothes, no more Chubbettes.

They took her to see Windflower. Paris sat on a chair at the top of a hill under a tree with her grandfather and watched the last of the dynamiting. It looked like a war movie she had seen. They told her the hill across the way had been twice as high, and the valley below had been much deeper, before they fixed them all up. Soon men were going to bring in truckloads of topsoil, and then lay lawn in big squares, just like you put down linoleum. Etta was screaming because she'd had her whole kitchen ripped out last spring and was still waiting for her first sight of the new equipment they'd ordered. Big foundations had been laid on top of the hill across the way, and the skeletons of two houses were just starting to rise. One of them would be for Paris.

Paris sat there missing the counselor she had had a crush on this summer. She wondered if this would be the last year she was in love with a counselor. If she didn't have someone to have a crush on then camp wouldn't be half as much fun. One of the two schools she would be interviewed at was coed, and the other was all girls. She didn't really care which one she went to until she saw the school. She couldn't stand boys her own age, and older boys never looked at her, not that she would know what to say or do if they did.

Her parents were going to look for an apartment near the school when she made her choice, or when the school made its choice. Maybe the schools wouldn't take her. It wasn't so easy to get into a good private school. But she had good marks, she wasn't afraid. She had always thought New York was very glamorous. The few times her parents had taken her to see Aunt Cassie and Uncle Andrew she was very impressed. Paris didn't have any idea how to be sophisticated or glamorous, but she wanted to be both. If you lived in New York you were already on your way to learning how. People in New York were different from other people, just the way Aunt Cassie was different from her other aunts.

Next summer she was going to go back to that same camp because she loved it, and her parents would move into their new apartment in New York, and fix up their new house in Windflower, and then when Paris came back everything would have been done for her. She would say goodbye to the subway and start taking the bus—that was one sophisticated thing already! And she would be a freshman in high school. That was another sophisticated thing. She could hardly imagine it. But right now she had her eighth-grade year to finish, and they were the highest class in the school, the leaders, the big kids. She might as well enjoy it, because after that she would have to start being a little kid all over again. But somehow she couldn't believe that. Paris knew now that she was finished with being a little kid. She hadn't missed her parents all summer, and she knew she was on her way to being a grownup. The question was, did anyone else know it, could they tell? The family still talked around her like she wasn't there, or talked about her right in front of her as if she was a baby, or talked Yiddish when they didn't want her to understand something they thought she was too young to know.

No, the family didn't know she wasn't a kid any more. But she knew. And right now, that was all that mattered. The rest would take care of itself.

ELEVEN

Melissa didn't like that Lavinia was going to move to New York without her, she didn't like it at all. They had always been so close, just down the block in winter and then in the same house in summer until Lavinia and Jonah went trailing off to camp those years, and now Lavinia was going to leave her. It just didn't seem right. Melissa began looking at her apartment, the place where she and Lazarus had been so happy all these years, and now she found things wrong with it. That bathroom looked out on a court, so dark and gloomy. The tiles were chipped, too. The fish decals she'd put on the tiles so lovingly when they were all the rage looked tacky now and Melissa was darned if she knew how to scrape them off. As for those bookcases she'd been so proud of, now they were overflowing with Lazarus' books and he was always complaining.

The neighborhood wasn't what it used to be either. Not that it was bad, but it no longer thrilled her. She was tired of it. This fall she had to paint again, which was a messy boring job, and the living room furniture needed to be reupholstered. It would be easier to move, after all, than go through all that boring work here. The more she thought of it, the better the idea sounded.

New York had all the theaters, the good restaurants, the places to go. Lazarus could go to work on the subway the way he always did; it would just be a few extra stops. And there was the opera, she mustn't forget that. They had season tickets as always. It would be nice to have dinner in New York and go to the opera, without worrying about getting there and back and without having her usual fight with Lazarus because she wouldn't take the subway at night and he said a cab was too expensive. She always won, but they always had their fight, and she hated that they had to go to New York on the subway even though they came home in a taxi. If you got all dressed up to go to something like the opera it was depressing to have to sit on the subway with all those slobs. Oh, and they could go to the symphony all the time, and all those wonderful concerts. Rain and snow couldn't keep them away if they lived in New York, it would all be so close and so convenient.

Everett would be going away to college next year, if any college was willing to take him with his bad marks, so there would just be the two of them. They could take a small apartment in midtown. When Everett came home for holidays he could sleep in the living room on a convertible sofa. Then Lazarus couldn't complain about the high rent because New York apartments cost so much more than Brooklyn ones. And after all, Everett would be getting married someday and he would want to live in his own apartment. He didn't seem to know any girls yet, or if he did he was too shy to ask them out, but when he went to college he would meet girls. He was still young, only seventeen. A seventeen-year-old boy wasn't interested in girls yet it seemed. In her day, she remembered, seventeen-year-old boys were always hanging around her when she was seventeen, but today young people were different. Maybe that was because they had to go out on formal dates and the boy had to pay for things and act like a man. Maybe Everett was just scared. He certainly wasn't either poor or stingy; she always gave him lots of pocket money, but instead of using it to take a girl out dancing he would just buy more and more electrical equipment, his junk as they all called it, or go to a movie all by himself. Everett would spend every cent she gave him on himself, and then beg for more.

It was a shame about Everett's bad marks, but she really couldn't blame him too much because she had been a bad student too. Everett said that the courses were too easy for him, too boring, and that he knew more than the teachers. He did know more than the science teachers, and he was good at math, but his English was terrible, even she could see that. His handwriting was illegible and he could hardly spell. She'd never seen such spelling on a grown boy from a good home and a good school. That was the trouble with sending him to that progressive school, they didn't make him work hard enough. They said he had a very high IQ. They said he was a genius. But they let him write like a five-year-old. With that handwriting he'd make a good doctor, scribbling prescriptions no one could decipher, and Lazarus had always rather hoped that Everett would become interested in medicine, but Everett wasn't interested in being a doctor at all. He was only applying to colleges because his parents were forcing him to. He said he wanted to be an inventor!

Did Thomas Edison go to college, he asked her. How did she know? She wasn't supposed to know things like that.

One day a month, a Wednesday, Melissa always went to a matinee in New York with a girlfriend. This afternoon she was going with Stella Greenglass to see a new hit play, *Foreign Affair*, which they'd written away for tickets to about three months ago. Although Melissa preferred musicals she liked to see everything, just to keep her hand in. It seemed so long ago that she was a silly girl who wanted so badly to go on the stage. What a lifetime of misery she would have had! She was lucky she came to her senses when she met Lazarus. Lazarus had his little foibles, but he was a perfect husband. He was so brilliant, and he loved her so much, and she was so proud of him. He was still the best catch in her whole crowd.

Melissa and Stella arrived at the theater early so they would have a chance to read the whole playbill before the play started. Melissa particularly enjoyed reading the biographies of the players. Sometimes then, even though it was silly, she would daydream and pretend it was her, and make up a fantasy biography for herself, all the shows she had starred in.

Stella had bought a box of chocolate-covered peppermints, but Melissa regretfully declined one because she was watching her figure. It was funny how she used to be able to eat as many sweets as she wanted—and what a sweet tooth she'd had!—and now she had to watch every bite to stay thin. That was what growing older meant. She didn't have a gray hair on her head, all of it was the same golden blonde it had been when she was a girl, and she had hardly a wrinkle that you could see, but she had to get on that bathroom scale every day to make sure the pounds didn't sneak up on her. Lazarus had a doctor's scale, of course, which was mean of him, because you could read every quarter of a pound and you *knew* it was accurate.

She had read nearly all of the actors' biographies when she came to a short one near the end, of an actor with a small part. He was Scott Brown, and one of the first plays he had been in was *All My Daughters*. He was her Scott Brown! Oh goodness, she hoped she wasn't blushing. It was so funny to think that here he was, after all those years, and she was going to see him right up there on that stage. She wondered if he was still handsome. It said in the biography that he had been in Canada for many years doing repertory. Was Canada good? He certainly wasn't a star; he had a small part in *Foreign Affair* and she hadn't even seen him in anything else. He'd always meant to be a star. Melissa could hardly wait for the play to start so she could see what Scott Brown looked like now, but at the same time she was afraid to see him because he might be a disappointment. He had been so handsome. She really had never considered throwing her life away on him. Why, it would have been a tragedy! She would never have been married to Lazarus, with her perfect life, and sitting here in her lovely pale green wool suit with the little golden fox around her neck, her nails all manicured and her hair all set, in an orchestra seat. She would have broken nails from scrubbing floors, and her hair would probably be all gray from worry and poverty.

She enjoyed the play, but Scott Brown didn't appear until the end of the first act and then he had only two lines. He was in the second act again and had a short scene, but that was all. He was still handsome, only older and more dignified-looking. It was a shame he had never made it. It was because he looked like . . . just anybody. That was why, so many years ago, she'd thought he looked like someone she knew and had felt comfortable with him. Scott Brown looked like someone everybody knew.

She wondered if she should go backstage. No, she really didn't want to speak to him. She tried to imagine Scott Brown at Windflower and the thought was so grotesque that it made her actually sick to her stomach. He wouldn't fit in at Windflower at all. Lazarus would be perfect at Windflower. Lazarus deserved Windflower.

That night at dinner Melissa broached the subject of moving to New York to Lazarus. He was not pleased, but he was not as resistant to the idea as she had expected. If that schoolteacher Jonah could afford it, he certainly could. Melissa asked him if she could begin looking for apartments when Lavinia began looking, so maybe they could live in the same building, and Lazarus told her to go ahead, looking was free.

She could hardly wait to telephone Lavinia after dinner and tell her the good news. They were well into a good chat about the kind of apartments they would like to look at when the maid came into the bedroom.

"Can I talk to you, Mrs. Bergman?"

"Yes, Ruby. Lavinia, I'll call you back."

The schvartze was standing there looking both pleased and regretful, a little smile on her face. "I'm quittin', Mrs. Bergman."

"You're leaving me? *Why?*"

"I'm gonna work in a war plant. Help the war effort. I'm gonna be a riveter."

"A riveter?" Melissa said, horrified. "That's a man's job!"

"Used to be a man's job. All the men in the Army now. I'm gonna get twice what I make here and help our country."

"You want a raise?" Melissa asked.

Ruby shook her head. "No, Ma'am. Thank you, but I'm gonna be Ruby the Riveter." She chuckled. "Maybe they'll write a song about me too, huh?"

"Oh, Ruby, you can't leave me! I need you too much."

"I'll come back after the war's over," Ruby said cheerfully.

"Well, that's very kind of you."

Ruby nodded, the sarcasm completely wasted on her. "I'll finish my week and then go."

"I can't talk you out of it?"

"No."

Melissa sighed. "Do you have a friend who wants your job here?"

"All my friends workin' in the war plants. That's how I got the idea."

"Oh, Ruby."

"You'll get along." She smiled and went back to the kitchen.

Melissa had developed a terrible headache. She took two aspirin and called Lavinia back. "Lavinia, you won't believe it. My schvartze is leaving me to work in a war plant."

"I'm not surprised," Lavinia said. "They make a fortune there."

"But what will I do?"

"You'll make do. You'll cook and you'll clean, and Lazarus can help out too. He's a man but he's not a cripple. Jonah helps me."

"Jonah's a lot younger," Melissa said indignantly. "I can't ask Lazarus to do housework."

"Jonah makes his own breakfast every morning and washes the dishes."

"Well, Lazarus can't cook."

"He can eat cornflakes standing over the sink like he does

anyway. It's not such a tragedy."

"Oh, I'm so upset," Melissa said. "You know what I'm going to do? I just decided. We're going to live in a housekeeping hotel, with room service and a hotel maid. We can live in the Edwardian." The Edwardian was Papa's hotel, he had finished it just before the war started and he owned it. "Papa can get us a good suite and a special rate. I've made up my mind."

"Enjoy yourself," Lavinia said.

"What's the matter with a hotel?"

"A hotel is fine. And the Edwardian is a first-class hotel. But for myself, I'd rather be carted off than live in a hotel. I have to have a real home."

"Well, that's you. I like hotels."

"Then enjoy yourself."

"Lavinia, why are you always so negative?"

"Did I say you shouldn't live in a hotel?"

"Oh, you're so impossible, Lavinia!"

Melissa hung up. She went into the living room and pulled Lazarus away from his favorite evening radio program.

"What's the matter, Toots?"

"Lazarus, I want us to live in a housekeeping hotel. I want to live in the Edwardian."

He pondered that. "We can get a cut rate from Papa, and get rid of the schvartze. That might be a good idea, Toots."

"I knew you'd like it."

He nodded. "Yes, I think it's a good idea."

"Well then, instead of signing the lease and painting we'll just move."

"It's all right with me."

TWELVE

The family had worried that Hazel, with her limitations, might have trouble taking care of her little son, Richie, but everything seemed to be going along fine.

Now that Richie was four years old, Hazel could take him with her wherever she went. She most liked to take him shopping with her. All day long she would wander through the air-conditioned new stores, enjoying the coolness, buying whatever took her fancy, dragging Richie along by the arm. He was a docile and pretty little boy, with a sweet smile. Everything pleased him. It never occurred to Hazel that he should have friends to play with because in her mind, while he was her prized son, he was also somehow her little doll baby from her youth, and he belonged to her. He did whatever she told him to. He was a good doll baby.

She would stand in the fitting room for hours, trying on new gowns to wear to the dinners Herman took her to, having them fitted, and Richie would sit quietly on the chair nearby, watching her. Sometimes he fell asleep, if it was late in the afternoon. Since he could sleep anywhere, it never occurred to her to take him home for a nap. Doll babies went to sleep whenever you told them to—they just shut their eyes—and Richie was the same. She bought him lots of clothes too, because she liked to dress him up. He didn't get dirty like other little boys she had seen on the street. His little sandals stayed white.

Sometimes she took him to the cabana club and let him dig in the sand. He liked grownups better than children, and always rewarded any admiring grownup with his sweet smile. Children seemed to frighten him. He would look at them as if he wanted to play with them, but he never got too close.

Hazel was looking forward to the summer when she would take him to Windflower, and they would spend the whole summer with the family. Herman was going to take them there and stay for a few days, and then he had to come back to Florida for business, but he said he would come to visit them once during the summer, or maybe even twice if he could get away. Hazel knew that Herman was very important, and that all the business he did bought her and Richie all their nice things, so she never complained if Herman couldn't be with her even though she would have liked him to. For that summer she was going to take Richie's baby nurse, who was still with him, so the nurse could make his meals and feed him and give him his baths just like she did here in Miami Beach. He was getting a little old to have a baby nurse, and Hazel felt she could do a lot of those things for him by herself, but nobody ever let her do anything. Herman said she should keep the nurse for this year anyway, but Hazel didn't like the way the nurse tried to tell her what to do. The nurse said she shouldn't give him Rice Krispies every night, that he had to have meat and vegetables. Hazel thought that was all right if the nurse cooked all those things, but on the nurse's nights off she gave him Rice Krispies because he liked them and you didn't have to cook them. Hazel knew that if the nurse would just mind her own business she could get along fine. She didn't like being told what to do, and she decided to get rid of that nurse next year no matter what.

Herman was a good father. He would sit down with Richie and talk to him man to man.

"Here's a hundred-dollar bill, Richie," he would say, handing it to him. "See, it has my picture in the middle of it. Someday you'll have lots of these, real ones."

Richie would look at his father solemnly, taking in every word, although it was hard to tell if he understood.

"Your stocks went up again today, Richie," Herman would say. "Wartime makes good business. You have steel stocks, and they're booming. You're going to be a very rich young man someday."

Sometimes Herman would take Richie in the car and show him places in and around Miami Beach. "See that hotel, Richie? Your daddy built that hotel, and he owns it. People pay rent to us for using that hotel. See that land over there, all empty? I own that land, and that means you own it too. Real estate is good business, Richie. I'm in real estate, and someday you'll be in real estate too."

Richie would listen to all this solemnly. Four years old, and so smart! Herman liked to take Richie on these car trips and show him everything they owned, and he liked to talk to Richie about business. He didn't know how to talk to Richie about little kid things, and he didn't like to play sports, so he treated Richie just like a good friend. Hazel knew he was very proud of his son.

From the start Herman had complained about the house Papa was building for Hazel at Windflower. He didn't see why he and Hazel had to share a house with Rosemary and Jack, why they couldn't have their own house. Hazel told him patiently that it was so she could have company and wouldn't be lonely. If Herman was away so much, then she would have Rosemary to talk to. Herman complained that the house was too small, and that there was no place for him to entertain his business friends when he came up north.

"How does it look if I invite my friends to a two-family house?"

"It's big, Herman."

"It's not big enough. Our house here is just as big, and we live here just the three of us. We should have had a house like The Big House."

Hazel didn't argue with him, but she knew Papa was always right. They had sent her photos of the houses when they were nearly finished, and of the rest of the place, with the lake and the pretty waterfall, and it looked very big and very nice. It was nicer than the house in Brooklyn. It didn't matter if Herman didn't like it; he would hardly ever be there anyway. What was he talking about, entertaining business friends? They never entertained at home, except once a year when they had a cocktail party and a lot of caterers did the whole thing. They always entertained Herman's business friends out, at restaurants and night clubs, and they went to all those charity dinners. Their house was scary at night, when Herman had to go to a meeting without her and she had to stay alone with Richie. That was the only time she was glad they had the nurse. There was always a sleep-in maid, but she was downstairs so far away. Herman liked everything to be the best, he said. He didn't go out to business meetings without her more than once a week, so Hazel didn't really mind, and she could always do her crossword puzzles to pass the time.

In the spring, when it stayed light longer after dinner, Hazel liked to take Richie in the car and drive down the road alongside the beach hotels so they could look at all the people dressed up. There was always a new hotel, and always so many people to look at. Richie liked to ride in the car. He would go, "Brrr, pup-pup-pup," and pretend he was turning a steering wheel. He was so smart. Hazel would just rubberneck along, driving slowly, having a good time. When Herman was out at one of his business meetings Hazel would have her little adventures, but she never told Herman because she knew he worried about her going out alone at night. He didn't think women should go out at night without their husbands. But if their husband was out without them, why couldn't they go out without him? It was just for fun, and if he didn't know it wouldn't hurt him.

One evening in late spring she was driving along with Richie beside her and she was sure she saw Herman. He was just getting out of a big chauffeur-driven limousine in front of a night club, with another man she had seen before with Herman and two young girls she had never seen. The girls were pretty and had good figures, but they had on too much makeup and she was sure they bleached their hair. One of them had lemon-yellow hair and the other one had her hair all piled up on top of her head and it was pink. Hazel knew nobody had pink hair. It really looked strange. Herman put his arm around the waist of the girl with pink hair and said something to her that made her laugh, and then the four of them went into the night club.

Richie pointed. "There's Daddy!"

"Is that Daddy?"

He nodded. "Yes."

"You sure?"

"Yes."

Then it must have been Herman if they both thought so. But Herman had told her he had to go to a business meeting. She didn't know they took girls to business meetings. She didn't like it, either. He could have taken her along if he was going to let girls come too. She didn't have to stay in the house alone. It wasn't fair. She had always thought a business meeting meant just men, smoking cigars in a room and talking about things she wouldn't understand. If Herman had a business meeting in a night club, why couldn't she come? She would be quiet as a mouse and watch the floor show and never interrupt. Who were those girls, anyway? That man was married too, and he hadn't let his wife come along.

That night Hazel waited up until Herman came in. It was two o'clock in the morning. He tiptoed into their bedroom and she said, "Herman."

"Oh," he said, surprised, "did I wake you up? I'm sorry."

"I wasn't asleep."

"Oh?"

"Who was that girl with pink hair?"

"Who?"

"I saw you with two girls and Mr. Levee."

"Where?" he asked.

"In front of the Flamingo Club. You went in."

"What were you doing in front of the Flamingo Club, Hazel?"

"I went for a ride."

"I told you never to go out alone at night! Why did you disobey me?"

Hazel pouted. "You went out. Why can't I?"

"Because you're a woman! Women should never go out at night alone! What would people think about me if my wife goes gallivanting around all alone at night? How does that look?"

"Who was that girl?"

"What girl?"

"The girl with the pink hair."

"Oh, her," Herman said, as if he had just remembered her. "She's Hy Levee's niece."

"Who's the other one?"

"His other niece."

"I thought you had business."

"I did," Herman said. "You know I do business with Hy Levee. His nieces came to town and he wanted to take them to a night club, and he didn't want them to go out with strange boys, so we took them."

"Oh," Hazel said. "Why couldn't I come?"

"Because the girls are very shy."

"You know boys for them," Hazel said.

"He won't let them go out with boys. They're too young."

"They didn't look so young."

"How could you tell in the middle of the night, from a car?" Herman said, very angry. "Is that how you drive? Looking out the window and not watching the road? Do you want to get killed? Do you want Richie to be an orphan?"

"I had Richie with me."

"You took Richie?" Herman yelled. His face was red. "You took that little baby out at night when he should have been in bed? What kind of a mother are you? Where is your sense of motherhood?"

Hazel started to sniffle. She didn't want Herman to be mad at her and have his face so red it looked like he was going to explode, and he had no right to tell her she was a bad mother. She was a good mother. He was mean. But she also knew he was right. Other mothers didn't take their babies for rides in the car at night. A four-year-old should have been asleep in bed.

"Don't cry," Herman said. His red face started to fade until it was its normal shade of pink. "You'll never, never do that again, will you Hazel? Do you promise?"

She nodded.

"You are my wife and the mother of my son," Herman said. "You represent me. You must always be a model of perfect behavior. The community respects you. I want you to stay home at night when I have to go out."

"Okay," Hazel said. She blew her nose into a tissue from the box on the night table between their beds.

"I don't enjoy going out with Hy Levee and his two boring nieces," Herman said. "But that's the sort of thing I have to do in order to do business. That's what a man does. He's nice to people, he entertains visitors and strangers. That's business."

"Oh."

"Go to sleep now, Hazel."

He turned off the light and she could hear him getting into his bed. She was glad Herman wasn't mad at her any more. She wasn't mad at him any more either. He probably didn't like going out with Hy Levee's two boring nieces. It must have been hard to talk to them. They didn't look like the nice girls other people she knew had for nieces. They looked like two floozies. Herman must have been very ashamed to be seen with them.

THIRTEEN

The family was going to move into Windflower in May. Etta's kitchen had finally come: the stove, the refrigerator, the new linoleum floor, the big country kitchen table and chairs to set around it. All the wallpaper had been put up in Lavinia and Melissa's house except for the large downstairs center hall, and in the middle of putting it up the decorator announced that the store had run out of paper in that pattern and they would have to wait six months for more to be made. Melissa was delighted, because she had decided when the first strip of paper was glued on that she hated it. Now she said to Lavinia, "The heck with the expense, let's rip it all off and get something else."

So they chose another paper that they both liked much better, and put it on instead. The inside of the house would be dignified but warm, like a gracious English country estate house. There were soft sofas and dignified but gay floral wallpapers, lovely antique reproduction furniture, and some real antique silver pieces put here and there on tables. Melissa had to have a piano, and Lavinia wanted a lot of plants. It was a house you could be comfortable and happy in.

Rosemary had decided on modern for her house. She was young, and modern was young. She was so sick of living in that tacky furnished room, cooking sneakily on a forbidden hot plate, that she wanted an airy, stark, modern home. Although she was the pianist in the family, Jack didn't have any money at the moment, so she decided to play Melissa's piano until they could afford one of their own. She would be stuck here in the sticks until the war was over, and who knew when that would be?

Jack had managed to get a weekend pass for the opening of Windflower, and Papa was going to have a big dinner party at his house, for just the family of course, and it looked as if all of them would be there. Hazel would take the train from Florida with Richie and his nurse and her housekeeper (whom Hazel kept calling the maid) and Herman would fly because he couldn't spare the time to take the train. Herman would hire temporary help in Miami Beach for the summer, probably just a cleaning woman, because he ate out every night anyway.

Lavinia and Melissa had investigated the shops in town where they would buy their food, and had opened a charge account, in Lavinia's name because she was the older. At the Winsor-Nature house the charge account was opened in the name of Winsor. Before the families moved in, the larder was stocked with all the canned goods that could be found, and at least two year's supply of toilet paper. The tradespeople in town didn't know what to think of them. Wartime hoarders, of course. But who hoarded toilet paper?

Everett's junk had been banished to the country. Melissa and Lazarus certainly weren't going to have it cluttering up their nice new hotel apartment. His room was full of electrical equipment, rolls of wire, tools, a soldering iron, who knew what else? It was all a mess, and what he couldn't jam into his room he put into the garage. This precipitated a fight, because everyone thought his junk was unsightly in the nice new garage next to Papa's limousine, and Everett said if he put it into the tool shed the weather would ruin it. Finally Everett won, only because he convinced

Lazarus that his junk cost money, and Lazarus didn't like to waste money.

Paris was going back to the camp she'd loved last year. Lavinia had to move all their things from Brooklyn to New York, and she didn't want to have to worry about the child underfoot. But this would be Paris' last year at camp. She would stay at Windflower from now on. There was enough for her to do: tennis, swimming, and walks, and she could even ride her bicycle. Paris didn't mind. To her this meant that they had discovered that she was no longer a child, and was too old for camp. She had been accepted at both the New York schools, and had chosen the all-girls one because it was more permissive. The other one was little and the teachers looked like fuddy-duddies. At the girls' school the math teacher let one of the girls throw an eraser at him, and he just laughed and tossed it back. She could just imagine her father letting one of his students get away with that! She didn't tell her parents about the incident, however; she said she liked the school because the facilities were better (they even had a swimming pool). It had always been intended that she would go to college so that she could make something of herself. She wanted to work on a magazine and then be a writer. She was the only one of all her friends who knew what she wanted to do when she grew up, except of course for the girls who knew they wanted to get married. She had gone over the possibilities in her mind—painting, drawing, acting, writing—and had decided that writing was what she had the best chance of succeeding at. The important thing was to have something to do that she loved. In order to be a writer she would have to go to college, and that meant she would have to do well in high school, so that meant no boys. Big deal. She couldn't stand boys anyway.

Lavinia had found a nice apartment only a block away from Paris' school. That had two advantages; Paris could walk to school and perhaps, for once, wouldn't be late, and also Lavinia could watch her from the window and see that she was safe. She couldn't walk a high school student to school, but she didn't want her wandering around the city either.

Everett had finally been accepted at the University of Miami. He refused to live in the dorm. He was afraid he wouldn't make friends, but he said it was because he couldn't stand to be with a lot of other boys. He was too good for a dorm. Papa said he could live with him and Etta in their house in Miami Beach. There was plenty of room. There really was no other solution, for you couldn't let a young boy fend for himself in a furnished room. He would have all his meals provided for him if he lived at his grandfather's, and he would have someone who would make him study. Etta was not one bit pleased about this arrangement, and even less pleased because no one had consulted her. Any relative of Papa's was welcome at his home, and now she had that sloppy, antisocial teenaged boy in her house. If they had consulted Etta she would have said no. But you couldn't cross Papa.

Everett would spend the whole summer at Windflower with his parents. Paris would be there for May and part of June until camp started, and then she would be there for September too because her school didn't open until October first. Poor kids at public school, they had to go so much longer because the schools were so overcrowded. But a small private school with only four kids in some of the classes was much more efficient. They could teach the kids in much less time, and they got to have longer vacations.

Paris' room at Windflower was exactly as she had imagined it, and she loved it. Little red carnations on a white background for the wallpaper, red and white gingham bedspreads on the two twin beds, and a white shaggy cotton rug because she was allergic to wool. She had her own bathroom, naturally, and a closet almost as big as a room . . . well, anyway, it was the biggest closet she had ever seen. You really could just go in there and sit if you wanted to. Everett had an ugly gray bedroom. It made her depressed just to look at it. And the decorator had put a ship's model on top of his dresser, which was silly considering that Everett had no interest whatever in ships.

There was one closet in the upstairs hall which Lazarus had appropriated for his very own. He had a lock installed on it, and he had the only key, which he hid. No one knew what was in there. Everyone was curious, but they assumed it had something private to do with his business as a doctor—drugs maybe, or patients' records. What else could it be? What it was, as only Lazarus knew, was his liquor. Bottles and bottles of whiskey, some of it left over from Prohibition days with the sticker with the skull and crossbones on it, saying "For Medicinal Use Only," his investment. His thing of value, salvaged from the crash of 1929. The crash had been long ago, and this was the boom time of 1943, but it didn't matter. Liquor was money. Remember how much he had paid for that bottle of Scotch during Prohibition? Why, it was as much as a workingman's wages for a whole week. And Lazarus owned cases of Scotch. Someday he might need it again. Who knew? So he locked it away in his closet and didn't tell anybody. It was his secret, his insurance.

Lavinia and Melissa interviewed couples, and finally hired one that Cassie sent them. They were colored, of course. The family didn't like to hire white help any more, they were low class and you couldn't trust them. A lot of them drank. You couldn't get the kind of nice white help you could in the old days. The immigrants who had come to this country eager to make something of themselves had disappeared; now there was riffraff, just knocking around from one job to another, with no ambition, dirty, filthy. Colored help was the best. This couple was named Ben and Mae. Ben was little and skinny and Mae was enormous. She would be the cook and he would be the butler; he would also clean, and he could drive a car, which was very useful because Jonah was the only one who could drive a car now. Melissa had forgotten how, or so she claimed. Everett zipped around in an awful hot rod he had bought and put together. Try to get him to do anybody a favor, like take them to town to do the grocery shopping, just try. He was so lazy and selfish that it ended up with Jonah doing all the chauffeuring for that family. It would be good to have Ben.

Of course they could always order meat and fish and groceries on the phone. You never knew what kind of quality they would send you if you didn't actually pick it out, feel it and sniff it, but it was good for emergencies. Hazel's housekeeper would order everything by phone. Etta had to order everything by phone too, because Papa would take his limousine and chauffeur to the city every day when he went to the office. Etta couldn't drive either. She had to come along in Jonah's car with Lavinia and Melissa, and then there was hardly enough room to put all the groceries on the way back. It was lucky for Etta that she had Henny, who could always cook something presentable from whatever the store sent.

When the family was ready to move into Windflower it meant that Windflower was completely ready to be moved into. The new dishes were all washed and neatly stacked on their shelves, the new linens and towels were neatly piled in the communal linen closet of each house.

Adam had bought a table with three leaves for his dining room. When the leaves were in, the table stretched the length of the entire room and could accommodate not only the immediate family but any relatives they decided to invite. Tonight, the opening party night, it would be only thirteen: Papa and Etta, Lavinia and Jonah and Paris, Melissa and Lazarus and Everett, Hazel and Herman (leaving little Richie in the house with his nurse because it was too late for him), Rosemary and Jack, and Basil.

Basil. He had been the silent outsider through all this, not offering suggestions, not really caring. His suite had been so thoroughly decorated for him that all he had to do was move in his clothes and toilet articles. The decorator had even chosen the etching to hang over the bed, a sea scene of course. Basil brought no books, no favorite print, no little memento to make his desk personal, and he didn't smoke. He didn't plan to spend much time there anyway. Weekends. He wasn't going to let that place cut into his social life, and he couldn't bring any of his girlfriends there because she would have to sleep in a separate room, and everyone would look at her and make comments on her, either encouraging him to get serious or telling him to drop her because she wasn't good enough. Basil didn't bring his girls home unless it was absolutely necessary, just once in a while to prove there really was a girl and she wasn't trash. He would bring home a nice refined widow, only a year or so older than himself, or a young girl who was the daughter of a friend of the family, and after he had presented her he would whisk her away again and concentrate on the women he really liked. He knew that his money as well as his sleek good looks attracted women, but there was no point in going too far and taking them to Windflower. One look at that place and the girl would think he was a millionaire, and she'd really try to get her hooks in him. There was an inevitable point where they all always started nagging about marriage, women were that way, but only a fool or a braggart would hasten that inevitable point. After all, it wasn't easy to break up with a girl, it was messy. They hung on, they pursued you, and sometimes you missed them a little and gave in and saw them again, which only started the whole messy business all over again. It wasn't easy being a bachelor. It was, however, easier than being a married man.

Everyone dressed up in their nicest summer party clothes. The crystal chandelier above the white linen tablecloth sparkled, the best dishes and silver and goblets were set out. Henny had been in the kitchen since the crack of dawn whipping up delicacies.

Lavinia handed Paris a carton of Camels. "Here," she said, "run into the kitchen and give these to Henny. Tell her they're a present from you."

"Why?"

"Because help resent kids, and this way she'll like you."

Paris took the carton of cigarettes into the hot kitchen. Henny was mixing a huge bowl of batter for a cake. Etta was going to let them have a home-made cake tonight, oh boy! The ever-present Camel drooped from Henny's upper lip as she mixed, and some ashes dropped into the batter but she efficiently stirred them right into it with her wooden spoon so they became invisible.

"Here, I brought you a present," Paris said, holding out the carton.

Henny looked at her and smiled with what looked to be genuine friendliness. "Thank you," she said.

"You're welcome."

There was nothing else to say, so Paris went back to join the others in the living room where they were all chattering and waiting for dinner, which was still an hour away. Some of them were sipping sweet sherry, and Adam had his small glass of schnapps. He was joined in a drink by Lazarus and Basil. Andrew and Cassie were going to drop by after dinner to visit, because even though they were not part of Windflower they were still an important part of the family.

At last Etta summoned them in to dinner. It was seven, and they were used to eating at six, and they were all hungry. They had fresh melon balls—honeydew and cantaloupe and water-melon—a huge, rare, standing roast ribs of beef, fresh asparagus dripping with butter, fresh stringbeans, oven-roast potatoes, green salad with tomatoes in it and a glutinous orange dressing (Etta got a minus for that, but the rest of the meal was superb), and for dessert there was the cake Henny had made, neatly iced, with little soft florettes of icing all around the border. Paris noticed a tiny speck of cigarette ash nestled in the center of one of the florettes and smiled to herself.

There were also macaroons and cookies from a good local bakery, because at parties you always had more than one dessert. And there were silver plates of mints and salted nuts. There was coffee or tea, and skim milk for Paris, which she declined, saying she was too full. Everett lit a Chesterfield and Etta gave him a dirty look because she hadn't bothered to put any ashtrays on the table.

"Go get an ashtray, Everett," Etta said.

Everett pushed back his chair and nearly knocked over one of the maids who had just entered carrying a large tray containing champagne glasses and a huge just-opened bottle of champagne, frosty mist still rising from the neck.

"Sit down, Everett," Melissa said.

"Ooh, champagne!" Rosemary said.

"I'll get ashtrays," Herman offered expansively, having just lit up one of his famous stinkadoros. Lavinia gave him a dirty look.

When everyone had a glass of champagne, an ashtray if it was needed, and they all were seated, Adam stood up and raised his glass in a toast.

"Speech, speech!" Lazarus said.

Adam smiled down at all of them. "Well," he said, "here we are. My family together, with me. My dream has come true. May we always be as happy as we are today."

PART III

Windflower

ONE

Paris loved living in New York, she loved being twelve and free, and she hated high school. Her mother had told her to expect that she would hate high school; everyone did. She was an adolescent now, which meant that she was going to do all sorts of unpredictable and irrational things. She waited for this unreasonable weirdness to overtake her. She also waited for the promised pimples. Her hands flew over her face with a will of their own, touching the spots where a pimple might appear, covering her mouth with the awful braces, hiding everything that might be ugly. All the girls wore bangs, so Paris cut bangs, the better to hide more of her face. The best bangs were worn long, almost over the eyes, like a sheepdog. She slouched in her school uniform, the better to be invisible.

The adults made it clear that teenagers were a sort of plague. Rule: It is forbidden to go outside the school in your uniform, because when you wear your uniform you represent the school. Meaning: Anything you do is bound to be disgraceful, therefore we don't want to admit we know you. The girls wore their uniforms outside the school anyway, and were as raucous and outrageous as they wanted to be.

Dalton, Paris' school, was divided into three parts: the primary, the middle, and the high school. Boys were allowed to go through the middle school and then sent away. She discovered immediately that the girls who had gone through the middle school together considered themselves an elite, both intellectually and culturally, and she as an outsider (especially from Brooklyn) was considered an upstart.

She didn't mind so much that the girls who had known each other all their lives couldn't understand how she had managed to obtain an adequate education anywhere else but at their school, but she deeply resented the attitude of some of the teachers, who felt the same way.

She would come home after school and tell her mother all the slights, insults, grievances she had accumulated during the day. Her mother would sit on the chaise longue in Paris' bedroom, listening sympathetically as Paris poured out this hoarded collection of wrongs. She had come to this school to learn and get into college, and they were against her. The English teacher wouldn't tell her how to make her stories better. What good was a dumb teacher who wouldn't teach you?

"Schools are completely geared for the average person," her mother would say, as annoyed as Paris was angry. "They have no place for the superior student. It's easier to make everyone average."

Every month the girls got their assignments in all their subjects for the whole month, with a chart to be initialed by each teacher each week showing that the student had done her work. If you didn't do your work and didn't get the initials on your chart by the end of the month, your only penalty was that you didn't get your assignment for the next month. Paris knew one girl, a sixteen-year-old freshman, obviously nearly retarded, who had been doing the same first month assignment for the whole term. Nobody cared. You had to be at school at eight-forty-five in the morning, where you went to the "house" where you had been assigned for the term, a small group consisting of a teacher and girls from each of the four high school classes. This was supposed to be the "unity-promoting" time where you had a friendly constructive meeting and got to know the girls from the other classes. Actually, it was the fifteen-minute period where the latecomers could rush in and where everyone sat around looking at each other's socks and shoes because everything else was covered up by the uniform so they would not become clothes-conscious. Paris, who had just become interested in clothes, was developing quite a shoe fetish.

Penny loafers were the best. Platform shoes with ankle straps and stockings meant you had a date after school and were sophisticated. High heels with angora socks were disgusting. Saddle shoes and white socks were fine; colored socks were totally tasteless. Paris had saddle shoes with autographs from stage stars on them, her own idea and a big hit. Because she was a big girl now and had an allowance of a dollar fifty a week she could go to Saturday matinees every once in a while with a friend and buy standing room. Too timid to go backstage, she and the friend would lurk right outside the stage door in the street and accost the star, requesting an autograph. If the star agreed, up went the foot with the saddle shoe on it, out went the hand with the fountain pen in it, already uncapped and waiting. She usually had success.

From nine o'clock to eleven in the morning the school had what was called lab time, which meant you could contact the teachers on your own and ask for help with problems, or collect their initials on your completed work. No one wanted extra assistance because that meant extra work, so the time was spent either waiting around to get initials or else fooling around in the halls. Paris spent part of her time hanging around in the halls and part of it in the library reading books that were not on her assigned list. She discovered Truman Capote in a magazine, and John O'Hara and F. Scott Fitzgerald in books, and they became her favorites.

Some mornings they had gym. The worst thing about gym was that the high school girls weren't allowed to use the elevators, and the gym was on the tenth floor, so you had to walk up ten flights and then play basketball. Paris liked basketball, however, now that she was thin and fast. She played guard, which she liked because it seemed more aggressive.

She had already chosen her friends, or rather they had chosen her. They were outsiders like herself. One was a newcomer from California, which was even more remote than Brooklyn although not as disgraceful. Another was too smart, a greasy grind like herself, but without humor, a girl who picked her nose all day. And the third, who had come all the way up from the primary school, was still an outsider because she was strange: she was fourteen and still had a governess, her home clothes looked like uniforms, her parents were rich and famous and she hardly ever saw them, and she had mad crushes on girls. But a friend was someone to hang around on the street with after school, to have adventures with, to explore the museums with and go to the movies with and sit at the drugstore counter with and eat sundaes and tell secrets with, to hang around stage doors with, to talk to on the phone at night.

Classes continued until three o'clock in the afternoon, with a break for the inedible lunch, and then everyone had to stay until four-thirty to do something creative. You could study painting or sculpture or acting, or play a musical instrument. You were only excused from this creative activity if you had to go to the dentist to have your braces adjusted. Paris studied painting. The teacher was a famous artist who had fallen on hard times because of his political beliefs, and there were only three girls in the class including Paris.

She drew cartoons for fun and painted huge oil paintings. Her teacher said she could be an artist. But writing interested her more. It was a shame that there was no decent English teacher. There had been one, briefly, but he had been fired. He was a strange man, who smoked in class and possibly drank too much outside it, but he told her she had great talent and she liked him. Then he was fired in the middle of the term and no one knew why, and replaced by a simpy little woman with pink spots on her face who had only a BA from some college no one had ever heard of and kept telling Paris she was wonderful. Paris knew that a compliment from this simp was not the same as one from that strange, tough man.

She wrote stories at home and showed them to her mother. Her heart pounding, she would stand there and try not to breathe too loudly while her mother lay on the chaise longue in Paris' bedroom and read the story. Then, the verdict.

"This isn't up to your usual elegant style."

"What's wrong with it?"

"This sentence is awkward. That word doesn't make sense. And I don't understand this line."

"How's this, better?"

"Yes, that's fine. Now it's a very good story."

"You didn't like it because it had three mistakes?" Paris would say, indignant.

Her mother would look bewildered. Three mistakes was three too many. A story had to be perfect. What else was criticism for?

Near the end of Paris' first year the school board voted to accept Negro students into the school, starting with the primary school, so they could grow up with the white students and become friends naturally. Paris' friend who had the governess and the two rich famous parents was yanked right out of school by her mother and registered at boarding school for the next year. There really hadn't been any hope for Janie anyway, because she had been the one who had asked at the students' meeting: "Do you mean they're going to be allowed to use the *swimming pool?*"

"It doesn't come off, you know," Paris told her, and Janie looked dubious.

Then her friend from California went back home. There went two friends. The nose-picker was very popular because she had come up from the middle school, so she had other friends besides Paris. The freshmen had already divided themselves into cliques. There were the older girls who went out with boys, and the younger ones who didn't know any or didn't like boys yet. There were the loud, vulgar outsiders who had obviously been taken into the school for their money. There were the longtime students, who had known each other since they were four years old. There were the WASP ballet students, whose parents lived in town houses and had dogs. There were the English girls who had been sent to America to escape the bombing. There were the Chinese girls whose parents had come to America to escape the communists. By the end of the freshman year the groups tended to loosen up and overlap.

Then the lifetime New York girls decided Paris really wasn't as bad as some of the new girls who didn't even have Brooklyn as an excuse. They started asking her for Saturday lunch dates. That was the big thing; Saturday lunch dates, at your house or hers, and then you went to the movies. You made dates weeks in advance. You even made dates with girls you hardly knew. It made you look and feel popular. It also broke down the barriers and some of the girls actually became friends at last. By the end of the first year Paris had a lot of friends, some of whom she liked more than others, of course, and she began to feel comfortable. She didn't see her old friends from Brooklyn at all any more. They were busy at their school, and they had all their new friends, and although her mother talked to some of their mothers on the phone they never made any plans for their daughters to meet. It was funny, Paris thought, she really didn't miss her old friends very much. They seemed so far away now, so remote. She was glad she had chosen to go to an all-girls school because she was too young to like boys. All her friends were going to Viola Wolff's dancing class. Paris adamantly refused to go.

"If you don't go, how will you meet nice boys for later?" her mother asked.

"I don't want to meet nice boys for later. I hate boys."

"You'll like them later."

"Then I'll meet them later."

Paris compromised by asking her Aunt Rosemary to teach her

how to dance one week when Jack had a leave and they came home to stay at Grandpa's house. Rosemary taught her the Foxtrot and the Charleston. Now there was absolutely no need to go to Viola Wolff's class and have to undergo the agony of dancing with boys.

Paris also refused to go to Sunday school and be confirmed. Since she had read the entire Bible herself three times by the time she was eleven years old her parents didn't protest too much. Being confirmed was another part of social life, the same as going to dancing school. Paris was invited to a group confirmation at Temple Emanu-El, which was very chic, and to the parties afterward, where you had to give a gift. The only moment of regret she had for not being confirmed was when she presented her friends with the little sterling silver pins she had bought all of them, and realized nobody was going to give her anything. Still, what was a silver pin compared to all those years of having been bored?

Paris' parents' maid had gone off to a war plant a long time ago, and every night she and her parents ate at Schrafft's, which was right in their apartment building and very convenient. They had a permanent six o'clock reservation and they always had the same table. The only night they had to eat elsewhere was Sunday, when Schrafft's was closed. Sunday was Grandpa day, when he was in the North. They either went to his house in Brooklyn, or else he and Etta came to New York and Paris and her parents and Aunt Melissa and Uncle Lazarus all ate together at Longchamps. Grandpa was thinking of selling his house in Brooklyn and moving to New York to the same hotel where Aunt Melissa and Uncle Lazarus lived. After all, he was in Florida all winter, and at Windflower during the summers, so who needed a house for two or three months a year? Then they could all visit him in the hotel on Sundays and eat in the hotel dining room on Sunday nights, which would be more cozy and familylike. Uncle Basil could have an adjoining apartment in the hotel, just an efficiency apartment of course, since he was still a bachelor.

The family always asked Paris how she liked school, and she always lied and said she liked it very much, giving a big hypocritical smile and showing her braces. Her mother had told her to say she liked school. Besides, it was just too boring to have to go into the long story of why she hated school so much.

Once in a while, on a Sunday night, they saw Aunt Cassie and Uncle Andrew. That was a big occasion to Paris because Aunt Cassie was so lively. Uncle Andrew hardly ever said anything and seemed shy. He asked her how school was. They had another baby now, a girl, named Blythe. Blythe Lucy Saffron. Blythe because they liked the name, and Lucy after Paris' dead grandmother whom she couldn't remember. The three children would stay at home with the governess, and Aunt Cassie and Uncle Andrew would eat at Longchamps with the rest of the family. Everyone ate at the same restaurant even when Grandpa was in Florida. Both Paris' father and Uncle Lazarus were very distrustful of new restaurants. They were sure they were going to be poisoned. Sometimes Uncle Andrew managed to drag them off to a Chinese restaurant and that was really an occasion. Uncle Lazarus always had plain broiled chicken. Her father worried about whether or not they were sneaking pork into his food. And Paris stayed up all night drinking water afterward because Chinese food made her so thirsty.

All in all, living in New York and going to high school was a lot more interesting and exciting than living in Brooklyn had been. Sometimes it was hard to imagine herself growing up, like when they had the horrible school dances and the whole high school was there, the awkward funny-looking freshmen and the sleek, sophisticated seniors, and none of the boys would dance with her. She nearly died of embarrassment then. Who would want to dance with her, a twelve-year-old girl, well, nearly thirteen, but with braces and not much figure and nothing at all to say to a boy? If only she had long swinging blonde hair and a black velvet dress! Then she would be sophisticated. But look at her, with her frizzy cold wave and her sheepdog bangs, and that pimple on her nose with about an inch of pancake makeup only making it look bigger, just not so red. Who would want her? They shouldn't let the seniors come to the dances if they had freshmen there. It was unfair competition. Then she discovered that the girl who was so popular was only a sophomore and she really wanted to kill herself. How could she change that much in one year? She would never look like that. Of course, that girl must be fifteen. Paris was the youngest girl in the high school. When she was fifteen she would be a senior. There was so much to worry about, what with trying to learn to be a writer and hoping to get into college, that having straight blonde hair was at the bottom of her list. Still, it was there. It had to do with a whole other world she didn't know anything about, but she intended to find out.

TWO

Everett had two lives, his real life and the life he pretended to everyone he was having. He liked Miami because he could ride around in his jalopy with the top down, and he liked the university because it was so big that no one could keep track of him, or so he thought. He went to classes when he felt like it. He lived with Papa (he never called him Grandpa, only Papa, because it seemed more grown up) and Etta in their house and had breakfast and dinner there. He was supposed to have lunch in the school cafeteria, between classes.

Twice, he had tried to have lunch in the cafeteria, but the moment he walked into that huge room full of strangers he knew he was done for. When he walked in some of the faces turned to look at him, blank masks judging him, and he wanted to run away. Most of the students just ignored him, busy with their friends, and perhaps that was worse. Everett knew no one. He forced himself to get on line in front of the steam tables, pushing his metal tray, not wanting any of that foul-smelling food but having to chose something or look like a fool. He pointed at something, took a cup of coffee, and looked around for a table. People were at all the tables as far as he could see, and how could he walk up to a stranger and ask to share? It was impossible. Tray in hand, feeling enormous and ridiculous, he walked across the room, sweating, looking for an empty table.

There was one empty table in the corner. The couple who had been sitting there were just getting up. Should he chance it? Out of the corner of his eye Everett saw two other people heading for it from the other side and he quickly calculated that they would get there at the same time as he would, thus precipitating a confrontation. He couldn't cope with that. Casually, as if he was finished, he went to the place where they collected the dirty dishes and put his untouched tray down with the garbage and walked out of the cafeteria.

He had a lump in his throat and thought he was going to cry. Why was it always so hard just to speak to people, just to have them look at him? His shyness was like a malignancy. He wanted to disappear, to drop through the floor, to be invisible, like that character in the comic books he had read as a kid. But on the other hand he was suffocating from loneliness. He walked to the parking lot and got into his red jalopy, gunned it up to seventy, and sped away toward the beach.

Near the beach he bought a hot dog and a paper cup of coffee from a stand. He ate in his car. Look at those fools on vacation, all strutting up and down, dressed up, staring and wanting to be stared at! He hated them. Tall, skinny, and innocuous in his college clothes he hoped he looked like a million other kids. He didn't want to stand out . . . yet, if only someone would notice him, speak to him, be his friend . . .

At eighteen, Everett was six feet tall, weighed a hundred and fifty pounds, and looked like a fox. His face was long with high cheekbones, his pale eyes (green like his mother's, but so light they seemed bleached out by the sun) looked out from a fringe of thick, long eyelashes and bushy fox-colored brows. They were frightened eyes, but looked devious. His hair was sandy, silky, like the hair of a red fox. His movements were quick but graceless. He seldom smiled. He had never been out with a girl.

He was consumed with the thought of sex. It haunted him; lust and curiosity and fantasy, girls. He bought girly magazines and kept them in his room. He yearned for some of the girls he saw on the campus and made up stories about his exploits with them, in case anyone should ever ask, but no one would. No one cared whether Everett Bergman had been to a gang-bang, had enjoyed a night of wild passion with a blonde senior, had been picked up by a stewardess, a nurse, a waitress. He had all these fantasy stories at the ready, but no one asked and no one cared because he had no friends.

It was bad enough to be a virgin, but there were other boys his age who were virgins. What was worse was to be unable to talk to a girl at all. His tongue would dry up in his mouth, he would develop amnesia, speech would leave him.

There was a beautiful red-haired girl in his compulsory freshman

English class with a lot of fuzzy sweaters which she filled as well as any girl in Everett's girly magazines, whom he longed for. No, lusted for was better, he saw her in all his lonely fantasies. He wanted to put his hands on her. She didn't have a steady boyfriend and he could have tried to ask her to have a cup of coffee with him. But his thoughts were so hot he was afraid they burned through his eyes. Maybe it would have been better if they had, then at least she would notice him. One day she was trying to get past him in the row of seats—he always sat on the aisle for a quick getaway—and she stepped on his foot.

"Oh, I'm *sorry!*" she said, looking him right in the eyes and smiling.

"S'okay," Everett murmured grumpily, looking over her shoulder. God, there were those angora-covered boobs, right up against him, practically in his face, and it was all he could do not to make a lunge for them. He shrank inside his own sweater and sat on his sweaty hands. She pushed on past him to an empty seat, and later he saw her glance at him with a puzzled look and then shrug. He looked away. The next time he saw her she was in the hall in an animated conversation with two handsome guys and she didn't even seem to recognize him.

He was hopeless. He stopped going to English class because it bored him, even though it was compulsory to pass, and at midterms he got a D. What did he expect, when he hadn't done the reading and had only gone to a few of the classes? He was lucky he hadn't gotten an E. It was only because he was so smart. The hell with them all.

Every evening at six o'clock sharp Everett had to appear for dinner at Papa's. He could see that Etta resented him. Her sharp, sarcastic voice whenever she deigned to address a question to him gave her away. "And what did the genius do today?"

She knew the genius had cut classes and was tinkering with his electrical equipment in his room. Henny must have told her. The two of them were thick as thieves. Everett thought Etta had a screw loose. Who would spend her days betting on horses with a nigger? It was a good thing they made all those colored live out of the beach area. They had to have an identification card to walk around after dark or the cops would get them. It kept the crime down. The Southern attitude, which he had never encountered in Brooklyn, which was full of well-meaning Jewish liberals like his family, gave Everett someone to hate. Not that he would ever dare to say a word to their faces, but he thought it, murmured it under his breath. "I'm wise to you, you schvartze . . ."

His father was the only person Everett had ever known who wasn't a do-good liberal. He said it right out about all the no-good bums he treated in that slum where he went to practice every day, all the minority groups who didn't pay their bills and were always sick because they didn't know how to eat right. That chink, what did he expect, eating hazerei? That wop, stuffing himself with spaghetti and garlic. That schvartze, frying everything in lard. Even his own people didn't escape Lazarus' scorn. That yiddel, poisoning himself with chicken fat.

As the school year wore on, Everett attended fewer and fewer classes, using the excuse that they were boring. He had not made a single friend. He would never have lived in the dormitory because he was too frightened to live with strangers. Share a bathroom with strangers? Have to talk to strangers? He knew he would never have friends, and as long as he didn't live in the dorm no one would know he was friendless. He was almost invisible. Only his jalopy was visible, bright red and emitting loud noises, zoom, zoom, varoom! People looked at it admiringly. It was his status symbol. If only some sexy, pretty girl would ask him for a ride in his car! But none of them ever did. They just gave him dirty looks when he sped by too close to them.

His inventions were his only solace. In his room he was putting together an intercom telephone system for the whole house. A private system. Actually, none of his inventions were original, they were copies of things he had read about in his magazines, but even the fact that he could put them together showed that he had ability. He knew his life work would be in something like that, inventing, or working with electrical or mechanical things. He knew he would never go into the family business and he would never work for anyone. He would be no one's slave. He would be the master, the boss, self-employed. The garage in back of Papa's house was filled with Everett's things, his inventions, the things he was working on, half-finished. His tools were there, his rolls of wire, his equipment, all the same things he had lovingly bought and put in the garage at Windflower. These were new things, new equipment, new inventions, which he had as lovingly bought with his own money here in Miami Beach. The garage was his major workshop. His room was only for the one work in progress. Etta had already insisted on that, furious.

"I won't have you messing up this room," she had said. "You're a guest here. This isn't your house. If your parents want to send you to me, okay, I'll take you, but not your junk. Get that stuff out of here!"

He had argued with her, and finally, because he had lied and said that the work was a project for school, she had agreed to let him keep just one in the bedroom. The rest had to stay in the garage. Many nights when the rest of the household was asleep, Everett went to the garage, where he worked for hours, playing his radio softly for company, lost in the beauty of creating things that worked. It was the only time he was happy. Electrical sparks were beautiful, more beautiful than poetry. He hated poetry. He hated words. They strangled him. But the human voice coming out of wires and cables was magic. He could speak for hours to strangers on his ham radio set because their voices and his voice uniting through the air via the magic of electricity was a union of perfect friendship. He couldn't talk to a neighbor on the phone without hemming and hawing and wishing to hang up, but when he sent his call out over the air on his ham radio set he felt like a part of the entire universe.

Now his ham radio set was his only social life. He had put it in the garage because people could hear him if he used it in his room. There was no privacy in that house. He would no more put his ham radio set into his room and communicate on it than he would bring a girl into his room and lay her right under the noses of his family.

His mother kept nagging him about school. How was he doing? Was he buckling down to work more? She knew about his bad marks at midterm, the D in English, the F in French—at that rate he should have had an A in advanced applied science, but he had a C minus. He knew more than the teacher, so why go to class to do what he already had learned at home? Was it his fault they had taken attendance, or that they had sprung a test on the class one day when he wasn't there? He could have gotten an A on that test. The hell with them all.

Why did everyone tell him he had to make something of himself? What did they think he was going to make? He wasn't God. On weekends Everett either fooled around in his room or else went riding around in his car. Sometimes he put the car in the driveway and practically took it apart, cleaning each piece lovingly, and put it together again. He wanted to keep it in such perfect condition that it would be a collector's model, at least until he had the money to buy a really good, powerful car. Papa was home from the office during the day on weekends, and from his attempts at conversation Everett could tell that Papa wanted to talk to him about the family business. He tried to listen because it was only polite, but he didn't want to be sucked into that thing. He wasn't meant for a desk job. After a while Papa seemed to understand and stopped trying to talk to him. Papa seemed to think it was an honor to go into the family business, and Everett supposed for some of the relatives it would be, but not for him.

He got along with Papa usually, but Etta made his life miserable. She was always complaining about him and picking on him. She said his room was a pigsty. Everett said what did she care, they had maids didn't they? The maids could stay out, for all he cared. He would prefer it. Then no one would encroach on his territory.

Now that he had grown up Everett had a ravenous appetite, a far different person from the little noneater he had been as a child, but no matter what he wolfed down he stayed thin. Etta always complained that he ate too much. It seemed that whatever he put into his mouth, that was the one morsel Etta decided she had been saving for Papa. "You took the last bagel!" "You had to grab the last piece of lox?" "I bet that boy ate a pound and a half of roast beef all by himself."

"Oh, it doesn't matter," Papa would say. "Thank God we can afford it."

"You're not the only person in this house, you know," Etta would snap at Everett. She would grab away the plate of tiny Danish with a swift, practiced, ladylike movement, and put it on the other side of the table where Everett couldn't reach it. Then he would have to ask for it. "Another?" she would say. "You had five already, but who's counting?"

"Oh, forget it," Everett would snarl under his breath. He knew he could go into the kitchen after lunch and eat whatever was left.

One Saturday at lunch Papa looked up from his cold borscht and said, "Today, Everett, you should clean out the garage."

"What?"

"Clean out your junk. There isn't any more room for anybody else."

"It's in the corner," Everett said, and when he glanced at Etta she had a smug look on her face. She loved it when anyone was making his life miserable.

"You call it the corner," Papa said. "I call it the whole garage. Clean it."

"Oh all right." He knew what "clean it" meant. Many times he'd been forced to clean up his room by his parents, and it just meant arrange everything neatly in boxes, but it took forever. It would take his whole weekend, and today of all days he'd been meaning to go to the sale at Sears Roebuck. Nobody around here cared about him. First he would go to the sale, and then he would pick up some empty boxes, and then he could work on the garage all night. It would be something to do when all the other college kids were whooping up and down the beach in their cars, tops down, out on dates, going to beer parties and dances and the movies, feeling each other up in parked cars, having Saturday night fun. Everett hated Saturday nights. By Saturday morning he had that heavy feeling in his throat which meant another Saturday night was going to be lost, another sexual encounter passing him by, another night of his youth wasted. Better to stay in the garage and feel he had something important to do.

But when he went to Sears he found browsing around there so engrossing that he spent the whole afternoon and also a hundred and seventy-two dollars. Now he was broke. He put his new purchases into the trunk of his car and went to the back of the largest market in town, where he picked up several thrown-out cardboard boxes and put them into the back seat. Then he drove back to the house. It was time for dinner.

"So?" Papa said, looking up from his steak. "You didn't clean up your junk this afternoon."

"I'll do it tonight."

"Good."

After dinner Everett took his new purchases into the garage and unpacked them lovingly. How could he resist not trying them out, not playing with them? He sat on the floor of the garage and began happily putting everything together the way it should be, because everything always came packed separately and unassembled from the store. It was true, he did have a lot of stuff, but everyone was entitled to a hobby. Could he help it if his took up space? Besides, it was more than a hobby, it was his future life's work.

It was midnight by the time he had finished fooling around. He still hadn't started putting anything away and now he was tired. He should have had another cup of coffee at dinner, but he'd been too full after two big pieces of Henny's delicious key lime pie. Well, at least he would get the boxes out of his car and put them into the garage, and then tomorrow bright and early he would get to work.

When he had put the boxes into the garage Everett looked at his ham radio and wondered if anyone was calling at this hour. The air was probably full of messages at only a little after midnight on a Saturday night. He couldn't resist turning it on and making a call. They didn't have dates either, those people, and they were much more interesting than those stupid college kids. He found a man on a yacht to talk to, and then a thirteen-year-old boy who was confined to his home with paralysis from polio and had been making ham calls since he was eleven. Obviously a genius. Everett enjoyed talking to him. He had a lot in common with the kid, both of them loners and outsiders. The poor kid was paralyzed from the waist down and in a wheel chair, but he had put together his whole ham set by himself, just the way Everett had when he was young. They talked about mechanical things and Everett was very impressed with the kid's knowledge. Then the kid said his mother was nagging him to go to bed and Everett laughed because it reminded him of when he was that age. They signed off, and then to his surprise Everett found a woman calling, so he had a good talk with her for about half an hour. She was an older woman and she had become interested in ham radio through her husband's interest, and then when he had died she had continued.

It was really late when Everett signed off, and he stumbled back to the house and fell into bed. Well, there was always Sunday to clean up the garage and make his equipment look presentable.

As usual, Everett slept late. It was past noon when he came downstairs to the dining room, too late for breakfast, too early for lunch. Henny gave him a cup of coffee in the kitchen and didn't look too happy about it. He lit a cigarette and walked out to the back porch with the cup of coffee in his hand. It was another perfect, hot, sunny day. He certainly wasn't looking forward to cleaning up the damn garage, it would be hot as hell in there. He smoked his cigarette and drank his coffee, left the empty cup on a table and walked slowly out to the garage to survey his unwelcome task.

The garage was completely empty except for Papa's car.

It was as if he had entered someone else's garage by mistake. Everett couldn't believe it. The coils of wire were gone, his tools were gone, his partly completed inventions were gone, the new things he'd bought on sale yesterday were gone, and even his ham radio set was gone. His ham radio set! He felt his stomach turn over, the sour taste of the coffee and cigarette in his mouth. His heart was pounding and he started to tremble. Where was all his stuff? He ran outside to the driveway and there was his red jalopy, right where he had left it last night, but it was empty. Behind the garage? No, nothing.

He ran around the outside of the garage like an idiot, flapping his arms, trying to croak something, and then he raced back to the house and ran in, slamming the screen door behind him.

"Papa! Etta!"

Papa came into the living room with the Sunday paper in his hand. He looked at Everett calmly. "Nu, so what's the screaming?"

"My stuff is gone!" Everett said. "My stuff, from the garage."

"I threw it out."

Everett looked at his grandfather to see if he was kidding. But there was no trace of a smile on the old man's face, nor anger either. Just that calm; a job needed to be done and he had done it.

"You threw it *out?*" Everett was aware that his voice had cracked, the way it hadn't done since he was an adolescent. "Where is it?"

"I left it for the junkman and he took it."

"You threw it out for *garbage?*"

Papa sat down in his favorite comfortable chair and opened the Sunday paper. Etta came cheerfully into the room as if she hadn't heard a word of Everett's anguished screaming.

"Lunch is ready," Etta said pleasantly.

"Oh, good," Papa said, and refolded the paper neatly.

Everett looked at both of them and ran out of the house before they could see him cry. He got into his car and gunned it away, sobbing, tears blinding him. He wanted to hit, to kill. His life, his love, it was gone. Where could the garbage collector have taken it? If he could just find out, maybe he could get back his ham radio set at least. But he knew it was hopeless. They collected trash early in the morning. That diabolical old man must have been up at the crack of dawn, as usual, and when he saw all the "junk" as he thought of it, he must have lost his temper. Everett remembered the story of his grandfather chopping the stone gargoyles off the fireplace with an ax. The old man had probably picked up each and every one of his beloved things and tossed them all out into the street, a tangled mess of junk for real. They would be resting now in the back of some smelly filthy garbage truck along with the remains of last night's dinner, smashed beyond repair. Maybe they had been put into the town garbage dump already, lost, destroyed. Everett was crying openly in the safety of his car, sobbing like a child and wishing he was dead. He could never go back to that house, never again.

He rode up and down side roads he had never seen and finally made his way to the beach. Up the road past where the hotels were, to the open places where no one lived. The air was cool even though the sun was hot, and he squinted his faded eyes against the sun, looking for a place to park. He drove up on to the shoulder of the road and stopped the car. The beach was broad and clean and empty. The sea rocked peacefully, the waves slapping symmetrically against the sand and spreading the surf out like a tablecloth. Everett went to the edge of the ocean and urinated into it, and then he walked over to a soft mound of sand and lay down. He wondered if he could live on the beach like a bum. No, he wouldn't like to sleep here, and he didn't like the sun either. He would go back downtown, to a rooming house.

He counted the money left in his pants pocket. He had seven dollars. He could take a five-dollar room and that would leave enough for food, and then he could call his mother collect and tell her to send him some money.

He drove back downtown, and through the side streets where the old, retired couples lived in little run-down rooming houses. He stopped in front of a three-story greenish house that had a sign in front that there were reasonable rooms to let, and went inside. It was only five dollars a night, and would be cheaper if he took the room by the month. No meals. An old woman ran the house, and when he told her he was a college student she seemed impressed. Education always impressed the members of the varicose vein set. There was a phone in the hall for the entire floor, but that didn't bother Everett because he didn't plan to get any calls. He paid for the room in advance and told her he would pick up his luggage later.

As soon as the landlady left he telephoned his mother, but there was no one home. Where would they go on Sunday? Maybe visiting. He wasn't going to call anyone else looking for her, she'd come home. He felt hungry so he got back into his car and drove around until he found a cheap place to eat and had bacon and eggs and toast. Everything tasted greasy, but food was food. He wondered if Papa and Etta were worried about him yet. It was nearly supper time. Would they wait, or would they just go on and eat without him? Etta wouldn't care, but Papa would care; after all, it was he who'd driven his own grandson out of the house. Well good, let them suffer.

When his watch said six o'clock Everett telephoned his mother again. She was still out. Damn her, probably eating out because it was Sunday night. Well, they always came home early.

The walls of his little room seemed to suffocate him. He didn't even have a radio. He got into his car again and realized he was almost out of gas. It was either gas or supper, and naturally Everett chose gas. Freedom was more important than food any day. He drank a coke from the machine in the gas station and then drove around in the balmy evening until the air got too chilly. He hadn't even brought a sweater. When his mother sent him the money he could buy some new clothes. He would never go back to that house. Papa could throw out his clothes the way he'd thrown out his equipment, if that was all Everett meant to him.

He wondered if he should tell his mother the great wrong that had been done to him. Would she take her father's side the way she always did, or would she side with her son? Maybe she wouldn't want to send him the money when she heard he'd run away. Maybe it would be a smart thing just to tell her to wire the money to him at the bank and then after it was safely in his hand he could call her and explain why he had left. That way at least she wouldn't be able to do anything about it. He needed money either way, wherever he lived.

He finally caught her at home at ten o'clock at night. He was annoyed at her, and his voice was petulant.

"Everett, you don't have to whine. When did I ever refuse you money?"

"Will you send it first thing in the morning?"

"Did you spend all the money I gave you *already?*"

"I had to. I have expenses."

"I hope you didn't buy any more junk, Everett. I want you to go out and enjoy yourself with your friends."

"I do."

"Well, that's good. How is Papa?"

"Fine."

"And Etta?"

"She's fine too."

"I want you to try to be neat around the house and not make a pest of yourself."

"Yes." Oh boy, he was glad he hadn't told her about the scene today with Papa and his "junk."

"You be nice to Etta. Maybe you should buy her a little present, some handkerchiefs or something, or some nice candy. She has to go to extra trouble for you."

"Okay," Everett said, bored. He sighed. He would buy Etta nothing. "I better go now, this is costing you money."

She laughed. "Since when did you ever worry about that?"

"Goodbye, Mom. Say hello to Dad."

Well, at least he'd attended to his financial affairs. Now for a good night's sleep. Everett went into the little room and turned back the covers on the bed. He lay down in his underpants, his customary sleeping garment, and stared at the ceiling. How could anybody live in this little box? He heard a senile cough from the next room and winced. Fossils. It was as bad as a dormitory. A sink in his room and the public toilet down the hall, one for men, one for women. A bathtub on claw feet in the bathroom. It was a good thing he seldom bathed. He didn't have a toothbrush but he hardly ever bothered to brush his teeth anyway. Tomorrow when he got the money he'd buy a razor, or maybe he'd just grow a beard. Ha! That'd shake them up. Maybe he'd never go back to college at all, just hang around and pretend he was going to college. He could loaf until Christmas vacation that way, and then he'd go back to New York to visit his parents, and then he'd come back here and . . . He was so bored and lonely he wanted to cry again. The future seemed endless. Just until Christmas vacation seemed endless. Even tonight seemed endless. If an hour was so long, how long would a year be, a lifetime? It was bad enough to live anywhere, but to live here was hopeless. His grandfather always said a man shouldn't have to live alone, and he was right. Loneliness was the worst thing in the whole world.

The next morning Everett got into his car and drove back to Papa's house. Nobody acted surprised to see him, nobody made any cracks. He put on a fresh shirt and opened a fresh pack of cigarettes, and when he went into the kitchen Henny gave him a freshly made cup of coffee. Papa went off to the office in his limousine, driven by Maurice, and the garage was completely empty. Everett could see that someone had hosed down the cement and swept up the place very neatly. If he wanted to he could even park his own car in there.

He felt as if he had died.

THREE

Everyone moved to Windflower for the summer on the same day in May. Lavinia closed up her city apartment very carefully, putting covers on the chairs and sofa, on the drapes, on the lampshades, after having prudently unplugged the lamps and removed the bulbs so there would be no chance of fire. She wrapped each bulb in tissue paper and put them all into a big cardboard box on the closet shelf. Melissa did the same.

Adam had sold his house in Brooklyn, smelling change in the air. The neighborhood was going down, and he wanted to get out while the property still had value. The good things, the heirloom furniture (as he thought of the things he had bought during the past twenty years), were moved up to his house in Windflower and arranged there lovingly by Etta, who now thought of all of them as hers. The not-so-good things, the worn-out and cheap things, were distributed among his poor and deserving relatives. And a few things went with him and Etta to their new apartment in the Edwardian Hotel. Adam was now a resident of New York City.

Hazel came to Windflower with the housekeeper and Richie. Richie was five years old now, and finally Hazel had managed to fire the nurse. She was really a baby nurse anyway, and she didn't care for older children if she could help it. Older children were too wild. The firing of the nurse had actually been by mutual consent, but Hazel liked to think it was her doing because it made her feel like the boss in the house.

In Virginia, Rosemary envied all of them their nice country summer, and she and Jack wrote joint letters still trying to find some humor in their long dreary Army stint.

It was Paris' first whole summer at Windflower. Carefully she put out her bottle of hand lotion, her new tube of toothpaste, her new toothbrush, her little jar of deodorant, her baby powder, her comb and brush, and arranged them in the medicine cabinet. Her mother had bought her some summer country dresses, and they were hung neatly in the huge closet. Picture postcards and stationery to write to friends went in the night table drawer, her portable typewriter and paper went into the closet, and her drawing materials as well.

Melissa took Mae the cook-maid on a tour of Paris' room and bathroom when Paris wasn't there. "Look how neat she is!" Melissa said, opening Paris' medicine cabinet and displaying the things neatly lined up on the shelves. "She's always that way. You'll never find any clothes on the floor from that child, no." It was Melissa's way of apologizing for Everett, her bribe to the help.

Everett was ensconced in his gray room amid his mess. His red jalopy stood in the driveway next to Jonah's sedan. Nobody but Adam bothered to use the garage because it was far away from the houses and a nuisance, but of course Adam had a chauffeur. Paris kept her new English racing bike in the garage too. Rosemary had won it in a raffle, the only thing she'd ever won, and since she couldn't ride it around the streets she gave it to Paris.

The girls—Lavinia and Melissa and Hazel—and Etta were very conscious of their new role as the ladies of a country estate, and had bought suitable new clothes. No longer the casual dresses of their beach house days, now they wore pastel linen dresses with cashmere sweaters to match, girdles and stockings, clean white high-heeled sandals, and summer jewelry made of mother of pearl and the new plastic. Their good winter jewelry went into the vault at the bank. Adam had found a small vault in the back of one of the closets in his bedroom, where perhaps Mrs. Crazy Russian had kept her jewels, but of course no one used it. A private safe was the best way to encourage burglars in the country. Everyone knew that help talked. Better not to show too much wealth, it gave people ideas.

Adam and Lazarus and Jonah wore what they pleased, because they were men. Old sloppy sweaters, baggy pants, comfortable shoes, were suitable for hard-working men who had to get dressed up every day to go to their offices. Lazarus arose at the crack of dawn to attend to his ablutions, ate a hearty breakfast consisting of half a grapefruit, hot oatmeal, two soft-boiled eggs, toast with jam, coffee, a banana, and a tall glass of buttermilk, and then Ben the butler drove him to the station to catch the seven-fifty-eight. From Grand Central Station, where his train arrived half an hour later (it was the crack express), Lazarus took the subway to his office in Brooklyn. He was always there before nine, in time to greet his first patient. Because he had eaten such a good breakfast he was never hungry for lunch, and thus saved at least a dollar and a half. He could get by with just a container of coffee, and see an extra patient besides.

Jonah went into the city with Adam in the limousine. Although he also was an early riser, he waited for Adam, who never left before nine-thirty because he felt he had earned his few moments of ease by this time in his life. Jonah was usually up by six, and took a brisk walk around the estate before a spartan breakfast. He went to the office with Adam and had lunch with him and Andrew and Basil.

Basil came to Windflower for long weekends. During the week he stayed in the city, where he conducted his social life. Everyone hoped he would find a nice girl to marry and settle down.

Weekdays for Lavinia and Melissa meant running the house. They had to plan the menus, hopefully without too many arguments, and attend to the shopping, and Lavinia was busy working on her flower garden with Tim Forbes. Both Lavinia and the caretaker had green thumbs, and all three houses were always filled with fresh flowers.

Everett had been forbidden to come downstairs to breakfast in his underwear, but he persisted in horrifying everyone by wearing his dirty old trousers with no shirt. Luckily he got up so late that no one had to look at him, and he ate breakfast alone. Paris slept right through breakfast and got up for lunch. No matter how Lavinia nagged her, she insisted on wearing blue jeans and shirts instead of a pretty dress. At least she was always clean.

"Why can't you wear a dress and set your hair?" Lavinia would say. "I got you all those nice dresses."

"Who's going to look at me?"

"We are. The family."

"Won't they like me if I'm not dressed up?"

"That has nothing to do with it. You should dress up for yourself. You should take pride in your appearance."

"I do. I like looking this way."

On weekdays lunch was served on the screen porch at the Mendes-Bergman house, Hazel ate with Richie, and Etta ate at her house. On weekends, when the men were home for lunch, everyone ate down at the lake. Ben would load the charcoal grill and the food into Jonah's car, and drive it down to the lake. There were metal tables and chairs down there, and Ben would set up the grill and cook hamburgers while those who wished could swim and sun and those who disliked swimming and suntans could wait in the pavillion for their food. Although Lavinia was displeased at the tire tracks Ben left in Papa's lovely, expensive new lawn, there was really no other way to get all that gear down there except by car. No one could carry it that far.

After dinner, whether on weekdays or weekends, the ritual was always the same: everyone went to Adam's house and sat in the living room. Etta set out a big bowl of fruit and it was just like the old days back in Brooklyn, a little stilted, but cheerful and safe. It was hard to think of things to say when you saw each other every day, all day, and every night. They were all always running in and out of each other's houses or on the phone to each other, and now here they were, dressed up, sitting there playing at being visitors. Paris was bored and gorged herself with fruit.

"Stop pulling the grapes off the stems," Etta would snap. "Cut off a bunch with the scissors."

"I only want one grape."

"You know you're going to end up eating them all."

"Diet and starve yourself all day," Lavinia would say. "Then come over here and stuff yourself. You'd think we don't have fruit at home."

At ten o'clock, when Lazarus was snoring in the corner in the easy chair and Adam looked as if he were about to doze off himself, everyone got up and said good night. There was a great to-do about who had the flashlights, and then they would all walk back to their own houses. Adam had had a street light installed between his house and the other two, but still everyone was a little afraid of the dark. Their houses were all lit up, and there were searchlights on the roofs. Paris liked to walk in the dark. She imagined there were prowlers and burglars lurking about. But if she couldn't see them then they couldn't see her either, and she was safe. Still, there was a delicious little thrill in imagining the danger.

The "next door" neighbors, who lived about a mile away, had come the previous summer to pay their respects. They were an elderly couple, German Jews, and very rich. It was because of them, and the Saffron family, and a Jewish banker across the way, that The Valley had become known to local people as The Polish Corridor. The Saffron family was a little intimidated by their neighbors, who had been there before them. After the courtesy call Etta, Lavinia, and Melissa had nagged Papa to go visit them back, but he never did. He put it off and put it off, and finally it was too late. Now the only time he saw the neighbors was when they were having an argument with him about the right of way.

People thought the new inhabitants of Windflower were strange. It was such a large family, and they kept to themselves, never tried to know anyone, no one saw them. A car would drive out of the gate and go away, then a car would return, but the only people you ever saw on the road were Molly Forbes and her two little boys, walking to the mailbox to gather up the clan's mail. Everyone in The Valley had horses, even the children, and everyone rode, but not the people in Windflower. No one knew what they did to entertain themselves.

The family thought they had plenty of things to do. Everett tinkered with his inventions in his room, the same as he did anywhere he was. He had gotten another ham radio. Paris rode her bicycle on the driveway on the grounds (never on the road outside because there were cars sometimes and you could get killed) and walked by herself through the woods. At the lake there were two gargoyles set into the stone of the pavilion (The Crazy Russian must have loved gargoyles) and Paris took her water colors down there and colored them in bright colors. It made them look more like cheerful elves. She also persuaded Hazel to let her take care of Richie some of the time. Richie was a quiet, sweet little boy, and he and Paris spent many hours wandering around the property, not saying anything. She wondered if he was old enough to think yet, and if so, what he thought. She couldn't remember what she thought when she was five. She made his supper and gave him his bath and secretly thought she was a much better baby sitter than Hazel was. Hazel gave him Rice Krispies all the time. Paris had had nutrition at school in her biology class, and she gave him meat and vegetables. Hazel certainly was dumb.

Paris wanted to invite some of her old friends from Brooklyn to visit her at Windflower, but her mother said no, they might be intimidated by all this splendor and feel badly. Actually it was Lavinia who was intimidated by the space and luxury of Windflower, they all were. It looked like a millionaire's estate. It was one thing to have money, but another thing to show it. Of course they would dress nicely, they would never stint on food, but one had to be careful not to be showy. You didn't invite people who were less fortunate than you were and rub their noses in it; it wasn't fair. It would be all right if Paris invited a nice friend from Dalton to come visit. But her friends from high school were either at camp or else their families had their own places for the summer, so it was hard to get anyone to come. That was the trouble with knowing rich kids.

Feeling slightly guilty, the family economized in little ways. Mae didn't change both sheets at the same time; she put the bottom one into the laundry, put the used top one on the bottom, and put a fresh one on the top. Lazarus brought piles of little wrapped cakes of guest soap from the Edwardian Hotel and he and Melissa used that. It didn't matter to him that it was Papa's hotel and therefore Papa paid for the soap; he, Lazarus was paying rent and therefore *he* was paying for the soap, so they might as well use it at Windflower.

Eating his lima beans carefully one at a time and masticating them the proscribed length of time, Lazarus launched into a story. "At the office today, this chink came in and . . . what are you kicking me for, Toots?"

Caught, Melissa would blush. "Don't say chink."

"This Chinaman came in, and . . . why are you kicking me now?"

"I didn't kick you that time," Melissa said.

"Then that rotten kid is kicking me." Lazarus glared at Paris, sitting across from him at the wide, long table.

"I can't kick you, my legs don't reach," Paris said.

"You kicked me."

"I didn't."

"Please eat, Lazarus, we're all waiting," from Melissa, prompted by Lavinia's impatient glance.

Dessert finally came. "Ooh, chocolate cake!" Everett said with malicious glee. "Paris can't have any because of her pimples. I'll have hers."

"Pig," Paris said.

"Let me count your pimples: one, two, three, four . . ."

"Shut up, Everett!"

"Don't say 'shut up,' " Lavinia said. "Be quiet, Everett."

"I don't think it's nice to talk about Paris' pimples," said Melissa.

"Will you all shut up about my pimples?" Paris said.

"I'll bet none of you knows what 'hirsute' means," Lazarus said. He had been studying the dictionary as usual, expanding his vocabulary.

"Hairy," Paris said.

Lazarus glared at her. Paris glared at Everett, who was wolfing down his second huge piece of chocolate cake.

"I got some nice fruit for you, Paris," Lavinia said.

"I don't want fruit."

"Wait till tonight when she stuffs herself over at Papa's," Lazarus said.

"So what?" Lavinia snapped. "She has a right."

Jonah sat there almost asleep, the dormouse at the tea party. He always tried to be invisible when they started squabbling. He didn't know why they had to snap at each other when they all loved each other. Families should be kind to each other.

"Can we go to the movies tonight?" Paris asked, as usual, the pest.

"No," Lavinia said. "We're going to Papa's."

For all their squabbles, Paris and Everett were good friends anyway, mainly because they had no one else at Windflower to be friends with. At last in his cousin Everett found an audience for his sex fantasies. She believed everything he told her. No matter that there were a few details of the gang-bang that were inaccurate; she didn't know the difference and she was impressed. She wasn't shocked. She thought Everett was a man of the world. For her he wove tales of his sexual conquests in Florida, the girls who chased him and found him irresistible, and she believed those too. It didn't seem strange to her that Everett never went out with a girl while he was here in the North. He didn't have to. A life of adventure was waiting for him whenever he chose to indulge in it, and after all, everyone knew that you led a different life in front of your parents than you did when you were free. It was only respectful. Even sophisticated Uncle Basil, who goodness knows everyone knew about, put on the act of being a shy shnook when he was with the family.

Paris supposed that someday if neither she nor Everett found anyone they liked, they would probably have to marry each other. It wasn't so unusual for cousins to marry. It had happened before in the family. It was nice to feel secure and know there would be a husband waiting for her when she would be old enough to have to marry. It meant she didn't have to go out with those awful boys they dragged to school dances. She couldn't imagine herself ever going out with one of them.

Sometimes when her mother and Aunt Melissa went into the town to buy groceries they let her come along so she could go to the library. She had gotten a library card first thing, and she took out piles of books: novels and short stories. Her favorite writers were still F. Scott Fitzgerald and John O'Hara, and she was in love with the Twenties. She had asked her mother about the Twenties, but her mother hadn't been a flapper, she had missed it all. How could someone have missed it all when they were the right age? It was a shame she herself had been born too late.

She had started writing children's books and illustrating them. It started because one day she said she was bored. There wasn't anything interesting to read in that house and she had finished all her library books, no one wanted to go swimming with her, her father was in the city so she had no one to play tennis with, and she was sick of listening to the grownups talk.

"You're bored?" her mother said. "Go write a book."

So Paris did. She didn't intend to send it to a publisher, but it was something to do. It was easy to write a children's book because it was short, so she wrote another one. They were fantasies; one about a lonely little boy and another about an outcast fish. Neither of them had friends so they had to fend for themselves. The little boy had an invisible midget to play with and the fish went around looking for friends but all the other fish rejected him. Her favorite subject matter was loneliness.

She was allowed to lock the outside door from her room to the hall, because there were men in the house and they had a male butler who might walk in on you with the vacuum cleaner in his hand while you were undressed, but she was not allowed to close the door which led to her parents' room. Her mother said it kept the air from ventilating and made it too hot. Paris knew better. There was no privacy in that house, not for children anyway. A child had the same status as a privileged pet. She was something to be watched with curiosity and amusement and exasperation, something to be talked about and over as if she couldn't hear or understand, something to amuse the adults. That was why people had children and made a family, so they would have built-in entertainment. But the children were expected to be good pets; to be obedient, respectful, neat and clean, polite, and talented; do tricks; get good marks. She could hear her father snore at night and she hoped that her parents didn't decide to have sex together because then she would hear them and it would be disgusting. So far they had behaved themselves and done nothing.

Sex was still something to be sorted out in her mind. She knew what people did, but she didn't know what they thought, how they felt. Why, for example, would her parents want to keep their door open? Why did she have a strange suspicion whenever Everett twisted her arm to tease her that he really wanted to kiss her? Sometimes Everett did make her let him kiss her on the mouth, when she had to bribe him to take her into town to the post office, or let her come to the movies with him. She didn't like it when he kissed her. It was a chaste kiss with closed lips, but there was nothing sexy or friendly about it, it was sort of desperate. Everett thought she was a pet too, just like the grownups did. Why didn't he kiss a girl his own age? She would yell at him, "Incest!" and that made him furious. He would hit her and twist her arm until she shrieked, and then her mother and his mother would come running into the room and her mother would yell at him that Paris had thin bones and not to break her arm.

"I don't know why those kids always have to fight," Melissa would say.

Paris knew. But she wasn't telling. Your first loyalty in matters of sex came to the person nearest your own age, whether you liked him or not. The older people wouldn't understand.

FOUR

The war was over. Jack Nature, still a sergeant and still untouched, got his honorable discharge, and he and Rosemary came back to New York and moved into the apartment Papa had gotten for them in the Edwardian. It was hard to get a place to live, and Rosemary considered herself lucky, even though the apartment wasn't as big as she would have liked. It was hers, and it was a home. She had never been much of a housekeeper or a cook, and she liked the built-in maid service the hotel gave its tenants, plus the nearness of all sorts of restaurants where she and Jack could eat dinner. He went right back to his father's dry cleaning company. Old Natelson was ailing and semiretired; he had just been waiting for his only son to come home from the war. A month after Jack was settled into his old job at the company, feeling comfortable and managing well, his father had a stroke, lingered a few days, and died. Jack complained about the responsibilities and the hard work, but Rosemary knew he was pleased to be the boss.

Jack didn't believe in spending any more money than you had to. Rosemary didn't mind, since it bothered her a little that she had more money than he did. Not that anyone outside the family knew it, but still, the man was supposed to support the wife, not the other way around. They were frugal. It wasn't good to be showy. And besides, now they would start a family, and that took a lot of money.

While the war was on and they had been holed up in that hotel room near the Army base it hadn't bothered Rosemary too much that she hadn't become pregnant. They had sometimes forgotten to use anything but nothing happened. Other Army wives were having babies and then their husbands were sent overseas and killed or maimed. It seemed ironic that she was here in the States, so safe, and she hadn't become pregnant. But where could a baby sleep in their room, in the dresser drawer? But now the war was over, they had a nice apartment, and she was well into her thirties. She'd better hurry before it was too late.

She and Jack had already decided that they would go against convention and have only two. Both of them had known what it was like to be the youngest in a large family and they wanted their children to have what they had missed. They hoped they would have a boy and a girl. But if they had two boys or two girls they would stop anyway. Who wanted to keep trying and have six of one kind? Two kids was convenient. You could take them with you on vacations. You could send them to private schools and college without going barefoot to pay for it. You could live in a reasonable-size apartment, not a big barn. Two was perfect. But where was the first?

In May Rosemary and Jack moved into their new house in Windflower. It was such a beautiful place, so big, so beautifully landscaped. They played tennis every day when Jack came home from work, and on weekends they played both morning and afternoon. They swam in the lake. Rosemary had never looked or felt healthier. She still wasn't pregnant.

Jack drove to work every day so he rented a car for her. She was much in demand among the family because she could drive. She decided she would drive to the grocery store every day to do the food shopping and Hazel made a fuss. Hazel felt that the reins of authority had been snatched from her. It was darned annoying, Rosemary thought, to have to consult with Hazel every day about what they would have for dinner, just as if Hazel was a functioning grownup, but if she didn't then Hazel would sulk. It was unfair that she had to live with Hazel anyway. Nobody had consulted her. At least Herman hadn't shown his face yet, and with any luck his visits would be brief. Imagine, after running away from Herman all that time, here she was living in the same house with him. Their kid, Richie, looked like a very cute version of Herman. It was almost impossible to imagine Herman Winsor as a child, but here he was in front of her own eyes, a baby Herman, but cuddly. Still, there was already something about Richie that reminded her of an old man. He was a strange, serious little boy. He said he had a wife in the attic who no one could see but him. Imagine a seven-year-old dreaming up a wife! Richie was an old man all right.

"How's your wife, Richie?" Rosemary would ask.

"She's fine."

"Why don't you let her come down?"

"Oh no, she has to stay in the attic."

"Don't you think that's mean? Maybe she'd like to come down."

"No," Richie would say solemnly, "she likes it there."

When Rosemary had a baby then Richie would have a real child to play with. She hoped he wouldn't be too old by then.

Dinner with Hazel every night was no pleasure. Rosemary would be talking to Jack and Hazel would butt in. Hazel still hated to be left out, just as she'd been when she was young. Richie ate with them at the dinner table now. He never talked unless you asked him something.

Jack seemed to have become friends with Everett. The two of them would sit outside at night, telling dirty jokes, until the mosquitoes drove them in. Jack had a whole collection of unsavory jokes he'd learned in the Army. Everett seemed to love them. Rosemary couldn't take much of it and then she'd find something to do in the house.

Even after all these years and coming back here as a happily married woman, it still made Rosemary cringe inside when they had to go over and see Etta. She still remembered how she'd felt when Papa had brought Etta home and she was still living at home and had to go right on living there with Etta in Mama's place. It was funny how you never outgrew the things you felt when you were young. They didn't hurt so much, they went further away, but they were still there inside you.

Papa looked older. He looked young for his age but Rosemary couldn't help noticing that he was a middle-aged man. He loved his work and would never retire. He went into the city every day. This place was his dream, and even though there were things about living there that none of then liked—this community living was difficult—they had to do it for his sake. He had worked hard for it. All their money had come from him, and they should be darned grateful. Rosemary had never made a cent in her life, yet she was rich.

Papa was always doing things for people. He'd built the loveliest little house for the caretaker and his family. It looked like the drawings of dream houses Rosemary had seen in magazines during the war, when everyone was dreaming of coming home to a little white house with rambler roses and a white picket fence, and a lawn and a vegetable garden and two kids and a family dog. There it all was, and the caretaker and his family were living in it, complete with the family dog, a mutt. Tim Forbes worked hard, though. No matter how early she woke up, Rosemary would see him working out on the grounds, sitting on his tractor with the cigarette drooping between his lips, bent over his prize roses, up on a ladder pruning a huge tree, spraying trees, clipping hedges, building a stone wall to make sure Steiglitz didn't intrude on their right of way, painting the metal furniture down at the pavilion, cleaning dead leaves out of the drainpipe, repairing screens, moving the sprinkler system that watered the huge lawns as the sun moved in the sky. There was no end to the work. A man had to love nature to spend so much time worrying about keeping things alive.

The man was so busy that he hadn't bothered to go to the doctor even though he'd been complaining all summer about his bad back. Papa had told him to take the day off, your health came first, but Tim would keep putting it off. Maybe he was afraid to go to the doctor. Lots of men were. They'd just keep hoping it would go away by itself. He'd go in the fall, he said, when the family moved back to the city and there wasn't so much work to do on the gardens.

It was the middle of September and they were planning to move back because Paris and Everett had to go to school. Tim Forbes had already rolled up the awnings and taken the terrace furniture in. Rosemary thought he looked very tired and thin, quite awful in fact. He and his wife were Irish Catholics and they had only the two kids. She wondered if they kept a calendar. Here she was thinking about their kids, wondering about their private life, wondering about everybody's private life who had kids. Catholics didn't use birth control. It must be easier not to have kids than everyone thought. All her life she'd thought if she ever did it once she'd get pregnant, and it wasn't until she got married and lost her virginity that she discovered it wasn't so. Maybe she should have tried to have a baby right from the start of her marriage, when she was younger, and then perhaps she'd have had a chance. Sometimes she saw Molly Forbes shepherding her two little boys and Richie down to the lake to play, or for a run across the hills, or across the road to see the horses, and she wished it were she with her own little kids. What did it take to have a kid? Lavinia used to say, "Any cow can have a calf," whenever any of her friends acted as if the very act of birth made them a kind of madonna, but sometimes Rosemary was sure that what was true for cows and all the rest of nature had nothing whatsoever to do with human beings.

It was Indian summer, hot. Rosemary went over to Lavinia's house to sit on the screened porch. Every afternoon Lavinia and Melissa sat on their cool porch and talked and ate fruit, and Rosemary and Hazel often joined them, Hazel knitting or doing her puzzles. The grass was dry and brown from the heat spell and there were clumps of algae on the lake. You couldn't swim, it was awful-looking.

"Tim Forbes is in the hospital," Lavinia said.

"The hospital?" Melissa said. "When did you hear that?"

"He finally went to the doctor and they gave him a chest x-ray, and it's . . ." She lowered her voice and looked around. "Cancer."

"Ooh!" Melissa bit her knuckle.

"He got worse fast, just like that. The doctors think he's done for."

"At his age?" Melissa said.

"Gee, she's got those two young kids," Rosemary said.

"Oh, let's not talk about it, it's too gruesome," Lavinia said. She had been very fond of Tim because they both loved flowers the same way and talked about them the same way, as if flowers were human.

The next month, when the family was back in the city, Tim Forbes died. Rosemary heard about it later. Papa went up to Windflower where the young widow was bewildered and in tears. This place was the only home she and her children had known in America. It had all happened so fast, and now she was alone.

Papa told her she could stay in her house forever, rent free. Her sons would continue to go to the local school. She would be the caretaker. Papa would hire a gardener-handyman from outside to come in and do day work. At first Molly Forbes couldn't believe it, but Papa insisted he meant it. When he went away and drove back to New York she seemed in a kind of shock that her life, which had been so suddenly torn apart, should be so quickly arranged again.

"Isn't that just like Papa?" Lavinia said proudly.

"He's a wonderful person," Jonah said. "One in a million."

I'll never envy her having kids again, Rosemary thought. Still, there was the rest of the world to envy. What was a woman without children? A man and wife weren't a family, they were just a couple. What would she do if God forbid something happened to Jack? She would be all alone. If she had kids . . . Kids made a house warm. Kids gave a life purpose. No matter that she and Jack had everything in common and got along so well together, there was something missing. What had she ever done that she had to be so punished?

FIVE

In a school that gives no marks it is impossible to tell if you will get into college until your senior year, when the principal tells you what the teachers have known all along and have kept a secret. The girls in Paris' class were very nervous, trying to make a joke about getting into some junior college that would take anyone, and worrying themselves sick that they would be the one who had to go there. Paris sent for some college brochures. She knew her parents would decide which was the best college for her to go to after the principal gave her the alternatives. She was sure she wouldn't have to go to the joke junior college, but beyond that it didn't really matter. It just had to be a college. College had the mystique, names didn't matter.

When she and her parents went to see the principal for the news Paris was very surprised when the principal said she could go to any college she wanted to. It had never occurred to her that the field would be wide open for her. In her trimonthly reports the teachers had always complained she was not working to her "full capacity." She had assumed that meant she wasn't getting As. It hadn't.

"Where do you think you would like to go?" the principal asked. Paris looked at her mother.

"We want her to go to Radcliffe," her mother said.

"What's Radcliffe?" Paris asked her.

"It's the girls' part of Harvard," her mother said. Her father nodded his approval.

"I want to go to Radcliffe," Paris said.

"Good," the principal said. "Very good. I'm sure you can get in. There is one thing you might consider though. You're only going to be sixteen next year. Maybe you would want to stay out for a year, take some sort of courses here at home, and become more mature, older. Then you could start college nearer to the age of the other girls."

"I agree with that," her mother said.

"What courses?" Paris said. "If I can get into college now, why do I need courses?"

"But you would be so far away from home, all alone," her mother said. "We just want you to stay home for a year so you can grow more mature."

"Do people get more mature automatically? I thought you got more mature from living."

"You'd be living," her mother said.

Paris thought of the tall shelves of books in the living room, the classics she hadn't read yet, her mother's college textbooks. She could stay home and read all of them and get an education no one else had. She knew when it came down to it they would never let her take courses. Her mother would keep her home in the apartment to be a friend and companion. They would have lunch at Schrafft's with Aunt Melissa and Aunt Cassie. All her friends from high school would be in college, living in other cities, and there would be no one left to be her friend. No one left her age. Her friends were her age, even though they were older chronologically. Her mother and aunts weren't her age. They wanted to make an oddity of her, half old woman like them, half permanent child kept at home to rot. It was tempting to think of reading all those books, tempting to put off a strange new experience until she was older and stronger, but she also sensed that if she stayed home she would never go to college. Oh, they thought she would get to college all right. But her mother clutched her with bonds stronger than claws. If she stayed at home with her mother and no friends for an entire year she would become so shy, so beaten down, so dependent, so strange, so unable to function, that she would be a better candidate for a mental institution than for Radcliffe.

"I want to go to college now," Paris said firmly.

"Why don't you think about it for a while," her mother said.

"I know I want to go to college now. I am old enough."

287

"They'll be eighteen," he mother said, "and you've never even been out with a boy."

"There are plenty of boys to meet at college and none here," Paris said.

"I'm sure she can handle the work," the principal said. "The only question is whether she feels she can handle the rest of it. Perhaps you'd like to consider a New York school."

"Where is Radcliffe?" Paris asked.

"Cambridge, Massachusetts," her father said.

"I want to go to Radcliffe," Paris said firmly.

If I don't go to Radcliffe, she thought, I'll never be a writer, and if I can't be a writer I'll kill myself.

They let her go up to Radcliffe for an interview. The dean of admissions said she certainly looked a lot older than fifteen. Paris' parents were impressed with the school. They hoped she would be accepted. Even though they wanted her to stay out for a year they wanted her to be the one who was able to say no or yes, not the school. It would not do to be rejected anywhere in life, if possible.

During the next few months Paris' mother several times brought up the subject of staying out and Paris rejected it. Eventually Paris realized she had won; her mother was waiting as eagerly as she was for the letter of acceptance to arrive in the mail. She was the only girl in her class to have applied to only one school. Everyone else had applied to at least four. It was a gamble, her friends told her, and she was crazy, and good luck. Paris really wasn't afraid that she wouldn't get in. After all, if a school knew they were the only school you had applied to, wouldn't they be flattered?

The letter of acceptance finally came. Everyone was pleased and relieved, but not as relieved as Paris was. For the first time she realized the terrible gamble she had taken. If she hadn't been accepted then she would have had to stay home after all.

When her parents told her grandfather the good news he was so pleased that he sent Paris a check for the entire first year's tuition. He didn't like to be bothered remembering birthdays, and he didn't believe in Christmas, so this was the first present he'd given her since she was a baby. Paris knew he was proud of her. *He* wouldn't have wanted her to stay home and rot! He was a progressive old man and he respected her. You didn't have to have long conversations with someone to know how he felt about you. It was a new era in fashion: the New Look. Paris owned only one dress, two skirts, and three blouses, because she wore school uniforms every day except weekends. Wasn't she lucky that all the styles changed just this year when she had to buy everything new for college? She would buy long circle skirts with waist cinchers and lots of cashmere sweaters and a plaid wool suit with a straight skirt and a matching hat with a feather in it to wear to football games. Her mother said they could shop up in Connecticut while they were at Windflower. She had already bought Paris three new silk blouses and carefully put in dress shields. Paris hated dress shields. She could hardly wait to get up to college and rip them out. Her mother was going to put dress shields in all her new cashmere sweaters too. Paris bought a pair of small scissors.

Cambridge would be cold so she and her mother had bought flannel pajamas with tight cuffs, and woolen bed socks. Paris already had a fur coat, mouton. She'd had it since her sophomore year in high school. She knew she would love college even though everything about college was still a mystery. In the movies college kids belonged to fraternities and sororities and acted like jerks, but at Radcliffe they didn't have that. It was more sophisticated. Embarked on another step toward her master plan for life, Paris was beginning to feel sophisticated herself. She had just turned sixteen. No one dared give her a sweet sixteen party. She was a college girl (almost).

When the family moved up to Windflower that June, right after her graduation from high school, Paris suggested that they buy tickets to the local summer theater. It was the first time anyone had suggested that the family do anything outside their own grounds. Lavinia and Jonah, Melissa and Lazarus, Paris and Everett would go every week to see the plays. Since Paris couldn't drive yet, her parents dropped her off at the playhouse on their way to do the grocery shopping, gave her money for tickets to that week's performance so they could see if they liked the idea, and arranged to pick her up when they'd gotten the shopping done.

Paris really hadn't meant to ask for a job. When she walked into the lobby all she meant to do was buy tickets and see how much it cost for the season. But the first thing she saw was an unflattering photograph of that week's star, standing in a frame in the lobby, and the next thing she saw was the door to the auditorium was open, the stage curtains were open, and kids her age were doing things with scenery. She suddenly felt an excitement she had never known before. She had been in plays at high school, but this was real, this was professional theater. It even smelled different, like a real theater, not like a school full of kids. Everybody looked very informal and she wasn't in the least frightened, only fascinated. She asked who was in charge, and someone directed her to a fat young man in shirtsleeves.

"That photo in the lobby is awful," Paris told him. "In New York we have caricatures of the stars that we put in the lobby each week."

"Who's we?"

She blithely ignored him and went on. "I'm a professional artist, and I would be glad to make the caricature for you every week if you would let me work here. It would help your business a lot. You wouldn't have to pay me. Just let me help paint scenery and so on."

"Pay you?" the fat young man said, amused. "The apprentices here pay us for the privilege."

"Why?"

"They get acting classes and a chance to act in plays when we need someone to fill in."

"Oh, I'd love that," Paris said.

"Well, if you're really an artist, bring in a picture and then I'll see."

"I'll draw one right now of that actor in the photo. Do you have any paper?"

One thing she could do was make a fast sketch that really resembled the person. She had done caricatures of her whole graduating class for their senior yearbook. She made a sketch and showed the man, and he was impressed.

"Okay," he said pleasantly. "You can start work here tomorrow. I'll give you the advance publicity photos to work from, or if you want I'll let you meet the stars and you can sketch from life if they let you."

"And can I be an apprentice too?"

"You'll have to do a lot of dirty work. Paint scenery, run errands, take notes, but you'll learn a lot too."

"And I won't have to pay?"

"No."

"Wonderful!"

"What's your name?" he asked.

For a moment Paris tried to think of a glamorous stage name but she couldn't manage to make any name but her own pass her lips. Her throat just dried up with the fear of being a hypocrite. "Paris Mendes," she said. He would probably think it was a terrible name.

"Made that up, huh?"

"No, it's mine."

"Okay, Paris. I'm Andy."

She went to the box office and bought tickets, and then she waited in front of the theater until her parents and Aunt Melissa came to get her.

"Here are your tickets and I have a job."

"A what?"

"I'm going to work at the playhouse drawing caricatures of the stars that they'll put in the lobby every week."

"You always were good at drawing," her mother said.

"And they'll let me be an apprentice. I'll learn all about the theater and even get to be in a play."

"Oh!" Melissa said. All sorts of expressions crossed her face: pleasure, longing, disapproval.

"That's fine," her mother said, "as long as you don't have to go there all the time."

"But I have to go there every day."

"Who's going to take you?" Melissa said.

"There's always somebody going to town. There are cars."

"We're not taking you every day," her mother said.

"Then I'll take a taxi."

"With what for money?"

"Please can't somebody take me? Everett has nothing to do. You could take turns. I'd drive if I could, you know that."

"Well, I could take her," her father said.

"You'd have to take her home too."

"Maybe I could get a ride home," Paris said.

"You are not going in cars with strangers," her mother said. "That's out."

"Your good-natured old father, recruited again," her father said. He seemed rather pleased. Paris thought he would probably like

291

to be an apprentice too if he could. Who wouldn't? It was the most exciting thing that had ever happened to her. A real job! It suddenly hit her what she had done. If she'd thought of how important it was she never would have had the courage to ask for the job, but something had just come over her, and it had all happened so easily. If she'd planned on it she never would have done it, never.

They teased her at Windflower about being stage struck, and they grumbled about who would drive her to work, but she managed to get there most days without too much begging. Every night she prayed that they would let her go the next morning, that someone would finally volunteer. Everett was the worst. He had to extract his price from her first; she had to let him kiss her and rub his hands over her breasts and try to get at her crotch. He was certainly disgusting. Paris dressed in jeans deliberately now, and shapeless shirts, to keep Everett away. When he tried to get his hand between her legs he was foiled because of the jeans. She would never wear a dress in his presence, even though her mother's nagging was becoming incessant. If her mother or his mother happened to come into the room while Everett was mauling her he would immediately change the sex play to horseplay, twisting her arm, and Paris would scream, the mother would scream, Everett would let her go, and then there was that awful moment when Everett had to decide whether or not he had been cheated of his price. If he hadn't been cheated, he would drive her to the playhouse. If he had been cheated, then he wouldn't drive her anywhere, and letting him kiss and maul her had all been wasted.

She and Everett were so different, and it was a shame *he* was the one who had a car and a driver's license. He was twenty-two years old, and after finally getting to be a junior at college he had dropped out. He'd been kicked out of college twice for getting bad marks and failing his tests, and both times Grandpa had gone to the dean or the trustees or someone and donated a big amount of money to the college and then they had taken Everett back on probation. Now Everett just lounged around Windflower, lazy and selfish. No job was good enough for him, he said. He wouldn't go into the family business, not that it would be any great loss not to have a jerk like him, and he wouldn't work for anyone else either. What Everett wanted was for his mother to set him up with a radio repair shop in Miami. He called it "the radio business." Aunt Melissa probably would—she never refused him anything, and at least he'd be working. He didn't even go out on dates with girls. Paris had begun to realize that Everett really didn't know any girls, in spite of all the wild stories he used to tell her when she was younger and gullible. A twenty-two-year-old boy had no business jumping on his little cousin who was practically his little sister. He was too old for that. But the trouble was, she was just getting old enough for that, and he was more interested in her than ever. She had decided she would never marry him. He didn't attract her. She would have to marry nobody. It didn't matter now, her days were full with the playhouse and her struggles to get there.

If she went to the playhouse in the morning her mother made her come home for lunch, and then no one wanted to drive her back for the afternoon. She could hardly blame them; it was hot in the afternoon. But she wasn't allowed to bring her lunch in a paper bag, because as her mother and aunt said, they were paying the help good money to serve their lunch and Paris could eat it with the family like a human being. The alternative, which she usually chose, was to go without lunch and cadge as much free candy and orange drink as she could from the candy concession in the theater. The apprentices ran the concession anyway, and a box of chocolate-covered almonds, while they were on the forbidden list for Paris' skin, made a satisfactory lunch. She told her mother they gave lunch to the apprentices. That wasn't a lie; candy was lunch.

She loved the playhouse. She had met several stars and had made caricatures of them. All the stars liked the drawings except one, who said it wasn't flattering enough. The others were very sweet to her. She was allowed to watch rehearsals and take notes for the producer, and although they hadn't yet had any promised acting lessons Paris felt that being around the plays in production served as acting lessons. She thought maybe it was all a fake, they took the kids' money and then never gave them acting lessons at all, and she was glad she didn't have to pay. Whatever she got was a bonus. She was the only one who didn't want to be a professional actor and who was going on to college in the fall. They were all friendly and nice to her.

One evening Paris and her family were just sitting down to

dinner when a girl phoned her from the playhouse.

"Can you dance?"

"No," Paris said.

"That's all right, we'll teach you. It's just social dancing, you know, ballroom."

"Oh, I can do that."

"Do you have a long dress?"

"No," Paris said.

"That's all right, we'll borrow one to fit you. One of the girls is sick and we need an extra girl for one scene tonight. Can you be here in an hour?"

"Me? You want me?"

"Yeah. Can you do it"

"Sure I can!" Paris said, and raced to tell the family.

They all had to come to see her make her professional debut. She felt like a star. So what if it was only one scene, it was a scene the star was in, and he actually touched her in it, bumped into her in fact, so that made her a real part of the scene. There was the audience, laughing and having a good time. Paris wasn't the least bit nervous. The boy she was dancing with was a nervous wreck, but she thought he was probably very stupid. This was just summer theater after all, and half those people in the audience were their neighbors even though they didn't know each other, so how could it be scary? It was wonderful!

She knew the family thought it was nothing. Her part was nothing. They weren't in the least impressed although they were polite. Foo on them.

The next day the producer spoke to her for the first time. "I think I might have another part for you," he said. "I'm trying to get the rights to a musical, if it's not too expensive. I'm going to let you audition for a speaking part. You have a flair for comedy. I'll let you know when in a week or so."

Paris told her mother, who didn't seem at all impressed. It was strange how they seemed to think this summer theater was absolutely nothing. They thought she was crazy to want to work during the summer when she could be at a nice place like Windflower enjoying herself.

"Why do you want to work when you don't have to?" her father said. "You don't need the money."

"They don't pay me anyway."

"Why should you work? You can work later on when you grow up."

"I *like* this, it's fun."

They had changed the bill after the one night of Paris' professional theatrical debut, and now they were doing a murder mystery. There wasn't much to do and the apprentices were hanging around the lobby in the afternoon when Aunt Rosemary came to drive Paris home. She was the only one who didn't live at the theater. She said goodbye to her friends and trotted off after Aunt Rosemary.

"Who was that boy?"

"Which boy?" Paris asked.

"The one who had his arm around you."

Which one was that? Oh, yes, him. "None of them are famous," Paris said. "They're just the other apprentices."

"Is he your boyfriend?"

"No."

When they got back to the house Aunt Rosemary told Paris' mother that there was a boy with his arm around Paris. He was an older boy, Rosemary said, at least eighteen, and you never knew what was going on in that place when a boy put his arm right around her shoulders.

After that no one would ever drive Paris to the playhouse again. They said they were too busy, even Everett. Her father tried to make it up to her by playing tennis with her, but Paris didn't want to play tennis. She wanted to be at the playhouse. She was very lonely.

"Ha! I heard about that place, all the sex going on," Everett said to her.

"What sex?"

"Rosemary saw."

"She saw nothing," Paris said, indignant.

"You don't need to know those people," her mother said. "They're not for you."

Now she would never audition for the musical, never get the part. She would sit here and rot, they would have their way. There was no sex at the playhouse. What did the family know about anything anyway? Everett lured her down to the lake when no one was there and said he would show her what the college boys would try to do to her when she got to college. She had to fight him off. He kept trying to show her and she kept telling him she would find out when she got there. Him with his flying hands and long bony fingers, mean fox mouth, and sneaky ways. But the family was afraid a boy at the playhouse had put his arm around her and would try to get her into trouble. They should only know.

SIX

Adam had always been a Republican, in fact he was the only one in the family who had actually voted for Alf Landon instead of Franklin Delano Roosevelt. Lazarus and Jonah were Republicans because they both believed the Republican Party was for business. Andrew and Basil were Democrats and liberals, although neither of them had to mingle with the underprivileged people they were so outspoken about helping. Herman was a Southern Democrat and a conservative. Jack, reluctantly, was a Democrat because it seemed to him the lesser of two evils. In point of fact, he hated everybody and thought they were all out to do him no good. Everett, who had voted for the first time, was a conservative Southern Democrat and an outspoken bigot. No party was really conservative enough for him, but he did the best he could. The wives voted with their husbands.

They all read different newspapers, and whenever they had an argument on issues of the day each one quoted the newspaper he read, which always elicited the same comment from his opponent: "What do you expect, reading that propaganda?" The only one whose taste in newspapers was eclectic was Lazarus, who read whatever he could pick up free on the seat of the subway or the commuter train, left behind by the previous occupant. *Wall Street Journal* or *Daily Worker*, it didn't matter if it was free.

But of all the family, Basil was the most involved in issues of the day. At forty he had aged well, his body trim, his hair still sleek and black. His face was no longer pretty, it had "character." Basil always had the luck to look like whatever was the ideal for the decade. Israel had become a nation, and Basil was a Zionist.

He spent a good deal of time helping to raise funds for Israel and the Jewish refugees who emigrated there. Other people gave money to plant trees, but Basil wanted to build hospitals and schools. He had made quite a name for himself among the other fund raisers as a generous and rich man, as well as an enthusiastic worker. It was rather unusual to see a bachelor of his age working for the cause. Most of them were younger, or else were married men. The married women thought it was a shame that Basil was not interested in meeting their daughters. Some of them would even have foisted their granddaughters on him if they could. Such a catch! Such a good family, so handsome and well educated, so dedicated to the cause! He's Adam Saffron's son, you know. The bachelor son. Such a waste!

There was one woman co-worker who interested Basil. She was French, a Jewish refugee herself, and her name was Nicole Wolfe. She was a blonde giantess in her early thirties, an inch taller than he was, with broad shoulders and craggy cheekbones. Her fingernails, covered with dark polish, looked like ten plums. She had straight posture and a loud, authoritative voice. She was an authority on everything. Her strong French accent only seemed to make her sound more authoritative to Basil.

"Art?" Nicole would say disdainfully. "You call American art Art? It's illustration. French artists are the only real artists. You compare a Norman Rockwell with a Marc Chagall? An Andrew Wyeth with a Picasso? Ridiculous!"

"But Chagall is Russian," Basil would say lamely. "And Picasso is Spanish."

"They live in France; they are French. Besides Chagall is a Jew, and all Jews are one. What American Jew has become famous in art, tell me that, eh? In France the Jewish artist is respected."

Basil, whose knowledge of the arts was rather limited, would always end up losing any discussion to her.

"Do you tell me this slop is food?" Nicole would say. "If you want to eat real food, you go to Lyons, you go to Paris. There you eat well. Here the food is a joke."

"There are some good French restaurants in New York," Basil said.

"Oh, I don't believe it."

"Yes, Nicole, really."

So he ended up taking her to one, where she ordered the food and the wine, complained about the quality, told Basil she would take him to an art gallery and show him a "real" painter, and accepted his invitation to go to another French restaurant the following night. He took her to the symphony, where she lectured him on music, to the ballet, where she reeled off names of dancers she preferred to the "klutzes" on the stage there, to the theater, where she told him if he had not seen French theater in the original French (which he did not understand) he had not really seen theater at all. She made him take a French course at Berlitz. She laughed at his accent. She took an English course, but Basil did not laugh at her accent, he complimented her. He was quite in awe of her. He had never met a woman like her before. They were always trying to please him, so servile and obvious in their efforts to prove what good companions and eventually good wives they could be, but Nicole lived only to "improve" him. She had fled the Germans without a sou, but she didn't ask him for anything. When he tried to give her gifts she had to be persuaded to take them. She in turn gave him lists of books he had to buy and read and a list of wines he had to buy for his closet "wine cellar," and made him change his barber.

Basil ordinarily did not spend much money on women, and he was surprised to discover that when he had known Nicole for six months he had managed to redecorate her one-room apartment, buy her six prints and one piece of sculpture (all French), and given her a gold wristwatch, a string of pearls, and a fur jacket. It was the only thing she was willing to accept that was not French; it was Russian broadtail.

She made him take her skiing. She was an excellent skiier. Basil fell down and sprained his ankle on the way from the ski lodge to the chair lift. He was sure he had done it subconsciously on purpose because he had never skied in his life and was terrified, and when Nicole accused him of just that he cringed. The only place she did not criticize him was in bed; there she only criticized the other women he had been with and said they had all lacked the soul and heart and fire of a Frenchwoman.

Finally, in desperation to find something she would not criticize, Basil took Nicole to Windflower that summer for a day. She was the first date he had ever taken there. She put on her bathing cap, and in her regulation Olympic swimsuit she made a perfect swan dive into the lake, swam to the float and back, and climbed out, not even breathing hard.

"A beautiful place, Basil," she said. Triumph!

The family did not like Nicole. She didn't like them either. They all had dinner at Papa's house that night, and then Basil drove Nicole back to New York because he was ashamed to make her sleep in the guest room. She would have laughed at him and said that Americans were prudes and hypocrites, as she had told him many times before.

"They are all manipulating you, your family," Nicole said on the way back to the city. "No wonder you've never married. They want to control you."

"They'd love for me to get married," Basil protested.

"Zut! You're so naïve."

"But why would they want to keep me single?"

"No one is good enough for them. They wouldn't like any woman you brought into their world. They're provincial. They need a good breath of fresh air."

Basil frowned. He didn't like it when anyone dared to criticize his family. Nicole gave him a sharp look and lit a cigarette. He had given her a gold lighter from Cartier, because Cartier was French. "I like your father though," she said. "That man is a genius."

Basil felt the tightened muscles at the back of his neck and shoulders begin to relax. Even Nicole realized how special his father was.

"You *should* get married, you know," Nicole said thoughtfully.

"Why?"

"You need your independence from them. You're not a child any more. You should get away, lead your own life, and the only way you can do that is with a strong woman on your side."

"But I don't want to get away from them. I love them."

"I don't mean tear the roots," she said. "I mean you should travel, see the world, be a mensch. Ah, comment peut-on parler avec un idiot?"

"Were you calling me an idiot?"

"Sartre was. He and Simone de Beauvoir have a perfect relationship. They are together but they live separately."

"Well, so are we," Basil said.

"That doesn't work in America. Here it's all two by two like Noah's ark. For me, I'd rather be free. But I think you should marry."

"Why should I get married if you don't want to?" Basil said. "You're a woman, you're supposed to get married. Why haven't you ever married anyway?"

She shrugged. "No man was ever good enough for me."

"Then why do you waste your time with me?"

"I don't know. I suppose because I love you."

She had never said she loved him before. She had said she was fond of him, that they got along well together, that she had tender feelings toward his little stupidities, but never that she loved him. Basil waited for the familiar thrill and letdown of conquest, but it didn't come. He had not conquered, she had. He was waiting around for her approval, but whenever she gave him a scrap of it he felt only relieved, not triumphant. Who was Nicole Wolfe anyway? An education gotten on the run, a life of peril, no money, no background, who even knew if she would be as chic in Paris as she claimed to be here in New York among the barbarians. Perhaps on her own ground she would be merely another pushy bourgeoise. How did he know her clothes were chic? Because she said so. How did he know she was even quoting Sartre or anyone else for that matter? He hadn't read them. But she fascinated him, she could make him do whatever she wanted him to, and Basil realized he was in love with her.

That weekend he went to Windflower alone. No one mentioned Nicole. Finally he couldn't stand the suspense. They were all sitting in Papa's living room after dinner.

"Well, I'm glad you met Nicole," Basil said to the room at large. "She's a fascinating woman."

"You're serious about that one?" Papa asked casually.

"I could be."

"I hope you know better."

Permission having been given, the dam broke. They all had something to contribute. Nicole was obviously a fortune hunter. The way she looked around the houses, practically taking inventory. Those clothes, atrocious. Those manners, so loud, so conceited. Such a know-it-all! Nothing was good enough for her. Such an accent, who could understand her? Didn't she know she was in America now? It was French this, French that, and everything American was no good according to her. Let her go back and live in France if everything was so perfect there. Always criticizing Basil, right in front of his own family! Wasn't he insulted? They were certainly insulted. What did he know about her anyway? Who was she? Where was she from? What made her think she was so much better than any of them? The way she went prancing around in that bathing suit, you'd think she was a movie star. She was a giantess. She looked like a man. She thought she was gorgeous. What was the matter with Basil anyway, had she hypnotized him?

"She's good for me," Basil said.

"Then you don't need our opinion, do you?" Papa said.

"I want your approval."

"For that I have to wait and see," Papa said.

Did that mean there was a chance? What did that mean? Basil decided to be hopeful. He invited Nicole up to Windflower the following weekend. She was totally unlike herself: sweet and smiling and complimenting everyone. Basil hardly recognized her. She hugged and kissed Richie and said how much she loved children. Basil had never heard her even mention children in all the time he had known her, except to say it was a good idea the Israelis had: to bring up their children in a separate dormitory on the kibbutz so the parents didn't have to be bothered with them. She acted very interested in all Lavinia's and Melissa's clothes, asking them which were their favorite stores. When they told her they had their things made she wrote down the names of all the places. She complimented Etta on the meals, and went into the kitchen to compliment Henny after dinner. She never stopped raving over the beauty of the estate, the gardens, the trees, the waterfall, the woods. Basil thought how nice it would be if she were always this compliant. But then she wouldn't be Nicole. Still, maybe she could change a little. He had changed for her, catering to her every wish. He could picture himself married to this new, nice Nicole. If he managed to be everything she wanted, then there would be nothing left for her to criticize, and then she would be nice. Look how nice she was already, trying to make the family like her.

"Do you think they liked me a little more?" she asked after the weekend was over. It was the first time Basil had ever seen her show doubt about anything.

"I don't see how they could have resisted you," he said.

"Oh, they're polite. But they still don't approve of me."

"But you'll see, they'll learn to love you."

"Yes? Perhaps."

He asked them again what they thought of her. They all looked at him as if he were a simpleton. Who did she think she was fooling, they asked. What an act! No one could be that sweet.

"No one can ever please you!" Basil said angrily to the family. He told Nicole they had liked her. He didn't see why everyone had to collaborate on trying to drive him crazy. All he wanted was for Nicole and his family to get along. If everyone got along, then he could ask her to marry him.

By fall nothing had changed. The family criticism was now stony silence. They were just biding their time, waiting for Basil to tire of her as he had of so many other women. Basil was depressed and worried. He would never give her up, but they had to like her. He couldn't marry someone they didn't like.

He took her to Papa's for the dinner that broke the Yom Kippur fast. No one ever brought an outsider to these family religious things, only an announced fiancée. He told Papa it would be nice to give Nicole a real home Yom Kippur evening for a change, poor Nicole, so far from home and without family. It started out as a mistake and grew rapidly worse. Nicole was horrified that no one but herself had fasted all day, and then she was horrified that the family did not observe both the evening before and the night after. She told them they were bad Jews, heathens.

"This service is not to socialize, it's to pray to God to forgive your sins," she said.

"You're not the only one who owns God," Lavinia said.

"The family! The family! All you all ever think of is the family," Nicole said. They had managed to struggle through dinner and now were in the living room, except for Paris and Everett, who were playing Chinese checkers in the bedroom the way they always had in the back room when they were children in Brooklyn.

"But what else is there but the family?" Papa said, amused. "What good is gelt, success, fame, if you don't have the love of your good family?"

"Basil doesn't need you," Nicole said. "He needs me. I will

be his family. Why can't you let him be a man?"

Basil couldn't look at any of them; he left the apartment. In the hall he could still hear Nicole's strident voice berating his family, berating his *Papa*! He cringed, but at the same time he listened with a pounding heart, as if he were a child eavesdropping on his parents fighting over him.

"Let Basil marry me," Nicole said. "I am the best thing that ever happened to him. He is unhappy all the time. If he married me he would be healthy and happy, and you would see no more sad, quiet little Basil in the corner. You would see a real man. Let him grow up!"

He heard them murmuring then, and after a few moments the sounds of their voices seemed unthreatening, pleasant. He ventured to come back into the apartment again. Nicole walked to his side and took his hand in hers.

"We are going to get married, Basil," she said. "Your father wants to give you his blessing."

Basil looked at Papa. He couldn't tell what Papa was thinking, but at least he didn't look angry.

"May I have your blessing, Papa?" he asked.

Papa nodded thoughtfully. Nicole kissed Basil on the mouth in front of everyone.

"Good yuntif!" she cried. "Happy New Year!"

The family was all murmuring good yuntif to each other and looking a little in shock still, as if none of this could possibly have happened to them in this safe, quiet place. Nicole went over to Papa and kissed him right on the mouth. One of the women gasped. Even Papa looked quite horrified at this imposition.

"I am your new daughter, Papa," Nicole said happily. She went back to Basil and put her arm around him. "My husband," she said.

"Future husband," Basil said. He was surprised he had managed to get the words out because he was still in such a nervous state. Future husband. Husband. He was going to marry Nicole! He was very happy. He tried to remember when he had first proposed to her and he realized he never really had. They had simply understood each other. It was as if she had read his mind. That was what a husband and wife should be, one mind, one body. He was glad he had waited for her. She was quite a woman.

SEVEN

In the fall of 1947 Paris went off to college, decided to major in English literature since there was no creative writing major, and fell in love with four boys at once. For the first time in four years instead of being the new kid at school she was only one of many new kids, and therefore not an outsider at all. All the freshmen were as anxious to please and to make new friends as she was. But she discovered something very strange: a lot of the girls were not there to get an education; they were there to meet and marry Harvard men.

There were two girls down the hall in her dorm who roomed together and were both Jewish, Dottie and Selma. "You aren't going to go out with him, are you?" Dottie asked, horrified.

"Sure. Why not?"

"He's not Jewish."

"So what?" Paris said.

"So it won't last. You'll be wasting your time. I'd never go out with a boy who isn't Jewish."

"Well, I'm only sixteen, I'm not worried," Paris said.

"You're wasting your youth," Dottie said.

There were two other girls who roomed together and were Catholic, Agnes and Bernadette, and having already dated most of the football team they were planning to transfer to Holy Cross for their sophomore year. "There aren't enough Catholic boys at Harvard," Agnes said. "I don't want to end up an old maid."

One of the boys Paris was in love with lived in New York, and he asked her if she would go out with him during Christmas vacation. He would be her first real date in New York, imagine! He said he would take her to a night club. The only time she had been to a night club was in Miami Beach with her whole family, and that didn't count. His name was Spencer Kimberly and her friends made fun of him and called him Kimberly Spencer because he had two last names instead of a first name and a last name. He looked a little like a mouse, and he hadn't yet kissed her, but Paris loved him anyway. She had met him on a blind date.

On their first date they both said they were never going to get married to anyone and decided that when they graduated they would live together in Europe.

"I'm listed in the Social Register," said Spencer Kimberly Spencer.

"That's nice," Paris said. She didn't have the faintest idea what the Social Register was but she thought she'd better not ask.

"What church do you go to in New York?" he asked her.

"I don't go to church."

"Oh. Well, I don't go so often myself," he said.

"You didn't tell him you go to synagogue?" Dottie said later, aghast. "You'll be sorry."

"But I don't go to synagogue either."

"You should have told him you're Jewish. You'll be sorry."

"I would if he'd asked," Paris said. But she was glad he hadn't asked. Already she was discovering that there were people who had never met a Jew and thought being Jewish was inferior. It was strange, because her own family thought *not* being Jewish was inferior. Here, however, she was in the minority, and she wondered if her parents were right and that was how the world was going to be when she emerged into it.

Some of the society girls were the worst. Selma had a friend who was a debutante and a High Church Episcopalian, which was apparently fancy, and since both she and Selma came from New York they planned to see each other during Christmas vacation. But the debutante said she had to meet Selma on the street corner because her mother wouldn't let her be friends with Jews. Selma said she wouldn't see her at all in that case.

"See!" Dottie said.

"Oh, it's just her, she's a nut," Selma said.

"You'll see," Dottie said.

Paris could see it getting to some of the girls. It could be something as simple as someone asking your name and giving her just your first name because your last name would give you away. She saw other girls doing it, the gulp, the hesitation, and trapped at last, murmuring, "Bernstein." Paris determined it would never get to her; those girls who were ashamed were crazy and the girls who looked down on them were crazy too.

But when she got to New York for the holidays her parents acted peculiar. Suddenly her father was using a lot of Yiddish expressions in front of her boyfriends when they came to see her, and her father never used to talk like that. It was as if he wanted to make it perfectly clear that his daughter came from a Jewish household, in case the boy had any other ideas. The boys, who had come from fancy prep schools and led sheltered lives with their social but provincial families didn't seem to know what to make of it. It all went completely over their heads. The phone was always ringing, boys were crawling out of the woodwork, and then Paris' mother began the attack.

"You shouldn't waste your time on those boys," she said. "They won't be your lasting friends."

Even her mother was planning her future . . . already! It was frightening.

"Why don't you go to the Hillel Society when you go back to school? You'll meet some nice Jewish boys for a change. It's about time. Why don't you go to the Blind Dance next week? The boys from the nicest families go there, and you'll meet some boys who will take you out in the city."

"I go out every night."

"But with what?"

Six months ago she hadn't even liked boys, there hadn't been one boy she could stand. Now she liked them all and the world was closing in on her, picking and choosing for her, trying to match her up for life. Paris didn't want anyone to pick a husband for her. She wanted to fall in love in her own time, meet a hundred boys, marry when she was ready. But she knew that Spencer and she would never live together in Europe. Spencer would go his way and she would go hers, and by the time they graduated they probably wouldn't even be seeing each other at all. He was as much a dreamer as she was. His family would probably marry him off to some little mouse-faced debutante who looked just like him. He was too short for a horsy one. She would be blonde, of course. Everything had been preordained. Paris couldn't stand the blind dates her mother and Aunt Melissa got for her, the sons of their friends. Those boys were as gauche and strange to her as if they came from the moon. She wanted to date the boys she met in school; then at least they had something to talk about. She couldn't imagine kissing a boy whose mother was a friend of her mother's. Would he go home and tell his mother? Ugh.

She was lying on the chaise longue in her mother's room one

day during Christmas vacation, talking to her mother through the open door of the bathroom, where her mother was taking a bath in her customary three inches of water so she wouldn't drown, and suddenly Paris realized that she would never marry anyone. She was doomed to be an old maid. The realization was like a physical blow; it was as if someone had hit her in the pit of her stomach. No one she liked would ever like her. Her parents and the girls at school had made it abundantly clear. You couldn't choose the boy you wanted, he was to be chosen for you, and she would never marry anyone who was chosen for her. So no one would ever marry her, and she would never marry anyone, and she would be alone all of her life. Thank God for college. There were so many boys there that she couldn't be lonely. She would make the most of it. Afterward, when she had graduated, she would be doomed.

She was lucky she was going to be a writer. She had something to do with her life. All the girls at college had mapped out their lives already: go steady in your senior year, get engaged at graduation, get married afterward, have a lot of children. If they couldn't find someone to marry at college then they would go to work after they graduated, but only to have something to do until they found a husband. If you had an interesting job you could attract a better class of men. Only Paris absolutely knew she didn't want to get married for a long, long time, even if anyone ever wanted her, which she doubted. Oh, drips and jerks would want her—there were always those. Every girl she knew had a drip after her whom she rejected constantly with no success.

Her mother liked to tell her how brave she had been to marry her father, he who was so different from herself, so religious, so poor, with such a demanding, possessive family that they had never forgiven Lavinia to this day for stealing their Jonah away from them. But what was so brave about marrying a man like Jonah Mendes? A girl would have to be an idiot not to see his good qualities right away. No, the whole family had done their little dance, done what was expected of them. But she, poor Paris, wasn't given any credit for having any sense or taste at all. They wanted to plan her life as if this was still the Middle Ages. Any unconventional thought she had was a threat to everyone, she could see that already. Why couldn't she keep her mouth shut and keep her thoughts to herself? Then she wouldn't always be fighting with her mother. It was just that she wanted her mother to agree with her for once, to approve of her. Her mother was stubborn and she was stubborn, and neither of them would ever give in. Paris supposed it would get worse as time went on. She was the trophy in a war.

Her mother kept saying, "I let you go to college," as if going away to college were something really brave and adventurous and grown up. Actually, life in the dorm was very regimented. Freshmen could only stay out until one o'clock in the morning two nights a week. You usually saved those for weekends. Other nights you had to be back in the dorm at ten o'clock. On Sunday night you got to stay out until eleven. You had to sign out and in in a book which was placed near the door. You also had to say where you were going. There was to be no cheating. If you were one minute late you were called up to a kangaroo court and made to tell your excuse, which short of death or an automobile accident resulting in a rush to the hospital was not accepted, and you were put on Social Pro, which meant that you were banished upstairs every night after dinner for a specified time (a week or two or three) with no phone calls allowed.

There was one telephone on each floor, with several push buttons. Each girl had a buzzer in her room and a light above the door. When the buzzer rang and the light flashed you rushed to a house phone on the wall in the hall where the switchboard girl told you what line your phone call was on. Then you ran to the phone on your floor, which was usually occupied, and then you ran from one floor to another until you found a phone which was not occupied, hoping meanwhile that the mysterious caller would not hang up. When you arrived finally at an available phone, out of breath and frantic, it was a great disappointment to find it was only your parents. The phones, except for one on the first floor in a phone booth, were situated in the floor laundry rooms, so while you were trying to have a private conversation with the boy you had a crush on at the moment, several girls were standing there ironing and listening.

The phone system was called "Bells." One girl had to stay on the switchboard (which was located in the front hall of the dorm near the door) for two hours, and they took turns. If you were a freshman you had to work in the kitchen and wait on table. Only upperclassmen had the privilege of being on Bells. Besides answering the phones and announcing the calls, the girl on Bells also announced Callers. Any pimply eighteen-year-old roaming around looking for a blind date qualified as a Caller. No men were allowed above the first floor. You had to receive Callers in the living room. Of course, you could also go outside with him, provided you came back before your curfew. If someone telephoned or came by to see you the girl on Bells left a note in your mailbox (a wall of cubbyholes on the first floor) that said "Mr. X called." Unless, of course, Mr. X was kind enough to leave his name. Many girls cried and had hysterical fits when they returned from the coffee shop on the corner to discover that the boy they had been waiting weeks to hear from had finally phoned when they were out. Because, of course, you could not call him back; that was unthinkably aggressive. You had to wait patiently for him to call again when he felt like it. Many girls stayed glued to their rooms because of this social rule, afraid to miss the phone call from the love of their lives. But no matter how much you loved him, you could not call him back. A girl didn't do that.

If a boy wanted to take you out on Saturday night it was proper to phone on the Monday before. You could usually tell what type he was right away. A jerk called on the Monday before so he could trap you before you made another date, also because he was a stickler for convention. The boys you liked the best, the ungallant, charming, unpredictable ones, usually called near the end of the week (unless they had tickets to a football game) or even called on Friday for Saturday, which was humiliating. Sometimes they just showed up to see if you were there. You went right out with them if you liked them, insulted or not. It was difficult to keep your social life the way you wanted it because the drips and jerks always asked you to the big football games two or three weeks in advance, and you would accept out of fear of having no date at all, and then the boy you liked would call later, when you had to turn him down because a nice girl didn't break dates, even with a boy she hated. Paris had been forced to turn Spencer down for four big football games because she was already stuck with boys her mother would have approved of but whom she found boring and unsexy.

There was no honesty and no communication between the girls and the boys. Everything was a game. The girls pretended to be interested in what the boys liked, talked about what the boys liked, and never dared ask them why they hadn't called for such a long time, when they would call again, or if there was any hope for the relationship. You simply kept your fingers crossed. What you were wanting was a love affair with a stranger, so naturally the entire experience was shrouded in mystery. If the boys had been friends or even real people, it would have been easy to understand, predict, and make work. The girls were no more real to them than they were to the girls. A girl was fun or not fun, easy to make out with or not easy, or impossible, but never a human being.

The girls' dorms were chaperoned by a house mother, with whom no one ever had a conversation. Her whole function was to see that the couples necking on the porch at curfew stopped and separated. Perhaps the college had intended she have another function—guidance, kindness, friendship—but none of the girls was aware of it and she never displayed any indication that she was capable of it. One night in winter Paris, who had a bad cold, began to have an asthma attack. She often had asthma attacks with colds, and knew she needed a vaporizer of some kind, so she went downstairs to the kitchen to find a pot to boil water in to make steam, but the kitchen was always locked after meals so none of the girls would steal food. She then found the house mother, who was dressed in her customary Army surplus camouflage robe and annoyed expression. By this time Paris was wheezing very badly and her lips and fingernails were turning blue.

"May I please have a pot? I need to make steam for my asthma."

"A pot?" the house mother said. "If you knew you had asthma you should have brought a pot from home." And she went away, never to return.

So Paris waited for morning when they would let her into the Health Center, fighting for breath, and finally passed out from lack of air.

She never did bring a pot to college for her asthma, because the house mother wouldn't have let her use the kitchen stove in any case. The function of the house mother was to keep the school rules and protect the girls' virginity, not keep them alive.

"It's nice you have a house mother," Paris' mother said. "You have someone to go to if you have a problem."

"Sure," Paris said. She didn't tell her mother about the incident; she didn't want her parents yanking her out of school.

It was cold that winter, freezing cold, and snow was piled up waist high in the streets. No one cleaned the streets in Cambridge; they just cleared a little footpath and left the rest of the snow until spring, when it would melt naturally. It was so cold that even the peeping toms and men who exposed themselves in the Common disappeared. Paris had never seen a man expose himself, even one of her dates. The boys she went out with were all shy. She was afraid of the pushy ones. She knew for a fact that some of the older girls, and even a few in her class, weren't virgins any more, because they talked about it openly among themselves, but most of the girls pretended they were. Paris' best friend, Rima Gold, adamantly insisted that every girl in the dorm was a virgin, and there was nothing Paris could say to convince her otherwise.

Rima and Paris had everything in common and also were complete opposites, which was why they got along so well. Both of them were only sixteen. Both of them were Jewish. Rima came from the Bronx, and although Paris had been living in New York for four years she considered that she really came from Brooklyn. Both of them had gone to progressive private schools. Neither of them had had a date before coming to Radcliffe, but both of them were now boy crazy. They both liked the same boys, but luckily not at the same time. At the start of their friendship they made a pact that neither of them would ever steal the other's boyfriend, and neither of them would go out with a boy the other was dating (no matter how he pestered her) until the one who had him first had declared she was through with him. For some reason both Rima and Paris were sought out by the prep school–Social Register boys, the ones with the profiles like Greek gods and lockjaw accents, who wore old raccoon coats and drove around in funny cars, the boys none of the other Jewish girls would even talk to because they were so strange, so forcign, definitely not husband material; not that they had a chance. Rima spent a lot of time knitting six-foot long scarves for her latest crushes. Perhaps the boys sought them out for the same reason Paris and Rima sought them out; they were cxotic and different, safe, not serious, adventurous and immature, laughed easily, liked silly things, and didn't want to get married right away. Most of the boys, having gone to all-boys schools deep in the country, had hardly been out with any girls before coming to Harvard, so they were virgins and naïve too. They liked to kiss. So did Paris and Rima. Rima had already gotten a rather bad reputation for being wild because she let boys kiss her on the first date. She was very romantic, and fancied herself Madame Bovary or Lady Hamilton, ready to die for love. But despite the fact that Paris and Rima went out almost every night, both of them got straight As.

Rima studied hard. She was an English major too, a good, shy, gentle girl, very high strung, too frail, with dark hair and pale skin and a closet full of expensive clothes. She loved to read poetry, and also wrote poetry, but hid it. She wanted to work in publishing when she graduated.

"Do you know what the dean told me?" she said to Paris. "She asked me what I wanted to major in and I told her English because I wanted to be an editor someday, and she said: 'We don't train girls for *jobs* here. This isn't a *trade school*. Radcliffe girls are expected to marry Harvard men and be better wives and mothers.'"

"I'm lucky I told her I wanted to be a writer. Everybody thinks you can be a writer while you're home taking care of your twelve kids."

"I'll never forget what she said," Rima said angrily. "Never." "What do you care? You'll never even see her again."

Paris also wrote poetry, but she sent it to the literary magazine, where it was promptly rejected. She also drew caricatures of all the girls in the dorm. She had decided not to send any stories to national magazines because they would probably be rejected and that would depress her. Part of her life plan was to enjoy college as much as possible and worry about her profession when she was prepared for it. One day, in desperation at having her stories as well as her poems rejected by the college magazine, she wrote the worst story she could, purposely obscure because it had no meaning, and it was promptly accepted. When it ran in the college literary magazine many girls came up to her to congratulate her and tell her how meaningful the symbolism had been to them.

"I have now learned that the last thing I ever want is to be judged by a jury of my peers," Paris told Rima. "They're all idiots."

Although things affected her deeply, Paris passed them off as a joke. The last thing she wanted was for anyone to know she was hurt. Rima, on the other hand, shook with emotions, wept hysterically over a missed phone call from a current love, and was secretly strong as steel. Both of them knew they were intelligent, but only Rima dared admit, even insist, that they were superior.

"It's not that those boys are dumb," she would say to Paris, "it's just that they're not as smart as we are, so they seem dumb to us."

"Don't ever say that to anybody," Paris said. She knew girls were supposed to act dumb if they weren't. It was death to be intelligent or intellectual. No one attractive would ever like her if she showed her mind. She would be stuck with a greasy grind, spending their Saturday nights studying together instead of in Cronins drinking beer and seeing everyone and being seen.

Rima never went out with a boy she didn't like, after one disastrous date where the boy tried to run her over with his car after she refused to kiss him. Paris, on the other hand, went out with every boy who asked her, although not more than once if he was terrible. Her mother had told her over and over to "give them a chance," so she did, although it made her feel used, like a thing instead of a person. A boy never seemed to care if you didn't like him, if you found him physically repulsive; all he cared about was whether or not he found you attractive to him. But she "gave them a chance." She even accepted a blind date from Dottie, who took her to the famous necking palace in the Boston suburbs. It was a huge room, like a coliseum, with a tiny dance floor in the center and rows and rows of loveseats set on tiers rising up toward the ceiling. The lights were very dim and blue, to further romance and anonymity. The couples sat there, about five hundred people in all, and necked and petted in the dim light, all together, pretending to be alone, mauling and slurping and knowing they were safe because no one would go all the way in public. Drinks were served, and a few people even danced, which is to say rubbed up against each other and swayed in a romantic death grip. Paris did not like her date, and as soon as she had clocked enough time to be polite, while pushing him away and chattering, she made him take her home. It was so hard to get away from that "giving them a chance" indoctrination that she almost had to give herself psychosomatic cramps in order to lie and say she felt too sick to stay any longer.

Dottie couldn't figure out why she hadn't liked the boy; after all, he had a car, and he had taken her to an expensive place. But she had a few more in reserve, if Paris was interested. Rejects . . .

Perhaps, Paris sometimes thought, she was too young to go to college, too inexperienced, too unsophisticated, but there had been no alternative. She'd had to get away from home. It wasn't her fault she'd started school young and then had been skipped. She wouldn't have become more sophisticated at home, that was for sure. There were other sixteen-year-olds in the freshman class, and they seemed more grown up than she was. Their lives had been different. And there were girls who were older who were babies compared to her. Their lives had been different too. There shouldn't be rules for what you should want in life at a particular moment—it was different for everybody. But everyone seemed scared to death not to conform to a particular ideal. College was supposed to open up the world and make it more accessible, not present you with a form you had to squeeze yourself into. It wasn't the school's fault, it was the girls' fault, their own fault. They could have taken their destiny in their own hands, but of course it never occurred to any of them to do so.

EIGHT

Everett had his own business in Miami Beach that winter, his own radio repair shop. His mother had finally given in and financed him. He was still living at Papa's house because he wasn't making a profit yet, and to tell the truth he was afraid of being lonely in a furnished room. The thought of renting and furnishing an entire apartment terrified him. Now that he had finished college and was a working man Papa and Etta treated him differently. No longer was anyone responsible to see that he studied and did not flunk out. He could go and come as he pleased, using the demands of his work as an excuse. They also assumed he was dating girls. He wasn't.

It wasn't for lack of desire; it was for lack of courage. Girls sometimes brought their radios into the shop for repair, but Everett always found something wrong with the girl—her teeth were funny, her eyes were funny—because he was afraid she would reject him. He had hired a woman to answer the phone and take care of the place while he was out on house calls, a large, motherly woman named Lorraine, whom the employment agency had sent, and he didn't like the idea of her watching him talk to the girls who sometimes came in. He was afraid Lorraine wanted him to be suave and make out, and this made him all the more tongue-tied. Sometimes he fantasized that Lorraine was in love with him. Big fat cow! She was probably alone and frustrated, dying to invite him to her apartment for a drink and drag him down on the sofa.

When Lorraine said she was leaving to take care of her sick sister, Everett wasn't at all disappointed. He didn't like having a substitute mother sitting there all day spying on him. He decided not to accept anyone the employment agency sent this time unless she was younger than he was.

They sent a blonde girl named Frances Riley, "Frankie." She looked athletic and told him she was twenty-one and came from Vermont. She liked Florida but hated the beach. Her skin was paper white and paper thin, the sort that would probably get red in the sun and was already dry so that it crinkled around her blue eyes when she smiled. She had a smart, shrewd face and slightly crooked teeth, and a crisp Eastern accent that sounded a lot better to him than the drawl he was used to and had started affecting himself.

"How come you left Vermont?" he asked her.

"I like adventure. I'm just moving on."

A twenty-one-year-old-girl with the courage to move on interested him. Her clothes were shabby and he figured she had been on her own for quite a while.

"Did you go to college?" he asked her.

"Do you think I'd be working here if I did?"

"Why not?" Everett asked, insulted. "My last operator was a college graduate."

"Well, she left, didn't she?"

He noticed with satisfaction that her blonde hair had black roots. "You need a new dye job if you're going to work here," he told her.

"Then advance me my salary if you're so smart," she said.

"I thought you did it yourself."

"Are you kidding?"

She was his employee and she didn't scare him a bit. He even thought she was rather pretty. He liked her straight nose and the way everything about her was so goyish: no ass, and flat-chested, and those muscles in her calves, nothing full-blown or ripe about her, just kind of skinny and mean and tough.

"Where do you live?" he asked her.

"With a bunch of stewardesses."

He couldn't picture Frankie Riley living with a bunch of stewardesses; she was so casual and they were all so neat and trim and perfect. She glanced at him and seemed to know what he was thinking. Her thin penciled eyebrows drew together in annoyance.

"It's cheap, and they're never there," she said.

"How come you never became a stewardess?"

"Because you always have to be somewhere when they want you to. You get calls in the middle of the night to be on some plane because the regular girl is sick. Who needs that?"

"I thought you liked adventure."

"My kind," Frankie said. "Not somebody else's kind."

"How would you like to go to dinner with me?" Everett said. The words popped out before he realized he had said them, and then he was pleased with himself. Why not? He was the boss, she ought to be flattered.

She looked him over. "Okay," she said.

Frankie Riley was Everett Bergman's first date. He was twenty-three years old and she was the first girl he had ever felt comfortable with except for his jerky little cousin Paris, who didn't count as a girl anyway even though he necked with her sometimes when he was desperate. He took Frankie to Howard Johnson's, the one that had booths and tables in back at night, and he bought her fried clams and six scotch and sodas. He had only one scotch and soda because he didn't drink very well, and after dinner he drove her along the beach until he got to his favorite place, the one where there were no houses and no people, and he tried to kiss her.

"I don't kiss men on the first date," she said.

He was disappointed because he was hoping she was drunk. She plucked his hand off her shoulder and he noticed that her little hand was very strong. She removed his other hand from her knee and smoothed her pastel cotton dress. For a moment Everett thought of getting tough with her and forcing her, the way he did with Paris, and then he realized you didn't do that with girls on a date, at least not if you ever expected to see them again.

"Okay," he said to her. "I respect that."

"Good."

"I guess I'll drive you home now. Show me where."

She lived in a pea green stucco house that reminded him of the one where he'd spent that terrible night when he'd run away. It seemed very long ago now, but still too close not to make him feel sick about it. Frankie didn't seem like a girl who would ever be lonely. She could take care of herself. She got out of the car and didn't ask him in. She gave him a little half-salute with her hand like a soldier, smiled her crooked smile, and headed for the door.

"Don't be late tomorrow," he called after her.

"You neither. Don't cruise around all night."

Cruise around all night! She thought he was going to get his rocks off by picking up another girl! The thought made him feel so good that he whistled all the way home. He wondered what she did on the second date. He fantasized about her and he really wanted her. He had started thinking about her as very desirable. He wanted to get his hands on that boyish body, to make her shrewd little face turn soft for him. He wished he knew more. He'd read every sex book he could get his hands on, and dirty books too, but that wasn't the same as doing it. If he could just get his hands on Frankie he would do every last thing he'd read about in the marriage manuals, from A to Z. Before he turned into his driveway he turned the car around and drove over to the all-night drugstore and bought a package of condoms, just in case, feeling very proud when he asked the clerk for them.

Frankie wouldn't let him kiss her until the fifth date and then she wouldn't open her mouth. She was efficient in the office, and every time Everett asked her out she went with him, but the condoms remained unused and drying up in his wallet. Whenever he tried to touch her body she pried his hands off. He kept a blanket in the trunk of his car just in case some night he'd be able to talk her into going on his deserted stretch of beach with him under the stars, and he even kept a pint of whiskey there too, but she never would set one foot outside his car except to go home and he'd be damned if he was going to waste his seduction whiskey on her if she wasn't. As for getting her to do anything in the car, that was hopeless. He was strong, but she was just as strong as he was.

"I studied judo," she said, "so don't start with me."

"Why would you study judo?"

"To keep off guys like you."

"Don't you like me?"

"Sure I like you," she said. "I'm just not that kind of a girl. I know you're rich and I'm poor, so you think I'm easy. Well, I'm not."

"I never thought you were easy," Everett said. "You're about as sexy as a buzz saw."

"Thanks a lot."

"Well, after all, I'm not a monster, am I?"

"I don't have to go to bed with you to prove you're not a monster. Poor, poor little Everett. Ums thinks ums a monster, so ums wants to cuddle and feel reassured. Don't think I haven't heard that line before."

"Are you a virgin?"

"Yes."

"Isn't that a little outdated?" he said.

"Oh, come off it."

"None of the girls I know are virgins," Everett said.

"Then why do you waste your time with me when you could be with them?"

"I sort of like you. You're like a little sister."

"If I'm nothing but a sister to you then I think I'll quit this job and be moving on."

"You're kidding, aren't you?" Everett said. He suddenly realized he would miss her if she left.

"No, I'm not kidding."

"Well, I was kidding. You're not like my little sister. I think you're all girl."

"Good. Then I'll stay a while. Let's go bowling."

"I don't know how," Everett said.

"I'll teach you. It's fun. I won three trophies in high school; my team did anyway. I was captain."

He took her to the Bowladrome and in between games he bought her six paper cups of scotch and soda. She still bowled better than he did, but he was really terrible. Most of the balls he tried to roll down the alley wiggled away at a crawl and died against the side before they got near the pins. Everett was glad he had money in his pocket because at least that showed he was a man even if he couldn't bowl. He stood there chain-smoking cigarettes and watching Frankie destroy him.

"Come on," he said. "I'm bored, let's go for a ride."

She shrugged and followed him out to his car. He drove her to the fancy section of Miami Beach where he lived with Papa and

Etta. He had never taken Frankie there before because there was simply no reason to; they always went out somewhere and he dropped her off at her house. She had no idea where he lived, or how. He stopped in front of the house. Papa had put floodlights in the garden in front of the house, illuminating the graceful giant palms and all the carefully tended foliage. There were lights on in the house and it looked enormous. The street was very quiet and peaceful, safe, the rich people protected behind thick walls. There was a nearly full moon and the whole thing looked like something out of a Hollywood movie.

"This is where I live," Everett said to her.

"Here?"

"Yes. It's my grandfather's house."

"*Jee*sus!"

"Nice, isn't it?"

"Yeah, I'd say so."

"It's nothing compared to the little place we have in Connecticut. Fifty-five acres. Lake, waterfall, lagoon, river, and we're going to build a swimming pool. Everybody has their own house."

"Who's everybody?"

"My parents and some aunts and uncles."

"You mean it's like a ranch or something," she said.

"More like a little town."

"Wow," Frankie said.

"And we have a tennis court, and woods, and there are a lot of horses in the field but they don't belong to us."

"Do you ride?" she asked.

"Nope."

"You play tennis?"

"No."

"Boy, what a waste."

"I shoot, though."

"Shoot what?"

"Guns. In the woods. At targets."

"Are you good?"

"Pretty good."

"I hate people who kill living things," Frankie said.

"I don't kill living things."

"Good. I'd hate you if you did."

"Well, I don't."

"I don't know why you want to live here when you could live there," she said.

"It's boring there," Everett said.

"It wouldn't bore me."

"Yes it would."

She sighed and chewed at a nail. He glanced at her from the corner of her eye. Let her eat her heart out. He knew he had something that she didn't have, that she'd never had and maybe never would have, and that was money. Well, maybe it wasn't his money, it was his parents', but still he had some of it. And that made him feel warm and comfortable with her.

A man had to be better than the woman and a man had to be the boss. But Frankie was tough, and Everett liked that. If she just wouldn't be so insistent on being a nice girl it would make life a lot easier for him. He'd told her a million times that he would respect her anyway and she'd said that she didn't care, what about the next guy? It made him feel insignificant that she thought of him as only a way station on her life of dating; it was insulting. She ought to be after him. What he really ought to do, Everett thought, was go out with another girl. But he didn't know another girl. Even though he saw Frankie a good part of the day at work and then almost every night, he never got tired of her. Everything about Frankie was alien to him, and Everett liked that. She was just the kind of girl his parents would hate.

NINE

That winter Nicole and Basil were married, in a simple ceremony in New York, attended by the groom's immediate family. The bride did not have family in America. Basil had thought it might be nice to have a spring garden wedding at Windflower, but Nicole did not want to wait. Besides, she told him, they were going to Europe for their honeymoon and only tourists and fools went to Europe in the tourist season, and of course since he was marrying her he would see Europe the way the natives did. They would go to London and Paris, spend a month traveling all over

France, and go to Monte Carlo and the Riviera. Andrew was not pleased that Basil was going to spend so long away from the office, leaving the burden of work on him and Papa, but it was good that Basil was getting married at last, not that Andrew liked Nicole. He thought she was awful, and couldn't imagine what his brother saw in her. Cassie was tiny and pretty and charming, but Nicole was huge and loud and went out of her way to insult people. It gave Andrew a headache when Nicole was in the room. He withdrew into the corner and looked at her out of his soft eyes, wondering how two brothers from the same home could have such different taste in women.

Nicole was not family. "Poor Basil," Lavinia said. "She'll give him a hard time." Now that Basil had gotten his punishment, a lifetime contract with someone who would torture him, Lavinia had her revenge, and along with it the guilt, and so she had decided that her brother was a saint. "He's so good to her, he waits on her hand and foot. He's such a good, kind person," Lavinia said in her vehement, clipped, schoolteacher tone, the one she used when reciting the list of wrongs inflicted on a member of the family, or good deeds performed by same. It was as if she knew her words would fly up to heaven to be written in the Holy Book, and wanted to be sure God spelled everything right.

Paris was the maid of honor at the wedding. The new dress she bought for the occasion fell apart during the reception and she had to return it the next day. Paris took that as a sort of augury for the marriage, a kind of symbolism. She had never before had a dress that fell apart in a few hours.

Nicole had told her there was nothing wrong with a girl not being a virgin, that she herself had not been a virgin when she got married. Since Paris considered Nicole middle-aged, she was not at all surprised. When she was in her thirties she certainly expected to be an ex-virgin too. She did not, however, tell her mother what Nicole had said. There was no point in adding fuel to the fire.

Virginity or the lack of it was one of the favorite topics of discussion at college in Paris' second year. Whenever she suspected that one of her friends might have done it with her steady boyfriend she tactfully refrained from asking. There was a certain embarrassment about the subject. She knew that Rima was a virgin. She was too. She was much too frightened of becoming pregnant to go all the way, and besides, the minute you did the word got around and you were marked, and all the boys called you up for just one thing. A girl had to go steady just to have the license to pet. The boy had to say he loved her, and she had to say she loved him and pretend to herself that she really did, or else a wrongly buttoned blouse on the return to the dorm could create a scandal. It was all so silly, she thought: the freshly applied bright red lipstick just so you could walk through the living room and pass the scrutiny of the jealous girls who had no dates that night. She had done so much kissing in parked cars with the radio on that she secretly feared she would always associate music with sex, like one of Pavlov's dogs, and when she got married she would always have to go to bed with the radio on.

One of her best friends at college was a commuter named Elizabeth Hamilton, who had been going steady with the same boy since they were both fourteen. They even looked alike. It was assumed that when she graduated she would marry him. Because she lived with her parents instead of in the dorm, and because her social life was settled, Elizabeth was different from most of the girls Paris knew. Their relationship was less incestuous. They had met in an art class (Elizabeth was an art major) and they often hung around the Square together, having lunch in a restaurant, or just coffee, talking, taking walks. They didn't talk about people they knew in common, they talked about things. Coming from a family that was always on top of each of its members, and then living in a dorm with no privacy, Paris relished that. She and Elizabeth often went to museums, and in good weather they sat on the steps of the library with their sketch pads and drew pictures. Elizabeth had never been to New York, and Paris had invited her to spend a week with her that summer at Windflower and go on trips to museums in the city. Elizabeth was slender and neat, with straight hair that Paris envied and Elizabeth hated. She looked like one of the girls in a junior fashion magazine. Everything she put on looked good on her, no matter how little it cost.

Rima Gold's parents had moved to Scarsdale from the Bronx, "for her." Scarsdale meant a different life, different opportunities, the kind of country club boys all the parents wanted their daughters to meet. It was too bad that Rima couldn't play tennis or golf, kept her head out of the water when she dog-paddled, and thought the best way to spend a Sunday afternoon was in her own back yard lying motionless under the sun. Paris wouldn't be caught dead at a country club either, although there were several within driving distance, and she had invited Rima to visit her every weekend. Rima's mother had agreed to drive her. It wasn't far. That summer Paris was going to take driving lessons even though she didn't have a car.. She was looking forward to the summer because she would have friends and something to do.

She always looked forward to the summer and then something always went wrong. The first day she would arrange all her things neatly in their places, breathe in the fresh country air, let her skin soak in the sun and wind, and then somehow as time went on everything changed. Time started to go slowly. She began to have nightmares at night. Her mother and aunts talked about her in her presence as if she weren't there. Should she keep that blouse she'd bought or return it? The color wasn't bad, but the workmanship was shoddy, it wasn't worth the money, and not all that becoming. She should return it. Nobody asked *her*. No one wanted to go anywhere. The grocery store was the limit of their adventurousness. No one went to summer theater any more; no one went to the movies. Uncle Lazarus listened to his favorite radio programs, and whenever one of them was on at the same time as lunch or dinner it had to be turned on full blast in the library so they could hear it in the dining room. Of course, at these times, conversation was impossible. Not that conversation was so interesting anyway, when all the family seemed to talk about was dieting and food, while they were stuffing themselves. The only reason her mother let Paris take driving lessons was that everyone knew that boys sometimes got fresh and told a girl she'd have to neck with them or walk home, or sometimes a boy got too drunk at a party to be able to drive, and so she should have a driver's license. Then she could escape and save herself. No one thought how useful it would be if she could drive; then she could go places and take them places too. Now that Everett was in business he didn't spend the whole summer at Windflower, just part of it for his vacation, so an extra car and driver was badly needed. But no one thought of Paris that way; she was still just a child to them. She felt smothered. How could they all be so content to sit there, all dressed up and their hair all done and makeup on, and then do nothing at all but sit on the porch and talk to each other, eat meals, sit at Grandpa's and talk to each other?

Thank goodness for Rima every Saturday. Her mother was different from Paris' mother; she drove a car and smoked cigarettes and was always doing something or going somewhere. Oh, was there a good farm down the road? Then she'd stop off and buy vegetables to take home. Was there an antique fair? Only an hour away? Then by all means she would investigate it. She did her own cooking and walked the dog and even did setting-up exercises for half an hour every morning. It was ironic that she had a daughter who couldn't drive and had no wish to learn, hated to cook, couldn't come near touching her toes, and whose favorite hobbies were reading poetry and sleeping. Paris and Rima always had something to talk about. They went into Paris' room and shut the door that led to her parents' room.

"You mother doesn't like me," Rima said.

"Don't be silly."

"No, she doesn't."

Paris always thought of Rima's presence as a buffer between herself and her mother; Rima liked to talk to her mother about growing flowers, and when she was around no one bothered Paris at all.

"Why wouldn't my mother like you?" Paris said.

"Because she doesn't trust me. She doesn't think I'm your real friend. I can tell."

"Does it make you uncomfortable?"

Rima shrugged. "Maybe in a couple of years she'll get to like me."

It was true that when her friend was there Paris spent little time with her mother, but that was what friends were for, to be your age. A mother was different. Even though a mother tried to be a friend, or at least said she did, she had the balance of power. A friend had to be equal. Her mother had friends of her own, let her invite them up. But her mother said she didn't want to invite their old friends from Brooklyn because the sight of all this luxury would make them uncomfortable.

"I don't want you to let Rima influence you," Paris' mother had said.

"Influence me in what?"

"In anything. Remember, you are you. You are the way I brought you up, and I don't want you to listen to your friends."

"About *what?*"

"Anything. Remember, in the long run your mother is the only person you can really trust."

On the Saturdays when Rima couldn't come to Windflower Paris was bored. She spent them with her mother, or wandering around alone. Uncle Basil and Nicole were living in Basil's suite at Grandpa's house, but during the week Nicole often went into the city with Basil because she didn't like to sit still. She was pregnant, but she didn't let it stop her. She took courses in the city, and when she was in the country she still swam and played tennis, flaunting her strong body. Paris didn't think it was very attractive to see that bulging belly in the Olympic swimsuit, but Nicole said it was "natural." It still looked like she'd eaten an extra large meal, but soon, Paris knew, Nicole's vanity would overcome her desire to prove how natural she was, and she would buy maternity clothes. At least, she hoped so.

Elizabeth came to visit in August. She loved the lake and looked just like a junior model standing there against the greenery in her new orange bathing suit with her hair straight and perfect no matter how hot and humid it was. She seemed awed by the place and the family. Paris realized that people who had never seen Windflower before might be overwhelmed. But to her the family was just a family; she knew how shy they were with strangers, how afraid they were that they might be lacking in social graces. Elizabeth was no one to be afraid of. She was just a college girl, too poor to go to a school away from home, a girl with simple tastes who loved to go to museums and look at pictures.

Elizabeth was supposed to stay for the whole week, but the third day when they were at the Museum of Modern Art, she said, "I have to go home tomorrow."

"Why?" Paris asked, very surprised and disappointed.

"I don't have any more money."

"What do you need money for?"

"I just don't feel comfortable without money."

Paris knew that was a lie; Elizabeth had hardly spent anything and she had seen her counting plenty of money the night she arrived. "You miss Jimmy, is that it?"

"Oh no, not really. I just have to go home."

"I wish you wouldn't. We don't have to go anywhere, just stay in the country if you want."

"No, I've already called my mother. Collect," Elizabeth added hastily.

That night Elizabeth packed and Paris watched her sadly, wondering what had gone wrong. Had someone hurt her feelings? Could the family have scared her that much? Had she been secretly spending money, was it really true? Maybe Elizabeth was just a hick after all, as Paris had heard her mother telling Aunt Melissa, and New York had scared her as much as Windflower had.

Elizabeth took the train back to Cambridge. "Well," Paris' mother said that night with a sigh of relief, "I'm glad she's gone."

"You are?"

"I looked—she had mildew in her suitcase. I don't want you bringing any more of those girls from school. They'll bring mildew in their suitcases and we'll get it all over the house."

TEN

In August of that summer Nicole finally gave in and started wearing maternity clothes. The men in the family were particularly relieved, for they had been embarrassed and repelled, seeing more of Nicole's body during this sacred time than they cared to. And, in her seventh month, she had ballooned, but she would not admit it.

"I don't really need these," she said, stroking her maternity blouse with her huge hand. Gulliver among the Lilliputians, she looked down at her in-laws and smiled. "I just wear them because it's fun to play pregnant woman for a change. I'll let Basil wait on me. Basil, bring me some ice cream and a dill pickle."

Basil started to rise, not sure if she was joking or not, and Nicole laughed. "Oh, sit down, Basil. I can get my own pickle if I want it. I can still do everything I used to do. I'm in such good shape that nothing has changed."

They were all at Papa's, after dinner, as usual. Nicole rose and strode to the center of the living room floor. "Look at me, everybody!" she cried in her loud voice. "Look! I'm seven months pregnant and I'm going to stand on my head."

There was a shocked intake of breath from the women and then silence as Nicole tossed her legs upward and performed a perfect handstand, walking a few steps on her hands for good measure. Her skirt flopped down over her face, revealing her maternity girdle, panties, stockings, and belly full of child. Jonah looked nauseated and averted his eyes. Lavinia wanted to rush over and cover Papa's eyes, but she figured he could take care of himself. Etta, who had turned out to be a prude after all, despite her beginnings, blushed. Melissa gave a little shriek and looked at Lazarus, as if he might be called on to do an emergency delivery right that moment on Etta's pastel rug. Hazel looked confused. And Basil pretended he thought it was admirable.

Nicole returned to an upright position and gave a triumphant crow: "There! What did you think of that?"

"You'll be lucky if the baby isn't born upside down," Lazarus said with distaste. "You'll have a breech birth, mark my words."

"Oh, don't be silly," Nicole said. "I'm strong as a horse."

"And act like one," Lavinia muttered to Jonah.

Rosemary, who had watched all this feeling it was only one more scene in her life of daily pain, really disliked Nicole at that moment. The woman had no idea how lucky she was to be pregnant, to have been able to conceive so quickly, almost at will, and at her age, too! And then to make such light of it, to threaten the baby just to show off, she had to be not right in the head. Nicole's pregnancy had made Rosemary even more conscious of the empty gap in her own family. There was even an empty room in the house for a child. It wasn't fair.

When she and Jack went back to their house that night and were safely in their bedroom where they could talk, Rosemary broached the subject of adoption.

"No," Jack said. "I won't."

"But if we can't have a baby of our own, we could get a wonderful little baby who has all the qualities of the two of us. They match them up. It would even look like you, and it would be musical. We would feel it's our own right away, everyone says you do. It would be just like having a baby except I wouldn't have to be pregnant. I'd just go to the hospital and bring home a little baby."

"I won't have a stranger in my house," Jack said.

"It wouldn't be a stranger. It'd be ours."

"Do you know how much a kid costs? Food, clothes, shoes, school, then they have to have music lessons, they want to go out, they want an allowance, they want a car, they want to go to college . . . A fortune! I'm not spending a fortune on someone else's kid."

"It would be our kid, Jack!"

"Not to me it wouldn't."

There was no way she could sway him. An adopted child was a threat to him, not just as a stranger but as a threat to his identity, his masculinity.

"What do you want some illegitimate baby for?" he asked Rosemary. "Who knows what kind of dumb girl the mother was, getting herself in trouble with some dumb boy in the back of a car. Who wants their kid?"

"You wouldn't ever love it, would you?" Rosemary said sadly.

"No. But I won't have to, because I won't have one here and that's that."

He had never been really adamant about anything before and Rosemary knew him well enough to know he would never give in. There was only one other avenue open to her. Not artificial insemination—thank God she was the one with problems, not him, because even she thought artificial insemination was nauseating—no, there was an operation the doctor had told her about. They blew air through the tubes and opened them up. Sometimes it worked. She would do it. If they had told her to eat worms she would. She had already taken hormones and they had only made her feel sick, but not with genuine morning sickness. All right, she'd have her tubes blown out. She knew it would hurt, and maybe it wouldn't work, but she would do it. She had been putting off the operation out of fear that this last chance wouldn't work either, and then she would be left without any hope at all.

"If somebody left a baby on our doorstep," Rosemary said sleepily, "Would you take it?"

"That Paris will probably come home pregnant," Jack said. "Off at college, doing who knows what, boy crazy. I see her with her girls friends, giggle-giggle, whisper-whisper, all about boys. I bet she gets knocked up."

"Oh, Jack!"

"That's who'll leave a baby on our doorstep. On Jonah and Lavinia's doorstep." He laughed, pleased with himself. "Can't you see them die of shock, those prudes."

"Lavinia always tried to bring Paris up well," Rosemary said. "It's not her fault."

"We're lucky we don't have a daughter," Jack said. "But a son is worse. I pity Lazarus and Melissa with that Everett. I never saw a kid so horny. But I think all he does is talk about it. And wish."

Jack Nature was not family. He knew it; Rosemary sensed it. They had gotten to know him, judged him, and found him wanting. His jokes were too crass, his mind too petty, he was stingy, they didn't like his old car and older clothes. Despite the new blue suit he'd bought after the war he still went around in his pre-war garb, baggy and beige. He complained about every cent he and Rosemary spent in the commune, even though most of it was hers, and he made fun of everyone behind their backs.

Rosemary knew that Jack was good with children. He got along better with Richie than he did with the adults in the family, although Jack wasn't too crazy about Richie. He told Richie corny jokes and Richie laughed, which was more than the rest of them did. But Richie was only ten years old. No matter that she was a grown woman now, Rosemary thought, the family still thought of her as the young one, the least, the one who got the leftovers. She knew they thought they were better than she was, more poised, more charming. And in a way, they were right. Look at Cassie—she gave the kind of dinner parties Rosemary could never dream of giving in a million years. She had good and loyal help, a gourmet cook, and Rosemary had trouble with help (her girl and Hazel's were always fighting in the one maid's room and one of them always stalked off to catch the next train to the city), and Rosemary couldn't cook at all. Cassie knew where to get floral arrangements that stunned you. Cassie served avocado stuffed with crab and Russian dressing for a first course; Rosemary served tomato juice. Rosemary's salad dressing came from a bottle. Rosemary served cake made from a mix, or usually just fruit, but Cassie's cook made seven-layer cake and Sacher torte and strudel and even home-made doughnuts. Cassie had finger bowls with China flowers in them and water goblets with eight-inch stems. Rosemary used the glasses the cheese spread came in for every-day, why break the good ones? She had the same good things as all the girls, but this was the country, wasn't it? And in the city for just the two of them it didn't seem worth the bother. And on top of all these worldly gifts, Cassie even had three wonderful children. No problems with those kids! They were beautiful, healthy, all-American kids like you saw in the movies or magazines, but never belonging to your friends.

The next day Rosemary called her doctor and made the appointment for the operation. It was really not so bad after all. She'd have to be ready for a lot worse—labor pains, if this thing worked. She felt calm and resigned, even cheerful, waiting to see what would happen. After she came back from the hospital and was lounging around at Windflower, the long quiet days stretched on, with Rosemary in a state of suspended animation, waiting for her identity.

Melissa was upset. Everett had told her on the telephone that he was coming to Windflower with his fiancée. Everett was engaged! The girl's name was Frankie Riley, the shicksa who answered his telephone. Now he was bringing her up to meet the family, and he planned to get married in the fall in Miami Beach. Apparently the girl didn't have any family she cared about and Everett was too shy for a big wedding.

"This Riley," Melissa asked Everett on the phone, "is she a Catholic?"

"No, she's nothing," Everett said.

"Well, then, would she become Jewish for us?"

"Why should she? I'm not Jewish."

"Everett!"

"Well, I don't practice any religion and neither does she. We're going to be married by a judge."

"And your children," Melissa said, "what are they going to become, judges?"

Everett chuckled. "They could do worse."

Frankie Riley would sleep in Everett's bedroom and Everett would have to sleep on the convertible couch in the downstairs library. It was too bad Everett's room was such a mess, but if the girl intended to marry him she'd have to get used to it. They would take her to a restaurant in the town the first night to entertain her. After that they would lead their normal lives and she could see what she was expected to fit into.

So Everett's getting married, Paris thought. She remembered

how as a child she had always thought she would marry Everett. Well, now it was final, and she was being thrown out into the world. Goodbye, Everett. No loss for her. She was looking forward to seeing the girl. It would be nice to have someone near her age around for a change. Someone had cleaned up Everett's room, probably Ben and Mae. Help thought a messy house reflected on them, not the occupants. Paris picked some flowers from the wild place near the river, tiger lilies, daisies, Queen Anne's lace, and some pink stuff, and put them into a small vase on Everett's bureau for Frankie Riley. It made the bedroom look less gray and masculine.

"Wear a dress and set your hair," Lavinia told her.

Set your hair—set your hair—set your hair—ugh. It put her teeth on edge to hear that all the time. Paris put on a dress and did not set her hair.

Lavinia was absent-mindedly combing the back of Paris' hair with her own comb. She could not bear to keep her hands off the child.

"Stop that!" Paris said, and jerked away. "Don't comb my hair!"

"Well, you just left out a place."

"My God, she's not coming here to marry *me*."

"I want you always to make a good impression. Even if the person you're making it on isn't worth a bean, it's better that you be the one to reject them, not them reject you."

Paris went into her room and put on lipstick and mascara. She heard the car drive up and saw it from her window. Everett and Frankie had taken the plane and he had rented a car at the airport. He was no fool. You didn't come to Windflower without a car if you were under ninety years old unless you liked solitary confinement. She rushed down the stairs.

Everett had the bags. Aunt Melissa was hovering around, shy and nervous but hiding it well. No one else was anywhere in sight.

Frankie looked like Everett, Paris thought, she had a fox face too. She had bleached hair with black roots and her crinoline was hanging out from her dress in the back. The hem had come down from the dress and she had fixed it with a safety pin. Each of them had brought only one small suitcase so evidently they weren't going to stay very long. Aunt Melissa had said maybe a week, unless the pressures of business made Everett rush back sooner. Aunt Melissa always talked about Everett's business as if the world couldn't go on if his radio repair shop were closed for a single day.

Everett kissed Paris hello on the mouth, as usual, and Frankie shook hands. She had a small, hard hand. Melissa shepherded them to their rooms to wash up and get ready to meet the rest of the household. Paris went back into her room and waited for a while, then, as she noticed Frankie had left Everett's door open she went across the hall and knocked on the door frame.

"Can I come in?"

"Sure," Frankie said. She was sitting on one of the twin beds in the same blue dress she had worn on the plane, and had partially unpacked her small suitcase. She had a jewel box on the bed beside her, the kind you bought in the five and ten, and it was nearly empty. She was looking through it like a child playing. She looked up and sized up Paris. "So you're Paris. My new cousin-to-be."

"Yes."

"Sit down." Paris did. "What's there to do here?"

"We swim and play tennis," Paris said. "Can you ride?"

"No. Can you?"

"No. Can you swim?"

"Sure. Can you bowl?"

"I did a few times in high school," Paris said.

"Is there a place to bowl around here?"

"I don't know."

"Well, I'll find one." Frankie was poking through her jewel box. She found a pin, a pair of silver wings, and held it up. "This is a pair of stewardess' wings," Frankie said. "A friend of mine gave them to me. Would you like to have them?" She held them out to Paris.

She thinks I'm a child, Paris thought. "I really hardly ever wear jewelry," she said. "I couldn't take them. Really. Thanks anyway."

"Okay," Frankie said and shrugged. She put the silver wings back into her jewel box and shut the lid. "What time is the cocktail hour around here?"

As it turned out, there actually was a cocktail hour that evening. Lazarus unlocked his secret closet and brought out a pint of whiskey, bearing the Prohibition label that said, "For Medicinal Purposes Only," and opened it with great ceremony on the screened porch. The whiskey was very old and extremely strong. "Wow!" Everett said. "A hundred and eighty proof. It looks like maple syrup. You must have had this for a long time."

"That is very valuable whiskey," Lazarus said. "It improves with age." He sipped at his little glassful appreciatively.

Jonah coughed and made a face, and Lavinia and Melissa put theirs down after the first sip to be polite. Paris didn't drink it at all; she hated whiskey and there was no point in wasting something so expensive. Let Frankie drink it. Frankie was the only one who was obviously enjoying it.

"Don't drink that, Jonah," Lavinia said. "You'll get sick."

"I guess we have to drink it, eh, Lazarus?" Frankie said cheerfully. Lazarus looked displeased at not being addressed as Doctor Bergman by this stranger.

"I think it's good," Everett said. He held his glass up to his father in a toast. "To us."

"To your health," Lazarus said.

"L'haim," Frankie said. "Isn't that what you say?"

"Yes, l'haim," Melissa said.

"Love, money, and the time to enjoy them," Frankie added. "Santé, amour, é dinero."

"Santé means health, not time," Lazarus said. "And it's French. Dinero is Spanish for money. You can't have a toast with French and Spanish in the same sentence."

"Why not?" Melissa said, trying to be nice even though Frankie, poor girl, was so ignorant.

"Who cares anyway?" Frankie said. She helped herself to another shot of the Prohibition whiskey.

"It's incorrect and inaccurate," Lazarus said.

"Then I'll give you an old English toast," Frankie said, holding up her glass. "Up yours."

Everett choked with laughter and tried to look serious. He was already high from the hundred-and-eighty-proof whiskey. "Hey, what else have you got in that closet?" he asked his father.

"Never you mind," Lazarus said. "That closet stays locked. This whiskey was a special treat."

"Well, we have some sherry in the closet downstairs," Lavinia said, "if anyone wants it. And I think we might even have some gin, or scotch. Which one is the scotch, Paris?"

"The brown one," Paris said. "The gin is colorless."

"Oh, that shows how much I know about drinking," Lavinia said cheerfully.

"I'll have a little sherry," Melissa said to be polite. "Lazarus, would you get it, please?"

Lazarus went off to get the sherry, the dispensing of alcoholic beverages being his province. He gave a small glassful each to Melissa and Lavinia. Paris went to the closet that doubled as a bar and got some gin. In the kitchen she made herself a gin and tonic. She hated whiskey but she liked gin; all the kids at college did.

"What's that?" Lavinia asked when she came back.

"Gin and tonic."

"Ooh, drinking gin? Do you drink?"

"Sometimes."

"You'll get high."

"I'm having *one drink*."

"Do the girls at college drink?"

"Of course."

Frankie was looking at all of them as if they were Martians. The pint of Prohibition whiskey was empty. "Where's that gin, Paris?" Frankie asked.

"I put it back in the closet."

"We never leave liquor in the kitchen," Melissa whispered, glancing toward the house to make sure the help was not within earshot. "You know how *they* are when they get near liquor. No point in tempting them."

"Who's 'they'?" Frankie asked.

"Schvartzes," Lazarus said loudly.

"Shh!" Melissa said.

"What are you shushing me for, Toots? They don't know they're shvartzes."

"What are shvartzes?" Frankie asked. "Maids?"

"Yeah, maids," Everett said, and laughed.

Frankie went off and came back with the bottle of gin, some ice, some bottles of tonic, and some glasses on a tray. She set the tray efficiently on the side table and mixed herself a drink. "Drink, anyone? Jonah?"

"No thank you," Jonah said. "Lavinia won't let me drink."

Frankie looked surprised. She sat down and drank her gin and tonic and lit a cigarette.

"Can you drink that after the whiskey?" Melissa asked. "Won't you get sick?"

"I never get sick," Frankie said.

"My goodness."

Lavinia looked at her watch. "We made a reservation for six o'clock. After that it gets crowded and the service isn't so good. Anybody who has to get ready better start doing so. Paris?"

"I'm ready," Paris said.

"Well you might have to . . ." Lavinia lowered her voice to an intimate whisper, "go to the bathroom."

Everyone got up, except Frankie and Everett. Both of them had looked at their watches too. "There's plenty of time," Everett said.

"I'm all ready," Frankie said. "There's just time for one last drink." She went to the side table and mixed it.

"Oh, Frankie," Melissa said, "you need to sew that hem."

Frankie looked down. "What hem?"

"The place with the pin in it. You can't go like that. We're going to a nice restaurant. You should sew it or change your dress."

"Oh."

"I have a sewing box upstairs," Lavinia said.

"Who's going to see the pin?" Frankie said. "I'm going to be sitting down."

"Oh, you just can't," Melissa said. "I'll sew it for you."

"Sewing is a wonderful convenience," Lavinia said.

"Not if you hate it," said Frankie.

Melissa and Lavinia took Frankie upstairs to be repaired, feeling like kind-hearted martyrs. Imagine, such a slob, coming to visit looking like that, and expecting to go out in that torn dress! Poor Everett, what had he gotten himself into? If she kept house the way she dressed . . . Not that Everett would notice. They were two slobs. What a pair.

Lazarus put the gin back into the downstairs closet so philistine hands would not defile it. That girl was the worst thing he had ever seen. She looked like a maid. But Everett had never had good taste in anything, so why should he have expected better?

335

It was a good thing they were going to be far away in Florida.

Jonah was hungry. He was trying to decide whether he should have the lobster or the sirloin steak tonight. He liked to plan ahead and decide what he was going to eat before he got to the restaurant. Everything in its place, planned and orderly.

"What are you going to eat tonight, Paris?" he asked.

"I don't know."

"I think I'll have the lobster."

They went to the restaurant in Everett's rented car. At the table Frankie and Everett decided they were going to have a highball.

"Ooh, so much drinking," Lavinia said.

They were all scrutinizing the large menus. "Why don't you have the lobster, Frankie," Melissa said kindly. "I'm sure you've never had lobster before."

"Actually," Frankie said in an uppity tone, "I'm very fond of lobster."

She's probably overwhelmed by all this, Melissa was thinking. She's not very gracious, but she's probably uncomfortable and shy. She just sticks out like a sore thumb.

Melissa is an angel, Lavinia was thinking. Any girl would be the luckiest girl in the world to get her for a mother-in-law. That girl probably doesn't even know how lucky she is.

Oh good, Frankie's going to make trouble, Paris was thinking.

Everett was hoping everyone would get along all right after a while. He had daydreamed of a confrontation in which Frankie really gave the family a hard time, but now that he had actually brought her here he realized he was anxious that she make a good impression. He knew that if his mother and the rest of them pushed her she would fight back, and he was a little afraid of that. Why couldn't she just keep her mouth shut? But then she wouldn't be his Frankie.

"I'm going into the television business," Everett said to his mother. "That's going to be the new thing. More and more people are buying sets. I'm going to be the first one in the neighborhood in TV repair."

"I think that's a very good idea," Melissa said. "You were always right on top of things, Everett."

"Television," Lazarus said scornfully. "If God had meant man to watch television . . ."

"Oh, you said that about radio too," Melissa said.

"He would have what?" Frankie asked.

"What?"

"If God had meant man to watch television, He would have what?"

"Invented it," Lazarus grumbled, caught.

"Well, He did!" Lavinia said, and laughed. "God gave someone the intelligence to invent it."

Paris had seen television once, at Selma's house. It had a tiny screen in a huge box and Selma's father had put a blurry magnifying glass over the tiny screen so she couldn't figure out what was happening on it, especially since they were watching a baseball game and she hated baseball. But a lot of Selma's neighbors had come over to watch the game, so she figured a lot of people probably thought television was wonderful.

"I made a set for myself already," Everett said. "I just bought the parts and put them together."

"He's very talented," Frankie said.

"My goodness, I should say so!" Melissa said admiringly.

"In the long run it cost me about three times as much as buying a set because of all the mistakes I made," Everett said: "But now I can fix anything."

"Then it was a good investment," Melissa said.

"I've been watching the television industry," Jonah said. "There are some good growth stocks."

"Oh, do you know about the stock market?" Frankie asked. "I'd like to learn about it."

"Fat chance," Lazarus said.

"What does that mean?"

"It takes years," Lazarus said.

"Does it take years, Jonah?" Frankie asked.

"I have to study it all the time," Jonah said.

"Well then you can just give me tips for when I'm rich," she said, and smiled.

That girl should have had orthodontia, Lavinia thought. Poor people never do.

She thinks she's going to be rich when she marries Everett, Melissa thought. I wonder what stories he told her. Well, maybe he seems rich to her. I hope she doesn't think all this she sees around here belongs to him.

ELEVEN

Hervé Saffron was born feet first, as Lazarus had predicted, but the obstetrician reached into his mother's body and turned him around, as one would a baby colt, so he came out properly. Hervé was an enormous baby, eleven pounds, squalling, with his mother's size and face and his father's dark hair. His hands were not a baby's hands, he was not cute, and he was hyperactive. His parents worshiped him.

Everett Bergman and Frances "Frankie" Riley were married in Miami in November. Nobody in the family approved, but when Melissa went to Papa for his word of judgment he took the young couple's side.

"Let them get married," Papa said. "If it doesn't work out they can always get divorced."

The old man certainly was abreast of the times, everyone said, not actually calling him "the old man," as that would have been disrespectful. To them, Papa was ageless. He was still vital, still went to the office every day, and still made all the major decisions in the family. But now he was the modern one, not flinching at the idea of bringing a goy into the family, not flinching at the thought of divorce. He was more liberal with his grandchildren than he had been with his children, but he knew the world had changed and these young people would have to be a part of it. He would not be there, but his plan would survive and so his family would be together, in as close a facsimile of his image as he could manage, and so he could watch the seasons pass without fear.

That winter Rosemary became pregnant at last. She was radiant. The baby was a girl, named Barbara Lucy Nature, nicknamed Buffy. Barbara was for Jack's dead mother, Bathsheba, and Lucy was for Rosemary's dead mother, Lucy. Buffy was an alert and happy infant, and Jack took many photographs of her, one of which Paris carried in her wallet.

Everett was so busy with his new TV repair business, which was taking more time than he had expected to get off the ground, that he and Frankie could only spend a two-week vacation at Windflower, but there were four grandchildren at Windflower now: Paris, Richie, Hervé, and Buffy.

Adam's sons and daughters had presented him with a television set. It sat in state in the living room at Windflower, and now when the family came over after dinner they watched programs. Everyone enjoyed this, except for Nicole.

"Television!" Nicole would say scornfully. "For morons. Why can't you talk to each other, have a good conversation? I myself wouldn't have a television set in the house. I prefer to read a good book."

Nicole and Basil and baby Hervé and his nurse (French, of course) were all staying downstairs in Basil's suite in Papa's house. As soon as the family started watching a favorite television program Nicole, who would not deign to join them, would pop out of the suite and put her finger to her lips.

"Shh. Turn that lower, the baby can't sleep."

They would turn the sound lower, which Adam did not like because in his later years his hearing was not as acute as it had been when he was younger. But Nicole would pop out again anyway.

"Shh! Lower! You're waking the baby."

Finally, in desperation, they would turn off the set and settle for conversation. No sooner had they found a subject of mutual interest, which was getting harder all the time, then out would pop the ever-present Nicole, finger to lips.

"Shh! You just woke up the baby."

"What's the matter with him, anyway?" Adam said in annoyance. His children had slept through anything when they were infants: a house full of relatives and greenhorns all babbling at once, family games, singing, arguments, laughter. What was wrong with that baby, anyway? His mother probably made him nervous. She certainly made Adam nervous.

Etta would make a prune face and then smile. "Hoo ha! I thought I was too old to have a baby in the house, but it seems I'm stuck with one all over again."

Everett and Frankie came to Windflower for their vacation, bringing photographs of their new dog, Daisy, a Doberman. It had long been Everett's dream to have a killer dog that only he could control, the Toughie of his childhood fantasy, and when

Frankie said she liked dogs too, he bought Daisy.

"Next year I'll bring her," he told his mother.

"No, you won't. I'm scared of dogs."

"Scared of Daisy? Everett smiled his fox smile. "Why? She won't hurt anyone unless I tell her to."

"You should be afraid to keep a dog like that in your house," Melissa said.

"She's guarding the house until we get home."

"Well, you just leave her there," Lavinia said. "Dogs are dirty. I don't want a dog here. Paris is allergic to dogs."

"How much does a dog that size cost to feed?" Lazarus asked.

"Oh, she just eats dog food," Everett said. "Although she loves to lick our toes when we're lying in bed. I call it toe jam."

"Ugh," Paris said. "You certainly are getting worse since you've been living in Florida."

"Everett, really," Melissa said. "Can't you control yourself?"

"I tell him," Frankie said. "He doesn't listen to me either."

Frankie was bored at Windflower. She hated the sun, so in the long afternoons she would sit on the carpeted stairs that led to the second floor, in the cool half-darkness, and drink. Lavinia always pulled down the blinds and closed them against the afternoon sun, so it would not fade the furniture and rugs. In this silent, subterranean darkness, Frankie was almost invisible. She and Everett both had keys to the car, his own car this time, which they had driven up north to save money, taking turns driving and making the trip in only a day and a half. She would take the car into the nearby village and buy scotch, and then she would drink it herself because no one wanted to join her.

"Talk to me, Jonah," she would say, whenever she could find him alone. "You and I are the only two intelligent people around here."

"I have to move some stones on the road," Jonah would say. Or, fix the wall, or mend the dam, or roll the tennis court. Anything to get away from her.

"Paris," Frankie would say, "come on, let's you and me go to the roadhouse."

"We can't go to a roadhouse in the daytime," Paris would say. "How does it look?"

"It looks nothing. We'll have a couple of beers, watch TV . . ."

"No, I have to do something."

Everett wouldn't go to the roadhouse either. He wanted to talk business with his mother, or Jonah, or tinker with his junk. His junk followed him everywhere, and grew like something from a science fiction movie: Everett's Junk. He was now building a television set for the family, in the bedroom that had once been his and now he shared with Frankie. There were still the twin beds with the night table separating them. Frankie wore boy's pajamas, striped, with a drawstring at the waist, and he slept in his undershorts. Frankie put a bathrobe over her pajamas for breakfast with the family, but Everett still appeared in only his underpants from time to time, just to test them. His mother always sent him back to his room to dress.

"You'll have to be careful with this TV set," Everett told the family, cheerfully sadistic. "I didn't put a case on it, so if you touch the wrong thing you'll get electrocuted."

Paris was so bored that she was always glad to see Everett, even though he drove everyone crazy. Actually, his driving them crazy was part of the entertainment. But he didn't stay the whole two weeks, after all. He said the family was driving him crazy. So he went back home with Frankie to the little house his mother had bought them in Florida.

"Come visit us," Frankie said to Paris. "I don't know how you stand it here."

"You can sleep on the living room couch with Daisy," Everett said.

"She's not going," Lavinia said.

Paris could hardly wait for fall, when she could go back to college. She still had Rima to visit her, but she missed the rest of college, the kids, the lively activity, the intellectual stimulation, and the boys. She had been going steady this past year, but now that her senior year was coming she had broken up. It would be her last chance to date a lot of boys, and she meant to take advantage of it. She knew she was going against the universal plan. You were supposed to go steady, then get engaged, then get married after graduation. She would rather kill herself than marry Fred. He was a handsome, prep school type, with a rich family and bland good looks, and she had to admit he was stupid. He had little to say to her. She liked him because he liked her and because everyone else was going steady, but that was all fun and makebelieve. She knew the difference between that and life. Not that Fred would marry her, as he wasn't Jewish. But still, he was the sort of passive boy who might even be persuaded to marry her if she really wanted him. She had tried to break up with him twice at the end of the term and he had cried, and she had been so touched that she had stayed with him, but finally the last week she had made it final. It was easier just before summer vacation. Maybe he had met another girl during the summer, and was in love again. She hoped so. Her friends didn't really understand why she had broken up with him. It was more than leaving him, it was going to something more. She didn't expect or want to meet a boy she would fall in love with and marry this last year. She just wanted to have a busy social life. She would be only nineteen. When she graduated she might never have a date she liked again, judging from what her parents had planned for her. She didn't know how to fight them, didn't have the courage to make a break, but at least she could make a compromise. It would be possible to live two lives if she had to.

TWELVE

Paris and Elizabeth were having dinner in a restaurant in Harvard Square. Paris was having her meals out of the dorm more and more in this, her senior year. The dorm seemed too regimented now.

"Don't go home when you graduate," Elizabeth said. "You're a very special person, very talented. Your family will destroy you."

"Where else could I go?"

"You could stay here and go to graduate school. Your parents wouldn't object. Or you could get an apartment in Cambridge and a job, and write."

It sounded so tempting, and just as unreal a dream as living in Europe. Now that the war was long over and the bombed cities were being rebuilt, many of the kids she knew were going to Europe for summer vacation the year they graduated, or even to stay for a year and find a job or just explore on their parents' money, but that dream was for boys and some lucky girls, but not for Paris. Her parents would never allow her to go anywhere alone and she didn't have the courage to oppose them. But to stay in Cambridge . . . to be able to sit around and have long talks with other people who were interested in the same things she was, to take writing courses, to write and try to sell to magazines . . . not to have to dress up and go on blind dates and to charity dances and try to find a husband who would please the family, but simply to live her own life the way she wanted, for her work and her thoughts and her interests and needs . . .

To be here in Cambridge with people of her own age was happiness, but the tough struggle that would get her where she wanted to be, Paris knew, was in New York. In New York she could work for a magazine or publishing company, learn the trade, meet people who would have things to teach her. She had to go to New York.

"I've met your family," Elizabeth said. "I'm so afraid they'll destroy you."

"I know they'll try," Paris said, "but I won't let them. I have to be in New York."

Elizabeth's life was settled. After having been engaged to Jimmy since she was fourteen years old, one day in this last year at college she saw a boy in the museum and fell in love with him at first sight. They spoke, and he asked her out. She sneaked out with him for coffee, they talked, and then she confessed to Paris with fear and emotion that she had really fallen in love this time, that she had to tell Jimmy it was over; she was in love with Allen. Allen felt the same way about her. So Elizabeth told Jimmy, and began seeing Allen, a tall, handsome boy who played football and the cello and loved art as much as she did. He came from a small town in the Midwest and was on scholarship. It would have seemed that Elizabeth, at twenty, had finally begun to date, but instead she and Allen decided to get married in the Harvard chapel when they both graduated this spring. She had given up her future for him, and so he had offered her one with him instead. To both of them it was only right and honorable, also logical. To Paris it was too romantic and unreal, but she hoped it would work out.

Senior year was the best year at Radcliffe because if your marks were good you could stay out every night until two o'clock without writing where in the book in the front hall. Other girls had blithely lied about their whereabouts in many cases, but Paris had been so conditioned to tell the truth by her mother (you could never fool her mother; Lavinia could look into her face and she would crumble) that she told the truth to everyone. So it was good to have this freedom now. Paris had made Dean's List every term. She was getting good marks on her stories and sending stories and poems regularly to the literary magazine, of which she was art editor, and they were always accepted. She had so much control on the magazine now that she had even put herself on the cover: a photo of a Radcliffe girl looking longingly at the new Lamont Library at Harvard, which was for men only with no girls allowed. She was active in the fight the girls were putting up to be allowed to use the same good library facilities as the men. "The boys," Paris still called them. Why should they be men, not boys, when she and her friends were all called "girls," not women? All right, she wasn't twenty-one yet, and a "woman" had to be twenty-one, but some of the girls were, and some of the boys were younger than twenty-one and still called men. How could you call those silly children, who got drunk and threw up in the bushes, whose only ambition in life was to get their hands in a girl's pants and eventually go to work in a bank, how could you call them men? Ectoplasms or schmoos or teddy bears maybe, but not men. How could anybody want to work in a bank? It was impossible for Paris to imagine any of the boys she knew as dignified bankers; she saw them more as tellers, all dressed up in their gray flannel suits and striped ties and button-down shirts, counting out someone else's money.

For her own career, she didn't mind that she would be living with her parents, because she was lucky they already lived in New York. She had read the help wanted ads in the newspapers and knew that a girl started out at forty dollars a week, fifty if she was lucky, and everyone wanted the few jobs in publishing. She could never have afforded to live in New York alone. If you lived with your parents and they fed and clothed you, fifty dollars a week was an enormous amount of money. She would save as much of it as she could so that someday, when she was older and braver, she could have her own apartment.

"Allen got his scholarship to grad school," Elizabeth said.

"Oh, good. I'm not surprised."

"Neither am I. I'm going to get a job to help support us while he's studying. A lot of the stores need salesgirls. I'd rather work in the museum, but they don't pay as much, and everybody wants the same job I do. It won't be easy for a few years, but as long as we don't have any children we can manage. And we *won't* have any children for a long time."

"Good," Paris said. Everyone in the class seemed to be competing in the baby race. Some of the girls were already married, most of those were pregnant, and it was a close race between two of them who would deliver first. It looked as if both of them might give birth right in the middle of final exams, which didn't seem like very good timing.

"I'll tell you the truth," Elizabeth said, "I just don't feel maternal yet. I know this would shock everyone but you, but I don't want a baby. I don't know what I'd do with it. Maybe later, when we have a decent-sized apartment and some money, I'll feel different."

"I don't feel one bit maternal," Paris said. "I feel like a kid. Kids shouldn't have kids."

"What do you say when people ask you how you feel about it?"

"I lie, of course."

Elizabeth sighed. "So do I. Except, of course, to Allen, and to our parents. They would kill us if we had a baby. They would have to support it, and they can't even afford to support us."

"We'll have to keep in touch after we graduate," Paris said.

"You bet. We'll write to each other. And you have to promise to come visit us. You won't mind sleeping on the couch, will you?"

"Of course I won't mind. It's got to be better than my bed in the dorm." They both laughed, and then they were sad for a minute. Who knew if they would see each other again after graduation? Their lives would be different, in different places. They would try to keep in touch, of course, but their lives would be full, each with her own problems and struggles.

"I can't wait to graduate," Elizabeth said.

"Neither can I. I'm not going to graduation, by the way."

"*You're not?* Why not?"

"I don't want to. It's silly."

"But it's one of the most important moments in your life."

"I don't have a date for the dance," Paris said. "And everyone who's going has a date. I can't stand to be there all alone, with

345

my parents. Rima's not going either."

"You can be with us," Elizabeth said.

"No. I'm just not going."

"Not to any of it?"

"Just the luncheon the first day. Then I'm leaving."

But as it turned out, Paris went to graduation, all of it. At the farewell luncheon the speeches and good will suddenly filled her with a rush of school spirit. As a going-away present each girl was given a cheap little keyring with the Radcliffe seal on it, and holding it in her hand Paris was filled with emotion for her school and everything it had meant to her. She telephoned her parents and told them to come see her graduate, and rented the cap and gown. She would go to everything.

The dance was held outdoors, in the quadrangle between the girls' dormitories, because it was a warm night. Paper lanterns swung from the trees, a band played, and her classmates with their dates wandered from porch to porch saying goodbye to old friends. Paris sat on the stone railing of her dorm with her parents, feeling embarrassed and sad and left out. She knew this was how it would be if she chose to stay alone; she would always be embarrassed and sad and left out.

"Dance with her, Jonah," her mother said.

"No," Paris said. "Nobody here is dancing with her father."

"Well, it's your own fault. You could have had a date. Nobody you knew was good enough for you."

"That's not true. They were going home."

"Well, if you had wanted to go steady you could have had a date for the dance too. Everybody here is going steady or engaged." There was pride in her mother's voice, not censure.

"Would you rather I was engaged, mother?"

"You know I always told you that was up to you."

"She's too young to get married," her father said, sounding perplexed.

"Of course she is," her mother said. She turned to Paris. "When you come home, we'll go to Windflower, and then in the fall when we're back in the city, please God, you'll keep up with your writing and you'll do some charity work."

"I'm getting a job," Paris said.

"All right. I had a job once. But you should do some charity work too. Grandpa always said that people should do for others."

"I could work in the foundling hospital a couple of nights a week after work, or maybe weekends."

"Don't be silly. You'll go to luncheons with me, you'll meet people. It's very important to become a part of the community. You don't need to work in the foundling hospital; they have all kinds of diseases there."

"Luncheons?" Paris said in horror.

"Yes, indeed," her mother said. "You'll meet my friends and they have nice sons and daughters you can become friends with. You can be on a committee for a dance or a benefit, and you'll meet more nice people."

"No luncheons," Paris said.

"Don't be silly. You'll go with me. You can still have a job. They give you a lunch hour, don't they?"

"Luncheons are for old people."

Her mother was furious. She took on her clipped tone. "There are many, many lovely young girls your age who go to charity luncheons with their mothers. They are humanitarians. They don't waste their lives with people who won't mean anything to them in a few years."

"Let's discuss it another time," Paris said. "This is my graduation dance. I'm supposed to be having a good time."

"Isn't that that friend of yours who was up at Windflower?" her father asked.

"Yes, Elizabeth," Paris said.

"Who's the guy?"

"Her fiancé. They're getting married next week."

"He's not much," her mother said. "But she's not much either."

Paris looked at Elizabeth and Allen and their parents, and wondered if Elizabeth would come over to say hello to her while her parents were there. She knew Elizabeth was afraid of her mother. Maybe Elizabeth hadn't seen them, hiding there in the shadows. She wanted to go over and say hello to their group and suddenly she felt a new shyness, a diffidence, a strangeness. She could see everything through her mother's eyes, as her mother must be seeing it, and Elizabeth and her family and fiancé and his family seemed like strangers. It was as if they were fading from sight, out of her life, like an old snapshot. Paris was suddenly afraid of them.

Her mother had a power over her, she knew it, and it was beyond anything she could understand intellectually. She could be so sure of something that she wanted, and then her mother would start to hammer at her and she would not be so sure. She would want it, but she would also want her mother to say it was all right. She was too old to be so influenced, and yet the older she became the stronger her mother's power seemed to be. That was why they fought. If Paris had been sure of what she wanted she would simply have done it, but she always let—no, made—her mother be part of it. She told herself it was because she wasn't yet twenty-one and had no legal rights, she told herself it was because she had no money, but the truth was she had no courage in the face of her mother's steely disapproval. Any extreme horror fantasy was better, more believable, than the withdrawal of her mother's love and approval. Sometimes she hated her mother for making life so difficult, and hated her father for not taking her side against her mother. Were all parents and children so tied together in love and hate and need? Paris doubted it. She felt she was a freak, and that they were freaks too. People either accepted everything their parents wanted or they broke away. But she was locked in mortal combat. If she chopped off one of her mother's tentacles she knew her mother would grow another, instantly, magically.

But she had her own strength around her soft inner core. Little Porcupine, her mother had called her as a child. She was still the little porcupine, protecting what was hers. Lavinia Saffron Mendes knew that soft core was there, partly an inheritance from Jonah: goodness, softness, and a dogged stubbornness, all of which Lavinia had seen and conquered in Jonah. But Jonah had chosen to be conquered. Paris had not.

PART IV

The Beginning

ONE

Richie was twelve, and his mother was driving him crazy. He knew that the other kids at school didn't get along so well with their mothers either, but his really got on his nerves. He couldn't communicate with her at all. He couldn't talk to her, reason with her. He was always fighting with her. She was so dumb, dumb, dumb. She followed him around the house when he was home and dragged him with her when she went out, and treated him like a pet. His father was working in his office all day, and in the evenings his parents went out to one of their charity affairs, or a business dinner, or else his father went out alone to a business meeting, so Richie never had a chance to broach the subject to him. Anyway, how could you tell your father that your mother was a pest and that she embarrassed you? His father said he was to respect his mother, sons should revere their parents. When his father did have time to talk to him it was always about business. Richie knew he would inherit his father's business someday, and could even go into it when he graduated from college and business school if he wanted to. He also knew that he would someday own a part of his mother's family's business, and so it was important that his father have these little man-to-man talks with him to prepare him for the future. Treated thus like a man, how could he turn around with a childish whine and complain about his mother? No, he couldn't. So he tried to avoid her as much as he could. That was very hard to do; she sought him out with her own radar.

"Richie? Whatcha doin'?"

He had read that certain kinds of whales and dolphins had a sort of radar, sonar actually, where they could bounce sounds off objects in the depths of the ocean and thus "see" them. It was as if his mother were some great whale, calling out, finding him. She was big on top and little on the bottom, and in her fishtail blue sequinned evening gown that trailed off into a little ruffle at the floor she even looked just like a whale.

Richie was a lonely child. He had few friends at school, and none of them was a close friend except for one extrovert boy, Iggie, who was friends with everybody. Except for Iggie, who was a slob, Richie never invited his friends home after school because he was embarrassed and guilty about the way he felt ashamed of his mother. It was wrong to be ashamed of your mother. You should respect her. But she said such dumb things sometimes, and she pestered his friends. He wanted a mother like he saw on TV and in the movies, helpful, wise, graceful, but if he couldn't have that because they only existed in the movies then he would like to have one like Iggie's mother. She was a yenteh, but she let him alone.

Once a week, in the afternoon, Richie's mother went to the beauty parlor, and she didn't make him go. That was wonderful. He played records in his room, or did his homework, or wandered around the house if he felt restless, feeling free for once. She went on Thursdays. This particular Thursday he decided to explore his parents' room. Your parents' room was forbidden territory, but since his mother felt free to explore his, Richie felt it was about time he availed himself of a comparable privilege. They had a wonderful big bedroom with twin beds in it, and a television set, and a dressing room and a huge bathroom. There were a million closets. His mother had a lot of clothes. His father had a lot of clothes, too. The maid kept the room really neat.

On the big triple dresser there were several silver framed photos of Richie, from the time he was a baby until now, so he assumed that was his mother's dresser. There was a matching chifferobe, and on top of that was a humidor containing his father's cigars, so he knew whose that was. You could see the back garden and the palm trees from the bedroom window. They really lived in a nice house. Richie listened carefully to hear if the maid was coming. Other people's maids had every Thursday off, but not their maid, because his mother had to go to the beauty parlor on Thursday and wouldn't dream of leaving him alone, so their maid had Wednesdays off. When his mother was having her hair done the maid was very contented in her room or in the kitchen preparing dinner, and she never went upstairs to see if he was getting into trouble. The maid, at least, respected him as a grown-up twelve-year-old, nearly a teenager, not a baby any more.

He opened the top drawer of his mother's dresser. Holy cow, what a mess! Everything was just thrown in; scarves, stockings, magazines. It looked like some kid's dresser drawer, worse than his. The maid knew better than to arrange her employer's dresser drawers, those things were private.

The magazines, Richie noticed, were his mother's beloved cross-word puzzle magazines. If she wasn't knitting she was working on her puzzles. He picked up one of them and idly leafed through it. She had apparently been working on it as all the pages had filled-in puzzles on them. Then he saw something that scared him half to death. None of the puzzles was really done, not the way you were supposed to with the letters written in the boxes to make words. She had made a big D that covered four boxes, then a C, then some other letters, and none of it made any sense at all. She hadn't even filled in the three-letter words, dog and cat. It was as if a three-year-old had been pretending to be a grownup, a three-year-old who couldn't read yet but could imitate.

But his mother could read! He knew she could read. Sometimes she read things aloud to him from the movie gossip column in the daily newspaper. It was just that she couldn't . . . couldn't reason. She couldn't actually do a crossword puzzle, but she liked pretending that she could because then people thought that she was just like everybody else, capable, with a hobby.

Richie grabbed the other puzzle magazines from his mother's drawer and looked through them. They were all the same, a mess. He stood there with the crossword puzzle magazines in his hand and began to cry.

His mother wasn't like other people's mothers. He had been right about that. She was retarded. He had always thought retarded was those scary Mongoloid children you saw on the charity telethon on TV, the ones who grinned and drooled and looked at you out of little piggy uncomprehending eyes, but his mother was retarded too. She didn't look queer, and she didn't drool or let her tongue flop around, but she could hardly talk straight and she played tricks on people and games like a child. She bought all those dumb silly things at the store and thought they were funny, those tricks and gags, and now Richie knew why.

Why didn't his father know?

His father always just went along acting as if his mother was perfectly normal. If his mother did something particularly weird or stupid his father just laughed it off, saying that was what women did. His father believed women were inferior to men, particularly wives, and it amused him that his wife was so helpless and passive, that she could never park the car right, that she forgot where she had put it, that she brought home jokes and tricks and gags she thought were funny. His father didn't like his wife to talk when he was holding forth in a group, and he felt a wife should be an ornament and credit to her husband, expensively dressed, neat, hair done, glittering with jewelry. So his mother sat there and didn't say anything, and looked like all the other wives, and his father was happy. His father didn't know his mother was retarded because *he didn't care.*

But I care, Richie thought, tears streaming down his cheeks. I care.

He knew it wasn't inherited. He was smart and got good marks in school, and his father was smart and did well in business. His aunts and uncles were smart. He particularly liked Uncle Basil, who was always very nice to him and seemed so gentle. Did the rest of them know about his mother? They always acted as if she was just like the rest of them, just like everybody else. Sometimes Aunt Rosemary yelled at her when she wanted her own way, because his mother could be very stubborn and Aunt Rosemary liked to argue about things. But that seemed normal in a house. With everybody living together the way they did at Windflower, no wonder they had fights. His parents, alone, never had fights. Whatever his father said in his own house was law.

Richie blew his nose in one of his mother's handkerchiefs and wiped his eyes. Then he threw the dirty handkerchief into her hamper in the bathroom for the maid to take away. He put the crossword puzzle magazines back into the drawer where he had found them. In a way he was sorry he had ever looked, and in another way he was glad. Now he was truly a man. The rabbi who gave him his Hebrew instruction said he would be a man next year when he was thirteen and had his bar mitzvah, but Richie knew differently. A man was a person who had to be alone and could survive. He was alone now. He didn't have a mother any more, he just had another kid in the house, one who was allowed to be boss over him because everybody had played a trick on her. They had pretended she was fine, just like anyone else, and she believed it. But even as he grieved for the lost, warm mother who had ceased to exist when he was about four years old, Richie was also glad, because now he didn't have to respect her and he could respect himself, depend on himself.

When his mother came back from the beauty parlor he acted just the same as ever. He told her she looked nice with her hair done and she was pleased. He even let her kiss him. There was some time before his father came home for dinner so he went into his room and started reading the Torah. When his mother came to the door he held it up and said, "Hebrew lesson tomorrow," and she withdrew. The Torah said a lot of things about man, how he should behave, and about women. It was better to be a man than a woman. Men were smarter, stronger. And if you obeyed the laws of God He would help you more.

That night at dinner Richie said to his father, "Tomorrow night I want us to light the candles."

"You do?" his father said. He seemed pleased. "How come?"

"I think we should. We're a Jewish household and we should behave like good Jews."

"I think that's a good idea," his father said. "Don't you, Hazel?"

"Do we have candles?" his mother said, bewildered.

"We'll buy some!" his father said. Why not? He had bought cars, houses, diamonds, furs, so what were a few candles? "Richie will buy them, since it's his idea."

"And I want to say the prayers too," Richie said. He knew his mother was supposed to light the candles and say the prayers, but she obviously couldn't, so he would.

"My little Hebrew student," his father said. "My scholar."

"I want to light the candles every Friday night from now on," Richie said. "And on Saturday, I don't want you to go to work."

"What do you mean? You're telling me not to go to work?" His father laughed. "A lunch meeting isn't work."

"It's Saturday," Richie said. "I want to go to temple."

"You go to Sunday school."

"I want to go to temple with the men."

"You can go to temple with the men when you're a man.

Meanwhile you go to Sunday school and take your Hebrew lessons and get ready for your bar mitzvah, and I'll go to my lunch meeting."

"You're going to Hialeah," Richie said accusingly.

"So what?"

"That's a race track. It's a sin."

His father laughed. "Now we have a religious fanatic in the house."

"I'll take him, Herman," his mother said.

"I don't want to go with you. I want to sit with the men."

"Now the temple isn't orthodox enough for you either?" his father said. He was taking it all as a big joke. After all, he was not an irreligious man, and it was good that his son should have an idea of his heritage, but enough was enough. Teenagers!

"I'm shocked that there is so little religion in this house," Richie said.

"What does he want?" his mother asked his father.

"It's all right, Hazel, it's a phase they all go through before they're bar mitzvahed. I went through it myself. He'll outgrow it."

Richie was poking at his dinner with his fork. "What's this?"

"What's what?" his mother asked.

"This."

"That's liver and bacon. You like it."

"That's *tref!*" Richie screamed.

"Don't scream," his father said, amused.

"It's pork, pig, tref!" Richie said. "I want another plate."

"What's the matter?" his mother asked.

Richie went into the kitchen and got another plate. The maid looked at him with surprise. He took the plate back to the dinner table and helped himself to some vegetables and potatoes. He would not eat the liver after it had been contaminated by touching the bacon. He would not eat unclean pig. He chewed his broccoli and felt strangely relieved and calm. It was better to know your path. He was so abysmally ignorant of the proper ways of observing the laws, but he would study and then he would obey. It would be good to find God and be able to speak to Him. He would be a true and faithful friend to God, and then God would be a true and faithful friend to him. Whatever tribulations had been put here on this earth for him to endure had only been put here to test him.

TWO

On summer evenings at Windflower Frankie would wander along the lawn, taking in the view, a glass of scotch and ice in her hand. "Don't wander away," Melissa would warn. "Dinner is promptly at six."

How scared they were of the maids! If it was my house, Frankie thought, I'd either have no maid or else one I could boss around. Who ever heard of eating when the maid says you have to eat? Rich people should have a cocktail hour and then eat at seven-thirty like anybody else. Dinner on the table smack at six o'clock was for poor people, blue-collar workers, the man of the house home from the factory starving and screaming for his meat. Six o'clock dinner was for oilcloth on the table; seven-thirty was for linen tablecloths they kept telling you were heirlooms, and real silverware with the family's initials on it, and a crystal chandelier over the table. She wasn't even hungry yet at six o'clock. They ate lunch all afternoon, it seemed like.

There was the Winsor-Nature house, and there through the picture window Frankie could see Richie wearing his skullcap, lighting the candles. He was so solemn and serious, such a little old man. The candlelight made a soft glow on his face and it looked like a religious picture. There was so much about being a Jew that Frankie didn't know, and she would have liked to know, but Everett didn't seem to know anything either, or else he didn't want to talk about it. Everett seemed to resent his heritage. Frankie wasn't too crazy about hers either, but you were stuck being what you were and at least you should be able to talk sensibly about it if someone asked you questions.

In the lower field the horses were frolicking. They always played before dinner, in the quiet, cool hour when the mist began to rise. That Valley was really weird, like a Gothic novel. At night the fog seemed to close everything in and the family seemed more isolated than ever. Frankie was lonely at Windflower. She felt trapped.

She had gone into this marriage with Everett with her eyes

open, planning to get him, and getting what she had gone out for, and now it was her own fault. First of all, he wasn't rich; it was all his parents' money and he got an allowance. Second, he spent everything on himself because he was selfish. Third, he worked like a dog and never seemed to make any money of his own. She was still working for him, answering the phones in the TV repair shop, having nothing better to do with her time. At least she made him pay her the same salary she'd gotten when she was single. She wasn't slave labor even if she was his wife.

They had nothing in common. Everett hated sports. He had wheedled some money out of his mother to buy some stocks he'd heard about, and the stocks had gone up and he'd made a big profit. Frankie wanted to put a down payment on a better house, and Melissa said Everett ought to ask Jonah about stocks and start building up a portfolio, but no, Everett had gone out and spent every damn cent on a private plane. It looked like a toy. He'd taken flying lessons and he went up in it every day after work. He'd taken Frankie up a few times, but she didn't see any reason to get killed just to prove to him she wasn't chicken. Then Etta's son, Stanley, the airlines pilot, had come to visit with his own private plane, and Stanley had started taking Etta up in it and giving her flying lessons. Old Etta, with her blue hair, flying a plane! Frankie had to give the old gal credit. It really looked jazzy, the lawn with the two little planes sitting on it. Etta said she'd never have the courage to fly all by herself, so she only went up with her son on the dual controls. When Stanley went away there was Everett's plane, but Etta wouldn't fly with him. She said she didn't trust him, he wasn't a professional. But Everett had a license. Frankie didn't like it the way everybody around Windflower treated Everett like a jerk, and he took it.

The plane was too small to fly back to Florida unless they planned to take a year doing it, so Everett was toying with the idea of either selling it or storing it. He was really stupid about money, even Frankie could see that. Everything he did was wrong, a waste, a mistake.

Frankie liked to go bowling; Everett refused. Frankie liked to drink; Everett thought it was a waste of time except at a party. Frankie liked to go to the movies; Everett said he was too tired. Everett never read any kind of book he could discuss with Frankie, just those magazines about mechanical things. What Everett wanted was to go to bed with Frankie and take advantage of his marital rights. And Frankie hated that.

She'd always known she wouldn't care for it, but she hadn't realized that every night would be a battle; the "headache," the "stomach ache," the "cramps," the period that she managed to invent a couple of extra times because Everett was too dumb to count. It wasn't that giving Everett his marital rights made her sick or anything; she just didn't like it, it was boring, messy, and she felt used. She didn't want any man getting that close to her. He didn't own her. He was rough, but by the clock it didn't take so long that she couldn't have put up with it; it was just that she was stubborn and she didn't feel like getting started in the first place. She told him once a week, Saturday night, that was it. That was what he would get. And if she didn't feel well on Saturday night then he'd get a raincheck. Thank God Everett was so nervous sleeping in his parents' house that he never jumped on her at all when they were at Windflower. If the rest of being at Windflower wasn't so boring Frankie would have liked to stay all summer just for that reason alone.

And, oh boy, was it boring here! Paris sat in her room all day writing; a book, she said. She was always writing some kind of a book, or rewriting it. Frankie could hear her portable typewriter going click-clack all day long, whenever she passed in the hall. Paris had put a big sign on the outside of her closed door with a skull and crossbones drawn on it: "Do Not Disturb! ! !" The only person who was anywhere near Frankie's age and she never emerged except for meals.

This estate was the most beautiful place Frankie had ever seen, just right for a party. But did this family ever give a party? Ha ha. Fat chance. If somebody in the family had a birthday they'd get all dressed up as if they were going into the city or someplace, and then they'd all go to the house of the person whose birthday it was and have a big, fancy dinner with roast beef and creamed sweetbreads in a rice ring, and two kinds of cake, birthday cake and ice cream cake, and cookies, and then they would all sit around and eat candy and talk about how they had to go on a diet. That was the worst idea for a party that Frankie had ever heard of. She'd been to a wake that was more fun than that.

She started drinking before lunch (right after breakfast, actually, but she considered it before lunch, which it was too), and then she kept on freshening her drink all day long, keeping just that nice edge on so that she could stand it here. She knew none of them liked her. She wasn't sure they liked Everett. It was hard to tell. You were In or you were Out around here. She knew she was definitely Out. She was an outsider. All her dreams about making a rich marriage and having a lot of money seemed meaningless when she considered that she was sitting here in the middle of more wealth than she'd ever seen in her life and nobody was having a good time, least of all her.

Everett must have complained to his mother about Frankie rejecting him in bed, because one day Melissa had gotten her aside for a walk in the garden and had the gall to conduct the following conversation.

MELISSA: I hope you and Everett are getting along all right.

FRANKIE: Sure, why shouldn't we be?

MELISSA: I mean . . . I mean, uh, you do sleep together, don't you?

FRANKIE (*Very coldly*): I do my duty.

Frankie told Everett for that little caper he wasn't going to get anything for a whole month. What did he think she was, telling his mother their own private business? They had a big, screaming fight about that, but not so much bigger or louder than the fights they often had. It was easy to fight with Everett. He really got on Frankie's nerves. She liked the dog, Daisy, the best of anyone in their whole household. Everett had promised to bring Daisy to Windflower, but at the last minute he'd chickened out. He was afraid his mother wouldn't pay for their plane tickets if they brought the dog. Daisy had been trained as a guard dog, and she was capable of killing an intruder, but she would never hurt Frankie or Everett. You could take a piece of meat right out of her mouth, and even though she could bite your hand off if she wanted to, she'd just look at you and wait to see if you were playing a game or what. Of course, if a stranger tried that trick he would be minus a hand. Frankie felt a kinship with Daisy. They were both alike in a way: tough, strong, loners, but trapped in life as possessions. They both belonged to Everett because he had bought them. They could both kill him if they wanted to, but they wouldn't.

THREE

When little Hervé had just started to run around, getting into everything, Nicole had her second child: a girl, Geneviève Lucy. Geneviève was an exquisite baby, like the drawing in the baby food ads, with dimples and curls and huge eyes. Basil and Nicole brought her to Windflower that summer, to stay in their suite at Papa's house. Hervé and Geneviève were in cribs, the nurse had the bed which had replaced the sofa last summer, and of course Basil and Nicole had the adjoining room. It was nice, everyone thought, that Geneviève and Rosemary's little Buffy were so close in age that they could play together when they were old enough, more like sisters than cousins.

"It's too bad poor Buffy is so homely," Nicole said. "My Geneviève looks like a little princess. Buffy looks like a monkey. I suppose she'll be jealous."

"Why don't you just shut up about it?" Rosemary snapped.

"Truth is truth," Nicole said calmly. "She'll find out when she's older."

"Maybe when they're older Buffy will be the beauty and Geneviève will lose her looks," Rosemary said.

"There's always plastic surgery," Nicole said. "In Europe they do miracles."

"Oh, Europe, Europe," Jack grumbled. "Why doesn't she go there?"

That was, in fact, what Nicole was planning to do. As soon as the children were a little older she and Basil would take them on many trips to France, give them culture, keep them from being crass Americans. In the meantime, as far as summers were concerned, Windflower was beautiful, but there was no excitement there. Nicole wanted Basil to buy a house in East Hampton, on Long Island, near the beach, where they could hobnob with intellectuals: writers, painters, people in publishing and theater and the television business. Nicole would give cocktail parties for all the local celebrities and have a chance to exercise her mind, as well as take long walks on the beach and invigorating swims in the cold ocean and exercise her body.

Basil had driven with Nicole and a couple she knew, a psychiatrist and his wife, to East Hampton, where they looked at houses. Basil knew there was a piece of land waiting for him at Windflower, on the hill overlooking the lake, where he was expected to build his house whenever he was ready. But he did not want to build his house there, never had wanted to. The houses in East Hampton really appealed to him. He loved the beach, the smell of the salt water and the feel of the hot sun, the social life, so many parties, and all the small restaurants. He didn't mind the drive. Nicole and the children could stay there all summer and he would take long weekends. Whatever made her happy made him happy, if only because it kept her from nagging him. When Nicole wanted something, she got it. But then, he wanted what she wanted; he just sometimes didn't realize it until she had pointed it out to him. But the problem was, what would Papa say?

While Basil was working up his courage to broach the subject to Papa, Papa surprised him by bringing it up himself. Papa and Basil were taking a little stroll around the property after lunch on a balmy Saturday afternoon. The babies were napping, and Nicole was swimming her afternoon mile.

"How blue is the sky," Papa said, looking up.

"Not a cloud," Basil said.

"A paradise here, isn't it." It was a statement, not a question. "Here is your hill, Basil, where I hope someday you'll build your house."

"Er . . ."

"It takes a long time to build a house," Papa went on. "You should be making plans. My house, it's a big house, but it's not big enough for two babies and a nursemaid. It's not good, shush-shush all the time. I'm an older man, I've had my children, now I want quiet in the daytime and cheerful noise at night, but with babies in the house it's just the opposite. In the daytime they cry, they run around, at night they have to sleep; there's not enough room."

"We saw a house in East Hampton we want to rent," Basil blurted out.

Papa nodded. He looked pleased. "So? You can stay there while you're building your house. A good idea."

"I . . . I might not build the house for a while," Basil said.

"No?"

"Nicole likes East Hampton."

Papa nodded again. "She might like to stay there and you wouldn't build here?"

"How would you feel about that, Papa? Tell me the truth."

"I think East Hampton would be good for Nicole. But you, Basil? Where do you want to live?"

"I don't know."

"So you'll rent in East Hampton, you'll see, and if you like it maybe you'll buy there?"

"That's what we thought we might do," Basil said. He was surprised at how easy it was. Papa, as always, seemed to anticipate what he was going to say, and actually seemed to be encouraging him. "We'll visit you, of course. Very often. And we hope you'll visit us."

"I went to the beach many years," Papa said. "I've had enough with the beach. You can visit me."

"Oh, we will!"

"Of course, if you want to live there, you'll have to become a part of the community, make friends."

"We already know some people who have houses there," Basil said.

"Good. It's a long drive, isn't it, for you every day?"

"Nicole and the children would stay there all summer and I would take four-day weekends, or three-day weekends if you need me at the office."

"If I need you? Of course I need you. You'll take three-day weekends."

Papa needed him! Basil smiled his gratitude and pleasure. "I'm always here for you, Papa," he said.

"So, this house you like, when can you have it?"

"We were hoping for next summer."

"It's gone already this summer?"

"I don't know. It was still available last week, but now it's the beginning of June so I don't know."

"What's wrong with it, they can't rent it?"

"It's expensive."

"Is it worth it?"

"We think so."

"We! We! What about you, you? Do you think it's worth it?"

"Yes, Papa, I do."

"You're not poor, you can afford it."

"Do you think I should take it this summer if it's still on the market?"

"Why not? So late in the season maybe the price has gone down."

"Let's walk back to the house. I'll call them!"

"And remember, if the price hasn't gone down, don't hondel. You're Adam Saffron's son. Adam Saffron's son doesn't have to hondel."

"Yes, Papa."

The house in East Hampton which Basil and Nicole had liked was, miraculously, still available. A large, modern house with big, airy windows, a large lawn, and only a block from the beach. You could see the ocean from the bedroom windows. It was very expensive. It was lucky Papa hadn't asked exactly how expensive it was. When Basil finished his negotiations on the phone he ran all the way down the hill to the lake to tell Nicole the good news.

The following week Basil and Nicole drove to East Hampton to close the deal and make lists of what they would have to buy or bring from the city. The house was completely furnished, but there were always personal things you wanted that they forgot to supply. Of course sheets and towels were not included, and none of the special utensils that Nicole wanted for her French cooking were there. But there was even a cook included with the rental of the house.

That very next weekend Basil and Nicole, little Hervé and baby Geneviève, the French nurse, and the new East Hampton cook were all ensconced in their wonderful big beach house. It occurred to Basil that Papa had been singularly easy to convince. Perhaps it was true that, as he had suspected, Papa had never been able to warm up to Nicole, even now that she was a member of the family. No, that was silly. How could anyone not like Nicole? It was just that Papa was a practical man. The Big House at Windflower wasn't meant for babies. Papa needed his peace and quiet, as he had said. East Hampton was for young people, young couples with little children, lively people who loved sports and social life. Their big, sprawling house would be casual and friendly. Children could spill ice cream on the deck chairs if they wanted to and no one would yell at them. Nicole believed in bringing up children permissively. Her friend the psychiatrist and his wife believed in letting their children do anything they wanted to so they would not become frustrated. Basil didn't want his own children to become frustrated either. Better a few spots and stains on the living room furniture than a child who had social problems in his later life.

In East Hampton that Saturday afternoon Nicole and Basil bought green and white striped sheets and towels, large beach towels, and a set of Sabatier knives. At Windflower that same day Maurice, the chauffeur, huffing and puffing, brought the sofa back upstairs from the cellar where it had been stored under plastic wraps, and put it where it belonged in what had been Basil's old study. The nurse's bed was given to Maurice for his own chauffeur's cottage, as it was time he had a new one. Hervé had broken the ship model that used to stand on the desk, but Etta put a large vase of freshly cut garden flowers in its stead. The cribs were gone to East Hampton with the children, and Etta had arranged for the cleaners to come on Monday to pick up the carpet to be cleaned.

"It's funny how a house where there were babies always smells like vomit," Etta said.

"Turn up the sound on the TV," Adam said. Etta, Rosemary, Lavinia, and Melissa rushed to comply.

"What's so good in East Hampton?" Paris asked.

"Nothing *you* want," Lavinia said.

FOUR

It was the day of Richie's bar mitzvah. Today he was a man. His prayers had all been learned, and the rabbi said he was a prize student. He was so fervent, so painstakingly proper in every detail, was it possible he might be considering going on to study to become a rabbi himself someday? No, Richie said politely, he was going to go to business school so he could become a businessman like his father. But of course, he added, he would always live the religious life and keep the faith and laws of his people. It was important to be a good Jew. He was only regretful that the rest of his family had forgotten so much of their beautiful heritage.

Thirteen years old and such a serious little boy, although a young man now. He walked around in a daze, lost in his own thoughts, and never answered when you said good morning. The happy smile was gone. It was a bashful smile, and he hung his head and wouldn't look you in the eye unless he was giving a lecture on religion. He was unpredictable: one moment a child, the next an old man. He would walk into a room where a radio was playing and snap it off.

"What are you doing?" the outraged owner of the radio would cry.

"You're interfering with my studies," Richie would answer in a calm tone, sure that right and God were on his side.

"So go in your room."

"I can still hear you."

There was only only one television set in the Winsor-Nature house, and it was in the living room. It belonged to Jack Nature, who had bought it wholesale from a friend. Hazel didn't care what program they watched, and Herman was never there, but Richie would walk over to the set in the middle of a program he didn't like and change the channel. Jack and Rosemary would scream.

"You're a *child* around here," Rosemary would say, "and don't you forget it."

Sometimes Richie was kind to Buffy, patiently playing with her and telling her stories, and then suddenly his mood would change and he would beat her up, twist her arm, sit on her until she cried.

"Why did you do that?" she would ask him.

"I don't know."

Only two years old, she was bright and astonishingly verbal. Her physical coordination was precocious too. She loved to run. Whenever she could escape the watchful eyes of the family she would run all the way down the hill, across the wide expanses of lawn, down the road, around the turnabout, up the hill again, to the edge of the lake, the edge of the woods. She was like a little puppy, so fast and tireless. They had started to call her The Runner. She knew her boundaries; anything outside the stone walls and electrified barbed wire of Windflower was forbidden. There were cars on the road that could hit and kill a child. Strange maniac men lurked in the dark bushes down the road to kidnap little girls.

Richie loved Buffy. He thought of her as the little sister he had never had. He didn't know why he sometimes turned on her. It was just that sometimes the tensions, the anger and bewilderment, and even the growing sexual frustrations inside him became too much to handle, and then he wanted to wrestle, and there was no one to wrestle with. He was not athletic, and he never invited friends to Windflower. He used to play with Timmy and Mike, the caretaker's sons, but the past year he had become self-conscious with them, feeling that they were beneath him. They went to the local public school, had their own friends, and treated him with polite deference. They were planning their lives now, hoping to get scholarships to college or attend a free state college. Their mother had taught them to be very polite to the family, and now, although they never went so far as to call him Mister Richie, they treated him differently than they treated their own friends, partly because Richie treated them differently too. The three little boys who had run along the banks of the lagoon with Molly Forbes so long ago were three teenagers, separate people. He would not invite them to his bar mitzvah. They were not family.

For two days now, workmen had been putting up a huge green and white striped tent, laying a wooden dance floor, and putting a wood floor inside the tent as well, covering the floor with artificial grass. There would be a small orchestra to play for dancing, and for background music while everyone feasted. Two long buffet tables would line two walls of the tent, and the sides of the tent could be rolled down in case God forbid it rained. Maurice would direct all the cars to the parking lot near the garage and chauffeur's cottage. Inside the tent would be dining tables with tablecloths and flower arrangements on them. It had been decided to have several very long tables instead of a lot of small round ones, so no one would feel he or she had been discriminated against because of whom they had to sit with. Some of the relatives, especially on Herman Winsor's side, were nearly strangers.

Herman had come up from Florida for the whole week. Hazel was proud of her son and happy that her husband was with her. Whenever all three of them were together she felt that there was nothing more wonderful for life to offer her. She had never stopped feeling lucky from the very day Herman proposed. Now here was her wonderful son, so handsome, who had learned all that Hebrew, all those foreign words and prayers, and was so smart that the rabbi had complimented him specially. She had bought Richie a new suit for the occasion, and Herman had picked out a gold wrist-watch from the two of them for their son, with an inscription on the back: *Richard Winsor, 1952, from his loving parents.* It was a very big watch, to get all those words on the back. She had bought a new dress for herself, and Herman said it was very pretty. She was the mother of the bar mitzvah boy! Everyone would look at her, so it was important to look specially nice today. Usually in the summer she left her diamonds and other expensive jewelry in the bank vault in Florida, because no one wore fancy things like that in the country, but this year Hazel had brought them with her. She wanted to wear all her diamonds to Richie's bar mitzvah party. She was the bar mitzvah mother, wasn't she! Besides, Herman had invited many of his relatives, and he wanted her to wear the diamonds: the necklace, the earrings, the pin, the bracelets, and the cocktail ring.

Presents for Richie were pouring in. Most of them, luckily, were savings bonds.

"How many fountain pens did you get, Richie?" Jack asked.

Richie smiled self-consciously. "Only eleven."

"You know the joke—the bar mitzvah boy gets up to make his speech and he says: 'Today I am a fountain pen.' "

In the morning there would be the ceremony at the temple in the next town (there was no temple in their town) and then everyone would attend the celebration luncheon, which would last all afternoon. It had been decided to hold the celebration at Windflower even though Richie's main temple was the one in Florida, because it was easier for everyone to come here than to go down there. Many of the relatives were old, Papa's surviving sisters, for example. Richie had never even seen them.

The bar mitzvah day had perfect summer weather, sunny, warm, but not uncomfortably hot. There was not the remotest possibility of rain. The caterers had put the finishing touches on the tent: leaves and ribbons wound around the tent poles. It looked very festive and pretty sitting there in the middle of the lawn between the two houses, under the great old trees.

"Can we keep it?" Buffy asked her father.

"No."

"Why?"

"It costs money."

When the first cars started driving up Buffy was suddenly shy and hid in the kitchen. Paris was all dressed up in a new dress and rather shy and self-conscious too. She didn't like having to kiss all those people, most of whom she hardly knew, but it was part of her family personality, kiss kiss. Her mother had told her to be friendly, that no one loves a porcupine, that if she wasn't nice to the family they wouldn't understand, they wouldn't like her. Basil and Nicole had come from East Hampton, with their kids, and Hervé was screaming to go swimming. He was just a little kid but he was big for his age and looked almost four years old. Nicole had bought him a lot of gold jewelry: a chain around his neck with some discs and charms on it, a bracelet, and two rings.

"She'd better watch out," Lavinia muttered darkly. "Putting all that jewelry on a boy, she'll make a fairy out of him."

"Isn't he handsome?" Nicole said over and over again. "Show everybody how handsome you are, Hervé mon fils."

Little Geneviève, toddling about, was all white ruffles and dimples. Cassie and Andrew had arrived, with their three children, Chris, Paul, and Blythe. Although Paul and Richie were near enough in age to be friends they didn't know each other at all. Richie couldn't think of a thing to say to his cousin, but luckily everyone was making such a fuss over him that he wasn't required to say much of anything.

"Don't kiss people on the face," Cassie whispered to Paris. "You'll get lipstick on them and mess up their hair. Just pretend, like this." She kissed the air. "Besides, what do you need to kiss some of those old horrors for anyway?" They both laughed and winked. "Hell-o, Nicole darling!" Cassie cried, and kissed the air next to Nicole's cheek. She led her reluctant little daughter toward huge Nicole. "Blythe, here's your Aunt Nicole."

"Hello, Blythe," Nicole boomed heartily. Blythe ventured to look up and gave a shy little smile. "Why don't you give her a permanent?" Nicole asked Cassie.

"Don't be silly," Cassie said.

"It's too bad she doesn't have hair like my Geneviève," Nicole said. "Ah, there's Jonah! Hello, Jonah!"

"Oooh, that woman gives me a migraine," Cassie whispered when Nicole was gone.

"Mommy, when can we go home?" Blythe asked.

"We just got here."

Now the cars were arriving from Brooklyn and the Bronx, with Adam's sisters and their grown children. Hepzibah and Zipporah, ancient and tiny, their husbands long dead, still speaking Yiddish, their wrinkled faces bearing the same lineage as the children who stood here now, so tall, so American. Zipporah, white-haired, delicate, still lovely, looking as Melissa might look someday. Hepzibah, her face more broad and peasant, smiling, sweet, looking much like her cousin Lucy, Adam's second wife, had looked, and as in some distorted way Hazel looked now. And Becky, Adam's youngest sister, old now too, her husband Isman as pale as paper, he walking with a cane, and she ill but smiling through her pain with the joy of seeing the whole family together again. Her face was the most like Adam's, but delicate, with shrewd little eyes, a face much like Lavinia's would be when she was old. Paris remembered Aunt Becky from when she was a child, and her mother often spoke of her, and spoke to her on the telephone, but the other nieces and nephews had never seen any of the great-aunts. When someone in the family died, some distant cousin or other, the older ones knew who it was, but they didn't bother to tell their children. Why worry children with tales of death when there was so much to worry about already?

"What ever happened to that uncle with the candy store?" Paris asked her mother once.

"Oh, he died a long time ago," her mother said, sounding a little surprised.

Everett and Frankie had come up to Windflower for their two-week vacation earlier than usual this summer because of Richie's bar mitzvah. Frankie had never been to a bar mitzvah in her life and didn't even know what one was. She walked around saying hello to the relatives she knew, trying to be friendly. There was Everett, in the corner as usual, not bothering to introduce her to anyone.

There was an open bar with a bartender, because Herman Winsor, at least, was sophisticated. Frankie had already fortified herself with a scotch or two at the house before venturing out into this crowd, and now she made a beeline to the bar and asked for a double on the rocks. She always felt more at home with bartenders than she did with party guests. They were working people, outsiders, like herself. She felt like she should be passing the trays of hors d'oeuvres along with the colored maids instead of standing here all dressed up with a fake smile on her face and a glass in her hand. The little bitty napkin they gave you to hold around the glass was sopping wet already. She drained her drink and held it out to the understanding bartender for a refill. Better just to get smashed and forget about the whole thing. She wasn't too crazy about Richie. He was a nasty kid. Nobody ever gave her a party when she was thirteen years old, and look at this one! It must have cost more than any of her relatives ever made in an entire year. More than Everett made, maybe. She knew his mother was giving him money. They wouldn't have two cars if his mother wasn't helping.

She took a pack of cigarettes out of her purse and the bartender reached forward in a flash and offered her a match. Bartenders were definitely better than this family. None of them ever lit her cigarettes, even Everett, who smoked like a chimney himself. She'd told him a million times: "Everett, light my cigarette," "Everett, hold the door open for me," "Everett, hold my chair at the table," "Everett, a man walks on the outside of the street," but would he ever listen? She had picked up bits and pieces of etiquette during her life and held on to them, hoping to better herself, and now she had bettered herself in the eyes of the world but in truth she was married to a slob. Maybe rich people didn't have to have manners. Their money made them look good no matter what they did.

Frankie had a secret this summer, and she wasn't going to tell any of them. She had made Everett promise not to tell until it showed, claiming modesty. Frankie was pregnant. She knew if her mother-in-law and the rest of them knew it they wouldn't give her a moment's peace: "Frankie, don't drink," "Frankie, don't smoke," "Frankie, you should eat more," blah blah. They'd have her upstairs taking afternoon naps and having her meals on a tray like a cripple, protecting their precious grandchild. Her baby would be Adam's great-grandchild. Maybe the family would respect her then. The baby would be half Everett's, but it would be half hers, too. She knew the family history, they'd told her often enough. Adam Saffron was once a nobody, just like her family, worse even because he didn't speak English and had to learn it. And look at him now! Maybe her kid would be a genius, like Adam.

Lavinia sat down in a chair on the lawn, tired from all the

things she had to do at a social affair like this. There were so many relatives to be greeted—mustn't leave anyone out and hurt their feelings—and she had to be sure Paris was doing her part and being nice to everyone, especially all her young cousins. It was so important to keep up with the family, be close to them, especially the ones who you didn't see all the time. Family, in the long run, was all you had. She'd told Paris many times, and hoped it had finally sunk in, that your family was your best friend. Next to your mother, of course. She was Paris' best friend and always would be. The family cared, some more than others. You had to be close to the ones who cared because they would be on your side in later life, and you had to make friends with the others so they wouldn't be against you. You saw who was bright and who was not, who was worth bothering with, and you made your moves, gathering them all in together, "keeping up" as they say, keeping close.

Paris was so careless, so remote. She didn't care about anything but her work. You could hardly ever drag her to lunch with her aunts; first she said she was looking for a job, and now that she had finally found one at that trashy paperback publishing company, she said she had only an hour for lunch. Jonah was the only one who could get close to her. He went to her office and picked her up, took her to lunch at the Stork Club, which both of them thought was very glamorous, and at least he had a chance to talk to her. He talked to her about the stock market. That was Jonah's favorite subject, and he said Paris seemed interested in it too. He hoped someday she would write some articles about the market.

Melissa came over and sat down beside Lavinia. "My goodness," she said, "I'm certainly glad to see Aunt Becky. I didn't think she'd make it, sick as she is."

"I think the doctor gave her some kind of pain killer," Lavinia said.

"Between her and Isman, poor things, I don't know who's holding up who."

Lavinia shook her head. "He looks terrible."

"Where's Andrew? I haven't seen him."

"Jonah took him down to where we're going to put in the swimming pool. He wanted to ask Andrew's advice. Andrew designed their pool house, you know, top to bottom."

"Oh, we wouldn't want such a big one, would we?" Melissa asked.

"I suppose not. We don't have all that company they do."

Melissa looked around and lowered her voice. "Listen, do you think Frankie's getting fat?"

Lavinia looked toward where Frankie was standing by the bar under the trees. "What do you expect, the way she drinks?"

"I think I should tell her to wear a girdle," Melissa said.

"Tell her to stop drinking."

"Oh, sure. Do you think she listens to me about anything? Do you think she even listens to Everett?"

"Does Everett tell her to stop drinking?" Lavinia asked.

"He doesn't seem to care."

"Then it's his problem," Lavinia said, dismissing them both. "It's his wife, let him worry."

At the projected site for the pool Andrew was trying to persuade Jonah to make the family put in a heated pool. The water would come from their own artesian well, and it would be as icy cold as a mountain stream. But the family had decided that a heated pool was an extravagance. The lake was cold, wasn't it? They managed to swim in it, didn't they? It was extravagant even to have a pool as well as a lake and a river and a lagoon, but all right, if everyone wanted a pool they would build a pool, but heating it was just too much.

"You'll be sorry," Andrew said.

"They voted against it."

"You can always put in a heater later," Andrew said. "But we get so much pleasure out of our pool, everyone swims all day. We turn it up to eighty. I can't imagine swimming in freezing cold water."

"Hardly any of them swim anyway," Jonah said. "Just the kids, and me, and I don't care."

"Not Rosemary and Jack?"

"Oh yes. I forget about them."

Jonah often forgot about them, at least as often as he could. He liked to forget about everyone but his own Lavinia and Paris, and Papa. It was hard to live here on this kibbutz with so many different people with so many different tastes. In a family everyone was different and it was often hard to get along. He knew; he had come from a large family. Now he only saw them all together once a year when they went to pay their respects to their parents' graves. Sometimes he spoke to one or another of his brothers on the phone. But he had always gotten along with all of them. He was always the peacemaker. It was pointless to fight with your loved ones. There were enough problems outside in the world, making a living, just trying to stay alive and well, that you shouldn't fight with your family. He had never fought with his family; he had just become separated from them, and them from him, with their own children and jobs and lives. Lavinia's family had taken him in with so much love and warmth that he felt he was one of them. All families were the same. It was Papa who made the difference. Papa made all of them special. Jonah would do anything in the world for Papa, who was such a wonderful man and had given him so much.

Jonah and Andrew walked back up the hill and joined the others, who were just going into the tent to start their enormous meal. It was buffet, with servants to whisk away used plates. Richie, looking proud and solemn, was sitting in the seat of honor, flanked by his parents. This thing must be costing a lot of money with so many people and so much food. Herman always said a party wasn't any good unless you had to throw out a lot of leftovers, but Jonah still couldn't bear to waste food. It hurt him in his heart. So many people were poor and hungry, the way he had been once, and much, much worse. This was a far cry from his own bar mitzvah. How serious and religious he had been then! In his heart he was still the same. It was just that you made adjustments to what life demanded of you. Richie seemed serious and religious too. Jonah wondered if he would keep it up. He doubted it.

FIVE

In New York, Paris was living with her parents, well established in her job and in her double life. Several times a week young men she had met at parties or on arranged dates, or because their mothers knew her mother, came to call for her, sat in the living room for ten or fifteen minutes talking to her father about business while she put the finishing touches on her appearance in her bedroom with her mother's help, and then Paris and the acceptable young man went out to dine or dance or drink at some expensive place and made the most superficial of small talk. She made it clear to these young men that they were not to touch her, never even kiss her goodnight—sometimes by her cold attitude and agile footwork at her front door, sometimes by actually telling them—and they accepted this, believing she was a virgin of exceptional purity and a good future wife. Then, several times a week, Paris called her mother and said she would not be home for dinner because she was going out with a group of her co-workers from the office, and then she met her married lover, an advertising man fifteen years older than she, and they had drinks and dinner and went to a borrowed apartment where they made love.

She found her lover fascinating, because he was older and more sophisticated, because he had been in this New York world longer than she had, because he had a wife and five children, which was wicked, and because he claimed he adored her. She was able to talk to him about herself, her feelings, her dreams, and he didn't laugh at her. He didn't think that her ambition to write a novel someday and see it published was ridiculous. And most wicked of all, making him as inaccessible as even having the wife and five children, was the fact that he was not Jewish. Her parents had made it clear she was to marry a Jewish boy. She still kept up with boys she had dated at college who weren't Jewish, but they were friends, and often she used their names as ploys to get out of the house and meet her lover. Some of them had turned out to be homosexual, and although Paris knew little about that life and was rather shocked and disappointed when she discovered that their roommates were also their lovers, they were good friends to her and enjoyed being vicarious participants in what they thought was her very sophisticated and exciting affair.

How funny, she thought, if her mother only knew that the reason her former college boyfriends would never be her "lasting friends," which meant potential husbands, was that they preferred boys, not because they didn't like Jewish girls.

It was husband-hunting time in New York, and probably all over the nation, but it was also wife-hunting time. The boys Paris dated with her parents' blessing made it quite clear that they either resented her ambition to become a novelist or else they thought it was an absurd girlish dream. They didn't want to talk about it or know about it. They wanted to talk about their own ambitions, to become a lawyer or a doctor or an accountant, to have two children and live in the suburbs. The only boy who didn't resent her ambition was an Israeli who was a cousin of a girl she'd gone to high school with, and he planned to go home soon anyway. He was quite proud of her ambition and talent. Maybe girls in Israel were treated differently than they were here, more as equals.

Her two steadiest dates were also her two worst. Paris couldn't decide if her parents thought so little of her that they could imagine either of these horrors as a son-in-law, or whether they thought she actually cared about them. One was the son of a woman who was her mother's friend, a sharp-tongued nasty woman who terrorized her son and therefore made him easy for Paris to handle. He was enormously tall and fat, and he stammered, particularly when he had to say her name. He called her "Pppppperry." Whenever he took her out dancing he got an erection which hit her chest. She found him repulsive. The other one she met at a Halloween party. Trick or treat, and he was the trick. He was fat too, but short, and although she knew he was very clean he always looked greasy. He perspired whenever he set eyes on her. His mother was asthmatic and possessive. Whenever she thought her precious son was serious about a girl his mother would throw herself down on the rug and have an asthma attack, swearing she would die and it would be all his fault. Since his mother sensed that Paris was not interested in her son (although she couldn't understand why not) she never made any trouble.

The few times she had dated an acceptable boy who wasn't bad, who attracted her, she found he ran away in terror when she complimented him or let him get too far while necking on the couch in her safe parents' apartment. Those boys were all so conscious of husband-hunting time, they were suspicious of everything. You could never be spontaneous with them; they didn't know how to react. They were zombies. Tell a boy you liked him, tell him he was sexy, and he fled. Tell him not to touch you, act too precious to be human, and you couldn't get rid of him. It was enough to turn a girl into a snow maiden if she wasn't one to start with.

Perhaps that was the main reason Paris preferred her married lover. It was fun to feel wicked, but it was more fun to be able to feel human and act warm and affectionate without being worried every minute that you were committing a social gaffe. Of course, she never mentioned marriage. That was the death knell, that word. She knew that because her friend Rima, who was also working in New York (and commuting to her parents' home in the suburbs), had an older married lover too, her second. The first had fled when Rima suggested that if his wife was as horrible as he always said and didn't care if she ever saw him, why didn't he divorce her so they could get married.

"You don't want me," he had said to Rima then. "You just want to get married; you want a house with chairs in it. Go find someone else, someone who'll buy you chairs."

"What did he mean, 'chairs'?" Rima had asked Paris. "What's so awful, so symbolic, about chairs?"

"I don't know."

Paris and Rima met for lunch or dinner and a movie once a week. Paris' mother didn't like Paris wasting her time going out at night with girls when she could be home getting phone calls from boys. "All right," her mother would say coldly, "go, but you'll miss an important phone call."

"So you can take a message."

"You should be *here.*"

Rima had taken a speedwriting course, and was a secretary to a television executive. She had wanted a job in publishing, but so far there was nothing available. Both she and Paris were surprised that hardcover publishing houses were so small, with so little staff. All your life you read books, knew there were more books published than you could ever manage to read, and all that was put out by a handful of lucky editors. Paris had taken the job at the paperback company, Paperback Originals, because she had applied everywhere and it was the only one offered to her. She was a reader. She made fifty dollars a week, which after withholding taxes gave her thirty-six dollars to take home. The girls she knew who had their own apartments all had roommates or were older than she was, making more money, and living in one room in a scary old walkup with garbage in the halls. Close as they were, best friends, even having similar affairs, it never occurred to Paris and Rima to leave their parents and get an apartment of their own to share. They were still afraid, and Paris' family was violently against it. None of their friends' daughters left home until they were married. Even the sons who left home—after all, a boy was different—came home to their mothers nearly every night for a good home-cooked dinner, and always brought their dirty laundry with them. If you came from out of town, all right, you had to live away from your parents if you wanted to work in New York, but if you came from New York, why leave? What would people say? They would say you couldn't get along with your parents, that you were wild, neurotic. Everyone knew that a girl took her own apartment for only one reason: to sleep with men.

Paris didn't agree. She thought it would be nice to have a place of her own where she could cook if she wanted to, eat when she wanted to, play her records as loud as she wanted, have a drink, ask friends in, and never have to date anyone she didn't like. It would be nice to have furniture that belonged to her, that she had picked out herself. Maybe Rima's ex-boyfriend had been right about the chairs. But it didn't mean you had to be married to have them.

Rima's new married boyfriend was an executive in the company where she worked. She said that all the young girls she knew who were going with married men had met these men where they worked. Married executives were always chasing the young girls. It was easy to feel popular. It was funny, Paris thought, after worrying all through college that she'd never have another date when she got out, here were all these married men flirting with her, trying to impress her, almost waiting on line for her to become available again. This was what her mother feared. But there was just as much danger from the single ones. There were a lot of single men who would never ask a girl out again if they discovered by the second date that she would never go to bed with them. By never, they meant a month or so. None of them had time. Where was someone who wanted to *know* her? Paris didn't feel like a person at all any more, she felt like a thing, a dating doll, dress it up, wind it up, and send it out until it runs down. Tick tock.

Grandpa and Etta had gone to Florida for the winter. Their old cook, Henny the chain smoker, had deserted them, preferring to stay north. She had promised to come back to Windflower, though, for the summer, so Etta didn't mind. Grandpa always paid such good wages that Etta never had any trouble getting help. Henny's daughters had stayed north with her. To this day, Paris couldn't keep them straight—there were so many of them and they kept appearing and disappearing. She wondered how many children Henny actually had.

On Sunday nights, when their cook was off, Paris and her parents went to a restaurant with Aunt Melissa and Uncle Lazarus. Paris' parents had finally bought a television set for the apartment, and then Aunt Melissa got one too, a store-bought one, not one with an open back like Everett had made that would kill you. Sometimes after dinner they would go back to Aunt Melissa and Uncle Lazarus' hotel apartment to watch TV.

"Look," Aunt Melissa said during a commercial for false teeth fixative, "I know that actor!"

"How come?" Paris' mother asked.

Aunt Melissa turned pink. "I mean, I knew him once, not very well. He went to school with me."

There he was again, doing a soap commercial. Paris remembered having seen him in several other commercials too, something for colds, and another one, she forgot what. He looked just like anybody and it was easy to forget him. That was probably why he was such a big success doing commercials, he was everyman.

"He struggled for so many years," Aunt Melissa said. "He wanted to be an actor. I'm glad he's doing well now."

"You call that stuff 'well'?" Uncle Lazarus grumbled. "That's not acting."

"It's a job," Paris' mother said.

"What's his name?" Paris asked.

"Oh . . . Scott Brown."

Life certainly was different today for young women, Paris thought. There was Aunt Melissa, so thrilled that a boy she'd gone to school with a million years ago was doing a false teeth commercial that she even remembered his name. She probably thought he was glamorous. She herself had already met so many interesting people that she wouldn't even be awed if she met a movie star. She would be very pleased, but not awed. Poor Aunt Melissa, dating all those dull boys on the block, meeting Uncle Lazarus, thinking he was the cat's pajamas, as he would say. How she would faint to know about her niece's double life.

But no matter how hard she tried to control her life and her feelings, Paris discovered that it was not possible. It had been fun and nice to be the one who was loved in her affair instead of the one who loved, but eventually she found she was in love with her lover, or at least it seemed so. She had never cared so much about any man before. And, being honest and feeling secure, she told

379

him she loved him. His attitude became noticeably cooler after that; although he still called her every morning at her office and whined baby talk into the phone he said he had to work late, or he had to go home more often than he had before. She supposed she had made a great mistake, that he liked only girls who didn't like him, but there was no point in pretending if she loved him; after all, wasn't honesty the only thing that made love worthwhile? To get someone to love you because you played games and lied was what she hated about dating. She couldn't let that same falseness come into her affair or it would be worth no more than just her casual dates. She started phoning him. It was now equal; he wasn't chasing her.

Then one evening in a dark, romantic bar, she made the fatal mistake, the one she had vowed never to make. She said, "If your wife is so horrible and she doesn't care if she never sees you, why don't you get divorced and marry me?"

He looked at her in horror. "You're crazy. You know that, don't you? You're crazy. You ought to go to a psychiatrist. Pick out a psychiatrist and I'll pay for him."

"Why am I crazy?"

"To want me."

"But you wanted me to want you," she said.

"That was different. You don't understand."

"Then explain it to me."

Instead, he drove her home, in his commuter's car, made her get out on the corner near her parents' apartment, and sped off to the safety of his "horrible" wife and five children in the suburbs. He never called her again. Paris called him every day for two weeks but he was always "out," so she gave up. She told herself that he was a masochist, that she would indeed have been crazy to want him, but her heart felt broken, it actually hurt. She walked down the street with a pain in her heart, she sat in her office in a daze or stared out the window at the street twenty-six stories below, and her pain was all she knew. Other girls had the same problem of being ditched by their boyfriends, she knew that, but their boyfriends hadn't been married and so they could talk about it. Thank God for Rima. She had been through the same disaster. The two of them felt like pariahs. It was funny how guilty you felt, how used and victimized, when the good part was over.

If you fell in love with a bachelor and made the mistake of

proposing, as so many of her school friends had done, and then he ran off in fear, at least you could say you had tried and now you wouldn't be wasting any more of your valuable time on him. These were supposed to be your few good years; every one that passed made you a little less desirable in the husband hunt. But if you fooled around with a married man because you weren't looking for a husband, and then you fell in love with him and changed your mind, that was stupid. Paris had learned that lesson.

With free time and a broken heart she devoted herself to her writing. Writing made her forget her humiliation and feel like a person again. She sent stories to magazines, and now they were coming back with encouraging letters from the fiction editors themselves. Finally she sold her first story to a national magazine. It was a detailed, funny story about one of her horrible blind dates. Her parents were very proud of her. She got two hundred and fifty dollars, more money than she'd ever seen in her life. How wonderful it would be to sell a story every month and not have to go to that office!

She liked her job and her boss, but there were things she did not like. She hated that the men in her department who weren't as smart as she was got paid more money just because they would have to support wives someday. She hated that she wasn't given an expense account because her boss said authors wouldn't respect a young girl and wanted to be taken to lunch by a man or a much older woman. Everyone assumed she was going to leave when she got married and so she had to fight for every little raise, every little step up in status. It didn't bother her to have to go into the boss' office and ask for a five-dollar raise; after all, they thought she was a sweet little kid and a joke, so she could ask for anything she wanted to. She asked for a raise regularly every six months. She was so underpaid to start with that they always gave it to her with no trouble.

Writing stories regularly, she sold two more within six months. She got five hundred dollars for each of them. This was incredible! She really could live as a writer if her luck held out. But so many stories were rejected, and there were so many articles she wrote that brought her only fifty dollars. It certainly wasn't a secure life. Her father put every cent she made into the stock market for her. They both agreed that if she was going to be a writer she would have to have an income from somewhere else.

"After all," her father said, "you might want to marry a nice boy who doesn't have any money of his own."

"A boy going to medical school," her mother added quickly. "An investment. Or a professor who might win the Nobel Prize someday."

Then why did they make her go out with those horrors? None of them was ever going to win anything. "He might have a nice friend," her mother would say. Didn't she know horrors never had nice friends? Her mother told her over and over how superior she was, how beautiful, how talented, and yet her parents were willing to see her sold off to some terrible boy she couldn't stand, who didn't want her to be a writer. Her parents didn't see what it was like on a date; only she did. They thought those boys were nice because they put up a good front in the living room. Her mother kept nagging her to quit her job, which was supposed to be throwing her into an unsavory environment, and stay home to write full time. That would be the kiss of death. When she became a full-time professional writer, Paris knew, it would be to attain her complete independence.

Meanwhile she drifted into another affair with another married man, eighteen years older than she, a writer. It started with lunches and graduated to lunches in borrowed apartments. He told her she needed an agent and got her one. He told her she was exceptionally talented. His stories and books were published all the time. He actually lived off his income as a writer. He was both lover and friend to her. This time she knew enough never to mention the forbidden word.

SIX

That winter Andrew was forty-seven years old. His round, boyish eyes that looked at everyone so appealingly now seemed incongruous in his lined, serious, adult face. His hair was completely gray. He tried to eat very sparingly of the delicious desserts their cook made for them every night but still he was no longer slim— not fat, but he had what Papa called "a corporation," and Andrew hated it. He had his suits made by the best tailor to disguise it, and was glad that he could afford to indulge his fastidious taste in clothes. He was nearly fifty, nearly old. No matter how he tried to disguise what age had done to him, his life was more than half over. What had he done with it? He had a lovely wife whom he loved very much, three good children, popular and devoted, a spacious apartment in the city that was a showplace, and an estate in the country that grew more beautiful every year. He had a responsible job in the family business, Papa's right hand so to speak, a six-figure income, and he was respected in the community for his work in behalf of charity. He should be happy that he was so lucky. But he was miserable.

His life was more than half over and it meant nothing. Each morning it was harder and harder to drag himself out of bed, so wrapped in misery that he seemed swaddled; he could hardly move. He stared at the wall for twenty minutes, then forced himself to take a shower and go to the breakfast table, where he would stare unseeing at his cup of coffee until it grew cold. He no longer took the subway to the office because the subway was a frightening maze full of strangers who meant him harm; he took a cab. But the cabs gave him as much claustrophobia as the subways did. The apartment was the only place where he felt safe.

On weekends the family always went to the country, but this winter Andrew did not feel up to the trip, even though Cassie always drove the station wagon to spare him because he had worked hard all week. The apartment was safe.

The kids enjoyed the country but they didn't mind staying in the city this winter because they had an active social life and many places to go with their friends. They had always brought friends up to the country, but they were freer here, with buses to take them anywhere they wanted to go. Besides, they loved to watch television, and most of the time they sat with their friends in the den watching football games and anything else that was on. His sister Lavinia thought that was terrible.

"Your children are going to grow up to be illiterate," she often told him. "They never read. Do you have a book in the house?"

Cassie liked to be with the children and watched television with them. She had even become a football fan. Andrew sat in his bedroom, thinking and worrying, or not thinking of anything at all. How could he afford all this? His expenses were enormous.

All right, his salary was enormous too, but still, the cost of living was going up, and in ten years he would be an old man. What would he have done with his life? Who would remember him? Where was the young artist who was going to study and paint in Paris, where were all his young dreams? They were silly dreams, but still, he might have made paintings that people would care about after he was gone. He never drew or painted any more. His pool house, his landscaping, the little details of the new office buildings the family built, working along with the architect, that was his art. So what? If he had been a painter, probably he would have been a failure and have starved. He needed all the material things he had in his life; he wanted them. One had to make money to have them. Money was essential. One had to work to earn money. Andrew could not leave the house any more to go to work.

His misery was all-encompassing and mysterious. He really wasn't sure why he felt sad, only that he did, that life seemed hopeless, each hour an eternity spent in fear and sorrow and loss. He had heard of men his age who had nervous breakdowns, jumped out of windows, had to be sent away, just because they were approaching middle age. Hadn't Nathan Seltzer, only forty-six, a year younger than he, spent a year sitting in a chair in his apartment, watched every minute by his frantic wife and sister so he wouldn't commit suicide? Male menopause, they called it. Menopause! That was for women.

He was sweet with Cassie and the children, but he moved like a robot. He could force a smile, a word, but his heart was breaking and he didn't know why. What would happen to them if he became incapacitated? He couldn't even think about it, and yet he couldn't stop thinking about it. All his life had been spent in responsibility. For pleasure you have to pay. You don't get something for nothing. But was it worth it?

Papa called him from the office.

"So, Andrew, you're still sick?"

"Hello, Papa."

"You haven't been to the office for two weeks. Last week you said you had a virus. You're sure it isn't worse?"

"No, Papa, it's better."

"Did you see a doctor?"

Andrew sighed. "No."

"Why not?"

"It's getting better."

"I'm coming to see for myself."

That afternoon, after work, Papa appeared. Andrew had not even been able to force himself to dress. Wearing his silk robe, unshaven for the past five days, he sat on the chaise longue in the huge bedroom he shared with Cassie. The maid had made the bed and put the bedspread on. After all, he wasn't sick. Papa gave his coat and hat and scarf to the maid and went into the bedroom. Cassie, who had greeted him at the door, stayed outside the bedroom, eavesdropping, hoping Papa might have more success with Andrew than she had had.

"Hello, Papa," Andrew said.

"Such a sad voice, like the mewing of a cat. Who died?"

Andrew forced a smile. "I'll be better soon."

"You have a headache, a stomach ache, what?"

"I don't know."

"You look terrible. Have Cassie call the doctor."

"All right."

"I don't understand it, a man who has everything—a good family, a good life, good health—he should let himself get like this."

"I have headaches, Papa."

"Headaches? Good. You see the doctor. A headache can be cured."

Oh God, how could he betray this man who had been so good to him? How could he lie to his father, and worse, not be there when his father needed him, pretending to be sick? But he *was* sick. Not all sickness meant virus and fever. How could he explain his pain that lodged in no particular part of his body and yet seemed to pervade all of it? He hadn't been able to explain it to Cassie, who would fuss over him and cater to him, how could he explain it to his father who only expected the best of him?"

Papa went to the bedroom doorway. "Cassie! Call the doctor now and make an appointment."

Cassie entered the room, glanced at Andrew, and went to the phone. She spoke quietly, then she turned and said: "He'll see you at nine o'clock tomorrow morning."

Maybe it would be good to go to the doctor. Maybe he had a brain tumor, or thyroid trouble, or even cancer. Who knew? Andrew felt a slight relief. He wondered why he hadn't thought of going to the doctor before, and then he knew. He had been afraid the doctor would find out there was nothing wrong with his body, that it was his mind which was sick.

"See he goes," Papa said to Cassie. He went to the hall closet to find his coat and hat.

"You're not going so soon?" Cassie said. "You just got here! Let me give you some tea, at least. The children will feel very badly that they missed you."

"Where are they at this hour?"

"Chris has football practice, Paul has a date with some boys in his class, and Blythe has her ballet lesson."

Papa smiled. "Ballet. Melissa was a dancer too when she was a little girl. Greek dancing, with veils."

"Oh, this week it's ballet, next week it might be the recorder. Blythe never knows what she wants to do."

"That's good too," Papa said. "When you're young you should try to learn everything. When you're old you don't have time."

You don't have time, Andrew thought. *You don't have time. You don't have time.* The words sounded like a death knell in his head. There would never be any more time for anything.

He went to the doctor the next morning and had a complete physical examination. The results came back at the end of the week; he was fine. Occasional migraines, as always, but that was nothing new, and he had pills for that. The doctor suggested that Andrew see a psychiatrist. He gave him the names of three he knew, and recommended one as his first choice.

"Psychiatrists are for crazy people," Andrew told Cassie.

"Don't be silly. Everybody's going nowadays. You might as well see him once, it can't hurt."

"I don't want anybody to know."

"They won't know if you don't tell them," Cassie said cheerfully.

He called the first-choice psychiatrist from the list and made an appointment for the following week. It would be a month that he had been sitting in the apartment by the time he saw the psychiatrist. Beyond that fact, and the fact that he could not bring himself to go to the office or do anything else but sit in the apartment, he had nothing to tell.

The psychiatrist's office was on Park Avenue, in a large, old, dignified building with a doorman. The office was as dignified as the building, with thin, old, Oriental carpets on the floor. The doctor seemed calm and unthreatening, older than Andrew, with gray hair. There was a leather couch with a clean little linen cloth on the part where a patient would lay his head, but Andrew had no intention of lying on that couch and trying to remember something horrible from his childhood that he had forgotten. He knew about psychiatrists. You lay on that couch for years and years, talking about anything that came into your head, and then suddenly you remembered some trauma from your childhood and you had a breakthrough and went into hysterics and then everything was different from then on. He'd seen *that* movie.

"Sit down, Mr. Saffron," the psychiatrist said. To Andrew's great relief he indicated a comfortable armchair facing the desk behind which he was sitting. Andrew looked at the chair, the desk, the psychiatrist, and the door through which he had just entered and through which he intended to escape. He remained standing.

"I'll tell you one thing, Doctor," Andrew said. "If you tell me that I hate my wife or my father, I'm leaving."

In his months of analysis, lying on the couch and discussing his dreams, both his sleeping and waking ones, five mornings a week, Andrew began to learn things about himself. He learned that no one is perfect or "normal," and that it was normal to worry, but one should not have to worry overmuch. He was relieved to find that remembered traumas and hysterical breakthroughs occurred much more often in movies than in real life. He learned that it was quite normal at his time of life to reassess what one had accomplished and where one was going, and often to feel depressed. He learned also that there was no reason for him not to have his cake and eat it too: so he started to take painting lessons with a private teacher every morning after he went to the psychiatrist, before he went to the office. He got up at seven, went to the psychiatrist at eight, had his painting class at nine, and was in the office at half past ten, just a few minutes later than he used to get there when he had nothing to do in the morning but choose which suit to wear.

The doctor said it was probably going to take five years. That was the usual length of time for a successful Freudian analysis. The den in Andrew's apartment was no longer just the television room for the children; now it was also his artist's studio, where he could paint all evening while the kids were in their rooms struggling with their homework. At first Andrew had been ashamed to paint at home, fearing he wasn't good enough, but his teacher told him he had talent, and finally he dared. Cassie thought he was brilliant, and soon framed oil paintings by Andrew Saffron replaced all the ones he and Cassie had bought through the years. Everyone in the family wanted one, but Andrew couldn't bear to give any of them away. They were his, and all irreplaceable. He made some for his children's rooms, but that was different, because they remained in his house. He had a studio in the country too so that he could paint on weekends and not miss the two days. Cassie began buying art books, and she and Andrew went to art galleries and to museums. Then they stopped going to other people's exhibits; Andrew's painting was his own expression of his own feelings and he didn't want to compare them with anyone else's. His analysis would take five years, but his painting would continue forever.

After a while he wasn't even embarrassed any more about going to an analyst. It was the thing to do, everyone was going, and many of those who didn't go needed it most. The family knew. It wasn't something to be spread around, because there were ignorant people in the world who thought you were crazy if you sought help, but still it was more something to be proud of than ashamed of. A man who would go to a doctor for his problems was a wiser man than one who would seek no help at all when he was sick. Yes, you had to be intelligent to go to a psychiatrist. And you had to be rich; it cost a fortune. That was one expediture Andrew was not going to worry about at all.

SEVEN

Frankie and Everett's baby was a boy and they named him John. John: a good, solid, Anglo-Saxon name, a little old-fashioned. Frankie had gone to public school with twelve boys named John, but Everett had never even known one. An active, nervous baby from the start, he looked a little like Everett. Frankie was sorry he looked like Everett; she had hoped he would look different from both of them, better, but certainly she would have preferred he look like her, because she had started to dislike Everett heartily and it was no pleasure to have a tiny facsimile of him in the house.

Melissa doted on John. "He looks just like Everett did at that age," she kept saying.

Frankie was waiting for the presents Jewish husbands were supposed to shower on their wives for presenting them with precious heirs. From Everett she got nothing, but her mother-in-law gave her a pearl necklace and a gold bracelet. Her mother-in-law always gave her nice presents for her birthday and just for no reason at all: a new coat, a set of decent dishes, a new carpet for their bedroom. She also bought all John's baby furniture. Frankie had painted his room herself. She saw no reason to waste the money, and besides, she was bored.

She didn't want to nurse him because no one did that any more unless they were a fanatic, so she gave him a bottle, which he usually spit up. Everett said he had done the same thing as a baby and Paris had been worse. It was some kind of allergy. Fine, Frankie thought grimly, he's even got the Bergman-Saffron allergies, but what has he got from me?

John was going to be her entree into the family. Precious gift of her womb, she brought him to Windflower and waited. Buffy's old crib was set up in the downstairs library, and all the relatives trooped in to observe this wonder, this curiosity, ahing and cooing at him. John looked at them out of his huge blue eyes and spit up. The family fussed and fawned and told Frankie what to do, criticized her, admonished her, warned her, and she waited. He was so little, it was only natural. Soon she would get the attention and the love. As soon as he was older and they saw how good he was, how much he loved her, then they would realize how important a mother was.

By the summer of 1956, when John was three, Frankie realized that not only would her plan never come true but fate had been even nastier than she had imagined. She was still the outsider. But John, her son, also son of Everett and great-grandson of Adam, was an insider. He was totally absorbed into the family, totally theirs. They resented her as if she were a kind of inferior nursemaid.

"John doesn't need steak," Frankie would snap at the cook. "He can eat weiners."

"John will eat steak like the rest of us," Melissa would say firmly.

Frankie gave John a crew cut so he would look masculine. The family protested. "He has such lovely hair," Melissa said. "Why can't you let it grow? You could part it on the side."

"My son is going to grow up to be a real man," Frankie would snarl. How they annoyed her!

She wanted John to learn to swim as soon as possible. In Florida the children started taking swimming lessons as young as two, because many people had swimming pools and they didn't want their kids to fall in and drown. Frankie took John to the pool at Windflower every morning and threw him in. He screamed and cried with fear and hatred of the icy cold water. Why was he screaming so? He had his life jacket on. Frankie would stand at one end of the pool—the short side of the shallow end, she wasn't a murderess, after all—and force him to swim to her. He had no other recourse. She wouldn't let him out. He would scream with fear until he was hysterical, but he would be dog paddling too, and he would finally make it. The family was very upset. They told her to stop, she was cruel, he was too young.

"My son is going to learn to swim," Frankie would snap at them. She would show them, she would make her son a real person, better, not a spoiled rich sissy like his father.

When John finally learned how to swim and actually began to enjoy it, Frankie began teaching him how to dive. He feared diving as much as he had feared swimming, but she forced him, making him kneel at the edge of the pool, head down, arms stiffly straight parallel to his ears, and then roll him in. He was going to be the best swimmer in the family, she would see to that.

He was going to have a lovely little body. Already he had small round muscles in his legs and arms although he was born skinny and would stay that way. He had lovely smooth skin with blondish down on it, thick dark eyelashes, and a mischievous grin. He was a tease. He liked to run full tilt at some member of the family, his little almost-shaved head like a bullet, and ram his head into the grownup's stomach. Standing there, knowing he was going to have the breath knocked out of him by this child, the hapless victim would have only one other recourse: to dodge aside at the last minute and let John crash himself into the wall. He was running so fast he couldn't stop, so sure that the victim would not escape, and the victim chose to be victimized instead of escaping, because you couldn't let a child give himself a concussion.

John was always active. And how he could eat! He never spit up any more. He ran around all day and then ate as much as the grownups at dinner. They let him sit at the dinner table with them, which Frankie did not approve of. They took him to restaurants with the family on the cook's night off, and they let him run around the room and get under the table to bite people's legs. He could do anything he wanted to. Frankie hit him. She spanked him and slapped him and yelled at him, but all he would do was cry and shut himself into the bathroom while the family yelled at her, telling her how mean she was, such a strict mother, so unfeeling.

"You love your mother, don't you, John?" Frankie would say whenever she knew they were listening. "You'll never leave me, will you? When I'm old, you'll make a lot of money and take care of me, won't you?"

John loved her. He would do anything she told him to. From someone, certainly not her, certainly not his father, he had a kind and gentle spirit. He could knock the breath out of an aunt or uncle or cousin, but if that same person hurt a toe John would get right down on the floor to kiss it, tears in his eyes. He kissed cuts and sores and bee stings, looking as pained as the people who had them.

"Such compassion," Lavinia marveled.

"Maybe he'll be a doctor like Lazarus," Melissa said.

A doctor wouldn't be bad, Frankie thought. Or a lawyer, or maybe an architect . . . But she would let him be what he wanted to be, not what they wanted him to be. She couldn't stand the way they had taken him over, but she would have been able to stand it if they had not taken him in so completely while still keeping her out. She was nothing to them, the vessel. Crack the mold, who needs it any more? She would fix them. When he got older, John was going to go to church.

In the meantime, Everett would dump her and John at Windflower, stay a few days, and then scurry back to Florida, claiming he couldn't be away from his business. He had hired another girl to take her place. She had to stay home with the kid now. She could hardly wait until John was old enough to go to school and be off her neck. She hated to sit in the house. At Windflower

they all wanted to take care of him and fuss over him, and sometimes she let them. Now they were all marveling how John swam
like a fish, such a little fellow, and loves the water so he won't
get out until he turns blue. Yet at the beginning of the summer
they were all calling her cruel. Did they ever give her credit, say
how clever she was for teaching him to swim? Not them. She was
stuck here for the whole summer. Everett said it was the least he
could do for his mother. Who cared about her, Frankie? She was
supposed to be grateful to be stuck here with nothing to do, no
place to go, waited on by maids.

She drank all day.

By afternoon Frankie was always drunk now, and by dinner-
time she would be in a rage at John, smacking him, picking on
him, not because he was any more naughty than any other child
but because he was an insider and she was an outsider and she had
been cheated. He was supposed to help her, not ruin her chances.
Before, they had just resented her because she was a stranger, but
now they resented her because they had the bad luck to have her
come along in the package deal with John. Everett telephoned
long distance every night. Money meant nothing to him, as long
as he was spending it on himself. He had had the decency to leave
her the car and fly back. She sometimes took John on a ride to
the Westchester County Airport and let him watch the small
planes land and take off. He liked that. There was a small snack
bar at the airport and Frankie could sit there and drink beer
while the kid watched his planes. Buffy wanted to come too, and
Frankie would have been glad to take her, but Rosemary said no.

"I'm not letting her take *my* child in a car," Rosemary would
say. "You can smell liquor on her breath."

Frankie knew Rosemary better than that. She wouldn't let
Frankie take her child anywhere, drunk or sober. Buffy was Rosemary and Jack's property. Frankie had never seen a family with
such jealous ownership of their children. Had they all gotten
together and decided to have just one apiece? It was really funny
how they had arranged that, building their houses with just the
right number of rooms and having just the right number of children to fit into them. They were so precise, they planned everything, no moment just happened for them. Even Paris had everything planned. Every morning she got up at the crack of dawn to
commute into New York on the train with Lazarus, she went

to her job, and then she came back with Lazarus in time for
dinner, and then at night she stayed in her room with the typewriter going tap-tap-tap. You'd think she came from a poor family,
you'd think they were starving, the way she worked so hard when
she didn't have to. In a way, Frankie admired her. At least she
had a goal that meant something. Maybe she'd never get what
she wanted, but at least she was trying hard as hell to get it.

EIGHT

Paris was not commuting with Lazarus because she liked him;
she was taking the same train because someone (usually her
father) had to drive them to the station and there could be only
one trip. Lazarus arose at five because it took him so long to get
ready. He had to shave twice, with an old-fashioned straight razor,
to be sure no trace of shadow remained on his perfect face. His
hot shower took a certain number of minutes, and then his cold
shower a certain number of minutes, and he never deviated. He
had to consume his enormous breakfast, chewing slowly the prescribed number of times. As he grew older he was slower. He
insisted on being at his office at nine o'clock, and as it was in
Brooklyn he had to take the train and then the subway, so he had
to catch the seven-fifty-eight. To catch the seven-fifty-eight they
had to leave the house at seven-thirty. So Paris had to get up at
six-thirty, which she detested, and then she always got to her
office by eight-thirty, the train being an express, and the doors
were locked until nine. She was not given a key to the office, not
being an executive, so she would wait in the coffee shop downstairs, cursing all of them and wishing she were still in her cool
bed asleep. Lazarus made her so mad that she wouldn't even sit
in the same car of the train with him. When they got to the station Paris would make a beeline for the smoking car. Lazarus
hated smoke and gave long lectures on the hazards of that filthy
habit tobacco. Paris didn't smoke herself, but she would rather
breathe in the foul air than sit next to the villain who made her
get up at half-past-six in the morning when the thing she hated

most in the world, had always hated most, was getting up early.

For years Aunt Melissa had pleaded with Lazarus to get an office in New York, closer to their hotel, closer to the country, but Lazarus couldn't; his old patients were all in that Brooklyn slum, they needed him, they knew him, and he needed them. He was too old to start over. Why then, Aunt Melissa would ask, didn't he retire? He wouldn't think of it.

Paris' office let her out at five o'clock. She would dart out the minute the hands of the clock hit the hour and run all the way to Grand Central Station because she and Lazarus always took the five-twenty-nine express. In the summer she didn't have drinks with friends after work. If she didn't take the train with Lazarus she wouldn't have her free ride from the station, and a taxi cost a dollar and a half. She was now making sixty-four dollars a week take-home pay after taxes. Every penny of that except for meager diet lunches went into the bank. Money meant escape. Besides, as long as she was going to have to be in the country she might as well enjoy it. It was nice to be where everything was so green, so cool, where it smelled so fresh and a sunset was a sight worth watching. She would lie on the cool thick grass before dinner and look at the hills and trees she remembered from so many summers and she would be filled with a mixture of love and hate— love because of the beauty, hate because of always feeling trapped here and so lonely. The beauty of Windflower only made the loneliness worse. This was a place where you should be with a lover, with friends, looking at the water and the graceful hills and being happy together. To lie here alone and watch the sky or sit on the hill and watch the riderless horses frolicking in the lower field was sad.

Lazarus (Paris no longer called him "Uncle" because they were both working adults) always found a discarded newspaper on the seat of the train and brought it to Windflower in triumph. He was so weird. Look what this place cost him, and then he was so happy to get a five-cent newspaper free. He never let anyone touch it until he was finished. There was always a paper in the house which Paris' father had bought, so she didn't care. She could read that one.

Nothing disturbed the rhythm of their summer days until the scandal, and even then there were those who tried to pretend it had never existed. One day the butcher in town told Aunt Melissa and Etta that Henny, Etta's cook, and her daughters, if indeed they were all her daughters, had been running a successful and well-known whorehouse in town during the winters when Grandpa and Etta were in Florida. "They been giving it away free anyhow," Henny had said philosophically, her cigarette bobbing from her upper lip, "so might as well get paid for it."

Adam Saffron's cook the madam of a whorehouse! Etta didn't know what to do. A good cook was hard to find nowadays, big salary or not, and how could she get along without Henny? She was used to Henny. Henny was used to her, to the house, to Papa's ways. After all, so what if the butcher knew, and therefore also the grocer and the baker and the candlestick maker and God knew who else? They were only tradespeople. Who would they tell? The Saffron family had no friends in this town. Who were the clients of Henny's alleged whorehouse anyway: help, butlers, chauffeurs, subservients? No one knew them socially. They wouldn't tell the people they worked for. It was best, Etta finally decided, to pretend she hadn't heard about it at all. Let Henny do what she pleased during the winters. In the summer she was still the superb cook, and her daughters slunk around the house in shapeless uniforms and house slippers, looking highly unlike courtesans or ladies of the evening. Maybe these were the ugly daughters, and the sexy ones were still working at the whorehouse? Or maybe the whorehouse shut down during the summers? Henny wouldn't let a profitable business operation go on without her personal supervision. No, Etta pretended it was all a lie. And Aunt Melissa (and Paris' mother, whom she had told instantly) also said it was a lie. "A damned lie!" Paris' mother said, rising to the defense of her family, whose help were of the highest moral caliber.

Then why did Maurice, Grandpa's fat colored chauffeur, give Henny those knowing looks, and she give them back, as if they had outwitted the enemy? "What looks?" said Etta. Her son, Stanley, and his wife and two children were visiting for the weekend, and tonight Etta was having all the Windflower relatives over for dinner. Who else but Henny could or would make dinner for eighteen people without protest?

And besides, Etta said, and they all agreed, the final truth: Who cares what "they" do?

Paris hoped it was true. She would have loved a scandal. It

would have been so much more interesting than life usually was here. She was still in love with her married writer, and he with her. Since she was a virtual prisoner here at Windflower every night, and he had a wife, it was convenient for both of them to confine their affair to lunchtime trysts. He telephoned her every day, even weekends when she was at home with her parents. Her parents didn't scare him. He felt he was a friend of hers, which he was, and therefore perfectly free to call whenever he wanted to talk to her.

When they were together she was less interested in having him tell her he loved her than in having him tell her she was a person, that she existed. Sometimes, with the family, she felt herself floating away as if she were nothing at all.

"Say I'm a person," Paris would plead to her lover. "Am I a person?"

"Of course you are. You're a person. You're a person. You're a person."

His soothing voice calmed her. It was not to be sexy she wanted, not to be beautiful or rich or talented or popular or clever, but to be a person. A whole human being, someone who mattered. Bits of her were being torn away, gobbled up, molded and formed to another's will, ever since she could remember. There had to be something left, something others could see and then she herself could see.

They didn't always make love when they had their lunch dates; sometimes they went to a restaurant and really had lunch. They tried to make their time together as spontaneous and normal as possible under the constricting circumstances. He made her feel safe. She could talk to him without always getting an argument the way you did at Windflower with everyone butting in and offering an opinion without being asked. The word "because" had become a permanent part of almost every sentence she spoke with her mother, because whatever she said was answered by "why?" Paris no longer said, "I want to do this," or "I'm going to do this," she said "I want to do this because . . ." There always had to be a good reason. If she were a real person, she knew, she would never have to say why. The fact that a person wanted to go somewhere or do something was enough reason.

One summer day Paris woke up with a cold. There was no hiding it from her mother; she was coughing a little and her nose was stuffed. She had a lunch date with her lover that day.

"You're not going to the office," her mother said.

"I'm not sick."

"Yes you are. Get in bed."

"It's an allergy," Paris said.

"I know a cold when I see one."

"I have to go to the office. I have an important lunch date."

"Cancel it."

Her mother's word was law. No one would drive her to the station. She could have called for a cab but it didn't even occur to her. She was entirely tied to her mother's will. Paris felt the familiar anger choking her and her throat closed the way it had when she was younger and had asthma. The asthma closed in on her then, along with the rage, forcing off her breathing, choking her, locking her in; all the protest she wanted to shriek out turned inward. She was suffocating with rage, and with impotence.

"See," her mother said, "now you're getting an asthma attack. Call your lunch date and cancel him."

Him! She knew, she must have known. Paris telephoned him (she was as free to call him at his home as he was to call her at hers) and told him she had a cold. He was regretful and said he would see her as soon as she was well.

"Tell your office you won't be in," her mother said. Paris obeyed.

That fall, when the family moved back from Windflower, Paris went to see Cassie. Cassie and Andrew lived near enough to her parents that she could go there after work and be back in time for dinner. Paris' mother liked that Paris was close and friendly with Cassie.

"Such a big sigh!" Cassie said. Paris was sitting on the chaise longue in the bedroom.

"I didn't even know I sighed."

"You sigh all the time."

"It's the only way I can breathe sometimes. Cassie, do you know a psychiatrist I can go to?"

"Well, there's Uncle Andrew's, but he won't take two people from the same immediate family."

"Can you ask him to recommend someone else?"

"Yes, I'll ask him."

"I want to go to a psychiatrist," Paris said. "I'm so unhappy."

"I think it's a very good idea," Cassie said cheerfully.

"But don't tell my mother. She won't understand and she'll get upset."

"She won't know unless you tell her," Cassie said.

So began the hushed secret phone calls and the slipping out of the house without saying goodbye or giving a reason. Paris went to the psychiatrist three times a week, during her lunch hours, and now she had someone on her side. Her mother had never let her shut her bedroom door and got upset when Paris tried to. "You're shutting me out," her mother would say. "Why do you have to shut your door? No one in this house spies on you." Paris told the analyst, and he said she should shut the door because he told her to. She was aware that she was substituting one authority for another, but at least this one was on her side. Her mother was hurt, and she remained intrepid. *He* had given her permission to shut her door.

Finally she decided to tell her mother she had been going to an analyst. It was hard to tell her in the apartment; somehow it was her parents' territory and Paris needed some neutral place. She asked her mother to have lunch with her at Schrafft's.

"You may have noticed I've changed a little," Paris said, over the dessert.

"Yes, I have. I've been worried."

"It's because I've been going to a psychiatrist."

"Oh." Her mother thought a moment, then brightened. "Your father and I were afraid you were falling under the influence of some man."

"No, just a shrink."

"Where did you get him?"

"From Uncle Andrew's doctor."

"Oh. But why do you need a psychiatrist?"

"You're not supposed to discuss that when you're in treatment."

"Who is he? What's his name? Can I go to see him?"

"Why do *you* want to go to see him?" Paris asked.

"Well, there might be something from your childhood that you forgot that I could tell him. I'm sure I could be of help."

"I'm supposed to tell him, not you."

"You were so sick as a child, all those allergies," her mother said. "Maybe they caused a trauma . . ."

"No."

"But you were such a happy child. Always laughing and giggling. I never saw such a happy child."

"Look, let's not discuss it, okay?"

"I hope you don't sit there and tell him it's all my fault," her mother said.

"Nothing's anybody's fault," Paris said. "I'm not crazy, you know. I just want to work out some things."

"I don't see why you couldn't have just come to me," her mother said, "and we could have worked them out together."

That winter Rima got a job in publishing at last, as the secretary to the editor-in-chief of a hardcover publishing company. Paris' stocks were bringing in some dividends, and with the money she had hoarded and saved she realized she could quit her job to write full time and still be able to pay the analyst. She'd been working at that office for nearly six years and still was nowhere. She wanted to write her own novel. Nights and weekends weren't enough time. She gave her boss her notice and the staff gave her a going-away party. She had told them all that she was going to write a novel; now she really had to. She still met her married lover for lunch. She had told him about the psychiatrist and he was both glad and saddened.

"You won't love me any more after a while," he said sadly. "But it will be good for you."

She supposed that like all married men he thought the only girl who could love him must have something wrong with her head.

She polished the novel she had been working on for years and sent it everywhere, and it was rejected everywhere. Her mother came into her room every morning to read what she had written and criticize it. Her mother liked the elegant language of Paris' novel and couldn't understand why it kept being sent back. The editors always wrote little notes, saying there was no plot and the characters had no feelings. *Just like me and my life*, Paris thought. *All locked in. I'll have to get away to really be a writer.*

Then the editor whom Rima worked for sent back the book with a note saying she should come in and have a talk with him.

"Oh, isn't that the place where Rima works?" her mother said. "She'll be jealous and she'll put the kibosh on the whole thing."

"Mother, Rima is the least jealous person I've ever met in my life. She is *thrilled* about my book."

"Hmm," her mother said, protective, suspicious, and dreamer of nightmares.

Paris went to see the editor. He was a distinguished-looking middle-aged man. "You could be a helluva writer," he told her. "But this one isn't the book. It's the kind of book people describe as 'having promise.' Nothing happens in it."

"I know," Paris said. "Nothing ever happens in life."

"Why don't you write a real novel, about something you know about? You could write about your contemporaries, your friends. No one has written a novel yet about being young in the Fifties."

"I've worked for years on this book," Paris said, holding her thin manuscript protectively. "Years and years. It's like you're killing my baby and telling me to go have another one."

"Well, think about it," he said kindly. "If you want to give me the first fifty pages, I'll give you a contract."

They shook hands. Rima walked her to the elevator. "You've got to do it!" Rima said, all excited. "Don't you realize what a chance this is? This is the best publisher in America."

"A contract . . . someone wants to give me a contract . . . I can't believe it. I'll have to leave home. I can't write at home. The new book would be just like the old one, all fake."

"You could write the first fifty pages in two weeks," Rima said. "I know you. And then when you got the contract they would give you an advance. Get an apartment. You're always talking about it. Your parents won't let you starve. They'll pay the rent."

"That's what you think."

"I know your parents. They'll scream, but once you've done it they won't let you down."

"I wish he'd publish *this* book," Paris said, cuddling it.

"But only three people would buy it. Do you want that?"

"Yes," she said. "I would still be thrilled."

So Paris began to look at apartments, from ads in the Sunday *Times*. She quickly discovered that they were either hovels where the person who showed them was very nice to her, or good, expensive apartments where the sleazy super thought she must be a call girl to be able to afford the rent and made lewd remarks and winked. Obviously, a girl of her age, in her midtwenties, single, who wanted to rent a nice apartment, had to be up to no good. She finally asked her father to have lunch with her, alone.

They went to a steak house. "I can't live at home any more,"

Paris said. She saw that he looked hurt and bewildered. "I have to get my own apartment. I've been looking, but they treat me like dirt. I need your help."

"Why can't you live at home?" he asked, his eyes so sad and yet beginning to question, ready to help.

"I can't. I'm going to get an apartment anyway, but if you came with me it would be easier."

"All right," he said.

"And don't tell mother yet. When we find something nice then we'll surprise her."

He told her mother of course, he always told her everything, but her mother didn't take the two of them seriously. It was too horrible a thought to contemplate, so she chose to ignore it for the moment. Paris spent the weekend at Rima's parents' house in the suburbs, and in the Sunday *Times* they saw an apartment that looked perfect. On Monday Paris and her father went to look at it. It was three small rooms, but it looked enormous to her, and just right to her father.

"It's such a nice new building," he said happily, "and it's right across the street from the temple."

"I don't go to temple."

"But it's so pretty to look at. And maybe you'll change your mind."

They took the apartment, with her father cosigning the lease. Next time, Paris thought, I'll sign my own lease because I'll have the money. Her father was as pleased and thrilled as if it were his own new apartment and he was young again. He imagined visiting her in this nice clean place. He had rationalized it all immediately: his daughter was a writer and kept odd hours, she needed peace and quiet, therefore she needed a place of her own to do her work. What he didn't realize was that his rationalization happened to be the truth. There was only one thing Paris intended to do in that apartment: write her book.

Her mother didn't care for the apartment and didn't tell any of her friends that her daughter had left home before she was married. She had to tell the family, but she told them Paris needed a place to write "because she works all night." She then turned around, as Rima had said she would, and took Paris to wholesale houses with her old decorator from Brooklyn, paying for all her daughter's furniture. Whenever anyone criticized Paris for moving away from home her mother came swiftly to her defense. Her father even acted proud.

Paris knew this was the greatest gamble of her life. As long as her parents paid her rent they still had the power to make her come home. She had to write the book and make her own money, as quickly as possible. The furniture wouldn't come for months: she had only a bed, a lamp, her dresser from home, her typewriter, and a borrowed bridge table and chairs. That was enough.

When her married lover came to visit her in her new apartment Paris realized she couldn't stand to have him touch her. She kept away from him, not even letting him take her hand. Suddenly she didn't like him; he frightened and repelled her. He seemed like a stranger in this life. He realized it immediately.

"I knew this would happen," he said sadly. He went to the door. "I'll keep in touch, I'll call you. Call me if you need anything. I love you. Goodbye."

How could he say he loved her? He hadn't married her, had he? He didn't love her enough for that. She realized that he had only been her way of rebelling against her parents and their values, and now she didn't have to rebel any more.

She lit the one lamp, on the bridge table next to her typewriter, and continued to work.

NINE

When Gilda Finkel was born her parents named her Golda, after her father's dead mother, thinking they could call her Goldie for short. But when she was a little girl, with long red curls, her parents went to the movies on the Grand Concourse, to see Rita Hayworth in *Gilda*, and when they got out her mother said to her father: "Do you know who our Goldie is going to grow up to look like?"

"Who?"

"Rita Hayworth, that's who. From now on we're calling her Gilda. Golda's a name for an old lady anyhow."

Gilda was an only child, and lived with her parents in an old apartment building in the Bronx, which year by year grew more dilapidated. Her father was a salesman, but he didn't do very well. It was her mother's ambition that Gilda become a star of some kind. She had tap dancing lessons, but as she was fat—zoftig, they called it—she despised them and eventually her mother decided to give her singing lessons instead. Gilda had a fine set of pipes, everyone said. She had a loud voice, anyway, a real belter, and she had the build to be an opera singer.

Gilda's father wanted her to go to college. At NYU she could meet a nice boy, better than the type that was starting to move into this neighborhood. More than half the kids in her high school were colored and Puerto Rican. If Gilda went downtown to NYU she could meet a nice Jewish boy with brains who was studying for a profession.

All Gilda wanted was to have fun. But she was a bright girl, bright enough for college, and she figured if she got away from home she could do what she wanted and maybe meet a couple of people who would help her with her career. It was her mother who was stage struck, but Gilda wasn't adverse to having a singing career if it wasn't too much work. At eighteen she was a nice-looking girl with a lot of red hair cascading down to her shoulders in waves and ringlets, too fat (but some men liked that), and had a cute little baby face. She had a problem focusing her eyes, so you never knew if she was looking at you or not, and it gave her a myopic, innocent, even sometimes idiotic look.

She liked NYU and loved the Village, where she spent most of her time. She made a lot of friends immediately, and most nights she stayed downtown in somebody's apartment because shlepping back up to the Bronx on the subway was a big drag. Her parents didn't mind. They didn't ask if who she was staying with was a boy or a girl; they assumed it was a girl. Sometimes it was.

Now that she was in college she had a lot of work to do, so she didn't take singing lessons any more. She did take a music course, and was trying to decide whether she should major in English or drama. Mostly, though, she just enjoyed herself. There were lots of things to do in the city, lots of parties, lots of just hanging out and having laughs. She took things as they came, no real plans. It was great to be away from home, even though she supposedly still lived there.

If the place where you lived was the place where you kept your clothes, then Gilda wasn't sure where she lived. She had clothes all over the place, at different friends' apartments, just in case. She carried a big shoulder bag with her hairbrush and her toothbrush in it, along with her wallet and makeup and stuff, so she'd always be ready for anything.

One day she was walking along the street downtown with her girlfriend Angelita Lopez, whose cousin Gilda had gone with for about two months at the beginning of the term, and Angie said, "Hey, I know a boy who lives in that house right there. He's very boring but he's very rich, and we could go up to see him and maybe get a fancy dinner."

"Okay," Gilda said. "What's his name?"

"Richie Winsor."

Gilda had heard of him. In a school as big as this there were still small cliques, and you knew of certain people by reputation. "Richie Winsor is very boring but very rich." "Gilda Finkel sleeps with Puerto Ricans." Etc., etc. Apparently, the word went, Richie Winsor had a fancy apartment and an expensive sports car, and he would take a girl to any restaurant she wanted, plus a supper club, and spend all kinds of money, but he never said a word. You would have to do all the talking, all night. The only time he opened his mouth was to tell you how rich he was, what his family owned, something like that. Nobody ever went out with him more than once or twice; it was just too tiring.

"Let's go ring the housephone," Angie said. The house was a big, new high rise, very expensive. They were just going in the door when a little blue Alfa Romeo sports coupe came zipping around the corner and parked, and out came a young guy.

"That's him!" Angie said. Gilda nearly fell down on the sidewalk laughing because they'd just been dishing him and there he was.

"Hi, Richie!" Angie said. "I want you to meet my friend Gilda Finkel."

"Hello," Richie said. He didn't look like much, not very tall, with a self-conscious look on his face and dandruff on the collar of his expensive sports jacket. Gilda wanted to brush it off; she could hardly keep her hands off it.

"Hi, Richie," Gilda said. "We were just coming up to visit you."

"Oh," he said, and stood there.

"Why don't you invite us up for a drink and show Gilda your paintings?" Angie said.

Richie nodded and led the way into his apartment house.

"Mr. Personality," Gilda whispered to Angie, and nearly choked trying not to laugh again.

Richie Winsor's apartment was very expensively decorated and very dull. It was all done in shades of brown and had about as much personality as he did. He showed them various paintings and graphics on his walls and said who had made them and how much they cost, and Gilda acted interested. It was a big apartment for a college boy, even for anyone. She and her parents didn't live in one any bigger, and their building was a slum compared to this. Finally he offered them a drink. He had a bar that lit up when you opened the door and had mirrors inside. Gilda couldn't stand it. It was like something out of a movie about a swinging bachelor, which this guy certainly was not.

"I don't drink anything but wine," Gilda said.

"Oh, I have wine," he said. He went to a closet and opened it and there were two cases of wine, one white, one red, lying on wine racks. Angie gave Gilda a look, as if to say: See? "Red or white?" Richie asked.

"Red," Angie said.

"White," Gilda said, just to be difficult.

Richie selected a bottle of red wine from the closet, then he closed the door and went into the kitchen where he opened the refrigerator and chose a bottle of chilled white wine. He opened them both with a horrible corkscrew with a man's head on top of it; the man was carved out of wood and had his tongue stuck out.

"Where did you get that corkscrew?" Gilda asked.

"My mother gave it to me."

They sat on the couch and drank their wine. Angie chattered away about the English class she and Richie both went to, and then Gilda took over when Angie ran out of things to say. She talked about her singing, and about music, and asked Richie questions which he answered with either a yes or a no. She thought maybe they were interrupting something; he certainly didn't seem to be trying to entertain them.

"I guess we'd better go," Gilda said. "You're probably busy."

"Oh, no," he said, sounding as if he meant it. "Stay."

"We're not keeping you from anything?"

"No."

"You really mean it?"

"Yes."

"Okay," she said cheerily. She held out her glass. "Why don't you just refill this and put on some records?"

He had only classical records and some opera. He put on the classical. That meant they had to keep on making conversation. As far as Gilda was concerned that wasn't too difficult because she liked to talk anyway. She had plenty of opinions on everything. It was weird talking to Richie because he hardly responded at all, but he kept looking at her so she knew he was listening. He must be shy; nobody could be that boring. It was too bad that a boy with all his money had such a case of social ineptitude. He was a sophomore, a year older than she was, but he acted like some eleven-year-old on his first date. When she ran out of things to say to him Gilda got up and looked at his books in the bookcase, and then she made comments on them and asked him questions, which again he answered with a yes or a no.

"It's seven o'clock," Angie said, looking at her wristwatch. "I better call my mother and tell her if I'm coming home to dinner or not." Since Mrs. Lopez lived uptown and worked nights, and Angie hardly ever bothered to come home at all, much less for the nonexistent dinner, that was her way of finding out if Richie intended to take them out or if they were going to have to scrounge somewhere else.

"I'm hungry," Gilda said.

"I'll take you girls out to dinner," Richie said. It was the first complete sentence he had uttered in several hours.

"Oh," Gilda said, "that would be lovely."

"I'll just go in the bedroom and call my mother, if that's all right with you," Angie said.

"And I'll go brush my hair," Gilda said, tossing her mane so he'd be sure to notice it if he hadn't already.

In the bedroom the two girls fell on each other's necks, giggling. "Shh! Ooh, isn't he just what I said?" Angie whispered.

"Where should we make him take us?"

"Let him pick," Angie whispered. "He's got a list *this* long."

"I look like a shlump."

"So what?"

Gilda brushed her hair and put on some lip pomade. His bedroom was as impersonal as the living room, not even a photo of his parents or a girl or anybody. He had a big bed. She wondered how often he ever got anybody into it. According to rumor, never. Poor Richie. She would be nice to him. A kid like that deserved a break. She could just see all those yentehs in the neighborhood if she came zipping up to her house in that blue Alfa Romeo of his. Her parents would be thrilled. Gilda met a nice, rich Jewish boy for a change. A college boy, a catch. No more Josés and Raouls with black leather jackets hanging around her doorstep. Richard Winsor. Some fancy.

TEN

When Paris' novel was published in the fall of 1958 it was an immediate best seller, climbed up the best-seller list, and was sold to paperback and the movies. She was interviewed on all the television talk shows, interviewed and photographed by the newspapers, and taken on a cross-country tour to promote the book. Seeing her picture in bookstore windows, seeing girls her age carrying her book in the street, none of it seemed real to her. It had all happened so fast it was like a dream. She was still the solitary person she had always been, but this time the solitary person was invited to parties filled with the rich and famous, the collectors and the hangers-on, and she was terrified. She felt as if she were on display, expected to say something important or interesting to justify her presence there, and since she couldn't think of anything she got drunk instead. The phone didn't ring any more than it had before she had become famous. She was waiting for the magic prince to appear, the perfect man to become her perfect husband, the reward for all this work, but he never did. She met more married men, more homosexuals, and more sons or nephews or cousins of women who had known her mother or her aunts and who now wanted to meet the celebrity. These new young men were as incompatible to her as the former ones had been, if not worse, because she was older and wanted someone who shared her interests. Was that too much to ask? Apparently it was. Her mother's friends said that because she was now famous and independently wealthy she would never be able to find a husband. A nice boy would be afraid of her. But she had always been rich, hadn't she? At least the family was. But that wasn't money she had earned, and therefore was not threatening.

Paris had never expected her novel to be a best seller. She had written about being young and single in the Fifties, her friends, herself, Rima, the girls she knew in her office and the boys they all dated, the men they fell in love with: their double life. She had thought she and her friends were freaks, but she had written about their struggles, and to her amazement all the other young people in the world seemed to be saying that they were just like her. It had been time to get the truth out in the open and display the hypocrisy they all lived by. But her family was shocked. Trash! How could she write those things? Her parents, faced with a fait accompli, defended her. The only ones who were really proud of her were Hazel, who hadn't read the book but liked the publicity, especially the idea of all those movie stars in the film, Melissa, and her grandfather, who was eighty years old now with failing eyesight. His daughter Lavinia protected him, reading to him a passage from Paris' book which happened to deal with love, marriage, and religion in a way which would make any grandfather proud. She told him not to bother to try to read the book; it was too long and the print was too small. He wanted someone to read it to him, but on the other hand it *was* a long book, and he had never been much for fiction. He was satisfied that his granddaughter was such a success. He was proud of her.

So Paris was now embarked on what would be her life. She was already trying to think of a subject for her second novel, while the controversy and praise for the first was at its height. Her stories and articles were not only accepted by magazines, they were asked for. Editors took her and her agent to lunch. She got fan mail, some of it friendly, some of it hostile, some from lunatics, some from strange men proposing marriage. It frightened her. She had her telephone number unlisted after several phone calls from an unknown man in a phone booth who told her what he would like to do to her. She still went to her analyst. She was still a solitary person and wondered if that was just the way she was, if her family life had shaped her that way and that was the way she would have to stay, terrified of parties and strangers, comfortable only with her own few friends, not demanding more, not even wanting it. She still went to Windflower in the summer, and slept in her old room next to that of her parents, this time with the connecting door closed and locked, the key removed and put into her own night table drawer. Except for Rima, she had no guests.

Rima, too, had embarked on what would be her life. She had met a married politician, twenty years older than she, and they had vowed to spend the rest of their lives together although he would live with his wife and children and she would live alone. He put her in an apartment a block away from the one where he lived with his family, and he visited her every night for a few minutes. He could not take her out to dinner, he could not be seen with her, because people would recognize him. He filled Rima's tiny apartment with antiques and engraved bibelots so that it looked like a museum. She bought many at-home clothes and only a few daytime things to wear to the office. She never went out. She only waited for him. Everyone told her she was crazy and she replied that she wanted it this way. The only time she had him to herself was during the summer, when he put his wife and children into their large home on Long Island and moved Rima into his New York apartment. He was quite fearless about that, almost hoping his wife would discover them. When his wife finally did, it made no difference. There would be no divorce. A divorce would ruin his career. His wife and children continued to spend summers on Long Island, where he visited them every weekend, and Rima spent weekends at Windflower with Paris. Even Paris told her she was crazy, but it was her life. Everyone settled for what they really wanted, didn't they?

Rima believed in compromise; Paris did not. Yet, wasn't her own life a compromise? Still tied to the family, hurt by whatever they said to criticize her, waiting for the approval that never came without some parenthesis or clause to take away the joy, giving clever interviews that made her out to be a brave and self-sufficient person because it was what she wanted the world to think, while in her private life she was lonely and vulnerable and frightened and even sometimes shocked by things. Whenever something affected her she wrote about it. It was her only escape. There was no one to talk to so she talked to strangers she would never meet who would read what she was saying. They couldn't interrupt, criticize, argue with her. They could complain afterward, but while she was saying what she felt they were silent, a silence she never found in the family. How could a place where there was all that talk be so lonely? There were so many people there, and yet the loneliness was like a physical pain.

That summer they were all there. Richie had brought Gilda Finkel, his girlfriend, to meet the family. He was trying to decide if he should marry her. Herman had come up from Florida to see what he thought of this Gilda Finkel, and he was horrified. At heart Herman was a great prude. Gilda was supposed to sleep in the downstairs library, which had grudgingly been made into a guest room for her, but she would go upstairs to Richie's room while everyone was sitting on the porch after lunch and shriek demandingly: "Richie! You come up here this minute."

Then they would shut the door and not come out for two hours. Everyone was afraid to think about what they were doing, but they all knew. That girl was using the wiles of her body to entrap poor Richie. He trotted after her with a hypnotized look on his face. She was too fat, she was falling out of the top of her bathing suit, she was loud, she had no class, but worst of all, she was going to bed with Richie right under the noses of his horrified parents. It was a wonder she didn't give Herman a stroke. Herman was in a state; he didn't know what to do. He told Richie he refused to let him marry that girl. He went back to Florida. Richie told his mother he wanted to marry Gilda.

"I love her," he told his mother. "I want her to be my wife and the mother of my children."

"He loves her," Hazel told the family.

Hazel, who had never before been taken into Richie's confidence or treated as a person of any intelligence at all, was touched. Still, this Gilda, no one liked her, did they? And Gilda yelled at Richie, and they had fights, and sometimes she slapped him. How could he be happy with a girl like that? A man was supposed to be the boss in a marriage.

What did Papa think? This time they had protected Papa from the outsider. He had taken Frankie's side, or perhaps it was Everett's side, but Gilda was really too much. Frankie had been cold, but Gilda was too hot. You couldn't tell Papa about the things that were going on upstairs in the Winsor-Nature house. They didn't let Gilda go to The Big House. The only time Papa walked to the pool was during the cool of the afternoon, to take a look at his family having a good time, and that was when Gilda had Richie trapped upstairs in the bedroom. Papa had a golf cart to travel the long distance to the lake, and to inspect the estate, and Etta sat beside him and took turns driving it.

"Who's that girl?" he asked her.

"Oh, some friend of Richie's," Etta said.

"Good. He should have company. He's too shy."

The end of Gilda's visit was not the end of Gilda. Richie had his apartment in the city, and there he could do what he pleased. She was living with him. Sometimes they had fights and Gilda went back to her parents in the Bronx; then Richie, contrite, would go after her, parking his blue Alfa Romeo in front of her run-down apartment building while the neighbors leaned out of their windows and the kids stole his hubcaps. Richie had already lost eight hubcaps to his reconciliations with Gilda, but his relationship with her was the most exciting thing that had ever happened to him in his life. He didn't know if he loved her or not. All he knew was that when she wasn't there he missed her. She was the only person who had ever made him feel comfortable. There was nothing frightening or phony about Gilda. She said what she wanted, asked for what she wanted, got what she wanted. He didn't have to worry about impressing her. She was so unimpressed with him and what he had to offer her that he had to come to the conclusion that it was he himself she wanted. He knew she wasn't in love with him either. Yet, she stayed with him. Maybe they were both lonely. He had everything money could buy, and it only gave him pleasure to give her things. He couldn't imagine the bleakness of his life without Gilda. This could grow into love. He could imagine being married to her and having her for a best friend. The truth was, although Richie thought he was lucky to have such a convenient bed partner after years of having no one at all, what he really liked best about Gilda was that she was his friend. She talked to him, and eventually he found that he could talk to her. Everyone thought it was the sex that bound him to her, that sexy, zoftig girl with the long flowing red hair and the dumb look in her eyes, but the truth was the sex wasn't so special. What was so special was that Gilda Finkel was Richie

Winsor's first, best, and only really close friend.

Frankie and Everett came up that summer with John, and with their killer dog, Daisy. Everett kept the dog on a leash most of the time, but the family cowered and his mother wouldn't let him keep Daisy in the same room she was in. They were all relieved that he wasn't going to stay long, because when he left he would take the dog with him.

As far as Everett was concerned, his marriage was dead. He and Frankie didn't sleep together any more, and they couldn't even have a conversation without fighting. Whatever it was he had been so attracted to a few years ago was gone. He felt older and wiser. She wasn't even pretty. She drank all the time and her eyes were bloodshot, the wit was dulled into a nasty disposition, and she was vicious to John. But what could he do? He told his mother, he asked her for advice, and his mother went to his grandfather, who had started the whole thing by giving Everett his permission to marry Frankie, and Papa said why didn't they get a divorce?

"What do I need a divorce for?" Frankie asked Everett. "You haven't any money to give me, and I'm perfectly happy as I am. If you want a divorce, I keep John."

He couldn't let her keep John. Yet, how could he keep him, alone, working all day? He had to stick with Frankie, if only because John needed someone. He looked at that kid, so smart, so loving, so inquisitive, and he understood why people had children even though it meant spending the rest of their lives trapped in a loveless hell of a marriage. He wouldn't have wanted to miss having John. What was it he had seen and liked about Frankie anyway, and where had it gone? Whose fault was it? Maybe marriage itself was a lost cause. People weren't like his parents, staying together forever no matter what, devoted and loving. His contemporaries were all getting divorced. You had to be blind not to see that. Frankie had all sorts of divorced girlfriends. The only thing Everett couldn't figure out was why anyone had married them in the first place.

John was five years old and he could mix a perfect martini for his mother's guests. When they were at home in Florida he got up every morning and took his milk from the lower shelf of the refrigerator where he could reach it and the cold cereal from its

412

box in the food cabinet, and made his own breakfast. He got dressed and waited outside the house until the school bus came to take him to first grade. He was too young to go to public school so Grandma had given his father money so he could go to private school. John didn't like school much. He could do everything for himself, and when they went to Windflower in the summer he packed his own suitcase.

"Anything you forget, it's your own tough luck," his mother would tell him.

He would pack everything he could remember, but it didn't matter if he forgot anything because whenever they got to Windflower his grandmother would say how dreadful and shabby his clothes were and take him to the store and buy him all new ones. When he had his new clothes, everything from underwear to shoes and pants and shirts and even a bow tie, everyone made a big fuss over him and said how handsome he looked. John liked people to tell him he was handsome and make a big fuss over him. No one ever did that at home in Florida. His mother just yelled at him a lot and made him water the lawn, and then if he didn't come in to supper the minute she called him she would lock him out of the house and make him stay out until his father came home from work and rescued him. By then it would be cold because the sun would have gone down, and John was always glad to see his father. He liked to be with his father because his father let him watch him work and fix things, and showed him how to fix things too. When he grew up, John wanted to fix television sets like his father did. They could have a store together.

His father was nice to him and never hit him the way his mother did. But John loved his mother too. The more she got mad at him the more he tried to make her like him. He saved his allowance and bought her things from the drugstore, like soap and bubble gum, so she would like him. He wanted her to smile and kiss him and tell him he was her big handsome boy, which sometimes she did. She told him that when he grew up he was going to have to make a lot of money and take care of her, because she would be old then. He intended to make a lot of money and take care of both his parents, because they would both be old, and he loved them both. He knew his parents didn't like each other much. They had a lot of fights. He hoped it wasn't his fault. Sometimes when they fought they mentioned his name, and then he would hide his head under the pillow so he couldn't hear what they were saying.

He knew his father didn't like that his mother drank so much. Sometimes John would take the empty bottles and hide them in the trash before his father got home so he wouldn't see them. His mother didn't care if his father knew she was drunk or not, but John did. When she was drunk she was mad at everybody and she made everybody mad at her. She had a lot of friends over and she always let John taste all their drinks. John liked the way they tasted. But he was careful never to drink enough to get drunk, because after all, he was only five years old.

Buffy, The Runner, Rosemary's only child, was eight. They were all used to her daily routine and hardly even noticed her as she ran. She was so fast now that one minute you would see her starting out from the front porch in her shorts and sneakers and the next minute you would see her as a tiny figure far away. She didn't really know why she felt compelled to run. It was something she did with herself, competing with herself, trying to do better and better each day, get stronger, run faster. She didn't need a car, she didn't need grownups. Her legs could take her anywhere she wanted to go. They were her escape. But she stayed within the confines of Windflower, running around and around as if on a track that had no end. She had a little gadget her father had bought her that you hung from your belt and it told how many miles you had gone. She also had a wristwatch that told seconds as well as minutes. It was what she had wanted for her birthday and her parents had given it to her. She did lengths and times and made herself go faster and faster, made her lungs fill with air and keep her going, feeling her heart pounding as if it would burst. She knew she was fast.

She watched the track meets on television in the afternoons. She had decided that when she got older she would be a track star. She didn't tell anybody what she was going to be when she grew up because she knew they would hate it. Her father laughed at the girl track stars on TV and said they were "a bunch of dikes," whatever that was. He said they were men dressed up in women's clothes. How could he tell, when the men and the women wore the same thing, shorts and shirts? Buffy knew it just meant he thought they were ugly. She didn't care; people thought she was funny-looking anyway.

She had always known she wasn't pretty because all her life everyone said how beautiful her cousin Geneviève was and how *she* needed to have a lot done to improve herself. Geneviève and Buffy were nearly the same age, so their mothers made them play together. Buffy was very jealous of Geneviève, especially when Aunt Nicole was around, because Aunt Nicole was always saying what a beauty Geneviève was. When Buffy and Geneviève were left alone to play they got along all right, although Buffy wasn't too crazy about her. She liked her school friends better. At school Buffy was a champion athlete. She was good at everything in gym. Geneviève didn't like gym much; she liked boys. At eight years old all the boys hated all the girls, except for Geneviève. The boys actually liked her, and she actually liked them. Some of them even invited her to their birthday parties, and everyone knew that was expressly forbidden. You didn't invite—ugh!—boys to your birthday party, and they wouldn't dream of inviting you. Geneviève was so sweet and such a little lady. Buffy, on the other hand, was a tomboy, and they hated her.

She looked a little like her mother and a little like her father. From her father she had inherited her forgettable beigeness, a drab and colorless texture that made her fade away in a crowd. She had her mother's frizzy hair, but it was beige, not reddish, and she had a sprinkling of her mother's freckles. She was little and stocky and strong, with long legs for her height. When she was old enough she would go to a real track and practice, just like those girls did. She wanted to win medals and trophies and bring them home, and then people would make a fuss over her like they did over Geneviève, only she would be unique. Lots of girls were born pretty, but how many made something of themselves by working hard for it? When she grew up and was a runner she could go all over the world like those girl track stars did, and see places and meet people from other countries. It would be exciting and fun.

The only sport Buffy didn't like was horseback riding. No one at Windflower ever rode a horse, and they were all scared of horses. Uncle Andrew's kids all rode. Her cousin Blythe had her own horse and rode it all summer and every weekend in the winter. Buffy couldn't think of one thing to say to Uncle Andrew's kids.

She was stricken dumb with shyness when she saw them. They seemed to come from another world, where everybody knew what to say and what to do. One time Buffy's mother put her up on a rented horse and Buffy was scared to death and screamed until they took her off. The horse seemed so high. Buffy liked things where you depended on yourself, like running or swimming. It wasn't natural to sit on a horse's back. The horse couldn't like it much. She would watch the neighbors' horses running around and playing in the lower field and hope they wouldn't escape and come over to Windflower. That summer one of them had, the mean stallion. He was some kind of prize horse but a little crazy, and his name was America. He belonged to the boy down the road. Aunt Melissa, who was a sweet little old lady with pink and white skin and always wore clean, pretty pastel dresses, was sitting in a chair on her front lawn under a tree when America came running by. Aunt Melissa was too startled to even scream, and then America ran on past the house and disappeared into the woods, where there was a bridle path. Then the boy who owned him came running by and asked Aunt Melissa if she'd seen his horse. She said she had. And the boy said: "Well, if he comes back will you hold him and call me?"

Everybody thought that was such a funny story they told it and told it. Imagine Aunt Melissa holding on to the mean stallion while someone called that boy on the phone to come and get him! It was just impossible to imagine. That huge horse would kick her to death, he would bite her hand off, he would kill every one of them. If you happened to see him, the best thing to do would be to get out of his way as fast as possible and let that boy worry about it.

At Windflower Buffy didn't have any friends but she liked Paris and Richie, even though they were much older than she was. Paris was always nice to her and listened to her talk and always seemed interested. Buffy wondered if Richie was going to marry Gilda Finkel. He'd never brought a girl home before. If he married her then maybe they'd have a baby and she could play with it. Buffy loved babies. When she was too old to run any more then she would take care of babies, but that was a thousand years from now and too far ahead to even think of. She didn't want her own parents to have a baby. She liked being an only child. Her parents always made a big fuss over her and took her everywhere they went. They took her to eat in restaurants and let her help pick which one. When John was a baby Buffy had loved to play with him, but now that he was a little kid it wasn't fun any more. He was too young to be her friend and too old to be a toy. Everybody at Windflower was the wrong age. There really wasn't anybody who was the right age for anybody else to play with. She was lucky she had something she liked to do that she could do all by herself.

ELEVEN

Richie Winsor married Gilda Finkel in New York, and everyone in the family, like it or not, attended the wedding and the reception. They went to the Bahamas for their honeymoon, and then returned to live in Richie's apartment while both of them continued their college educations. When Richie graduated from college he entered law school—Columbia, like his uncles—and he and Gilda spent summer weekends at Windflower in the house with his mother, Rosemary, Jack, and Buffy. Herman, who had never reconciled himself to Gilda as a daughter-in-law, came up for occasional visits as usual. Hazel was very happy to have her son with her, because she never saw him in the winter except for Christmas vacation and then he and Gilda went out every night to a restaurant or night club and spent every day at the beach so she hardly saw them at all even though they were staying in her own house.

Frankie found Gilda a kind of curiosity. There was Gilda, an outsider like herself, but Gilda couldn't care less. She made no effort whatsoever to make anyone like her. She and Richie invited up hordes of their loud, unattractive friends from the city, and had cookouts and swimming parties. Frankie thought they were probably Gilda's friends, since Richie had never invited anyone before. Now he was the grand host, inviting the world. There were two sides of the swimming pool now: one for Richie and Gilda and their company, and the other side for the rest of the family. Richie had never been known to introduce anyone or to observe any other social amenity, so no one talked to the strangers. They didn't talk to the family either. They probably thought the family was as strange as the family thought they were—such a timidity and lack of joy, such dressed-up old ladies, so fastidious, as if they were going to tea in town instead of on a stroll around the grounds. Melissa and Lavinia wouldn't go to the pool because they were shy; Jonah and Lazarus wouldn't swim with the company because they thought the strangers made the water dirty. John, who was seven, swam like a fish, and Frankie didn't have to watch him. Rosemary and Jack braved the presence of the strangers because the pool cost money and they felt they should get their good use out of it. They went to swim every day, especially when Buffy was at the pool. Hazel wandered down a few times, but nobody talked to her so she would sit in the shade by the pool house and knit or do her puzzles.

Paris had gone to Europe. Her second book was coming out in the fall, and now a magazine had assigned her a story to do in Rome, and then she was going to travel to Venice and Capri with some people she had met. The magazine was paying for her first-class plane fare and her hotel in Rome, and giving her enough spending money so that it would nearly cover the rest of her vacation as well. What a deal, Frankie thought enviously. She wished she could be a writer. She never got to go anywhere except here at Windflower, stuck here summer after summer, going crazy. She wouldn't lower herself to talk to Richie and Gilda's friends, who were all fat and frumpy and overdressed. The girls wore bathing caps with rubber flowers all over them, and false eyelashes at the pool. The guys were repulsive. None of them had ever done a day's exercise in their lives. Their flabby stomachs made them look forty years old, not twenty-two or whatever Richie and his friends must be now. Spoiled, rich kids, Frankie thought with disgust. And Gilda was sitting there at the edge of the pool like Cleopatra, ordering her Marc Antony around. "Richie, start the fire," "Richie, make the hamburgers," "Richie, get some more wine from the house, and some ice, Richie, *ice!*" The last word would be shouted after Richie's already retreating obedient form.

The only person who wasn't afraid of those loud outsiders was John, who was used to strangers from seeing all Frankie's friends in the house in Florida. He was friendly and fearless, and Richie and Gilda's company thought he was cute. They would give him hamburgers and admire his dives from the board when he demanded they look. They'd better admire him, Frankie thought. My kid is the only one in that bunch who knows how to dive! Still, she didn't like him hanging around those people, taking their handouts like he never got fed at home. When she caught him at it she would grab the hamburger away and smack him. He had to learn. He would eat anything, go anywhere to get scraps, and he was so skinny nobody knew where he put it. He burned it up. She'd been skinny like that when she was young. Now that she had left her carefree twenties and was a mother it wasn't so easy to keep skinny. Once you were thirty, good luck. Your waistline said goodbye and went its own way, whether you liked it or not. She wore loose-fitting shirts now over her slacks because she had a pot from drinking. Somebody once asked her if she was pregnant again and it shocked her so much that she cut out all her beer and went exclusively to scotch. And no desserts, ever, not any more.

The one person in that family whom Frankie admired was Papa. The old man was eighty-two years old, and he still went to the office. He wasn't what he had been, but he was still sharp for an old man, and you could see he was still the boss around here. Every night after dinner the whole bunch of them trooped over to The Big House, where Papa would be lying on the sofa in the living room, and they would all sit there and pay court to him until he yawned and said it was time to go home. Most of the time he didn't even bother to talk to anyone; he just lay on the sofa and watched and listened, half-dozed sometimes if he was bored, then woke up, and spoke to anyone who came over to sit on the edge of the sofa or kneel at his side. Frankie's mother-in-law and Lavinia talked about him a lot, about the good old days, and Frankie was sorry that she hadn't known him then and that John really wouldn't know him at all. To John, his great-grandfather was a strong old man who hurt him with his moustache when he kissed him.

Frankie thought that maybe if she'd met Papa when he was younger he might have liked her more. He was always polite— Papa was never rude to anyone—but he didn't pay attention to her. He wouldn't sit and talk to her. He intimidated her so that after making a little small talk she would retreat. Well, what the hell did she have to say to him anyway? He knew so much more than she did, and what could she ask him about? When he was a kid in Russia? How to make a million dollars? He would think she was crazy.

The family was getting ready to go to some big dinner party at Andrew and Cassie's country place. They never went there more than once a year, if that, because it was far away, and Cassie had decided that it was about time she invited them all over to see how she'd redecorated the house around Andrew's paintings. So naturally, since they never went anywhere, the Windflower contingent all talked about this coming event for weeks, what should they wear, who would sit with who in the big car, who would drive the other car, what should they buy for a hostess gift, etc., etc. It was making Frankie nervous. She didn't want to go at all. She was intensely uncomfortable in Cassie's presence because she was so ritzy. When Cassie looked at her Frankie always wondered if her black roots were showing or if there was a stain on her blouse. She didn't want to go to their fancy place and eat their fancy dinner, especially since she was sure they wouldn't think to serve booze, or at least not enough, and she didn't see how she could get through the ordeal without it.

"John isn't going," Frankie told Melissa.

"Why not?"

"He's too young. He'll get too excited and I don't want him out late."

"Oh, he should get to know his young cousins," Lavinia said, interrupting as usual with her big loyalty-to-the-family number.

"John can sleep in the car on the way back," Melissa said.

"He's my son and he's not going," Frankie said. "I'll stay here with him."

"Oh?" Maybe, they were thinking, Frankie wasn't such a bad mother after all, really concerned about her child. Little did they know.

"Well, Rosemary's taking Buffy," Melissa said, but it was really just a last token protest.

"Buffy's *ten*," Frankie said firmly.

"He'll be awfully disappointed," Lavinia said.

Frankie didn't even bother to answer her. John would do what she said and that was that. He could stay up late and watch television. They wouldn't all be there hovering over him and telling him to go to bed. He wouldn't be very disappointed not to go. She would let him have at the candy box that Lazarus always locked up. Boy oh boy, the way they locked up things in this house! The booze locked up so the maids wouldn't get at it, the candy locked up so the kids couldn't get at it, and the key hung on a nail which any child could reach as soon as he was old enough to drag a chair to it. Every night after dinner Lazarus would go into the closet where the candy was locked up and stand there hunched over the whole box, picking out piece after piece with his long bony fingers, chewing thoroughly, totally absorbed, and if you tried to come in he got all embarrassed and annoyed as if you had caught him zipping up his fly. According to Lazarus, the only time it was medically recommended to eat sweets was after a meal, and since he was against sweets in principle anyway, he got furious with guilt if you discovered that in his old age he had become a candy freak.

It was finally the famous night of Cassie and Andrew's family dinner party. Richie was taking Gilda. When Frankie realized that, she almost had a change of heart. She wasn't as bad as Gilda. If that fat slob could show up, why couldn't she? Gilda had a tight white dress and a feather boa and rhinestone drop earrings. It was really outrageous. But that was Gilda: jeans or feathers.

When Frankie saw the rest of them trooping out of their houses to the cars she realized Gilda hadn't been too outrageous after all. They were all wearing cocktail dresses! For dinner in the country, after a two-hour drive cramped in a crowded car! Frankie was glad she had decided not to go.

"Don't let John stay up too late," her mother-in-law said, the pest.

"Have a good time," Frankie said.

"There are Good Humors in the freezer. Don't let him eat more than one; I saw him eating one this afternoon."

"They're all gone. Lazarus ate them," Frankie said.

"I did not! That's a damned lie!" Lazarus' face was purple with rage because it was a lie; she had just made it up to bug him.

"Come on, Melissa," Lavinia said, "don't keep Papa waiting." Lavinia had managed to get herself, Jonah, Melissa, and Lazarus seats in the big car with Papa and Etta. The chauffeur was driving, so everyone could relax. Jack was driving Hazel's big car with

Rosemary, Hazel, Buffy, Richie, and Gilda. If I'd gone, Frankie thought, I would have had to drive my Volkswagen anyway, and who needs that?

When they all drove away Frankie made herself a nice big scotch on the rocks and sat on the screened porch in solitary splendor. John was in the living room watching TV. It was late afternoon, and nice, and very quiet. The maids had gone down to the lake to fish since they didn't have to prepare dinner. Later they would bring the fish back up to the house and fry it. Frankie hoped they would catch enough for her and John too. She was sick and tired of all those la-de-la dinners they had around here. Sometimes she just wanted to drive to Howard Johnson's and get some fried clams.

She made another drink and sat there sipping it and thinking of all the kinds of food she would like if she didn't have to watch her waistline. Fried clams. A cheeseburger with French fried potatoes with lots of catsup and a pitcher of draft beer. Key lime pie. Irish coffee. Bratwurst with sauerkraut and German beer and a big plate of hash brown potatoes on the side, and a couple of scotches and then coffee with a couple of brandies. A lemon-filled sugar donut. Two fried eggs on top of hash brown potatoes the way they used to make it in the diner when she was helping her mother. How she used to hate that diner, but how she missed their fried eggs on top of hash browns! They were made just right, not too greasy. Codfish cakes with cream sauce. Chicken croquettes with gravy. It was all that cheap restaurant food she had been brought up on and thought she would never miss, and now she hadn't had it for so long she did miss it. The only thing she liked from her new life was caviar. Frankie really liked caviar. The other stuff, the gefilte fish and the matzo balls and the borscht made her sick just to taste them. All Everett ever wanted was steak. Steak every night, blood rare, and he would never eat vegetables or salad or even take a vitamin pill. Someday he would just fall apart. You couldn't just live on half-raw meat and black coffee. Frankie liked her steak very well done, with a lot of A-1 sauce on it to kill the taste.

She could hear the maids coming back from the lake. Then she heard the fat sizzling and smelled the lovely smell of frying fish. She made another drink and went into the kitchen.

"What'd you get?"

"Just two little porgies. Ain't nothin' biting tonight."

"Oh, that's a shame," Frankie said, and left.

"Miss Frankie?"

"What?"

"What did you intend for John to have for supper?"

Frankie turned back. "I don't care. What've you got?"

"His grandmother got a nice broiler for him. For you too."

"Then will you fry them, please?"

"Fried?" The cook was surprised and pleased. Nobody in that house would eat anything fried.

"Yes, fried," Frankie said. "For both of us."

By the time the fried chicken was ready Frankie was starving. The hell with her diet. She would have a good time. Naturally she and John couldn't eat in the living room in front of the television set because they might get stains on the rug, so they had to eat in the dining room. She hated that. It made her depressed to sit all alone at that big table in that big dining room with the kid. It was like some movie about rich people, all bored and stuffy and alone, not saying a word at the table because they were so far away from each other they would have to scream, and rich stuffy people didn't do that.

"Do you want the rest of my chicken, John?"

"Oh, yes, please, Ma'am."

She had brought him up well, she decided, pleased. He always called her Ma'am, even when overcome with emotion at the prospect of stuffing himself with an unexpected bonus of fried chicken.

What she would do tonight, to cheer herself up, was drive to the roadhouse and have a couple of drinks and play the jukebox and maybe even find somebody to talk to. That would be fun. John would be safe; the maids were here. She would just go scoot off after dinner and have herself a pleasant evening for once, and she'd be back in the house before any of them came back so they'd never know she'd been gone. The maids always went into their room after dinner, and anyway, they wouldn't tell. She'd make John go to bed and then he wouldn't tell either, because he wouldn't know. Ah, if she only had some friends here to invite, the way Richie and Gilda did. She would really know how to use this place. But since she couldn't, then she would just have to go elsewhere to find her amusement. To each his own.

John went to bed without much more protest than usual, and

Frankie brushed her teeth and put on lipstick and powder. She brushed her hair and put on some cologne. She put Everett's old sweater over her shirt and slacks because the night had turned chilly, and added her charm bracelet to look nice, and then she got into her car, checked the gas to see if there was enough, and drove down the long driveway out of Windflower toward freedom.

She liked the roadhouse. It was small, and it wasn't much, but she felt comfortable and relaxed there. They knew her; she fit in. She had a couple of scotches and bought a pack of cigarettes from the machine and settled in for a pleasant few hours. It wasn't crowded, even though it was Saturday night,. because not many of the people around here went anywhere, and when they did they went to the country club. Mostly people had parties in their own homes. Kids on dates just went to someone's house, or to a dance at the club. Not many people went to the roadhouse, and it was a wonder it managed to stay open, but it was small and cozy and beloved of the few regulars, so it struggled along. It had been here ever since she had been coming to Windflower and it had never changed.

The nice thing about the roadhouse was that people came there to drink and not to pick each other up or get fresh. It was where you went to relax. Frankie felt perfectly safe. If she wanted to talk to the bartender or the waitress, both of whom she knew, she could, and if not, then she didn't have to. A man drinking alone would have his snort and go home, not bothering her. He would have a wife and kids at home, and this was a way station, not a pickup joint. There were some young couples on dates, too. Frankie didn't know why the family was so shocked at the idea of her going to the roadhouse, so that the only time she could come here was when she could sneak away. Also, they kept screaming about drinking and driving, because they didn't drink and they didn't know how to drive, so both those things seemed very mysterious and dangerous to them. She could hold it. She'd had more than she could count and she wasn't too drunk. You had to be used to drinking in order to be a good drinker.

She looked at the clock over the bar. Damn, the evening had gone too fast! Now she'd better hurry home before all the vultures returned and really laid her out. Oh boy, if they found John all alone and her gone, would they yell! Frankie called for the check, paid it, and left.

The fog had risen during the evening and the road was ghostly
. . . ghastly? no, ghostly . . . with this strange cottony mist all
around the car and her headlights cutting a tiny tunnel through
it. It was lucky, Frankie thought, that she knew the way so well.
A stranger would get hopelessly lost. With all the lakes and streams
and rivers around here sending up moisture, and then the valley
holding it in, you were surrounded by heavy mist every night. Tonight was one of the worst ones. She wanted to hurry, but she
knew that if she drove too fast she might miss the road and go off
on the shoulder, or even miss her own turnoff entirely and then
she would get lost. The big trees arched over her head and made
a mysterious world of their own underneath them. She had her
headlights on bright and still she couldn't see more than about
four feet. She wasn't scared, just a little nervous because she'd
stayed longer at the roadhouse than she'd meant to and she hoped
she would get home before the family did. She crossed the bridge
and then she knew she was nearly there. The stables were down
the road, and then their own property started, and then there
would be the Windflower entrance with the lanterns burning on
top of the stone wall and she would be home safe. Home safe . . .
that was funny, to think of Windflower as home. It had never
been her home, never would be, yet it was all she had up north,
so maybe it was her home. Home was where her bed was, how
about that? Her kid was there, too. Frankie squinted into the fog
and tried to see where she was. Boy, would she be glad to get
there! She couldn't see *anything*. She started whistling through
her teeth, the way she had when she was a kid, so she wouldn't
be nervous any more. Maybe she'd passed it? Maybe the family
was home and they'd turned off the lanterns. If they had, she
would never be able to find the entrance to turn off.

Suddenly, rising up out of the mist right in front of her was an
enormous stallion, terrified by her little car, rearing up on his hind
feet, his front hooves flying toward her windshield, whinnying
with terror. Frankie turned the wheel frantically to get away from
him, this lost night monster, great black shrieking creature, and
crashed head-on into the stone wall right outside Windflower.

The family decided Frankie should be buried in Vermont, with
her own people. Everett made all the arrangements and accompanied the body. He wanted to take John with him, but his

425

mother and the others talked him out of it: John was too young; it was too morbid. He had taken his mother's death badly, as was expected, so whenever he had an outburst of wildness or brattiness, they understood. Poor little boy! What would become of him now? He couldn't stay with Everett because who would take care of him after school while Everett was at work? A maid, a house-keeper, some ignorant hired stranger? He couldn't stay with his grandparents either; Everett wouldn't hear of it, and to tell the truth both Melissa and Lazarus were too old to have a wild child in their house at this stage of their lives. It was wonderful to have John for two months or so in the summer, but not all year in the city. They all thought the best thing to do would be to send John to some nice boys' boarding school in Florida, near enough to home so that he could spend weekends with Everett. Boarding schools took boys as young as seven, children of divorce, of be-reavement, of parents who just didn't want them around.

Lavinia felt John's grief as if it were her own. She still remem-bered, although only vaguely, how she had felt as a lonely child without a mother. Or perhaps she only imagined she remembered? She had been only a baby, and John was seven and bright for his age. He must be suffering terribly. She hadn't cared for Frankie any more than any of them, but still, it was a shame. A mother, even a rotten one, was still a mother, and John loved Frankie. Poor little thing. He would be less lonely at boarding school than with Everett. At least he would have other boys his age to play with, and kind teachers to be father surrogates.

John thought they were sending him away to get rid of him. He didn't tell any of them that, but he knew it. They didn't want him. What was it about him that they didn't like? He wasn't so awful, was he? Maybe they just didn't like kids, that was all. His father didn't even put up a fight to keep him. It was obvious that his father didn't care. Why didn't he care? John had always been sure his father loved him.

The family thought that Frankie had crashed her car into the wall because she had been drunk, so they hushed the whole inci-dent up and no one ever mentioned it. It was "the accident." Lazarus said that small foreign cars were a menace, and if God had meant man to drive a car . . . and for once no one tried to make him finish the sentence to tease him. Jack said what could you expect from a car made by Nazis? Lavinia told Jonah not to drive any more, he was getting too old, they should let someone else drive. Jonah had always been a wild driver anyway. Eventually Frankie's death became, in the eyes of the family, a sort of Revenge of the Machines. It was as if the only thing Frankie had had to do with it at all was that she happened to be there.

Everett didn't miss Frankie. He was alone in his small house in Florida, going every day to work and then home again to heat up a TV dinner, and he was used to being alone. He drew into himself, relieved not to have her around. He made more trips to Windflower that summer to see John, and thought it was a good thing he was putting the kid in boarding school in the fall because his family would drive the poor kid crazy and ruin him. John didn't mention his mother any more, and Everett wondered what he was thinking.

The last night John and Everett were there before Everett took John back down south to be enrolled in the school, the family asked John what he wanted to have for dinner.

"It's your last night here, so you can have anything you want," Melissa said. "You pick it. Roast beef? Steak? Lobster?"

"I want fried chicken," John said.

"Fried chicken?" She was appalled. "Why in the world would you want fried chicken?"

"You said I could have what I want. I want fried chicken."

Melissa shrugged and went to the kitchen to tell the cook to make fried chicken, except for Lazarus, of course, who would eat only broiled.

At dinner they all tried to be cheerful and told John how much he would enjoy his new school. The maid came out with a huge silver platter piled high with crisp pieces of fried chicken. When John had taken his share he couldn't eat any of it. He poked it with his fork and then he put his fork down and tears filled his eyes.

"You wanted it, now you don't want it," Melissa said. "What's the matter with you?"

John looked away, out the window, over the hills, withdrawing from them, and when he looked back his blue eyes were calm as sheets of glass. "My mother and I had fried chicken together the night she went away," he said cheerfully, a comment, a matter of information.

No one had mentioned Frankie for a long time now, and her

name came as an interruption, almost an imposition. When would he forget? When would she go away? John was eating now, with his customary good appetite. Maybe it was better for him to talk about her. He seemed all right.

TWELVE

Richie graduated from law school and passed his bar exams with no difficulty. Everyone expected him to settle down to the practice of law, but instead he entered divinity school to study to be an Orthodox rabbi. He had found a school in the mountains of Pennsylvania that was so religious no one had ever heard of it. Gilda had to wear a sheitel, and dresses with high necks, long sleeves, and hems down to the ground so no part of her body would show. Makeup was of course forbidden. Having to wear a sheitel didn't bother her; she'd always thought wigs were jazzy anyway, so she bought a blonde one and a black one so that when she got tired of being Rita Hayworth she could be Marilyn Monroe or Elizabeth Taylor. She didn't take Richie's calling too seriously. She figured he was just going to school until he was too old to be drafted.

The religious community was isolated and like a very small town. Everyone knew everyone's business, and from the start they were all shocked by the behavior of Richard Winsor's wife. Everyone at the school took their religious laws very seriously. There was even a mikvah, although each house had modern central plumbing. Small private houses had been converted into apartments, but since Richie could afford it he rented an entire house for himself and Gilda. In the bedroom there were twin beds separated by a sink. It was one of the laws of the school that upon rising in the morning one must not walk more than a certain number of steps before washing oneself, and therefore the oddly placed sink. It was also necessary to wash before and after the marital act, which was most blessed when performed on Friday night. Gilda thought it was all hilarious. She would have shoved the beds together but everything was built in.

Their house was only partially furnished, since most couples liked to bring their own things from home to make it more comfortable. Gilda couldn't be bothered, and Richie didn't seem to mind that their living room, which was right on the street, had neither curtains nor shades. In the evenings, when no public appearance was required of her, Gilda would shuck her puritan dress and put on her jeans and hand-painted tee shirt, and she and Richie would sit in the living room and play their collection of records. Gilda had added some rock to Richie's classical, and the strains of some depraved English group would sail out into the pious night and horrify the community. Looking into the living room windows they would see Richard Winsor's wife dressed in that outrageous fashion, makeup on her face, her black sheitel (her favorite) still on her head.

There were complaints. Richie finally made Gilda buy curtains. He studied hard, and when he and Gilda returned home for Thanksgiving, he refused to answer any questions put to him by his parents. His whole demeanor was serious and deeply religious. Since Richie had always been silent, no one tried too hard to make him talk about his new call to the religious life. Hazel was confused and Herman was disappointed. Herman would have been able to reconcile himself to the idea of his son as a rabbi, although it seemed a waste, but such a religious nut? Richie had always been religious, but this was too much. Some of the things they did at that school Herman had never even heard of before.

"I'd like a grandchild," Hazel said to Gilda. "So, when?"

"We're going to have at least six children," Gilda said sincerely, and while she was in Miami Beach she took the opportunity to go to the drugstore and renew her supply of birth control pills. The school was adamantly against birth control of any kind, and if she'd gone to the local drugstore the community would have found out about it and had her head on a platter.

"You're not going to be able to support six children on what a rabbi makes," Herman told Richie.

"You know I'm rich."

"Somebody's going to have to handle the business. I won't be here forever. You can't just leave it. Everything I did, I did for you."

"I feel my spiritual life comes first," Richie said.

Herman rearranged some of his business affairs so that Richie would have to pay a minimal amount of attention to them and the income would still come pouring in. He hoped they didn't teach them at that school to give everything away like in some of those nutty priest schools. He put everything in trust so that Richie could enjoy his income but not dip into the principal and dispose of it. Oh, what a thankless son to grieve his father so! It was one thing to tell his friends that his son the lawyer was studying to be a rabbi now, but what kind of a rabbi? What kind of a school was that? Gilda chattered on, laughing, about the things they made them do at the school and Herman felt sick. He didn't understand his son at all. What kind of wife would Gilda make for an Orthodox rabbi? A chorus girl she looked like, not a rebbetzin.

Richie was happy in his marriage and content at the school. He had always enjoyed studying and learning new things. Gilda was his best friend and he always liked being with her. He was never lonely any more. Whenever she did anything outrageous he loved it because it was something he would have liked to do if he had thought of it but would never have dared to do even if he had. She was the only person who could make him laugh. She never shocked him. When the religious community got together and Gilda made some faux pas, as she invariably did, Richie couldn't look at her, not because he was embarrassed but because he knew she was holding in her giggles and if he looked at her she would make him giggle too. She was so alive. He wanted to give her the world.

John was at school too, settled in. He had made many friends and was a natural leader. He hated to study. His grandmother had told him that she hated to study when she was a little girl, and his father had told him that he had hated schoolwork too, so John knew it ran in the family. When he applied himself, which he did if the subject interested him, he did very well. The headmaster said his tests showed that he was brilliant, but his behavior showed that he was lazy. John still thought that when he grew up he would work in the shop with his father, and since his father would teach him everything he needed to know, what difference did it make if he didn't study hard at school? On the other hand, his father shouldn't have sent him away. Maybe he didn't want to work in TV repair with his father after all. Maybe he would be a scientist, and discover something like a cure for cancer, or maybe he'd be a famous lawyer like Perry Mason on TV. He might even be a school teacher, like Stan, his adviser, whom John liked very much. Stan was only twenty-nine, and he was handsome and athletic and nice. He wasn't at all like those dried-up old ladies John had had for teachers in school before. Stan taught English and football. John liked football because the younger boys like himself played touch football and you didn't have to hurt anybody, and he was a good player. He had always disliked English, but with Stan teaching it he tried hard and realized he was good with words. He found it easy to write a story or a composition and he got good marks. Maybe he could even be a writer like his cousin Paris. There were a lot of good things to do instead of staying in the TV repair shop with his father. When he grew up he wouldn't need his father. He would have better friends.

They had all kinds of awful rules at his school which John and the other boys found ingenious ways to avoid. You had to get up at a quarter to seven in the morning and take a cold shower. All the boys turned on the showers, threw water on the floor, wet their towels and their hair, and avoided bathing altogether. You had to eat everything on your plate before you could leave the dining room, so the boys simply filled their napkins with whatever they disliked, put the napkins into their pockets, and disposed of them down the toilet after dinner. If it was too big to go down the toilet you could bury it. You had to spend two hours in the library doing homework every night, but any boy knew that you could put your favorite magazine into your school book and read that instead until the time was up.

The younger boys like John slept in a big dormitory, and the older ones had rooms of their own with a roommate. All the boys in John's dorm wanted to be his roommate for later. John thought it was too bad that the boys couldn't live with the teachers and their families instead. He would have liked to live with Stan, who had a pretty wife and a baby girl. They would have been just like a family. He wasn't really jealous of Stan's wife either, because she was always so nice to him. Sometimes Stan invited some of the boys he advised to come to his house for Sunday dinner, which was at noon. John really loved that. At those times he was sure that he would rather be a teacher than anything. You could live in a nice little house and have a pretty wife and a cute baby and invite

431

lots of kids to come and visit. He had never lived in a house like that before, where everyone was so calm and so sweet to each other.

On weekends John went home to stay with his father, who took him places with him. They went to the store to buy things his father wanted, and they went to the grocery to buy food for breakfast, and they went to restaurants for their other meals. Sometimes they went to a movie. His father didn't seem to have any friends. He didn't like to play baseball or any other sport either. John told his father about sports and his father told him about fixing things. Most of the time they just sat in the house and watched television. They never saw Aunt Hazel and Uncle Herman, even though they lived right there in Miami Beach. John didn't mind; he didn't feel he knew them at all. He wondered if his father went out with any ladies during the week when he was at school, and if he was going to get married again. He supposed it wasn't fair to hope that his father would never marry anybody, because his father was all alone, but he was relieved that his father never called any ladies when he was around and none ever called him. His father never introduced him to any girlfriends of his either, so maybe he didn't have any. One of the boys at school, whose father had been married twice, told John that they dragged you places with the future wife so you would get to know her before they made her your stepmother. He said any fool could tell who was going to be his future stepmother because she was always around and made a big fuss over you and sat through baseball games with you and your father. John couldn't imagine his own father ever doing anything like that. His father had never taken him to a ballgame in his life, and as long as some lady didn't come along to start them going to ballgames he knew he was safe.

In New York that winter Buffy was training seriously to be a runner. She bought track magazines, and her gym teacher told her that there was a good track at Columbia where they sometimes let people practice even thought they weren't students. She took the bus up there every day after school, telling her mother she was going to a friend's house. She was thirteen, and all the girls went to each other's houses after school, gossiping and playing records and talking about boys. Except Buffy; she went to Columbia and ran around the track. She had bought the proper track shoes and a track suit for cold weather. She was the youngest person there, and the older kids, who seemed to be all boys, treated her as a kind of mascot. During rest breaks some of the older boys talked to her and told her things she wanted to know about training, and about where she should go to college. She also learned there was no such thing as professional. Professional was a dirty word. You were an Amateur runner, and you tried to compete in the Nationals. Naturally everyone's dream was to be in the Olympics, but you had to be trained for that all your life, and Buffy's parents weren't going to get her a trainer and she couldn't do it by herself. If she got into the Nationals, she could travel. You could go all over the world to compete in meets if you were a winner. It was the best life she could think of.

On Saturday mornings her parents made her go to Sunday school, and Saturday afternoons she had to go to the Youth Group, where you had planned, supervised activities with boys your age. Most of the time Buffy didn't go; she started out from her parents' apartment and then just went right up to Columbia. If her parents saw the cute boys there, compared to the creepy, pimply-faced boys her age in the Youth Group, they certainly wouldn't think she was a social misfit. Not that any of those older boys ever considered her anything but another ambitious runner. But Buffy wasn't interested in boys yet anyway. Running was her whole life. It was the only way she could think of to get what she wanted. She didn't want to grow up like her parents. It was all right for them, they seemed to like it, but she felt sorry for them. They never went anywhere, never did anything, and her mother didn't even have a job. Buffy couldn't see how they could be happy. Maybe older people had to compromise because when they were growing up they had been taught to do a certain thing and they didn't know anything else. She was being taught to do a certain thing too, but she didn't intend to do it. She was different. She thought for herself.

Three months before Richie was to be ordained as an Orthodox rabbi he turned twenty-six. He was no longer eligible to be drafted. He told the school that he had decided he didn't really have the calling after all, and he and Gilda packed up and left. They went to Europe for six months, traveling with knapsacks on their backs. He told his parents that when he came back he would settle down to work. They didn't mind; after all, it was such a relief that he had come to his senses again. The only thing they couldn't figure out was why he and Gilda wanted to travel around like two hippies. Richie could afford to go first class. When had his parents ever denied him anything? It was that Gilda. She came from poverty, she was a hippie, and she didn't know any better. She had influenced him.

"Next time we'll go the conventional way," Richie told Gilda. "But this time I want to see the country like the people do."

That was fine with her.

THIRTEEN

Adam Saffron was eighty-six, and he was beginning to feel like an old man. On his eightieth birthday the family had given him a big party, and he had enjoyed it. Father's Day, too, had always been an occasion, with a huge dinner and a cake and someone taking photos for the family albums. But during the last few years he had felt the motor running more slowly. He didn't want a big birthday party, he didn't feel up to a Father's Day celebration; just his family around him was enough. Now he didn't go to the office every day; he went for only a few hours each day in the winter and in the summer he hardly went at all. Once a week, perhaps, the appearance of Adam Saffron would cause the buzzing among the employees that the arrival of a visiting dignitary would. He would see that everything was all right, have lunch with the boys, and go home. He was tired, and content to rest, although he still kept control of everything, had reports, knew what was going on. He was glad that Andrew and Basil were so good in the business. He wondered which of the younger generation would follow them.

Not Everett, he was hopeless. Everyone had known at the start that Everett had no head for business, and no interest in it. Not Richie; he was off on some trip again, making up for the childhood he had never had. The solemn little old man he was at thirteen was now in his twenties (Adam could never remember exactly how old any of them were) and had turned into a child. Fun and adventure was all he thought about. Well, he would just have to grow up more slowly than the others. Then there were Andrew's boys, Chris and Paul. Chris had been serving his apprenticeship working for a friend of Adam's, learning real estate. The man was shrewd, and Chris was learning well. Adam did not believe in paying people to learn, especially not family. It made for ill will. Let Chris start elsewhere, not exactly at the bottom, mind you, and serve his time, and then when he had learned all he had to know he could come into the business and work alongside his father as a young contributor, not someone who got the job as a favor.

Chris enjoyed real estate, and loved competition. As a little boy he had been an athlete, and still was, but the competitive spirit he had shown in sports he now transferred to business deals. He had a good head on him. As for Paul, his younger brother, he was willing but reluctant to come into the business. His interests lay elsewhere. No one, even Paul, knew for sure where they were. Perhaps the stock market? He seemed to like that the best, and was working for a Wall Street firm. There was nothing wrong with that, Adam thought. It was good to have a stockbroker in the family. The main thing was to do something well. As long as someone in the family had his hand in the business and the employees were well chosen, intelligent, and faithful, the business could run. It was no longer necessary for Adam to watch every detail. Andrew and Basil had learned everything. They weren't what he had been, but he was tired now and not about to get upset about it. There had been a time when his skill and foresight had been indispensable; now they were a good thing to have but the world would not collapse without them. He could relax and leave the main part of the business to the boys.

What was to become of Hervé, Basil's son? He had no interest in the business at the moment, and Adam was rather relieved. The boy spent so much time in France that he was only half American. Nicole insisted on bringing her children up to be half French, half American. To Adam this was peculiar. In his day every person wanted to be an American, would give anything for the privilege, and this woman wanted to take her children away. She even had them chattering in French at the dinner table so they would not forget it. Hervé wanted to be a movie star. What kind of craziness was that? But if he had his heart set on it, then let him try. Adam really didn't care very much. The boy was so conceited he got on everyone's nerves. So let there be a movie star in the family, and when the boy failed, then let there be either a playboy, or perhaps eventually a reformed playboy who would let his father teach him something. Basil was too soft, too sweet. He should take a firm hand with his son, make a man of him. But Adam was tired, and he wasn't going to butt in.

John—now, there was a bright little boy who might grow up to be a credit to them all. Even though there were a few branches not so wonderful, the line went on, sturdy and strong. Adam could tell that John had potential, he with the self-defeating father and the alcoholic mother who had unfortunately gone to an early death. Adam had a feeling about John.

It never occurred to Adam to consider that any of his granddaughters should go into the business. Business was for men. Paris had surprised everybody by becoming such a well-known writer, but when Adam had heard he was not surprised. He had always known the child would do something in the arts. Always drawing, writing her poems and little stories, chattering away when she was so tiny; she had talent and two intelligent parents who encouraged it. It was good to have such a talented granddaughter, who could make her own money, and she could write her books even after she was married and had children. She didn't have to work, but she wanted to. As for the other girls, Blythe and Buffy and Geneviève, he supposed they would go to college and then find some interesting temporary work to do until they got married. He was glad that all of them had a good future before them with no money worries. It was good that they wouldn't have to go to work unless they wanted to. They were all three nice girls, and three nice boys would be lucky someday to get them. He was glad that Geneviève, who was as pretty as a movie star, didn't have the slightest desire to be one. It was her crazy brother with that ambition. His mother had probably put the idea into his head.

Ah! Crazy world today! So much of it good and so much of it meshuggah. People today didn't know what they wanted. They had so much of everything to choose from they just sat in the middle, like a child in a roomful of playthings, and cried. Adam had no patience with people who complained and whined. America was the good land, where a man with a mind and a will could work hard and get anything he wanted. Adam didn't go to the

movies any more; he fell asleep in the movies. The theater didn't
interest him. Television wasn't bad, but it wasn't good either. He
liked to watch the news, but the stories they had on afterward were
so silly they made him sick. Variety shows, comedy, they were good
for Etta. She loved to watch television. It usually put Adam to
sleep. What he missed most of all, with his failing sight, were his
newspapers. You could always find a world in the newspapers,
news, human interest, business, everything. Now he could read
the headlines, and some of the stories, but it was a strain and he
couldn't sit there for hours enjoying his newspapers the way he
had in the old days. Yes, man was a machine that ran down, and
no amount of parts you added could ever make him as good as
new. You put on eyeglasses; they helped, but not enough. You
gave him a cane if he got tired walking, but it didn't give him new
legs. His heart grew tired, beating, beating, beating, all those years,
like an old clock.

His children looked older. They were middle-aged. There was
Etta, who had once been his young bride, and she didn't look out
of place among his children; she had gray hair and a lined face
and so did they. He had to give Lazarus credit, the old goat.
Lazarus lied about his age and got upset if you tried to find out
how old he really was, but Adam guessed Lazarus was nearly as old
as he was. He was certainly closer to eighty than seventy. But
Lazarus crept to his office and crept home, studied his huge dictionary through his thick glasses, and carried on.

It was just as well he couldn't read the newspapers the way he
used to, Adam thought. Every time he looked at the obituary page
it seemed as if another one of his old cronies had died. There
wasn't anyone left any more, just himself and maybe one or two
others he had forgotten. The surprise was when you picked up
the paper and saw that someone had died and you thought he'd
died years ago. All his sisters and brothers had died, even little
Becky. Poor little Becky, so sick and in such pain for so long
that her death had seemed like a blessing. Her husband had gone
before her; all the husbands of his sisters had left them widows.
Men died sooner. Women were strong. They tried to fool you and
act weak, but most of the women he had known in his lifetime
had outlasted their men. It wasn't good to think about death; it
was depressing and you couldn't keep it away anyhow, but when
you got older it seemed to be all around you.

437

Everett should remarry. A man shouldn't be alone. If he had been younger, his old self, Adam would have done something about that. He would have arranged something, found someone, had a talk with the boy, explained to him that it wasn't good for John to be in a boarding school so young, that the child should have a home. Melissa said Everett did nothing but work in his shop and go home alone. It wasn't right. Maybe this winter when they went back to Miami Beach, he would have a talk with Everett. He couldn't talk to him this summer here at Windflower; Everett hadn't even come up. John was in summer school, taking a course in reading—reading? at his age?—making up something he hadn't done well in. No, it wasn't the reading he had done badly at; it was math. John was good at reading. It was hard to remember these things because they didn't seem to matter so much any more. You had an instinct, a feeling about a person, and you knew it would work out. When you had lived a long time you saw that you could keep trying to stuff knowledge into an onion and it remained an onion, but a smart person . . . They said John was coming up for two weeks at the end of the summer after his summer school was over, and maybe Everett would come with him and they could talk then. Otherwise, they would talk in Florida. A few months wasn't going to make such a difference.

Adam's heart attack came to him as a betrayal. When he felt the pain he knew right away, and all he could think was: *It's too soon.* Etta called the doctor, and the doctor insisted he go to the hospital right away in an ambulance. Adam, in his bed in his familiar bedroom upstairs in his house at Windflower, refused. He wouldn't go to the hospital, he couldn't go, he was afraid to go. He knew you died in the hospital. He had been in hospitals before, to visit other people, even once himself when they took out his appendix, but this time it was different. He knew that this time if he let them put him into the hospital he would never come out alive.

"No hospital!" Adam said. "No hospital!" His strong voice sounded so strangely weak, not at all the way he had meant it to. It was quavering. "No hospital!"

"Come on, Papa," they all said. His daughters, his wife, his sons-in-law, even his granddaughter Paris, they were hovering around him, strength in numbers, and two young doctors put him into the ambulance on a stretcher and rushed him off into the night. Safe country night, passing lighted homes of relaxing people, torn out of his own safe home and forced here to this too brightly lit white hospital, put into a small hard bed, dressed in an ugly rag of a hospital gown, stuck with needles and tubes, encased in an oxygen tent, shut off from the world behind this plastic curtain and attached to machines, a human robot. Adam tried to talk, to protest, but his voice was so faint only he could hear it. They were all taking over, his children, making him the child and them the grownups. Andrew was there, and later Basil, who must have been driving for hours. They spoke to the nurse, who was a child, not much older than thirty, and she spoke to them, and all of it was so soft that Adam couldn't hear. They were taking his power away from him. If he had had the strength he would have ripped off all those tubes and gadgets and gotten up, told them who was still the boss. His own doctor came then, the doctor he knew and trusted, the betrayer who had insisted he come here to this hospital. Adam hoped the doctor would say it was a mistake, he could go home, but he knew that would never happen. He could see from the doctor's face. The doctor was telling him to be still, to rest, to relax. Ordering him, as if he were a child, to do what he was told. To do what his nurse told him? Only a child had a nurse. And his children, hovering there, going out of the room to talk secrets with the doctor, running everything, taking away his power, forgetting who he was, that he was the boss, that he was Papa, that none of them would be here today or be anything at all if it weren't for him, that *they needed him.* Why then was he unable to speak, unable to make anyone hear him or understand him? Was this what it was like at the end of a man's life, to be turned into an infant again as you were at the start of it all?

PART V
Horizons

ONE

The Big House stood empty. It stood empty for the rest of the summer the year Adam died, and it stood empty the summer after. No one went near it except the new Japanese gardener/caretaker/handyman, who went inside once in a while to make sure everything was all right. Etta had gone to live in Texas, near her son, Stanley, who was a senior pilot. No one tried to stop her. She had never been real family, not even after nearly thirty years of marriage to Papa. Her son from her first long-ago marriage was her real family, his children were her real grandchildren, and she felt so too. She was very rich now, and no one had to worry about her. They sent her birthday cards.

The Big House was the first one you saw when you drove up the long driveway, and it stood at the highest point of the hill, so it seemed to be guarding the others, just as Papa had guarded his family when he was alive. He was gone, but his presence was there, and none of them could bear to go into The Big House because it sent them off into a renewal of their grief and loss. Once in a while one of them crept in to retrieve some article of sentimental or material value. Rosemary crept in to get her Mama's old vase. Lavinia took the clock. Did Etta grab anything? She can have her own things, but we get Mama's. Buffy was afraid to go near the house at all; she thought it might be haunted.

Ivy and vines grew thickly along the stone walls and up and around the big chimney. The hedges grew high and were trimmed by the Japanese gardener. The roses bloomed in the flower garden, and died. Bees hummed in the thick, syrupy heat of July afternoons, feasting undisturbed on flowers. Birds nested in the chimney, sat on eggs, had young, flew away. Only the sound of the power lawn mower disturbed the stillness. The grass must not be allowed to grow too high. The house would be kept up, but no one would go into it, no one would live there. No one could bear to call it Papa's house; it was The Big House, spoken with just a pause, a gasp.

Anything of worth or particular emotional value was taken to the other houses, put into city apartments, gathered up. Furniture remained, enough for any family, but it was all furniture that Etta and the decorator had chosen. It didn't matter. The flowers on the wallpaper and draperies and furniture covers had faded, the carpets were streaked by years into a soft moiré pattern, and no one cared. In bright sun you could see these things, but the drapes were always kept drawn. The dishes in the kitchen cupboard were Etta's dishes, her everyday set. The good dishes were gone, and the silver too. Only forks with twisted tines, knives with bent blades, spoons with the silver worn off, remained in the kitchen drawer. No one wanted them. When Papa had been alive there had been such warmth in that house that no one had noticed the flowers were faded, the rugs were worn, time had passed. They had all thought everything would go on forever. Now everything hung suspended, between a breath and a breath, no one able to make a decision, no one even able to think.

Paris was in Hollywood, where they were making a movie of her third book. She had rented a bungalow at the Chateau Marmont, with her expense money from the movie company, and filled it with her crazy friends: hopefuls, fakers, failures, hangers-on, a few minor successes, all lonely and grouping together to have fun and forget their troubles. She had parties. Her analyst thought it was good for her to see people and didn't make her pay for the time she was out of town. She had a car which she never drove because she was afraid of the fast Los Angeles traffic. She used it only to go to the supermarket, to buy more food for her parties. Liquor was no problem. She had an admirer who sent her two cases of wine every week (on his expense account) and most of her friends didn't drink anyway; they took pills and smoked pot. Paris drank the wine herself, two bottles every day, and didn't take pills or smoke pot because they didn't interest her. She wandered through her days and nights, listening to her tapes that played rock music unceasingly, talking to her friends, laughing, watching them steal each other's lovers and throw scenes, and none of it touched her. She was still locked into her private self, the observer. She had no artistic control over the movie and everything was going wrong. She doubted if it would ever be made,

444

but they were paying her expenses and so she stayed, dutifully turning in the revisions the producer told her to write, watching him mangle her book, frustrated, furious, ashamed. She decided never to come to Hollywood again, but meanwhile it was keeping her away from Windflower, and there were people here her age, lively people. They were weird, but at least they kept her from being lonely. She had a lot of boyfriends. It was like college again in a way and made her forget for a while that she was getting older, that time was passing and it was destined that she always be alone.

She wondered sometimes what good it did you to be a writer. If you stayed home and wrote books you never saw anyone, and if you went to Hollywood to write a movie a lot of stupid people with big egos tried to take your work away from you and make it theirs, destroying it in the process and so destroying you. And always at the back of this problem was the more basic one, the pull of her family, the phone calls, the letters, the demands to come home, the questions: What was she doing that she couldn't do at home? It had been the same every time she went to Europe. There were her parents at the airport when she came back. "Well, I'm glad you got that over with," her mother would say, as if she'd been suffering in London or Paris or Rome, instead of having a wonderful time. Her mother seemed to think that "they" were forcing her to go away, her wicked publisher, her wicked agent, all the "exploiters," tearing her away from her family and sending her off to some foreign country to work too hard. She didn't need the money. Fame only made life more difficult. Why did she go away? She couldn't explain because she hated herself for having to defend something that shouldn't have to be defended: her right to have a free adult life. So she let them think she was being overworked and exploited. It was easier for them to accept and understand.

There was no one at Windflower for Buffy to be with this summer, no one near her age that is, and she spent all her time training, sprinting down the long gravel driveway. Whenever there was a track meet on TV she watched it. She had a crush on a Russian Olympic star now, whose name was Yuri, and she bought everything written about him she could find. She wondered if he spoke any English. He was twenty-one; she was fifteen. He competed not only in the Olympics but also in the Nationals, and traveled all over the world. If she were a runner she might be able to meet him. She fantasized about this meeting, dreamed of him, and was relieved to read that he had no special girlfriend. Russian runners were allowed to compete for years, until they were too old. Yuri would always be somewhere where she could follow his triumphs, worship him, and know he might someday, somehow, be accessible.

Richie and Gilda were in Israel. He felt it was important to see the holy land of his people, every bit of it. He had wanted Gilda to work with him on a kibbutz, but she had refused, and so they were touring the country instead. It was very quiet at Windflower with them gone. No one had company. Everyone was subdued, sad. This big, beautiful place—it seemed such a waste that the young people weren't here to enjoy it, to sit on the porch at night and watch the sunset, to swim in the pool, to make the tennis court ring with the sound of volleying balls and shouts and laughter. The Japanese gardener watered and rolled the en-tout-cas court regularly, hoping it would be used, and sometimes Rosemary and Jack went down to use it, playing more slowly now, not running around, hitting the balls directly to each other. Jack complained constantly about the expenses, but he and Rosemary were really the only ones who got any use out of the facilities. The family had finally given in and gotten a heater for the pool. But Jack kept turning it off to save money, so no one would go in, even Buffy. As for the electric bills, they stayed the same because Jack couldn't seem to understand the principle of a thermostat that turned the heater off when the water was comfortable enough, and the amount of power needed to heat a pool from scratch. The Japanese gardener/caretaker was confused by all this turning on and turning off, so he stayed away from the heater entirely, confining his pool care to vacuuming the pool.

Herman came up for three days, looking grayish and not well. His doctor had warned him to diet and cut out his cigars, but he was not a good patient, preferring to enjoy himself. He refused to take a vacation and sit around Windflower, and rushed right back to Florida. As far as anyone knew, Herman had never taken a vacation. He and Hazel had never been to Europe, or even to the Catskills. When they were together in Florida they still went out every night. During the summers, it was Hazel who had the vacation, sitting in Windflower and feeling sorry for Herman, who was working so hard in the hot Southern summer. But Herman loved being in Miami Beach, going out, seeing his friends. Three days at Windflower was the most he could stand.

It was Rosemary who answered the telephone when the doctor called from Florida to tell Hazel that Herman had had a stroke and was in a coma. Hazel flew right down to Florida, Rosemary with her. You couldn't let her go alone, and Rosemary as The Good Soul insisted it was her place. Jack stayed at Windflower with Buffy, waiting to hear what would be. Meanwhile, Lavinia and Melissa tried to find Richie, who was somewhere in Israel. They first tried all the big hotels, and luckily managed to find him registered at one of them. They had wanted to phone him, to spare him the full brunt of the shock, but he was never in. Now the doctor in Florida said Herman was dying. Poor Hazel! Poor Richie! What a mess! At last, in desperation, Lavinia and Melissa sent Richie a cable.

"COME HOME. YOUR FATHER IS DYING."

And Richie cabled back: "I CAN'T. I HAVEN'T SEEN MASADA YET."

Richie and Gilda came back in time to attend to Herman's funeral arrangements. No one in the family could understand Richie, the religious fanatic, so cruel, so heartless. Slowly, they were turning against him, pushing him out. He'd better be nice to his mother now; he was all she had. Why couldn't he stay put like a normal person?

Hazel was sad and bewildered by the speed with which her happy life had fallen apart. First her father had been taken away, then her husband. But she still had Richie, and she insisted that he and Gilda move into the big house in Florida with her. There was so much room, and it was so lonely. Richie agreed, but he was not pleased with the arrangement. He and Gilda went out to dinner nearly every night, and instead of spending time with Hazel they spent time with each other. He refused to sell the little house Herman had bought for him and Gilda to live in, which still was only partly furnished and not really half as nice as Hazel's house. He went to his father's office to attend to his business, and discovered that he was now even richer than he had dreamed.

The farmland which Herman had bought so long ago for Richie was now valuable real estate. Miami was expanding, bigger and bigger. Richie's Farm was worth twenty million dollars. Richie

447

was the richest person in the whole family. He didn't see any reason why it should change his life. He had always lived well. Gilda went out and bought a set of plastic-upholstered living room furniture for their house. She said it was easy to keep clean. She didn't demand a fur coat or diamonds. She wanted to travel, to have an interesting life. That was what Richie wanted too. He didn't know what to do with his mother. She and his father had had a million friends when his father was alive, and now it appeared that they had only been business friends. The house was empty. No one came to visit Hazel. The wives had all been just wives of Herman's friends; they had not been her friends. Day and night Hazel sat in her lonely big house and waited for friends to come to visit her, to console her in her bereavement, but only one or two came, and only once, as a courtesy. Letters poured in, but no one telephoned, no one invited her anywhere, no one came to see her. Gilda was getting annoyed with Hazel, who got on her nerves. She had never known anyone like Hazel before. Hazel kept following her around. That woman was going to drive her nuts!

Since they would be stuck here for a while anyway, Richie and Gilda decided to start their family. Gilda became pregnant more easily than she had expected, considering that she'd been on the pill and she thought that threw something off for a while, and as soon as she was pregnant she insisted that Richie let her live in her own house again. Richie agreed. He promised his mother he would visit her every day, or at least phone her, and he and Gilda moved back into their own small house. After all, a pregnant woman needed peace of mind, and his wife and future child came first. He was the man of the family and he had to take care of them.

That winter, after some thought, Paris asked her mother if she and Rima could rent The Big House at Windflower for the following summer. Lavinia called a family conference and they agreed. It seemed a waste to have the house stand empty, lonely and depressing, and as long as Paris was willing to pull her own weight in the financial department, why not? Lavinia bought sheets and blankets and towels and moved the furniture around, trying to make it more cheerful. She was so relieved to have her daughter back again that she would give her anything.

"Don't worry about the laundry," she told Paris, "I'll pay for it. And I'll get a cleaning woman to come once a week and I'll pay her too."

"She can come during the week when I'm not there," Paris said.

"You're only coming *weekends?*"

"I have to work."

"You can work in the country. No one will disturb you."

"I have a boyfriend."

"Ahh? Who is he?"

"Just no one."

"But he must be someone."

"I mean he's no one to get excited about."

"Then why can't you come to the country?"

"I'm not that unexcited about him."

"Oh, you!" her mother said, and laughed.

Paris had felt her grandfather's presence with her ever since he had died. Sometimes, in California, she had wondered if he was there too, and she had talked to him in her head. Some people had told her she was living in James Dean's bungalow and it was haunted. She knew that if anyone haunted it, it was her grandfather. She knew he was in his house, too. There was no Heaven. If someone died, he lived on if the people who lived on remembered him. She thought he wouldn't mind that she was using his house. Her life style wasn't exactly his, but he would understand. She hoped The Big House wasn't jinxed. It was silly to be afraid. Still, there was a certain amount of respect due to it. She wondered what the dead expected of the living, and was glad her mother had moved the furniture around and that the family had taken so much of it away, because it helped the house to look different.

TWO

There were two sides of the pool again, one for the family and the other for Paris and her peculiar friends. Reports went back up the hill to the two houses—someone had taken the top off her bikini, they're all wearing costumes and making a movie, someone went down to the deserted lake and took all his clothes off, there are motorcycles in the driveway. Jack bought a high-powered telescope and spent his weekends spying on Paris' freaks. "She's breaking her mother's heart," he told Rosemary again and again. "She ought to be sent back to her parents' house and her friends kicked out. Poor Jonah and Lavinia. They're prudes, but this is too much for anybody."

The first summer there were just Paris and Rima and the nice Jewish boy Paris was trying to get to marry her, a thirty-six-year-old bachelor whose attention span never lasted longer than six months and whose interest in Paris was now purely platonic. He and Rima loathed each other. Rima told Paris he was a faggot because all Don Juans were repressed homosexuals, and he told Rima she was a trollop because she was going with a married man. Whenever he was in the room, Rima left it delicately, with her nose in the air, like a cat. The only place they were forced to be together was in the dining room at dinner, and it was there he told his same old funny stories over and over and neither Paris nor Rima laughed. Paris wondered what she had seen in him, and supposed it was just her own stubbornness. She still couldn't stand to be rejected; she had been brought up to believe a girl was ruined forever if she had an affair, and even though she knew it was nonsense because she had seen so many of her friends first live together and then make it legal, she couldn't shake off all the guilt even with the analyst's reassurance, and so part of her felt she should marry every man she went to bed with. She'd seen those marriages too, the arranged-by-guilt ones, and she knew they didn't work. It was difficult to be living in this time, to be a mature young woman in a time and place where everything was changing except your past indoctrination.

The second summer it was more or less open house. Paris' friends were in the theater, or on the fringes of it. Actors whom Buffy recognized with delight played tennis on the court, and later got drunk in the kitchen. Hairdressers in black leather came roaring up on huge motorcycles, and as soon as they were in the driveway in front of The Big House they immediately dismantled their bikes and cleaned each part lovingly and then put them together again. It was not an uncommon sight to see a man all dressed in black leather roaring through the woods on a giant motorcycle, with a girl in a tiny bikini on the seat in back of him, her pale white skin gleaming in the leafy darkness of the woods, like some ethereal forest creature, all vulnerable. She usually got covered with scratches and poison ivy. She was never Paris.

One weekend a psychologist, two hairdressers, and an assistant district attorney all dropped acid in the living room and one of them freaked out for a few hours. Paris, who never touched acid, comforted him.

Paris was always cooking huge meals and Rima was always washing mountains of dishes, and no matter what the guests were or weren't doing, no one was having the orgy the family suspected they were. Paris didn't think it was strange that she hardly knew these people. Some of them she knew better than others, some were regular visitors, one was always her own special boyfriend. She liked having a lot of people around because it made it easier to entertain them. They could entertain each other. Every evening she played cards for hours, but never for money. They usually played Hearts. She had renamed it Hate. You could get all your hostility out by ganging up on one person, usually the one who annoyed you by playing the slowest. She had made a rule that if anyone brought strangers with them they also had to bring food. The house was filled with things like caviar and spaghetti. Sometimes someone brought a dirty movie up from the city and they rented a projector and showed it on a wall. Everyone laughed and made catcalls.

There was no problem of where to sleep. Rooms were not assigned except to the regulars. The others could sleep where they fell.

"A house should be used," Paris said to Rima. "People should enjoy this place."

"Yes, but are we enjoying it?" Rima asked.

"I suppose so. What else is there?"

"I always see myself washing those millions of dishes."

"Then we'll get paper plates."

The next summer there were less people, but the rooms were all used. It was important to fill all the bedrooms. There had been too many wasted years, too many memories of lonely summers, too much to make up for. The family still stayed away from The Big House, but now for a different reason than when it had been empty. Now it was too full. Only Jonah walked over in the evening, after he and Lavinia and Melissa and Lazarus had finished dinner and Paris and her company were still having before-dinner cocktails. Jonah liked the liveliness in the house. He thought most of Paris' friends were strange, but at least she seemed to be having a good time, and that was good. He saw now how sad and lonely she had been all those years, wandering around Windflower alone, and he regretted it. But who had known at the time that it wasn't such a good idea? Who knew she had wanted company? They had thought the family was enough. Now he saw her surrounded by all her strange friends and he wondered if she was happy. He doubted it. But still, it was better than it had been before, and he was glad to be able to report to Lavinia with perfect honesty that there was no hanky-panky going on at The Big House, no matter what the nasty rumors were, and no, he hadn't had a drink, just something nice and mild Rima had made for him with tomato juice, called a Bloody Mary.

Sometimes Paris wondered what drew her back, summer weekend after summer weekend, to Windflower, when really she hated it. It was too filled with unhappy memories, and whenever she dared to come alone during the week, to stay a few days and write, her mother came over and hovered, driving her crazy. Her mother nagged her to have dinner at the Mendes-Bergman house, as it was incomprehensible that Paris would want to eat alone, and that meant the evening too. And of course her parents walked her home, with so many admonitions from her mother that Paris ended up locking all the windows and leaping up at any odd sound. There were other places she could go on summer weekends. People she knew had rented houses at East Hampton and said they loved it, invited her to visit. She could have rented her own house. After the first summer her parents were overcome with guilt at the idea of Paris having to pay rent to live on her own family's estate, so they paid the corporation her share as well as their own. Her mother wanted her to stay. "If Paris goes," she would threaten, "then I'll go." But Paris knew that wasn't true. Her mother had stayed when she had been in Europe, in California. They always knew she would come back. Why did she come back?

Did she stay on because this was a beautiful place, convenient to New York, and it was free? She wasn't that cheap. You didn't pay in money, but you paid in other ways, emotionally, and besides, it was costing her a fortune to feed all those freeloaders and keep them supplied with wine and vodka.

Windflower intimidated her boyfriends. Whenever she was involved with a young man he always wanted her to stay in the city with him, he wanted to call the shots, and she cajoled and begged and nagged until he agreed to come to Windflower instead. Her boyfriends didn't like to be with so many people; they hardly ever saw her alone. They felt kept. They were usually unsuccessful writers, so-so actors, all struggling, all uncomfortable in the face of such obvious wealth. She kept explaining it wasn't her money, it was the family, she didn't even have a piece of paper saying the house was hers; but it didn't matter, they were still resentful, making her fetch and carry for them to make up for being the dominant one financially. She knew she needed either someone who was more successful than she was, or a contented gigolo. She always lost her boyfriends after she dragged them to Windflower. They couldn't stand the strain. Then why did she make them come? Why couldn't she do what they wanted to do, even if it meant spending the summer in the hot city? They always had air conditioning, television; they could go to movies, theater, bars, restaurants, parties, see friends. Her boyfriends said it would be romantic. Paris thought it would be a waste of Windflower. There it was, that beautiful place, and the family kept talking about how expensive it was to keep up until she felt guilty for not being there to enjoy it.

But what did "enjoying it" mean? Just being there, at the expense of her personal life, her emotional life, her very ego? At the center of a hurricane of guests she was the calm eye that had nothing to do with the rest of them, the almost invisible one. She was the one who had brought them together there, and yet if she disappeared it wouldn't really matter. People kept saying what a good hostess she was because she never organized anything, they were so relaxed in her house, they felt so at home.

Everett had escaped, and spent the summers in Florida where he had to run his business. John had made friends at boarding school and spent most of the summer visiting them and their families. He never brought any of them to Windflower, just came up with his father for the brief mandatory visit. His grandparents went to Florida to visit him for a few weeks during the Christmas holiday and stayed at a hotel. Lazarus complained it was expensive. But her grandson and son were all Melissa had, so every year she managed to drag grumbling Lazarus to Florida. When he got there he liked it.

Even though Hazel spent her summers at Windflower, Richie and Gilda didn't. Hazel had Rosemary, Richie figured, so he and Gilda took trips. Gilda had had a baby boy, named Harrison after Herman. The family had only seen him once. He had reddish hair, like Gilda's, and he slept. They all took turns holding him, all except Hazel, who wasn't allowed to because she was shaky now and they were afraid she would drop him. They passed the placidly sleeping baby around as if he were a doll, and Hazel looked on sadly, her arms held out, waiting for her turn that never came.

"I'm the only one who can't hold him," she protested. When they had taken the baby away she took out his baby pictures and looked at them.

Richie and Gilda couldn't decide whether to take the baby with them on a camping trip through the American West, or leave him with her parents in the Bronx while they went on a safari to Africa. It was dangerous to bring a little baby to Africa, such strange food and water. Finally they decided to go to Africa, and Harrison went to the Finkels in the Bronx.

Harrison Winsor was Adam Saffron's great-grandson. It was hard to believe. Papa had never seen him, he had never seen Papa, and when he grew older Papa would only be a family legend, not a real person to him at all. Already, John was forgetting his great-grandfather. It was natural. Buffy said she didn't remember him too well either. She had been a baby when he was in his prime, and she had only known him as a tired old man who loved his grandchildren and was content to kiss them, not shape their destiny.

There were less of them left, and so they drew in tighter, closing the circle. Lavinia held on for dear life, telling and retelling old family stories, praising her sisters and brothers, reminding Paris that your family was all you had. Melissa remembered her girlhood fondly. Ah, the fun, the parties, the get-togethers, the happy friends! It made Paris wonder how she ever found time to get married. She doted on Lazarus, and he on her, in many ways like a father and daughter. He was visibly much older than she was now, and frailer, and she worried about him. If he didn't tell his old stories, she did. She knew all of them by heart. Lazarus and Lavinia still bickered, but not as furiously. He didn't have the energy, and she was more mellow. The old were entitled to be eccentric.

Like pioneer families in the long winter nights on the plains, this family drew together for protection during their long Wind-flower summers, sitting together on the screened porch, entertaining or boring each other with the old tales they knew so well. They did not read or go to the movies. They lived off each other, their companionship, their irritation, and their memories. Paris wondered if she would end up like them. It was a prospect that depressed her profoundly. Yet she couldn't see herself doing anything else except as a fond daydream, and she knew perfectly well that the only thing keeping her trapped here was her own self. She who had done everything she had set out to do, the determined one, the achiever, was still ambivalent and therefore powerless to take this one last step.

THREE

What were they to do with Hazel? Since Herman's death her condition had deteriorated rapidly with what the doctor said was a series of little strokes to the brain and hardening of the arteries cutting off the blood supply. She lost her balance and fell down, she was forgetful, and you couldn't leave her alone because whenever she felt ill she took her little pills, and the doctor had said those little pills were dangerous if not taken properly. Worst of all, she drove them crazy, following them, wanting to join them, demanding their attention. She was not their responsibility, she was the responsibility of her son. Children were meant to take care of their parents when they were old and sick. But did Richie care? Did Gilda care? No, they were going off on another of their trips, this time to the Scandinavian countries, with little Harrison in tow. Richie wanted his son to see snow. For this he deserted his mother, for snow?

Rosemary said she and Jack couldn't stand to have Hazel with them another summer at Windflower. It wasn't fair; she wasn't a nurse. The family got together with Richie before he left and demanded that he do something. He was the man of the family now, they told him, he had to make decisions. And they had decided the decision he must make was to hire a companion for Hazel, part nurse, part watchdog, to live with her. Richie agreed. They also thought he should make his mother sell that huge house; it was too big and empty and lonely for one person, and there were all those stairs for her to tumble down. They rejected the idea of putting in a chair-elevator, since Hazel would undoubtedly misuse it. No, she should get a nice apartment.

Richie agreed to all of it. He sold the big house in Miami Beach and bought his mother a good cooperative apartment with two bedrooms and two bathrooms, although as it turned out the nurse had to sleep in the same room with Hazel because she often got up in the middle of the night to go to the bathroom and forgot where she was. It had been difficult to get a nice nurse because people nowadays didn't want to be companions. They finally found a middle-aged widow, three hundred pounds and never stopped talking, worse than Hazel they all agreed, if you had to pick one of them you'd rather be with, but what could they do? She was a trained nurse, and she was willing to spend twenty-four hours a day with Hazel, and she could squeeze herself into the driver's seat of Hazel's big car and take her around. In her better moments Hazel still enjoyed looking through the stores.

Having arranged everything neatly so the family would stop being mad at him, Richie took his wife and son away on their long trip.

Rosemary felt it wasn't fair that she was the one who had to live with Hazel at Windflower. They all should have had their own houses; but it was too late now. Sometimes Hazel was just fine, sitting for hours watching television, but other times she would turn around and say to Rosemary: "Did you know my husband?" as if they hadn't lived in the same house for more summers than Rosemary cared to remember. Jack hated every minute of it. Hazel wasn't even his relative, just his sister-in-law, and since he never liked anybody it was easy for him to find many things to be annoyed about now. The nurse and Hazel ate with them at the dinner table, and the nurse talked too much and ate too much, even gobbling the food out of Hazel's plate, and you'd at least think that with her mouth full she would shut up, but no. He began taking Rosemary and Buffy out to restaurants to eat, leaving Hazel alone with the nurse.

"It would be better for everybody," Buffy told Paris, "if she'd just die."

"Shame on you!" Paris said. "How would you like it if you were old and someone said that about you?"

Buffy thought about it. "I guess you're right," she said.

"You'd better have sympathy for old people," Paris said. "Someday you're going to be old, but you'll still have feelings."

"But she isn't old," Buffy said. "She's younger than your mother, and Aunt Melissa. She just looks old."

"That's because she's sick."

"Well, it's awful for my parents," Buffy said.

She lives too much in the head, that one, Paris thought. It was as if Buffy had placed all her feelings into compartments of cool, clear logic. The only people she felt emotional about were her parents and herself. Everyone else she filed away neatly and disposed of in the neat compartments of her mind. She thought everyone in the family was crazy except her parents. File under C for Crazy. She adored her father and had ambivalent feelings about her mother, with whom she was always fighting, so she had filed them neatly under E for Escape. Otherwise they would interfere with her master plan to see the world. No matter what anyone said she had quietly and secretly filed Hazel away under E too, for Euthanasia.

"You just don't know what it's like to have to live with her," Buffy kept saying, and when her father didn't take her to a restaurant she ate out of the refrigerator and refused to come to meals.

"Oh, the poor girl," Lavinia said of Hazel, "she's so sick." Now that Hazel was so helpless and yet so annoying, Lavinia seemed to see her as a girl again, the way she had been when they were all growing up and she had been different from them. "Poor Hazel," Lavinia would say, "her husband and her son were her whole life . . . There never was a better wife and mother."

"I don't think she should come up here next summer," Rosemary said. "I'm going to tell her. I can't go through another summer like this one."

"Why don't you send her to the Catskills?" Melissa suggested.

457

"Send her to a nice resort hotel."

"She doesn't want to go."

"She'd have friends," Melissa said. "She'd have things to do."

"She only wants to be with the family."

Hazel hadn't wanted to sell her house. It was her own house, and she had been happy there with Herman and Richie. But the family told her she had to sell it, and Richie was a man now, and he said she had to sell it too. She let them tell her what to do but she didn't like it. She missed her house. It was hers. She knew she was sick because she felt sick. Sometimes she was light-headed, and sometimes her heart pounded too hard, and most of the time she had a headache. When she said she felt sick Mrs. Barkis said: "Oh, no, you're not sick, dear. It's all in your head. Positive Thinking, dear."

Hazel didn't like Mrs. Barkis. She was always talking about Positive Thinking and making faces behind Hazel's back. Hazel knew. She'd say she had a headache and then Mrs. Barkis would wink and screw up her face and make all kinds of funny faces like she was in a TV cartoon and didn't want anyone to miss what she was trying to show. It made Hazel so mad! But she didn't say anything. She just sat there and wondered why none of the family seemed to love her any more. They never wanted to see her. At first, at the beginning of the summer, Hazel had started off to the other house to visit with her sisters, and she could see everybody disappearing off the screened porch. They just ran away from her. They thought she didn't know. After a while the headaches got worse and she was too tired to walk to the other house. There wasn't any reason if they didn't want to see her.

Mrs. Barkis made her take walks. "Come on, dear," she would say, grabbing Hazel's arm as if she were a little kid. "We'll take a little walk now. You'll be surprised how much better you feel when you're up and out. Nothing like exercise. Positive Thinking, dear." The two of them, Hazel and that big fat woman with the blonde curls on top of her head and the two rouge spots on her cheeks, would walk slowly around the grounds. Mrs. Barkis would be huffing and puffing but Hazel would just be feeling dizzy. She couldn't wait to sit down, and then when she finally sat down she would feel sad. The days were so long. She lost track of days, of weeks, of time. Why wasn't Richie here? Was he at camp? No,

Richie never went to camp. Where was he? A little boy shouldn't be away from home.

Herman was gone. She knew he was gone, he was dead. That was one thing Hazel never forgot. If Herman were here he would save her. She wouldn't have to stay with that nurse she hated who told her what to do and made fun of her behind her back. Hazel told Rosemary a million times that she didn't like Mrs. Barkis, and Rosemary told her, "Oh, she's not so bad." How would Ro know? Nobody made faces behind her back and called her "dear" in that mean tone of voice.

Sometimes Hazel got away from her nurse. That was fun, like an adventure, like the things she used to do when she was young. She would wait until Mrs. Barkis was having her afternoon nap, which she had every day, and then she would sneak out of the bedroom and try to get downstairs without anyone catching her. Sometimes she fell. If she fell down she couldn't get up by herself, but she didn't want anyone to know she'd fallen down so she just waited until someone came along and then she'd ask them to help pick her up as if it was very natural. She liked it best if the maid found her because she wouldn't yell at her. Rosemary yelled at her and asked why she'd gone out of her room without her nurse.

"She's asleep," Hazel would say.

Then Rosemary would yell at Mrs. Barkis, which was fun. There was so little fun in that house. Nobody had a good time. It was such a big place but most of the time Hazel couldn't find anybody to talk to. They disappeared. But it was worse in Florida. In Florida she didn't have anybody except Mrs. Barkis, whom she couldn't stand. All day long Mrs. Barkis talked at her, even when Hazel didn't say a word back. After a while Hazel just stopped listening. Mrs. Barkis talked about trips she had taken when she was younger, all kinds of trips, to all kinds of foreign countries, and Hazel wasn't interested in that. She would have liked to talk about babies. She had the photos of her grandson, Harrison, in her purse, and she took them out all the time and looked at them, and tried to show them to Mrs. Barkis, just to be friendly.

"Oh, I saw those, dear," Mrs. Barkis would say, shoving Hazel's hand away. "Those are old pictures. He's much older now."

Older? How much older? How old was Harrison? Where was he? Was he all right? Would he know she was his grandma? Why couldn't she remember how old he was? Why didn't Richie give her new pictures?

"Where's Richie?"

"You know he's on his vacation, dear."

Vacation from what?

Mrs. Barkis had hidden all Hazel's pills but Hazel knew where they were. When they used to be in the medicine chest in the bathroom Hazel could take them by herself, but now she had to wait to take them until her nurse gave them to her. She didn't like that no one trusted her. She could count. She could take her pills by herself. She knew they were dangerous if you took too many. They could kill you. She wasn't stupid, even though everybody acted as if she was. She wouldn't take a whole lot of pills that were dangerous and going to kill her. Why did everybody think she was stupid? That hurt. She was good and let Mrs. Barkis dole out her pills, but it hurt her feelings, just like all the other things everyone did to make her feel like she wasn't in her right mind. The family had always thought she wasn't as smart as they were, and that hurt, but when she married Herman everyone knew she was just as good as they were. Her Richie was smarter than anybody, going to all those schools and graduating with good marks. Hazel still had her puzzles, but now she looked up the answers in the back and wrote the words in the spaces in her shaky printing and left the puzzle books open on tables so everyone would see how smart she was. She'd gotten the idea of looking up the answers from Mrs. Barkis, who did it. It was a good idea. Hazel wondered why she'd never thought of it before.

She had been so lonely in Florida that all winter she had looked forward to coming to Windflower to be with the family, and then when she got there it wasn't anything like she'd expected. Everybody acted different. Sometimes Hazel forgot that Papa wasn't alive any more, and she would try to go over to The Big House, but then someone would always stop her. Then she'd remember he was gone. If he was here, he would make them all treat her nice, the way he used to when they were kids and the others tried to leave her out.

"Who lives in that house?" Hazel asked Melissa.

"Paris."

"I want to see Paris."

Paris came to see her. Hazel looked at her and thought how

different she looked than what she'd expected. "You look older," she said.

"I *am* older," Paris said cheerfully.

"You look thirty," Hazel said, disappointed. She had thought Paris would still be a baby. "I guess I look old, huh?"

"No," Paris said, "you're looking well." Hazel knew she was lying. "A little thinner, that's good."

"She's getting better all the time, aren't you, dear?" Mrs. Barkis interrupted. "Positive Thinking, right, dear?"

"The doctor wants me thin," Hazel said.

"I think that's a good idea," Paris said.

"Did you see the pictures of Harrison?" Hazel asked, fumbling through her pocketbook, which she always kept with her so she wouldn't lose it.

"Oh, you showed them to her last year," Mrs. Barkis said.

"I can't find them," Hazel said, and snapped shut her purse.

"So Richie must be in Denmark by now," Paris said.

"Denmark?"

"Oh, and at the end of his trip he's going on to Moscow," Mrs. Barkis said. "I personally wouldn't want to go to Moscow. I hear the food is just terrible there. A friend of mine went there recently on a tour and she said she couldn't eat anything but the bread. Their black bread is simply delicious. But the meat was tough, she said, and you couldn't get a vegetable unless it was canned, and then it wasn't very good. Of course, in the Scandinavian countries he'd get all that wonderful smoked fish. My favorite is herring in mustard sauce."

"Richie's coming back in September," Hazel said.

"Oh, that's good," Paris said.

"She *thinks* he's coming back in September," Mrs. Barkis said.

"I have a headache," Hazel said.

"Oh, no you don't," said Mrs. Barkis. "It's all in your mind, dear. Positive Thinking. You know, Paris, I was in Copenhagen myself once. It's a most delightful city. They eat smorgasbord, you know, and drink aquavit. My goodness, I put on about twenty pounds when I was there. They have a bread there called limpa, which has just a taste of licorice. It's delicious." She went on and on and Hazel just stopped listening.

After a while Paris got up to go and Hazel wanted to go to the door with her so she could tell her a secret. They went to the door with Mrs. Barkis following them, still talking, and Hazel looked at her niece clear in the eyes, trying to see if she could understand, if she would believe her. "Pa . . . ?"

"Yes?"

Hazel leaned close and whispered in Paris' ear. "I can't stand her."

"I know."

"I want to go home."

"Secrets, secrets! What are you whispering about?" the nurse said. Hazel snapped her mouth shut and looked away. Oh, she didn't like that nurse at all, she didn't want her around, she didn't see why they made her have her. It wasn't fair.

"I'll see you tomorrow," Paris said, and went away toward her house. Hazel tried to go after her but she couldn't keep up. She knew Paris wouldn't come back to see her tomorrow; people always said they'd come back and then they didn't.

And Paris didn't come back.

Hazel didn't remember how long she had been at Windflower this summer, if it had been weeks or months or days. Every day was so long, and she got confused. She wanted to go home. She was lonely in her apartment in Miami Beach and she didn't have any friends, but at least she didn't have to know that the family was trying to run away from her. She remembered how she used to chase after Rosemary when they both were young, when Ro used to go ice skating in the park and didn't want to take her. But she got to go along anyway until Mama decided she was a big girl and should stay home with the grownups. Hazel missed Mama. She hadn't seen her in years and years and hadn't even thought about her much. Mama had been dead for a long time. Had Mama ever met Herman? Hazel tried to remember. She wondered if Mama had known she got married. She hoped so, because Mama would have been glad.

Everybody had somebody but her. She had Mrs. Barkis, but that was worse than nobody. Paris didn't have anybody. Paris never got married, Hazel remembered that. She should have asked Paris when she was going to get married, but she'd forgotten to and now it was too late. Paris better get married before she was too old. Hazel didn't understand anybody who didn't want to get married. Somebody must have asked Paris—everybody got asked sometime. She just didn't understand Paris at all. Even Mrs.

Barkis had a husband once. If somebody wanted *her* . . .

Hazel told Rosemary she wanted to go home. Rosemary was glad and told Mrs. Barkis to pack.

"We're going home now, dear," Mrs. Barkis said to Hazel, just as if it wasn't Hazel's own idea. She made Hazel take a last walk with her around the grounds. "Don't you want to have a last look, dear?"

No, Hazel didn't want to have a last look. What was there to look at? It didn't make her happy to look at the view, it made her sad. It made her remember when things were different.

"Was that pool always there?" Hazel asked.

"Well, I don't know, dear."

"Why do you call me dear?"

"What?"

"You always call me dear," Hazel said. "But you don't like me."

Mrs. Barkis made a mean face and glared at her. What she looked like, Hazel thought, was a cookie lady. You made a big round face from a sugar cookie, and then you put two little raisins in for the eyes and a half a maraschino cherry for the mouth and you had a cookie lady. The cook used to make them for Richie when he was little. How he used to love them! He would always ask for cookie ladies. Hazel wondered if he remembered. She hardly ever got to see Richie any more. She would like to tell him to have somebody make cookie ladies for Harrison.

"She's getting hostile," Mrs. Barkis told Rosemary that evening when she thought Hazel wasn't listening. "Hostile and paranoid. I'd call the doctor if I were you and get her some tranquilizers. She turned on me down at the swimming pool today for no reason, just turned on me."

"What did she say?" Rosemary asked.

"I'd rather not say. I don't want to upset you. It doesn't matter. But when they start to get hostile and paranoid, the next step is they get depressed, and we wouldn't want Mrs. Winsor getting all depressed now, would we?"

"You can certainly tell me what she said," Rosemary said.

"Well," Mrs. Barkis said in a grieved tone, "She said I didn't like her. Now you know that's not true. I wouldn't stay with her if I didn't like her. It certainly isn't the money. I hardly get enough to get by on."

"Why, you get a lot!" Rosemary said.

"Oh, it's not easy, not easy at all. I'd just like a little gratitude. It's not easy when you give everything for a person and then that person turns on you. It's very upsetting. Why, I could get a dozen other jobs that pay more, and I wouldn't have to work so hard either. You know I'm up and down five or six times a night with her, just making sure she gets to the bathroom all right, and in between I can hardly sleep for fear she might need me. I'd like to be able to put away something for my own old age, you know, but I just don't see how I can with what I'm being paid now."

"I'll talk to the family," Rosemary said coldly.

"Oh, I hated to ask you, really," Mrs. Barkis said, "but I just had to. Inflation you know, dear."

Ro doesn't care about me, Hazel thought. She knows that woman doesn't like me and she doesn't care.

When they got back to Florida the doctor gave Hazel some pills he said would make her feel happier. They only made her sleepy. She could hardly drag herself around, and when Mrs. Barkis talked at her it was easier than ever to shut her out. Hazel knew that the nurse wanted her to take those pills so she wouldn't be any trouble. She didn't feel happy; she felt sad. The doctor shouldn't have lied to her. She trusted him. If she could have taken a pill that made her feel happy she would have been glad to have it. There was nothing to be happy about any more.

"What month is this?" Hazel asked Mrs. Barkis one day.

"Why, October, dear. October first."

"Richie was coming back in September."

"Well, he'll be back soon, dear. Here's your happy pill now."

"It makes me sad," Hazel said.

"Don't be silly. It makes you happy. Positive Thinking, dear. Drink it down."

"I want to call the doctor."

"Now, what would you say to him?"

"Tell him I feel sick."

"Oh, you feel fine. Now why don't you watch a little TV?" Mrs. Barkis switched on the set and settled herself down to watch her game shows. She loved game shows. She watched every one of them. She said it was "just like a college education." Hazel didn't understand the game shows and didn't like them. She liked the prizes the people won and liked seeing how happy they were to get them. It was nice to see that people were so glad to get a present. There wasn't any present Hazel could think of that she wanted any more, except maybe to see her grandson just once and hold him.

"C'n we go to the store?" Hazel asked.

Mrs. Barkis looked pleased. "The store? You want to go to the store?"

"I said that."

"Well, we'll go this afternoon after our naps, dear."

"Why can't we go now?"

"Well, what do you need that's so important?"

"For Harrison. A present for Harrison."

"Oh, all right," Mrs. Barkis said. She hoisted herself out of her easy chair with great difficulty. "I need some stockings anyway. They just don't last any more like they used to. I think it's the air pollution. That smog just eats away the nylon. They say if you stand in front of the exhaust of a car your stockings just fall apart, and I believe it." On and on, blah blah. Hazel didn't mind this time. She had her secret.

At the store they went to the toy department and Hazel bought a big, cuddly baby doll, just the same size as Harrison was the last time she remembered him. It had on blue sleepers with feet, and it had reddish hair just like her grandson. Hazel let them wrap it. Back in the apartment she put the gift wrapped box into her own closet and shut the door. It was her closet and Mrs. Barkis wasn't allowed in there. She was so excited she could hardly wait until after lunch when Mrs. Barkis lay down for her afternoon nap and soon was snoring. Then Hazel went into her closet and unwrapped the package, folding up the gift paper and ribbon neatly, and took the baby doll in her arms to the living room.

She sat on the chair and held the baby doll tenderly, rocking it. It felt good in her arms, not as heavy as she remembered Richie when he was that age, but soft like a baby. It had rubber baby skin and she put her cheek against the baby doll's cheek and felt how nice it was.

"Sleep, baby," she said. "Sleep."

Mrs. Barkis found her that way when she woke up from her nap and came into the living room: sitting in the chair asleep with the baby doll cuddled in her arms. "Oh my," Mrs. Barkis said, but then she didn't say anything else.

Richie called on the phone. He was back! Hazel wanted him to come over right away, to let her go to see him, but he said no, they were very tired from their trip and he and Gilda both had stomach trouble from drinking all those different kinds of water in all those different countries, even though you ordered bottled water you couldn't always trust them in the out-of-the-way places. But Harrison was fine. Richie said he would see her as soon as he felt better.

Hazel waited. She didn't know how many days it was. It was a long time. Then one day Richie came to see her and brought her a new picture of him and Harrison and Gilda standing in front of a building he said was the Kremlin, in Moscow, Russia.

"Papa came from Russia," Hazel said.

"You mean Grandpa."

"Your grandpa. Papa. He came from Russia."

"I know," Richie said.

"Then why would you want to *go* there?" Hazel asked, bewildered.

"Why, it's historical." Richie said. "It's broadening. Travel is educational."

Hazel studied the photograph. "Harrison looks so big."

"He is big," Richie said proudly.

"When can I see him?"

"Soon. I'll bring him over soon."

"Where do you live?" she asked.

"You know where I live, Mother."

"No. I forgot."

"I live where we've always lived. Same house."

"The little house?"

"Yes."

"We should all be together in our old house," Hazel said.

"I have to go to the office now," Richie said.

"Office?"

"I have to take care of things. All our family business." He reminded her of Herman. She smiled at him.

Richie left. "Oh," Mrs. Barkis said, "you forgot to give him the present for your little grandson."

"What present?"

"The doll."

"Harrison's too big," Hazel said angrily. "I know that. You think I'm dumb. That doll is *my* doll."

466

She waited and waited for Richie to come back. He had promised her he'd come back. Richie wouldn't break a promise. Sometimes he called on the phone to ask the nurse if she was all right. If she knew it was him Hazel would make Mrs. Barkis let her talk to him. She always asked Richie when he would come to see her and he always said he would come soon, but he didn't come. Hazel thought maybe he couldn't stand to look at her. She looked at herself in the mirror over the bathroom sink and she knew she looked awful. She was so old and skinny and her face didn't go together right. Her mouth seemed to go one way and her chin another, and she trembled. She looked ugly. It must make Richie sad to see her look so ugly. She wished she looked better. She had stopped wearing her bridge because it hurt her gums, and now when she talked nobody could understand her at all, not that there was anybody to talk to. But Mrs. Barkis couldn't seem to understand her and that made Hazel feel so alone it was scary.

She didn't have anything any more. She felt sadder and lonelier every day. She was so lonesome it hurt her chest to breathe. She felt like crying all the time, but she wouldn't give Mrs. Barkis the satisfaction. Time went by so slowly. Sometimes she remembered lots of things and other times she would look around the apartment and wonder what she was doing there. She should be in her own house, doing all the things she had to do, picking out which dress to wear when she went out tonight with Herman, seeing that Richie was all right; what was this place? Who was that woman? Then she would remember. Everything was gone. She would be better off dead.

At night Hazel took her baby doll to bed with her. She put it to sleep under the covers, with its head on the pillow, and then she lay very quietly beside it until they both fell asleep. She wished it would make her be young again. When she was a girl she'd had a doll. When she looked back she thought she had been happy then. She used to think she was lonesome but she didn't know what it was to be lonesome until now. Richie was never going to come to see her. He was too busy. Even if he did see her, it wouldn't make things the same as they were before. It wouldn't bring back her husband and her little boy and her happy life with all their friends in the winters and then the happy summers with the family in the country. That was all gone. There wasn't anything left.

Hazel knew where Mrs. Barkis hid all the pills. The pink ones were the dangerous ones, the ones that could kill you if you took too many. They were her heart pills. She could take them all and she would go to sleep and when she woke up everything would be all right again. If she could just go to sleep for a long, long time, years and years, it would be all right afterward. If she died, Hazel knew, everyone would be sorry, and then they would be nicer to her. She knew she wouldn't ever wake up if she died, but somehow it didn't seem real. Dying meant not having to be here, always so sad and lonely and waiting for something good to happen that never did. She couldn't imagine herself not being anywhere. But she could imagine this great lump of loneliness rising off her chest, and being peaceful.

She waited until one afternoon when Mrs. Barkis was having her afternoon nap. Mrs. Barkis was so tired from having to get up all night that she slept very hard in the afternoon and nothing bothered her. Hazel waited until the snores were even and deep and then she went into Mrs. Barkis' bathroom, the one she wasn't allowed to use, and looked into the medicine chest. There was a plastic bag with a zipper on top, like a makeup bag, only she knew Mrs. Barkis had a great big box for her makeup, and sure enough, inside that little plastic bag were all Hazel's pills. The white ones were the happy pills. The blue ones were something else, she wasn't sure. There were some other white ones she took whenever her ankles swelled. And there were the pink ones!

There was a whole bottle of pink pills because Mrs. Barkis had just had the prescription refilled. Oh, Hazel wasn't so dumb. She had heard Mrs. Barkis on the phone the other day calling the drugstore. A whole bottle of those pink pills would be enough to make her die. Hazel took the bottle into her own bathroom, tiptoeing, and drank them all down with a big glass of water.

She lay down on the living room couch with her doll because she didn't want to go into that bedroom. She didn't feel like it was her own bedroom because Mrs. Barkis slept there at night in the other bed. The other bedroom was Mrs. Barkis' bedroom, where she kept all her clothes and had her afternoon nap, so that wasn't Hazel's either. Nothing in that apartment was really hers. She just lived there. The living room couch was a good place for a visitor. She was a visitor. She wouldn't be there long. She was glad. The afternoon sun was streaming in through the windows and she could hear cars going by down below in the street. It was hard to hear them because of the air conditioning. The room was too cold. Hazel's fingers were all numb and she dropped the doll, but she didn't know it till she heard it thump because she couldn't feel it. She felt funny, but she wasn't scared, she was happy. Her heart was pounding like she was getting ready to go on a big adventure.

Everyone said it was terrible about Hazel accidentally taking an overdose of her medicine. She must have been feeling unwell and had stumbled into the bathroom and taken more pills than she should have. She had dropped some on the sink and on the floor because her hands were shaking, so it never occurred to anyone that it was anything but an accident. Mrs. Barkis said she felt so guilty, but you couldn't watch her twenty-four hours a day. They should have had a relief nurse. The family regretfully agreed. Poor Hazel always tried to be so independent, didn't want to be a bother to anybody, must have thought she'd just take a pill and forgot and took more.

Richie insisted on a very Orthodox funeral. The family didn't object because they knew that when she was alive Hazel had always agreed with anything her son had wanted to do, and whatever he had wanted she had wanted.

FOUR

When Buffy was in her senior year of high school she wrote to the New York chapter of the Amateur Athletic Union for her AAU card and entered her first track meet. After some thought she had decided to be a long-distance runner, because girls could continue in long-distance running much longer than sprinting, until they were even thirty years old. She wanted a long career. Besides, she liked the idea of distance. Distance meant escape.

All her classmates were applying to colleges, and Buffy had already decided to go to Bakersfield, because they had track meets there and it was one of the colleges where runners went. This first meet which she had entered would qualify her to get into Bakersfield if she met the standard. She knew she could.

"Bakersfield?" her parents said. "What kind of college is that?"

"It's the University of Southern California."

"Oh, California," her father said. "You want to be a hippie."

Buffy just shrugged. Let him think she wanted to be a flower child, at least he would think it was better than being a runner.

At the last minute before the meet began she was a little nervous. Maybe these girls were better than she had thought. So much depended on winning. It was all she had wanted, all she had thought about, for all these years, her first step on her life plan. But when she started to run everything became familiar and she wasn't afraid at all. Buffy and her body were friends; she had taught it and forced it and developed it until it responded exactly the way she wanted it to. If she didn't keep after it, it might fail her. But it respected her will, and she respected its will, and she had made it give in to her terms. She was leaving all the other girls behind her, but that didn't mean anything if they were too slow. But at the end of the race she found that she was not only first, but had bettered the standard.

The girls were socializing now, being friendly, but Buffy wasn't interested. She walked away, drying her wet face with a towel, and then she went home.

Her mother wanted to buy her a new wardrobe for college. Skirts, sweaters, even pants if she insisted, and nice clothes for dating.

"People don't date any more, Mother," Buffy said.

"What do you mean they don't date? They sit home?"

"No, I mean a boy doesn't call you up and ask you out for next Saturday night, and you don't put on a black dress and go dancing. Boys and girls are more like friends today. You just go out when you feel like it, and you don't dress up. You wear jeans, you go to the movies or something."

"Well, I certainly didn't expect you to do more, at your age," her mother said. "I expect you to be friends. We were always friends, when I was your age. I don't expect you to fall in love and get married at eighteen, you know. But you need some nice dresses. I never heard of a girl going off to college without some nice dresses."

She let her mother buy her whatever she wanted. As long as it was her mother's money who cared? She then shortened the "nice dresses" until her mother screamed that she could see Buffy's underpants, which was fine with Buffy because she knew her long, well-shaped legs were her best feature. She'd had her frizzy beige hair straightened, and now it was sort of reddish and the ends looked as if she'd been electrocuted. She wanted to grow it long and her mother wanted her to go to the hairdresser and get it trimmed, and finally Buffy gave in and said she would let him trim the frayed ends. The bastard nearly gave her a crew cut. Now she really looked like those dikey runners her father was always making fun of. Everybody in the family said it was a big improvement and looked cute. Thank God for eye makeup. At least people knew she was a girl.

Her parents drove her to the airport from Windflower. They were still up there, and her father said it was easier. Buffy had all new clothes and some new suitcases. She'd made her mother buy her very light suitcases, for air travel. She was no fool: when she got to travel all around Europe when she was a runner she would need to travel light. She had her clock radio under her arm, but her father had to ship her hi-fi and records air freight.

"You're supposed to study, you know," her father said, "not listen to that rock 'n' roll."

"I know." She also knew he would give in, because he always did.

The school seemed so big after her high school. There were so many people, so many buildings. But there was really only one thing Buffy was interested in, and that made it all seem smaller and not so frightening. She registered for some courses that sounded like fun. She didn't have the faintest idea what she was going to major in, but neither did most of the other kids. You didn't have to decide right away. One of the courses she signed up for was Russian Films—just in case she ever met Yuri, they could have something to talk about.

She still had her crush on Yuri. She decided not to fall in love with any of the boys at school because you could get hurt that way. Most of the girls and boys slept together when they went out and Buffy knew it didn't mean anything and if you fell in love with a boy you were seeing you could be hurt very badly when he went on to another girl. Everybody *said* they were in love, but they just said it. Also, girls were very ashamed about being virgins. It was like being a virgin meant they were neurotic or something. On the other hand, you wanted to say you'd only had a very few boys you'd actually slept with. You could go to bed with a boy and do everything else, but if you didn't actually screw then it didn't count as a bona-fide affair or whatever they were calling it this week. There were all those dumb rules that didn't make any sense at all. She ended up having a lot of friends. It was easier. She had a couple of romances, and of course you had to tell your friends that sex was great, although she didn't think it was so wonderful. Those boys didn't even know what they were doing. One boy, who was so shy he'd never done anything with a girl before, she actually had to tell him what to do. It was a disaster. She wondered if it would have been different if she had been born beautiful, or if it would have been worse.

Sex, Buffy thought, was highly overrated, but what else was there to do on Saturday night when neither of you had any money?

There were frequent all-comers track meets, where anybody who showed up could compete, and Buffy competed in all of them. She always came in in the first three, and people were beginning to notice her and know who she was. That made everything else worthwhile. She trained every day, and if she ever missed a day she felt so guilty it almost made her feel sick.

Then she entered the national championship. You had to come in first or second to qualify for the national team, the one that got to tour all over Europe during the summer, competing in track meets. This was the big one, the one Buffy had been waiting for. She was ready. She entered the 880, as always, and came in second. Her dream was going to come true, and the only thing that spoiled it was that she had wanted to come in first. It had been so close she was almost first. It really annoyed her not to be first, the best, even though being second was just as good because it meant she made the team and that was really what she wanted. She wouldn't be going to Windflower this summer, for the first time in her life; she would be going to West Germany and Italy and Paris. And someday, maybe even Moscow! All those countries, with all those kids her age, guys as well as girls, seemed like paradise.

Her parents might not like it, but that was too bad. It wouldn't cost them anything, and she was a grownup now and could go wherever she wanted.

When she went home at midterm, a boy she'd been sleeping with named Lee, who wanted to be a newspaperman, invited Buffy to a party for the team of Russian runners who had been touring the indoor track circuit. He knew she would really appreciate it, but he didn't know how much. Yuri was on the team. At last, if everything went well, she would meet him.

The minute she and Lee entered the crowded hotel room she saw Yuri. He stood out from everybody else, his fair hair, his smile, that handsome familiar face she had been dreaming of all these years; it was as if there was a glow around him. Buffy's heart turned over. Her mouth was dry. What could she say to him? Suppose he didn't speak English?

"Get me a ginger ale," she said to Lee. He trotted off to the bar and Buffy walked up to Yuri. He was with two men, so she was ahead already.

"Hi," Buffy said.

Yuri nodded his head and smiled at her. "Hi," he said.

"Do you speak English?"

"Little."

"I'm a big fan of yours," she said. "A big admirer."

"Oh, fan. Thank you."

"My name is Buffy Nature."

Faced with this juggernaut the two men who were with Yuri smiled knowingly and moved away to join another group. Buffy found herself alone with him. He looked her up and down. "You have nice legs," he said.

"Thank you."

Lee took just that moment to come over with her glass of ginger ale and Buffy could have killed him. She took the glass and gave him a fierce look. He knew she was a track fanatic so he went over to another girl and started talking to her, glancing at Buffy to see what progress she was making. Lee seemed more amused than jealous, for now.

"That man your husband?" Yuri asked.

"Oh, no. A friend. Are you married?"

He laughed. "No, no married. I don't like marriage."

"Neither do I," Buffy said.

"You come my room?"

She could hardly believe she had been so honored. "Yes," she said.

"I have three roommates. Must get key another room," Yuri said. "You wait here."

"I have to get away from my friend," Buffy said. "Let's meet somewhere."

He thought a moment. "You know where is laundry room?"

"No."

"Down hall, this side." He gestured. "Small room with door open. We meet there. I get key to friend's room."

"Okay," Buffy said. "Hurry."

When he left her Buffy glanced at Lee and then walked very casually out of the living room into the bedroom, as if she were going to the bathroom, and then darted out the bedroom door into the hotel corridor. The laundry room was not far, and the door was open as Yuri had said. The maids were probably making up the rooms for the night. Buffy went into the laundry room and hid in the corner. Her heart was pounding. *He'd better show up,* she thought. That would be the worst thing that ever happened to her, to be stood up in a laundry room. At least no one would know, but what humiliation! Now she was sorry she hadn't gone to the bathroom, because she was so nervous she really had to go. She'd just have to go in his room. It wouldn't be very romantic, but Russians knew the facts of life just as well as anybody else. She took her mirror out of her purse and checked her makeup. Oh, hurry up, Yuri!

Yuri appeared at the door of the laundry room with a big smile on his face and a hotel room key dangling from his hand. They sprinted down the hall together and he opened the door to an empty room. There were two twin beds, neatly turned down for the night, the curtains were closed, and a soft night-light made it all romantic and cosy. He locked the door and began to take off his clothes.

"Excuse me," Buffy said, and went into the bathroom. Whew, now she felt better. When she came out of the bathroom he was already in one of the beds with the covers up to his chest, lying there waiting for her. She thought he looked gorgeous. She took off her clothes and dropped them on the floor and slipped into the narrow bed next to his silky body. Then he kissed her, and she just couldn't believe this marvelous thing was really happening to her, after all those years of wishing.

He was perfect in bed. Buffy was so thrilled she just couldn't get over it. It was the best thing that had ever happened to her in her entire social life. Yuri had taken one look at her and had been overcome with passion and had whisked her right off to bed with him. Buffy's ego had just gone up about one thousand percent. She would never think she was ugly again. Yuri had picked *her*!

Yuri looked at his wristwatch. "Is late. Must go back."

Buffy turned his wrist toward her and looked at his watch. It was wonderful how going to bed with someone could make you feel so at ease with him afterward. Before, she wouldn't even have dared touch his wrist, now she was just as proprietary as if he was anybody. They had been in the room for twenty minutes. She hoped that jerk who had brought her to the party wouldn't start looking for her. Gee, she had *liked* Lee. He hadn't seemed like such a jerk before. Well, everything was relative.

When they were dressed she gave Yuri a last kiss. He smiled at her "Very nice girl," he said.

"Very nice boy."

"Not boy. Twenty-four years old."

"Very nice *man*," Buffy said.

"You go first, I lock door."

"See ya," she said wistfully, peered outside the door to be sure the corridor was empty, and darted back to the party.

Lee didn't seem to have missed her. She saw Yuri come in then and go over to talk to some people, and she thought: *I know him better than anybody here even guesses.* He was so gorgeous! She felt fine. She wondered if she would get pregnant. They hadn't bothered to use anything. Wouldn't that be something, having Yuri's baby! No, it would be awful; it would ruin her career. Buffy was sure she wouldn't get pregnant. It wasn't a dangerous day, and besides, nothing bad had ever happened to her in her life.

That spring Buffy trained as hard as she could, even working out in the gym with weights to build up strength. She wrote Yuri a letter, but he never answered it and she wondered if he even got it. If it was meant for them to meet again they would, if not, she had her whole life ahead of her. If she'd gotten him in two seconds, imagine what adventures lay ahead of her in Europe! She could hardly wait.

Her European tour that summer with the American team was the most exciting thing that had ever happened to her. She kept winning. She loved to run and she loved to win, and the only event she didn't much care for was the relay race because you were doing it for the team, not for yourself. Buffy didn't care at all about the team, she only cared about herself. Being at the head of the pack, running on your own, knowing you had left the others behind, that was bliss.

The guys and girls from different countries didn't mingle much socially. You dated the boys on your own country's team, and went out in groups with the boys and girls from your own team, so Buffy was glad she hadn't wasted her time studying any foreign languages. She liked all the American boys and slept with two of them.

Her parents were not pleased about her career, although they were glad she was getting a chance to see the world, as long as she gave it all up at the end of the summer. Buffy had no intention whatsoever of giving it up at the end of the summer, or ever. She no longer felt as if she lived in her parents' apartment, or at Windflower. She lived in the college dorm, and she lived in a series of European hotels. She was never going back home, except to drop off clothes from one season and pick up clothes from another. She was never going back to Windflower. She didn't have to.

She knew that when she graduated she would be invited to enter meets all winter long, and would be touring winter as well as summer. When she graduated she would get her own apartment. Probably it wouldn't be in New York. New York was too expensive. She might even live with a guy if she was in love at the time. She knew from traveling with the team that living with one boy would be infinitely preferable to living with messy girls.

Windflower had become like an old half-forgotten dream, one you wanted to forget. She had been dreaming all the years she had lived there, lost in fantasies, dreaming up her future. Now her future was here, and it was real. She supposed she'd see her parents once in a while. If she ever ran at Madison Square Garden they could watch her win. They were so cheap they wouldn't go anyplace else, like Europe. But you never knew. They might reform, or her father might find a really low-priced package tour. If anyone could, he could. Buffy didn't really care. They were the ones who wanted to see her, not she them. But they'd probably stay at Windflower. They'd probably enjoy having the house all to themselves. They were the only ones who really seemed to use the facilities at Windflower. She could never be so easily satisfied. She wanted exactly the life she had now, and would have, and she had done it *herself*. Buffy felt proud.

FIVE

Everett was forty-two years old that winter, and in his own way he had found his manhood, his contentment, peace of mind, and what passed for happiness. He had settled into his ways, a routine, a regimented untidiness, a life style, and he had found friends. He still lived in the same little house, that seemed big now because he was alone in it. John was fourteen and away at a ritzy New England prep school. Frankie had faded into a memory. The furniture was worn and torn and used, just the way Everett liked it. Daisy, his beloved Doberman, had been killed by a car, and he had replaced her with another killer dog; this one he named Bluebell. She had a sweet face, and she obeyed him. He liked the way she terrified intruders and kept his privacy intact.

He worked long hours in his television repair shop, not because his mother would ever let him starve, but because he really enjoyed it. A girl answered the phone, a young plump girl, not his type, with a moustache. Everett was gruff with her and she brought him coffee in the mornings from the diner across the way, in a damp paper cup, with a cruller: his breakfast. She had a boyfriend who picked her up at the shop at the end of the working day in a pickup truck.

At the end of his working day Everett had gotten into the habit of stopping off at a neighborhood bar called The Stoney End. It was a dark, pleasant bar, patronized mostly by men who would never consider taking their wives there because their wives were supposed to be home taking care of the house. They all knew a woman's place. The Stoney End smelled faintly of beer, the television set above the bar was black and white and was always tuned to sports events, except when it was time for the six o'clock news. Everett liked to get there in time for the six o'clock news, drink a Miller, and talk to his cronies. There were no seasons in The

Stoney End, no world, except that at Christmas time some plastic poinsettias graced the windows and after Christmas a silver paper banner proclaimed Happy New Year. The air conditioning was always at the same temperature, not quite cold enough, and the men sat there in their shirtsleeves, comfortably bantering with the owner-bartender.

"Hey, Ray, when ya goin' ta getcha self a decent machine there, huh?"

"When you skinflints start spendin' some money," Ray would shoot back.

There wasn't even a bowl of free peanuts on the bar. You could buy a package of potato chips for a quarter; there was a cigarette machine, and a jukebox that sometimes played quietly under the roar of the boxing match or football game on the TV. No one really listened to either the jukebox or the TV, except for the few avid sports fans. Who, after all, would come to a bar to watch a dinky nine-inch screen in black and white when he could be home watching the game on a big screen in color, his wife handing him cold beers? No, they came to the bar for companionship, for peace, to get away from the wife and kids or, as in Everett's case, to get away from the nothingness that awaited them at home.

They weren't all bums or barflies, no, not by a long shot. Everett had met his best friends in that bar. One was a chemistry professor, another owned a used-car lot, and a third was a would-be writer. One was even a cop. They had long discussions, but never arguments. Even though a couple of the guys were intellectuals, they weren't pinkos. Parlor liberals reminded Everett of his own ineffectual family. He himself was a solid conservative. He felt proudly that he was a part of the mainstream of American life, of the come-up-the-hard-way-and-do-it-yourself school. He didn't believe in helping the poor, who were all shiftless and lazy. The help his family had given him he preferred to put out of mind, considering that it was the least they could have done since they were family. It was different from giving to strangers. His mother was paying for John's school, but Everett made John work during the summers. He wouldn't give the kid any money. And actually, John liked to work. It had disappointed Everett that John had decided not to work for him, but the kid said he made more working for that big company, so what the hell? He was right, it was good to make as much money as you could if you were doing what you liked to do.

He tried to be friends with John, the few times he saw the kid. He watched carefully to be sure John wasn't developing any of those weird, smart-ass ideas the other kids his age had, wasn't smoking pot or hanging around with rabble-rousers and communists. Fourteen wasn't too young to start watching. John seemed polite, well groomed, and private. He wasn't a hippie or a weirdo, which was one of the reasons Everett had been worried about the fancy Eastern school at first, because they put funny ideas into kids' heads back up north. Superintellectual liberals, how he hated them! But John seemed okay. He wore a tie; his hair was too long for Everett's taste but at least it didn't hang down to his shoulders like a girl. Hell, he wore a tie more often than Everett did!

Everett's mother had stopped nagging him to find another wife. He and his mother were good friends now that he didn't have to see her or live with her. They talked on the phone together every day. He called her, sometimes collect. They talked about business mostly, and Everett supposed she was his best friend. When he phoned he usually asked after his father's health, but never asked to speak to him. They had nothing to say to each other. But Everett liked his mother. She enjoyed things. He was sorry he hadn't taken after her more, that he'd turned out dour and serious like his father, but still, he enjoyed things more now. This was probably the most contented time of Everett's life.

The bar was his life. It was like a social club. The men there didn't bother to socialize outside the bar, to invite each other home to meet the wife and kids, to go to a movie or bowl or go out to eat. What for? Inside the bar they were safe; it was theirs. The other things, the dragging the yammering kids to the hamburger joint, the movie on Saturday night with the wife, the parties, the PTA, those were the things you *had* to do. But sitting around The Stoney End just relaxing with the guys, that was something you *wanted* to do. Everett had never been much of a drinker and he still wasn't. A Miller or two, he liked that. It was the companionship that brought him to The Stoney End night after night, not the booze.

There were four booths in the back where you could get a pretty fair meal if you wanted. Everett ate there sometimes, alone, and had a steak, nearly raw the way he liked it and had trained the Cuban cook to make it for him. It wasn't great meat but it was a helluva lot easier than going to the supermarket and shopping and cooking and then having to wash dishes. Sometimes, if he was tired, he would just have a beer and then go home, lie down, watch a little TV, read the evening paper or look through a magazine, and then if he got bored he would get up and go back to The Stoney End to see what was happening there. He knew there would always be someone he knew, or someone who would talk to him even if they didn't know each other, because Ray the owner-bartender was always wisecracking and making people feel friendly and good.

He remembered that roadhouse Frankie used to go to up at Windflower and how mad he'd get because he didn't see why she had to go to some cheap bar when they had everything she could want at home. Maybe she had found that kind of friendship and companionship at the roadhouse, like he found here. But what the hell, Frankie was a damned drunk! Still, maybe he could have tried to understand her better. He sure had tried, but she never seemed interested in understanding him either. She'd been in his life so long ago that the sharp edges were beginning to wear off in his memory, and now he could say to the guys that he'd once had a wife who got killed in an accident and he had a great kid, and what the hell, everybody had some kind of tragedy in their lives, right? You just had to make the best of it.

He hadn't been to Windflower for years. Everybody understood. They were used to his ways. He had to work, and he couldn't take time off, and besides, there were memories. His parents used to come to visit him and John every Christmas, but now his father was older and not feeling too well and couldn't make the trip, so his parents stayed home. He and his mother had their phone calls. She saw John a couple of times a year, for a day, when he came through New York on his way to Florida or to visit a friend in the East. John had a million friends. Everett couldn't figure out who the kid took after. Maybe his grandmother, Everett's mother. She said she'd had a million friends too when she was young. It was too bad, Everett thought, that she was tied down nursing his father, but she seemed to like it. Yep, she was a good ol' girl.

Everett knew that when his father died he'd have money. It didn't mean much to him. He couldn't really think of anything he'd like to spend a lot of money on. He didn't want to expand his business, he didn't want to travel, he didn't care about a better house or clothes or even putting in a swimming pool. The only thing he spent money on was his car, and he always had enough for that. Even though he lived in Florida he was always pale white. Suntans were for tourists. He had thought once it might be fun to buy a small yacht, but then he'd decided against it. It would be enjoyable to work on it, fix it, maintain it, but he really didn't like the water. No, he had everything he wanted right here, right now. Maybe he was creeping toward middle age and settling down. There was nothing wrong with that.

John, at fourteen, was mature for his age, tall and strong, with a quiet, sure charm and a fairness of outlook that made him the acknowledged leader in his class. He liked Exeter, and hoped to go to a good Eastern college where he could major in psychology and then came back and teach it. He wanted to be a teacher, he had decided, in a boys' prep school just like this one, up north, and never go back to Florida. He had no ties back in Miami. He was fond of his father, but in a rather removed way, as if his father were an eccentric older brother, a bit odd, with some weird ideas, set in his ways, conservative, hicky even. His father wore funny sloppy clothes and liked to sit around in a bar and never read a book. His father was so full of prejudices it was funny. He had a bad word to say about everybody, from minorities to the very rich. John was more amused than annoyed. It didn't concern him, really; he was too far away to be affected by it and could smile politely and say, "Yes, Sir," the way he'd been taught by his mother when he was a child, and then his father would be pacified.

His interest in psychology had started because of his own personal problems. Before that he'd thought of being a writer, or of teaching English, or maybe some sport. But as he grew older he became aware of certain conflicts he had in his mind about his mother and the way he felt about her. On the one hand he missed her very much, and on the other he remembered how badly she'd treated him and how mad he'd been at her sometimes, and then he sometimes felt guilty about her death as if it had relieved him of some burden. That terrified him. So he had gone to his adviser, who had sent him to talk to a doctor in town who was associated with the school in some way, and through their talks John had realized that what he felt was normal and natural because his mother had, after all, been a human being with faults, not a goddess, and being dead didn't wipe out all her faults as if they'd never existed. John also realized that when he had been with the family at Windflower he had felt a little guilty about loving his mother because everybody there seemed to dislike her. Like he'd say, "My mother says . . . ," and their faces would turn stony, turn away from him, and he wanted them to like him. It was so interesting that a person could have so many different conflicting feelings about the same person: love, hate, anger, respect, embarrassment, fondness, annoyance, and even confusion and incomprehension. He knew that a lot of boys had those feelings about their parents, and it would be good for them to understand what they were feeling and make some sense out of it. Psychology would help. He didn't want to be a doctor or a psychologist, he just wanted to teach the stuff, and be there as an adviser if some of the kids wanted to talk to him. He felt he could help because he understood. And he liked the sheltered academic life in a prep school community. It was like a big family. He'd even thought for a while of teaching something in a boarding school for younger kids, but then he'd thought no, he wanted to teach on a more advanced level, and besides there were still unhappy memories lurking even though he'd liked his old school. He realized now that he'd been unhappy when he was young, but now he felt good about himself and about his life. He would never have had this independence, this security, if he hadn't been sent away from home so young.

He went to visit his grandparents as infrequently as possible. He liked the physical aspects of Windflower, but whenever he went there his grandmother drove him crazy. She treated him as if he were four years old. It was "Eat this," and "Eat that," and "Do this," and "Don't do that," and "Be careful" until it was coming out his ears. She was afraid of everything. The whole world seemed menacing to her. She worried where he was, and if he left the house to go next door to visit Paris she was frantic that something bad had happened to him. He made one-day visits to his grandmother now, out of courtesy, because he couldn't stand more. After being on his own all his life since he could remember it was very irritating to be hovered over and smothered like that.

He wondered if she'd treated his father like that when he was young.

It was impressive, John thought, that two of his cousins had become so famous. Paris was a writer and Buffy was a runner, and he followed both their careers with loyalty and interest. He thought it was funny that the "old folks," as he thought of his grandparents and aunts and uncles, were sort of shocked about Paris' books and Buffy's choice of career. He thought they were both terrific. The old folks had such old-fashioned ideas. Even his father was shocked, but then his father was one of the worst of the old folks sometimes, even though he tried to pretend to be modern.

The only thing John had in common with his father was that they were both crazy about cars. When they were together that was the main thing they talked about. Now John was working after school and during the summer to save money to buy his own car. When he told his father that he was working for Canco because he made a lot of money there his father had seemed to assume that John intended to spend his life there. That was really a laugh, working in the shipping department of a canning company! But what else could you get when you were fourteen? People thought the only thing you were good enough to do was lift boxes. He just wanted the car, that was all. And a little spending money, to go out with his friends, see movies, and go skiing. John had learned to ski up north and he loved it. He figured that by the time he was old enough to get a driver's license (even though he had a Florida learner's permit now) he would have enough money to buy his car, and then he could buy a good pair of skis. He had a cheap pair now, that he'd bought with Christmas and birthday money he'd saved from the family. Then he'd get a good hi-fi. There were a lot of nice things he wanted like that, and he knew he'd never be rich on a teacher's salary, but it didn't matter if getting them took longer. He'd get them all eventually.

Some of his teachers had been the most important people in his life. He still remembered Stan, his adviser when he'd been just a little kid, and how much it had helped to have a friend like him. Maybe people who weren't in the academic community didn't think teachers were so important, and maybe some teachers were jerks, but there was a lot of good to be done in education. John wondered why his father had never thought of teaching people all the things he knew about making things and fixing things. His father didn't like people. That was too bad. Meeting new people, getting to know them, having friends, was one of the best things in life. No one should ever have to be alone.

SIX

Now that he was very old Lazarus had become quiet. No longer did he regale the family with the same old stories, with new words he had discovered, with new medical theories. He dozed, woke with a start as if surprised, and dozed again. He did not like the world as it was; he preferred the past. Sometimes he had a wild look in his eyes, almost of anger, of being offended by this new unseemly world that pushed its way into his old safe one through the medium of his television set, his radio, and even on the street. No, it wasn't safe to walk on the street any more. There were no movies to go to; they were all shocking. The people on the street were dirty-looking, unkempt, unhealthy. He took his daily walk with Melissa now, leaning on her arm for support, peering out at his street with contempt and annoyance. All that garbage piled up! Dog filth! Hippies! Cars honking, buses hooting, exhausts breathing out poison. The air itself was poisoned, dropping little crisp black dots of poison on his window sill, his clothes, his very person. He wore a hat, he put his collar up, he leaned on Melissa, and he wondered why he drove himself to take his healthful constitutional when the world he took it in was so filthy it would only do him harm. He appreciated Windflower, it was so clean and silent, except for the restful sounds of nature, the waterfall, the leaves rustling in the trees, the occasional chirping of birds. Not disease-carrying pigeons but polite country birds that kept their distance.

It was very quiet at Windflower that summer of 1967. Lazarus sat under his favorite tree, his unabridged dictionary on the metal table in front of his chair, and read a little with a magnifying glass, but it made him sleepy and often he just looked out over the vista until he nodded off into a nap. Jonah took solitary walks around the property for hours. Lavinia puttered in her garden and arranged flowers for the houses. Bringing an armful of fresh-cut garden flowers to Paris and arranging them for her was Lavinia's excuse to see her child, who was always locked away upstairs in her bedroom typing. Lavinia knew better than to interrupt her, but she always hoped she would arrive when Paris was in the kitchen having a meal. Rima was usually at the pool, baking herself in the sun and giving herself wrinkles. Lavinia was glad Paris didn't spend much time in the sun. Sun gave you cancer. She left long notes in the kitchen for Paris, pages and pages. She brought fresh vegetables from the farm down the road and washed them and left them with more notes.

"Oh, your poor mother," Rima said, "washing all those vegetables."

It bothered Paris that her mother sneaked in and out like a fan, an admirer, hoping for a glimpse of her. But what could she do? She still couldn't bring herself to go over there often to see them, and she kept coming here to her own house, her borrowed house, and then hiding in it like a hermit. It was ridiculous. She should go away altogether. But her mother said she would miss her, and after all, she had a book to write, as usual, and what better place to write it than this place where nothing happened to distract you?

Paris had stopped having weekend guests, except for Rima, who was still involved with her married man. Now Paris invited people for dinner, six and eight at a time, and she and Rima cooked. Their friends were respectable: married couples, mostly business associates, a few old friends who sometimes brought houseguests or a relative from out of town with them. Paris had become a good cook and she enjoyed it.

Buffy was away in Europe, running with her team. Rosemary and Jack needed only one maid now, who also had to cook because Rosemary hated cooking. They ate meals at odd hours: lunch at three o'clock. Everyone wondered how they had found such a docile cook.

Melissa was the only one who was constantly busy, because she was afraid to leave Lazarus out of her sight for long. She had been nursing him for so long that she had almost become him. Now it was she who told his old stories, who imparted tidbits of medical advice, "Lazarus says . . ." He no longer ate his huge breakfasts, feeling that older people should eat more sparingly, and besides, he really had no appetite. She was always at her wit's end trying to find something that would tempt him. Caviar? Too salty, he said. Custard? Too sweet, he said. A cookie? Too rich, he said. This cookie then? Too dry, he said. She hovered over him, cutting his meat, trying to find the choicest bits, removing the fat, offering him his vegetables, coaxing him to eat as she had done to Everett so long ago. He was her baby. If he spent too long in the shower she worried that he had fallen or had a heart attack, forgetting that Lazarus always took long showers. She rapped on the bathroom door: "Are you all right, Toots?" She took him for his walks around the grounds, adjusting her quick step to his slow one, until finally she walked slowly all the time, even when he was not with her, leaning slightly to one side as if the heavy burden of his body were still pressed against her.

"What's the matter with you?" Lavinia would say. "Stand up!"

Melissa wanted to be old, she wished herself old. He was so much older than she, how much? Eighteen years? Seventeen, perhaps, she had forgotten. That year she was sixty-four, and Lazarus was . . . eighty-seven! Why, he was twenty-three years older than she was. She remembered how sophisticated he had been once, so suave, so gallant, so wise and all-knowing about the world, and she such a frivolous girl. She didn't want to be a frivolous middle-aged woman, she wanted to be old and serene and wise, and because she couldn't bear the thought of being too different from him, she wanted to be tired too, and content to rest. She would have liked to go to the theater, but Lazarus hated it, and it was too much of an effort for him. He refused to hire a car and driver; too expensive he said. They never went to opera any more, or to concerts, and she tried not to miss them. When he took naps, she took naps. She slept all afternoon, beside him on the bed, waking occasionally to see if he was still all right. When he woke up she brought him cookies and milk, an eggnog, trying to tempt him, and when he turned the snack away, as he usually did, she consumed it herself. She had put on weight and almost become plump. It became her, everyone said, but she wasn't pleased with herself. She had always been proud of her trim figure. Now there were favorite clothes she couldn't squeeze herself into any more. But the added weight made her look older, more matronly, and she felt she should accept it. She was not a young woman. She was Dr. Lazarus Bergman's wife, and a grownup.

There were so many of her friends she hadn't seen for ages. It was a full-time job, taking care of Lazarus. He didn't go to the office any more; at least she had finally made him give that up. It was about time. He really wouldn't have retired except that most of his patients had died of old age. Besides, his office was in an impossible neighborhood, too dangerous even for a young man. Melissa watched with awe as husband after husband of her girl-friends died untimely deaths. Why they were her age, young men! Too young to die. Melissa and Lazarus were inseparable. It was how an old couple should be in their twilight years, growing old companionably together.

"Sixty-four isn't old," Lavinia would snap at her. "I'm older than you are and I live a normal life. Invite some company, or get a nurse for a couple of hours if you're so scared, and go out to a matinee with a friend."

"Oh, I wouldn't enjoy it," Melissa murmured, shocked at the very idea.

It was nice, Melissa thought, that Everett had turned out to be such a devoted son, telephoning her every day from Florida. She missed seeing him, but his phone calls were like little visits and she enjoyed them. She missed John more than she missed Everett, because Everett was always the same but John was constantly changing, growing up, getting smarter and more interesting and charming and devilish and she was missing so much of it. John was so sociable, with all those friends! The schools had been good for John, and she had to believe Everett had been a good father, because then that made her good; she was, after all, Everett's mother. She was glad John wanted to work and that Everett encouraged it. She had always encouraged Everett in his chosen career even though the rest of the family didn't seem to think much of it.

She had been lucky to have a long happy marriage when so many other people had their troubles. But sometimes now, when she lay in their bedroom while Lazarus napped, or when she leafed through a magazine while Lazarus dozed in the living room, she felt depressed. She was glad to have him there and it made her feel secure, but she was restless and a strange sadness filled her. She had indigestion, she had aches and pains, and sometimes she noticed a little twitch over one eyelid. Some days she and Lazarus hardly exchanged two sentences with each other. Mostly she cajoled him to eat or take his walk or stop walking because he seemed tired, and he said no. They didn't have discussions any more, or conversations. Sometimes Melissa felt lonely. But her love for him wrapped her warmly as she shivered in her heart, and she let her thoughts drift back to the old days, the happy days when they all had so much fun, so many friends, so many parties, on the go, always laughing and chattering and planning things to do. What had narrowed their lives so much? Not just age; it had started happening before Lazarus grew so old. It was partly Windflower. Having the family around her had made Melissa so content, so self-sufficient, that she really hadn't had time to be such a social butterfly. Those long summers when you didn't get around to inviting your friends, and then in the winter you were embarrassed about it and then they had their lives too, their children and grandchildren to worry about. And there had been the winter trips to Florida, so that cut out all the holiday parties in Brooklyn and New York. It had always been the family first, and eventually it had been only the family. And now, of course, she couldn't leave Lazarus for a moment, except once in the city when she ran to the doctor to get some tranquilizers. She had been so nervous leaving him alone for that short time, even though the maid was there and he was asleep, that when she finally got home she had to take two of the tranquilizers immediately. The doctor said they would keep her from being depressed and make her eyelid stop twitching.

Sometimes when she was lying down she pictured herself dancing, twirling and swaying in a sea-green dress, with a long chiffon scarf trailing gracefully behind her, and it was as restful as counting sheep. The little image danced across her sight under her closed eyelids like a little movie, a miniature, a tiny young Melissa. How golden her hair had been! She heard the music in her head, the old wind-up Gramophone, and she smiled. Such foolish dreams she'd had, and yet, they still made her smile.

At Windflower, that summer, a phrase kept running through Melissa's head and she couldn't figure out why. It was "The last of the Mohicans." It would pop into her head for no reason at all—"The last of the Mohicans"—and she thought it must have been something Lazarus had said once.

Lazarus died peacefully in his sleep, of natural causes, at age eighty-seven, that summer at Windflower.

Melissa was totally bereft. She had no one to take care of now, no one to look up to, and she was in a daze. Day after day she sat staring out over the hills, not really seeing them, not moving, not speaking, almost dead herself. Everett had come up for the funeral and stayed for two days. While he was there he went through some of his father's papers and found Lazarus' birth certificate. He hadn't been eighty-seven after all, he had been eighty-nine; he had lied about his age all these years for vanity's sake.

"He was almost ninety," Lavinia told Melissa consolingly. "He had a long happy life. Pull yourself together."

"He was a tough old guy," Jonah said admiringly. "Taking care of himself all these years paid off. Now you should start to take care of yourself, take a walk, don't just sit there."

Lavinia and Rosemary had to pull her up out of her chair, one on each side, holding her up, making her take a slow stroll around the grounds. It was as if Lazarus' soul had entered Melissa's body. She seemed frail, bent, her steps were slow, she faltered, and she still leaned as if she were supporting his body against hers. All these years, thinking only of him, how could she begin again?

In the fall the family moved back to the city. Melissa was afraid to sleep in her apartment alone. She had never been in any house alone in all her life. First she had lived with her sisters and brothers, then with her husband and child, and finally with her husband alone, but never by herself. She determined to manage. She had been tough once, strong, a spitfire, hadn't she? She would sleep alone.

Her friends phoned and came to call. There were dozens of them it seemed, all the girls she'd grown up with who were now old widows like herself, with married children, and they sat in her living room and chatted of old times. Melissa thought with surprise that most of them really didn't look too bad. They had kept in shape, their hair was either subtly streaked with gray or dyed a natural color, they wore stylish clothes, rouge, powder, perfume, their nails were done. They weren't bad at all, and she shouldn't have let herself go because it was too soon.

With no one to look after and feed, Melissa wasn't interested in food, and so she noticed with some pleasure that she had lost the extra weight she had put on the last few years and now her clothes fit again. Lavinia dragged her to the theater with her and Jonah. They went to a matinee once a month and insisted Melissa come too, and then Lavinia made Melissa send away for matinee tickets and go with her friends. Then there were the concerts, and the ballet. There was Blanche, who had been quite a musician in her day, and whose banker husband had died three years ago, and she insisted Melissa share her season tickets to a concert series. They would go Dutch, of course. And Ivy, who had been such a brain, married to a successful businessman who had died just last year, and she wanted Melissa to take piano lessons of all things! If not piano lessons, then how about a poetry course at the Y? Or what about flower arranging? Ivy was taking all of these. Her children were all married and she said once every week or two was plenty to see your grandchildren; after all, you didn't want to get in the way, and to tell the truth, what could you say to kids anyway?

And there was Jessica, whose son managed a travel agency, and who went on trips all the time. Her husband had died a long time ago, and while he was alive of course she had gone with him, so she knew her way around. Melissa had always admired Jessica's spirit. That winter Jessica signed up for a three-month European tour she would take in the late spring, to be crowned by a trip to Moscow to see the Bolshoi Ballet. She wanted Blanche and Ivy and Melissa to go with her.

"Moscow!" Melissa said. "It's so far."

"You can't mourn forever," Jessica said. "It'll be almost a year. Travel is the best remedy for grief, I've found. There'll be the four of us and we'll have fun, like four schoolgirls."

"Some schoolgirls," Melissa said. "Old hags."

"You can be an old hag," Ivy said, "but I'm not. I'm starting my exercise class again next week at the Y, now that my back is better."

"That's how you pulled it out in the first place," Melissa said, but she was tempted to join them on the trip. She had never been to Europe. She had never really been anywhere. All those places she had dreamed of and had never seen, all the plans and hopes deferred. There were always so many other people to think of first.

"Come with us," Jessica said. "Ivy is going. Blanche is going. You'll be sorry if you miss it. There's nothing to do in New York in the summer anyway."

"We always go to Windflower . . ." Melissa said.

"Do you want to go back there?"

Melissa thought about it. No, she didn't want to go back. It would be her first summer there without Lazarus, and so lonely.

But more than that, she hadn't wanted to go there for years, not since Papa died. She'd never really admitted it to herself, but she hadn't wanted to; she'd wanted to go other places, do other things, live. She had so many things to make up for. Life was so short. She wasn't too old, only sixty-four. At Windflower she would be the fifth wheel. She didn't want everybody to feel sorry for her, tolerate her. She wanted to run her own life, have adventures, see new things. Jessica was such a seasoned traveler, and with her son in charge of all their travel arrangements, everything would be first class and perfectly safe.

"I'll go with you on the tour," Melissa said.

"Hurray! You won't regret it, believe me."

Lazarus would have been glad, Melissa thought. He would have been proud of her, to see her seeking culture, standing on her own two feet. She missed him so much, but she mustn't feel guilty for entering life again. That was what life was for. And maybe, if this trip worked out, she could take one every summer, just the way Jessica and other women did. It was perfectly respectable. It was expensive, but she could afford it. She had thought for a while that maybe she would go down south to see Everett, but that was silly. Let Everett come to see her. What would she do down south anyway? She didn't even know anybody there. No, she had friends and she would travel, see things. She wouldn't say anything about it to Lavinia or Rosemary, but Melissa knew that she would never go back to Windflower again. Never. Let them laugh at her if they wanted and say this was her second childhood, and she would laugh right with them and agree. She felt reborn. How interesting to find yourself reborn in such a different time, when a woman could do exactly what she wanted to do and no one could tell her no.

SEVEN

That summer Lavinia and Jonah and Paris were the last of the Mohicans. Buffy was away running in Europe, and now that she was gone Jack grumbled constantly about how expensive Windflower was, such a waste of money, and finally Rosemary began to agree with him because Windflower didn't interest her any more now that her daughter was gone. It was as if Buffy had run away from her, right out of her life.

There were Andrew and Cassie, happily in their kibbutz, with their three children all married and all coming up every weekend, winter and summer, except when they went on a trip to ski or get some winter sun. And there were Rosemary and Jack, with a stranger for a child.

"Cassie must have done something right," Rosemary kept saying. "I wish I knew what it was."

It was beyond her comprehension. Chris, Cassie's oldest boy, the athlete, had married an athletic girl, but they spent their weekends jogging around Andrew's place; they didn't run away to be professionals like crazy Buffy. And all week Chris worked in the family business, right with his father, a help and a credit. He was rich and lived well; he liked it. Buffy could have been rich; she could have married some boy who liked to run if she loved it so much. And there was Paul, Cassie's second son, a stockbroker, with a wife who liked staying home and taking care of their three children and was no fool either. Cassie was a happy grandmother. As usual, Rosemary thought, Cassie gets it all and I miss out.

And last there was Blythe, Cassie's shy little girl, who had married a boy who looked exactly like her, a shy little boy of twenty-nine who made a hundred thousand dollars a year, as if Blythe needed it! They rode horses together, Blythe and her husband, like two characters from an English novel. Blythe had a job too, and she couldn't wait for Friday night when she could go to the country. She *wanted* to be there! Rosemary wracked her brains to discover what Cassie had done that she hadn't, but she couldn't think of anything and so she gave up.

Rosemary and Jack went to Chautauqua for two weeks that summer, to hear the concerts and the lectures, and they enjoyed it so much they made arrangements to rent an inexpensive cottage for the entire following summer. Okay, Rosemary thought, now I'll think of myself, do for myself; it's about time. She and Jack would wallow in the music, meet compatible friends, do what they liked for a change. When she thought of all the money she would save by not going to Windflower, and not hiring an expensive cook-maid, and not renting two cars, she felt warm all over. After all, she thought, we only went to all that trouble and expense of spending summers at Windflower because it was good for Buffy.

Melissa sent happy postcards from her European tour. Brief cards, always scribbled in haste because she was coming from one delightful event and hurrying to another. She bubbled like a schoolgirl. "You won't believe it," she scribbled to Lavinia, "a man actually flirted with me! Ooh la la, those French! But he was too *old* for me! ! ! Ha ha."

"Meshuggah," Lavinia said, shrugging. "But it's good for her, poor thing."

Lavinia had fixed up Paris' house during the winter, had some of the rooms painted, because goodness knows it needed it. The flowers on the wallpaper had all faded. Maybe next year she'd get new wallpaper, if she could only get her hands on Paris long enough to go with her to pick it out. To Lavinia it was "Paris' house" now, and she always called it that to make sure her claim on it was understood. No one could have that house, she would see to that. Paris had to have a place to stay. If Paris didn't come up to Windflower, why Lavinia didn't know what she would do. It was all for her, for Paris, that was what everything was for. What did she need to be in Windflower for without Paris? She bought a new stove for Paris when the old one broke; she even got a new refrigerator when Paris complained the food was spoiling. And what did Paris do? She accepted invitations all over the place and no one ever saw her. First it was East Hampton, for an entire week, and then two weeks in California at Malibu, and then she got an assignment to write an article in London and away she went. Why did she have to work in the hot summer? She didn't need the money. Her agent was exploiting her. No matter how Lavinia tried to talk her out of it, Paris went anyway. And then when she had been in London for two weeks she wrote to Lavinia that she was going to spend a week or two visiting friends who had a house in the South of France.

"I hope they're nice friends," Lavinia wrote back. She didn't even know who they were. Paris never told her anything any more. It was that analyst; it was his fault. He had made Paris secretive.

When Paris finally graduated from the analyst, stopped throwing away her money on that quack and letting him influence her, Lavinia was very relieved. When Andrew had gone to an analyst so long ago he had gone every day and gotten it over with, but there was Paris hanging on year after year, and then taking all sorts of long trips in between. Her analyst never made her pay for the time she missed; in fact he encouraged it. He wanted her to go away. He wanted to make her a stranger from her mother. Why did analysts try to make enemies out of families? Lavinia knew the answer to that one. They wanted to hang on to someone who was perfectly well and convince him he was sick so they could get paid all that money every week forever and ever. Oh, it was a crime! But anyway, Paris had come to her senses and stopped going, so things would be all right now. Lavinia only hoped the doctor hadn't done too much damage.

Paris and Rima were thirty-seven that year. They had decided that when they were forty they would start to lie about their ages, but they would always have to pretend to the same age because everyone knew they had gone to school together. "What age are we now?" Rima would ask, and they would laugh.

"I like getting older," Paris said. "I really don't mind it."

"Well, I mind it," Rima said. She had spent ten years with her married lover, ten years of waiting for him to visit her and donate a scrap of his time, ten years of eating dinner alone on a tray, ten years of feeling her heart turn over with frantic nervousness at the sound of his key in the lock, and then when he went away too soon, always too soon, feeling her throat close and the tears start coming out of her eyes. She cried every time he left, every time for ten years, and she didn't know why because she ought to be used to it by now. He never stayed long enough for her to tell him all the things she wanted to say. She was nervous when he arrived because there was so much to say and so little time, and she always forgot something, remembering it only after he had left. What kind of a relationship was that? That was no life. She was tired of it and she resented it. She had chosen it, but she had been young then and foolish, an innocent, she had thought she would never grow old. She hadn't dreamed what loneliness could be.

Rima was a senior editor now, at last. Her job was her life. Every night she took home manuscripts and read them, and was fond of saying: "A married woman could never have the job I have. It takes too much time. You have to be single, with no responsibilities."

And then one evening at a business party she went to only because her married lover was out of town and so she was free, Rima met a man. He was a magazine editor, divorced, Southern, all soft-spoken Southern charm and an impish wit. He was only two years older than she was; a baby, she thought delighted. He asked her to dinner and she went, feeling as if she were sneaking out, cheating. She liked feeling that way. They liked each other, and she began sneaking out to be with him more and more, at first terrified her lover would find out and then not caring at all.

Within two weeks they were in love. He had his own apartment, which was convenient, since Rima's lover had a key to hers and could walk in any time. She felt she should tell her politician and break it off, since deceit was never her strong suit, but she was afraid to hurt him, and so she went along recklessly, enjoying herself for the first time in years.

"He makes me laugh," she told Paris rapturously. "He makes me feel so young. He makes me want to go to the country and throw snowballs."

Her new lover saw no reason why he and Rima couldn't live together. She told him about her politician. He still saw no reason why they couldn't live together, since the other was over, wasn't it? Rima thought maybe it had been over for years, maybe it had never existed. She waited for her old lover as usual, but this time when she heard his key in her lock her heart was pounding because she knew she would tell him what she had to say, and this time she would make him listen.

She told him it was over and she was moving out. He wouldn't have to worry about scandal any more, he wouldn't have to sneak away from his wife and children and the electorate. He took it staunchly, with tears in his eyes, but did not make a scene. He never made a scene about anything. He had trained himself never to do anything dangerous. He said he was sorry to lose her but happy she had found an unmarried man who could give her a more suitable life. He said he would always be her friend.

The next day while Rima was at the office her politician let himself into her apartment with his key and carefully removed every photograph and snapshot of himself, all his love notes, letters, and anything with his handwriting on it.

"Typical," Rima said. She picked up the empty silver picture frame and looked at the blank glass. "That's his real picture," she said. Then she packed her clothes, gave her museum furniture to charity for a tax deduction, and moved in with her new love. "It was old lady furniture," she said. "I decided I hated it."

Weekends she spent in East Hampton, where her lover had a small house. Paris came up and spent a week while they were on vacation, and they promised to come to Windflower. "You should see it," Rima told him. "It's the most beautiful place in the world. It's really something to see."

They went to Windflower for one weekend. Paris was hardly ever there; she was always traveling or visiting someone. The leaves were very thick and green on the huge trees, and tiny white windflowers sprinkled the grass on the acres and acres of rolling hills. Molly Forbes, the caretaker, prematurely white-haired now but still as slim and lithe as she had been twenty years ago, ran down the hill surrounded by her dogs. Paris remembered when Richie had been a child, Molly running down the hill with Richie and her two little boys; all of them grown up now and gone away.

"What ever became of Basil?" Rima asked Paris. She knew all of the family and remembered their names, even the ones she had seen only once or twice when they came to visit. "He was so handsome," she told her lover. "I used to joke and say I'd marry him if he ever got divorced. Are you jealous?"

"Nope."

"He's fine," Paris said. "His son Hervé is in Budapest working for a movie director on location there. He's a chairgetter."

"What's a chairgetter?"

"You know: the director says, 'Hervé go get a chair,' and Hervé does."

"Didn't he once want to be a movie star?"

"Yes, well, now he wants to be a director. And Geneviève, Basil's daughter, is going to college and going steady with supposedly a very nice boy. They're both at summer school now."

"Wouldn't it be great to be young now?" Rima said. "Boys and girls can be *friends*. We could go to summer school and live in a coed dorm. It was horrible being young when we were young."

"I think it must always be horrible being young," Paris said.

This summer there was a purpose to Paris' traveling, more than the usual one of work or vacation. All her life she had planned, quietly, secretly, stubbornly, to get what she wanted, and now she wanted the next great step in her life plan. She didn't think of it as "the last step" because it was more a beginning than an end. She was looking for a place to spend her future summers.

It seemed to her that all her life her parents had been telling her it was the wrong time to be happy, at least on other terms than theirs. First she was too young, it was improper, what would people think? If you were free when you were young you were throwing your life away out of ignorance, because you should be planning for your Real Happiness, whatever that was. Probably they meant a kind of security, safety, achieved through a sensible husband who would enter the family circle and close it behind him and Paris so they would be safe in the fortress evermore. But when she got older, and was not married, her parents began worrying about her old age, so now they spoke of saving money, putting money away for the future, for her old age, and although they never spoke the dreaded words they meant "your lonely old age." She wasn't even forty yet and her mother spoke of nice homes for the elderly where wealthy people could go when they were alone so they could be cared for. Her mother was already thinking of her as if she were ninety! Where was her life, the life she had planned for and waited for, her maturity? Where was the enjoyment of now? There was only fear of the future, while now disappeared in a succession of lonely days. Paris didn't want to be an old lady with a young gigolo on the Riviera, she wasn't a fool, but she didn't want to end up in an old-age home either. She wanted to enjoy something now. This was to be her last summer at Windflower. She would find a house and buy it, and spend her summers there. She told no one but Rima, knowing her parents would get hysterical.

She had investigated various places. East Hampton and Malibu were out, as was the rest of America, because she was single and it was too difficult to live a normal life as a single woman. Either there were the singles complexes, the pleasure mini-cities where the unattached paired and mated frantically as quickly as seals and then parted to find other momentary partners, enjoying the new sexual freedom, or there were the less homogeneous communities where she would already be too old. She would be a leftover, a castoff: "Why haven't you ever married?" She didn't want to be known as a single, an unmarried woman, she wanted to be Paris Mendes, writer, and what do you do? In Europe at least they would start out by knowing her as an American, and that label would be so strong that the fact that she didn't have a husband would be as unimportant as the fact that she had brown eyes.

She liked London. She had always felt at home there. But London was no place to buy a summer home because it was a city. She wanted to be in a beautiful summery place, near water, a country place. So when a couple she knew invited her to spend a few weeks in their house in St.-Paul-de-Vence, she went with delight and hope. She liked France, but she had been frightened of the Riviera because there were too many phonies, too many millionaires and fake millionaires, too many seventeen-year-old girls with beautiful bodies, long straight blonde hair (the nemesis of her high school days), bikinis, golden unmarked youthful skin, and ancient eyes. She didn't want to go anywhere where she had to compete in order to find friends. She wanted a place that was natural, where there were writers and artists and friendly people who would accept her simply because she happened to live in their town. She wanted a town square, where people could sit and have a drink in the late afternoons after working or playing, where they could become friends, and then meet each other as friends, demanding nothing, not competing, not showing off, just enjoying their lives. She wanted other Americans, but not a tourist place, at least not a notoriously tourist place where magazines came to take pictures of what everyone was wearing this summer. She wanted it to be near enough to the sea so that she could drive there whenever she wanted to. She wanted good weather, old houses, and a view. She wanted it to look like a painting she had seen once. She didn't know if she would ever find it.

The moment she saw the ancient walled city on top of the mountain her heart sank. Walls! Windflower had walls, and people left there feet first. She hated walls, and electrified barbed wire, and fear. But then when she was inside, looking down at the incredible view, and around her at the colors, the quality of preserved beauty, she realized it wasn't like Windflower at all. St.-Paul-de-Vence was the opposite of Windflower because it was old, it had a history, while Windflower was only a place where people waited. There were little squares here, and there were writers and artists and Americans, and some tourists, and you could walk from one end of the town to the other if you had the strength, and certainly drive it, and you could drive to the sea. Her friends, an art dealer and his wife, who was a painter, both Americans, knew a lot of people and introduced her. It seemed good, it seemed right. Paris waited, and hoped.

In the mornings when she woke up she opened the shutters and looked out, breathing in the clear air, and every morning she felt the same rush of happiness as if something new was beginning. There were no memories here. It was a joy to turn a corner, to see an old wall of a building, or a tree, and not to feel a sad memory. There was a past here but it was not hers. Here, for her, was only a future. Her two friends were good-hearted and open and warm, they liked people and food and conversation, and every kind of artistic endeavor their friends were interested in interested them. Their friends, who became Paris' friends, were the same. Their houses were completely informal and yet they cared; you could tell in the way plants grew and things they loved and had collected were displayed to be enjoyed. It could be a painting or a shell, or a dozen of each.

Near the end of the season there was a small house available. It was just big enough for Paris and two houseguests. Rima had already promised to come visit her wherever she was, and Paris thought perhaps there would be other people she wanted to invite who would want to come, but if they didn't she wouldn't be lonely anyway. She felt at home here now. She rented the house for a month with the understanding that she might buy it. First you had to live in a house to see if it was the right house for you.

From the beginning she knew it was right. Every day she planned ways she would decorate it, simply, but in her own way to make it hers. When you are planning to redecorate a house you know you already feel you own it. She wondered if she would be lonely, but she didn't feel lonely, she felt happy.

Her friends found her a maid who came every day for two hours to clean and was willing to cook whenever needed. Paris wanted to shop and cook herself, to entertain new friends who had entertained her, and she realized that in this particular house with these particular friends "entertain" was the wrong word; it was a word from Windflower. What she wanted was to enjoy her friends, and have them enjoy her and her new home.

At the end of the month her friends helped her with the arrangements to buy the house. Paris felt strange. She had never bought or owned anything in her life, except her car, and that had been bought for her by her parents, who then made her too frightened to drive it because they worried so that she might be killed. She had always saved her money and she could afford the little house, but it wasn't that which felt strange, it was having responsibility for the first time. She wondered if it would frighten her. It didn't. She liked owning the house; she wanted to do everything in it herself, even put down the tiles on the patio floor.

She knew her parents would be horrified, full of worries about how she had been cheated, how the house would fall down around her ears, how she would die without a doctor (but there was a doctor in the town, he just wasn't their family doctor), and how she couldn't be trusted to act like an adult person, wasn't this the proof of it? Buying was so permanent. She was going away from them, going away from Windflower. She knew her father would understand, because secretly he had always harbored a wish for adventure but had put it away in favor of practicality. She also knew her mother would finally have to accept it, and would eventually even defend her decision, as her mother finally had with everything Paris had done on her own. Paris didn't care any more if they approved or not, but now she just didn't want to hurt them. It was the sign she had finally grown up. She was the one with the power now. It always happened at a certain time between parents and children, this reversal.

EIGHT

In March Lavinia and Jonah went to Windflower to see that everything was all right, to close things up, because no one would be coming up that summer. Since Paris had bought her house in St.-Paul-de-Vence (who had influenced her to do such a crazy thing?) Lavinia had no real wish to go to Windflower for the summer, and Jonah had finally persuaded her to spend six weeks in Israel, his dream. Part of the persuasion had been the fact that Paris had invited them—was allowing them?—to visit her for a week and stay in her newly decorated guest room.

"It's very simple," she told Lavinia. "Don't expect anything luxurious."

Luxurious! As if Lavinia cared! All she wanted was to see her daughter, to see the house, to be sure everything was all right. Paris was so pleased and proud of her new possession. Lavinia remembered her own pride in her new house in Windflower, despite all the difficulties getting the things they needed during wartime, and she almost felt excited herself.

Jonah was excited about going to Israel. For years he had talked longingly of seeing Israel, telling Lavinia the names of friends of his who had been there not just once but many times, and she had ignored him, but now she was going to go there with him. They had booked everything the best, air-conditioned hotels, a guide, an air-conditioned car the guide would drive while he showed them the historical and new sights. Lavinia would like it, he was sure. He had made sure she wouldn't be uncomfortable for a minute, sparing no expense. What was he to do with his money after all, now that he was a middle-aged man? Jonah never thought of himself as old. An old man didn't walk five miles every day the way he did, winter and summer, and his doctor had told him he had the body of a man twenty years younger. Lavinia was the one who was fragile, who hated hot weather and uncomfortable beds not her own, so he would be sure that she enjoyed this trip and then perhaps she would be willing to go with him to other places and do other things. Ah, Israel! Jonah was so proud of the Israelis, the Jewish people taking an active role in building a new land, the poor babies who had been orphaned by Hitler now grown up and secure in their own country with healthy children of their own. The past and present melded sometimes in his mind, and he would never forget those photographs he had seen after the war. He had given up the formal aspects of his religion for Lavinia, but he had never given up his strong identity as a Jew. A person could worship in his heart; he didn't have to go to temple.

They had hired a car and driver for the day to go to Windflower. Lavinia had not let Jonah drive a car for years, except to go to the supermarket in the summers. In the summers they rented a car. Who wanted to own a car, such a problem and a nuisance?

The driver waited for them in the turnabout, leaning against his long black car, smoking, while they went to their house to do what they had to do.

"How desolate it is here!" Lavinia said to Jonah, looking down at the huge expanse of bare land, the black leafless trees, the huge, full, rushing waterfall swollen with melted snow. "I wouldn't want to live in the country all year round." She shivered.

"I don't know why Andrew and Cassie want to go to the country every weekend in the winter," Jonah said. "Of course, theirs is an all-year-round house."

"Ours could be too," Lavinia said. "I just wouldn't like it. Andrew loves it. For me, it's so boring, nothing to do, just sit around and eat too much." She thought of Andrew and Cassie in their country house, their married children coming up every weekend, summer and winter, and she wondered what made some people love the country and others not. But she knew it wasn't the country, it was more, it was the family. She was no fool. "Why?" she said. "I wonder."

"Why what?"

"Why do Cassie's children stay and all of ours leave? All right, Everett is a poor soul, but Melissa did the best she could. And Richie, who could ever understand him? Buffy is strange. But Paris, what did we do wrong? What didn't we do? I always made her get to know the family. I wanted her to have a sense of the family. We went to Papa's every Sunday, and every holiday, and it was Cassie who never brought her children. I used to say: 'Your children won't ever have a sense of family.' Do you remember how every Thanksgiving we all got together and Cassie's children were never there? They were always at their school dance, or with friends, or on a date, or at a party. Cassie let them go off with their friends instead of being with the family, and I used to think they'd never get to know us. I always *made* Paris come to family get-togethers, I wanted her to know the family. And now she goes off and Cassie's children have all come back. I don't understand it."

"Maybe . . ." Jonah said thoughtfully, "Maybe we were unfair to her to make her commute all those years. All those summers here alone, maybe she was lonely and we didn't know it. We always thought just being here was enough."

"It was enough for me when I was young," Lavinia said. "I was so happy being with my family, my brothers and sisters, my parents. We all had such good times together. We had friends. Paris never wanted friends. When did she ever invite company? I put two beds in her room so she could have company, but she never wanted any. It wasn't my fault."

"Nobody says it's your fault, Lavinia."

"It was Papa's dream for us to have this place . . ." How lucky they had all felt when they moved into this beautiful estate! Lavinia remembered it now in all its good parts, the warmth of being together, the safety, the beautiful afternoons under the striped lawn umbrellas in Papa's garden, all of them young, hopeful, grateful for having the money to do this, despite the little inconveniences of having to share a house. All right, sometimes it wasn't so easy to get along all in the same house, but they had managed. And Paris had seemed so glad not to have to go to camp any more. She had loved her room. She had seemed difficult at times, brooding, but all adolescents acted that way, Lavinia knew that. Paris had seemed so close to her then. She remembered when Paris was twelve and going to her first school dance, and had asked her: "Mother, do I have to dance cheek to cheek?" And hadn't Lavinia answered her: "You do exactly what you want to, and you don't have to dance cheek to cheek if you don't want to." Why, she had always told Paris to be her own person. She had never forced her to do anything! So why was she such a villain that Paris had to run away?

She wished Paris would get married to some nice man who would take care of her. What would happen to Paris when they were gone? She would have enough money, thank God, but she would be all alone, who would take care of her? She needed a husband, a companion. It wasn't too late. Paris could get married and she didn't have to have children if she didn't want to. She could adopt children. Why didn't Paris want to get married?

Cassie's children had each moved into their own apartment when they graduated from college, and then each of them had been married within a year. Paris had her own apartment, Lavinia had let her; hadn't she furnished it with all the best, paid for everything, been a friend and a mother at the same time? Why, she remembered one time when Paris wanted to buy a table and had said: "Mother it's so expensive, it's a hundred and fifty dollars," and hadn't Lavinia told her to go right ahead and buy it?

She hadn't been a villain. Why had Paris run away?

She had been independent too. She remembered when she had asked Papa if she could quit her job and come to work in the office with him. How well they had always gotten along, she and Papa! He had told her she was just like him. That was the highest compliment she had ever been given, could ever hope for. To be like Papa, the genius, the philanthropist, the visionary. He was a great man among little men. Would he have said let Paris have her house in France? Would he have been saddened to see them go away from Windflower, one by one, or would he have understood the need of each to find his own frontier the way he, Papa, had when he was young? But Papa had done it all for them. He had sought out a new frontier so he could make a home for his family, not so he could seek adventure for adventure's sake. It was different now. People were different. What did they want?

Carefully, Lavinia checked each lamp to make sure it had been unplugged from the wall, and then she pulled out the plug of the television set. They said it was better for the set to do that if you didn't use it for a long time. Should they take it to the city? No, they would be back someday soon, and those things didn't spoil. She knew they would be back. Paris would get tired of her house in France, she would be lonely, she would find it too much trouble. All her life Paris had had things done for her, so she would hate having to do for herself. In a strange country, in a strange language, she would find it too hard. She would come back. She had to come back!

Lavinia went into the kitchen and checked to see that the refrigerator was unplugged and a fresh box of charcoal still rested inside on a shelf so it would stay fresh and sweet. Those canned goods in the cupboard, she would have to phone Molly Forbes and tell her to take them. You shouldn't keep those things around too long. They always left a few things, just to have something for the first day, but they could bring new supplies up with them when they came back.

Upstairs in her bedroom Lavinia looked through the closets to see if there was anything she wanted. There were a few dresses she liked, but they were quite old and maybe she should leave them here and get new ones for Israel. She wanted to look nice there; they would be eating out every night and staying in the best hotels. She went into Paris' room and looked through the closets. There were some dresses from . . . oh, it must be about 1952. Nice country cocktail dresses, ones she had bought for Paris to wear to family dinners so she could look pretty. And there was the straw basket Paris had bought once on a trip to Mexico. Lavinia didn't like to throw things out because you never knew when you could use them again or give them to somebody. The wallpaper was so faded she could hardly see the pattern. She remembered how thrilled with it Paris had been when she saw it. "Just what I wanted!" she had cried happily. It was like being a detective, going back into memories and trying to find out when it all first started coming apart. How could you tell which was the first moment, if that moment would have mattered if it hadn't been followed by others?

"Should I take this jacket?" Jonah called to her through the open door of the suite. After Paris had moved into The Big House Lavinia had found the key and opened the door again between their two rooms.

"Wait a minute, let me look. No, that's for the country. We'll get you some nice new clothes. Leave that here for when we come back."

Come back, come back. Would they come back? Of course they would. The place would be empty this summer but then everything would straighten out. Lavinia would keep after Paris; she wouldn't give up. She never gave up, and finally she always got what she wanted, didn't she?

They had lunch in the kitchen, sandwiches and fruit Lavinia had brought in a paper bag from the city, and she made instant coffee she had brought too. Their driver went into the nearby town to have lunch at the new Howard Johnson's, or was it McDonald's? Lavinia couldn't remember because they never went to those places. They were nice for people with young children, but she had no need of them. She wrapped up the garbage carefully to take back with them in the car to the city because there was no garbage collection during the winter except for Molly Forbes' house, and Lavinia didn't want to bother her. She put on her coat and went out to the front porch. There was Molly, her nose reddened from the cold, running down the hill toward the icy stream with her dogs. How those dogs loved her! It was nice for her that she had the dogs during the desolate winters. Soon, in a month, the place would start to look more alive, more livable, as those dead-looking trees began to wake up and the ground turned from frozen stone to wakening earth. There would be green things. Who would take care of her garden?

Lavinia went back into the house and checked the thermostat. She had turned it up when they came in so they could take off their coats, and now she turned it down again, just warm enough so the water pipes wouldn't freeze and burst. The drapes were drawn against the sun that would come back in the spring and fade the carpets. She had covered the furniture with clean sheets the way she always did at the end of every summer, and it all looked colorless and anonymous. It made her impatient to be out of there. It didn't look like her house this way. All her plants were in her apartment in the city, and this house seemed so still, waiting, asleep like the winter ground outside. What had she forgotten? Her past was there, memories, but she would never forget them. She would take them with her wherever she went.

She went out to the car after carefully closing the door so she could hear the lock catch. Now where was Jonah? What a nuisance! Then she saw him, striding cheerfully toward the house, his cheeks pink and healthy from the chill air.

"The ice is melted in the river," he said happily, "and I saw fish."

"Well? We always had fish."

"Remember when I used to take Paris fishing, when she was a little girl?"

"I still would never trust that fish enough to eat," Lavinia said. "You never know where it's been."

"Molly is fishing," Jonah said. "I saw her."

"Let her." Molly was a country woman. She would know which fish were fit to eat and which were not. If she wanted to take chances that was her business.

"We didn't lose any trees this winter during the snow," Jonah said. "Except one and it was dead anyway."

"We'll use it for firewood in Paris' house," Lavinia said. "Paris likes a fire."

"Firewood is better when it's aged a while," Jonah said, nodding.

There would still be the three of them, Lavinia was thinking. If everyone in the family wanted to go their separate ways, let them, but there would still be she and Jonah and Paris. She would keep them together. She would talk to Paris on the phone all spring and fall and winter in New York, and they would get together. If they just could have dinner together once a week, she wouldn't demand more, although she would have liked more. Her own little family, the three of them, was the most important. And she would keep up with the others as she always did, on the phone. Someone had to hold the family together. Someone had to care. You had to work at it, you had to hold on, you could never give up. She'd always said that.

Lavinia and Jonah settled into the back seat of the black car and the driver started down the long driveway away from Windflower. When she looked back out of the window the last house she could see, as always, was The Big House. It looked so sturdy there against the white sky, at the top of the hill. She imagined to herself that Papa still lived there, and for a moment she felt happy.

Epilogue

Almost half of The Valley belongs to one deserted estate: Wind-flower. There is the sign, "Windflower—Service," and then much later, "Windflower," although you can see no house, only a road that seems to stretch for miles. On either side of the main entrance are stone walls, then there are the acres of grass surrounded by the electrified barbed wire that could stun a large animal and kill a small one. The grass is high now in the outer field, studded with the tiny white flowers that gave the estate its name. "No Trespassing" signs are tacked up on the large trees near the entrance, but no one pays much attention to them any more. Most people think the place is a public park. The families who live in the new houses along Hill Avenue come to picnic here sometimes, or to ride their sleds down the hills in winter. The pond is fine for ice skating on cold winter days, and in summer the little boys come to fish in the lake and to dare each other to walk across the slippery stones on top of the waterfall.

The houses are empty here, except for the one where the caretaker lives, and they have been empty for so long that the local people just ignore them, as if they were another useless convenience like the pool house by the empty swimming pool or the ivy-choked pavilion by the lake. The tennis court has no net and no tapes, but sometimes there are little paw prints in the en-tout-cas, what is left of it. Small animals live here freely now, skunks and woodchucks and rabbits and raccoons. Nobody ever kills them except occasionally a car on the road in the fog. Once there were timid deer that came to drink from the edge of the lake at dawn, but they are long gone, and so are the horses that ran and played in the lower field. The stables across the road are still there, that boarded the neighborhood horses, but now there is only one horse in the corral, wearing a muzzle and fixing you with a mean eye.

The horses from the riding academy on Green Street still cut across the bridle path that runs along the edge of the woods in Windflower. The bridle path came with the estate, and the Saffrons left it open as a gesture of good will, although no one ever knew it belonged to anybody because the estate was so large.

It is summer now, and the trees are in full leaf, enormous trees, old but still rich with sap. It has not been an excessively hot summer yet, so the waterfall is still full, and in the stillness you can hear it clearly. A little car comes up the road and turns in at the Windflower entrance. At the sound of it there comes another sound from somewhere behind the top of the hill, the barking of dogs to announce the presence of strangers. A young man is driving the car: John Bergman, and he is nineteen years old and it is his car, his first car, bought with his own money, carefully saved. With him are two other young men, his friends from college. They have brought fishing rods with them, and an assortment of lures and hooks, because John has told them that he knows a place where the fishing is good, where he used to come around sometimes when he was a kid. Their names are Terry and Peter, and they, like everyone else at school, look up to John because he has about him a quality of leadership, of differentness. There are secrets in him. He is golden. If John tells you he knows a place where there are fish you know you will catch them.

John parks his car in the driveway beside an enormous deserted house. The house is so covered with ivy that you cannot even peer into the windows. There are tufts of wild grass growing between the chunks of broken gravel in the driveway, and almost without thinking John reaches down and plucks one out.

"Hey, this is some place!" Terry says admiringly. "That looks like a haunted house."

"It's definitely haunted," John says, and laughs.

The three of them start walking down the hill with their fishing gear and a woman comes toward them from somewhere, surrounded by lively dogs. She is Molly Forbes, and when she sees John she recognizes him even though she hasn't seen him for years and years, and her face lights up with pleasure at what a fine young man he's turned out to be. He motions to his friends to stay there and walks up to her quickly, just as she is about to greet him.

"Pretend you don't know me," John whispers. She nods. She understands.

The dogs are jumping all over him now in greeting, and Molly is telling them: "Stop it, stop it, down now, you be good, sit pretty, sit." She and John glance at each other and years of memories pass between them in that moment, different for each of them and yet much the same. He smiles at her and goes back to his friends.

"She said it was okay," he tells them, and they go down to the lake.

Too fascinated to fish, Terry and Peter lay their gear down on the cracked cement of the old pavilion floor and go chattering through the ruins. "Look at the gargoyles," Terry says, pointing at two funny faded statues which might be gargoyles or elves, depending on your point of view. "Somebody must have painted them once, look, you can still see the colors."

"They had electricity here," Peter remarks, pointing out the remains of old wires. "I wonder if they lived here."

"No, they couldn't have lived here. It has no sides. They would have lived in those three houses up on the hill. They must have just had parties here."

"What a great place to have parties!"

John is kneeling at the edge of the lake, looking down into the depths to see where the fish are hiding. He sees them, and stands up, pleased. "It's full of fish," he says. "I think they're bass."

"We could cook them in that fireplace," Peter says.

Terry is looking at the waterfall, leaning over the iron railing, almost hypnotized. He pulls his glance away and looks out over the vista; the river, the little curved wooden bridge, the broad expanse of rolling hills covered now with long, thick grass and tiny white flowers. He has never seen such a place and is sorry he didn't bring his camera. You could get some good shots here. It's really beautiful. "Why don't we go look at the houses?"

"I don't want to do that," John says.

"Okay."

John and Peter are baiting their hooks now, deciding which is the best place to start to fish. Terry is still looking admiringly at the view.

"I wonder if they had a good time here," he says, and then he shrugs, because after all it has nothing to do with him, and he goes to join his friends.